In Search of
Lost Time

IN SEARCH OF
LOST TIME

VOLUME V

THE CAPTIVE
THE FUGITIVE

MARCEL PROUST

TRANSLATED BY
C. K. SCOTT MONCRIEFF AND TERENCE KILMARTIN
REVISED BY D. J. ENRIGHT

THE MODERN LIBRARY

NEW YORK

LIBRARY OF CONGRESS CATALOGING-IN-PUBLICATION DATA
Proust, Marcel, 1871–1922.
[Prisonnière. English]
The captive; The fugitive/Marcel Proust; translated by C. K. Scott
Moncrieff & Terence Kilmartin; revised by D. J. Enright.
p.   cm.—(In search of lost time; 5)
Includes bibliographical references.
ISBN 0-375-75311-7
I. Scott-Moncrieff, C. K. (Charles Kenneth), 1889–1930.
II. Kilmartin, Terence. III. Enright, D. J. (Dennis Joseph), 1920– .
IV. Proust, Marcel, 1871–1922. Albertine disparue. English. 1993.
V. Title. VI. Series: Proust, Marcel, 1871–1922.
À la recherche du temps perdu. English; v. 5.
PQ2631.R63P713   1993
843´.912—dc20   93-15168

MARCEL PROUST

Marcel Proust was born in the Parisian suburb of Auteuil on July 10, 1871. His father, Adrien Proust, was a doctor celebrated for his work in epidemiology; his mother, Jeanne Weil, was a stockbroker's daughter of Jewish descent. He lived as a child in the family home on Boulevard Malesherbes in Paris, but spent vacations with his aunt and uncle in the town of Illiers near Chartres, where the Prousts had lived for generations and which became the model for the Combray of his great novel. (In recent years it was officially renamed Illiers-Combray.) Sickly from birth, Marcel was subject from the age of nine to violent attacks of asthma, and although he did a year of military service as a young man and studied law and political science, his invalidism disqualified him from an active professional life.

During the 1890s Proust contributed sketches to *Le Figaro* and to a short-lived magazine, *Le Banquet,* founded by some of his school friends in 1892. *Pleasures and Days,* a collection of his stories, essays, and poems, was published in 1896. In his youth Proust led an active social life, penetrating the highest circles of wealth and aristocracy. Artistically and intellectually, his influences included the aesthetic criticism of John Ruskin, the philosophy of Henri Bergson, the music of Wagner, and the fiction of Anatole France (on whom he modeled his character Bergotte). An affair begun in 1894 with the composer and pianist Reynaldo Hahn marked the beginning of Proust's often anguished acknowledgment of his homosexuality. Following the publication of

Emile Zola's letter in defense of Colonel Dreyfus in 1898, Proust became "the first Dreyfusard," as he later phrased it. By the time Dreyfus was finally vindicated of charges of treason, Proust's social circles had been torn apart by the anti-Semitism and political hatreds stirred up by the affair.

Proust was very attached to his mother, and after her death in 1905 he spent some time in a sanatorium. His health worsened progressively, and he withdrew almost completely from society and devoted himself to writing. Proust's early work had done nothing to establish his reputation as a major writer. In an unfinished novel, *Jean Santeuil* (not published until 1952), he laid some of the groundwork for *In Search of Lost Time,* and in *Against Sainte-Beuve,* written in 1908–9, he stated as his aesthetic credo: "A book is the product of a different self from the one we manifest in our habits, in society, in our vices. If we mean to try to understand this self it is only in our inmost depths, by endeavoring to reconstruct it there, that the quest can be achieved." He appears to have begun work on his long masterpiece sometime around 1908, and the first volume, *Swann's Way,* was published in 1913. In 1919 the second volume, *Within a Budding Grove,* won the Goncourt Prize, bringing Proust great and instantaneous fame. Two subsequent sections—*The Guermantes Way* (1920–21) and *Sodom and Gomorrah* (1921)—appeared in his lifetime. (Of the depiction of homosexuality in the latter, his friend André Gide complained: "Will you never portray this form of Eros for us in the aspect of youth and beauty?") The remaining volumes were published following Proust's death on November 18, 1922: *The Captive* in 1923, *The Fugitive* in 1925, and *Time Regained* in 1927.

CONTENTS

Numerals in the text refer the reader to explanatory notes while asterisks indicate the position of textual addenda. The notes and the addenda follow the text.

THE CAPTIVE

At daybreak, my face still turned to the wall, and before I had seen above the big window-curtains what shade of colour the first streaks of light assumed, I could already tell what the weather was like. The first sounds from the street had told me, according to whether they came to my ears deadened and distorted by the moisture of the atmosphere or quivering like arrows in the resonant, empty expanses of a spacious, frosty, pure morning; as soon as I heard the rumble of the first tramcar, I could tell whether it was sodden with rain or setting forth into the blue. And perhaps these sounds had themselves been forestalled by some swifter and more pervasive emanation which, stealing into my sleep, diffused in it a melancholy that announced snow or else (through a certain intermittent little person) burst into so many hymns to the glory of the sun that, having first of all begun to smile in my sleep, having prepared my eyes, behind their shut lids, to be dazzled, I would awake finally to clarion peals of music. It was, in fact, principally from my bedroom that I took in the life of the outer world during this period. I know that Bloch reported that, when he called to see me in the evenings, he could hear the sound of conversation; as my mother was at Combray and he never found anybody in my room, he concluded that I was talking to myself. When, much later, he learned that Albertine had been staying with me at the time, and realised that I had concealed her presence from everybody, he declared that he saw at last

1

the reason why, during that phase of my life, I had always refused to go out of doors. He was wrong. His mistake was, however, perfectly excusable, for reality, even though it is necessary, is not always foreseeable as a whole. People who learn some correct detail about another person's life at once draw conclusions from it which are not accurate, and see in the newly discovered fact an explanation of things that have no connexion with it whatsoever.

When I reflect now that, on our return from Balbec, Albertine had come to live in Paris under the same roof as myself, that she had abandoned the idea of going on a cruise, that she was installed in a bedroom within twenty paces of my own, at the end of the corridor, in my father's tapestried study, and that late every night, before leaving me, she used to slide her tongue between my lips like a portion of daily bread, a nourishing food that had the almost sacred character of all flesh upon which the sufferings that we have endured on its account have come in time to confer a sort of spiritual grace, what I at once call to mind in comparison is not the night that Captain de Borodino allowed me to spend in barracks, a favour which cured what was after all only a passing distemper, but the night on which my father sent Mamma to sleep in the little bed beside mine. So true is it that life when it chooses to deliver us once more from sufferings that seemed inescapable, does so in different, at times diametrically opposed conditions, so much so that it seems almost sacrilegious to note the identical nature of the consolations vouchsafed!

When Albertine had heard from Françoise that, in the darkness of my still curtained room, I was not asleep, she had no qualms about disturbing me as she washed herself in her bathroom. Then, frequently, instead of waiting until later in the day, I would go to my own bathroom, which adjoined hers and was a very agreeable place. Time was when a stage manager would spend hundreds of thousands of francs to begem with real emeralds the throne upon which a great actress would play the part of an empress. The Russian ballet has taught us that simple lighting effects, trained upon the right spot, will beget jewels as gorgeous and more varied. This decoration, already more ethereal, is not so pleasing, however, as that which, at eight o'clock in the morning, the sun substitutes for what we were accustomed to see when we did not rise before noon. The windows of our respective bathrooms, so that their occupants might not be visible from without, were not smooth and transparent but crinkled with an artificial and old-fashioned hoar-frost. All of a sudden, the sun would colour this muslin glass, gild it, and, gently disclosing in my person an earlier young man whom habit had long concealed, would intoxicate me with memories, as though I were in the heart of the country amidst golden foliage in which even a bird was not lacking. For I could hear Albertine ceaselessly humming:

> For melancholy
> Is but folly,
> And he who heeds it is a fool.

I was too fond of her not to be able to spare a smile for her bad taste in music. This song had, as it happened, during the past summer, delighted Mme Bontemps, who presently heard people say that it was silly, with the result that, instead of asking Albertine to sing it when she had company, she would substitute:

A song of farewell rises from troubled springs,

which in its turn became "an old jingle of Massenet's the child is always dinning into our ears."

A cloud passed, blotting out the sun; I saw the prudish, leafy screen of glass grow dim and revert to a grey monochrome.

The partition that divided our two dressing-rooms (Albertine's, identical with my own, was a bathroom which Mamma, who had another at the opposite end of the flat, had never used for fear of disturbing my rest) was so thin that we could talk to each other as we washed in double privacy, carrying on a conversation that was interrupted only by the sound of the water, in that intimacy which is so often permitted in hotels by the smallness and proximity of the rooms but which, in private houses in Paris, is so rare.

On other mornings, I would remain in bed, drowsing for as long as I chose, for orders had been given that no one was to enter my room until I had rung the bell, an act which, owing to the awkward position in which the electric push had been hung above my bed, took such a time that often, tired of feeling for it and glad to be left alone, I would lie back for some moments and almost fall asleep again. It was not that I was wholly indifferent to Albertine's presence in the house. Her separation from her girlfriends had succeeded in sparing my heart any fresh anguish. It kept it in a state of repose, in a semi-immobility which would help it to recover. But this calm which my mistress procured for me was an assuagement of suffering rather than a joy. Not that it did not enable me to taste many joys from which the intensity of my anguish had debarred me, but, far from my owing them to Albertine, who in any case I no longer found very pretty and with whom I was bored, with whom I was indeed clearly conscious that I was not in love, I tasted these joys on the contrary when Albertine was not with me. And so, to begin the morning, I did not send for her at once, especially if it was a fine day. For some moments, knowing that he would make me happier than Albertine, I remained closeted with the little person inside me, the melodious psalmist of the rising sun, of whom I have already spoken. Of the different persons who compose our personality, it is not the most obvious that are the most essential. In myself, when ill health has succeeded in uprooting them one after another, there will still remain two or three endowed with a hardier constitution than the rest, notably a certain philosopher who is happy only when he has discovered between two works of art, between two sensations, a common element. But I have sometimes wondered whether the last of all might not be this little mannikin, very similar to another whom the optician at Combray used to set up in his shop window to forecast the weather, and who, doffing his hood when the sun shone, would put it on again if it was going to rain. I know how selfish this little mannikin is; I may be suffering from an attack of breathlessness which only the coming of rain would assuage, but he pays no heed, and, at the first drops so impatiently awaited, all his gaiety forgotten, he sullenly pulls down his hood. Conversely, I dare say that in my last agony, when all my other "selves" are dead, if a ray of sunshine steals into the room while I am drawing my last breath, the little barometric mannikin will feel a great relief, and will throw back his hood to sing: "Ah, fine weather at last!"

I would ring for Françoise. I would open the *Figaro*. I would scan its columns and ascertain that it did not contain an article, or so-called article, which I had sent to the editor, and which was no more than a slightly revised version of the page that had recently come to light, written long ago in Dr Percepied's carriage, as I gazed at the spires of Martinville. Then I would read Mamma's letter. She found it odd, if not shocking, that a girl should be living alone with me. On the first day, at the moment of leaving Balbec, when she saw how wretched I was and was worried about leaving me by myself, my mother had perhaps been glad when she heard that Albertine was travelling with us and saw that, side by side with our own boxes (those boxes among which I had spent the night in tears in the hotel at Balbec) Albertine's too—narrow and black, having for me the appearance of coffins, and as to which I did not know whether they would bring life or death to our house—had been loaded on to the "twister." But I had never even asked myself the question, being all overjoyed, in the radiant morning, after the fear of having to remain at Balbec, that I was taking Albertine with me. But if at the start my mother had not been hostile to this proposal (speaking kindly to my friend like a mother whose son has been seriously wounded and who is grateful to the young mistress who is nursing him with loving care), she had become so now that it had been all too completely realised and the girl was prolonging her sojourn in our house, moreover in the absence of my parents. I cannot, however, say that my mother ever openly manifested this hostility to me. As in the past, when she had ceased to dare to reproach me with my nervous instability and my laziness, now she had qualms—which perhaps I did not altogether perceive or did not wish to perceive at the time—about running the risk, by offering any criticism of the girl to whom I had told her that I intended to make an offer of marriage, of casting a shadow over my life, making me in time to come less devoted to my wife, of sowing perhaps, for a season when she herself would no longer be there, the seeds of remorse at having grieved her by marrying Albertine. Mamma preferred to seem to be approving a choice which she felt herself powerless to make me reconsider. But all the people who saw her at that time have since told me that in addition to her grief at having lost her mother she had an air of constant preoccupation. This mental strife, this inward debate, had the effect of overheating my mother's brow, and she was constantly opening the windows to let in the fresh air. But she failed to come to any decision, for fear of influencing me in the wrong direction and so spoiling what she believed to be my happiness. She could not even bring herself to forbid me to keep Albertine for the time being in our house. She did not wish to appear more strict than Mme Bontemps, who was the person principally concerned, and who saw no harm in the arrangement, which greatly surprised my mother. All the same, she regretted that she had been obliged to leave us together, by departing just at that moment for Combray where she might have to remain (and did in fact remain) for many months, during which my great-aunt required her incessant attention by day and night. Everything was made easier for her down there thanks to the kindness and devotion of

Legrandin who, sparing himself no pains, kept putting off his return to Paris from week to week, not that he knew my aunt at all well, but simply, first of all, because she had been his mother's friend, and also because he knew that the invalid, condemned to die, valued his attentions and could not do without him. Snobbery is a grave disease, but it is localised and so does not utterly corrupt the soul. I, on the other hand, unlike Mamma, was extremely glad of her absence at Combray, but for which I should have been afraid (being unable to tell Albertine to conceal it) of her learning of the girl's friendship with Mlle Vinteuil. This would have been to my mother an insurmountable obstacle, not merely to a marriage about which she had meanwhile begged me to say nothing definite as yet to Albertine, and the thought of which was becoming more and more intolerable to myself, but even to the latter's being allowed to stay for any length of time in the house. Failing so grave a reason, of which she was not aware, Mamma, through the dual effect of the edifying and liberating example of my grandmother, according to whom, in her admiration of George Sand, virtue consisted in nobility of soul, and of my own corrupting influence, was now indulgent towards women whose conduct she would have condemned in the past, or even now had they been any of her own middle-class friends in Paris or Combray, but whose large-heartedness I extolled to her and whom she forgave much because of their affection for me.

However all this may be, and even apart from any question of propriety, I doubt whether Mamma could have put up with Albertine, since she had retained from Combray, from my aunt Léonie, from all her kindred, habits of punctuality and order of which my mistress had not the remotest conception. She would never think of shutting a door and, by the same token, would no more hesitate to enter a room if the door stood open than would a dog or a cat. Her somewhat inconvenient charm was, in fact, that of behaving in the household not so much like a girl as like a domestic animal which comes into a room and goes out again and is to be found wherever one least expects to find it, and she would often—something that I found profoundly restful—come and lie down beside me on my bed, making a place for herself from which she never stirred, without disturbing me as a person would have done. She ended, however, by conforming to my hours of sleep, and not only never attempted to enter my room but would take care not to make a sound until I had rung my bell. It was Françoise who impressed these rules of conduct upon her. She was one of those Combray servants, conscious of their master's place in the world, who feel that the least that they can do is to see that he is treated with all the respect to which they consider him entitled. When a stranger on leaving after a visit gave Françoise a tip to be shared with the kitchenmaid, he had barely slipped his coin into her hand before Françoise, with an unparalleled display of speed, tact and energy, had passed the word to the kitchenmaid who came forward to thank him, not in a murmur, but openly and clearly, as Françoise had told her that she must do. The parish priest of Combray was no genius, but he also knew what was right and proper. Under his instruction, the daughter of some Protestant cousins of Mme Sazerat's had been converted to Catholicism, and her family had behaved impeccably towards him. There was a question of her marrying a young nobleman of Méséglise. The young man's parents wrote to inquire about her in a somewhat arrogant letter, in which they expressed contempt for her Protestant origin. The priest replied in such a tone that the Méséglise nobleman, crushed and grovelling, wrote a very different letter in which he begged as the most precious favour to marry the girl.

Françoise deserved no special credit for making Albertine respect my slumbers. She was imbued with the tradition. From her studied silence, or the peremptory response that she made to a proposal to enter my room, or to send in some message to me, which Albertine had expressed in all innocence, the latter realised with astonishment that she was now living in an alien world, where strange customs prevailed, governed by rules of conduct which one must never dream of infringing. She had already had a forewarning of this at Balbec, but, in Paris, made no attempt to resist, and would wait patiently every morning for the sound of my bell before venturing to make any noise.

The training that Françoise gave her was also salutary for our old servant herself, in that it gradually stilled the lamentations which, ever since our return from Balbec, she had not ceased to utter. For, just as we were boarding the train, she had remembered that she had failed to say good-bye to the housekeeper of the hotel, a mustachioed lady who looked after the bedroom floors and barely knew Françoise by sight, but had been comparatively civil to her. Françoise insisted on getting out of the train, going back to the hotel, making her farewells to the housekeeper, and postponing her departure for Paris until the following day. Common sense, coupled with my sudden horror of Balbec, restrained me from granting her this concession, but my refusal had infected her with a morbid ill-humour which the change of air had not sufficed to cure and which lingered on in Paris. For, according to Françoise's code, as illustrated in the carvings of Saint-André-des-Champs, to wish for the death of an enemy, or even to inflict it, is not forbidden, but it is a horrible sin not to do the right thing, not to return a civility, to omit, like a regular churl, to say good-bye to the housekeeper before leaving a hotel. Throughout the journey, the continually recurring memory of her not having taken leave of this woman had dyed Françoise's cheeks with a scarlet flush that was quite alarming. And if she refused to eat or drink until we reached Paris, it was perhaps because this memory was a real "weight" on her stomach (every social class has its own pathology) even more than to punish us.

Among the reasons which led Mamma to write me a letter every day, a letter which never failed to include some quotation from Mme de Sévigné, was the memory of my grandmother. Mamma would write to me: "Mme Sazerat gave us one of those little luncheons of which she possesses the secret and which, as your poor grandmother would have said, quoting Mme de Sévigné, deprive us of solitude without affording us company." In one of my earlier replies I was inept enough to write to Mamma: "By those quotations, your mother would recognise you at once." Which brought me, three days later, the reproof: "My poor boy, if it was to speak to me of *my mother*, your reference to Mme de Sévigné was most inappropriate. She would have answered you as she answered Mme de Grignan: 'So she was nothing to you? I had supposed that you were related.' "

By this time, I would hear my mistress leaving or returning to her room. I would ring the bell, for it was time now for Andrée to arrive with the chauffeur, Morel's friend, lent me by the Verdurins, to take Albertine out. I had spoken to the latter of the remote possibility of our marriage; but I had never made her any formal promise; she herself, from discretion, when I said to her: "I don't know, but it might perhaps be possible," had shaken her head with a melancholy smile, as much as to say "Oh, no it won't," which meant: "I'm too poor." And so, while I continued to say: "Nothing could be less certain" when speaking of plans for the future, for the present I did everything in my power to amuse her, to make her life agreeable, with perhaps the unconscious design of thereby making her wish to marry me. She herself laughed at my lavish generosity. "Andrée's mother would pull a bit of a face if she saw me turn into a rich lady like herself, what she calls a lady who has 'horses, carriages, pictures.' What? Did I never tell you that she says that. Oh, she's quite a type! What surprises me is that she raises pictures to the same dignity as horses and carriages."

We shall see in due course that, in spite of stupid habits of speech which she had not outgrown, Albertine had developed to an astonishing degree. This was a matter of complete indifference to me, a woman's intellectual qualities having always interested me so little that if I pointed them out to some woman or other it was solely out of politeness. Céleste's curious genius alone might perhaps appeal to me. In spite of myself, I would continue to smile for some moments, when, for instance, having ascertained that Albertine was not in my room, she accosted me with: "Heavenly deity perched on a bed!" "But why, Céleste," I would say, "why deity?" "Oh, if you suppose that you have anything in common with the mortals who make their pilgrimage on our vile earth, you are greatly mistaken!" "But why 'perched' on a bed? Can't you see that I'm lying in bed?" "You never lie. Who ever saw anybody lie like that? You've just alighted there. With your white pyjamas, and the way you twist your neck, you look for all the world like a dove."

Albertine, even in the discussion of the most trivial matters, expressed herself very differently from the little girl that she had been only a few years earlier at Balbec. She would go so far as to declare, in connexion with a political incident of which she disapproved: "I consider that fearsome," and I am not sure that it was not about this time that she learned to say, when she wanted to indicate that she thought a book badly written: "It's interesting, but really, it might have been written *by a pig*."

The rule that she must not enter my room until I had rung amused her greatly. As she had adopted our family habit of quotation, and in following it drew upon the plays in which she had acted at her convent and for which I had expressed a liking, she always compared me to Assuerus:[1]

> And death is the reward of whoso dares
> To venture in his presence unawares . . .
> None is exempt; nor is there any whom
> Degree or sex can save from such a doom;
> Even I myself . . .

> Like all the rest, I by this law am bound;
> And, to address him, I must first be found
> By him, or he must call me to his side.

Physically, too, she had changed. Her blue, almond-shaped eyes—now even more elongated—had altered in appearance; they were indeed of the same colour, but seemed to have passed into a liquid state. So much so that, when she closed them, it was as though a pair of curtains had been drawn to shut out a view of the sea. It was no doubt this aspect of her person that I remembered most vividly each night on leaving her. For, quite contrarily, every morning the ripple of her hair, for instance, continued to give me the same surprise, as though it were some novelty that I had never seen before. And yet, above the smiling eyes of a girl, what could be more beautiful than that clustering coronet of black violets? The smile offers greater friendship; but the little gleaming coils of blossoming hair, more akin to the flesh of which they seem to be a transposition into tiny wavelets, are more provocative of desire.

As soon as she entered my room, she would spring on to my bed and sometimes would expatiate upon my type of intellect, would vow in a transport of sincerity that she would sooner die than leave me: this was on mornings when I had shaved before sending for her. She was one of those women who can never distinguish the cause of what they feel. The pleasure they derive from a fresh complexion they explain to themselves by the moral qualities of the man who seems to offer them a possibility of future happiness, which is capable, however, of diminishing and becoming less compelling the longer he refrains from shaving.

I would inquire where she was thinking of going.

"I believe Andrée wants to take me to the Buttes-Chaumont; I've never been there."

Of course it was impossible for me to discern among so many other words whether beneath these a falsehood lay concealed. Besides, I could trust Andrée to tell me of all the places that she visited with Albertine. At Balbec, when I had felt utterly weary of Albertine, I had made up my mind to say, untruthfully, to Andrée: "My little Andrée, if only I had met you again sooner, it's you that I would have loved! But now my heart is pledged to another. All the same, we can see a great deal of each other, for my love is causing me great unhappiness, and you will help me to find consolation." And now these same lying words had become true within the space of three weeks. Perhaps Andrée had believed in Paris that it was indeed a lie and that I was in love with her, as she would doubtless have believed at Balbec. For the truth is so variable for each of us, that other people have difficulty in recognising what it is. And as I knew that she would tell me everything that she and Albertine had done, I had asked her, and she had agreed, to come and call for Albertine almost every day. Thus I could without anxiety remain at home. Also, Andrée's privileged position as one of the girls of the little band gave me confidence that she would obtain everything I might want from Albertine. Truly, I could have said to her now in all sincerity that she would be capable of setting my mind at rest.

At the same time, my choice of Andrée (who happened to be staying in Paris, having given up her plan of returning to Balbec) as guide and companion to my mistress was prompted by what Albertine had told me of the affection that her friend had felt for me at Balbec, at a time when, on the contrary, I was afraid that I bored her; indeed, if I had known this at the time, it is perhaps with Andrée that I would have fallen in love.

"What, you never knew?" said Albertine, "but we were always joking about it. Do you mean to say you never noticed how she used to copy all your ways of talking and arguing? Especially when she'd just been with you, it was really striking. She had no need to tell us whether she had seen you. As soon as she joined us, we could tell at once. We used to look at one another and laugh. She was like a coalheaver who tries to pretend that he isn't one, although he's black all over. A miller has no need to say that he's a miller—you can see the flour all over his clothes, and the mark of the sacks he has carried on his shoulder. Andrée was just the same, she would twist her eyebrows the way you do, and stretch out her long neck, and I don't know what all. When I pick up a book that has been in your room, even if I'm reading it out of doors, I can tell at once where it's been because it still has a faint whiff of your beastly fumigations. It's only the tiniest thing—I can't really explain—but it's rather a nice thing really. Anyhow whenever anybody spoke nicely about you, seemed to think a lot of you, Andrée was in ecstasies."

Notwithstanding all this, in case there might have been some secret plan made behind my back, I would advise her to give up the Buttes-Chaumont for that day and to go instead to Saint-Cloud or somewhere else.

It was not of course, as I was well aware, that I was the least bit in love with Albertine. Love is no more perhaps than the diffusion of those eddies which, in the wake of an emotion, stir the soul. Certain such eddies had indeed stirred my soul through and through when Albertine spoke to me at Balbec about Mlle Vinteuil, but these were now stilled. I no longer loved Albertine, for I no longer felt anything of the pain I had felt in the train at Balbec on learning how Albertine had spent her adolescence, with visits perhaps to Montjouvain. I had thought about all this for long enough, and it was now healed. But from time to time certain expressions used by Albertine made me suppose—why, I cannot say—that she must in the course of her life, short as it had been, have received many compliments, many declarations, and received them with pleasure, that is to say with sensuality. Thus she would say in any connexion: "Is that true? Is it really true?" Of course, if she had said, like an Odette: "Is it really true, that thumping lie?" I should not have been disturbed, for the very absurdity of the formula would have explained itself as a stupid inanity of feminine wit. But her questioning air: "Is that true?" gave on the one hand the strange impression of a creature incapable of judging things by herself, who relies on your corroboration, as though she were not endowed with the same faculties as yourself (if you said to her: "We've been out for a whole hour," or "It's raining," she would ask: "Is that true?"). Unfortunately, on the other hand, this want of facility in judging external phenomena for herself could not be the real origin of her "Is that true? Is it really true?" It seemed rather that these words had been, from the dawn of her precocious nubility, replies to: "You know, I never saw anybody as pretty as you," or "You know I'm madly in love with you, you excite me terribly"—affirmations that were answered, with a coquettishly acquiescent modesty, by these repetitions of: "Is that true? Is it really true?" which no longer served Albertine, when in my company, save to reply by a question to some such affirmation as: "You've been asleep for more than an hour," "Is that true?"

Without feeling to the slightest degree in love with Albertine, without including in the list of my pleasures the moments that we spent together, I had nevertheless remained preoccupied with the way in which she disposed of her time; had I not, indeed, fled from Balbec in order to make certain that she could no longer meet this or that person with whom I was so afraid of her doing wrong for fun (fun at my expense, perhaps), that I had adroitly planned to sever, by my departure, all her dangerous entanglements at one blow? And Albertine had such extraordinary passivity, such a powerful faculty for forgetting, and for complying with one's wishes, that these relations had indeed been severed and the phobia that haunted me cured. But such a phobia is capable of assuming as many forms as the undefined evil that is its cause. So long as my jealousy had not been reincarnated in new people, I had enjoyed after the passing of my anguish an interval of calm. But the slightest pretext serves to revive a chronic disease, just as the slightest opportunity may enable the vice of the person who is the cause of our jealousy to be practised anew (after a lull of chastity) with different people. I had managed to separate Albertine from her accomplices, and, by so doing, to exorcise my hallucinations; if it was possible to make her forget people, to cut short her attachments, her taste for sensual pleasure was chronic too, and was perhaps only waiting for an opportunity to be given its head. Now Paris provided just as many opportunities as Balbec. In any town whatsoever, she had no need to seek, for the evil existed not in Albertine alone, but in others to whom any opportunity for pleasure is good. A glance from one, understood at once by the other, brings the two famished souls in contact. And it is easy for an astute woman to appear not to have seen, then five minutes later to join, the person who has read her glance and is waiting for her in a side street, and to make an assignation in a trice. Who will ever know? And it was so simple for Albertine to tell me, in order that she might continue these practices, that she was anxious to revisit some place on the outskirts of Paris that she had liked. And so it was enough that she should return later than usual, that her expedition should have taken an inexplicably long time, although it was perhaps perfectly easy to explain (without bringing in any sensual reason), for my malady to break out afresh, attached this time to mental pictures which were not of Balbec, and which I would set to work, as with their predecessors, to destroy, as though the destruction of an ephemeral cause could put an end to a congenital disease. I did not take into account the fact that in these acts of destruction in which I had as an accomplice, in Albertine, her faculty of changing, her ability to forget, almost to hate, the recent object of her love, I was sometimes causing great pain to one or other of those unknown persons with whom she had successively taken her pleasure, and that I was doing so in vain, for they would be abandoned but replaced, and, parallel to the path strewn with all the derelicts of her light-hearted infidelities, there would continue for me another, pitiless path interrupted only by an occasional brief respite; so that my suffering, had I thought about it, could end only with Albertine's life or with my own. Even in the first days after our return to Paris, not satisfied by the information that Andrée and the chauffeur had given me as to their expeditions with my mistress, I had felt the environs of Paris to be as baleful as those of Balbec, and had gone off for a few days in the country with Albertine. But everywhere my uncertainty as to what she might be doing was the same, the possibility that it was something wrong as abundant, surveillance even more difficult, with the result that I had returned with her to Paris. In leaving Balbec, I had imagined that I was leaving Gomorrah, plucking Albertine from it; in reality, alas, Gomorrah was disseminated all over the world. And partly out of jealousy, partly out of ignorance of such joys (a case which is extremely rare), I had arranged unawares this game of hide and seek in which Albertine would always elude me.

I questioned her point-blank: "Oh, by the way, Albertine, am I dreaming, or did you tell me that you knew Gilberte Swann?" "Yes; that's to say that she spoke to me once in class, because she had a set of the French history notes. In fact she was very nice and lent them to me, and I gave them back to her when I next saw her." "Is she the kind of woman that I object to?" "Oh, not at all, quite the opposite."

But, rather than indulge in this sort of interrogation, I would often devote to imagining Albertine's excursions the energy that I did not employ in sharing them, and would speak to her with the enthusiasm which unfulfilled designs can keep intact. I expressed so keen a longing to see once again some window in the Sainte-Chapelle, so keen a regret that I was not able to go there with her alone, that she said to me lovingly: "Why, my sweet, since you seem so keen about it, make a little effort, come with us. We'll wait as long as you like, until you're ready. And if you'd rather be alone with me, I'll just send Andrée home, she can come another time." But these very entreaties to me to go out added to the calm which enabled me to yield to my desire to remain indoors.

It did not occur to me that the apathy reflected in my thus delegating to Andrée or the chauffeur the task of soothing my agitation, by leaving them to keep watch on Albertine, was paralysing and deadening in me all those imaginative impulses of the mind, all those inspirations of the will, which enable us to guess and to forestall what a person is going to do. It was all the more dangerous because by nature I have always been more open to the world of potentiality than to the world of contingent reality. This helps one to understand the human heart, but one is apt to be taken in by individuals. Productive of suffering, my jealousy was born of mental images, not based on probability. Now there may occur in the lives of men and of nations (and there was to occur in mine) a moment when we need to have within us a chief of police, a clear-sighted diplomat, a master-detective, who instead of pondering over the possible contingencies that extend to all the points of the compass, reasons soundly and says to himself: "If Germany announces this, it means that she intends to do something else, not just 'something' in the abstract but precisely this or that or the other, which she may perhaps have already begun to do," or "If so-and-so has fled, it is not in the direction a or b or d, but to the point c, and the place to which we must direct our search for him is c." Alas, I allowed this faculty, which was not highly developed in me, to grow numb, to lose strength, to disappear, by letting myself be lulled as soon as others were engaged in keeping watch on my behalf.

As for the reason for my desire to remain at home, I should have been very reluctant to explain it to Albertine. I told her that the doctor had ordered me to stay in bed. This was not true. And if it had been true, his instructions would have been powerless to prevent me from accompanying my mistress. I asked her to excuse me from going out with herself and Andrée. I shall mention only one of my reasons, which was dictated by prudence. Whenever I went out with Albertine, if she left my side for a moment I became anxious, began to imagine that she had spoken to or simply looked at somebody. If she was not in the best of tempers, I thought that I must be causing her to miss or to postpone some appointment. Reality is never more than a first step towards an unknown on the road to which one can never progress very far. It is better not to know, to think as little as possible, not to feed one's jealousy with the slightest concrete detail. Unfortunately, in the absence of an outer life, incidents are created by the inner life too; in the absence of expeditions with Albertine, the random course of my solitary reflexions furnished me at times with some of those tiny fragments of the truth which attract to themselves, like a magnet, an inkling of the unknown, which from that moment becomes painful. Even if one lives under the equivalent of a bell jar, associations of ideas, memories, continue to act upon us. But these internal shocks did not occur immediately; no sooner had Albertine set off on her drive than I was revivified, if only for a few moments, by the exhilarating virtues of solitude. I took my share in the pleasures of the new day; the arbitrary desire—the capricious and purely solipsistic impulse—to savour them would not have sufficed to place them within my reach, had not the particular state of the weather not merely evoked for me their past images but affirmed their present reality, immediately accessible to all men whom a contingent and consequently negligible circumstance did not compel to remain at home. On certain fine days, the weather was so cold, one was in such full communication with the street, that it seemed as though the outer walls of the house had been dismantled, and, whenever a tramcar passed, the sound of its bell reverberated like that of a silver knife striking a house of glass. But it was above all in myself that I heard, with rapture, a new sound emitted by the violin within. Its strings are tautened or relaxed by mere differences in the temperature or the light outside. Within our being, an instrument which the uniformity of habit has rendered mute, song is born of these divergences, these variations, the source of all music: the change of weather on certain days makes us pass at once from one note to another. We recapture the forgotten tune the mathematical necessity of which we might have deduced, and which for the first few moments we sing without recognising it. These modifications alone, internal though they had come from without, gave me a fresh vision of the external world. Communicating doors, long barred, reopened in my brain. The life of certain towns, the gaiety of certain excursions, resumed their place in my consciousness. With my whole being quivering around the vibrating string, I would have sacrificed my dim former existence and my life to come, erased by the india-rubber of habit, for a state so unique.

If I had not gone out with Albertine on her long expedition, my mind would stray all the further afield, and, because I had refused to savour with my senses this particular morning, I enjoyed in imagination all the similar mornings, past or possible, or more precisely a certain type of morning of which all those of the same kind were but the intermittent apparition which I had at once recognised; for the sharp air blew the book open of its own accord at the right page, and I found before me, already marked, so that I might follow it from my bed, the Gospel for the day. This ideal morning filled my mind full of a permanent reality identical with all similar mornings, and infected me with a joyousness which my physical debility did not diminish: for, a sense of well-being resulting far less from the soundness of our health than from the surplus of our energies, we can achieve it just as well by restricting the scope of our activity as by increasing our strength. The activity with which I was overflowing and which I kept constantly charged as I lay in bed, made me pulsate and leap internally, like a machine which, prevented from moving from its position, turns over on itself.

Françoise would come in to light the fire, and in order to make it draw, would throw upon it a handful of twigs, the scent of which, forgotten for a year past, traced round the fireplace a magic circle within which, glimpsing myself poring over a book, now at Combray, now at Doncières, I was as joyful, while remaining in my bedroom in Paris, as if I had been on the point of setting out for a walk along the Méséglise way, or of going to join Saint-Loup and his friends on manoeuvres. It often happens that the pleasure which everyone takes in turning over the keepsakes that his memory has collected is keenest in those whom the tyranny of physical illness and the daily hope of its cure prevent, on the one hand, from going out to seek in nature scenes that resemble those memories and, on the other hand, leave so convinced that they will shortly be able to do so that they can remain gazing at them in a state of desire and appetite and not regard them merely as memories or pictures. But, even if they could never have been more than this for me, even if, in recalling them, I could see them as pictures only, they none the less suddenly re-created out of my present self, the whole of that self, by virtue of an identical sensation, the child or the youth who had first seen them. There had been not merely a change in the weather outside, or, inside the room, a change of smells; there had been in myself an alteration in age, the substitution of another person. The scent, in the frosty air, of the twigs of brushwood was like a fragment of the past, an invisible ice-floe detached from some bygone winter advancing into my room, often, moreover, striated with this or that perfume or gleam of light, as though with different years in which I found myself once more submerged, overwhelmed, even before I had identified them, by the exhilaration of hopes long since abandoned. The sun's rays fell upon my bed and passed through the transparent shell of my attenuated body, warmed me, made me glow like crystal. Then, like a famished convalescent already battening upon all the dishes that are still forbidden him, I wondered whether marriage with Albertine might not spoil my life, not only by making me assume the too arduous task of devoting myself to another person, but by forcing me to live apart from myself because of her continual presence and depriving me for ever of the joys of solitude.

And not of these alone. Even if one asks of the day nothing but desires, there are some—those that are excited not by things but by people—whose character it is to be personal and particular. So that if, on rising from my bed, I went to the window and drew the curtain aside for a moment, it was not merely, as a pianist for a moment turns back the lid of his instrument, to ascertain whether, on the balcony and in the street, the sunlight was tuned to exactly the same pitch as in my memory, but also to catch a glimpse of some laundress carrying her linen-basket, a baker-woman in a blue apron, a dairymaid with a tucker and white linen sleeves, carrying the yoke from which her milk-churns are suspended, some haughty fair-haired girl escorted by her governess—an image, in short, which differences of outline, perhaps quantitatively insignificant, were enough to make as different from any other as, in a phrase of music, the difference between two notes, an image but for the vision of which I should have dispossessed my day of the goals which it might have to offer to my desires of happiness. But if the access of joy brought me by the spectacle of women whom it was impossible to imagine *a priori* made the street, the town, the world, more desirable, more deserving of exploration, it set me longing, for that very reason, to recover my health, to go out of doors and, without Albertine, to be a free man. How often, at the moment when the unknown woman who was to haunt my dreams passed beneath the window, sometimes on foot, sometimes at full speed in a motor-car, did I not suffer from the fact that my body could not follow my gaze which kept pace with her, and falling upon her as though shot from the embrasure of my window by an arquebus, arrest the flight of the face that held out for me the offer of a happiness which, thus cloistered, I should never know!

Of Albertine, on the other hand, I had nothing more to learn. Every day she seemed to me less pretty. Only the desire that she aroused in others, when, on learning of it, I began to suffer again and wanted to challenge their possession of her, raised her in my eyes to a lofty pinnacle. She was capable of causing me pain, but no longer any joy. Pain alone kept my wearisome attachment alive. As soon as it subsided, and with it the need to appease it, requiring all my attention like some agonising distraction, I felt how utterly meaningless she was to me, as I must be to her. I was miserable at the thought that this state of affairs should persist, and, at certain moments, I longed to hear of something terrible that she had done, something that would keep us estranged until I was cured, giving us a chance to make it up and to reconstitute in a different and more flexible form the chain that bound us.

In the meantime, I relied on countless events, on countless pleasures, to procure for her in my company the illusion of that happiness which I did not feel capable of giving her. I should have liked, as soon as I was cured, to set off for Venice, but how was I to manage it, if I married Albertine, I who was so jealous of her that even in Paris whenever I decided to stir from my room it was to go out with her? Even when I stayed in the house all the afternoon, my thoughts accompanied her on her drive, traced a distant blue horizon, created round the centre that was myself a fluctuating zone of vague uncertainty.

"How completely," I said to myself, "would Albertine spare me the anguish of separation if, in the course of one of these drives, seeing that I had ceased to talk of marriage, she decided not to come back, and went off to her aunt's without my having to say good-bye to her!" My heart, now that its scar had begun to heal, was beginning to detach itself from hers; I could, in my imagination, shift her, separate her from myself without pain. No doubt, failing myself, some other man would be her husband, and in her freedom she would indulge in those amorous adventures which filled me with horror. But the day was so fine, I was so certain that she would return in the evening, that even if the idea of possible misbehaviour did enter my mind, I could, by an exercise of free will, imprison it in a part of my brain in which it had no more importance than the vices of an imaginary person would have had in my real life; manipulating the supple hinges of my thought, with an energy which I felt, in my head, at once physical and mental, as it were a muscular movement and a spiritual impulse, I had broken away from the state of perpetual preoccupation in which I had hitherto been confined, and was beginning to move in a free atmosphere, in which the idea of sacrificing everything in order to prevent Albertine from marrying someone else and to put an obstacle in the way of her taste for women seemed as unreasonable in my own eyes as in those of a person who had never known her.

However, jealousy is one of those intermittent maladies the cause of which is capricious, arbitrary, always identical in the same patient, sometimes entirely different in another. There are asthma sufferers who can assuage their attacks only by opening the windows, inhaling the high winds, the pure air of mountains, others by taking refuge in the heart of the city, in a smoke-filled room. There are few jealous men whose jealousy does not allow certain derogations. One will consent to infidelity provided he is told of it, another provided it is concealed from him, wherein they are equally absurd, since if the latter is more literally deceived inasmuch as the truth is not disclosed to him, the other demands from that truth the aliment, the extension, the renewal of his sufferings.

What is more, these two inverse idiosyncrasies of jealousy often extend beyond words, whether they implore or reject confidences. We see jealous lovers who are jealous only of the men with whom their mistress has relations in their absence, but allow her to give herself to another man, if it is done with their permission, near at hand, and, if not actually before their eyes, at least under their roof. This case is not at all uncommon among elderly men who are in love with a young woman. They feel the difficulty of winning her favours, sometimes their inability to satisfy her, and, rather than be deceived, prefer to allow into the house, into an adjoining room, some man whom they consider incapable of giving her bad advice, but not incapable of giving her pleasure. With others it will be just the opposite; never allowing their mistress to go out by herself for a single minute in a town they know, keeping her in a state of veritable bondage, they allow her to go for a month to a place they do not know, where they cannot picture to themselves what she may be doing. With regard to Albertine, I had both sorts of soothing quirk. I should not have been jealous if she had enjoyed her pleasures in my vicinity, with my encouragement, completely under my surveillance, thereby relieving me of any fear of mendacity; nor should I have been jealous if she had moved to a place so unfamiliar and remote that I could not imagine, had no possibility of knowing, and no temptation to know, her manner of life. In either case, my uncertainty would have been eliminated by a knowledge or an ignorance equally complete.

The decline of day plunging me back by an act of memory into a cool atmosphere of long ago, I would inhale it with the same delight as Orpheus the subtle air, unknown upon this earth, of the Elysian Fields. But already the day was ending and I would be overcome by the desolation of evening. Looking mechanically at the clock to see how many hours must elapse before Albertine's return, I would see that I still had time to dress and go downstairs to ask my landlady, Mme de Guermantes, for particulars of various pretty articles of clothing which I wanted to give Albertine. Sometimes I would meet the Duchess in the courtyard, going out shopping, even if the weather was bad, in a close-fitting hat and furs. I knew quite well that to a number of intelligent people she was merely a lady like any other, the name Duchesse de Guermantes signifying nothing, now that there are no longer any duchies or principalities; but I had adopted a different point of view in my manner of enjoying people and places. This lady in furs braving the bad weather seemed to me to carry with her all the castles of the territories of which she was duchess, princess, viscountess, as the figures carved over a portal hold in their hands the cathedral they have built or the city they have defended. But my mind's eyes alone could discern these castles and these forests in the gloved hand of the lady in furs who was a cousin of the king. My bodily eyes distinguished in it only, on days when the sky was threatening, an umbrella with which the Duchess did not hesitate to arm herself. "It's much wiser—one can never be certain, I may find myself miles from home, with a cabman demanding a fare *beyond my means*." The words "too dear" and "beyond my means" kept recurring all the time in the Duchess's conversation, as did also: "I'm too poor"—without its being possible to decide whether she spoke thus because she thought it amusing to say that she was poor, being so rich, or because she thought it smart, being so aristocratic (that is to say affecting to be a peasant), not to attach to riches the importance that people give them who are merely rich and nothing else and who look down on the poor. Perhaps it was, rather, a habit contracted at a time in her life when, already rich, but not rich enough to satisfy her needs considering the expense of keeping up all those properties, she felt a certain financial embarrassment which she did not wish to appear to be concealing. The things about which we most often jest are generally, on the contrary, the things that worry us but that we do not wish to appear to be worried by, with perhaps a secret hope of the further advantage that the person to whom we are talking, hearing us treat the matter as a joke, will conclude that it is not true.

But on most evenings at this hour I could count on finding the Duchess at home, and I was glad of this, for it was more convenient for the purpose of discussing at length the particulars that Albertine required. And I would go down almost without thinking how extraordinary it was that I should be calling upon that mysterious Mme de Guermantes of my boyhood simply in order to make use of her for a practical purpose, as one makes use of the telephone, a supernatural instrument before whose miracles we used to stand amazed, and which we now employ without giving it a thought, to summon our tailor or to order an ice cream.

The accessories of costume gave Albertine enormous pleasure. I could not resist giving her some new trifle every day. And whenever she had spoken to me rapturously of a scarf, a stole, a sunshade which, from the window or as they passed one another in the courtyard, her eyes, that so quickly distinguished anything connected with elegance of dress, had seen round the throat, over the shoulders, or in the hand of Mme de Guermantes, knowing how the girl's naturally fastidious taste (refined still further by the lessons in elegance which Elstir's conversation had been to her) would by no means be satisfied by any mere substitute, even of a pretty thing, such as fills its place in the eyes of the common herd but differs from it entirely, I would go in secret to ask the Duchess to explain to me where, how, from what model the article had been created that had taken Albertine's fancy, how I should set about obtaining one exactly similar, in what lay the maker's secret, the charm (what Albertine called the "chic," the "style") of its manner and—the beauty of the material having also its importance—the name and quality of the fabrics that I was to insist upon their using.

When I had mentioned to Albertine, on our return from Balbec, that the Duchesse de Guermantes lived opposite us, in the same building, she had assumed, on hearing the proud title and great name, that more than indifferent, that hostile, contemptuous air which is the sign of an impotent desire in proud and passionate natures. Splendid though Albertine's might be, the qualities that lay buried in it could develop only amid those trammels which are our personal tastes, or that bereavement of those of our tastes that we have been obliged to forgo, as in Albertine's case snobbery: in other words, what are called aversions. Albertine's aversion for society people occupied very little room in her nature, and appealed to me as an aspect of the revolutionary spirit—that is to say an embittered love for the nobility—engraved upon the obverse side of the French character to that which displays the aristocratic style of Mme de Guermantes. Albertine would perhaps not have given a thought to this aristocratic style, in view of the impossibility of achieving it, but remembering that Elstir had spoken to her of the Duchess as the best-dressed woman in Paris, her republican contempt for a duchess gave way to a keen interest in a fashionable woman. She was always asking me to tell her about Mme de Guermantes, and was glad that I should call on the Duchess to obtain advice about her own clothes. No doubt I could have got this from Mme Swann, and indeed I did once write to her with this intention. But Mme de Guermantes seemed to me to carry the art of dressing even further. If, on going down for a moment to see her, after making sure that she had not gone out and leaving word that I was to be warned as soon as Albertine returned, I found the Duchess swathed in the mist of a grey crêpe de Chine gown, I accepted this aspect of her which I felt to be due to complex causes and to be quite unalterable, and steeped myself in the atmosphere which it exhaled, like that of certain late afternoons cushioned in pearly grey by a vaporous fog; if, on the other hand, her indoor gown was Chinese with red and yellow flames, I gazed at it as at a glowing sunset; these garments were not a casual decoration alterable at will, but a given, poetical reality like that of the weather, or the light peculiar to a certain hour of the day.

Of all the outdoor and indoor gowns that Mme de Guermantes wore, those which seemed most to respond to a specific intention, to be endowed with a special significance, were the garments made by Fortuny from old Venetian models. Is it their historical character, or is it rather the fact that each one of them is unique, that gives them so special a significance that the pose of the woman who is wearing one while she waits for you to appear or while she talks to you assumes an exceptional importance, as though the costume had been the fruit of a long deliberation and your conversation was somehow detached from everyday life like a scene in a novel? In the novels of Balzac, we see his heroines put on this or that dress on purpose when they are expecting some particular visitor. The dresses of today have less character, always excepting the creations of Fortuny. There is no room for vagueness in the novelist's description, since the dress does really exist, its smallest details are as naturally preordained as those of a work of art. Before putting on one or another of them, the woman has had to make a choice between two garments that are not more or less alike but each one profoundly individual, and identifiable by name.

But the dress did not prevent me from thinking of the woman. Indeed, Mme de Guermantes seemed to me at this time more attractive than in the days when I was still in love with her. Expecting less of her (I no longer went to visit her for her own sake), it was almost with the relaxed negligence one exhibits when alone, with my feet on the fender, that I listened to her as though I were reading

a book written in the language of long ago. I was sufficiently detached to enjoy in what she said that pure
charm of the French language which we no longer find either in the speech or in the writing of the present day.
I listened to her conversation as to a folk song deliciously
and purely French; I understood why I should have heard
her deriding Maeterlinck (whom in fact she now admired,
out of feminine weak-mindedness, influenced by those literary fashions whose rays spread slowly), as I understood
why Mérimée had derided Baudelaire, Stendhal, Balzac,
Paul-Louis Courier, Victor Hugo, Meilhac, Mallarmé. I
was well aware that the critic had a far more restricted
outlook than his victim, but also a purer vocabulary. That
of Mme de Guermantes, almost as much as that of Saint-
Loup's mother, was enchantingly pure. It is not in the
bloodless pastiches of the writers of today who say *au
fait* (for "in reality"), *singulièrement* (for "in particular"),
étonné (for "struck with amazement"), and the like, that
we recapture the old speech and the true pronunciation of
words, but in conversing with a Mme de Guermantes or a
Françoise. I had learned from the latter, when I was five
years old, that one did not say "the Tarn" but "the Tar";
not "Béarn" but "Béar." The effect of which was that at
twenty, when I began to go into society, I had no need to
be taught there that one ought not to say, like Mme Bontemps, "Madame de Béarn."

It would not be true to say that the Duchess was unaware of this earthy and quasi-peasant quality that survived in her, or was entirely innocent of affectation in
displaying it. But, on her part, it was not so much the
false simplicity of a great lady aping the countrywoman,
or the pride of a duchess bent upon snubbing the rich

ladies who express contempt for the peasants whom they do not know, as the quasi-artistic preference of a woman who knows the charm of what she possesses and is not going to spoil it with a coat of modern varnish. In the same way, everybody used to know a Norman innkeeper, landlord of the "William the Conqueror" at Dives, who had carefully refrained—a rare thing indeed—from giving his hostelry the modern comforts of a hotel, and, albeit a millionaire, retained the speech and the smock of a Norman peasant and allowed you to enter his kitchen and watch him prepare with his own hands, as in a farmhouse, a dinner which was nevertheless infinitely better, and even more expensive, than in the most luxurious hotel.

All the local sap that survives in the old noble families is not enough; it must be embodied in a person of sufficient intelligence not to despise it, not to obliterate it beneath a society veneer. Mme de Guermantes, unfortunately clever and Parisian and, when I knew her, retaining nothing of her native soil but its accent, had at least, when she wished to describe her life as a girl, contrived for her speech one of those compromises (between what would have seemed too spontaneously provincial on the one hand or artificially literary on the other) which form the attraction of George Sand's *La Petite Fadette* or of certain legends related by Chateaubriand in his *Mémoires d'Outre-Tombe*. My chief pleasure was in hearing her tell some anecdote which brought peasants into the picture with herself. The historic names, the old customs, gave to these blendings of the castle with the village a distinctly attractive savour. Having stayed in contact with the lands where it was sovereign, a certain type of aristocracy remains regional, so that the simplest utterance unfolds un-

der our eyes a whole map of France, historical and geographical.

If there was no affectation, no deliberate effort to fabricate a special language, then this style of pronunciation
was a regular museum of French history displayed in conversation. "My great-uncle Fitt-jam" was not at all surprising, for we know that the Fitz-James family are proud
to boast that they are French nobles and do not like to
hear their name pronounced in the English fashion. One
must, however, marvel at the touching docility of the
people who had previously supposed themselves obliged
to pronounce certain names phonetically, and who, all of
a sudden, after hearing the Duchesse de Guermantes
pronounce them otherwise, adopted a pronunciation which
they could never have guessed. Thus the Duchess, who
had had a great-grandfather attending on the Comte
de Chambord, liked to tease her husband for having
turned Orleanist by proclaiming: "We old Frochedorf
people . . ." The visitor, who had always imagined that
he was correct in saying "Frohsdorf," at once turned his
coat, and ever afterwards might be heard saying "Frochedorf."

On one occasion when I asked Mme de Guermantes
who a young blood was whom she had introduced to me
as her nephew but whose name I had failed to catch, I
was none the wiser when from the back of her throat the
Duchess uttered in a very loud but quite inarticulate
voice: "C'est l' . . . i Eon, frère à Robert. He claims to
have the same shape of skull as the ancient Welsh." Then
I realised that she had said: "C'est le petit Léon," and that
this was the Prince de Léon, who was indeed Robert de
Saint-Loup's brother-in-law. "I know nothing about his

skull," she went on, "but the way he dresses, and I must say he does dress very well, is not at all in the style of those parts. Once when I was staying at Josselin, with the Rohans, we all went over to a place of pilgrimage to which peasants had come from pretty well every part of Brittany. A great hulking villager from Léon stood gaping at Robert's brother-in-law in his beige breeches. 'What are you staring at me like that for?' said Léon, 'I bet you don't know who I am.' The peasant admitted as much. 'Well,' said Léon, 'I'm your Prince.' 'Oh!' said the peasant, taking off his cap and apologising. 'I thought you were an *Englische*.'"

And if, seizing this point of departure, I led Mme de Guermantes on to talk about the Rohans (with whom her own family had frequently intermarried), her conversation would become impregnated with a hint of the melancholy charm of the Breton "pardons," the calvary processions, and (as that true poet Pampille would say) with "the pungent flavour of buckwheat pancakes cooked over a gorse fire."

Of the Marquis du Lau (whose sad end is familiar—when, himself deaf, he used to be taken to call on Mme H——who was blind), she would recall the less tragic years when, after the day's sport, at Guermantes, he would change into slippers before having tea with the King of England, to whom he did not regard himself as inferior, and with whom, as we see, he did not stand on ceremony. She described all this so picturesquely that she seemed to invest him with the plumed musketeer hat of the somewhat vainglorious gentlemen of Périgord.

But even in the mere designation of people Mme de

Guermantes, having remained herself a countrywoman—which was her great strength—would take care to distinguish between different provinces, and place people within them, as a Parisian-born woman could never have done, and those simple names, Anjou, Poitou, Périgord, re-created landscapes in her conversation.

To revert to the pronunciation and vocabulary of Mme de Guermantes, it is in this aspect that the nobility shows itself truly conservative, with everything that the word implies in the sense of being at once slightly puerile, slightly dangerous, stubborn in its resistance to change, but at the same time diverting to an artist. I wanted to know the original spelling of the name Jean. I learned it when I received a letter from a nephew of Mme de Villeparisis who signs himself—as he was christened, as he figures in the Almanach de Gotha—Jehan de Villeparisis, with the same handsome, superfluous, heraldic *h* that we admire, illuminated in vermilion or ultramarine, in a Book of Hours or in a stained-glass window.

Unfortunately, I never had time to prolong these visits indefinitely, for I was anxious, as far as possible, not to return home after Albertine. But it was only in driblets that I was able to obtain from Mme de Guermantes that information as to her clothes which was of use in helping me to order costumes similar in style, so far as it was possible for a young girl to wear them, for Albertine.

"For instance, Madame, that evening when you dined with Mme de Saint-Euverte, and then went on to the Princesse de Guermantes, you had a dress that was all red, with red shoes, you were marvellous, you reminded me of a sort of great blood-red blossom, a glittering ruby—now, what was that dress called? Is it the sort of thing that a young girl can wear?"

The Duchess, imparting to her tired features the radiant expression that the Princesse des Laumes used to wear when Swann paid her compliments years ago, glanced quizzically and delightedly, with tears of merriment in her eyes, at M. de Bréauté who was always there at that hour and who sat beaming behind his monocle with an indulgent smile for this intellectual's rigmarole because of the physical excitement of youth which seemed to him to underlie it. The Duchess appeared to be saying: "What's the matter with him? He must be mad." Then turning to me with a winning expression: "I wasn't aware that I looked like a glittering ruby or a blood-red blossom, but I do indeed remember that I had on a red dress: it was red satin, which was being worn that season. Yes, a young girl can wear that sort of thing at a pinch, but you told me that your friend never went out in the evening. It's a full evening dress, not a thing that she can put on to pay calls."

What is extraordinary is that of the evening in question, which after all was not so very remote, Mme de Guermantes remembered nothing but what she had been wearing, and had forgotten a certain incident which nevertheless, as we shall see presently, ought to have mattered to her greatly. It seems that among men and women of action (and society people are men and women of action on a minute, a microscopic scale, but action none the less), the mind, overtaxed by the need to attend to what is going to happen in an hour's time, commits very little to memory. As often as not, for instance, it was not with the object of deliberately misleading and making himself appear innocent of an error of judgment that M. de Norpois, when you reminded him of the prophecies he had uttered with regard to an alliance with Germany of which nothing had ever come, would say: "You must be mistaken, I have no recollection of it whatever, it isn't like me, for in that sort of conversation I am always most laconic, and I would never have predicted the success of one of those *coups d'éclat* which are often nothing more than *coups de tête* and habitually degenerate into *coups de force*. It is beyond question that in the remote future a Franco-German *rapprochement* might come into being and would be highly profitable to both countries; nor would France have the worse of the bargain, I dare say; but I have never spoken of it because the time is not yet ripe, and if you wish to know my opinion, in asking our late enemies to join with us in solemn wedlock, I consider that we would be courting a grave setback and would receive some unpleasant shocks." In saying this M. de Norpois was not being untruthful; he had simply forgotten. We quickly forget what we have not deeply considered, what has been dictated to us by the spirit of imitation, by the passions of the day. These change, and with them our memory undergoes alteration. Even more than diplomats, politicians are unable to remember the point of view which they adopted at a certain moment, and some of their palinodes are due less to an excess of ambition than to a deficiency of memory. As for society people, they remember very little.

Mme de Guermantes assured me that, at the party to which she had gone in a red dress, she did not remember Mme de Chaussepierre's being present, and that I must be mistaken. And yet, heaven knows, the Chaussepierres had been present enough in the minds of both the Duke and the Duchess since then. For the following reason. M. de Guermantes had been the senior vice-president of the Jockey Club when the president died. Certain members of the club who were not popular in society and whose sole pleasure was to blackball the men who did not invite them to their houses launched a campaign against the Duc de Guermantes who, certain of being elected, and relatively indifferent to the presidency which was a small matter for a man in his social position, paid no attention. It was urged against him that the Duchess was a Dreyfusard (the Dreyfus case was long since over, but twenty years later people would still talk about it, and so far only two years had elapsed) and entertained the Rothschilds, that too much consideration had been shown of late to certain great international potentates like the Duc de Guermantes, who was half German. The campaign found sympathetic ears, clubs being always jealous of men who are in the public eye, and detesting big fortunes. Chaussepierre's was by no means meagre, but nobody could be offended by it; he spent hardly a sou, the couple lived in a modest apartment, the wife went about dressed in black wool. A passionate music-lover, she did indeed give little afternoon parties to which many more singers were invited than to the Guermantes. But no one talked about these parties, which occurred without any refreshments, often in the absence of the husband, in the obscurity of the Rue de la Chaise. At the Opéra, Mme de Chaussepierre passed unnoticed, always among people whose names recalled the most "die-hard" element of the intimate circle of Charles X, but who were retiring and unsocial. On the day of the election, to the general surprise, obscurity triumphed over glitter: Chaussepierre, the second vice-president, was elected president of the Jockey, and the Duc de Guermantes was left sitting—that is to say, in the senior vice-president's chair. Of course, being president of the Jockey means little or nothing to princes of the highest rank such as the Guermantes. But not to be president when it is your turn, to be passed over in favour of a Chaussepierre, whose wife's greeting Oriane not only had refused to acknowledge two years earlier but had gone so far as to show offence at being greeted by such an obscure scarecrow, this the Duke did find hard to swallow. He pretended to be above such setbacks, asserting incidentally that it was his long-standing friendship with Swann that was at the root of it. Actually, his anger never cooled.

One curious thing was that nobody had ever before heard the Duc de Guermantes make use of the quite commonplace expression "well and truly"; but ever since the Jockey Club election, whenever anybody referred to the Dreyfus case, out would come "well and truly." "Dreyfus case, Dreyfus case, it's easy to say, and it's a misuse of the term. It's not a question of religion, it's well and truly political." Five years might go by without your hearing him say "well and truly" again, if during that time nobody mentioned the Dreyfus case, but if, at the end of five years, the name Dreyfus cropped up, "well and truly" would at once follow automatically. The Duke could not in any case bear to hear any mention of the case, "which has been responsible," he would say, "for so many misfortunes," although he was really conscious of one only: his failure to become president of the Jockey.

And so on the afternoon in question—the afternoon on which I reminded Mme de Guermantes of the red dress she had worn at her cousin's party—M. de Bréauté was none too well received when, for want of anything better to say, by an association of ideas which remained obscure and which he did not illuminate, he began, twisting his tongue about between his pursed lips: "Talking of the Dreyfus case . . ." (why the Dreyfus case?—we were talking simply of a red dress, and certainly poor Bréauté, whose only desire was to make himself agreeable, can have had no malicious intention, but the mere name of Dreyfus made the Duc de Guermantes knit his Jupiterian brows) ". . . I was told of a rather nice remark, damned clever, 'pon my word, that was made by our friend Cartier" (the reader may care to know that this Cartier, Mme de Villefranche's brother, had not the slightest connexion with the jeweller of that name), "not that I'm in the least surprised, for he's got wit enough and to spare."

"Oh!" broke in Oriane, "he can spare me his wit. I can't tell you how much your friend Cartier has always *bored* me, and I've never been able to understand the boundless charm that Charles de La Trémoïlle and his wife seem to find in the creature, for I meet him there every time I go to their house."

"My dear Dutt-yess," replied Bréauté, who had difficulty in pronouncing *ch*, "I think you're a bit hard on Cartier. It's true that he has perhaps made himself rather excessively at home at the La Trémoïlles', but after all he does provide Tyarles with a sort of—what shall I say?—a sort of *fidus Achates*, and that has become a very rare bird indeed in these days. Anyhow, what he's supposed to have said is that if M. Zola had gone out of his way to stand his trial and to be convicted, it was in order to enjoy the only sensation he had never yet tried, that of being in prison."

"And so he ran away before they could arrest him," Oriane broke in. "Your story doesn't hold water. Besides, even if it was plausible, I find the remark absolutely idiotic. If that's what you call witty!"

"Good grate-ious, my dear Oriane," replied Bréauté who, finding himself contradicted, was beginning to lose confidence, "it's not my remark, I'm telling you it as it was told to me, take it for what it's worth. Anyhow, it earned M. Cartier a proper dressing-down from that excellent fellow La Trémoïlle who, quite rightly, doesn't like people to discuss what one might call, so to speak, current events in his drawing-room, and was all the more annoyed because Mme Alphonse Rothschild was present. Cartier was given a positive roasting by La Trémoïlle."

"Of course," said the Duke, in the worst of tempers, "the Alphonse Rothschilds, even if they have the tact never to speak of that abominable affair, are Dreyfusards at heart, like all the Jews. Indeed that is an argument *ad hominem*" (the Duke was a trifle vague in his use of the expression *ad hominem*) "which is not sufficiently exploited to prove the dishonesty of the Jews. If a Frenchman robs or murders somebody, I don't consider myself bound, because he's a Frenchman like myself, to find him innocent. But the Jews will never admit that one of their co-citizens is a traitor, although they know it perfectly well, and never think of the terrible repercussions" (the Duke was thinking, naturally, of that accursed election of Chaussepierre) "which the crime of one of their people can bring even to . . . Come, Oriane, you're not going to pretend that it isn't damning to the Jews that they all support a traitor. You're not going to tell me that it isn't because they're Jews."

"I'm afraid I am," retorted Oriane (feeling, together with a trace of irritation, a certain desire to hold her own against Jupiter Tonans and also to put "intelligence" above the Dreyfus case). "Perhaps it's just because they are Jews and know themselves that they realise that a person can be a Jew and not necessarily a traitor and anti-French, as M. Drumont seems to maintain. Certainly, if he'd been a Christian, the Jews wouldn't have taken any interest in him, but they did so because they knew quite well that if he hadn't been a Jew people wouldn't have been so ready to think him a traitor *a priori*, as my nephew Robert would say."

"Women never understand a thing about politics," exclaimed the Duke, fastening his gaze upon the Duchess. "That shocking crime is not simply a Jewish cause, but *well and truly* an affair of vast national importance which may bring the most appalling consequences for France, which ought to have driven out all the Jews, whereas I'm sorry to say that the sanctions taken up to the present have been directed (in an ignoble fashion, which should be overruled) not against them but against the most eminent of their adversaries, against men of the highest rank who have been cast aside to the ruin of our unhappy country."

I felt that the conversation had taken a wrong turning and reverted hurriedly to the topic of clothes.

"Do you remember, Madame," I said, "the first time that you were friendly to me . . ."

"The first time that I was friendly to him," she repeated, turning with a smile to M. de Bréauté, the tip of whose nose grew more pointed, and his smile more tender out of politeness to Mme de Guermantes, while his voice, like a knife on the grindstone, emitted a few vague and rusty sounds.

". . . You were wearing a yellow dress with big black flowers."

"But, my dear boy, that's the same thing, those are evening dresses."

"And your hat with the cornflowers that I liked so much! Still, those are all things of the past. I should like to order for the girl I mentioned to you a fur coat like the one you had on yesterday morning. Would it be possible for me to see it?"

"Of course; Hannibal has to be going in a moment. You shall come to my room and my maid will show you everything. Only, my dear boy, though I shall be delighted to lend you anything you like, I must warn you that if you have things from Callot's or Doucet's or Paquin's copied by some small dressmaker, the result is never the same."

"But I never dreamed of going to a small dressmaker. I know quite well it wouldn't be the same thing, but I should be interested to hear you explain why."

"You know quite well I can never explain anything, I'm a perfect fool, I talk like a peasant. It's a question of handiwork, of style; as far as furs go, I can at least give you a line to my furrier, so that he shan't rob you. But you realise that even then it will cost you eight or nine thousand francs."

"And that indoor gown that you were wearing the other evening, with such a curious smell, dark, fluffy, speckled, streaked with gold like a butterfly's wing?"

"Ah! that's one of Fortuny's. Your young lady can quite well wear that in the house. I have heaps of them; you shall see them presently, in fact I can give you one or two if you like. But I should like you to see one that my cousin Talleyrand has. I must write to her for the loan of it."

"But you had such charming shoes as well. Were they Fortuny too?"

"No, I know the ones you mean, they're made of some gold kid we came across in London, when I was shopping with Consuelo Manchester. It was amazing. I could never make out how they did it, it was just like a golden skin, simply that, with a tiny diamond in front. The poor Duchess of Manchester is dead, but if it's any help to you I can write and ask Lady Warwick or the Duchess of Marlborough to try and get me some more. I wonder, now, if I haven't a piece of the stuff left. You might be able to have a pair made here. I shall look for it this evening, and let you know."

Since I endeavoured as far as possible to leave the Duchess before Albertine had returned, it often happened, because of the hour, that I met in the courtyard as I came away from her door M. de Charlus and Morel on their way to have tea at . . . Jupien's, a supreme treat for the Baron! I did not encounter them every day but they went there every day. It may, incidentally, be observed that the regularity of a habit is usually in direct proportion to its absurdity. Really striking things we do as a rule only by fits and starts. But senseless lives, of a kind in which a crackpot deprives himself of all pleasure and inflicts the greatest discomforts upon himself, are those that change least. Every ten years, if we had the curiosity to inquire, we should find the poor wretch still asleep at the hours when he might be living his life, going out at the hours when there is nothing to do but get oneself murdered in the streets, sipping iced drinks when he is hot, still trying desperately to cure a cold. A slight burst of energy, for a single day, would be sufficient to change these habits for good and all. But the fact is that lives of this sort are on the whole peculiar to people who are incapable of energy. Vices are another aspect of these monotonous existences which the exercise of will-power would suffice to render less painful. Both aspects were to be observed simultaneously when M. de Charlus came every day with Morel to have tea at Jupien's. A single outburst had marred this daily custom. The tailor's niece having said one day to Morel: "That's all right then, come tomorrow and I'll stand you tea," the Baron had quite justifiably considered this expression very vulgar on the lips of a person whom he regarded as almost a prospective daughter-in-law, but as he enjoyed being offensive and became intoxicated by his own indignation, instead of his simply asking Morel to give her a lesson in refinement, the whole of their homeward walk was a succession of violent scenes. In the most rude and arrogant tone the Baron said: "So your 'touch' which, I can see, is not necessarily allied to 'tact,' has hindered the normal development of your sense of smell, since you could allow that fetid expression 'stand you tea'—at fifteen centimes, I suppose—to waft its stench of sewage to my regal nostrils? When you have come to the end of a violin solo, have you ever in my house been rewarded with a fart, instead of frenzied applause or a silence more eloquent still since it is due to fear of being unable to restrain, not what your young woman lavishes upon us, but the sob that you have brought to my lips?"

When a public official has had similar reproaches heaped upon him by his chief, he is invariably sacked next day. Nothing, on the contrary, could have been more painful to M. de Charlus than to dismiss Morel, and, fearing indeed that he had gone a little too far, he began to sing the girl's praises in the minutest detail, tastefully expressed and unconsciously sprinkled with impertinent observations. "She is charming; as you are a musician, I suppose that she seduced you by her voice, which is very beautiful in the high notes, where she seems to await the accompaniment of your B sharp. Her lower register appeals to me less, and that must bear some relation to the triple rise of her strange and slender throat, which when it seems to have come to an end begins again; but these are trivial details, it is her silhouette that I admire. And as she is a dressmaker and must be handy with her scissors, you must get her to give me a pretty paper cut-out of herself."

Charlie had paid but little attention to this eulogy, the charms which it extolled in his betrothed having completely escaped his notice. But he said, in reply to M. de Charlus: "That's all right, my boy, I shall tell her off properly, and she won't talk like that again." If Morel addressed M. de Charlus thus as his "boy," it was not that the handsome violinist was unaware that his own years numbered barely a third of the Baron's. Nor did he use the expression as Jupien would have done, but with that simplicity which in certain relations postulates that a suppression of the difference in age has tacitly preceded tenderness (a feigned tenderness in Morel's case, in others a sincere tenderness). Thus, at about this time M. de Charlus received a letter worded as follows: "My dear Palamède, when am I going to see you again? I miss you terribly and think of you often . . . *etc.* Ever yours, PIERRE." M. de Charlus racked his brains to discover which of his relatives it could be who took the liberty of addressing him so familiarly, and must consequently know him intimately, although he failed to recognise the handwriting. All the princes to whom the Almanach de Gotha accords a few lines passed in procession through his mind for a few days. And then, all of a sudden, an address written on the back of the letter enlightened him: the writer was the doorman at a gambling club to which M. de Charlus sometimes went. This doorman had not felt that he was being discourteous in writing in this tone to M. de Charlus, for whom on the contrary he felt the deepest respect. But he felt that it would be uncivil not to address by his Christian name a gentleman who had kissed one several times, and thereby—he naïvely imagined—bestowed his affection on one. M. de Charlus was secretly delighted by this familiarity. He even brought M. de Vaugoubert away from an afternoon party in order to show him the letter. And yet, heaven knows M. de Charlus did not care to go about with M. de Vaugoubert. For the latter, his monocle stuck in his eye, would keep looking round at every passing youth. What was worse, shedding all restraint when he was with M. de Charlus, he adopted a form of speech which the Baron detested. He referred to everything male in the feminine, and, being intensely stupid, imagined this pleasantry to be ex-

tremely witty, and was continually in fits of laughter. As
at the same time he attached enormous importance to his
position in the diplomatic service, these deplorable snig-
gering exhibitions in the street were constantly interrupted
by sudden fits of terror at the simultaneous appearance of
some society person or, worse still, of some civil servant.
"That little telegraph messenger," he said, nudging the
scowling Baron with his elbow, "I used to know her, but
she's turned respectable, the wretch! Oh, that messenger
from the Galeries Lafayette, what a dream! Good God,
there's the head of the Commercial Department. I hope
he didn't notice anything. He's quite capable of mentioning it to the Minister, who would put me on the retired
list, all the more so because it appears he's one himself."
M. de Charlus was speechless with rage. At length, to
bring this infuriating walk to an end, he decided to produce the letter and give it to the Ambassador to read, but
warned him to be discreet, for he liked to pretend that
Charlie was jealous, in order to be able to persuade people
that he was loving. "And," he added with a priceless expression of benevolence, "we ought always to try to cause
as little pain as possible."

Before we come back to Jupien's shop, the author
would like to say how grieved he would be if the reader
were to be offended by his portrayal of such weird characters. On the one hand (and this is the less important aspect of the matter), it may be felt that the aristocracy is,
in these pages, disproportionately accused of degeneracy
in comparison with the other classes of society. Were this
true, it would be in no way surprising. The oldest families
end by displaying, in a red and bulbous nose, or a mis-
shapen chin, characteristic signs in which everyone recog-

nises "blood." But among these persistent and increasingly pronounced features, there are others that are not visible, to wit tendencies and tastes. It would be a more serious objection, were there any foundation for it, to say that all this is alien to us, and that we ought to extract poetry from the truth that is close at hand. Art extracted from the most familiar reality does indeed exist and its domain is perhaps the largest of any. But it is none the less true that considerable interest, not to say beauty, may be found in actions inspired by a cast of mind so remote from anything we feel, from anything we believe, that they remain incomprehensible to us, displaying themselves before our eyes like a spectacle without rhyme or reason. What could be more poetic than Xerxes, son of Darius, ordering the sea to be scourged with rods for having engulfed his fleet?

It is certain that Morel, relying on the influence which his personal attractions gave him over the girl, communicated to her, as coming from himself, the Baron's criticism, for the expression "stand you tea" disappeared as completely from the tailor's shop as, from a salon, some intimate acquaintance who used to call daily but with whom, for one reason or another, the hostess has quarrelled or whom she wants to keep out of sight and meets only outside. M. de Charlus was pleased by the disappearance of "stand you tea." He saw in it a proof of his own ascendancy over Morel and the removal of the one little blemish from the girl's perfection. In short, like everyone of his kind, while genuinely fond of Morel and of the girl who was all but engaged to him, and an ardent advocate of their marriage, he thoroughly enjoyed his power to create, as and when he pleased, more or less inoffensive little scenes, outside and above which he himself remained as Olympian as his brother would have done. Morel had told M. de Charlus that he loved Jupien's niece and wished to marry her, and the Baron enjoyed accompanying his young friend on visits in which he played the part of father-in-law to be, indulgent and discreet. Nothing pleased him better.

My personal opinion is that "stand you tea" had originated with Morel himself, and that in the blindness of her love the young seamstress had adopted an expression from her beloved which jarred horribly with her own pretty way of speaking. This way of speaking, the charming manners that went with it, and the patronage of M. de Charlus brought it about that many customers for whom she had worked received her as a friend, invited her to dinner, and introduced her to their friends, though the girl accepted their invitations only with the Baron's permission and on the evenings that suited him. "A young seamstress received in society?" the reader will exclaim, "how improbable!" If one thinks about it, it was no less improbable that at one time Albertine should have come to see me at midnight, and that she should now be living with me. And yet this might perhaps have been improbable of anyone else, but not of Albertine, fatherless and motherless, leading so free a life that at first I had taken her, at Balbec, for the mistress of a racing cyclist, a girl whose nearest of kin was Mme Bontemps who in the old days, at Mme Swann's, had admired in her niece only her bad manners and who now closed her eyes to anything that might rid her of the girl through a wealthy marriage from which a little of the wealth would trickle into the aunt's pocket (in the highest society, very well-born and very penurious mothers, having succeeded in finding rich brides for their sons, allow themselves to be kept by the young couples, and accept presents of furs, cars and money from daughters-in-law whom they do not like but whom they introduce to their friends).

The day may come when dressmakers will move in society—nor should I find it at all shocking. Jupien's niece, being an exception, cannot yet be regarded as a portent, for one swallow does not make a summer. At all events, if the very modest advancement of Jupien's niece did scandalise some people, Morel was not among them, for on certain points his stupidity was so intense that not only did he label "rather a fool" this girl who was a thousand times cleverer than himself, and foolish perhaps only in loving him, but he actually took to be adventuresses, dressmakers' assistants in disguise playing at being ladies, the highly reputable ladies who invited her to their houses and whose invitations she accepted without a trace of vanity. Naturally these were not Guermantes, or even people who knew the Guermantes, but rich and elegant middle-class women broad-minded enough to feel that it is no disgrace to invite a dressmaker to your house and at the same time snobbish enough to derive some satisfaction from patronising a girl whom His Highness the Baron de Charlus was in the habit, in all propriety of course, of visiting daily.

Nothing could have pleased the Baron more than the idea of this marriage, for he felt that in this way Morel would not be taken from him. It appears that Jupien's niece had been, when scarcely more than a child, "in trouble." And M. de Charlus, while he sang her praises to Morel, would not have been averse to confiding this secret

to his friend—who would have been furious—and thus
sowing the seeds of discord. For M. de Charlus, although
terribly spiteful, resembled a great many kind people who
sing the praises of some man or woman to prove their
own kindness, but would avoid like poison the soothing
words, so rarely uttered, that would be capable of putting
an end to strife. Notwithstanding this, the Baron refrained
from making any insinuation, for two reasons. "If I tell
him," he said to himself, "that his lady-love is not spot-
less, his vanity will be hurt and he will be angry with me.
Besides, how am I to know that he is not in love with
her? If I say nothing, this flash in the pan will soon subside, I shall be able to control their relations as I choose,
and he will love her only to the extent that I shall allow.
If I tell him of his betrothed's past transgression, who
knows whether my Charlie may not still be sufficiently
enamoured of her to become jealous? Then I shall by my
own doing be converting a harmless and easily controlled
flirtation into a serious passion, which is a difficult thing
to manage." For these reasons, M. de Charlus preserved a
silence which had only the outward appearance of discretion, but was in another respect meritorious, since it is almost impossible for men of his sort to hold their tongues.

Moreover, the girl herself was delightful, and M. de
Charlus, who found that she satisfied all the aesthetic interest that he was capable of taking in women, would have
liked to have hundreds of photographs of her. Not such a
fool as Morel, he was delighted to hear the names of the
respectable ladies who invited her to their houses, and
whom his social instinct was able to place, but he took
good care (wishing to retain his hold over him) not to say
so to Charlie, who, a complete oaf in this respect, contin-

ued to believe that, apart from the "violin class" and the Verdurins, there existed only the Guermantes and the few almost royal houses enumerated by the Baron, all the rest being but "dregs" or "scum." Charlie interpreted these expressions of M. de Charlus literally.

What, you will say, M. de Charlus, awaited in vain every day of the year by so many ambassadors and duchesses, not dining with the Prince de Croy because one has to give precedence to the latter, M. de Charlus spent all the time that he denied to these great lords and ladies with a tailor's niece! In the first place—the paramount reason—Morel was there. But even if he had not been there, I see nothing improbable in it, or else you are judging things as one of Aimé's minions would have done. Few except waiters believe that an excessively rich man always wears dazzling new clothes and a supremely smart gentleman gives dinner parties for sixty and travels everywhere by car. They deceive themselves. Very often an excessively rich man wears constantly the same jacket; while a supremely smart gentleman is one who in a restaurant hobnobs only with the staff and, on returning home, plays cards with his valet. This does not prevent him from refusing to give precedence to Prince Murat.

Among the reasons which made M. de Charlus look forward to the marriage of the young couple was this, that Jupien's niece would then be in some sense an extension of Morel's personality, and so of the Baron's power over him and knowledge of him. It would never even have occurred to him to feel the slightest scruple about "betraying," in the conjugal sense, the violinist's future wife. But to have a "young couple" to guide, to feel himself the redoubtable and all-powerful protector of Morel's wife, who, looking upon the Baron as a god, would thereby prove that Morel had inculcated this idea into her, and would thus contain in herself something of Morel—all this would add a new variety to the form of M. de Charlus's domination and bring to light in his "creature," Morel, a creature the more—the husband—that is to say would give the Baron something different, new, curious, to love in him. Perhaps indeed this domination would be stronger now than it had ever been. For whereas Morel by himself, naked so to speak, often resisted the Baron whom he felt certain of winning back, once he was married he would soon fear for his household, his bed and board, his future, would offer to M. de Charlus's wishes a wider target, an easier hold. All this, and even at a pinch, on evenings when he was bored, the prospect of stirring up trouble between husband and wife (the Baron had always been fond of battle-pictures) was pleasing to him. Less pleasing, however, than the thought of the state of dependence upon himself in which the young people would live. M. de Charlus's love for Morel acquired a delicious novelty when he said to himself: "His wife too will be mine just as much as he is; they will always behave in such a way as not to annoy me, they will obey my every whim, and thus she will be a sign (hitherto unknown to me) of what I had almost forgotten, what is so very dear to my heart—that to all the world, to everyone who sees that I protect and house them, to myself, Morel is mine." This testimony, in the eyes of the world and in his own, pleased M. de Charlus more than anything. For the possession of what we love is an even greater joy than love itself. Very often, those who conceal this possession from the world do so only from the fear that the beloved object may be taken from them. And their happiness is diminished by this prudent reticence.

The reader may remember that Morel had once told the Baron that his great ambition was to seduce some young girl, and this one in particular, and that to succeed in his enterprise he would promise to marry her, but, the rape accomplished, would "buzz off"; but what with the declarations of love for Jupien's niece which Morel had poured out to him, M. de Charlus had forgotten this confession. What was more, Morel had quite possibly forgotten it himself. There was perhaps a real gap between Morel's nature—as he had cynically admitted, perhaps even artfully exaggerated it—and the moment at which it would regain control of him. As he became better acquainted with the girl, she had appealed to him, he grew fond of her; he knew himself so little that he even perhaps imagined that he was in love with her, for ever. True, his initial desire, his criminal intention remained, but concealed beneath so many superimposed feelings that there is nothing to prove that the violinist would not have been sincere in saying that this vicious desire was not the true motive of his action. There was, moreover, a brief period during which, without his admitting it to himself precisely, this marriage appeared to him to be necessary. Morel was suffering at the time from violent cramp in the hand, and found himself obliged to contemplate the possibility of having to give up the violin. Since, in everything but his art, he was astonishingly lazy, he was faced with the necessity of finding someone to keep him; and he preferred that it should be Jupien's niece rather than M. de Charlus, this arrangement offering him greater freedom and also a wide choice of different kinds of women, rang-

ing from the apprentices, perpetually changing, whom he
would persuade Jupien's niece to procure for him, to the
rich and beautiful ladies to whom he would prostitute her.
That his future wife might refuse to lend herself to these
ploys, that she could be to such a degree perverse, never
entered Morel's calculations for a moment. However, his
cramp having ceased, they receded into the background
and were replaced by pure love. His violin would suffice,
together with his allowance from M. de Charlus, whose
demands upon him would certainly be reduced once he,
Morel, was married to the girl. This marriage was the urgent thing, because of his love, and in the interest of his
freedom. He asked Jupien for his niece's hand, and Jupien
consulted her. This was wholly unnecessary. The girl's
passion for the violinist streamed around her, like her hair
when she let it down, as did the joy in her beaming eyes.
In Morel, almost everything that was agreeable or advantageous to him awakened moral emotions and words to
correspond, sometimes even melting him to tears. It was
therefore sincerely—if such a word can be applied to
him—that he addressed to Jupien's niece speeches as
steeped in sentimentality (sentimental too are the speeches
that so many young noblemen who look forward to a life
of idleness address to some charming daughter of a bourgeois plutocrat) as the theories he had expounded to
M. de Charlus about the seduction and deflowering of
virgins had been steeped in unmitigated vileness. However, there was another side to this virtuous enthusiasm
for a person who afforded him pleasure and to the solemn
promises that he made to her. As soon as the person
ceased to cause him pleasure, or indeed if, for example,
the obligation to fulfil the promises that he had made

caused him displeasure, she at once became the object of an antipathy which he sought to justify in his own eyes and which, after some neurasthenic disturbance, enabled him to prove to himself, as soon as the balance of his nervous system was restored, that, even looking at the matter from a purely virtuous point of view, he was released from any obligation.

Thus, towards the end of his stay at Balbec, he had managed somehow to lose all his money and, not daring to mention the matter to M. de Charlus, looked about for someone to whom he might appeal. He had learned from his father (who at the same time had forbidden him ever to become a "sponger") that in such circumstances the correct thing is to write to the person whom you intend to ask for a loan saying that you have a "business matter to discuss with him," that you would like to make a "business appointment." This magic formula had so enchanted Morel that he would, I believe, have been glad to lose his money, simply to have the pleasure of asking for a "business" appointment. In the course of his life he had found that the formula did not have quite the magic power that he supposed. He had discovered that certain people, to whom otherwise he would never have written at all, did not reply within five minutes of receiving his letter asking to "talk business" to them. If the afternoon went by without his receiving an answer, it never occurred to him that, even on the most optimistic assumption, it was quite possible that the gentleman addressed had not yet come home, or had had other letters to write, if indeed he had not gone away, or fallen ill, or something of that sort. If, by an extraordinary stroke of luck, Morel was given an appointment for the following morning, he would accost his intended creditor with: "I was quite surprised not to get an answer, and I wondered whether there was anything wrong; but I'm glad to see you're quite well," and so forth. So, at Balbec, without telling me that he wished to talk "business" to him, he had asked me to introduce him to that very Bloch to whom he had been so unpleasant a week earlier in the train. Bloch had not hesitated to lend him—or rather to get M. Nissim Bernard to lend him—five thousand francs. From that moment Morel had worshipped Bloch. He asked himself with tears in his eyes how he could show his gratitude to a person who had saved his life. Finally, I undertook to ask on his behalf for a thousand francs a month from M. de Charlus, a sum which he would at once forward to Bloch who would thus find himself repaid within quite a short time. The first month, Morel, still under the impact of Bloch's generosity, sent him the thousand francs immediately, but after this he doubtless decided that the remaining four thousand francs might be put to more satisfactory use, for he began to speak extremely ill of Bloch. The mere sight of him was enough to fill his mind with dark thoughts, and Bloch himself having forgotten the exact amount that he had lent Morel, and having asked him for 3,500 francs instead of 4,000, which would have left the violinist 500 francs to the good, the latter took the line that, in view of so preposterous a fraud, not only would he not pay another centime but his creditor might consider himself very fortunate if Morel did not bring an action against him. As he said this his eyes blazed. Not content with asserting that Bloch and M. Nissim Bernard had no cause for resentment against him, he was soon saying that they might count themselves lucky that he showed no resentment towards them. Finally, M. Nissim Bernard having apparently stated that Thibaud played as well as Morel, the latter felt that he ought to take the matter to court, such a remark being calculated to damage him professionally; then, since there was no longer any justice in France, especially against the Jews (anti-semitism having been in Morel the natural effect of a loan of 5,000 francs from a Jew), took to never going out without a loaded revolver.

A similar splenetic reaction in the wake of keen affection was soon to occur in Morel with regard to the tailor's niece. It is true that M. de Charlus may have been to some extent unwittingly responsible for this change, for he was in the habit of declaring, without meaning a word of it, and merely to tease them, that once they were married he would never see them again and would leave them to fend for themselves. This idea was in itself quite insufficient to detach Morel from the girl; but, lurking in his mind, it was ready when the time came to combine with other related ideas capable, once the compound was formed, of becoming a powerful disruptive agent.

It was not very often, however, that I was fated to meet M. de Charlus and Morel. Often they had already gone into Jupien's shop when I came away from the Duchess, for the pleasure that I found in her company was such that I was led to forget not merely the anxious expectation that preceded Albertine's return, but even the hour of that return.

I shall set apart from the other days on which I lingered at Mme de Guermantes's one that was marked by a trivial incident the cruel significance of which entirely escaped me and was not brought home to me until long afterwards. On this particular evening, Mme de

Guermantes had given me, knowing that I was fond of them, some branches of syringa which had been sent to her from the South. When I left her and went upstairs to our flat, Albertine had already returned, and on the staircase I ran into Andrée, who seemed to be distressed by the powerful smell of the flowers that I was bringing home.

"What, are you back already?" I said.

"Only a moment ago, but Albertine had some letters to write, so she sent me away."

"You don't think she's up to any mischief?"

"Not at all, she's writing to her aunt, I think. But you know how she dislikes strong scents, she won't be particularly thrilled by your syringa."

"How stupid of me! I shall tell Françoise to put them out on the service stairs."

"Do you imagine Albertine won't notice the scent of them on you? Next to tuberoses they've the strongest scent of any flower, I always think. Anyhow, I believe Françoise has gone out shopping."

"But in that case, as I haven't got my latchkey, how am I to get in?"

"Oh, you've only got to ring the bell. Albertine will let you in. Besides, Françoise may have come back by this time."

I said good-bye to Andrée. I had no sooner pressed the bell than Albertine came to open the door, which she had some difficulty in doing since, in the absence of Françoise, she did not know where to turn on the light. At last she managed to let me in, but the scent of the syringa put her to flight. I took them to the kitchen, so that meanwhile my mistress, leaving her letter unfinished (I had no idea why), had time to go to my room, from which she called to me, and to lie down on my bed. Once again, at the actual moment I saw nothing in all this that was not perfectly natural, at the most a little confused, but in any case unimportant. She had nearly been caught with Andrée, and had snatched a brief respite for herself by turning out all the lights, going to my room so that I should not see the disorder of her bed, and pretending to be writing a letter. But we shall see all this—the truth of which I never ascertained—later on.

In general, apart from this isolated incident, everything would be quite normal when I returned from my visits to the Duchess. Since Albertine never knew whether I might not wish to go out with her before dinner, I usually found in the hall her hat, coat and umbrella, which she had left lying there in case they should be needed. As soon as I caught sight of them on opening the door, the atmosphere of the house became breathable once more. I felt that, instead of a rarefied air, it was happiness that filled it. I was rescued from my melancholy, the sight of these trifles gave me possession of Albertine, and I would rush to greet her.

On the days when I did not go down to Mme de Guermantes, so that time should not hang too heavy for me during the hour that preceded Albertine's return, I would take up an album of Elstir's work, one of Bergotte's books, or Vinteuil's sonata. Then, just as those works of art which seem to address themselves to the eye or ear alone require that, if we are to appreciate them, our awakened intelligence shall collaborate closely with those organs, I would unconsciously summon up from within me the dreams that Albertine had inspired in me long ago before I knew her and that had been quenched by the routine of everyday life. I would cast them into the composer's phrase or the painter's image as into a crucible, or use them to enrich the book that I was reading. And no doubt the latter appeared all the more vivid in consequence. But Albertine herself gained just as much by being thus transported from one into the other of the two worlds to which we have access and in which we can place alternately the same object, by escaping thus from the crushing weight of matter to play freely in the fluid spaces of the mind. I found myself suddenly and for an instant capable of passionate feelings for this wearisome girl. She had at that moment the appearance of a work by Elstir or Bergotte, I felt a momentary ardour for her, seeing her in the perspective of imagination and art.

Presently I would be told that she had returned; though there was a standing order that her name was not to be mentioned if I was not alone, and if, for instance, I had Bloch in the room with me, I would compel him to stay a little longer so that there should be no risk of his meeting my mistress in the hall. For I concealed the fact that she was staying in the house, and even that I ever saw her there, so afraid was I that one of my friends might become infatuated with her, and wait for her outside, or that in a momentary encounter in the passage or the hall she might make a signal and fix a rendezvous. Then I would hear the rustle of Albertine's skirt on her way to her own room, for, out of tact and also no doubt in the spirit in which, when we used to go to dinner at La Raspelière, she went out to great lengths to ensure that I should have no cause for jealousy, she did not come to my room when she knew that I was not alone. But it was not only for this reason, as I suddenly realised. I remembered; I had known a different Albertine then all at once she had changed into another, the Albertine of today. And for this change I could hold no one responsible but myself. Everything that she would have admitted to me readily and willingly when we were simply good friends had ceased to flow from her as soon as she had suspected that I was in love with her, or, without perhaps thinking of the name of Love, had divined the existence in me of an inquisitorial sentiment that desires to know, yet suffers from knowing, and seeks to learn still more. Ever since that day, she had concealed everything from me. She kept away from my room whether she thought my visitor was male or (as was not often the case) female, she whose eyes used at one time to sparkle so brightly whenever I mentioned a girl: "You must try and get her to come here. I'd be amused to meet her." "But she's what you call a bad type." "Precisely, that'll make it all the more fun." At that moment, I might perhaps have learned all that there was to know. And even when, in the little Casino, she had withdrawn her breasts from Andrée's, I believe that this was due not to my presence but to that of Cottard, who was capable, she doubtless thought, of giving her a bad reputation. And yet, even then, she had already begun to "freeze," confiding words no longer issued from her lips, her gestures became guarded. Then she had rid herself of everything that might have disturbed me. To those parts of her life of which I knew nothing she ascribed a character the inoffensiveness of which my ignorance conspired to accentuate. And now the transformation was completed; she went straight to her room if I was not alone, not merely from fear of disturbing me, but in order to show me that she was not interested in other people. There was one thing alone that she would never again do for me, that she would have done only in the days when it would have left me indifferent, that she would then have done without hesitation for that very reason, namely, confess. I should be for ever reduced, like a judge, to drawing uncertain conclusions from verbal indiscretions that were perhaps explicable without postulating guilt. And always she would feel that I was jealous, and judging her.

Our engagement was assuming the aspect of a criminal trial, and gave her the timorousness of a guilty party. Now she changed the conversation whenever it turned on people, men or women, who were not of mature years. It was when she had not yet suspected that I was jealous of her that I should have asked her to tell me what I wanted to know. One ought always to take advantage of that period. It is then that one's mistress tells one about her pleasures and even the means by which she conceals them from other people. She would no longer have admitted to me now as she had admitted at Balbec, partly because it was true, partly by way of apology for not making her affection for me more evident, for I had already begun to weary her even then, and she had gathered from my kindness to her that she need not show as much affection to me as to others in order to obtain more from me than from them—she would no longer have admitted to me now as she had admitted then: "I think it stupid to let people see who one loves. I'm just the opposite: as soon as a person attracts me, I pretend not to take any notice. In that way, nobody knows anything about it."

What, it was the same Albertine of today, with her

pretensions to frankness and indifference to everyone, who had told me that! She would never have expressed such a rule of conduct to me now! She contented herself, when she was chatting to me, with applying it by saying of some girl or other who might cause me anxiety: "Oh, I don't know, I didn't even look at her, she's too insignificant." And from time to time, to anticipate discoveries which I might make, she would proffer the sort of confessions whose very tone, before one knows the reality which they are intended to distort, to exculpate, already betrays them as lies.

As I listened to Albertine's footsteps with the consoling pleasure of thinking that she would not be going out again that evening, I marvelled at the thought that, for this girl whom at one time I had supposed that I could never possibly succeed in knowing, returning home every day actually meant returning to my home. The fugitive and fragmentary pleasure, compounded of mystery and sensuality, which I had felt at Balbec, on the night when she had come to sleep at the hotel, had been completed and stabilised, filling my hitherto empty dwelling with a permanent store of domestic, almost conjugal, ease that radiated even into the passages and upon which all my senses, either actively or, when I was alone, in imagination as I awaited her return, peacefully fed. When I had heard the door of Albertine's room shut behind her, if I had a friend with me I made haste to get rid of him, not leaving him until I was quite sure that he was on the staircase, down which I might even escort him for a few steps.

Coming towards me in the passage, Albertine would greet me with: "I say, while I'm taking off my things, I shall send you Andrée. She's looked in for a minute to say hello." And still swathed in the big grey veil, falling from her chinchilla toque, which I had given her at Balbec, she would turn from, me and go back to her room, as though she had guessed that Andrée, whom I had entrusted with the duty of watching over her, would presently, by relating their day's adventures in full detail, mentioning their meeting with some person of their acquaintance, impart a certain clarity of outline to the vague regions in which the day-long excursion had run its course and which I had been incapable of imagining.

Andrée's defects had become more marked; she was no longer as pleasant a companion as when I first knew her. One noticed now, on the surface, a sort of sour uneasiness, ready to gather like a swell on the sea, merely if I happened to mention something that gave pleasure to Albertine and myself. This did not prevent Andrée from being nicer to me and liking me better—and I had frequent proof of this—than other more amiable people. But the slightest look of happiness on a person's face, if it was not caused by herself, gave a shock to her nerves, as unpleasant as that given by a banging door. She could accept sufferings in which she had no part, but not pleasures; if she saw that I was unwell, she was distressed, was sorry for me, would have stayed to nurse me. But if I displayed a satisfaction as trifling as that of stretching myself with a blissful expression as I shut a book, saying: "Ah! I've just spent two delightful hours reading. What an enjoyable book!", these words, which would have given pleasure to my mother, to Albertine, to Saint-Loup, provoked in Andrée a sort of disapprobation, perhaps simply a sort of nervous discomfort. My satisfactions caused her an irritation which she was unable to conceal. These defects were supplemented by others of a more serious nature; one day when I mentioned the young man so learned in matters of racing, gambling and golf, so uneducated in everything else, whom I had met with the little band at Balbec, Andrée said with a sneer: "You know that his father is a swindler, he only just missed being prosecuted. They're swaggering now more than ever, but I tell everybody about it. I should love them to bring an action for slander against me. I'd have something to say in the witness-box!" Her eyes sparkled. In fact I discovered that the father had done nothing wrong, and that Andrée knew this as well as anybody. But she had felt spurned by the son, had looked around for something that would embarrass him, put him to shame, and had concocted a whole string of evidence which she imagined herself called upon to give in court, and, by dint of repeating the details to herself, was perhaps herself unsure whether they were true or not. And so, in her present state (and even without her brief, mad hatreds), I should not have wished to see her, if only because of the malevolent touchiness that surrounded with a sour and frigid carapace her warmer and better nature. But the information which she alone could give me about my mistress interested me too much for me to be able to neglect so rare an opportunity of acquiring it.

Andrée would come into my room, shutting the door behind her. They had met a girl they knew, whom Albertine had never mentioned to me.

"What did they talk about?"

"I can't tell you; I took advantage of the fact that Albertine wasn't alone to go and buy some wool."

"Buy some wool?"

"Yes, it was Albertine who asked me to get it."

"All the more reason not to have gone. It was perhaps a pretext to get you out of the way."

"But she asked me to go for it before we met her friend."

"Ah!" I would reply, breathing again. At once my suspicions were revived: she might, for all I knew, have made an appointment beforehand with her friend and have provided herself with an excuse to be left alone when the time came. Besides, could I be certain that it was not my former hypothesis (according to which Andrée did not always tell me the truth) that was correct? Andrée was perhaps in league with Albertine.

Love, I used to say to myself at Balbec, is what we feel for a person; our jealousy seems rather to be directed towards that person's actions; we feel that if she were to tell us everything, we might perhaps easily be cured of our love. However skilfully jealousy is concealed by him who suffers from it, it is very soon detected by her who has inspired it, and who applies equal skill in her turn. She seeks to put us off the scent of what might make us unhappy, and easily succeeds, for, to the man who is not forewarned, how should a casual remark reveal the false-hoods that lie beneath it? We do not distinguish this re-mark from the rest; spoken apprehensively, it is received unheedingly. Later on, when we are alone, we shall return to this remark, which will seem to us not altogether con-sistent with the facts of the case. But do we remember it correctly? There seems to arise spontaneously in us, with regard to it and to the accuracy of our memory, a doubt of the sort which, in certain nervous conditions, prevents us from remembering whether we have bolted the door, no less after the fiftieth time than after the first; it would seem that we can repeat the action indefinitely without its ever being accompanied by a precise and liberating memory. But at least we can shut the door again for the fifty-first time. Whereas the disturbing remark exists in the past, in an imperfect hearing of it which it is not within our power to re-enact. Then we concentrate our attention upon other remarks which conceal nothing, and the sole remedy, which we do not want, is to be ignorant of everything in order not to have any desire for further knowledge.

As soon as jealousy is discovered, it is regarded by the person who is its object as a challenge which justifies deception. Moreover, in our endeavour to learn something, it is we who have taken the initiative in lying and deceit. Andrée or Aimé may promise us that they will say nothing, but will they keep their promise? Then Bloch could promise nothing because he knew nothing. And Albertine has only to talk to any of the three in order to learn, with the help of what Saint-Loup would have called "cross-checking," that we are lying to her when we claim to be indifferent to her actions and morally incapable of having her watched. Following thus upon my habitual boundless uncertainty as to what Albertine might be doing, an uncertainty too indeterminate not to remain painless, which was to jealousy what that incipient forgetfulness in which assuagement is born of vagueness is to grief, the little fragment of an answer which Andrée had just brought me at once began to raise fresh questions; in exploring one sector of the vast zone that extended round me, I had succeeded only in pushing back still further that unknowable thing which, when we seek to form a definite idea of it, another person's life invariably is to us. I would continue to interrogate Andrée while Albertine, from tact and in order to leave me free (was she conscious of this?) to question her friend, prolonged her toilet in her own room.

"I think Albertine's uncle and aunt both like me," I would thoughtlessly remark to Andrée, forgetting her peculiar nature.

At once I would see her glutinous features change, like a mixture that has turned; her face would seem permanently clouded. Her mouth would become bitter. Nothing remained in Andrée of that juvenile gaiety which, like all the little band and notwithstanding her delicate health, she had displayed in the year of my first visit to Balbec and which now (it is true that Andrée was several years older) became so rapidly eclipsed in her. But I would make it reappear involuntarily before Andrée left me that evening to go home to dinner. "Somebody was singing your praises to me today in the most glowing terms," I would say to her. Immediately a ray of joy would beam from her eyes; she looked as though she really loved me. She avoided my gaze but smiled at the empty air with a pair of eyes that had suddenly become quite round. "Who was it?" she would ask with an artless, avid interest. I would tell her, and, whoever it was, she was delighted.

Then the time would come for her to leave me. Albertine would come back to my room; she had undressed, and was wearing one of the crêpe de Chine dressinggowns or Japanese kimonos which I had asked Mme de Guermantes to describe to me, and for some of which supplementary details had been furnished me by Mme Swann, in a letter that began: "After your long eclipse, I felt as I read your letter about my *tea-gowns* that I was hearing from a ghost."

Albertine had on her feet a pair of black shoes studded with brilliants which Françoise indignantly called clogs and which were modelled upon those which, from the drawing-room window, she had seen Mme de Guermantes wearing in the evening, just as a little later Albertine took to wearing slippers, some of gold kid, others of chinchilla, the sight of which gave me great pleasure because they were all of them signs (which other shoes would not have been) that she was living under my roof. She had also certain things which had not come to her from me, including a fine gold ring. I admired upon it the outspread wings of an eagle. "It was my aunt who gave me it," she explained. "She can be quite nice sometimes after all. It makes me feel terribly old, because she gave it to me on my twentieth birthday."

Albertine took a far keener interest in all these pretty things than the Duchess, because, like every obstacle in the way of a possession (in my own case the ill health which made travel so difficult and so desirable), poverty, more generous than opulence, gives to women far more than the clothes that they cannot afford to buy: the desire for those clothes which goes hand in hand with a genuine, detailed, thorough knowledge of them. She, because she had never been able to afford these things, and I, because in ordering them for her I was seeking to give her pleasure, were both of us like students who already know all about the pictures which they are longing to go to Dresden or Vienna to see. Whereas rich women, amid the vast quantities of their hats and gowns, are like those tourists to whom a visit to a gallery, being preceded by no desire, gives merely a sensation of bewilderment, boredom and exhaustion. A particular toque, a particular sable coat, a particular Doucet dressing-gown with pink-lined sleeves, assumed for Albertine, who had observed them, coveted them and, thanks to the exclusiveness and meticulousness that characterise desire, had at once isolated them from the rest against an empty background in which the lining or the sash stood out to perfection, and studied them down to the smallest detail—and for myself who had gone to Mme de Guermantes in quest of an explanation of what constituted the peculiar merit, the superiority, the stylishness of each garment and the inimitable cut of the great designer—an importance, a charm which they certainly did not possess for the Duchess, surfeited before she had even acquired an appetite, and would not, indeed, have possessed for me had I seen them a few years earlier while accompanying some lady of fashion on one of her wearisome tours of the dressmakers' shops.

To be sure, a woman of fashion was what Albertine too was gradually becoming. For, while each of the things that I ordered for her was the prettiest of its kind, with all the refinements that might have been added to it by Mme de Guermantes or Mme Swann, she was beginning to possess these things in abundance. But it mattered little, since she had admired them beforehand and in isolation. When we have been smitten by one painter, then by another, we may end by feeling for the whole gallery an admiration that is not frigid, for it is made up of successive enthusiasms, each one exclusive in its day, which finally have joined forces and become reconciled in one whole.

She was not, moreover, frivolous, read a great deal when she was alone, and read aloud to me when we were together. She had become extremely intelligent. She would say, quite falsely in fact: "I'm appalled when I think that but for you I should still be quite ignorant. Don't contradict. You have opened up a world of ideas to me which I never suspected, and whatever I may have become I owe entirely to you."

It will be remembered that she had spoken in similar terms of my influence over Andrée. Had either of them a real feeling for me? And, in themselves, what were Albertine and Andrée? To know the answer, I should have to immobilise you, to cease to live in that perpetual state of expectancy ending always in a different presentment of you, I should have to cease to love you in order to fix your image, cease to be conscious of your interminable and always disconcerting arrival, O girls, O successive rays in the swirling vortex wherein we throb with emotion on seeing you reappear while barely recognising you, in the dizzy velocity of light. We might perhaps remain unaware of that velocity, and everything would seem to us motionless, did not a sexual attraction set us in pursuit of you, O drops of gold, always dissimilar and always surpassing our expectation! Each time, a girl so little resembles what she was the time before (shattering, as soon as we catch sight of her, the memory that we had retained of her and the desire that we had proposed to gratify), that the stability of nature which we ascribe to her is purely fictitious and a convention of speech. We have been told that some pretty girl is tender, loving, full of the most delicate feelings. Our imagination accepts this assurance, and when we behold for the first time, beneath the woven

girdle of her golden hair, the rosy disc of her face, we are
almost afraid that this too virtuous sister, cooling our ardour by her very virtue, can never be to us the lover for
whom we have been longing. What secrets, however, we
confide to her from the first moment, on the strength of
that nobility of heart, what plans we make together! But a
few days later, we regret that we were so confiding, for
the rosy-cheeked girl, at our second meeting, addresses us
in the language of a lascivious Fury. As for the successive
facets which after pulsating for some days the roseate
light, now eclipsed, presents to us, it is not even certain
that a momentum external to these girls has not modified
their aspect, and this might well have happened with my
band of girls at Balbec. People extol to us the gentleness,
the purity of a virgin. But afterwards they feel that something more spicy would please us better, and recommend
her to show more boldness. In herself was she one more
than the other? Perhaps not, but capable of yielding to
any number of different possibilities in the headlong current of life. With another, whose whole attraction lay in a
certain ruthlessness (which we counted upon subduing to
our own will), as, for instance, with the fearsome jumping
girl at Balbec who grazed in her leaps the bald pates of
startled old gentlemen, what a disappointment when, a
new facet of her personality being presented to us, just as
we are making tender declarations fired by the memory of
her cruelty to others, we hear her telling us, by way of an
opening gambit, that she is shy, that she can never say
anything intelligent to anyone at a first introduction, so
frightened is she, and that it is only after a fortnight or so
that she will be able to talk to us at her ease. The steel
has turned to cotton wool, and there is nothing left for us

to attempt to break down, since of her own accord she has shed her hard integument. Of her own accord, but through our fault perhaps, for the tender words which we addressed to Harshness had perhaps, even without any deliberate calculation on her part, suggested to her that she ought to be gentle. (Distressing as the change may have been to us, it was not altogether maladroit, for our gratitude for all her gentleness may exact more from us than our delight at overcoming her cruelty.)

I do not say that a day will not come when, even to these luminous girls, we shall assign sharply defined characters, but that will be because they will have ceased to interest us, because their entry upon the scene will no longer be, for our heart, the apparition which it expected to be different and which, each time, leaves it overwhelmed by fresh incarnations. Their immobility will come from our indifference to them, which will deliver them up to the judgment of our intelligence. The latter's conclusions will not in fact be very much more categorical, for after deciding that some defect, predominant in the one, was happily absent from the other, it will see that this defect was offset by some precious quality. So that, from the false judgment of our intelligence, which comes into play only when we have lost interest, there will emerge well-defined, stable characters of girls, which will enlighten us no more than did the surprising faces that used to appear every day when, in the bewildering speed of our expectation, they presented themselves daily, weekly, too different to allow us, since their course was never arrested, to classify them, to award degrees of merit. As for our sentiments, we have said so too often to repeat it here, as often as not love is no more than the association of the image of a girl (whom otherwise we should soon have found intolerable) with the heartbeats inseparable from an endless wait in vain and her failure to turn up at the end of it. All this is true not only of impressionable young men in the face of changeable girls. At the stage that our narrative has now reached, it appears, as I later learned, that Jupien's niece had altered her opinion of Morel and M. de Charlus. My chauffeur, to reinforce her love for Morel, had extolled to her, as existing in the violinist, boundless refinements of delicacy in which she was all too ready to believe. And at the same time Morel never ceased to complain to her of the despotic treatment that he received from M. de Charlus, which she ascribed to malevolence, never imagining that it could be due to love. She was moreover forced to acknowledge that M. de Charlus was a tyrannical presence at all their meetings. And in corroboration of this, she had heard society women speak of the Baron's atrocious spitefulness. Lately, however, her judgment had been completely reversed. She had discovered in Morel (without ceasing for that reason to love him) depths of malevolence and perfidy, compensated it was true by frequent gentleness and genuine sensitivity, and in M. de Charlus an immense and unsuspected kindness mixed with incomprehensible asperities. And so she had been no more able to arrive at a definite judgment of what, each in himself, the violinist and his protector really were, than I was able to form of Andrée, whom nevertheless I saw every day, or of Albertine who was living with me.

On the evenings when the latter did not read aloud to me, she would play me some music or begin a game of draughts, or a conversation, which I would interrupt with

kisses. Our relations had a simplicity that made them
soothing. The very emptiness of her life gave Albertine a
sort of eagerness to comply with the few demands I made
on her. Behind this girl, as behind the purple light that
used to filter beneath the curtains of my room at Balbec,
while outside the concert blared, there shone the blue-
green undulations of the sea. Was she not, after all (she in
whose being there now existed an idea of me so habitual
and familiar that, next to her aunt, I was perhaps the person whom she distinguished least from herself), the girl
whom I had seen the first time at Balbec, beneath her flat
cap, with her insistent laughing eyes, a stranger still, slender as a silhouette projected against the waves? These effi-
gies preserved intact in our memory astonish us, when we
recall them, by their dissimilarity from the person we
know, and we realise what a task of remodelling is performed every day by habit. In the charm that Albertine
had in Paris, by my fireside, there still survived the desire
that had been aroused in me by that insolent and blossoming cortége along the beach, and just as Rachel retained in Saint-Loup's eyes, even after he had made her
abandon it, the glamour of her stage life, so in this Albertine cloistered in my house, far from Balbec whence I had
hurried her away, there persisted the excitement, the social confusion, the restless futility, the roving desires of
seaside life. She was so effectively caged that on certain
evenings I did not even ask her to leave her room for
mine, she whom at one time all the world pursued, whom
I had found it so hard to overtake as she sped past on her
bicycle, whom the lift-boy himself was unable to bring
back to me, leaving me with little hope of her coming, although I sat up waiting for her all night. Had not Alber-

tine been—out there in front of the hotel—like a great actress of the blazing beach, arousing jealousy when she advanced upon that natural stage, speaking to no one, jostling the habitués, dominating her friends? And was not this so greatly coveted actress the same who, withdrawn by me from the stage, shut up in my house, was now here, shielded from the desires of all those who might henceforth seek for her in vain, sitting now in my room, now in her own, engaged in some work of design or engraving?

No doubt, in the first days at Balbec, Albertine seemed to exist on a parallel plane to that on which I was living, but one that had converged on it (after my visit to Elstir) and had finally joined it, as my relations with her, at Balbec, in Paris, then at Balbec again, grew more intimate. Moreover, what a difference there was between the two pictures of Balbec, on my first visit and on my second, pictures composed of the same villas from which the same girls emerged by the same sea! In Albertine's friends at the time of my second visit, whom I knew so well, whose good and bad qualities were so clearly engraved on their features, how could I recapture those fresh, mysterious strangers who once could not thrust open the doors of their chalets with a screech over the sand or brush past the quivering tamarisks without making my heart beat? Their huge eyes had sunk into their faces since then, doubtless because they had ceased to be children, but also because those ravishing strangers, those actresses of that first romantic year, about whom I had gone ceaselessly in quest of information, no longer held any mystery for me. They had become for me, obedient to my whims, a mere grove of budding girls, from among whom I was not a little proud of having plucked, and hidden away from the rest of the world, the fairest rose.

Between the two Balbec settings, so different one from the other, there was the interval of several years in Paris, the long expanse of which was dotted with all the visits that Albertine had paid me. I saw her in the different years of my life occupying, in relation to myself, different positions which made me feel the beauty of the intervening spaces, that long lapse of time during which I had remained without seeing her and in the diaphanous depths of which the roseate figure that I saw before me was carved with mysterious shadows and in bold relief. This was due also to the superimposition not merely of the successive images which Albertine had been for me, but also of the great qualities of intelligence and heart, and of the defects of character, all alike unsuspected by me, which Albertine, in a germination, a multiplication of herself, a fleshy efflorescence in sombre colours, had added to a nature that formerly could scarcely have been said to exist, but was now difficult to plumb. For other people, even those of whom we have dreamed so much that they have come to seem no more than pictures, figures by Benozzo Gozzoli against a greenish background, of whom we were inclined to believe that they varied only according to the point of vantage from which we looked at them, their distance from us, the effect of light and shade, such people, while they change in relation to ourselves, change also in themselves, and there had been an enrichment, a solidification and an increase of volume in the figure once simply outlined against the sea.

Moreover, it was not only the sea at the close of day that existed for me in Albertine, but at times the drowsy murmur of the sea upon the shore on moonlit nights. For sometimes, when I got up to fetch a book from my father's study, my mistress, having asked my permission to lie down while I was out of the room, was so tired after her long outing in the morning and afternoon in the open air that, even if I had been away for a moment only, when I returned I found her asleep and did not wake her. Stretched out at full length on my bed, in an attitude so natural that no art could have devised it, she reminded me of a long blossoming stem that had been laid there; and so in a sense she was: the faculty of dreaming, which I possessed only in her absence, I recovered at such moments in her presence, as though by falling asleep she had become a plant. In this way, her sleep realised to a certain extent the possibility of love: alone, I could think of her, but I missed her, I did not possess her; when she was present, I spoke to her, but was too absent from myself to be able to think of her; when she was asleep, I no longer had to talk, I knew that I was no longer observed by her, I no longer needed to live on the surface of myself.

By shutting her eyes, by losing consciousness, Albertine had stripped off, one after another, the different human personalities with which she had deceived me ever since the day when I had first made her acquaintance. She was animated now only by the unconscious life of plants, of trees, a life more different from my own, more alien, and yet one that belonged more to me. Her personality was not constantly escaping, as when we talked, by the outlets of her unacknowledged thoughts and of her eyes. She had called back into herself everything of her that lay outside, had withdrawn, enclosed, reabsorbed herself into her body. In keeping her in front of my eyes, in my hands, I had an impression of possessing her entirely which I never had when she was awake. Her life was submitted to me, exhaled towards me its gentle breath.

I listened to this murmuring, mysterious emanation, soft as a sea breeze, magical as a gleam of moonlight, that was her sleep. So long as it lasted, I was free to dream about her and yet at the same time to look at her, and, when that sleep grew deeper, to touch, to kiss her. What I felt then was a love as pure, as immaterial, as mysterious, as if I had been in the presence of those inanimate creatures which are the beauties of nature. And indeed, as soon as her sleep became at all deep, she ceased to be merely the plant that she had been; her sleep, on the margin of which I remained musing, with a fresh delight of which I never tired, which I could have gone on enjoying indefinitely, was to me a whole landscape. Her sleep brought within my reach something as serene, as sensually delicious as those nights of full moon on the bay of Balbec, calm as a lake over which the branches barely stir, where, stretched out upon the sand, one could listen for hours on end to the surf breaking and receding.

On entering the room, I would remain standing in the doorway, not venturing to make a sound, and hearing none but that of her breath rising to expire upon her lips at regular intervals, like the reflux of the sea, but drowsier and softer. And at the moment when my ear absorbed that divine sound, I felt that there was condensed in it the whole person, the whole life of the charming captive outstretched there before my eyes. Carriages went rattling past in the street, but her brow remained as smooth and untroubled, her breath as light, reduced to the simple expulsion of the necessary quantity of air. Then, seeing that her sleep would not be disturbed, I would advance cautiously, sit down on the chair that stood by the bedside, then on the bed itself.

I spent many a charming evening talking and playing with Albertine, but none so sweet as when I was watching her sleep. Granted that she had, as she chatted with me, or played cards, a naturalness that no actress could have imitated; it was a more profound naturalness, as it were at one remove, that was offered me by her sleep. Her hair, falling along her pink cheek, was spread out beside her on the bed, and here and there an isolated straight tress gave the same effect of perspective as those moonlit trees, lank and pale, which one sees standing erect and stiff in the backgrounds of Elstir's Raphaelesque pictures. If Albertine's lips were closed, her eyelids, on the other hand, seen from where I was placed, seemed so loosely joined that I might almost have questioned whether she really was asleep. At the same time those lowered lids gave her face that perfect continuity which is unbroken by the eyes. There are people whose faces assume an unaccustomed beauty and majesty the moment they cease to look out of their eyes.

I would run my eyes over her, stretched out below me. From time to time a slight, unaccountable tremor ran through her, as the leaves of a tree are shaken for a few moments by a sudden breath of wind. She would touch her hair and then, not having arranged it to her liking, would raise her hand to it again with motions so consecutive, so deliberate, that I was convinced that she was about to wake. Not at all; she grew calm again in the sleep from which she had not emerged. Thereafter she lay motionless. She had laid her hand on her breast, the limpness of the arm so artlessly childlike that I was obliged, as I gazed at her, to suppress the smile that is provoked in us by the solemnity, the innocence and the grace of little children.

I, who was acquainted with many Albertines in one person, seemed now to see many more again reposing by my side. Her eyebrows, arched as I had never noticed them, encircled the globes of her eyelids like a halcyon's downy nest. Races, atavisms, vices reposed upon her face. Whenever she moved her head, she created a different woman, often one whose existence I had never suspected. I seemed to possess not one but countless girls. Her breathing, as it became gradually deeper, made her breast rise and fall in a regular rhythm, and above it her folded hands and her pearls, displaced in a different way by the same movement, like boats and mooring chains set swaying by the movement of the tide. Then, feeling that the tide of her sleep was full, that I should not run aground on reefs of consciousness covered now by the high water of profound slumber, I would climb deliberately and noiselessly on to the bed, lie down by her side, clasp her waist in one arm, and place my lips upon her cheek and my free hand on her heart and then on every part of her body in turn, so that it too was raised, like the pearls, by her breathing; I myself was gently rocked by its regular motion: I had embarked upon the tide of Albertine's sleep.

Sometimes it afforded me a pleasure that was less pure. For this I had no need to make any movement, but allowed my leg to dangle against hers, like an oar which one trails in the water, imparting to it now and again a gentle oscillation like the intermittent wing-beat of a bird asleep in the air. I chose, in gazing at her, the aspect of her face which one never saw and which was so beautiful. It is I suppose comprehensible that the letters which we receive from a person should be more or less similar to one another and combine to trace an image of the writer sufficiently different from the person we know to constitute a second personality. But how much stranger is it that a woman should be conjoined, like Radica with Doodica,[2] with another woman whose different beauty makes us infer another character, and that in order to see them we must look at one of them in profile and the other in full face. The sound of her breathing, which had grown louder, might have given the illusion of the panting of sexual pleasure, and when mine was at its climax, I could kiss her without having interrupted her sleep. I felt at such moments that I had possessed her more completely, like an unconscious and unresisting object of dumb nature. I was not troubled by the words that she murmured from time to time in her sleep; their meaning was closed to me, and besides, whoever the unknown person to whom they referred, it was upon my hand, upon my cheek that her hand, stirred by an occasional faint tremor, tightened for an instant. I savoured her sleep with a disinterested, soothing love, just as I would remain for hours listening to the unfurling of the waves.

Perhaps people must be capable of making us suffer intensely before they can procure for us, in the hours of remission, the same soothing calm as nature does. I did not have to answer her as when we were engaged in conversation, and even if I could have remained silent, as for that matter I did when it was she who was talking, still while listening to her I did not penetrate so far into the depths of her being. As I continued to hear, to capture from moment to moment, the murmur, soothing as a barely perceptible breeze, of her pure breath, it was a whole physiological existence that was spread out before me, at my disposal; just as I used to remain for hours lying on the beach, in the moonlight, so long could I have remained there gazing at her, listening to her. Sometimes it was as though the sea was beginning to swell, as though the storm was making itself felt even inside the bay, and I would press myself against her and listen to the gathering roar of her breath.

Sometimes, when she was too warm, she would take off her kimono while she was already almost asleep and fling it over an armchair. As she slept I would tell myself that all her letters were in the inner pocket of this kimono, into which she always thrust them. A signature, an assignation, would have sufficed to prove a lie or to dispel a suspicion. When I could see that Albertine was sound asleep, leaving the foot of the bed where I had been standing motionless in contemplation of her, I would take a step forward, seized by a burning curiosity, feeling that the secret of this other life lay offering itself to me, flaccid and defenceless, in that armchair. Perhaps I took this step forward also because to stand perfectly still and watch her sleeping became tiring after a while. And so, on tiptoe, constantly turning round to make sure that Albertine was not waking, I would advance towards the armchair. There I would stop short, and stand for a long time gazing at the kimono, as I had stood for a long time gazing at Albertine. But (and here perhaps I was wrong) never once did I touch the kimono, put my hand in the pocket, examine the letters. In the end, realising that I would never make up my mind, I would creep back to the bedside and begin again to watch the sleeping Albertine, who would tell me nothing, whereas I could see lying across an arm of the chair that kimono which would perhaps have told me much.

And just as people pay a hundred francs a day for a room at the Grand Hotel at Balbec in order to breathe the sea air, I felt it to be quite natural that I should spend more than that on her, since I had her breath upon my cheek, between my lips which I laid half-open upon hers, through which her life flowed against my tongue.

But this pleasure of seeing her sleep, which was as sweet to me as that of feeling her live, was cut short by another pleasure, that of seeing her wake. It was, carried to a more profound and more mysterious degree, the same pleasure as I felt in having her under my roof. It was gratifying to me, of course, that when she alighted from the car in the afternoon, it should be to my house that she was returning. It was even more so to me that when, from the underworld of sleep, she climbed the last steps of the staircase of dreams, it was in my room that she was reborn to consciousness and life, that she wondered for an instant: "Where am I?" and, seeing the objects by which she was surrounded, and the lamp whose light scarcely made her blink her eyes, was able to assure herself that she was at home on realising that she was waking in *my* home. In that first delicious moment of uncertainty, it seemed to me that once again I was taking possession of her more completely, since, instead of her returning to her own room after an outing, it was my room that, as soon as Albertine should have recognised it, was about to enclose, to contain her, without there being any sign of misgiving in her eyes, which remained as calm as if she had never slept at all. The uncertainty of awakening, revealed by her silence, was not at all revealed in her eyes.

Then she would find her tongue and say: "My—" or "My darling—" followed by my Christian name, which, if we give the narrator the same name as the author of this book, would be "My Marcel," or "My darling Marcel." After this I would never allow a member of my family, by calling me "darling," to rob of their precious uniqueness the delicious words that Albertine uttered to me. As she uttered them, she pursed her lips in a little pout which she spontaneously transformed into a kiss. As quickly as she had earlier fallen asleep, she had awoken.

No more than my own progression in time, no more than the fact of looking at a girl sitting near me beneath a lamp that shed upon her a very different light from that of the sun when I used to see her striding along the seashore, was this material enrichment, this autonomous progress of Albertine, the determining cause of the difference between my present view of her and my original impression of her at Balbec. A longer term of years might have separated the two images without effecting so complete a change; it had come about, this sudden and fundamental change, when I had learned that Albertine had been virtually brought up by Mlle Vinteuil's friend. If at one time I had been overcome with excitement when I thought I detected mystery in Albertine's eyes, now I was happy only at times when from those eyes, from those cheeks even, as revealing as the eyes, at one moment so gentle but quickly turning sullen, I succeeded in expelling every trace of mystery. The image which I sought, upon which I relied, for which I would have been prepared to die, was no longer that of Albertine leading an unknown life, it was that of an Albertine as known to me as it was possible for her to be (and it was for this reason that my love could not be lasting unless it remained unhappy, for by definition it did not satisfy the need for mystery), an Albertine who did not reflect a distant world, but desired nothing else—there were moments when this did indeed appear to be the case—than to be with me, to be exactly like me, an Albertine who was the image precisely of what was mine and not of the unknown.

When it is thus from an hour of anguish in relation to another person that love is born, when it is from uncertainty whether we shall keep or lose that person, such a love bears the mark of the revolution that has created it, it recalls very little of what we had previously seen when we thought of the person in question. And although my first impressions of Albertine, silhouetted against the sea, might to some small extent persist in my love for her, in reality, these earlier impressions occupy but a tiny place in a love of this sort, in its strength, in its agony, in its need of comfort and its resort to a calm and soothing memory with which we would prefer to abide and to learn nothing more of the beloved, even if there were something horrible to be known. Even if the previous impressions are retained, such a love is made of very different stuff!

Sometimes I would put out the light before she came in. It was in the darkness, barely guided by the glow of a smouldering log, that she would lie down by my side. My hands and my cheeks alone identified her without my eyes seeing her, my eyes that were often afraid of finding her changed; so that, by virtue of these blind caresses, she may perhaps have felt bathed in a warmer tenderness than usual.

On other evenings, I undressed and went to bed, and, with Albertine perched on the side of the bed, we would resume our game or our conversation interrupted by kisses; and in the physical desire that alone makes us take an interest in the existence and character of another person, we remain so true to our own nature (even if, on the other hand, we abandon successively the different persons whom we have loved in turn) that on one occasion, catching sight of myself in the mirror at the moment when I was kissing Albertine and calling her "my little girl," the sorrowful, passionate expression on my own face, similar to the expression it would have worn long ago with Gilberte whom I no longer remembered, and would perhaps assume one day with another if I were ever to forget Albertine, made me think that, over and above any personal considerations (instinct requiring that we consider the person of the moment as the only real one), I was performing the duties of an ardent and painful devotion dedicated as an oblation to the youth and beauty of Woman. And yet with this desire by which I was honouring youth with a votive offering, with my memories too of Balbec, there was blended, in my need to keep Albertine thus every evening by my side, something that had hitherto been foreign to my amorous existence at least, if it was not entirely new in my life. It was a soothing power the like of which I had not experienced since the evenings at Combray long ago when my mother, stooping over my bed, brought me repose in a kiss. To be sure, I should have been greatly astonished at that time had anyone told me that I was not extremely kind and especially that I would ever seek to deprive someone else of a pleasure. I must have known myself very imperfectly then, for my pleasure in having Albertine to live with me was much less a positive pleasure than the pleasure of having withdrawn from the world, where everyone was free to enjoy her in turn, the blossoming girl who, if she did not bring me any great joy, was at least withholding joy from others. Ambition and fame would have left me unmoved. Even more was I incapable of feeling hatred. And yet to love carnally was none the less, for me, to enjoy a triumph over countless rivals. I can never repeat it often enough: it was more than anything else an appeasement.

For all that I might, before Albertine returned, have doubted her, have imagined her in the room at Montjouvain, once she was in her dressing-gown and seated facing my chair or (if, as was more frequent, I had remained in bed) at the foot of my bed, I would deposit my doubts in her, hand them over for her to relieve me of them, with the abnegation of a worshipper uttering a prayer. All through the evening she might have been there, curled up in a mischievous ball on my bed, playing with me like a cat; her little pink nose, the tip of which she made even tinier with a coquettish glance which gave it a daintiness characteristic of certain women who are inclined to be plump, might have given her an inflamed and provocative air; she might have allowed a tress of her long, dark hair to fall over her pale-pink waxen cheek and, half shutting her eyes, unfolding her arms, have seemed to be saying to me: "Do what you like with me"—but when the time came for her to leave me, and she drew close to me to say good-night, it was a softness that had become almost familial that I kissed on either side of her sturdy neck which then never seemed to me brown or freckled enough, as though these solid qualities were associated with a certain frank good nature in Albertine.

"Are you coming with us tomorrow, old crosspatch?" she would ask before leaving me.

"Where are you going?"

"That will depend on the weather and on you. But have you written anything today, my little darling? No? Then it was hardly worth your while not coming with us. Tell me, by the way, when I came in this evening, you knew my step, you guessed at once who it was?"

"Of course. Could I possibly be mistaken? Couldn't I tell my little goose's footstep among a thousand? She must let me take her shoes off before she goes to bed, it will give me such pleasure. You're so nice and pink in all that white lace."

Such was my answer; amid the sensual expressions, others will be recognised that were peculiar to my grandmother and my mother. For, little by little, I was beginning to resemble all my relations: my father who—in a very different fashion from myself, no doubt, for if things repeat themselves, it is with great variations—took so keen an interest in the weather; and not my father only, but, more and more, my aunt Léonie. Otherwise Albertine could not but have been a reason for my going out, so as not to leave her on her own, beyond my control. Although every day I found an excuse in some particular indisposition, what made me so often remain in bed was a person—not Albertine, not a person I loved but a person with more power over me than any beloved—who had transmigrated into me, a person despotic to the point of silencing at times my jealous suspicions or at least of preventing me from going to verify whether they had any foundation, and that person was my aunt Léonie—my aunt Léonie, who was entirely steeped in piety and with whom I could have sworn that I had not a single point in common, I who was so passionately fond of pleasure, apparently worlds apart from that maniac who had never known any pleasure in her life and lay telling her beads all day long, I who suffered from my inability to actualise a literary career whereas she had been the one person in the family who could never understand that reading was anything other than a means of whiling away the time, of "amusing oneself," which made it, even at Eastertide, permissible on Sundays, when every serious occupation is forbidden in order that the whole day may be hallowed by prayer. And as if it were not enough that I should bear an exaggerated resemblance to my father, to the extent of not being satisfied like him with consulting the barometer, but becoming an animated barometer myself, as if it were not enough that I should allow myself to be ordered by my aunt Léonie to stay at home and watch the weather, from my bedroom window or even from my bed, here I was talking now to Albertine, at one moment as the child that I had been at Combray used to talk to my mother, at another as my grandmother used to talk to me. When we have passed a certain age, the soul of the child that we were and the souls of the dead from whom we sprang come and shower upon us their riches and their spells, asking to be allowed to contribute to the new emotions which we feel and in which, erasing their former image, we recast them in an original creation. Thus my whole past from my earliest years, and, beyond these, the past of my parents and relations, blended with my impure love

for Albertine the tender charm of an affection at once filial and maternal. We have to give hospitality, at a certain
stage in our lives, to all our relatives who have journeyed
so far and gathered round us.

Before Albertine obeyed and took off her shoes, I
would open her chemise. Her two little uplifted breasts
were so round that they seemed not so much to be an integral part of her body as to have ripened there like fruit;
and her belly (concealing the place where a man's is disfigured as though by an iron clamp left sticking in a
statue that has been taken down from its niche) was
closed, at the junction of her thighs, by two valves with a
curve as languid, as reposeful, as cloistral as that of the
horizon after the sun has set. She would take off her
shoes, and lie down by my side.

O mighty attitudes of Man and Woman, in which
there seeks to be united, in the innocence of the world's
first days and with the humility of clay, what the Creation
made separate, in which Eve is astonished and submissive
before Man by whose side she awakens, as he himself,
alone still, before God who has fashioned him! Albertine
would fold her arms behind her dark hair, her hip
swelling, her leg drooping with the inflexion of a swan's
neck that stretches upwards and then curves back on itself. When she was lying completely on her side, there
was a certain aspect of her face (so sweet and so beautiful
from in front) which I could not endure, hook-nosed as in
one of Leonardo's caricatures, seeming to betray the malice, the greed for gain, the deceitfulness of a spy whose
presence in my house would have filled me with horror
and whom that profile seemed to unmask. At once I took
Albertine's face in my hands and altered its position.

"Be a good boy and promise me that if you don't come out tomorrow you'll work," she would say as she slipped her chemise on again.

"Yes, but don't put on your dressing-gown yet."

Sometimes I ended by falling asleep by her side. The room would grow cold, more wood would be wanted. I would try to find the bell above my head, but fail to do so, after fingering all the copper rods in turn save those between which it hung, and would say to Albertine who had sprung from the bed so that Françoise should not find us lying side by side: "No, come back for a moment, I can't find the bell."

Sweet, gay, innocent moments to all appearance, and yet moments in which there gathers the unsuspected possibility of disaster, which makes the amorous life the most precarious of all, that in which the unpredictable rain of sulphur and brimstone falls after the most radiant moments, whereupon, without having the heart or the will to draw a lesson from our misfortune, we set to work at once to rebuild upon the slopes of the crater from which nothing but catastrophe can emerge. I was as carefree as those who imagine their happiness will last. It is precisely because this tenderness has been necessary to give birth to pain—and will return moreover at intervals to calm it—that men can be sincere with each other, and even with themselves, when they pride themselves on a woman's lovingness, although, taking things all in all, at the heart of their intimacy there lurks continuously and secretly, unavowed to the rest of the world, or revealed unintentionally by questions and inquiries, a painful disquiet. But this could not have come to birth without the preliminary tenderness, which even afterwards is intermittently necessary to make the pain bearable and to avoid ruptures; and concealment of the secret hell that a life shared with the woman in question really is, to the point of parading an allegedly tender intimacy, expresses a genuine point of view, a universal process of cause and effect, one of the modes whereby the production of grief and pain is rendered possible.

It no longer surprised me that Albertine should be in the house, and would not be going out tomorrow except with myself or in the custody of Andrée. These habits of shared life, these broad lines by which my existence was demarcated and within which nobody might penetrate but Albertine, and also (in the future plan, of which I was still unaware, of my life to come, like the plan drawn up by an architect for monuments which will not be erected until long afterwards) the remoter lines, parallel to these and broader still, by which, like an isolated hermitage, the somewhat rigid and monotonous prescription of my future loves was adumbrated, had in reality been traced that night at Balbec when, in the little train, after Albertine had revealed to me who it was that had brought her up, I had decided at all costs to remove her from certain influences and to prevent her from straying out of my sight for some days. Day after day had gone by, and these habits had become mechanical, but, like those rites the meaning of which History seeks to discover, I could have said (though I would not have wished to say) to anybody who asked me to explain the meaning of this life of seclusion which I carried so far as no longer to go to the theatre, that its origin lay in the anxiety of an evening and my need to prove to myself, during the days that followed, that the girl of whose unfortunate childhood I had learned should have no possibility, whether she wished to or not, of exposing herself to similar temptations. I no longer thought, except very rarely, of these possibilities, but they were nevertheless to remain vaguely present in my consciousness. The fact that I was destroying them—or trying to do so—day by day was doubtless the reason why I took such pleasure in kissing those cheeks which were no more beautiful than many others; beneath any carnal attraction at all deep, there is the permanent possibility of danger.

I had promised Albertine that, if I did not go out with her, I would settle down to work. But in the morning, just as if, taking advantage of our being asleep, the house had miraculously flown, I awoke in different weather beneath another clime. We do not begin to work as soon as we disembark in a strange country to the conditions of which we have to adapt ourselves. And each day was for me a different country. How could I even recognise my indolence itself, under the novel forms which it assumed? Sometimes, on days when the weather was beyond redemption, mere residence in the house, situated in the midst of a steady and continuous rain, had all the gliding ease, the soothing silence, the interest of a sea voyage; another time, on a bright day, to lie still in bed was to let the lights and shadows play around me as round a tree-trunk. Or yet again, at the first strokes of the bell of a neighbouring convent, rare as the early morning worshippers, barely whitening the dark sky with their hesitant hail-showers, melted and scattered by the warm breeze, I would discern one of those tempestuous, disor-

dered, delightful days, when the roofs, soaked by an intermittent downpour and dried by a gust of wind or a ray of
sunshine, let fall a gurgling raindrop and, as they wait for
the wind to turn again, preen their iridescent pigeon's-
breast slates in the momentary sunshine; one of those
days filled with so many changes of weather, atmospheric
incidents, storms, that the idle man does not feel that he
has wasted them because he has been taking an interest in
the activity which, in default of himself, the atmosphere,
acting as it were in his stead, has displayed; days similar
to those times of revolution or war which do not seem
empty to the schoolboy playing truant, because by loitering outside the Law Courts or by reading the newspapers
he has the illusion of deriving from the events that have
occurred, failing the work which he has neglected, an intellectual profit and an excuse for his idleness; days, finally, to which one may compare those on which some
exceptional crisis has occurred in one's life from which the
man who has never done anything imagines that he will
acquire industrious habits if it is happily resolved: for instance, the morning on which he sets out for a duel which
is to be fought under particularly dangerous conditions,
and he is suddenly made aware, at the moment when it is
perhaps about to be taken from him, of the value of a life
of which he might have made use to begin some important work, or merely to enjoy a few pleasures, and of
which he has failed to make any use at all. "If only I'm
not killed," he says to himself, "how I shall settle down to
work the very minute, and how I shall enjoy myself too!"
Life has in fact suddenly acquired a higher value in his
eyes, because he puts into life everything that it seems to
him capable of giving instead of the little that he nor-

mally demands of it. He sees it in the light of his desire, not as his experience has taught him that he was apt to make it, that is to say so tawdry. It has, at that moment, become filled with work, travel, mountain-climbing, all the splendid things which, he tells himself, the fatal outcome of the duel may render impossible, without thinking that they were already impossible before there was any question of a duel, owing to the bad habits which, even had there been no duel, would have persisted. He returns home without even a scratch, but he continues to find the same obstacles to pleasures, excursions, travel, to everything which for a moment he had feared that death would deprive him of; life is sufficient for that. As for work— exceptional circumstances having the effect of intensifying what previously existed in a man, work in the industrious, idleness in the lazy—he takes a holiday from it.

I followed his example, and did as I had always done since my first resolution to become a writer, which I had made long ago, but which seemed to me to date from yesterday, because I had regarded each intervening day as non-existent. I treated this day in a similar fashion, allowing its showers of rain and bursts of sunshine to pass without doing anything, and vowing that I would begin to work next day. But then I was no longer the same man beneath a cloudless sky; the golden note of the bells contained, like honey, not only light but the sensation of light (and also the sickly savour of preserved fruits, because at Combray it had often loitered like a wasp over our cleared dinner-table). On this day of dazzling sunshine, to remain until nightfall with my eyes shut was a thing permitted, customary, health-giving, pleasant, seasonable, like keeping the outside shutters closed against the heat. It was in such weather as this that at the beginning of my second visit to Balbec I used to hear the violins of the orchestra amid the blue-green surge of the rising tide. How much more fully did I possess Albertine today! There were days when the sound of a bell striking the hour bore upon the sphere of its sonority a plaque so spread with moisture or with light that it was like a transcription for the blind or, if you like, a musical interpretation of the charm of rain or the charm of sunlight. So much so that, at the moment, as I lay in bed with my eyes shut, I said to myself that everything is capable of transposition and that a universe that was exclusively audible might be as full of variety as the other. Travelling lazily upstream from day to day as in a boat, and seeing an endlessly changing succession of enchanted scenes appear before my eyes, scenes which I did not choose, which a moment earlier had been invisible to me, and which my memory presented to me one after another without my being free to choose them, I idly pursued over that smooth expanse my stroll in the sunshine.

Those morning concerts at Balbec were not long past. And yet, at that comparatively recent time, I had given but little thought to Albertine. Indeed, on the very first days after my arrival, I had not known that she was at Balbec. From whom then had I learned it? Oh, yes, from Aimé. It was a fine sunny day like this. The worthy Aimé! He was glad to see me again. But he does not like Albertine. Not everybody can like her. Yes, it was he who told me that she was at Balbec. But how did he know? Ah! he had met her, had thought that she was badly-behaved. At that moment, as I approached Aimé's story by a different facet from the one it had presented when he had told it to me, my thoughts, which hitherto had been sailing blissfully over these untroubled waters, exploded suddenly, as though they had struck an invisible and perilous mine, treacherously moored at this point in my memory. He had told me that he had met her, that he had thought her badly-behaved. What had he meant by bad behaviour? I had understood him to mean vulgar behaviour, because, to contradict him in advance, I had declared that she was most refined. But no, perhaps he had meant Gomorrhan behaviour. She was with another girl, perhaps their arms were round one another's waists, perhaps they were staring at other women, were indeed behaving in a manner which I had never seen Albertine adopt in my presence. Who was the other girl? Where had Aimé met her, this odious Albertine?

I tried to recall exactly what Aimé had said to me, in order to see whether it could be related to what I imagined, or whether he had meant nothing more than common manners. But in vain might I ask the question, the person who put it and the person who could supply the recollection were, alas, one and the same person, myself, who was momentarily duplicated but without any additional insight. Question as I might, it was myself who answered, I learned nothing more. I no longer gave a thought to Mlle Vinteuil. Born of a new suspicion, the fit of jealousy from which I was suffering was new too, or rather it was only the prolongation, the extension of that suspicion; it had the same theatre, which was no longer Montjouvain but the road upon which Aimé had met Albertine, and for its object one or other of the various friends who might have been with Albertine that day. It was perhaps a certain Elisabeth, or else perhaps those two girls whom Albertine had watched in the mirror at the

Casino, while appearing not to see them. She had doubt-less been having relations with them, and also with Es-ther, Bloch's cousin. Such relations, had they been revealed to me by a third person, would have been enough almost to kill me, but since it was I who imagined them, I took care to add sufficient uncertainty to deaden the pain. We succeed in absorbing daily in enormous doses, under the guise of suspicions, this same idea that we are being betrayed, a quite small quantity of which might prove fatal if injected by the needle of a shattering word. And it is no doubt for that reason, and as a by-product of the instinct of self-preservation, that the same jealous man does not hesitate to form the most terrible suspicions upon a basis of innocuous facts, provided that, whenever any proof is brought to him, he refuses to ac-cept the irrefutable evidence. Besides, love is an incurable malady, like those diathetic states in which rheumatism affords the sufferer a brief respite only to be replaced by epileptiform headaches. If my jealous suspicion was calmed, I then felt a grudge against Albertine for not hav-ing been tender enough, perhaps for having made fun of me with Andrée. I thought with alarm of the idea that she must have formed if Andrée had repeated all our conver-sations; the future loomed black and menacing. This mood of depression left me only if a new jealous suspicion drove me to further inquiries or if, on the other hand, Al-bertine's displays of affection made my happiness seem to me insignificant. Who could this girl be? I must write to Aimé, try to see him, and then check his statement by talking to Albertine, making her confess. In the mean-time, convinced that it must be Bloch's cousin, I asked Bloch himself, who had not the remotest idea of my purpose, simply to let me see her photograph, or, better still, to arrange for me to meet her.

How many persons, cities, roads jealousy makes us eager thus to know! It is a thirst for knowledge thanks to which, with regard to various isolated points, we end by acquiring every possible notion in turn except the one that we require. One can never tell whether a suspicion will not arise, for, all of a sudden, one recalls a remark that was not clear, an alibi that cannot have been given without a purpose. One has not seen the person again, but there is such a thing as a retrospective jealousy, that is born only after we have left the person, a delayed-action jealousy. Perhaps the habit that I had acquired of nursing within me certain desires, the desire for a young girl of good family such as those I used to see pass beneath my window escorted by their governesses, and especially for the girl whom Saint-Loup had mentioned to me, the one who frequented houses of ill fame, the desire for handsome lady's-maids, and especially for Mme Putbus's, the desire to go to the country in early spring to see once again hawthorns, apple-trees in blossom, storms, the desire for Venice, the desire to settle down to work, the desire to live like other people—perhaps the habit of storing up all these desires, without assuaging any of them, contenting myself with a promise to myself not to forget to satisfy them one day—perhaps this habit, so many years old already, of perpetual postponement, of what M. de Charlus used to castigate under the name of procrastination, had become so prevalent in me that it took hold of my jealous suspicions also and, while encouraging me to make a mental note that I would not fail, some day, to have things out with Albertine as regards the girl, or possibly girls (this part of the story was confused and blurred in my memory and to all intents and purposes indecipherable) with whom Aimé had met her, made me also postpone this inquest. In any case, I would not mention the subject to my mistress this evening, for fear of making her think me jealous and so offending her.

And yet when, on the following day, Bloch sent me the photograph of his cousin Esther, I made haste to forward it to Aimé. And at the same moment I remembered that Albertine had that morning refused me a pleasure which might indeed have tired her. Was that in order to reserve it for someone else, this afternoon, perhaps? For whom? Jealousy is thus endless, for even if the beloved, by dying for instance, can no longer provoke it by her actions, it may happen that memories subsequent to any event suddenly materialise and behave in our minds as though they too were events, memories which hitherto we had never explored, which had seemed to us unimportant, and to which our own reflexion upon them is sufficient, without any external factors, to give a new and terrible meaning. There is no need for there to be two of you, it is enough to be alone in your room, thinking, for fresh betrayals by your mistress to come to light, even though she is dead. And so we ought not to fear in love, as in everyday life, the future alone, but even the past, which often comes to life for us only when the future has come and gone—and not only the past which we discover after the event but the past which we have long kept stored within ourselves and suddenly learn how to interpret.

No matter, I was only too happy, as afternoon turned to evening, that the hour was not far off when I should be able to look to Albertine's presence for the appeasement which I needed. Unfortunately, the evening that followed was one of those when this appeasement was not forthcoming, when the kiss that Albertine would give me when she left me for the night, very different from her usual kiss, would no more soothe me than my mother's kiss had soothed me long ago, on days when she was vexed with me and I dared not call her back although I knew that I should be unable to sleep. Such evenings were now those on which Albertine had formed for the next day some plan about which she did not wish me to know. Had she confided it to me, I would have shown an eagerness to ensure its realisation that no one but Albertine could have inspired in me. But she told me nothing, and she had no need to tell me anything; as soon as she came in, before she had even crossed the threshold of my room, while she was still wearing her hat or toque, I had already detected the unknown, restive, desperate, uncontrollable desire. These were often the evenings when I had awaited her return with the most loving thoughts, and looked forward to throwing my arms round her neck with the warmest affection. Alas, misunderstandings such as I had often had with my parents, whom I would find cold or irritable when I ran to embrace them, overflowing with love, are as nothing in comparison with those that occur between lovers. The anguish then is far less superficial, far harder to endure; it has its seat in a deeper layer of the heart.

On this particular evening, however, Albertine was obliged to mention the plan that she had in mind; I gathered at once that she wished to go next day to pay a visit to Mme Verdurin, a visit to which in itself I would have seen no objection. But evidently her object was to meet someone there, to prepare some future pleasure. Otherwise she would not have attached so much importance to this visit. That is to say, she would not have kept on assuring me that it was of no importance. I had in the course of my life followed a progression which was the opposite of that adopted by peoples who make use of phonetic writing only after having considered the characters as a set of symbols; having, for so many years, looked for the real life and thought of other people only in the direct statements about them which they supplied me with of their own free will, in the absence of these I had come to attach importance, on the contrary, only to disclosures that are not a rational and analytical expression of the truth; the words themselves did not enlighten me unless they were interpreted in the same way as a rush of blood to the cheeks of a person who is embarrassed, or as a sudden silence. Such and such an adverb (for instance that used by M. de Cambremer when he understood that I was "literary" and, not having yet spoken to me, as he was describing a visit he had paid to the Verdurins, turned to me with: "*Incidentally*, Borelli was there!") bursting into flames through the involuntary, sometimes perilous contact of two ideas which the speaker has not expressed but which, by applying the appropriate methods of analysis or electrolysis, I was able to extract from it, told me more than a long speech. Albertine sometimes let fall in her conversation one or other of these precious amalgams which I made haste to "treat" so as to transform them into lucid ideas.

It is in fact one of the most terrible things for the lover that whereas particular details—which only experiment or espionage, among so many possible realisations, would ever make known to him—are so difficult to discover, the truth on the other hand is so easy to detect or merely to sense. Often, at Balbec, I had seen her fasten on girls who came past us a sudden lingering stare, like a physical contact, after which, if I knew the girls, she would say to me: "Suppose we asked them to join us? I should so enjoy insulting them." And now, for some time past, doubtless since she had succeeded in reading my mind, no request to me to invite anyone, not a word, not even a sidelong glance from her eyes, which had become objectless and mute, and, with the abstracted, vacant expression that accompanied them, as revealing as had been their magnetic swerve before. Yet it was impossible for me to reproach her, or to ply her with questions about things which she would have declared to be so petty, so trivial, stored up by me simply for the pleasure of "nit-picking." It is hard enough to say: "Why did you stare at that girl who went past?" but a great deal harder to say: "Why did you not stare at her?" And yet I knew quite well—or at least I should have known if I had not chosen instead to believe those affirmations of hers—what Albertine's demeanour comprehended and proved, like such and such a contradiction in the course of conversation which often I did not perceive until long after I had left her, which kept me in anguish all night long, which I never dared mention to her again, but which nevertheless continued to honour my memory from time to time with its periodical visits. Even in the case of these furtive or sidelong glances on the beach at Balbec or in the streets of Paris, I might sometimes wonder whether the person who provoked them was not only an object of desire at the moment when she passed, but an old acquaintance, or else some girl who had simply been mentioned to her and whom, when I heard about it, I was astonished that any-body could have mentioned to her, so remote was she from what one would have guessed Albertine's range of acquaintance to be. But the Gomorrah of today is a jigsaw puzzle made up of pieces that come from places where one least expected to find them. Thus I once saw at Rive-belle a big dinner-party of ten women, all of whom I happened to know, at least by name, and who, though as dissimilar as could be, were none the less perfectly united, so much so that I never saw a party so homogeneous, al-beit so composite.

To return to the girls whom we passed in the street, never would Albertine stare at an old person, man or woman, with such fixity, or on the other hand with such reserve and as though she saw nothing. Cuckolded hus-bands who know nothing in fact know perfectly well. But it requires more accurate and abundant evidence to create a scene of jealousy. Besides, if jealousy helps us to dis-cover a certain tendency to falsehood in the woman we love, it multiplies this tendency a hundredfold when the woman has discovered that we are jealous. She lies (to an extent to which she has never lied to us before), whether from pity, or from fear, or because she instinctively shies away in a flight that is symmetrical with our investiga-tions. True, there are love affairs in which from the start a woman of easy virtue has posed as virtue incarnate in the eyes of the man who is in love with her. But how many others consist of two diametrically opposite periods! In the first, the woman speaks almost freely, with slight modifications, of her zest for pleasure and of the amorous life which it has made her lead, all of which she will deny later on with the utmost vigour to the same man when she senses that he is jealous of her and spying on her. He comes to regret the days of those first confidences, the memory of which torments him nevertheless. If the woman continued to make them, she would furnish him almost unaided with the secret of her conduct which he has been vainly pursuing day after day. And besides, what abandon those early confidences proved, what trust, what friendship! If she cannot live without being unfaithful to him, at least she would be doing so as a friend, telling him of her pleasures, associating him with them. And he thinks with regret of the sort of life which the early stages of their love seemed to promise, which the sequel has rendered impossible, turning that love into something agonisingly painful, which will make a final parting, according to circumstances, either inevitable or impossible.

Sometimes the script from which I deciphered Albertine's lies, without being ideographic, needed simply to be read backwards; thus this evening she had tossed at me casually the message, intended to pass almost unnoticed: "I may go and see the Verdurins tomorrow. I don't really know whether I will go, I don't particularly want to." A childish anagram of the admission: "I shall go to the Verdurins' tomorrow, it's absolutely certain, I attach the utmost importance to it." This apparent hesitation indicated a firm resolution and was intended to diminish the importance of the visit while informing me of it. Albertine always adopted a dubitative tone for irrevocable decisions. Mine was no less irrevocable: I would see that this visit to Mme Verdurin did not take place. Jealousy is often only an anxious need to be tyrannical applied to matters of love. I had doubtless inherited from my father this

abrupt, arbitrary desire to threaten the people I loved best
in the hopes with which they were lulling themselves with
a sense of security which I wanted to expose to them as
false; when I saw that Albertine had planned without my
knowledge, behind my back, an expedition which I would
have done everything in the world to make easier and
more pleasant for her had she taken me into her confidence, I said casually, in order to make her tremble, that I
expected to go out the next day myself.

I began to suggest to Albertine other expeditions in
directions which would have made the visit to the Verdurins impossible, in words stamped with a feigned indifference beneath which I strove to conceal my agitation.
But she had detected it. It encountered in her the electric
power of a contrary will which violently repulsed it; I
could see the sparks flash from Albertine's pupils. What
use was it, though, to pay attention to what her eyes were
saying at that moment? How had I failed to observe long
ago that Albertine's eyes belonged to the category which
even in a quite ordinary person seems to be composed of
a number of fragments because of all the places in which
the person wishes to be—and to conceal the desire to
be—on that particular day? Eyes mendaciously kept always immobile and passive, but none the less dynamic,
measurable in the yards or miles to be traversed before
they reach the desired, the implacably desired meeting-
place, eyes that are not so much smiling at the pleasure
which tempts them as shadowed with melancholy and discouragement because there may be a difficulty in their
getting there. Even when you hold them in your hands,
such persons are fugitives. To understand the emotions
which they arouse, and which others, even better-looking,

do not, we must recognise that they are not immobile but in motion, and add to their person a sign corresponding to that which in physics denotes speed.

If you upset their plans for the day, they confess to you the pleasure they had concealed from you: "I did so want to go and have tea with so and so who I'm fond of." And then, six months later, if you come to know the person in question, you will learn that the girl whose plans you had upset, who, trapped, in order that you might set her free had confessed to you that she was thus in the habit of taking tea with a dear friend every day at the hour at which you did not see her, has never once been inside this person's house, that they have never had tea together, since the girl used to explain that her whole time was taken up by none other than yourself. And so the person with whom she confessed that she was going to tea, with whom she begged you to allow her to go to tea, that person, a reason admitted by necessity, it was not her, it was somebody else, it was something else still! What something else? Which somebody else?

Alas, the multifaceted eyes, far-ranging and melancholy, might enable us perhaps to measure distance, but do not indicate direction. The boundless field of possibilities extends before us, and if by any chance the reality presented itself to our eyes, it would be so far outside the limits of the possible that, knocking suddenly against this looming wall, we should fall over backwards in a daze. It is not even essential that we should have proof of her movement and flight, it is enough that we should guess them. She had promised us a letter; we were calm, we were no longer in love. The letter has not come; each mail fails to bring it; what can have happened? Anxiety is born afresh, and love. It is such people more than any others who inspire love in us, to our desolation. For every new anxiety that we feel on their account strips them in our eyes of some of their personality. We were resigned to suffering, thinking that we loved outside ourselves, and we perceive that our love is a function of our sorrow, that our love perhaps is our sorrow, and that its object is only to a very small extent the girl with the raven hair. But, when all is said, it is such people more than any others who inspire love.

More often than not, a body becomes the object of love only when an emotion, fear of losing it, uncertainty of getting it back, melts into it. Now this sort of anxiety has a great affinity for bodies. It adds to them a quality which surpasses beauty itself, which is one of the reasons why we see men who are indifferent to the most beautiful women fall passionately in love with others who appear to us ugly. To such beings, such fugitive beings, their own nature and our anxiety fasten wings. And even when they are with us the look in their eyes seems to warn us that they are about to take flight. The proof of this beauty, surpassing beauty itself, that wings add is that often, for us, the same person is alternately winged and wingless. Afraid of losing her, we forget all the others. Sure of keeping her, we compare her with those others whom at once we prefer to her. And as these fears and these certainties may vary from week to week, a person may one week see everything that gave us pleasure sacrificed to her, in the following week be sacrificed herself, and so on for months on end. All of which would be incomprehensible did we not know (from the experience, which every man shares, of having at least once in a lifetime ceased to love a woman, forgotten her) how very insignificant in herself a woman is when she is no longer—or is not yet—permeable to our emotions. And, of course, if we speak of fugitive beings it is equally true of imprisoned ones, of captive women whom we think we shall never be able to possess. Hence men detest procuresses, because they facilitate flight and dangle temptations, but if on the other hand we are in love with a cloistered woman, we willingly have recourse to a procuress to snatch her from her prison and bring her to us. In so far as relations with women whom we abduct are less permanent than others, the reason is that the fear of not succeeding in procuring them or the dread of seeing them escape is the whole of our love for them and that once they have been carried off from their husbands, torn from their footlights, cured of the temptation to leave us, dissociated in short from our emotion whatever it may be, they are only themselves, that is to say next to nothing, and, so long desired, are soon forsaken by the very man who was so afraid of their forsaking him.

I have said: "How could I have failed to guess?" But had I not guessed it from the first day at Balbec? Had I not detected in Albertine one of those girls beneath whose envelope of flesh more hidden persons stir, I will not say than in a pack of cards still in its box, a closed cathedral or a theatre before we enter it, but than in the whole vast ever-changing crowd? Not only all these persons, but the desire, the voluptuous memory, the restless searching of so many persons. At Balbec I had not been troubled because I had never even supposed that one day I should be following a trail, even a false trail. Nevertheless, it had given Albertine, in my eyes, the plenitude of someone filled to the brim by the superimposition of so many persons, of so many desires and voluptuous memories of persons. And now that she had one day let fall the name "Mlle Vinteuil," I should have liked, not to tear off her dress to see her body, but through her body to see and read the whole diary of her memories and her future passionate assignations.

Strange how the things that are probably most insignificant suddenly assume an extraordinary value when a person whom we love (or who has lacked only this duplicity to make us love her) conceals them from us! In itself, suffering does not of necessity inspire in us sentiments of love or hatred towards the person who causes it: a surgeon can hurt us without arousing any personal emotion in us. But with a woman who has continued for some time to assure us that we are everything in the world to her, without being herself everything in the world to us, a woman whom we enjoy seeing, kissing, taking on our knee, we are astonished if we merely sense from a sudden resistance that she is not at our entire disposal. Disappointment may then revive in us the forgotten memory of an old anguish, which we nevertheless know to have been provoked not by this woman but by others whose betrayals stretch back like milestones through our past. And indeed, how have we the heart to go on living, how can we move a finger to preserve ourselves from death, in a world in which love is provoked only by lies and consists solely in our need to see our sufferings appeased by the person who has made us suffer? To escape from the depths of despondency that follow the discovery of this lying and this resistance, there is the sad remedy of endeavouring to act, against her will, with the help of people whom we feel to be more closely involved than we are in her life, upon her who is resisting us and lying to us, to play the cheat in turn, to make ourselves loathed. But the suffering caused by such a love is of the kind which must inevitably lead the sufferer to seek an illusory comfort in a change of position. These means of action are not wanting, alas! And the horror of the kind of love which anxiety alone has engendered lies in the fact that we turn over and over incessantly in our cage the most trivial utterances; not to mention that rarely do the people for whom we feel this love appeal to us physically to any great extent, since it is not our deliberate preference, but the accident of a moment's anguish (a moment indefinitely prolonged by our weakness of character, which repeats its experiments every evening until it yields to sedatives) that has chosen for us.

No doubt my love for Albertine was not the most barren of those to which, through lack of will-power, a man may descend, for it was not entirely platonic; she did give me some carnal satisfaction, and moreover she was intelligent. But all this was supererogatory. What occupied my mind was not something intelligent that she might have said, but a chance remark that had aroused in me a doubt as to her actions; I tried to remember whether she had said this or that, in what tone, at what moment, in response to what words, to reconstruct the whole scene of her dialogue with me, to recall at what moment she had expressed a desire to visit the Verdurins, what word of mine had brought that look of vexation to her face. The most important event might have been at issue without my going to so much trouble to establish the truth of it, to reconstitute its precise atmosphere and colour. No doubt, after these anxieties have intensified to a degree which we find unbearable, we sometimes manage to calm them altogether for an evening. We too are invited to the party which the woman we love was to attend and the true nature of which has been obsessing us for days; she has neither looks nor words for anyone but us; we take her home and then, all our anxieties dispelled, we enjoy a repose as complete and as healing as the deep sleep that comes after a long walk. And no doubt such repose is worth a high price. But would it not have been simpler not to buy ourselves, deliberately, the preceding anxiety, and at an even higher price? Besides, we know all too well that however profound these temporary respites may be, anxiety will still prevail. Often, indeed, it is revived by a remark that was intended to set our mind at rest. The demands of our jealousy and the blindness of our credulity are greater than the woman we love could ever suppose. When, spontaneously, she swears to us that such and such a man is no more to her than a friend, she shatters us by informing us—something we never suspected—that he has been her friend. While she is telling us, in proof of her sincerity, how they had tea together that very afternoon, at each word that she utters the invisible, the unsuspected, takes shape before our eyes. She admits that he has asked her to be his mistress, and we suffer agonies at the thought that she can have listened to his overtures. She refused them, she says. But presently, when we recall her story, we wonder whether that refusal is really genuine, for there is wanting, between the different things that she said to us, that logical and necessary connexion which, more than the facts related, is the sign of truth. Besides, there was that frightening note of scorn in her voice: "I said to him no, categorically," which is to be found in every class of society when a woman is lying. We must nevertheless thank her for having refused, encourage her by our kindness to repeat these painful confidences in the future. At the most, we may remark: "But if he had already made advances to you, why did you accept his invitation to tea?" "So that he should not hold it against me and say that I hadn't been nice to him." And we dare not reply that by refusing she would perhaps have been nicer to us.

Albertine alarmed me further when she said that I was quite right to say, out of regard for her reputation, that I was not her lover, since "for that matter," she went on, "it's perfectly true that you aren't." I was not perhaps her lover in the full sense of the word, but then, was I to suppose that all the things that we did together she did also with all the other men whose mistress she swore to me that she had never been? The desire to know at all costs what Albertine was thinking, whom she saw, whom she loved—how strange that I should sacrifice everything to this need, since I had felt the same need to know in the case of Gilberte names and facts which now meant nothing to me! I was perfectly well aware that in themselves Albertine's actions were of no greater interest. It is curious that a first love, if by the fragile state in which it leaves one's heart it paves the way for subsequent loves, does not at least provide one, in view of the identity of symptoms and sufferings, with the means of curing them. Besides, is there any need to know a fact? Are we not aware beforehand, in a general way, of the mendacity and even the discretion of those women who have something to conceal? Is there any possibility of error? They make a virtue of their silence, when we would give anything to make them speak. And we feel certain that they have assured their accomplice: "I never say anything. It won't be through me that anybody will hear about it, I never say anything."

A man may give his fortune and even his life for a woman, and yet know quite well that in ten years' time, more or less, he would refuse her the fortune, prefer to keep his life. For then that woman would be detached from him, alone, that is to say non-existent. What attaches us to people are the countless roots, the innumerable threads which are our memories of last night, our hopes for tomorrow morning, the continuous weft of habit from which we can never free ourselves. Just as there are misers who hoard from generosity, so we are spendthrifts who spend from avarice, and it is not so much to a person that we sacrifice our life as to everything of ours that may have become attached to that person, all those hours and days, all those things compared with which the life we have not yet lived, our life in the relative future, seems to us more remote, more detached, less intimate, less our own. What we need is to extricate ourselves from these bonds which are so much more important than the person, but they have the effect of creating in us temporary obligations which mean that we dare not leave the person for fear of being badly thought of, whereas later on we would so dare, for, detached from us, that person would no longer be part of us, and because in reality we create obligations (even if, by an apparent contradiction, they should lead to suicide) towards ourselves alone.

If I was not in love with Albertine (and of this I could not be sure) then there was nothing extraordinary in

the place that she occupied in my life: we live only with
what we do not love, with what we have brought to live
with us only in order to kill the intolerable love, whether
it be for a woman, for a place, or again for a woman em-
bodying a place. Indeed we should be terrified of beginning to love again if a new separation were to occur. I had
not yet reached this stage with Albertine. Her lies, her admissions, left me to complete the task of elucidating the
truth: her innumerable lies, because she was not content
with merely lying, like everyone who imagines that he or
she is loved, but was by nature, quite apart from this, a
liar (and so inconsistent moreover that, even if she told
me the truth every time about, for instance, what she
thought of other people, she would say something different every time); her admissions, because, being so rare, so
quickly cut short, they left between them, in so far as
they concerned the past, huge blanks over the whole expanse of which I was obliged to retrace—and for that first
of all to discover—her life.

As for the present, so far as I could interpret the
sibylline utterances of Françoise, it was not only on particular points but over a whole area that Albertine lied to
me, and "one fine day" I would see what Françoise pretended to know, what she refused to tell me, what I dared
not ask her. It was no doubt with the same jealousy that
she had shown in the past with regard to Eulalie that
Françoise would speak of the most unlikely things, but so
vaguely that at most one could deduce therefrom the
highly improbable insinuation that the poor captive (who
was a lover of women) preferred marriage with somebody
who did not appear to be me. If this had been so, how, in
spite of her telepathic powers, could Françoise have come

to hear of it? Certainly, Albertine's statements could give me no definite enlightenment, for they were as different day by day as the colours of a spinning-top that has almost come to a standstill. However, it seemed that it was hatred more than anything else that impelled Françoise to speak. Not a day went by without her addressing to me, and I in my mother's absence enduring, such speeches as:

"To be sure, you're very nice, and I shall never forget the debt of gratitude that I owe you" (this probably so that I might establish fresh claims upon her gratitude) "but the house has become infected ever since niceness brought in deceitfulness, ever since cleverness has been protecting the stupidest person that ever was seen, ever since refinement, good manners, wit, dignity in all things, the appearance and the reality of a prince, allow themselves to be dictated to and plotted against and me to be humiliated—me who've been forty years in the family— by vice, by everything that's most vulgar and base."

What Françoise resented most about Albertine was having to take orders from somebody who was not one of ourselves, and also the strain of the additional housework which, affecting the health of our old servant (who would not, for all that, accept any help in the house, not being a "good for nothing"), in itself would have accounted for her irritability and her furious hatred. Certainly, she would have liked to see Albertine-Esther banished from the house. This was Françoise's dearest wish. And, by consoling her, its fulfilment would in itself have given our old servant some rest. But to my mind there was more to it than this. So violent a hatred could have originated only in an over-strained body. And, more even than of consideration, Françoise was in need of sleep.

*   *   *

Albertine went to take off her things and, to lose no time in finding out what I wanted to know, I seized the telephone receiver and invoked the implacable deities, but succeeded only in arousing their fury which expressed itself in the single word "Engaged." Andrée was in fact engaged in talking to someone else. As I waited for her to finish her conversation, I wondered why it was—now that so many of our painters are seeking to revive the feminine portraits of the eighteenth century, in which the cleverly devised setting is a pretext for portraying expressions of expectation, sulkiness, interest, reverie—why it was that none of our modern Bouchers or Fragonards had yet painted, instead of "The Letter" or "The Harpsichord," this scene which might be entitled "At the telephone," in which there would come spontaneously to the lips of the listener a smile that is all the more genuine because it is conscious of being unobserved.

Finally I got through to Andrée: "Are you coming to call for Albertine tomorrow?" I asked, and as I uttered Albertine's name, I thought of the envy Swann had aroused in me when he had said to me, on the day of the Princesse de Guermantes's party: "Come and see Odette," and I had thought how potent, when all was said, was a Christian name which, in the eyes of the whole world including Odette herself, had on Swann's lips alone this entirely possessive sense. Such a monopoly—summed up in a single word—over the whole existence of another person had appeared to me, whenever I was in love, to be sweet indeed! But in fact, when we are in a position to say it, either we no longer care, or else habit, while not blunting its tenderness, has changed its sweetness to bitterness.* I knew that I alone was in a position to say

"Albertine" in that tone to Andrée. And yet, to Albertine, to Andrée, and to myself, I felt that I was nothing. And I realised the impossibility which love comes up against. We imagine that it has as its object a being that can be laid down in front of us, enclosed within a body. Alas, it is the extension of that being to all the points in space and time that it has occupied and will occupy. If we do not possess its contact with this or that place, this or that hour, we do not possess that being. But we cannot touch all these points. If only they were indicated to us, we might perhaps contrive to reach out to them. But we grope for them without finding them. Hence mistrust, jealousy, persecutions. We waste precious time on absurd clues and pass by the truth without suspecting it.

But already one of the irascible deities with the breathtakingly agile handmaidens was becoming irritated, not because I was speaking but because I was saying nothing.

"Come along, I've been holding the line for you all this time; I shall cut you off."

However, she did nothing of the sort but, evoking Andrée's presence, enveloped it, like the great poet that a damsel of the telephone always is, in the atmosphere peculiar to the home, the district, the very life itself of Albertine's friend.

"Is that you?" asked Andrée, whose voice was projected towards me with an instantaneous speed by the goddess whose privilege it is to make sound more swift than light.

"Listen," I replied, "go wherever you like, anywhere, except to Mme Verdurin's. You must at all cost keep Albertine away from there tomorrow."

"But that's just where she's supposed to be going."

"Ah!"

But I was obliged to break off the conversation for a moment and to make menacing gestures, for if Françoise continued—as though it were something as unpleasant as vaccination or as dangerous as the aeroplane—to refuse to learn to use the telephone, whereby she would have spared us the trouble of conversations which she might intercept without any harm, on the other hand she would at once come into the room whenever I was engaged in a conversation so private that I was particularly anxious to keep it from her ears. When she had left the room at last, not without lingering to take away various objects that had been lying there since the previous day and might perfectly well have been left there for an hour longer, and to put on to the fire a log made quite superfluous by the burning heat generated in me by the intruder's presence and my fear of finding myself "cut off" by the operator, "I'm sorry," I said to Andrée, "I was interrupted. Is it absolutely certain that she has to go to the Verdurins' tomorrow?"

"Absolutely, but I can tell her that you don't want her to."

"No, not at all, but I might possibly come with you."

"Ah!" said Andrée, in a voice that sounded annoyed and somehow alarmed by my audacity, which was incidentally fortified as a result.

"Well then, good-night, and please forgive me for disturbing you for nothing."

"Not at all," said Andrée, and (since, now that the telephone has come into general use, a decorative ritual of polite phrases has grown up round it, as round the tea-tables of the past) she added: "It's been a great pleasure to hear your voice."

I might have said the same, and with greater truth than Andrée, for I had been deeply affected by the sound of her voice, having never noticed before that it was so different from the voices of other people. Then I recalled other voices still, women's voices especially, some of them slowed down by the precision of a question and by mental concentration, others made breathless, even interrupted at moments, by the lyrical flow of what they were relating; I recalled one by one the voices of all the girls I had known at Balbec, then Gilberte's, then my grandmother's, then Mme de Guermantes's; I found them all dissimilar, moulded by a speech peculiar to each of them, each playing on a different instrument, and I thought to myself how thin must be the concert performed in paradise by the three or four angel musicians of the old painters, when I saw, mounting to the throne of God by tens, by hundreds, by thousands, the harmonious and multiphonic salutation of all the Voices. I did not leave the telephone without thanking, in a few propitiatory words, the goddess who reigns over the speed of sound for having kindly exercised on behalf of my humble words a power which made them a hundred times more rapid than thunder. But my thanksgiving received no other response than that of being cut off.

When Albertine came back to my room, she was wearing a black satin dress which had the effect of making her seem paler, of turning her into the pallid, intense Parisian woman, etiolated by lack of fresh air, by the atmosphere of crowds and perhaps by the practice of vice, whose eyes seemed the more uneasy because they were not brightened by any colour in her cheeks.

"Guess," I said to her, "who I've just been talking to on the telephone. Andrée!"

"Andrée?" exclaimed Albertine in a loud, astonished, excited voice that so simple a piece of intelligence hardly seemed to call for. "I hope she remembered to tell you that we met Mme Verdurin the other day."

"Mme Verdurin? I don't remember," I replied as though I were thinking of something else, in order to appear indifferent to this meeting and not to betray Andrée who had told me where Albertine was going next day. But how could I tell whether Andrée was not herself betraying me, whether she would not tell Albertine tomorrow that I had asked her to prevent her at all costs from going to the Verdurins', and whether she had not already revealed to her that I had on several occasions made similar recommendations? She had assured me that she had never repeated anything, but the value of this assertion was counterbalanced in my mind by the impression that for some time past Albertine's face had ceased to show the trust that she had placed in me for so long.*

Suffering, when we are in love, ceases from time to time, but only to resume in a different form. We weep to see the beloved no longer respond to us with those bursts of affection, those amorous advances of earlier days; we suffer even more when, having relinquished them with us, she resumes them with others; then, from this suffering, we are distracted by a new and still more agonising pang, the suspicion that she has lied to us about how she spent the previous evening, when she was no doubt unfaithful to us; this suspicion in turn is dispelled, and we are soothed by our mistress's affectionate kindness; but then a forgotten word comes back to us; we had been told that she was ardent in moments of pleasure, whereas we have always found her calm; we try to picture to ourselves these passionate frenzies with others, we feel how very little we are to her, we observe an air of boredom, longing, melancholy while we are talking, we observe like a black sky the slovenly clothes she puts on when she is with us, keeping for other people the dresses with which she used to flatter us. If, on the contrary, she is affectionate, what joy for a moment! But when we see that little tongue stuck out as though in invitation, we think of those to whom that invitation was so often addressed that even perhaps with me, without her thinking of those others, it had remained for Albertine, by force of long habit, an automatic signal. Then the feeling that she is bored by us returns. But suddenly this pain is reduced to nothing when we think of the unknown evil element in her life, of the places, impossible to identify, where she has been, where she still goes perhaps during the hours when we are not with her, if indeed she is not planning to live there altogether, those places in which she is separated from us, does not belong to us, is happier than when she is with us. Such are the revolving searchlights of jealousy.

Jealousy is moreover a demon that cannot be exorcised, but constantly reappears in new incarnations. Even if we could succeed in exterminating them all, in keeping the beloved for ever, the Spirit of Evil would then adopt another form, more pathetic still, despair at having obtained fidelity only by force, despair at not being loved.

Tender and sweet though Albertine was on certain

evenings, she no longer had any of those spontaneous impulses which I remembered from Balbec when she used to say "How very nice you are, really!" and her whole heart seemed to go out to me unrestrained by any of those grievances which she now felt and which she kept to herself because she doubtless considered them irremediable, impossible to forget, unavowable, but which nevertheless created between us a significant verbal prudence on her part or an impassable barrier of silence.

"And may one be allowed to know why you telephoned to Andrée?"

"To ask whether she had any objection to my joining you tomorrow and paying the Verdurins the visit I've been promising them since La Raspelière."

"Just as you like. But I warn you, there's an appalling fog this evening, and it's sure to last over tomorrow. I mention it because I shouldn't like you to make yourself ill. Personally, I need hardly say that I'd love you to come with us. However," she added with a thoughtful air, "I'm not at all sure that I'll go to the Verdurins'. They've been so kind to me that I ought, really . . . Next to you, they've been nicer to me than anybody, but there are some things about them that I don't quite like. I simply must go to the Bon Marché or the Trois-Quartiers and get a white bodice to wear with this dress which is really too black."

To allow Albertine to go by herself into a big shop crowded with people perpetually brushing against one, provided with so many exits that a woman can always say that when she came out she could not find her carriage which was waiting further along the street, was something that I was quite determined never to consent to, but the thought of it made me extremely unhappy. And yet it did not occur to me that I ought long ago to have ceased to see Albertine, for she had entered, for me, upon that lamentable period in which a person, scattered in space and time, is no longer a woman but a series of events on which we can throw no light, a series of insoluble problems, a sea which, like Xerxes, we scourge with rods in an absurd attempt to punish it for what it has engulfed. Once this period has begun, we are perforce vanquished. Happy are they who understand this in time not to prolong unduly a futile, exhausting struggle, hemmed in on every side by the limits of the imagination, a struggle in which jealousy plays so sorry a part that the same man who, once upon a time, if the eyes of the woman who was always by his side rested for an instant upon another man, imagined an intrigue and suffered endless torments, now resigns himself to allowing her to go out by herself, sometimes with the man whom he knows to be her lover, preferring to the unknowable this torture which at least he knows! It is a question of the rhythm to be adopted, which afterwards one follows from force of habit. Neurotics who could never stay away from a dinner-party will eventually take rest cures which never seem to them to last long enough; women who recently were still of easy virtue live in penitence. Jealous lovers who, to keep an eye on the woman they loved, cut short their hours of sleep, deprived themselves of rest, now feeling that her desires, the world so vast and secret, and time are too much for them, allow her to go out without them, then to travel, and finally separate from her. Jealousy thus perishes for want of nourishment and has survived so long only by clamouring incessantly for fresh food. I was still a long way from this state.

I was now at liberty to go out with Albertine as often as I wished. As there had recently sprung up round Paris a number of aerodromes, which are to aeroplanes what harbours are to ships, and as, ever since the day when, on the way to La Raspelière, that almost mythological encounter with an airman, at whose passage overhead my horse had reared, had been to me like a symbol of liberty, I often chose to end our day's excursion—with the ready approval of Albertine, a passionate lover of every form of sport—at one of these aerodromes. We went there, she and I, attracted by that incessant stir of departure and arrival which gives so much charm to a stroll along a jetty, or merely along a beach, to those who love the sea, and to loitering about an "aviation centre" to those who love the sky. From time to time, amid the repose of the machines that lay inert and as though at anchor, we would see one being laboriously pulled by a number of mechanics, as a boat is dragged across the sand at the bidding of a tourist who wishes to go for an outing on the sea. Then the engine was started, the machine ran along the ground, gathered speed, until finally, all of a sudden, at right angles, it rose slowly, in the braced and as it were static ecstasy of a horizontal speed suddenly transformed into a majestic, vertical ascent. Albertine could not contain her joy, and would demand explanations of the mechanics who, now that the machine was in the air, were strolling back to the sheds. The passenger, meanwhile, was covering mile after mile; the huge skiff, upon which our eyes remained fixed, was now no more than a barely visible dot in the sky, a dot which, however, would gradually recover its solidity, its size, its volume, when, as the time allowed for the excursion drew to an end, the moment came for landing. And we watched with envy, Albertine and I, as he sprang to earth, the passenger who had gone up like that to enjoy in the solitary expanses of the open sky the calm and limpidity of evening. Then, whether from the aerodrome or from some museum or church that we had been visiting, we would return home together for dinner. And yet I did not return home calmed, as I used to be at Balbec by less frequent excursions which I rejoiced to see extend over a whole afternoon and would afterwards contemplate, standing out like clustering flowers, against the rest of Albertine's life as against an empty sky beneath which one muses pleasantly, without thinking. Albertine's time did not belong to me then in such ample quantities as today. Yet it had seemed to me then to belong to me much more, because I then took into account—my love rejoicing in them as in the bestowal of a favour—only the hours that she spent with me, whereas now—my jealousy searching anxiously among them for the possibility of a betrayal—it was only those hours that she spent apart from me.

Tomorrow, evidently, she was looking forward to a few such hours. I must choose to cease from suffering or to cease from loving. For, just as in the beginning it is formed by desire, so afterwards love is kept in existence only by painful anxiety. I felt that part of Albertine's life eluded me. Love, in the pain of anxiety as in the bliss of desire, is a demand for a whole. It is born, and it survives, only if some part remains for it to conquer. We love only what we do not wholly possess. Albertine was

lying when she told me that she probably would not go to
see the Verdurins, as I was lying when I said that I
wished to go. She was seeking merely to dissuade me from
going out with her, and I, by my abrupt announcement of
this plan which I had no intention of putting into practice, to touch what I felt to be her most sensitive spot, to
track down the desire that she was concealing and to force
her to admit that my company next day would prevent
her from gratifying it. She had virtually made this admission by ceasing suddenly to wish to go to see the Verdurins.

"If you don't want to go to the Verdurins'," I told
her, "there is a splendid charity show at the Trocadéro."
She listened to my exhortations to attend it with a doleful
air. I began to be harsh with her as at Balbec, at the time
of my first fit of jealousy. Her face reflected her disappointment, and in reproaching her I used the same arguments that had been so often advanced against me by my
parents when I was small, and that had appeared so unin-
telligent and cruel to my misunderstood childhood. "No,
in spite of your gloomy look," I said to Albertine, "I can't
feel sorry for you; I should feel sorry for you if you were
ill, if you were in trouble, if you had suffered some bereavement; not that you would mind in the least, I dare
say, considering your expenditure of false sensibility over
nothing. Besides, I'm not very impressed by the sensibility of people who pretend to be so fond of us and are
quite incapable of doing us the smallest favour, and whose
minds wander so that they forget to deliver the letter we
have entrusted to them on which our whole future depends."

A great part of what we say being no more than a

recitation from memory, I had often heard these words uttered by my mother, who (always ready to explain to me that one ought not to confuse genuine sensibility with sentimentality, what the Germans, whose language she greatly admired despite my grandfather's loathing for that nation, called *Empfindung* and *Empfindelei*) once, when I was in tears, had gone so far as to tell me that Nero was probably highly-strung and was none the better for that. Indeed, like those plants which bifurcate as they grow, side by side with the sensitive boy which was all that I had been, there was now a man of the opposite sort, full of common sense, of severity towards the morbid sensibility of others, a man resembling what my parents had been to me. No doubt, as each of us is obliged to continue in himself the life of his forebears, the level-headed, caustic individual who did not exist in me at the start had joined forces with the sensitive one, and it was natural that I should become in my turn what my parents had been to me. What is more, at the moment when this new personality took shape in me, he found his language ready made in the memory of the sarcastic, scolding things that had been said to me, that I must now say to others, and that came so naturally to my lips, either because I evoked them through mimicry and association of memories, or because the delicate and mysterious incrustations of genetic energy had traced in me unawares, as upon the leaf of a plant, the same intonations, the same gestures, the same attitudes as had been characteristic of those from whom I sprang. Sometimes, playing the sage when talking to Albertine, I seemed to be hearing my grandmother. Indeed it often happened to my mother (so many obscure unconscious currents caused everything in me even down to the tiniest movements of my fingers to be drawn into the same cycles as my parents) to imagine that it was my father at the door, so similar was my knock to his.

Moreover the coupling of contrary elements is the law of life, the principle of fertilisation, and, as we shall see, the cause of many misfortunes. As a rule we detest what resembles ourselves, and our own faults when observed in another person exasperate us. How much the more does a man who has passed the age at which one instinctively displays them, a man who, for instance, has maintained an expression of icy calm through the most aggravating moments, execrate those same faults if it is another man, younger or simpler or stupider, who displays them! There are sensitive people for whom merely to see in other people's eyes the tears which they themselves have held back is infuriating. It is excessive similarity that, in spite of affection, and sometimes all the more the greater the affection, causes division to reign in families.

Possibly in myself, as in many other people, the second man that I had become was simply another aspect of the first, excitable and sensitive where he himself was concerned, a sage mentor to others. Perhaps it was so also with my parents according to whether they were considered in relation to me or in themselves. In the case of my grandmother and mother it was only too clear that their severity towards me was deliberate on their part and indeed cost them dear, but perhaps even my father's coldness too was only an external aspect of his sensibility. For it was perhaps the human truth of this twofold aspect— the one concerned with the inner life, the other with social relations—that was expressed in a remark which seemed to me at the time as false in substance as it was commonplace in form, when someone said of my father: "Beneath his icy exterior, he conceals an extraordinary sensibility; the truth is that he's ashamed of his feelings." Did it not in fact conceal incessant secret storms, that calm of his, interspersed at times with sententious reflections and ironical comments on the awkward manifestations of sensibility, which now I too affected in my relations with everyone and above all never swerved from, in certain circumstances, with Albertine?

I really believe that I came near that day to making up my mind to break with her and to set out for Venice. What bound me anew in my chains had to do with Normandy, not that she showed any inclination to go to that region where I had been jealous of her (for it was my good fortune that her plans never impinged upon the painful zones in my memory), but because when I happened to say to her: "It's as though I were speaking to you about your aunt's friend who lived at Infreville," she replied angrily, delighted—like everyone in an argument who is anxious to muster as many points as possible on his side—to show me that I was in the wrong and herself in the right: "But my aunt never knew anybody at Infreville, and I've never been near the place." She had forgotten the lie that she had told me one afternoon about the touchy lady with whom she simply must go and have tea, even if by visiting this lady she were to forfeit my friendship and shorten her own life. I did not remind her of her lie. But it shattered me. And once again I postponed our rupture to another day. A person has no need of sincerity, nor even of skill in lying, in order to be loved. Here I mean by love reciprocal torture.

I saw nothing reprehensible that evening in speaking

to her as my grandmother—that mirror of perfection—
used to speak to me, nor, when I told her that I would
escort her to the Verdurins', in having adopted the
brusque manner of my father, who would never inform us
of any decision except in a manner calculated to cause us
the maximum of agitation, out of all proportion to the decision itself. So that it was easy for him to call us absurd
for appearing so distressed by so small a matter, our distress corresponding in reality to the perturbation that he
had aroused in us. And if—like the inflexible wisdom of
my grandmother—these arbitrary whims of my father's
had been passed on to me to complement the sensitive nature to which they had so long remained alien and,
throughout my whole childhood, had caused so much suffering, that sensitive nature informed them very exactly as
to the points at which they could most effectively be
aimed: there is no better informer than a reformed thief,
or a subject of the nation one is fighting. In certain untruthful families, a brother who has come to call without
any apparent reason and makes some casual inquiry on
the doorstep as he leaves, appearing scarcely to listen to
the answer, indicates thereby to his brother that this inquiry was the sole object of his visit, for the brother is
quite familiar with that air of detachment, those words uttered as though in parentheses and at the last moment,
having frequently had recourse to them himself. Similarly,
there are pathological families, kindred sensibilities, frater-
nal temperaments, initiated into that mute language which
enables the members of a family to understand each other
without speaking. Thus who can be more nerve-racking
than a neurotic? And then there may have been a deeper

and more general cause for my behaviour in these cases. In those brief but inevitable moments when we hate someone we love—moments which last sometimes for a whole lifetime in the case of people we do not love—we do not wish to appear kind in order not to be pitied, but at once as unpleasant and as happy as possible so that our happiness may be truly hateful and wound to the very soul the occasional or permanent enemy. To how many people have I not untruthfully maligned myself, simply in order that my "successes" might seem to them the more immoral and infuriate them the more! The proper thing to do would be to take the opposite course, to show without arrogance that we have generous feelings, instead of taking such pains to hide them. And this would be easy if we were capable of never hating, of always loving. For then we should be so happy to say only the things that can make other people happy, melt their hearts, make them love us.

True, I felt some remorse at being so insufferable to Albertine, and said to myself: "If I didn't love her, she would be more grateful to me, for I wouldn't be nasty to her; but no, it would be the same in the end, for I should also be less nice." And I might, in order to justify myself, have told her that I loved her. But the avowal of that love, apart from the fact that it would have told Albertine nothing new, would perhaps have made her colder towards me than the harshness and deceit for which love was the sole excuse. To be harsh and deceitful to the person whom we love is so natural! If the interest that we show towards other people does not prevent us from being gentle towards them and complying with their wishes, it is because our interest is not sincere. Other people leave us indifferent, and indifference does not prompt us to unkindness.

The evening was drawing to a close. Before Albertine went to bed, there was no time to lose if we wished to make peace, to renew our embraces. Neither of us had yet taken the initiative.

Meanwhile, feeling that in any case she was angry with me, I took the opportunity of mentioning Esther Lévy. "Bloch tells me," I said untruthfully, "that you're a great friend of his cousin Esther."

"I shouldn't know her if I saw her," said Albertine with a vague look.

"I've seen her photograph," I continued angrily. I did not look at Albertine as I said this, so that I did not see her expression, which would have been her sole reply, for she said nothing.

It was no longer the peace of my mother's kiss at Combray that I felt when I was with Albertine on these evenings, but, on the contrary, the anguish of those on which my mother scarcely bade me good-night, or even did not come up to my room at all, either because she was cross with me or was kept downstairs by guests. This anguish—not merely its transposition into love but this anguish itself—which for a time had specialised in love and which, when the separation, the division of the passions occurred, had been assigned to love alone, now seemed once more to be extending to them all, to have become indivisible again as in my childhood, as though all my feelings, which trembled at the thought of my not being able to keep Albertine by my bedside, at once as a mistress, a sister, a daughter, and as a mother too, of whose regular good-night kiss I was beginning once more to feel the childish need, had begun to coalesce, to become unified in the premature evening of my life which seemed fated to be as short as a winter day. But if I felt the same anguish as in my childhood, the different person who caused me to feel it, the difference in the feeling she inspired in me, the very transformation in my character, made it impossible for me to demand its appeasement from Albertine as in the old days from my mother. I could no longer say: "I'm unhappy." I confined myself, with a heavy heart, to speaking of inconsequential matters that took me no further towards a happy solution. I waded knee-deep in painful platitudes. And with that intellectual egoism which, if some insignificant fact happens to have a bearing on our love, makes us pay great respect to the person who has discovered it, as fortuitously perhaps as the fortune-teller who has foretold some trivial event which has afterwards come to pass, I came near to regarding Françoise as more inspired than Bergotte and Elstir because she had said to me at Balbec: "That girl will bring you nothing but trouble."

Every minute brought me nearer to Albertine's goodnight, which at length she said. But that evening her kiss, from which she herself was absent and which made no impression on me, left me so anxious that, with a throbbing heart, I watched her make her way to the door, thinking: "If I'm to find a pretext for calling her back, keeping her here, making peace with her, I must be quick; only a few steps and she will be out of the room, only two, now one, she's turning the handle; she's opening the door, it's too late, she has shut it behind her!" But perhaps it was not too late after all. As in the old days at

Combray when my mother had left me without soothing me with her kiss, I wanted to rush after Albertine, I felt that there would be no peace for me until I had seen her again, that this renewed encounter would turn into something tremendous which it had not been before and that—if I did not succeed by my own efforts in ridding myself of this misery—I might perhaps acquire the shameful habit of going to beg from Albertine. I sprang out of bed when she was already in her room, I paced up and down the corridor, hoping that she would come out of her room and call me; I stood stock-still outside her door for fear of failing to hear some faint summons, I returned for a moment to my own room to see whether she might not by some lucky chance have forgotten her handkerchief, her bag, something which I might have appeared to be afraid of her needing during the night, and which would have given me an excuse for going to her room. No, there was nothing. I returned to my station outside her door, but the crack beneath it no longer showed any light. Albertine had put out the light, she was in bed; I remained there motionless, hoping for some lucky accident which did not occur; and long afterwards, frozen, I returned to bestow myself between my own sheets and cried for the rest of the night.

But on certain such evenings I had recourse to a ruse which won me Albertine's kiss. Knowing how quickly sleep came to her as soon as she lay down (she knew it also, for, instinctively, before lying down, she would take off the slippers which I had given her, and her ring which she placed by the bedside, as she did in her own room when she went to bed), knowing how heavy her sleep was, how affectionate her awakening, I would find an excuse for going to look for something and make her lie down on my bed. When I returned she would be asleep and I saw before me the other woman that she became whenever one saw her full-face. But her personality quickly changed when I lay down beside her and saw her again in profile. I could take her head, lift it up, press her face to my lips, put her arms round my neck, and she would continue to sleep, like a watch that never stops, like an animal that stays in whatever position you put it in, like a climbing plant, a convolvulus which continues to thrust out its tendrils whatever support you give it. Only her breathing was altered by each touch of my fingers, as though she were an instrument on which I was playing and from which I extracted modulations by drawing different notes from one after another of its strings. My jealousy subsided, for I felt that Albertine had become a creature that breathes and is nothing else besides, as was indicated by the regular suspiration in which is expressed that pure physiological function which, wholly fluid, has the solidity neither of speech nor of silence; and, in its ignorance of all evil, drawn seemingly rather from a hollowed reed than from a human being, that breath, truly paradisiacal to me who at such moments felt Albertine to be withdrawn from everything, not only physically but morally, was the pure song of the angels. And yet, in that breathing, I thought to myself of a sudden that perhaps many names of people, borne on the stream of memory, must be revolving.

Sometimes indeed the human voice was added to that music. Albertine would murmur a few words. How I longed to catch their meaning! It would happen that the name of a person of whom we had been speaking and who had aroused my jealousy would come to her lips, but

without making me unhappy, for the memory that it
brought with it seemed to be only that of the conversations that she had had with me on the subject. One
evening, however, when with her eyes still shut she half
awoke, she said tenderly, addressing me: "Andrée." I concealed my emotion. "You're dreaming, I'm not Andrée," I
said to her, smiling. She smiled also: "Of course not, I
wanted to ask you what Andrée said to you this evening."
"I assumed that you used to lie beside her like that." "Oh
no, never," she said. But, before making this reply, she
had hidden her face for a moment in her hands. So her silences were merely screens, her surface affection merely
kept beneath the surface a thousand memories which
would have rent my heart, her life was full of those incidents the good-natured, bantering account of which forms
one's daily gossip at the expense of other people, people
who do not matter, but which, so long as a woman remains buried in the depths of one's heart, seem to us so
precious a revelation of her life that, for the privilege of
exploring that underlying world, we would gladly sacrifice
our own. Then her sleep would seem to me a marvellous
and magic world in which at certain moments there rises
from the depths of the barely translucent element the
avowal of a secret which we shall not understand. But as a
rule, when Albertine was asleep, she seemed to have recaptured her innocence. In the attitude which I had imposed upon her, but which in her sleep she had speedily
made her own, she seemed to trust herself to me. Her face
had lost any expression of cunning or vulgarity, and between herself and me, towards whom she raised her arm,
on whom she rested her hand, there seemed to be an absolute surrender, an indissoluble attachment. Her sleep

moreover did not separate her from me and allowed her to retain the consciousness of our affection; its effect was rather to abolish everything else; I would kiss her, tell her that I was going to take a turn outside, and she would half-open her eyes and say to me with a look of surprise—for the hour was indeed late—"But where are you off to, my darling——" (calling me by my Christian name), and at once fall asleep again. Her sleep was no more than a sort of blotting out of the rest of her life, an even silence over which from time to time familiar words of tenderness would pass in their flight. By putting these words together, one might have arrived at the unalloyed conversation, the secret intimacy of a pure love. This calm slumber delighted me, as a mother, reckoning it a virtue, is delighted by her child's sound sleep. And her sleep was indeed that of a child. Her awakening also, so natural and so loving, before she even knew where she was, that I sometimes asked myself with dread whether she had been in the habit, before coming to live with me, of not sleeping alone but of finding, when she opened her eyes, someone lying by her side. But her childlike grace was more striking. Like a mother again, I marvelled that she should always awake in such a good humour. After a few moments she would recover consciousness, would utter charming words, unconnected with one another, mere twitterings. By a sort of reversal of roles, her throat, which as a rule one seldom remarked, now almost startlingly beautiful, had acquired the immense importance which her eyes, by being closed in sleep, had lost, her eyes, my regular interlocutors to which I could no longer address myself after the lids had closed over them. Just as the closed lids impart an innocent, grave beauty to the face by suppressing all that the eyes express only too plainly, there was in the words, not devoid of meaning but interrupted by moments of silence, which Albertine uttered as she awoke, a pure beauty of a kind that is not constantly tarnished, as is conversation, by habits of speech, stale repetitions, traces of familiar defects. Moreover, when I had decided to wake Albertine, I would have been able to do so without fear, knowing that her awakening would bear no relation to the evening that we had passed together, but would emerge from her sleep as morning emerges from night. As soon as she had begun to open her eyes with a smile, she would have offered me her lips, and before she had even said a word, I would have savoured their freshness, as soothing as that of a garden still silent before the break of day.

The day after the evening when Albertine had told me that she might perhaps, then that she might not, be going to see the Verdurins, I awoke early, and, while I was still half asleep, my joy informed me that it was a spring day interpolated in the middle of the winter. Outside, popular themes skilfully transposed for various instruments, from the horn of the china repairer, or the trumpet of the chair mender, to the flute of the goatherd who seemed, on a fine morning, to be a Sicilian drover, were lightly orchestrating the matutinal air with an "Overture for a Public Holiday." Our hearing, that delightful sense, brings us the company of the street, of which it traces every line for us, sketches all the figures that pass along it, showing us their colours. The iron shutters of the baker's shop and of the dairy, which had been lowered last night over every possibility of feminine bliss, were now being raised, like the canvas of a ship that is getting under way and about to set sail across the transparent sea, on to a vision of young shopgirls. This sound of the iron shutters being raised would perhaps have been my sole pleasure in a different part of the town. In this quarter a hundred other sounds contributed to my joy, of which I would not have missed a single one by remaining too long asleep. It is one of the enchantments of the old aristocratic quarters that they are at the same time plebeian. Just as, sometimes, cathedrals used to have them within a stone's throw of their portals (which have even preserved the name, like the door of Rouen cathedral styled the Booksellers', because these latter used to expose their merchandise in the open air beside it), so various minor trades, but in this case itinerant, passed in front of the noble Hôtel de Guermantes, and made one think at times of the ecclesiastical France of long ago. For the beguiling calls which they launched at the little houses on either side had, with rare exceptions, little connexion with song. They differed from song as much as the declamation—scarcely tinged by even the most imperceptible modulation—of *Boris Godunov* and *Pelléas*; but on the other hand recalled the drone of a priest intoning his office, of which these street scenes are but the good-humoured, secular, and yet half-liturgical counterpart. Never had I so delighted in them as since Albertine had come to live with me; they seemed to me a joyous signal of her awakening, and by interesting me in the life of the world outside made me all the more conscious of the soothing virtue of a beloved presence, as constant as I could wish. Several of the foodstuffs peddled in the street, which personally I detested, were greatly to Albertine's liking, so much so that Françoise used to send her young footman out to buy them, slightly humiliated perhaps at finding himself mixing with the plebeian crowd. Very distinct in this peaceful quarter (where the noises were no longer a cause of lamentation to Françoise and had become a source of pleasure to myself), there reached my ears, each with its different modulation, recitatives declaimed by these humble folk as they would be in the music—so entirely popular—of *Boris*, where an initial tonality is barely altered by the inflexion of one note leaning upon another, music of the crowd, which is more speech than music. It was "Winkles, winkles, a ha'porth of winkles!" that brought people running to buy the cornets in which were sold those horrid little shellfish, which, if Albertine had not been there, would have repelled me, as did the snails which I heard being peddled at the same hour. Here again it was of the barely musical declamation of Moussorgsky that the vendor reminded me, but not of it alone. For after having almost "spoken" the refrain: "Who'll buy my snails, fine, fresh snails?" it was with the vague sadness of Maeterlinck, transposed into music by Debussy, that the snail vendor, in one of those mournful cadences in which the composer of *Pelléas* shows his kinship with Rameau: "If vanquished I must be, is it for thee to be my vanquisher?"[3] added with a singsong melancholy: "Only tuppence a dozen . . ."

I have always found it difficult to understand why these perfectly simple words were sighed in a tone so far from appropriate, as mysterious as the secret which makes everyone look sad in the old palace to which Mélisande has not succeeded in bringing joy, and as profound as one of the thoughts of the aged Arkel who seeks to utter in the simplest words the whole lore of wisdom and destiny. The very notes upon which the voice of the old King of Allemonde or that of Golaud rises with ever-increasing sweetness to say: "We do not know what is happening here. It may seem strange. Perhaps nothing that happens is in vain," or else: "You mustn't be frightened . . . she was a poor little mysterious creature, like everyone," were those which served the snail vendor to repeat in an end-less cantilena: "Only tuppence a dozen . . ." But this metaphysical lamentation scarcely had time to expire upon the shore of the infinite before it was interrupted by a shrill trumpet. This time it was not a question of victuals; the words of the libretto were: "Dogs clipped, cats doc-tored, tails and ears docked."

It was true that the fantasy or wit of each vendor or vendress frequently introduced variations into the words of all these chants that I used to hear from my bed. And yet a ritual suspension interposing a silence in the middle of a word, especially when it was repeated a second time, constantly evoked the memory of old churches. In his lit-tle cart drawn by a she-ass which he stopped in front of each house before entering the courtyard, the old-clothes man, brandishing a whip, intoned: "Old clothes, any old clothes, old clo . . . thes" with the same pause between the final syllables as if he had been intoning in plainchant: "*Per omnia saecula saeculo . . . rum*" or "*requiescat in pa . . . ce*" although he had no reason to believe in the im-mortality of his clothes, nor did he offer them as cere-ments for the eternal rest in peace. And similarly, as the

motifs, even at this early hour, were beginning to inter-
weave with one another, a costermonger pushing her little
hand-cart employed in her litany the Gregorian division:

> Tender and green,
> Artichokes tender and sweet,
> Ar . . . tichokes

although she had probably never heard of the antiph-
onary, or of the seven tones that symbolise, four the arts
of the quadrivium and three those of the trivium.

Drawing from a penny whistle, or from a bagpipe,
airs of his own southern country whose sunlight har-
monised well with these fine days, a man in a smock, carrying a bullwhip in his hand and wearing a Basque beret
on his head, stopped before each house in turn. It was the
goatherd with two dogs driving before him his string of
goats. As he came from a distance, he arrived fairly late in
our quarter; and the women came running out with bowls
to receive the milk that was to give strength to their little
ones. But with the Pyrenean airs of this benign shepherd
was now blended the bell of the grinder, who cried:
"Knives, scissors, razors." With him the saw-setter was
unable to compete, for, lacking an instrument, he had to
be content with calling: "Any saws to set? Here's the set-
ter!" while in a gayer mood the tinker, after enumerating
the pots, pans and everything else that he repaired, struck
up the refrain:

> Tan, ran, tan, tan, ran, tan,
> For pots or cans, oh! I'm your man.
> I'll mend them all with a tink, tink, tink,
> And never leave a chink, chink, chink,

and little Italians carrying big iron boxes painted red, upon which the numbers—winning and losing—were marked, and flourishing their rattles, issued the invitation: "Enjoy yourselves, ladies, here's a treat."

Françoise brought in the *Figaro*. A glance was sufficient to show me that my article had still not appeared. She told me that Albertine had asked whether she might come to my room and sent word that she had after all given up the idea of calling upon the Verdurins and had decided to go, as I had advised her, to the "special" matinée at the Trocadéro—what nowadays would be called, though with considerably less significance, a "gala" matinée—after a short ride which she had promised to take with Andrée. Now that I knew that she had abandoned her possibly nefarious intention of going to see Mme Verdurin, I said with a laugh: "Tell her to come in," and told myself that she might go wherever she chose and that it was all the same to me. I knew that by the end of the afternoon, when dusk began to fall, I should probably be a different man, moping, attaching to every one of Albertine's movements an importance that they did not possess at this morning hour when the weather was so fine. For my insouciance was accompanied by a clear notion of its cause, but was in no way modified thereby.

"Françoise assured me that you were awake and that I wouldn't be disturbing you," said Albertine as she entered the room. And since, next to making me catch cold by opening the window at the wrong moment, what Albertine most dreaded was to come into my room when I was asleep: "I hope I haven't done wrong," she went on. "I was afraid you'd say to me:

What insolent mortal comes to meet his doom?"

And she laughed that laugh which I always found so disturbing.

I replied in the same jesting vein:

Was it for you this stern decree was made?

And, lest she should ever venture to infringe it, added: "Although I'd be furious if you did wake me."

"I know, I know, don't be frightened," said Albertine.

To show that I was mollified, I added, still enacting the scene from *Esther* with her, while in the street below the cries continued, drowned by our conversation:

In you alone a certain grace I see
That always charms and never wearies me

(and to myself I thought: "Yes, she does weary me very often"). And remembering what she had said to me the night before, as I thanked her extravagantly for having given up the Verdurins, so that another time she would obey me similarly with regard to something else, I said: "Albertine, you distrust me although I love you and you place your trust in people who don't love you" (as though it were not natural to distrust the people who love you and who alone have an interest in lying to you in order to find out things, to thwart you), and added these lying words: "It's funny, you don't really believe that I love you. As a matter of fact, I don't *adore* you." She lied in her turn when she told me that she trusted nobody but myself and then became sincere when she assured me that she knew quite well that I loved her. But this affirmation did not seem to imply that she did not believe me to be a liar who spied on her. And she seemed to forgive me as though she saw these defects as the agonising consequence of a great love or as though she herself did not feel entirely guiltless.

"I beg of you, my darling girl, no more of that trick riding you were practising the other day. Just think, Albertine, if you were to have an accident!"*

Of course I did not wish her any harm. But how delighted I should have been if, with her horses, she had taken it into her head to ride off somewhere, wherever she chose, and never come back to my house again! How it would have simplified everything, that she should go and live happily somewhere else, I did not even wish to know where!

"Oh! I know you wouldn't survive me for forty-eight hours. You'd kill yourself."*

Thus did we exchange lying speeches. But a truth more profound than that which we would utter were we sincere may sometimes be expressed and announced by another channel than that of sincerity.

"You don't mind all that noise outside?" she asked me. "Personally I love it. But you're such a light sleeper."

I was on the contrary often an extremely heavy sleeper (as I have already said, but am compelled to repeat in view of what follows), especially when I only fell asleep in the morning. As this kind of sleep is—on an average—four times as refreshing, it seems to the awakened sleeper to have lasted four times as long, when it has really been four times as short. A splendid, sixteenfold error in multiplication which gives so much beauty to our awakening and gives life a veritable new dimension, like those drastic changes of rhythm which, in music, mean that in an andante a quaver has the same duration as a minim in a prestissimo, and which are unknown in our waking state. There, life is almost always the same, whence the disappointments of travel. Yet it would seem that our dreams are sometimes made of the coarsest stuff of life, but that stuff is as it were treated, kneaded so thoroughly—with a protraction due to the fact that none of the temporal limitations of the waking state is there to prevent it from tapering off into unbelievable heights— that we fail to recognise it. On the mornings after this good fortune had befallen me, after the sponge of sleep had wiped from my brain the signs of everyday occupations that are traced upon it as on a blackboard, I was obliged to bring my memory back to life; by an exercise of will we can recapture what the amnesia of sleep or of a stroke has made us forget, what gradually returns to us as our eyes open or our paralysis disappears. I had lived through so many hours in a few minutes that, wishing to address Françoise, for whom I had rung, in words that corresponded to the facts of real life and were regulated by the clock, I was obliged to exert all my inner power of compression in order not to say: "Well, Françoise, here we are at five o'clock in the evening and I haven't set eyes on you since yesterday afternoon." And seeking to dispel my dreams, giving them the lie and lying to myself as well, I said brazenly, compelling myself with all my might to silence, the direct opposite: "Françoise, it must be at least ten o'clock!" I did not even say ten o'clock in the morning, but simply ten o'clock, so that this incredible hour might appear to be uttered in a more natural tone. And yet to say these words, instead of those that continued to run in the mind of the half-awakened sleeper that I still was, demanded the same effort of equilibrium that a man requires when, jumping out of a moving train and running for some yards along the platform, he manages to avoid falling. He runs for a moment because the environment that he has just left was one animated by great velocity, and utterly unlike the inert soil to which his feet find it difficult to accustom themselves.

Because the dream world is not the waking world, it does not follow that the waking world is less real; far from it. In the world of sleep, our perceptions are so overloaded, each of them blanketed by a superimposed counterpart which doubles its bulk and blinds it to no purpose, that we are unable even to distinguish what is happening in the bewilderment of awakening: was it Françoise who had come to me, or I who, tired of calling her, went to her? Silence at that moment was the only way of revealing nothing, as when we are brought before a magistrate cognisant of all the charges against us when we ourselves have not been informed of them. Was it Françoise who had come, or was it I who had summoned her? Was it not, indeed, Françoise who had been asleep and I who had just awoken her? To go further still, was not Françoise contained within me, for the distinction between persons and their interaction barely exists in that murky obscurity in which reality is no more translucent than in the body of a porcupine, and our all but non-existent perception may perhaps give us an idea of the perception of certain animals? Besides, in the state of limpid unreason that precedes these heavy slumbers, if fragments of wisdom float there luminously, if the names of Taine and George Eliot are not unknown, the waking state remains none the less superior to the extent that it is possible to continue it every morning, but not to continue the dream life every night. But perhaps there are other worlds more real than the waking world. Even it we have seen transformed by each new revolution in the arts, and still more, at the same time, by the degree of proficiency or culture that distinguishes an artist from an ignorant fool.

And often an extra hour of sleep is an attack of paralysis after which we must recover the use of our limbs and learn to speak. Our will would not be adequate for this task. We have slept too long, we no longer exist. Our waking is barely felt, mechanically and without consciousness, as a water pipe might feel the turning off of a tap. A life more inanimate than that of the jellyfish follows, in which we could equally well believe that we had been drawn up from the depths of the sea or released from gaol, were we but capable of thinking anything at all. But then from the highest heaven the goddess Mnemotechnia bends down and holds out to us in the formula "the habit of ringing for coffee" the hope of resurrection. Even then, the instantaneous gift of memory is not always so simple. Often we have at our disposal, in those first minutes in which we allow ourselves to glide into the waking state, a variety of different realities among which we imagine that we can choose as from a pack of cards. It is Friday morning and we have just returned from a walk, or else it is teatime by the sea. The idea of sleep and that we are lying in bed in our nightshirt is often the last thing that occurs to us. The resurrection is not effected at once; we think we have rung the bell, but we have not done so, and we utter senseless remarks. Movement alone restores thought, and when we have actually pressed the electric button we are able to say slowly but distinctly: "It must be at least ten o'clock, Françoise. Bring me my coffee."

Françoise, *mirabile dictu*, could have had no suspicion of the sea of unreality in which I was still wholly immersed and through which I had had the energy to make my strange question penetrate. Her answer would be: "It's ten past ten," which made me appear quite rational and enabled me not to betray the fantastic conversations by which I had been interminably lulled (on days when a mountain of non-existence had not crushed all life out of me). By force of will, I had reintegrated myself with reality. I was still enjoying the last shreds of sleep, that is to say of the only source of invention, the only novelty that exists in story-telling, since none of our narrations in the waking state, even when embellished with literary graces, admit those mysterious differences from which beauty derives. It is easy to speak of the beauty created by opium. But to a man who is accustomed to sleeping only with the aid of drugs, an unexpected hour of natural sleep will reveal the vast, matutinal expanse of a landscape as mysterious and more refreshing. By varying the hour and the place in which we go to sleep, by wooing sleep in an artificial manner, or on the contrary by returning for a day to natural sleep—the strangest kind of all to whomsoever is in the habit of putting himself to sleep with soporifics—we succeed in producing a thousand times as many varieties of sleep as a gardener could produce of carnations or roses. Gardeners produce flowers that are delicious dreams, and others too that are like nightmares. When I fell asleep in a certain way I used to wake up shivering, thinking that I had caught the measles, or, what was far more painful, that my grandmother (of whom I no longer ever thought) was hurt because I had mocked her that day at Balbec when, in the belief that she was about to die, she had wished me to have a photograph of her. At once, although I was awake, I felt that I must go and explain to her that she had misunderstood me. But already my bodily warmth was returning. The diagnosis of measles was set aside, and my grandmother was so far away that she no longer made my heart ache.

Sometimes over these different kinds of sleep a sudden darkness fell. I was afraid to continue my walk along an entirely unlighted avenue, where I could hear prowling foot-steps. Suddenly an argument broke out between a policeman and one of those women whom one often saw driving hackney carriages, and mistook at a distance for young coachmen. Upon her box among the shadows I could not see her, but she was speaking, and in her voice I could read the perfections of her face and the youthfulness of her body. I strode towards her, in the darkness, to get into her carriage before she drove off. It was a long way. Fortunately, her argument with the policeman was prolonged. I overtook the carriage which was still stationary. This part of the avenue was lighted by street lamps. The driver became visible. It was indeed a woman, but large and old and corpulent, with white hair tumbling beneath her cap, and a strawberry mark on her face. I walked past her, thinking: "Is this what happens to the youth of women? If we have a sudden desire to see those we have met in the past, have they grown old? Is the young woman we desire like a character on the stage when, through the defection of the actress who created the part, the management is obliged to entrust it to a new star? But then it is no longer the same."

Then I would be overcome with a feeling of sadness. We have thus in our sleep countless images of pity, like Renaissance Pietà's, not, like them, wrought in marble, but on the contrary unsubstantial. They have their purpose, however, which is to remind us of a more compassionate, more humane view of things, which we are too apt to forget in the icy common sense, sometimes full of hostility, of the waking state. Thus I was reminded of the vow that I had made at Balbec that I would always treat Françoise with compassion. And for the whole of that morning at least I would manage to compel myself not to be irritated by Françoise's quarrels with the butler, to be gentle with Françoise to whom everyone else showed so little kindness. For that morning only, and I would have to try to frame a code that was a little more permanent; for, just as nations are not governed for any length of time by a policy of pure sentiment, so men are not governed for long by the memory of their dreams. Already this dream was beginning to fade away. In attempting to recall it in order to portray it I made it fade all the faster. My eyelids were no longer so firmly sealed over my eyes. If I tried to reconstruct my dream, they would open completely. We must constantly choose between health and sanity on the one hand, and spiritual pleasures on the other. I have always been cowardly enough to choose the former. Moreover, the perilous power that I was renouncing was even more perilous than one might suppose. Those dreams, those images of pity, do not fly away alone. When we alter thus the conditions in which we go to sleep, it is not our dreams alone that fade, but, for days on end, sometimes for years, the faculty not merely of dreaming but of going to sleep. Sleep is divine but by no means stable; the slightest shock makes it volatile. A friend to habit, it is kept night after night in its appointed place by habit, more steadfast than itself, protected from any possible disturbance; but if it is displaced, if it is no longer subjugated, it melts away like a vapour. It is like youth and love, never to be recaptured.

In these various forms of sleep, as likewise in music, it was the lengthening or shortening of the interval that created beauty. I enjoyed this beauty, but on the other hand I had missed in my sleep, however brief, a good number of the street cries which render perceptible to us the peripatetic life of the tradesmen, the victuallers of Paris. And so, habitually (without, alas, foreseeing the drama in which these late awakenings and the draconian, Medo-Persian laws of a Racinian Assuerus were presently to involve me) I made an effort to wake early so as to miss none of these cries. In addition to the pleasure of knowing how fond Albertine was of them and of being out of doors myself without leaving my bed, I heard in them as it were the symbol of the atmosphere of the world outside, of the dangerous stirring life through the midst of which I did not allow her to move save under my tutelage, in an external prolongation of her seclusion, and from which I withdrew her at the hour of my choosing to make her return home to my side.

Hence it was with the utmost sincerity that I was able to say in answer to Albertine: "On the contrary, they give me pleasure because I know that you like them."

"Straight from the boat, oysters, from the boat!"

"Oh, oysters! I've been simply longing for some!"

Fortunately Albertine, partly from fickleness, partly from docility, quickly forgot the things for which she had been longing, and before I had time to tell her that she would find better oysters at Prunier's, she wanted in succession all the things that she heard cried by the fish woman: "Prawns, lovely prawns, alive, alive-o . . . skate, nice fresh skate . . . whiting to fry, to fry . . . here comes the mackerel, freshly caught mackerel, my ladies, beautiful mackerel . . . who'll buy my mussels, fine fat mussels!"

In spite of myself, the warning: "Here comes the mackerel" made me shudder. But as this warning could not, I felt, apply to our chauffeur, I thought only of the fish of that name, which I detested, and my uneasiness did not last.[4]

"Ah! mussels," said Albertine, "I should so like some mussels."

"My darling! They were all very well at Balbec, but here they're not worth eating; besides, I implore you, remember what Cottard told you about mussels."

But my remark was all the more ill-chosen in that the next costermonger announced a thing that Cottard had forbidden even more strictly:

> Lettuce, cos lettuce, not to hawk,
> Lovely cos lettuce out for a walk.

Albertine consented, however, to forgo the cos lettuces, on the condition that I would promise to buy for her in a few days' time from the woman who cried: "Argenteuil asparagus, lovely green asparagus." A mysterious voice, from which one would have expected some stranger utterance, insinuated: "Barrels, barrels . . ." One was obliged to remain under the disappointing impression that nothing more was being offered than barrels, for the word was almost entirely drowned by the cry: "Glazier, gla-zier, any broken panes, here comes the gla-zier," a Gregorian division which reminded me less, however, of the liturgy than did the call of the rag-and-bone man, unwittingly reproducing one of those abrupt changes of tone in the middle of a prayer which are common enough in the ritual of the church: "*Praeceptis salutaribus moniti et divina institutione formati, audemus dicere*," says the priest, ending briskly upon "*dicere*." Without irreverence, as the pious of the Middle Ages used to perform farces and satires on the very threshold of the church, it was of that "*dicere*" that the rag-and-bone man reminded one when, after drawling the other words, he uttered the final syllable with a brusqueness befitting the accentuation laid down by the great seventh-century Pope: "Any old rags, any old iron, any . . ." (all this chanted slowly, as were the two syllables that followed, whereas the last concluded more briskly than "*dicere*") "rabbit . . . skins." The oranges ("Valencia oranges, lovely ripe oranges"), the humble leeks even ("Here's fine leeks"), the onions ("Threepence a rope") sounded for me as it were an echo of the rolling waves in which, left to herself, Albertine might have perished, and thus assumed the sweetness of a *suave mari magno*.

> Here's carrots for lunch
> At tuppence a bunch.

"Oh!" exclaimed Albertine, "cabbages, carrots, oranges. Just the things I want to eat. Do make Françoise go out and buy some. She shall cook us a dish of creamed carrots. Besides, it will be so nice to eat all these things together. It will be all the shouts we're hearing transformed into a good dinner. Oh, please, ask Françoise to give us instead skate *au beurre noir*. It's so good!"

"Very well, my little darling. But don't stay any longer, otherwise you'll be asking for every single thing on the barrows."

"All right, I'm off, but I never want anything again for our dinners, except what we've heard cried in the street. It's such fun. And to think that we shall have to wait two whole months before we hear: 'Green and tender beans, fresh green beans!' How true that is: tender beans; you know I like them as soft as soft, dripping with oil and vinegar, you wouldn't think you were eating them, they melt in the mouth like drops of dew. Oh dear, it's the same with the cream cheese, such a long time to wait: 'Good cream cheese, fresh cheese!' And the dessert grapes from Fontainebleau: 'Best *chasselas* for sale.'" (And I thought with dismay of all the time that I should have to spend with her before those grapes were in season.) "Wait, though. I said I wanted only the things that we had heard cried, but of course I make exceptions. And so it's by no means impossible that I may look in at Rebattet's and order an ice for the two of us. You'll tell me that it's not the season for them, but I do so want one!"

I was disturbed by this plan of going to Rebattet's, rendered more certain and more suspect in my eyes by the words "it's by no means impossible." It was the day on which the Verdurins were "at home," and, ever since Swann had informed them that Rebattet's was the best place, it was there that they ordered their ices and pastries.

"I have no objection to an ice, my darling Albertine, but let me order it for you, I don't know myself whether it will be from Poiré-Blanche's, or Rebattet's, or the Ritz, anyhow I shall see."

"Then you're going out?" she said with a look of mistrust.

She always maintained that she would be delighted if I went out more often, but if anything I said gave her to suppose that I would not be staying indoors, her uneasy air made me think that the joy she would evince on seeing me go out more often was perhaps not altogether sincere.

"I may perhaps go out, perhaps not. You know quite well that I never make plans beforehand. In any case ices are not a thing that's hawked in the streets, so why do you want one?"

And then she answered me in words which showed me what a fund of intelligence and latent taste had suddenly developed in her since Balbec, in words akin to those which, she maintained, were due entirely to my influence, to living continually in my company, words which, however, I should never have uttered, as though I had been somehow forbidden by an unknown authority ever to decorate my conversation with literary forms. Perhaps the future was not destined to be the same for Albertine as for myself. I had almost a presentiment of this when I saw her eagerness to employ in speech images so "bookish," which seemed to me to be reserved for another, more sacred use, of which I was still in ignorance. She said to me (and I was, in spite of everything, deeply touched, for I thought to myself: True, I myself wouldn't speak like that, and yet, all the same, but for me *she* wouldn't be speaking like that. She has been profoundly influenced by me, and cannot therefore help but love me, since she is my creation): "What I like about these foodstuffs that the pedlars cry is that a thing heard like a rhapsody changes its nature when it comes to the table and addresses itself to my palate. As for ices (for I hope that you won't order me one that isn't cast in one of those old-fashioned moulds which have every architectural shape imaginable), whenever I eat them, temples, churches, obelisks, rocks, a sort of picturesque geography is what I see at first before converting its raspberry or vanilla monuments into coolness in my gullet."

I thought that this was a little too well expressed, but she felt that I thought that it was well expressed and went on, pausing for a moment when she had brought off a simile to laugh that beautiful laugh of hers which was so painful to me because it was so voluptuous.

"Oh dear, at the Ritz I'm afraid you'll find Vendôme Columns of ice, chocolate ice or raspberry, and then you'll need a lot of them so that they may look like votive pillars or pylons erected along an avenue to the glory of Coolness. They make raspberry obelisks too, which will rise up here and there in the burning desert of my thirst, and I shall make their pink granite crumble and melt deep down in my throat which they will refresh better than any oasis" (and here the deep laugh broke out, whether from satisfaction at talking so well, or in self-mockery for using such carefully contrived images, or, alas, from physical pleasure at feeling inside herself something so good, so cool, which was tantamount to a sexual pleasure). "Those mountains of ice at the Ritz sometimes suggest Monte Rosa, and indeed, if it's a lemon ice, I don't object to its not having a monumental shape, its being irregular, abrupt, like one of Elstir's mountains. It mustn't be too white then, but slightly yellowish, with that look of dull, dirty snow that Elstir's mountains have. The ice needn't be at all big, only half an ice if you like, those lemon ices are still mountains, reduced to a tiny scale, but our imagination restores their dimensions, like those Japanese dwarf trees which one feels are still cedars, oaks, manchineels; so much so that if I arranged a few of them beside a little trickle of water in my room I should have a vast forest, stretching down to a river, in which children would lose their way. In the same way, at the foot of my yellowish lemon ice, I can see quite clearly postillions, travellers, post-chaises over which my tongue sets to work to roll down freezing avalanches that will swallow them up" (the cruel delight with which she said this excited my jealousy); "just as," she went on, "I set my lips to work to destroy, pillar by pillar, those Venetian churches of a porphyry that is made with strawberries, and send what's left over crashing down upon the worshippers. Yes, all those monuments will pass from their stony state into my inside which thrills already with their melting coolness. But, you know, even without ices, nothing is so exciting or makes one so thirsty as the advertisements for thermal springs. At Montjouvain, at Mlle Vinteuil's, there was no good confectioner who made ices in the neighbourhood, but we used to make our own tour of France in the garden by drinking a different mineral water every day, like Vichy water which, as soon as you pour it out, sends up from the bottom of the glass a white cloud which fades and dissolves if you don't drink it at once."

But to hear her speak of Montjouvain was too painful, and I cut her short.

"I'm boring you, good-bye my darling," she said.

What a change from Balbec, where I would defy Elstir himself to have been able to divine in Albertine this wealth of poetry, though a poetry less strange, less personal than that of Céleste Albaret, for instance. Albertine would never have thought of the things that Céleste used to say to me, but love, even when it seems to be nearing its end, is partial. I preferred the picturesque geography of her ices, the somewhat facile charm of which seemed to me a reason for loving Albertine and a proof that I had some power over her, that she loved me.

As soon as Albertine had gone out, I felt how exhausting was her perpetual presence, insatiable in its restless animation, which disturbed my sleep with its movements, made me live in a perpetual chill by her habit of leaving doors open, and forced me—in order to find excuses that would justify my not accompanying her, without, however, appearing too unwell, and at the same time seeing that she was not unaccompanied—to display every day greater ingenuity than Sheherazade. Unfortunately, if by a similar ingenuity the Persian storyteller postponed her own death, I was hastening mine. There are thus in life certain situations that are not all created, as was this, by amorous jealousy and a precarious state of health which does not permit us to share the life of a young and active person, situations in which nevertheless the problem of whether to continue a shared life or to return to the separate existence of the past poses itself almost in medical terms: to which of the two sorts of repose ought we to sacrifice ourselves (by continuing the daily strain, or by returning to the agonies of separation)—to that of the head or that of the heart?

In any event, I was very glad that Andrée was to accompany Albertine to the Trocadéro, for recent and on the whole fairly trivial incidents had persuaded me that—though I still had, of course, the same confidence in the chauffeur's honesty—his vigilance, or at least the perspicacity of his vigilance, was not quite what it had once been. It happened that, only a short while before, I had sent Albertine alone in his charge to Versailles, and she told me that she had had lunch at the Réservoirs; as the chauffeur had mentioned Vatel's restaurant, on discovering this contradiction I found an excuse to go downstairs and speak to him (it was still the same man, whose acquaintance we made at Balbec) while Albertine was dressing.

"You told me that you had lunch at Vatel's, but Mlle Albertine mentioned the Réservoirs. What's the explanation?"

The chauffeur replied: "Oh, I said I had my lunch at Vatel's, but I've no idea where Mademoiselle had hers. She left me as soon as we reached Versailles to take a horse cab, which she prefers when it isn't a long drive."

Already I was furious at the thought that she had been alone; still, it was only during the time that it took her to have lunch.

"You might surely," I suggested mildly (for I did not wish to appear to be keeping Albertine actually under surveillance, which would have been humiliating to myself, and doubly so, for it would have shown that she concealed her activities from me), "have had your lunch, I don't say at her table, but in the same restaurant?"

"But she told me not to bother to meet her before six o'clock in the Place d'Armes. I wasn't to call for her after lunch."

"Ah!" I said, making an effort to conceal my dismay. And I returned upstairs. So it was for more than seven hours on end that Albertine had been alone, left to her own devices. I could reassure myself, it is true, that the cab had not been merely an expedient whereby to escape from the chauffeur's supervision. In town, Albertine preferred dawdling in a cab, saying that one had a better view, that the air was milder. Nevertheless, she had spent seven hours about which I should never know anything. And I dared not think of the manner in which she must have spent them. I felt that the driver had been extremely maladroit, but my confidence in him was henceforth absolute. For if he had been to the slightest extent in league with Albertine, he would never have admitted that he had left her unguarded from eleven o'clock in the morning until six in the evening. There could be but one other explanation (and it was absurd) of the chauffeur's admission. This was that some quarrel between Albertine and himself had prompted him, by making a minor disclosure to me, to show her that he was not the sort of man who could be silenced, and that if, after this first gentle warning, she did not toe the line with him, he would simply spill the beans. But this explanation was absurd; it first of all presupposed a non-existent quarrel between him and Albertine, and then meant attributing the character of a blackmailer to this handsome chauffeur who had always shown himself so affable and obliging. In fact, two days later I saw that he was more capable than in my suspicious frenzy I had for a moment supposed of exercising over Albertine a discreet and perspicacious vigilance. Having managed to take him aside and talk to him of what he had told me about Versailles, I said to him in a casual, friendly tone: "That drive to Versailles you told me about the other day was everything that it should have been, you behaved perfectly as you always do. But if I may give you just a little hint, nothing of any great consequence, I feel such a responsibility now that Mme Bontemps has placed her niece in my charge, I'm so afraid of accidents, I feel so guilty about not accompanying her, that I'd be happier if it were you alone, you who are so safe, so wonderfully skilful, to whom no accident can possibly happen, who drove Mlle Albertine everywhere. Then I need fear nothing."

The charming apostolic motorist smiled a subtle smile, his hand resting upon the consecration-cross of his wheel.[5] Then he answered me in the following words which (banishing all the anxiety from my heart and filling it instead with joy) made me want to fling my arms round his neck.

"Never fear," he said to me. "Nothing can happen to her, for when my wheel isn't guiding her, my eye follows her everywhere. At Versailles, I went quietly along and visited the town with her, as you might say. From the Réservoirs she went to the Château, from the Château to the two Trianons, with me following her all the time without appearing to see her, and the amazing thing is that she never saw me. Oh, even if she had it wouldn't have been such a calamity. It was only natural, since I had the whole day before me with nothing to do, that I should visit the Château too. All the more so because Mademoiselle certainly can't have failed to notice that I've read a bit myself and take an interest in all those old curiosities." (This was true; indeed I should have been surprised if I had learned that he was a friend of Morel's, so far did he surpass the violinist in taste and sensitivity.) "Anyhow, she didn't see me."

"She must have met some of her friends, of course, for she has several at Versailles."

"No, she was alone all the time."

"Then people must have stared at her, such a dazzling young lady all by herself."

"Why, of course they stared at her, but she knew practically nothing about it; she went round all the time with her eyes glued to her guide-book, or gazing up at the pictures."

The chauffeur's story seemed to me all the more accurate in that it was indeed a postcard representing the Château, and another representing the two Trianons, that Albertine had sent me on the day of her visit. The care with which the obliging chauffeur had followed every step of her itinerary touched me deeply. How could I have supposed that this rectification—in the form of a generous amplification—of the account he had given two days earlier was due to the fact that in those two days Albertine, alarmed that the chauffeur should have spoken to me, had submitted and made her peace with him? This suspicion never even occurred to me. What is certain is that this version of the chauffeur's story, by ridding me of any fear that Albertine might have deceived me, quite naturally cooled my ardour towards my mistress and made me take less interest in the day that she had spent at Versailles. I think, however, that the chauffeur's explanations, which, by absolving Albertine, made her seem even more boring to me than before, would not perhaps have been sufficient to calm me so quickly. Two little pimples which she had on her forehead for a few days were perhaps even more effective in modifying the feelings of my heart. Finally, these feelings were diverted fur-

ther still from her (so far that I was conscious of her existence only when I set eyes on her) by the strange
confidence volunteered me by Gilberte's maid, whom I
met by chance. I learned that, when I used to go to see
Gilberte every day, she was in love with a young man of
whom she saw a great deal more than of myself. I had
had a momentary inkling of this at the time, and indeed I
had questioned this very maid. But, as she knew that I
was in love with Gilberte, she had denied the story, had
sworn that Mlle Swann had never set eyes on the young
man. Now, however, knowing that my love had long since
died, that for years past I had left all her letters unan-
swered—and also perhaps because she was no longer in
Gilberte's service—of her own accord she gave me a full
account of the amorous episode of which I had known
nothing. This seemed to her quite natural. I assumed, remembering the oaths she had sworn at the time, that she
had not been aware of what was going on. Not at all; it
was she herself who used to go, on the orders of Mme
Swann, to inform the young man whenever the one I
loved was alone. The one I loved then . . . But I asked
myself whether my love of those days was as dead as I
thought, for this story pained me. Since I do not believe
that jealousy can revive a dead love, I supposed that my
painful impression was due, in part at least, to the injury
to my self-esteem, for a number of people whom I did not
like and who at that time and even a little later—their attitude has since altered—affected a contemptuous attitude
towards me, knew perfectly well, while I was in love with
Gilberte, that I was being duped. And this made me wonder retrospectively whether in my love for Gilberte there
had not been an element of self-love, since it so pained

me now to discover that all the hours of tenderness which had made me so happy were recognised, by people I did not like, as downright deception on Gilberte's part at my expense. In any case, love or self-love, Gilberte was almost dead in me, but not entirely, and the result of this chagrin was to prevent me from worrying unduly about Albertine, who occupied so small a place in my heart. Nevertheless, to return to her (after so long a digression) and to her expedition to Versailles, the postcards of Versailles (is it possible, then, to have one's heart thus obliquely assailed by two simultaneous and interwoven jealousies, each inspired by a different person?) gave me a slightly disagreeable impression whenever my eye fell upon them as I tidied my papers. And I thought that if the chauffeur had not been such a worthy fellow, the accordance of his second narrative with Albertine's cards would not have amounted to much, for what are the first things that people send you from Versailles but the Château and the Trianons, unless the cards have been chosen by some sophisticated person who adores a certain statue, or by some idiot who selects as a "view" of Versailles the horse tramway station or the goods depot.

But perhaps I am wrong in saying an idiot, such postcards not having always been bought by a person of that sort at random, for their interest as coming from Versailles. For two whole years men of intelligence, artists, used to find Siena, Venice, Granada a "bore," and would say of the humblest omnibus, of every railway carriage: "There you have true beauty." Then this fancy passed like the rest. Indeed, I am not sure that people did not revert to the "sacrilege of destroying the noble relics of the past." At any rate, a first-class railway carriage ceased to be regarded as *a priori* more beautiful than St Mark's in Venice. People continued to say: "Here you have real life, the return to the past is artificial," but without drawing any definite conclusion. At all events, while retaining full confidence in the chauffeur, to ensure that Albertine would be unable to desert him without his daring to stop her for fear of being taken for a spy, I no longer allowed her to go out after this without the reinforcement of Andrée, whereas for a time I had found the chauffeur sufficient. I had even allowed her then (a thing I would never dare do now) to stay away for three whole days by herself with the chauffeur and to go almost as far as Balbec, such a craving did she have for travelling at high speed in an open car. Three days during which my mind had been quite at rest, although the rain of postcards that she had showered upon me did not reach me, owing to the appalling state of the Breton postal system (good in summer, but disorganised, no doubt, in winter), until a week after the return of Albertine and the chauffeur, so hale and hearty that on the very morning of their return they resumed their daily outings as though nothing had happened. I was delighted that Albertine should be going this afternoon to the Trocadéro, to this "special" matinée, but above all reassured by the fact that she would have a companion there in the shape of Andrée.

Dismissing these reflexions, now that Albertine had gone out, I went and stood for a moment at the window. There was at first a silence, amid which the whistle of the tripe vendor and the hooting of the trams reverberated through the air in different octaves, like a blind piano-tuner. Then gradually the interwoven motifs became distinct, and others were combined with them. There was also a new whistle, the call of a vendor the nature of whose wares I never discovered, a whistle that exactly resembled the whistle of the trams, and since it was not carried out of earshot by its own velocity, it gave the impression of a single tram-car, not endowed with motion, or broken down, immobilised, screeching at brief intervals like a dying animal.

And I felt that, should I ever have to leave this aristocratic quarter—unless it were to move to one that was entirely plebeian—the streets and boulevards of central Paris (where the greengrocery, fishmongering and other trades, established in big stores, rendered superfluous the cries of the street hawkers, who in any case would have been unable to make themselves heard) would seem to me very dreary, quite uninhabitable, stripped, drained of all these litanies of the small trades and itinerant victuals, deprived of the orchestra that came every morning to charm me. On the pavement a woman with no pretence to fashion (or else obedient to an ugly fashion) came past, too brightly dressed in a sack overcoat of goatskin; but no, it was not a woman, it was a chauffeur who, enveloped in his goatskin, was proceeding on foot to his garage. Winged messengers of variegated hue, escaped from the big hotels, were speeding towards the stations bent over their handlebars, to meet the arrivals by the morning trains. The whirring of a violin was due at one time to the passing of a car, at another to my not having put enough water in my electric hot-water bottle. In the middle of the symphony an old-fashioned tune rang out; replacing the sweet-seller, who generally accompanied her song with a rattle, the toy-seller, to whose kazoo was attached a jump-

ing-jack which he sent bobbing in all directions, paraded
other puppets for sale, and, indifferent to the ritual declamation of Gregory the Great, the reformed declamation of
Palestrina or the lyrical declamation of the moderns, warbled at the top of his voice, a belated adherent of pure
melody:

> Come along all you mammies and dads,
> Here's toys for your lasses and lads!
> I make them myself,
> And I pocket the pelf.
> Tralala, tralala, tralalee.
> Come along youngsters . . .

Making no attempt to compete with this lively aria,
little Italians in berets offered their statuettes for sale in
silence. Soon, however, a young fifer compelled the toy
merchant to move on and to chant more inaudibly,
though in brisk time: "Come along all you mammies and
dads!" Was this young fifer one of the dragoons whom I
used to hear in the mornings at Donciéres? No, for what
followed was: "Here comes the china restorer. I repair
glass, marble, crystal, bone, ivory and antiques. Here
comes the restorer." In a butcher's shop, between an aureole of sunshine on the left and a whole ox suspended from
a hook on the right, a young assistant, very tall and slender, with fair hair and a long neck emerging from a sky-
blue collar, was displaying a lightning speed and a
religious conscientiousness in putting on one side the
most exquisite fillets of beef, on the other the coarsest
parts of the rump, and placing them on glittering scales
surmounted by a cross from which there dangled a set of
beautiful chains, and—although he did nothing after-

wards but arrange in the window a display of kidneys, steaks and ribs—was really far more reminiscent of a handsome angel who, on the Day of Judgment, will organise for God, according to their quality, the separation of the good and the wicked and the weighing of souls. And once again the thin, shrill music of the fife rose into the air, herald no longer of the destruction that Françoise used to dread whenever a regiment of cavalry filed past, but of "repairs" promised by an "antiquary," simpleton or rogue, who, in either case highly eclectic and very far from specialising, applied his art to the most diverse materials. The little bakers' girls hastened to stuff into their baskets the long loaves ordered for some luncheon party, while the dairymaids deftly attached the milk-churns to their yokes. Could it, I wondered, be altogether warranted, the nostalgic view I had of these young creatures? Would it not have been different if I had been able to detain for a few moments at close quarters one of those whom from the height of my window I saw only inside their shops or in motion? To estimate the loss that I suffered by my seclusion, that is to say the riches that the day had to offer me, I should have had to intercept in the long unwinding of the animated frieze some damsel carrying her laundry or her milk, transfer her for a moment, like the silhouette of a mobile piece of stage décor between its supports, into the frame of my door, and keep her there before my eyes for long enough to elicit some information about her which would enable me to find her again some day, like the identification discs which ornithologists or ichthyologists attach before setting them free to the legs or bellies of the birds or fishes whose migrations they are anxious to trace.

And so I told Françoise that I wanted some shopping done, and asked her to send up to me, should any of them call, one or other of the girls who were constantly coming to the house with laundry or bread or jugs of milk, and whom she herself used often to send on errands. In doing so I was like Elstir, who, obliged to remain closeted in his studio, on certain days in spring when the knowledge that the woods were full of violets gave him a hunger to see some, used to send his concierge out to buy him a bunch; and then it was not the table upon which he had posed the little floral model, but the whole carpet of undergrowth where in other years he had seen, in their thousands, the serpentine stems bowed beneath the weight of their tiny blue heads, that Elstir would fancy that he had before his eyes, like an imaginary zone defined in his studio by the limpid odour of the evocative flower.

Of a laundry girl, on a Sunday, there was not the slightest prospect. As for the baker's girl, as ill luck would have it she had rung the bell when Françoise was not about, had left her loaves in their basket on the landing, and had made off. The greengrocer's girl would not call until much later. Once, I had gone to order a cheese at the dairy, and among the various young female employees had noticed a startling towhead, tall in stature though little more than a child, who seemed to be day-dreaming, amid the other errand-girls, in a distinctly haughty attitude. I had seen her from a distance only, and for so brief an instant that I could not have described her appearance, except to say that she must have grown too fast and that her head supported a mane that gave the impression far less of capillary characteristics than of a sculptor's stylised

rendering of the separate meanderings of parallel snow-
tracks on a mountainside. This was all that I had been
able to make out, apart from a sharply defined nose (a
rare thing in a child) in a thin face, which recalled the
beaks of baby vultures. It was not only the clustering of
her comrades round her that prevented me from seeing
her distinctly, but also my uncertainty whether the sentiments which I might, at first sight and subsequently, inspire in her would be those of shy pride, or of irony, or of
a scorn which she would express later on to her friends.
These alternative suppositions which I had formed about
her in a flash had thickened the blurred atmosphere
around her in which she was veiled like a goddess in a
cloud shaken by thunder. For moral uncertainty is a
greater obstacle to an exact visual perception than any defect of vision would be. In this too skinny young person,
who also struck one's attention too forcibly, the excess of
what another person would perhaps have called her
charms was precisely what was calculated to repel me, but
had nevertheless had the effect of preventing me from
even noticing, let alone remembering, anything about the
other dairymaids, whom the aquiline nose of this one and
her uninviting look, pensive, private, seeming to be passing judgment, had totally eclipsed, as a white streak of
lightning plunges the surrounding countryside into darkness. And thus, of my call to order a cheese at the dairy, I
had remembered (if one can say "remember" in speaking
of someone so carelessly observed that one adapts to the
nullity of the face ten different noses in succession), I had
remembered only the girl I had found unpleasing. This
can be enough to set a love affair in motion. And yet I
might have forgotten the startling towhead and might

never have wished to see her again, had not Françoise told me that, though still quite a nipper, she had all her wits about her and would shortly be leaving her employer, since she had been going too fast and owed money in the neighbourhood. It has been said that beauty is a promise of happiness. Conversely, the possibility of pleasure may be a beginning of beauty.

I began to read Mamma's letter. Behind her quotations from Mme de Sévigné ("If my thoughts are not entirely black at Combray, they are at least dark grey; I think of you constantly; I long for you; your health, your affairs, your absence: think how they must seem to me when the dusk descends") I sensed that my mother was vexed to find Albertine's stay in the house prolonged, and my intention of marriage, although not yet announced to the betrothed, confirmed. She did not express her annoyance more directly because she was afraid that I might leave her letters lying about. Even then, veiled as they were, she reproached me for not informing her immediately, after each of them, that I had received it: "You remember how Mme de Sévigné used to say: 'When one is far away, one no longer laughs at letters which begin: *I have received yours.*'" Without referring to what distressed her most, she expressed displeasure at my lavish expenditure: "Where on earth does all your money go? It is distressing enough that, like Charles de Sévigné, you do not know what you want and are 'two or three people at once,' but do try at least not to be like him in spending money so that I may never have to say of you: 'He has discovered how to spend and have nothing to show, how to lose without gambling and how to pay without clearing himself of debt.'"

I had just finished Mamma's letter when Françoise returned to tell me that she had in the house that same rather too forward young dairymaid of whom she had spoken to me. "She can quite well take Monsieur's letter and do his shopping for him if it's not too far. You'll see, she's just like a Little Red Ridinghood." Françoise went to fetch the girl, and I could hear her showing the way and saying: "Come along now, frightened because there's a passage! Stuff and nonsense, I never thought you'd be such a goose. Have I got to lead you by the hand?" And Françoise, like a good and faithful servant who means to see that her master is respected as she respects him herself, had draped herself in the majesty that ennobles the procuress in the paintings of the old masters, wherein the mistress and the lover fade into insignificance by comparison.

Elstir, when he gazed at the violets, had no need to bother about what they were doing. The entry of the young dairymaid at once robbed me of my contemplative calm; I could no longer think of anything except how to give plausibility to the fable of the letter that she was to deliver and I began to write quickly without venturing to cast more than a furtive glance at her, so that I might not seem to have brought her into my room to be scrutinised. She was invested for me with that charm of the unknown which would not have existed for me in a pretty girl whom I had found in one of those houses where they attend on one. She was neither naked nor in disguise, but a genuine dairymaid, one of those whom we picture to ourselves as being so pretty when we do not have the time to approach them; she was a particle of what constitutes the eternal desire, the eternal regret of life, the twofold current of which is at length diverted, directed towards us. Twofold, for if it is a question of the unknown, of a person who, from her stature, her proportions, her indifferent glance, her haughty calm, we suspect must be divine, at the same time we want this woman to be thoroughly specialised in her profession, enabling us to escape from ourselves into that world which a special costume makes us romantically believe to be different. Indeed, if we wanted to embody in a formula the law of our amorous curiosities, we should have to seek it in the maximum divergence between a woman glimpsed and a woman approached and caressed. If the women of what used at one time to be called the closed houses, if prostitutes themselves (provided that we know them to be prostitutes) attract us so little, it is not because they are less beautiful than other women, but because they are ready and waiting; because they already offer us precisely what we seek to attain; it is because they are not conquests. The divergence, there, is at its minimum. A whore smiles at us in the street as she will smile when she is by our side. We are sculptors. We want to obtain of a woman a statue entirely different from the one she has presented to us. We have seen a girl strolling, indifferent and insolent, along the seashore, we have seen a shop-assistant, serious and active behind her counter, who will answer us curtly if only to avoid being subjected to the jibes of her comrades, or a fruit-vendor who barely answers us at all. Whereupon we will not rest until we can discover by experiment whether the proud girl on the seashore, the shop-assistant obsessed with what other people will say, the aloof fruit-vendor, cannot be made, by skilful handling on our part, to relax their uncompromising attitude, to throw about our necks those arms that were laden with fruit, to bend towards our lips, with a smile of consent, eyes hitherto cold or absent—oh, the beauty of the eyes of a working-girl, eyes which were stern in working hours when she was afraid of the scandalmongering of her companions, eyes which shunned our obsessive gaze and which, now that we have seen her alone and face to face, allow their pupils to light up with sunny laughter when we speak of making love! Between the shopgirl, or the laundress busy with her iron, or the fruit-seller, or the dairymaid—and that selfsame wench when she is about to become one's mistress, the maximum divergence is attained, stretched indeed to its extreme limits, and varied by those habitual gestures of her profession which make a pair of arms describe, during the hours of toil, an arabesque as different as it is possible to imagine from those supple bonds that already every evening are fastened about one's neck while the mouth shapes itself for a kiss. And so one spends one's life in anxious approaches, constantly renewed, to serious working-girls whose calling seems to distance them from one. Once they are in one's arms, they are no longer what they were, the distance that one dreamed of bridging is abolished. But one begins anew with other women, one devotes all one's time, all one's money, all one's energy to these enterprises, one is enraged by the too cautious driver who may make us miss the first rendezvous, one works oneself up into a fever. And yet one knows that this first rendezvous will bring the end of an illusion. No matter: as long as the illusion lasts one wants to see whether one can convert it into reality, and then one thinks of the laundress whose coldness one remarked. Amorous curiosity is like the curiosity aroused in us by the names of places; perpetually disappointed, it revives and remains for ever insatiable.

Alas, as soon as she stood before me, the fair dairymaid with the streaky locks, stripped of all the desires and imaginings that had been aroused in me, was reduced to her mere self. The quivering cloud of my suppositions no longer enveloped her in a dizzying haze. She acquired an almost apologetic air from having (in place of the ten, the twenty that I recalled in turn without being able to fix them in my memory) but a single nose, rounder than I had thought, which gave her a hint of stupidity and had in any case lost the faculty of multiplying itself. This flyaway caught on the wing, inert, crushed, incapable of adding anything to its own paltry appearance, no longer had my imagination to collaborate with it. Fallen into the inertia of reality, I sought to spring back again; her cheeks, which I had not noticed in the shop, appeared to me so pretty that I was abashed, and to recover my composure said to the young dairymaid: "Would you be so kind as to hand me the *Figaro* which is lying there. I must make sure of the address to which I am going to send you." Thereupon, as she picked up the newspaper, she disclosed as far as her elbow the red sleeve of her jersey and handed me the conservative sheet with a neat and courteous gesture which pleased me by its swift familiarity, its fluffy appearance and its scarlet hue. While I was opening the *Figaro*, for the sake of something to say, and without raising my eyes, I asked the girl: "What do you call that red knitted thing you're wearing? It's very pretty." She replied: "It's my sweater." For, by a slight downward tendency common to all fashions, the garments and words which a few years earlier seemed to belong to the relatively smart world of Albertine's friends, were now the currency of working-girls. "Are you quite sure it won't be giving you too much trouble," I said, while I pretended to be searching the columns of the *Figaro*, "if I send you rather a long way?" As soon as I myself thus appeared to consider the job I wanted her to do for me somewhat arduous, she began to feel that it would be a nuisance to her: "The only thing is, I'm supposed to be going for a ride on my bike this afternoon. You see, Sunday's the only day we've got." "But won't you catch cold, going bare-headed like that?" "Oh, I shan't be bare-headed, I'll have my cap, and I could get on without it with all the hair I have." I raised my eyes to those flavescent, frizzy locks and felt myself caught in their swirl and swept away, with a throbbing heart, amid the lightning and the blasts of a hurricane of beauty. I continued to study the newspaper, but although it was only to keep myself in countenance and to gain time, while only pretending to read I nevertheless took in the meaning of the words that were before my eyes, and my attention was caught by the following: "To the programme already announced for this afternoon in the great hall of the Trocadéro must be added the name of Mlle Léa who has consented to appear in *Les Fourberies de Nérine*. She will of course take the part of Nérine, which she plays with dazzling verve and bewitching gaiety." It was as though an invisible hand had brutally torn from my heart the bandage beneath which its wound had begun to heal since my return from Balbec. The flood of my anguish came pouring out in torrents. Léa was the actress friend of the two girls at Balbec whom Albertine, without appearing to see them, had watched in the mirror, one afternoon at the

Casino. It was true that at Balbec Albertine, at the name of Léa, had adopted a particular tone of solemnity in order to say to me, almost shocked that anyone could suspect such a pattern of virtue: "Oh no, she isn't in the least that sort of woman. She's a very nice person." Unfortunately for me, when Albertine made an assertion of this kind, it was invariably a first stage in a series of different assertions. Shortly after the first would come this second one: "I don't know her." In the third phase, after Albertine had spoken to me of somebody who was "above suspicion" and whom (in the second place) she did not know, she would gradually forget first of all that she had said that she did not know the person and then, unwittingly contradicting herself, would inform me that she did. This first lapse of memory having occurred, and the new assertion been made, a second lapse of memory would begin, concerning the person's being above suspicion. "Isn't so and so," I would ask, "one of those women?" "Why, of course, everybody knows that!" Immediately the note of solemnity was sounded afresh in an assertion which was a vague echo, greatly reduced, of the first assertion of all. "I'm bound to say that she has always behaved perfectly properly with me. Of course, she knows that I'd soon send her about her business if she tried it on. But that's neither here nor there. I'm obliged to give her credit for the genuine respect she has always shown me. It's easy to see she knew the sort of person she had to deal with." We remember the truth because it has a name, is rooted in the past, but a makeshift lie is quickly forgotten. Albertine would forget this latest lie, her fourth, and, one day when she was anxious to gain my confidence by confiding in me, would open up to me with regard to the same person who at the outset had been so respectable and whom she did not know: "She took quite a fancy to me at one time. Three or four times she asked me to walk home with her and to come up and see her. I saw no harm in walking home with her, in front of lots of people, in broad daylight, in the open air. But when we reached her front door I always made some excuse and I never went upstairs." Shortly after this, Albertine would make some remark about the beautiful things that this lady had in her house. By proceeding from one approximation to another one would doubtless have succeeded in getting her to tell the truth, a truth which was perhaps less serious than I was inclined to believe, for, though susceptible to women, she perhaps preferred a male lover, and, now that she had me, might not have given a thought to Léa.

Already, in the case of quite a number of women at any rate, it would have been enough for me to gather together and present to my mistress a synthesis of her contradictory statements, in order to convict her of her misdeeds (misdeeds which, like astronomical laws, it is a great deal easier to deduce by a process of reasoning than to detect and observe in reality). But then she would have preferred to say that one of her statements had been a lie, the withdrawal of which would thus bring about the collapse of my whole system of deduction, rather than acknowledge that everything she had told me from the start was simply a tissue of mendacious tales. There are similar tales in the *Arabian Nights* which we find charming. They pain us coming from a person whom we love, and thereby enable us to penetrate a little deeper in our knowledge of human nature instead of being content to play around on its surface. Grief enters into us and forces us, out of painful curiosity, to probe. Whence emerge truths which we feel that we have no right to keep hidden, so much so that a dying atheist who has discovered them, certain of his own extinction, indifferent to fame, will nevertheless devote his last hours on earth to an attempt to make them known.

However, I was still at the first stage of enlightenment with regard to Léa. I was not even aware whether Albertine knew her. No matter, it came to the same thing. I must at all costs prevent her from renewing this acquaintance or making the acquaintance of this stranger at the Trocadéro. I say that I did not know whether she knew Léa or not; yet I must in fact have learned this at Balbec, from Albertine herself. For amnesia obliterated from my mind as well as from Albertine's a great many of the statements that she had made to me. Memory, instead of being a duplicate, always present before one's eyes, of the various events of one's life, is rather a void from which at odd moments a chance resemblance enables one to resuscitate dead recollections; but even then there are innumerable little details which have not fallen into that potential reservoir of memory, and which will remain for ever unverifiable. One pays no attention to anything that one does not connect with the real life of the woman one loves; one forgets immediately what she has said to one about such and such an incident or such and such people one does not know, and her expression while she was saying it. And so when, in due course, one's jealousy is aroused by these same people, and seeks to ascertain whether or not it is mistaken, whether it is indeed they who are responsible for one's mistress's impatience to go out, and her annoyance when one has prevented her from doing so by returning earlier than usual, one's jealousy, ransacking the past in search of a clue, can find nothing; always retrospective, it is like a historian who has to write the history of a period for which he has no documents; always belated, it dashes like an enraged bull to the spot where it will not find the dazzling, arrogant creature who is tormenting it and whom the crowd admire for his splendour and cunning. Jealousy thrashes around in the void, uncertain as we are in those dreams in which we are distressed because we cannot find in his empty house a person whom we have known well in life, but who here perhaps is another person and has merely borrowed the features of our friend, uncertain as we are even more after we awake when we seek to identify this or that detail of our dream. What was one's mistress's expression when she told one that? Did she not look happy, was she not actually whistling, a thing that she never does unless she has some amorous thought in her mind and finds one's presence importunate and irritating? Did she not tell one something that is contradicted by what she now affirms, that she knows or does not know such and such a person? One does not know, and one will never know; one searches desperately among the unsubstantial fragments of a dream, and all the time one's life with one's mistress goes on, a life that is oblivious of what may well be of importance to one, and attentive to what is perhaps of none, a life hagridden by people who have no real connexion with one, full of lapses of memory, gaps, vain anxieties, a life as illusory as a dream.

I suddenly realised that the young dairymaid was still in the room. I told her that the place was undoubtedly a long way off, and that I did not need her. Whereupon she also decided that it would be too much trouble: "There's a fine match this afternoon, and I don't want to miss it." I felt that she must already be in the habit of saying "Sport's the thing," and that in a few years' time she would be talking about "living her own life." I told her that I certainly did not need her any longer, and gave her five francs. Immediately, having little expected this largesse, and telling herself that if she got five francs for doing nothing she would get a great deal more for doing my errand, she began to find that her match was of no importance. "I could easily have taken your message. I can always find time." But I pushed her towards the door, for I needed to be alone: I must at all costs prevent Albertine from meeting Léa's girlfriends at the Trocadéro. It was essential that I should succeed in doing so, but I did not yet know how, and during these first few moments I opened my hands, gazed at them, cracked my knuckles, whether because the mind, when it cannot find what it is seeking, in a fit of laziness decides to halt for an instant during which it is vividly aware of the most insignificant things, like the blades of grass on a railway embankment which we see from the carriage window trembling in the wind, when the train stops in the open country—an immobility that is not always more fruitful than that of a captured animal which, paralysed by fear or mesmerised, gazes without moving a muscle—or because I was holding my body in readiness—with my mind at work inside it and, in my mind, the means of action against this or that person—as though it were simply a weapon from which would be fired the shot that would separate Albertine from Léa and her two friends. It is true that, earlier that morning, when Françoise had come in to tell me that Albertine was going to the Trocadéro, I had said to myself: "Albertine is at liberty to do as she pleases," and had supposed that in this radiant weather her actions would remain without any perceptible importance to me until the evening. But it was not only the morning sun, as I had thought, that had made me so carefree; it was because, having obliged Albertine to abandon the plans that she might perhaps have initiated or even realised at the Verdurins', and having reduced her to attending a matinée which I myself had chosen and with a view to which she could not have planned anything, I knew that whatever she did would of necessity be innocent. Similarly, if Albertine had said a few moments later: "I don't really care if I kill myself," it was because she was certain that she would not kill herself. Surrounding both myself and Albertine there had been this morning (far more than the sunny day) that environment which itself is invisible but through the translucent and changing medium of which we saw, I her actions, she the importance of her own life—that is to say those beliefs which we do not perceive but which are no more assimilable to a pure vacuum than is the air that surrounds us; composing round about us a variable atmosphere, sometimes excellent, often unbreathable, they deserve to be studied and recorded as carefully as the temperature, the barometric pressure, the season, for our days have their own singularity, physical and moral. The belief, which I had failed to notice this morning but in which nevertheless I had been joyously enveloped until the moment when I had looked a second time at the *Figaro*, that Albertine would do nothing that was not blameless—that belief had vanished. I was no

longer living in the fine sunny day, but in another day
carved out of it by my anxiety lest Albertine might renew
her acquaintance with Léa, and more easily still with the
two girls if, as seemed to me probable, they went to applaud the actress at the Trocadéro where it would not be
difficult for them to meet Albertine during one of the intervals. I no longer gave a thought to Mlle Vinteuil; the
name of Léa had brought back to my mind, to make me
jealous, the image of Albertine in the Casino watching the
two girls. For I possessed in my memory only a series of
Albertines, separate from one another, incomplete, a collection of profiles or snapshots, and so my jealousy was
restricted to a discontinuous expression, at once fugitive
and fixed, and to the people who had caused that expression to appear upon Albertine's face. I remembered her
when, at Balbec, she was eyed with undue intensity by
the two girls or by women of that sort; I remembered the
distress that I felt when I saw her face subjected to an active scrutiny, like that of a painter preparing to make a
sketch, entirely enveloped in it, and, doubtless on account
of my presence, submitting to this contact without appearing to notice it, with a passivity that was perhaps
clandestinely voluptuous. And before she pulled herself
together and spoke to me, there was an instant during
which Albertine did not move, smiled into the empty air,
with the same air of feigned spontaneity and secret
pleasure as if she were posing for somebody to take her
photograph, or even seeking to assume before the camera
a more dashing pose—the one she had adopted at Doncières when we were walking with Saint-Loup, and,
laughing and passing her tongue over her lips, she pre-

tended to be teasing a dog. Certainly at such moments she was not at all the same as when it was she who was interested in little girls who passed by. Then, on the contrary, her intense and velvety gaze fastened itself, glued itself to the passer-by, so adhesive, so corrosive, that you felt that, in withdrawing, it must tear away the skin. But that look, which did at least give her a certain gravity, almost as though she were ill, seemed to me a pleasant relief after the vacant, blissful look she had worn in the presence of the two girls, and I should have preferred the sombre expression of the desire that she may perhaps have felt at times to the beaming expression caused by the desire which she aroused. However much she tried to conceal her awareness of it, it bathed her, enveloped her, vaporous, voluptuous, made her whole face glow. But who knows whether, once my back was turned, Albertine would continue to suppress everything that at such moments she held in suspension within herself, that radiated around her and gave me such anguish, whether, now that I was no longer there, she would not respond boldly to the advances of the two girls? Certainly these memories caused me great pain; they were like a complete admission of Albertine's proclivities, a general confession of infidelity, against which the specific pledges that she gave me and that I wanted to believe, the negative results of my incomplete inquiries, the assurances of Andrée, given perhaps with Albertine's connivance, were powerless to prevail. Albertine might deny specific betrayals; but by words that she let fall, more potent than her declarations to the contrary, by those looks alone, she had confessed to what she would have wished to hide far more than any specific facts, to what she would have let herself be killed sooner than admit: her natural tendency. For there is no one who will willingly deliver up his soul.

In spite of the pain that these memories caused me, could I have denied that it was the programme of the matinée at the Trocadéro that had revived my need of Albertine? She was one of those women whose very failings can sometimes take the place of absent charms, and, no less than their failings, the tenderness that follows upon them and brings us that assuagement which, like an invalid who is never well for two days in succession, we are incessantly obliged to recapture in their company. Besides, even more than their faults while we are in love with them, there are their faults before we knew them, and first and foremost their nature. For what makes this sort of love painful is the fact that there pre-exists it a sort of original sin of Woman, a sin which makes us love them, so that, when we forget it, we feel less need of them, and to begin to love again we must begin to suffer again. At this moment, the thought that she must not meet the two girls again and the question whether or not she knew Léa were what was chiefly occupying my mind, in spite of the rule that one ought not to take an interest in particular facts except in relation to their general significance, and notwithstanding the childishness, as great as that of longing to travel or to make friends with women, of splintering one's curiosity against such elements from the invisible torrent of painful realities, which will always remain unknown to one, as have fortuitously crystallised in one's mind. Moreover, even if one succeeded in destroying those elements, they would at once be replaced by others. Yesterday I was afraid lest Albertine should go to see Mme Verdurin. Now my only thought was of Léa. Jealousy, which is blindfold, is not merely powerless to discover anything in the darkness that enshrouds it; it is also one of those tortures where the task must be incessantly repeated, like that of the Danaides, or of Ixion. Even if the two girls were not there, what impression might not Léa make on her, beautified by her stage attire, haloed with success, what thoughts might she not leave in Albertine's mind, what desires, which, even if she repressed them in my company, would give her an aversion for a life in which she was unable to gratify them!

Besides, how could I be certain that she did not already know Léa, and would not pay her a visit in her dressing-room? And even if Léa did not know her, who could assure me that, having certainly seen her at Balbec, she would not recognise her and make a signal to her from the stage that would enable Albertine to gain admission back-stage? A danger seems perfectly avoidable when it has been averted. This one was not yet averted, and because I was afraid that it might never be, it seemed to me all the more terrible. And yet this love for Albertine, which I felt almost vanish when I attempted to realise it, seemed somehow at this moment to acquire a proof of its existence from the intensity of my anguish. I no longer cared about anything else, I thought only of how to prevent her from remaining at the Trocadéro, I would have offered any sum in the world to Léa to persuade her not to go there. If then we prove our predilection by the action that we perform rather than by the idea that we form, I must have been in love with Albertine. But this renewal of my suffering gave no greater consistency to the image of Albertine that I retained within me. She caused

my ills like a deity who remains invisible. Making endless
conjectures, I sought to ward off my suffering without
thereby realising my love.

First of all, I must make certain that Léa was really
going to perform at the Trocadéro. After dismissing the
dairymaid, I telephoned to Bloch, whom I knew to be on
friendly terms with Léa, in order to ask him. He knew
nothing about it and seemed surprised that it could be of
any interest to me. I decided that I must act quickly, remembered that Françoise was dressed and ready to go out
and that I was not, and while I got up and dressed I told
her to take a motor-car and go to the Trocadéro, buy a
seat, search the auditorium for Albertine and give her a
note from me. In this note I told Albertine that I was
greatly upset by a letter which I had just received from
that same lady on whose account she would remember
that I had been so wretched one night at Balbec. I reminded her that, on the following day, she had reproached me for not having sent for her. And so I was
taking the liberty, I told her, of asking her to sacrifice her
matinée and to join me at home so that we might take the
air together, which might help me to recover from the
shock. But since it would be some time before I was
dressed and ready, she would oblige me, seeing that she
had Françoise as an escort, by calling at the Trois-
Quartiers (this shop, being smaller, seemed to me less
dangerous than the Bon Marché) to buy the white tulle
bodice that she required.

My note was probably not superfluous. To tell the
truth, I knew nothing that Albertine had done since I had
come to know her, or even before. But in her conversation
(she might, had I mentioned it to her, have replied that I

had misunderstood her) there were certain contradictions, certain embellishments which seemed to me as decisive as catching her red-handed, but less usable against Albertine who, often caught out like a child, had invariably, by dint of sudden, strategic changes of front, stultified my cruel attacks and retrieved the situation. Cruel, most of all, to myself. She employed, not by way of stylistic refinement, but in order to correct her imprudences, abrupt breaches of syntax not unlike that figure which the grammarians call anacoluthon or some such name. Having allowed herself, while discussing women, to say: "I remember, the other day, I . . . ," she would suddenly, after a "semi-quaver rest," change the "I" to "she": it was something that she had witnessed as an innocent spectator, not a thing that she herself had done. It was not she who was the subject of the action. I should have liked to recall exactly how the sentence had begun, in order to decide for myself, since she had broken off in the middle, what the conclusion would have been. But since I had been awaiting that conclusion, I found it hard to remember the beginning, from which perhaps my air of interest had made her deviate, and was left still anxious to know her real thoughts, the actual truth of her recollection. Unfortunately the beginnings of a lie on the part of one's mistress are like the beginnings of one's own love, or of a vocation. They take shape, accumulate, pass unnoticed by oneself. When one wants to remember in what manner one began to love a woman, one is already in love with her; daydreaming about her beforehand, one did not say to oneself: "This is the prelude to love; be careful!"—and one's day-dreams advanced unobtrusively, scarcely noticed by oneself. In the same way, save in a few comparatively rare

cases, it is only for narrative convenience that I have frequently in these pages confronted one of Albertine's false
statements with her previous assertion on the same subject. This previous assertion, as often as not, since I could
not read the future and did not at the time guess what
contradictory affirmation was to form a pendant to it, had
slipped past unperceived, heard it is true by my ears, but
without my isolating it from the continuous flow of Albertine's speech. Later on, faced with the self-evident lie,
or seized by an anxious doubt, I would endeavour to recall it; but in vain; my memory had not been warned in
time; it had thought it unnecessary to keep a copy.

I instructed Françoise to let me know by telephone
when she had got Albertine out of the theatre, and to
bring her home whether she was willing or not.

"It really would be the last straw if she wasn't willing
to come and see Monsieur," replied Françoise.

"But I don't know that she's as fond of seeing me as
all that."

"Then she must be an ungrateful wretch," went on
Françoise, in whom Albertine was renewing after all these
years the same torment of envy that Eulalie used at one
time to cause her in my aunt's sickroom. Unaware that
Albertine's position in my household was not of her own
seeking but had been willed by me (a fact which, from
motives of self-esteem and to infuriate Françoise, I preferred to conceal from her), she was amazed and incensed
by the girl's cunning, called her when she spoke of her to
the other servants a "play-actress," a "wily customer"
who could twist me round her little finger. She dared not
yet declare open war on her, showed her a smiling face
and sought to acquire merit in my eyes by the services

she did her in her relations with me, deciding that it was useless to say anything to me and that she would gain nothing by doing so, but always on the look-out for an opportunity, so that if ever she discovered a crack in Albertine's armour, she was determined to enlarge it, and to separate us for good and all.

"Ungrateful? No, Françoise, I think it's I who am ungrateful. You don't know how good she is to me." (It was so comforting to me to appear to be loved!) "Off you go."

"All right, I'll hop it, double quick."

Her daughter's influence was beginning to contaminate Françoise's vocabulary. So it is that all languages lose their purity by the addition of new words. For this decadence of Françoise's speech, which I had known in its golden period, I was in fact myself indirectly responsible. Françoise's daughter would not have made her mother's classic language degenerate into the vilest slang if she had stuck to conversing with her in dialect. She had never hesitated to do so, and if they had anything private to say to each other when they were both with me, instead of shutting themselves up in the kitchen they provided themselves, right in the middle of my room, with a protective screen more impenetrable than the most carefully closed door, by conversing in dialect. I supposed merely that the mother and daughter were not always on the best of terms, if I was to judge by the frequency with which they employed the only word that I could make out: *m'esasperate* (unless it was myself who was the object of their exasperation). Unfortunately the most unfamiliar tongue becomes intelligible in time when we are always hearing it spoken. I was sorry that it was dialect, for I succeeded in picking it up, and should have been no less successful had Françoise been in the habit of expressing herself in Persian. In vain did Françoise, when she became aware of my progress, accelerate the speed of her delivery, and her daughter likewise; there was nothing to be done. The mother was greatly put out that I understood their dialect, then delighted to hear me speak it. I am bound to admit that her delight was a mocking delight, for although I came in time to pronounce the words more or less as she herself did, she found a gulf between our two pronunciations which gave her infinite joy, and she began to regret that she no longer saw people to whom she had not given a thought for years but who, it appeared, would have rocked with laughter which it would have done her good to hear if they could have listened to me speaking their dialect so badly. The mere idea of it filled her with gaiety and nostalgia, and she enumerated various peasants who would have laughed until they cried. However, no amount of joy could mitigate her sorrow at the fact that, however badly I might pronounce it, I understood it perfectly well. Keys become useless when the person whom we seek to prevent from entering can avail himself of a skeleton key or a jemmy. Dialect having become useless as a means of defence, she took to conversing with her daughter in a French which rapidly became that of the most debased epochs.

I was now ready, but Françoise had not yet telephoned. Should I set out without waiting for a message? But how could I be sure that she would find Albertine, that the latter hadn't gone back-stage, that even if Françoise did find her, she would allow herself to be brought home? Half an hour later the telephone bell began to tinkle and my heart throbbed tumultuously with hope and fear. There came, at the bidding of an operator, a flying squadron of sounds which with an instantaneous speed brought me the voice of the telephonist, not that of Françoise whom an ancestral timidity and melancholy, when she was brought face to face with any object un-known to her fathers, prevented from approaching a tele-phone receiver, although she would readily visit a person suffering from a contagious disease. She had found Alber-tine in the lobby by herself, and Albertine, after going off to tell Andrée that she was not going to stay, had come straight back to Françoise.

"She wasn't angry? Oh, I beg your pardon; will you please ask the lady whether the young lady was angry?"

"The lady asks me to say that she wasn't at all angry, quite the contrary, in fact; anyhow, if she wasn't pleased, she didn't show it. They're now going to go to the Trois-Quartiers, and will be home by two o'clock."

I gathered that two o'clock meant three, for it was al-ready past two. But Françoise suffered from one of those peculiar, permanent, incurable defects which we call dis-eases: she was never able either to read or to express the time correctly. When, after consulting her watch at two o'clock, she said "It's one o'clock" or "It's three o'clock," I was never able to understand whether the phenomenon that occurred was situated in her vision or in her mind or in her speech; the one thing certain is that the phe-nomenon never failed to occur. Humanity is a very old institution. Heredity and cross-breeding have given insu-perable strength to bad habits, faulty reflexes. One per-son sneezes and gasps because he is passing a rose-bush, another breaks out in a rash at the smell of wet paint; others get violent stomach-aches if they have to set out on a journey, and grandchildren of thieves who are themselves rich and generous cannot resist the temptation to rob you of fifty francs. As for discovering the cause of Françoise's incapacity to tell the time correctly, she herself never threw any light upon the problem. For, notwithstanding the fury that her inaccurate replies regularly provoked in me, Françoise never attempted either to apologise for her mistake or to explain it. She remained silent, seeming not to hear, and thereby making me lose my temper altogether. I should have liked to hear a few words of justification, if only to be able to demolish them; but not a word, an indifferent silence. However, as far as today was concerned there could be no doubt; Albertine was coming home with Françoise at three o'clock, Albertine would not be meeting Léa or her friends. Whereupon, the danger of her renewing relations with them having been averted, it at once began to lose its importance in my eyes and I was amazed, seeing with what ease it had been averted, that I should have supposed that I would not succeed in averting it. I felt a keen impulse of gratitude towards Albertine, who, I could see, had not gone to the Trocadéro to meet Léa's friends, and who showed me, by leaving the matinée and coming home at a word from me, that she belonged to me, even for the future, more than I had imagined. My gratitude was even greater when a cyclist brought me a note from her bidding me be patient, and full of the charming expressions that she was in the habit of using. "My darling dear Marcel, I return less quickly than this cyclist, whose bike I should like to borrow in order to be with you sooner. How could you imagine that I might be angry or that I could enjoy anything better than to be with you? It will be nice to go out, just the two of us together; it would be nicer still if we never went out except together. The ideas you get into your head! What a Marcel! What a Marcel! Always and ever your Albertine."

The dresses that I bought for her, the yacht of which I had spoken to her, the Fortuny gowns—all these things, having in this obedience on Albertine's part not their recompense but their complement, appeared to me now as so many privileges that I exercised; for the duties and expenses of a master are part of his dominion, and define it, prove it, fully as much as his rights. And these rights which she acknowledged were precisely what gave my expenditure its true character: I had a woman of my own, who, at the first word that I sent her out of the blue, informed me deferentially by telephone that she was coming, that she was allowing herself to be brought home, at once. I was more of a master than I had supposed. More of a master, in other words more of a slave. I no longer felt the slightest impatience to see Albertine. The certainty that she was at this moment engaged in shopping with Françoise, that she would return with her at an approaching moment which I would willingly have postponed, lit up like a calm and radiant star a period of time which I would now have been far better pleased to spend alone. My love for Albertine had made me get up and prepare to go out, but it would prevent me from enjoying my outing. I reflected that on a Sunday afternoon like this little shopgirls, midinettes, prostitutes must be strolling in the Bois. And with the words *midinettes, little shopgirls* (as had often happened to me with a proper name, the name of a girl read in the account of a ball), with the image of a white bodice, a short skirt, since beneath them I placed an unknown person who might perhaps come to love me, I created out of nothing desirable women, and said to myself: "How delightful they must be!" But of what use would it be to me that they were delightful, seeing that I was not going out alone?

Taking advantage of the fact that I still was alone, and drawing the curtains together so that the sun should not prevent me from reading the notes, I sat down at the piano, opened at random Vinteuil's sonata which happened to be lying there, and began to play; seeing that Albertine's arrival was still a matter of some time but was on the other hand certain, I had at once time to spare and peace of mind. Lulled by the confident expectation of her return escorted by Françoise and by the assurance of her docility as by the blessedness of an inner light as warming as the light of the sun, I could dispose of my thoughts, detach them for a moment from Albertine, apply them to the sonata. I did not even go out of my way to notice how, in the latter, the combination of the sensual and the anxious motifs corresponded more closely now to my love for Albertine, from which jealousy had been for so long absent that I had been able to confess to Swann my ignorance of that sentiment. No, approaching the sonata from another point of view, regarding it in itself as the work of a great artist, I was carried back upon the tide of sound to the days at Combray—I do not mean Montjouvain and the Méséglise way, but to my walks along the Guermantes way—when I myself had longed to become an artist. In abandoning that ambition *de facto*, had I forfeited something real? Could life console me for the loss of art? Was there in art a more profound reality, in which our true personality finds an expression that is not af-

forded it by the activities of life? For every great artist
seems so different from all the rest, and gives us so
strongly that sensation of individuality for which we seek
in vain in our everyday existence! Just as I was thinking
thus, I was struck by a passage in the sonata. It was a
passage with which I was quite familiar, but sometimes
our attention throws a different light upon things which
we have known for a long time and we remark in them
what we have never seen before. As I played the passage,
and although Vinteuil had been trying to express in it a
fancy which would have been wholly foreign to Wagner, I
could not help murmuring "*Tristan*," with the smile of an
old family friend discovering a trace of the grandfather in
an intonation, a gesture of the grandson who has never set
eyes on him. And as the friend then examines a photograph which enables him to specify the likeness, so, on
top of Vinteuil's sonata, I set up on the music-rest the
score of *Tristan*, a selection from which was being given
that afternoon, as it happened, at a Lamoureux concert.
In admiring the Bayreuth master, I had none of the scruples of those who, like Nietzsche, are bidden by a sense of
duty to shun in art as in life the beauty that tempts them,
and who, tearing themselves from *Tristan* as they renounce *Parsifal*, and, in their spiritual asceticism, pro-
gressing from one mortification to another, succeed, by
following the most bloody of the stations of the cross, in
exalting themselves to the pure cognition and perfect adoration of *Le Postillon de Longjumeau*.[6] I was struck by how
much reality there is in the work of Wagner as I contemplated once more those insistent, fleeting themes which
visit an act, recede only to return again and again, and,
sometimes distant, dormant, almost detached, are at other

moments, while remaining vague, so pressing and so close, so internal, so organic, so visceral, that they seem like the reprise not so much of a musical motif as of an attack of neuralgia.

Music, very different in this respect from Albertine's society, helped me to descend into myself, to discover new things: the variety that I had sought in vain in life, in travel, but a longing for which was none the less renewed in me by this sonorous tide whose sunlit waves now came to expire at my feet. A twofold diversity. As the spectrum makes visible to us the composition of light, so the harmony of a Wagner, the colour of an Elstir, enable us to know that essential quality of another person's sensations into which love for another person does not allow us to penetrate. Then a diversity inside the work itself, by the sole means that exist of being effectively diverse: to wit, combining diverse individualities. Where a minor composer would claim to be portraying a squire, or a knight, while making them both sing the same music, Wagner on the contrary allots to each separate appellation a different reality, and whenever a squire appears, it is an individual figure, at once complicated and simplified, that, with a joyous, feudal clash of warring sounds, inscribes itself in the vast tonal mass. Whence the plenitude of a music that is indeed filled with so many different strains, each of which is a person. A person or the impression that is given us by a momentary aspect of nature. Even that which, in this music, is most independent of the emotion that it arouses in us preserves its outward and absolutely precise reality; the song of a bird, the call of a hunter's horn, the air that a shepherd plays upon his pipe, each carves its silhouette of sound against the horizon. True,

Wagner would bring them forward, appropriate them, introduce them into an orchestral whole, make them subservient to the highest musical concepts, but always respecting their original nature, as a carpenter respects the grain, the peculiar essence of the wood that he is carving.

But notwithstanding the richness of these works in which the contemplation of nature has its place alongside the action, alongside the individuals who are not merely the names of characters, I thought how markedly, all the same, these works partake of that quality of being—albeit marvellously—always incomplete, which is the characteristic of all the great works of the nineteenth century, that century whose greatest writers somehow botched their books, but, watching themselves work as though they were at once workman and judge, derived from this self-contemplation a new form of beauty, exterior and superior to the work itself, imposing on it a retroactive unity, a grandeur which it does not possess. Without pausing to consider the man who belatedly saw in his novels a *Human Comedy*, or those who entitled heterogeneous poems or essays *The Legend of the Centuries* or *The Bible of Humanity*, can we not say none the less of the last of these that he so admirably personifies the nineteenth century that the greatest beauties in Michelet are to be sought not so much in his work itself as in the attitudes that he adopts towards his work, not in his *History of France* nor in his *History of the Revolution*, but in his prefaces to those books? Prefaces, that is to say pages written after the books themselves, in which he considers the books, and with which we must include here and there certain sentences beginning as a rule with a: "Dare I say?" which is not a scholar's precaution but a musician's cadence.

The other musician, he who was delighting me at this moment, Wagner, retrieving some exquisite fragment from a drawer of his writing-table to introduce it, as a retrospectively necessary theme, into a work he had not even thought of at the time he composed it, then having composed a first mythological opera, and a second, and afterwards others still, and perceiving all of a sudden that he had written a tetralogy, must have felt something of the same exhilaration as Balzac when the latter, casting over his books the eye at once of a stranger and of a father, finding in one the purity of Raphael, in another the simplicity of the Gospel, suddenly decided, shedding a retrospective illumination upon them, that they would be better brought together in a cycle in which the same characters would reappear, and touched up his work with a swift brush-stroke, the last and the most sublime. An ulterior unity, but not a factitious one, otherwise it would have crumbled into dust like all the other systematisations of mediocre writers who with copious titles and sub-titles give themselves the appearance of having pursued a single and transcendent design. Not factitious, perhaps indeed all the more real for being ulterior, for being born of a moment of enthusiasm when it is discovered to exist among fragments which need only to be joined together; a unity that was unaware of itself, hence vital and not logical, that did not prohibit variety, dampen invention. It emerges (but applied this time to the work as a whole) like such and such a fragment composed separately, born of an inspiration, not required by the artificial development of a thesis, which comes to be integrated with the rest. Before the great orchestral movement that precedes the return of Isolde, it is the work itself that has attracted

towards itself the half-forgotten air of a shepherd's pipe.
And, no doubt, just as the orchestra swells and surges at
the approach of the ship, when it takes hold of these notes
of the pipe, transforms them, imbues them with its own
intoxication, breaks their rhythm, clarifies their tonality,
accelerates their movement, expands their instrumenta-
tion, so no doubt Wagner himself was filled with joy
when he discovered in his memory the shepherd's tune,
incorporated it in his work, gave it its full wealth of
meaning. This joy moreover never forsakes him. In him,
however great the melancholy of the poet, it is consoled,
transcended—that is to say, alas, to some extent destroyed—by the exhilaration of the fabricator. But then,
no less than by the similarity I had remarked just now between Vinteuil's phrase and Wagner's, I was troubled by
the thought of this Vulcan-like skill. Could it be this that
gave to great artists the illusory aspect of a fundamental,
irreducible originality, apparently the reflexion of a more
than human reality, actually the result of industrious toil?
If art is no more than that, it is no more real than life and
I had less cause for regret. I went on playing *Tristan*. Separated from Wagner by the wall of sound, I could hear
him exult, invite me to share his joy, I could hear the im-
mortally youthful laughter and the hammer-blows of
Siegfried ring out with redoubled vigour; but the more
marvellously those phrases were struck, the technical skill
of the craftsman served merely to make it easier for them
to leave the earth, birds akin not to Lohengrin's swan but
to that aeroplane which I had seen at Balbec convert its
energy into vertical motion, glide over the sea and vanish
in the sky. Perhaps, as the birds that soar highest and fly
most swiftly have more powerful wings, one of these

frankly material vehicles was needed to explore the infinite, one of these 120 horse-power machines—the Mys-
tère model—in which nevertheless, however high one
flies, one is prevented to some extent from enjoying the
silence of space by the overpowering roar of the engine!

Somehow or other the course of my musings, which
hitherto had wandered among musical memories, turned
now to those men who have been the best performers of
music in our day, among whom, slightly exaggerating his
merit, I included Morel. At once my thoughts took a
sharp turn, and it was Morel's character, certain peculiarities of that character, that I began to consider. As it happened—and this might be connected though not confused
with the neurasthenia to which he was a prey—Morel
was in the habit of talking about his life, but always presented so shadowy a picture of it that it was difficult to
make anything out. For instance, he placed himself entirely at M. de Charlus's disposal on the understanding
that he must keep his evenings free, as he wished to be
able after dinner to attend an algebra course. M. de Charlus conceded this, but insisted on seeing him after the
lessons.

"Impossible, it's an old Italian painting" (this witti-
cism means nothing when written down like this; but
M. de Charlus having made Morel read L'Education senti-
mentale, in the penultimate chapter of which Frédéric
Moreau uses this expression, it was Morel's idea of a joke
never to say the word "impossible" without following it
up with "it's an old Italian painting"), "the lessons go on
very late, and they're already enough of an inconvenience
to the teacher, who would naturally feel hurt . . ."

"But there's no need to have lessons, algebra isn't a

thing like swimming, or even English, you can learn it
equally well from a book," replied M. de Charlus, who
had guessed from the first that these algebra lessons were
one of those images of which it was impossible to decipher anything at all. It was perhaps some affair with a
woman, or, if Morel was seeking to earn money in shady
ways and had attached himself to the secret police, an expedition with detectives, or possibly, what was even
worse, an engagement as a gigolo whose services may be
required in a brothel.

"A great deal more easily from a book," Morel assured M. de Charlus, "for it's impossible to make head or
tail of the lessons."

"Then why don't you study it in my house, where
you would be far more comfortable?" M. de Charlus
might have answered, but took care not to do so, knowing
that at once, preserving only the same essential element
that the evening hours must be set apart, the imaginary
algebra course would change to obligatory lessons in
dancing or drawing. In this M. de Charlus could see that
he was mistaken, partially at least, for Morel often spent
his time at the Baron's in solving equations. M. de Charlus did raise the objection that algebra could be of little
use to a violinist. Morel replied that it was a distraction
which helped him to pass the time and to combat his
neurasthenia. No doubt M. de Charlus might have made
inquiries, have tried to find out what actually were these
mysterious and inescapable algebra lessons that were
given only at night. But M. de Charlus was too caught up
in the toils of his own social life to be able to unravel the
tangled skein of Morel's occupations. The visits he received or paid, the time he spent at his club, the dinner-

parties, the evenings at the theatre, prevented him from thinking about the problem, or for that matter about the malevolence, at once violent and underhand, to which (it was reported) Morel had been wont to give vent and which he had at the same time sought to conceal in the successive circles, the different towns through which he had passed, and where people still spoke of him with a shudder, with bated breath, never daring to say anything about him.

It was unfortunately one of the outbursts of this neurotic venom that I was destined to hear that day when, rising from the piano, I went down to the courtyard to meet Albertine, who had still not arrived. As I passed by Jupien's shop, in which Morel and the girl who, I supposed, was shortly to become his wife were alone together, Morel was screaming at the top of his voice, thereby revealing an accent that I hardly recognised as his, a coarse peasant accent, suppressed as a rule, and very strange indeed. His words were no less strange, and faulty from the point of view of the French language, but his knowledge of everything was imperfect. "Will you get out of here, *grand pied de grue, grand pied de grue, grand pied de grue,*" he repeated to the poor girl who at first had clearly not understood what he meant, and now, trembling and indignant, stood motionless before him.[7] "Didn't I tell you to get out of here, *grand pied de grue, grand pied de grue.* Go and fetch your uncle till I tell him what you are, you whore." Just at that moment the voice of Jupien, who was returning home with one of his friends, was heard in the courtyard, and as I knew that Morel was an utter coward, I decided that it was unnecessary to add my forces to those of Jupien and his friend, who in another moment would have entered the shop, and retired upstairs again to avoid Morel, who, for all his having pretended (probably in order to frighten and subjugate the girl by a piece of blackmail based perhaps on nothing at all) to be so anxious that Jupien should be fetched, made haste to depart as soon as he heard him in the courtyard. The words I have set down here are nothing, and would not explain why my heart was beating as I went upstairs. These scenes which we witness from time to time in our lives acquire an incalculable element of potency from what soldiers call, in speaking of a military offensive, the advantage of surprise, and however agreeably I might be soothed by the knowledge that Albertine, instead of remaining at the Trocadéro, was coming home to me, I still heard ringing in my ears those words ten times repeated: "*Grand pied de grue, grand pied de grue,*" which had so upset me.

Gradually my agitation subsided. Albertine was on her way home. I would hear her ring the bell in a moment. I felt that my life was no longer even what it could have been, and that to have a woman in the house like this with whom quite naturally, when she returned home, I would go out, to the adornment of whose person the energy and activity of my being were to be more and more diverted, made of me as it were a bough that has blossomed, but is weighed down by the abundant fruit into which all its reserves of strength have passed. In contrast to the anxiety that I had been feeling only an hour earlier, the calm induced in me by the prospect of Albertine's return was even vaster than that which I had felt in the morning before she left the house. Anticipating the future, of which my mistress's docility made me to all intents and purposes master, more resistant, as though it were filled and stabilised by the imminent, importunate, inevitable, gentle presence, it was the calm (dispensing us from the obligation to seek our happiness in ourselves) that is born of family feeling and domestic bliss. Familial and domestic: such was again, no less than the feeling which had brought me such peace while I was waiting for Albertine, that which I experienced later when I drove out with her. She took off her glove for a moment, either to touch my hand, or to dazzle me by letting me see on her little finger, next to the ring that Mme Bontemps had given her, another upon which was displayed the large and liquid surface of a bright sheet of ruby.

"What, another new ring, Albertine! Your aunt *is* generous!"

"No, I didn't get this from my aunt," she said with a laugh. "I bought it myself, since thanks to you I can save up ever so much money. I don't even know whose it was before. A visitor who was short of money left it with the proprietor of a hotel where I stayed at Le Mans. He didn't know what to do with it, and would have sold it for much less than it was worth. But it was still far too dear for me. Now that, thanks to you, I'm becoming a smart lady, I wrote to ask him if he still had it. And here it is."

"That makes a great many rings, Albertine. Where will you put the one that I am going to give you? Anyhow, this one's very pretty. I can't quite make out what that is carved round the ruby, it looks like a man's grinning face. But my eyesight isn't good enough."

"Even if it was better than it is it wouldn't get you very far. I can't make it out either."

In the past it had often happened to me, on reading a book of memoirs or a novel in which a man is always going out with a woman, or having tea with her, to long to be able to do likewise. I had thought sometimes that I had succeeded in doing so, as for instance when I took Saint-Loup's mistress out, to go to dine with her. But however much I summoned to my assistance the idea that I was at that moment actually impersonating the character I had envied in the novel, this idea assured me that I ought to find pleasure in Rachel's company and yet afforded me none. For, whenever we attempt to imitate something that has really existed, we forget that this something was brought about not by the desire to imitate but by an unconscious force which itself is also real; but this unique impression, which all my longing to taste a delicate pleasure by going out with Rachel had failed to give me, I was now experiencing, without having looked for it in the slightest, but for quite other reasons, reasons that were sincere and profound; to take a single instance, for the reason that my jealousy prevented me from losing sight of Albertine, and, the moment I was able to leave the house, from letting her go anywhere without me. I was experiencing it only now because our knowledge is not of the external objects which we want to observe, but of involuntary sensations, because in the past, though a woman might indeed be sitting in the same carriage as myself, she was not *really* by my side as long as she was not continually re-created there by a need for her such as I felt for Albertine, as long as the constant caress of my gaze did not incessantly restore to her those tints that need to be perpetually refreshed, as long as my senses, appeased perhaps but still freshly remembering, were not aware of the savour and substance beneath those colours, as long as, combined with the senses and with the imagination that exalts them, jealousy was not maintaining that woman in a state of equilibrium at my side by a compensated attraction as powerful as the law of gravity.

Our motor-car sped along the boulevards and the avenues, whose rows of houses, a pink congelation of sunshine and cold, reminded me of my visits to Mme Swann in the soft light of her chrysanthemums, before it was time to ring for the lamps. I had barely time to make out, being separated from them by the glass of the car as effectively as I should have been by that of my bedroom window, a young fruit-seller, or a dairymaid, standing in the doorway of her shop, illuminated by the sunshine like a heroine whom my desire was sufficient to launch upon exquisite adventures, on the threshold of a romance which I should never know. For I could not ask Albertine to let me stop, and already the young women whose features my eyes had barely distinguished, and whose fresh complexions they had barely caressed, were no longer visible in the golden haze in which they were bathed. The emotion that gripped me when I caught sight of a wine-merchant's girl at her cash-desk or a laundress chatting in the street was the emotion that we feel on recognising a goddess. Now that Olympus no longer exists, its inhabitants dwell upon the earth. And when, in composing a mythological scene, painters have engaged to pose as Venus or Ceres young women of the people following the humblest callings, so far from committing sacrilege they have merely added or restored to them the quality, the divine attributes of which they had been stripped.

"What did you think of the Trocadéro, you little gad-about?"

"I'm jolly glad I came away from it to go out with you. It's by Davioud, I believe."

"But how learned my little Albertine is becoming! It is indeed by Davioud, but I'd forgotten."

"While you're asleep I read your books, you old lazy-bones. As a building it's pretty lousy, isn't it?"

"I say, little one, you're changing so fast and becoming so intelligent" (this was true, but even had it not been true I was not sorry that she should have the satisfaction, failing others, of saying to herself that at least the time she spent in my house was not being entirely wasted) "that I don't mind telling you things which would generally be regarded as false but which correspond to a truth that I'm searching for. You know what is meant by impressionism?"

"Of course!"

"Very well then, this is what I mean: you remember the church at Marcouville-l'Orgueilleuse which Elstir disliked because it was new? Isn't it rather a denial of his own impressionism when he abstracts such buildings from the global impression in which they're included, brings them out of the light in which they're dissolved and scrutinises their intrinsic merit like an archaeologist? When he paints, haven't a hospital, a school, a poster on a hoarding the same value as a matchless cathedral which stands by their side in a single indivisible image? Remember how the façade was baked by the sun, how that carved frieze of saints at Marcouville floated on the sea of light. What does it matter that a building is new, if it appears old, or even if it doesn't? All the poetry that the old quarters contain has been squeezed out to the last drop, but if you look at some of the houses that have been built lately for well-to-do tradesmen in the new districts, where the stone is all freshly cut and still too white, don't they seem to rend the torrid midday air of July, at the hour when the shopkeepers go home to lunch in the suburbs, with a cry as sharp and acidulous as the smell of the cherries waiting for the meal to begin in the darkened dining-room, where the prismatic glass knife-rests throw off a multicoloured light as beautiful as the windows of Chartres?"

"How wonderful you are! If I ever do become clever, it will be entirely owing to you."

"Why, on a fine day, tear your eyes away from the Trocadéro, whose giraffe-neck towers remind one of the Charter-house of Pavia?"

"It reminded me also, standing up like that on its knoll, of a Mantegna that you have, I think it's of St Sebastian, where in the background there's a terraced city where you'd swear you'd find the Trocadéro."

"There, you see! But how did you come across the Mantegna reproduction? You're absolutely staggering."

We had now reached a more plebeian neighbourhood, and the installation of an ancillary Venus behind each counter made it as it were a suburban altar at the foot of which I would gladly have spent the rest of my life. As one does on the eve of a premature death, I drew up a mental list of the pleasures of which I was deprived by the fact that Albertine had put a full stop to my freedom. At Passy it was in the middle of the street itself, so crowded were the footways, that some girls, their arms encircling one another's waists, enthralled me with their smiles. I had not time to distinguish them clearly, but it is unlikely that I was overrating their charms; in any crowd, after all, in any crowd of young people, it is not unusual to come upon the effigy of a noble profile. So that these assembled masses on public holidays are as precious to the voluptuary as is to the archaeologist the disordered jumble of a site whose excavation will bring ancient medals to light. We arrived at the Bois. I reflected that, if Albertine had not come out with me, I might at this moment, in the enclosure of the Champs-Elysées, have been hearing the Wagnerian storm set all the tackle of the orchestra groaning, draw into its frenzy, like a light spindrift, the tune of the shepherd's pipe which I had just been playing to myself, set it flying, mould it, distort it, divide it, sweep it away in an ever-increasing whirlwind. I was determined, at any rate, that our drive should be short and that we should return home early, for, without having mentioned it to Albertine, I had decided to go that evening to the Verdurins'. They had recently sent me an invitation which I had flung into the waste-paper basket with all the rest. But I had changed my mind as far as this evening was concerned, for I meant to try to find out who Albertine might have been hoping to meet there in the afternoon. To tell the truth, I had reached that stage in my relations with Albertine when, if everything remains the same, if things go on normally, a woman no longer serves any purpose for one except as a transitional stage before another woman. She still retains a corner in one's heart, but a very small corner; one is impatient to go out every evening in search of unknown women, especially unknown women who are known to her and can tell one about her life. Herself, after all, we have possessed, and exhausted everything that she has consented to yield to us of herself. Her life is still herself, but precisely that part of her which we do not know, the things about which we have questioned her in vain and which we shall be able to gather from fresh lips.

If my life with Albertine was to prevent me from going to Venice, from travelling, at least I might this afternoon, had I been alone, have been making the acquaintance of the young midinettes scattered about in the sunlight of this fine Sunday, in the sum total of whose beauty I gave a considerable place to the unknown life that animated them. Are they not, those eyes one sees, shot through with a look behind which we do not know what images, memories, expectations, disdains lie concealed, and from which we cannot separate them? Will not that life, which is that of the woman passing by, impart a different value, according to what it is, to the frown on that forehead, the dilating of those nostrils? Albertine's presence debarred me from approaching them, and perhaps thus ceasing to desire them. The man who would maintain in himself the desire to go on living and a belief in something more delicious than the things of daily life, must go out driving; for the streets, the avenues, are full of goddesses. But the goddesses do not allow us to approach them. Here and there, among the trees, at the entrance to some café, a waitress was watching like a nymph on the edge of a sacred grove, while beyond her three girls were seated by the sweeping arc of their bicycles that were stacked beside them, like three immortals leaning against the clouds or the fabulous coursers upon which they perform their mythological journeys. I noticed that, whenever Albertine looked for a moment at these girls with deep attentiveness, she at once turned round towards me. But I was not unduly troubled, either by the intensity of this contemplation, or by its brevity which was compensated by that intensity; indeed, as to the latter, it often happened that Albertine, whether from exhaustion, or because it was an attentive person's way of looking at other people, would gaze thus in a sort of brown study either at my father or at Françoise; and as for the rapidity with which she turned to look at me, it might be due to the fact that Albertine, knowing my suspicions, might wish, even if they were unjustified, to avoid laying herself open to them. This attention, moreover, which would have seemed to me criminal on Albertine's part (and quite as much so if it had been directed at young men), I myself fastened upon all the midinettes without thinking it reprehensible for a moment, almost deciding indeed that it was reprehensible of Albertine to prevent me, by her presence, from stopping the car and going to join them. We consider it innocent to desire, and heinous that the other person should do so. And this contrast between what concerns oneself on the one hand, and on the other the person one loves, is not confined only to desire, but extends also to lying. What is more usual than a lie, whether it is a question of masking the daily weaknesses of a constitution which we wish to be thought strong, of concealing a vice, or of going off, without offending other people, to the thing that we prefer? It is the most necessary means of self-preservation, and the one that is most widely used. Yet this is the thing that we actually propose to banish from the life of the person we love; we watch for it, scent it, detest it everywhere. It distresses us, it is sufficient to bring about a rupture, it seems to us to conceal the gravest misdemeanours, except when it conceals them so effectively that we do not suspect their existence. A strange state, this, in which we are so inordinately sensitive to a pathogenic agent whose universal proliferation makes it inoffensive to other people and so baneful to the wretch who finds that he is no longer immune to it!

The life of these pretty girls (since, because of my long periods of reclusion, I so rarely met any) appeared to me, as to everyone in whom ease of fulfilment has not deadened the power of imagining, a thing as different from anything that I knew, and as desirable, as the most marvellous cities that travel holds in store for us.

The disappointment I had felt with the women I had known, or in the cities I had visited, did not prevent me from falling for the attraction of others or from believing in their reality. Hence, just as seeing Venice—Venice, for which this spring weather filled me also with longing, and which marriage with Albertine would prevent me from knowing—seeing Venice in a diorama which Ski would perhaps have declared to be more beautiful in tone than the place itself, would to me have been no substitute for the journey to Venice the length of which, determined without my having any hand in it, seemed to me an indispensable preliminary, so in the same way, however pretty she might be, the midinette whom a procuress had artificially provided for me could not possibly be a substitute for the gangling girl who was passing at this moment under the trees, laughing with a friend. Even if the girl I found in the house of assignation were prettier than this one, it could not be the same thing, because we do not look at the eyes of a girl we do not know as we would look at little chunks of opal or agate. We know that the little ray that colours them or the diamond dust that makes them sparkle is all that we can see of a mind, a will, a memory in which is contained the family home that we do not know, the intimate friends whom we envy. The enterprise of gaining possession of all this, of something so difficult, so recalcitrant, is what gives its attraction to that gaze far more than its merely physical beauty (which may serve to explain why the same young man can awaken a whole romance in the imagination of a woman who has heard somebody say that he is the Prince of Wales but pays no further attention to him after learning that she is mistaken). To find the midinette in the house of assignation is to find her emptied of that unknown life which permeates her and which we aspire to possess with her; it is to approach a pair of eyes that have indeed become mere precious stones, a nose whose wrinkling is as devoid of meaning as that of a flower. No, concerning the unknown midinette who was passing at that moment, it seemed to me as indispensable, if I wished to continue to believe in her reality, to face up to her resistance by adapting my mode of approach, challenging a rebuff, returning to the charge, obtaining an assignation, waiting for her outside her place of work, getting to know, episode by episode, everything that constituted the girl's life, experiencing whatever was represented for her by the pleasure I was seeking, and traversing the distance which her different habits, her special mode of life, set between me and the attention, the favour I wished to reach and win over—all this seemed to me as indispensable as making a long journey by train if I wished to believe in the reality of Pisa and not see it simply as a panoramic show in a World Fair. But these very similarities between desire and travel made me vow to myself that one day I would grasp a little more closely the nature of this force, invisible but as powerful as any belief or, in the world of physics, as atmospheric pressure, which exalted cities and women to such a height so long as I did not know them, and, slipping away from beneath them as soon as I had approached them, made them at once collapse and fall flat on to the dead level of the most commonplace reality.

Further on, another little girl was kneeling beside her bicycle, which she was putting to rights. The repair finished, the young racer mounted her machine, but without straddling it as a man would have done. For a moment the bicycle swerved, and the young body seemed to have added to itself a sail, a huge wing; and presently we saw the young creature speed away, half-human, half-winged, angel or peri, pursuing her course.

This was what the presence of Albertine, this was what my life with Albertine, deprived me of. Deprived me, did I say? Should I not have thought rather: what it presented to me? If Albertine had not been living with me, if she had been free, I should have imagined, and with reason, every one of these women as a possible or indeed a probable object of her desire, of her pleasure. They would have appeared to me like dancers in a diabolical ballet, representing the Temptations to one person, and shooting their darts into the heart of another. Midinettes, schoolgirls, actresses, how I should have hated them all! Objects of horror, for me they would have been excluded from the beauty of the universe. Albertine's servitude, by releasing me from suffering on their account, restored them to the beauty of the world. Now that they were harmless, having lost the sting that stabs the heart with jealousy, I was free to admire them, to caress them with my eyes, another day more intimately perhaps. By shutting Albertine away, I had at the same time restored to the universe all those glittering wings that flutter in public gardens, ballrooms, theatres, and which became tempting once more to me because she could no longer succumb to their temptation. They composed the beauty of the world. They had at one time composed that of Albertine. It was because I had seen her first as a mysterious bird, then as a great actress of the beach, desired, perhaps won, that I had thought her wonderful. As soon as she was a captive in my house, the bird that I had seen one afternoon advancing with measured tread along the front, surrounded by a congregation of other girls like seagulls alighted from who knew where, Albertine had lost all her colours, together with all the opportunities that other people had of securing her for themselves. Gradually she had lost her beauty. It required excursions like this, in which I imagined her, but for my presence, accosted by some woman or by some young man, to make me see her again amid the splendour of the beach, although my jealousy was on a different plane from the decline of the pleasures of my imagination. But in spite of these abrupt reversions in which, desired by other people, she once more became beautiful in my eyes, I might very well have divided her stay with me into two periods, in the first of which she was still, although less so every day, the glittering actress of the beach, and in the second of which, become the grey captive, reduced to her drab self, she needed these flashes in which I remembered the past to restore her colour to her.

Sometimes, in the hours in which I felt most indiffer-

ent towards her, there came back to me the memory of a
far-off moment on the beach, before I yet knew her,
when, not far from a lady with whom I was on bad terms
and with whom I was almost certain now that she had
had relations, she burst out laughing, staring me in the
face in an insolent fashion. All round her hissed the blue
and polished sea. In the sunshine of the beach, Albertine,
in the midst of her friends, was the most beautiful of
them all. It was this magnificent girl, who, in her familiar
setting of boundless waters—she, a precious object in the
eyes of the admiring lady—had inflicted this insult on
me. It was definitive, for the lady had returned perhaps to
Balbec, had registered perhaps, on the luminous and
echoing beach, the absence of Albertine; but she was unaware that the girl was living with me, was wholly mine.
The vast expanse of blue water, her obliviousness of the
predilection she had had for this particular girl and had
now diverted to others, had closed over the insult that Albertine had offered me, enshrining it in a glittering and
unbreakable casket. Then hatred of that woman gnawed
my heart; of Albertine too, but a hatred mingled with admiration of the beautiful, adulated girl, with her marvellous hair, whose laughter upon the beach had been an
affront. Shame, jealousy, the memory of my first desires
and of the brilliant setting, had restored to Albertine her
former beauty and worth. And thus there alternated with
the somewhat oppressive boredom that I felt in her company a throbbing desire, full of resplendent images and of
regrets, according to whether she was by my side in my
room or I set her free again in my memory, on the sea-
front, in her gay beach clothes, to the sound of the musical instruments of the sea—Albertine, now abstracted

from that environment, possessed and of no great value, now plunged back into it, escaping from me into a past which I should never get to know, humiliating me before the lady who was her friend as much as the splashing of the waves or the dizzying heat of the sun—Albertine restored to the beach or brought back again to my room, in a sort of amphibious love.

Elsewhere, a numerous band were playing ball. All these girls had come out to make the most of the sunshine, for these February days, even when they are as dazzling as this one, do not last long, and the splendour of their light does not postpone the hour of its decline. Before that hour drew near, we had a spell of chiaroscuro, because after we had driven as far as the Seine, where Albertine admired, and by her presence prevented me from admiring, the reflexions of red sails upon the wintry blue of the water, and a tiled house nestling in the distance like a single red poppy against the clear horizon of which Saint-Cloud seemed, further off still, to be the fragmentary, friable, ribbed petrifaction, we left our motor-car and walked a long way. For some moments I even gave her my arm, and it seemed to me that the ring which her arm formed round mine united our two persons in a single self and linked our destinies together.

Our shadows, now parallel, now close together and joined, traced an exquisite pattern at our feet. It seemed to me already wonderful enough, at home, that Albertine should be living with me, that it should be she who came and lay down on my bed. But it was the transportation of that marvel to the outside world, into the heart of nature, by the shore of the lake in the Bois which I loved so much, beneath the trees, that it should be precisely her shadow, the pure and simplified shadow of her leg, of her bust, that the sun delineated in monochrome by the side of mine upon the gravel of the path. And the fusion of our shadows had a charm for me that was doubtless more insubstantial, but no less intimate, than the contiguity, the fusion of our bodies. Then we returned to the car. And it chose, for our homeward journey, a succession of little winding lanes along which the wintry trees, clothed, like ruins, in ivy and brambles, seemed to be pointing the way to the dwelling of some magician. No sooner had we emerged from their shady cover than we found, leaving the Bois, the daylight still so bright that I thought I should still have time to do everything I wanted to do before dinner, when, only a few moments later, as the car approached the Arc de Triomphe, it was with a sudden start of surprise and dismay that I perceived, over Paris, the moon prematurely full, like the face of a clock that has stopped and makes us think that we are late for an engagement. We had told the driver to take us home. For Albertine, this also meant returning to my home. The presence of women, however dear to us, who are obliged to leave us to return home does not bestow that peace which I found in the presence of Albertine seated in the car by my side, a presence that was conveying us not to the emptiness of the hours when lovers are apart, but to an even more stable and more sheltered reunion in my home, which was also hers, the material symbol of my possession of her. True, in order to possess, one must first have desired. We do not possess a line, a surface, a mass unless it is occupied by our love. But Albertine had not been for me during our drive, as Rachel had once been, a meaningless dust of flesh and clothing. At Balbec, the imagination of my eyes, my lips, my hands had so solidly constructed, so tenderly polished her body that now, in this car, in order to touch that body, to contain it, I had no need to press my own body against Albertine, nor even to see her; it was enough for me to hear her, and, if she was silent, to know that she was by my side; my interwoven senses enveloped her completely and when, on our arrival at the house, she quite naturally alighted, I stopped for a moment to tell the chauffeur to call for me later, but my eyes enveloped her still as she passed ahead of me under the arch, and it was still the same inert, domestic calm that I felt as I saw her thus, solid, flushed, opulent and captive, returning home quite naturally with me, like a woman who belonged to me, and, protected by its walls, disappearing into our house. Unfortunately she seemed to feel herself in prison there, and—judging by her mournful, weary look that evening as we dined together in her room—to share the opinion of that Mme de La Rochefoucauld who, when asked whether she was not glad to live in so beautiful a home as Liancourt, replied: "There is no such thing as a beautiful prison." I did not notice it at first; and it was I who bemoaned the thought that, had it not been for Albertine (for with her I should have suffered too acutely from jealousy in a hotel where all day long she would have been exposed to contact with so many people), I might at that moment be dining in Venice in one of those little low-ceilinged restaurants like a ship's saloon, from which one looks out on the Grand Canal through little curved windows encircled with Moorish mouldings.

I ought to add that Albertine greatly admired a big bronze I had by Barbedienne which with ample justification Bloch considered extremely ugly. He had perhaps less reason to be surprised at my having kept it. I had never sought, like him, to furnish for aesthetic effect, to arrange rooms artistically. I was too lazy for that, too indifferent to the things that I was in the habit of seeing every day. Since my taste was not involved, I had a right not to modulate my interiors. I might perhaps, in spite of this, have discarded the bronze. But ugly and expensive things are extremely useful, for they possess, in the eyes of people who do not understand us, who do not share our taste and with whom we may be in love, a glamour which a fine object that does not reveal its beauty may lack. Now the people who do not understand us are precisely the people with regard to whom it may be useful to us to take advantage of a prestige which our intellect is enough to ensure for us among superior people. Although Albertine was beginning to show some taste, she still had a certain respect for the bronze, and this was reflected back upon me in an esteem which, coming from Albertine, mattered infinitely more to me than the question of keeping a bronze which was a trifle degrading, since I loved Albertine.

But the thought of my bondage ceased of a sudden to weigh upon me and I looked forward to prolonging it still further, because I seemed to perceive that Albertine was sorely conscious of her own. True, whenever I had asked her whether she was unhappy in my house, she had always replied that she did not know where it would be possible for her to be happier. But often these words were contradicted by an air of nostalgia and edginess. Certainly if she had the tastes with which I had credited her, this prevention from ever satisfying them must have been as

frustrating to her as it was calming to myself, calming to
such an extent that I should have decided that the hypothesis of my having accused her unjustly was the most
probable, had it not been so difficult to fit into this hypothesis the extraordinary pains that Albertine took never
to be alone, never to be free to go out with anyone, never
to stop for a moment outside the front door when she
came in, always to insist on being ostentatiously accompanied, whenever she went to the telephone, by someone
who would be able to repeat to me what she had said—
by Françoise or Andrée—always to leave me alone with
the latter (without appearing to be doing so on purpose)
after they had been out together, so that I might obtain a
detailed report of their outing. Contrasted with this marvellous docility were occasional gestures of impatience,
quickly repressed, which made me wonder whether Albertine might not be planning to shake off her chains.

Certain incidental circumstances seemed to corroborate my supposition. Thus, one day when I had gone out
by myself, I ran into Gisèle in the neighbourhood of
Passy, and we chatted about this and that. Presently, not
without pride at being able to do so, I informed her that I
saw Albertine constantly. Gisèle asked me where she
could find her, since she *happened* to have something to
say to her. "What is it?" "Something to do with some
young friends of hers." "What friends? I may perhaps be
able to tell you, though that needn't prevent you from
seeing her." "Oh, girls she knew years ago, I don't remember their names," Gisèle replied vaguely, beating a
retreat. She left me, supposing herself to have spoken with
such prudence that I could not conceivably have suspected anything. But falsehood is so unexacting, needs so

little help to make itself manifest! If it had been a question of friends of long ago, whose very names she no longer remembered, why did she "happen" to need to speak to Albertine about them? This "happen," akin to an expression dear to Mme Cottard: "It couldn't be better timed," could be applicable only to something particular, opportune, perhaps urgent, relating to specific persons. Besides, simply the way she opened her mouth, as though about to yawn, with a vague expression, when she said to me (almost retreating bodily, as she went into reverse at this point in our conversation): "Oh, I don't know, I don't remember their names," made her face, and in harmony with it her voice, as clear a picture of falsehood as the wholly different air, keen, animated, forthcoming, of her "I happen to have" was of truth. I did not cross-examine Gisèle. Of what use would it have been to me? Of course she did not lie in the same way as Albertine. And of course Albertine's lies pained me more. But they had obviously a point in common: the fact of the lie itself, which in certain cases is self-evident. Not evidence of the reality that the lie conceals. We know that each murderer, individually, imagines that he has arranged everything so cleverly that he will not be caught, but in general, murderers are almost always caught. Liars, on the contrary, are rarely caught, and, among liars, more particularly the woman with whom we are in love. We do not know where she has been, what she has been doing. But as soon as she opens her mouth to speak, to speak of something else beneath which lies hidden the thing that she does not mention, the lie is immediately perceived, and our jealousy increased, since we are conscious of the lie, and cannot succeed in discovering the truth. With Albertine, the

impression that she was lying was conveyed by a number
of characteristics which we have already observed in the
course of this narrative, but especially by the fact that,
when she was lying, her story erred either from inadequacy, omission, implausibility, or on the contrary from a
surfeit of petty details intended to make it seem plausible.
Plausibility, notwithstanding the idea that the liar holds of
it, is by no means the same as truth. Whenever, while listening to something that is true, we hear something that
is only plausible, that is perhaps more plausible than the
truth, that is perhaps too plausible, an ear that is at all
musical senses that it is not correct, as with a line that
does not scan or a word read aloud in mistake for another.
The ear senses it, and if we are in love, the heart takes
alarm. Why do we not reflect at the time, when we
change the whole course of our life because we do not
know whether a woman went along the Rue de Berri or
the Rue Washington, why do we not reflect that these
few yards of difference, and the woman herself, will be reduced to the hundred millionth part of themselves (that is
to say to dimensions far beneath our perception), if we
only have the wisdom to remain for a few years without
seeing the woman, and that she who has out-Gullivered
Gulliver in our eyes will shrink to a Lilliputian whom no
microscope—of the heart, at least, for that of the disinterested memory is more powerful and less fragile—can ever
again discern! However that may be, if there was a point
in common—mendacity itself—between Albertine's lies
and Gisèle's, still Gisèle did not lie in the same way as
Albertine, nor indeed in the same way as Andrée, but
their respective lies dovetailed so neatly into one another,
while presenting a great variety, that the little band had

the impenetrable solidity of certain commercial houses, booksellers for example or newspaper publishers, where the wretched author will never succeed, notwithstanding the diversity of the persons employed in them, in discovering whether or not he is being swindled. The director of the newspaper or review lies with an attitude of sincerity all the more solemn in that he is frequently obliged to conceal the fact that he himself does exactly the same things and indulges in the same commercial practices as he denounced in other newspaper or theatre directors, in other publishers, when he chose as his banner, when he raised against them the standard of Honesty. The fact of a man's having proclaimed (as leader of a political party, or in any other capacity) that it is wicked to lie obliges him as a rule to lie more than other people, without on that account abandoning the solemn mask, doffing the august tiara of sincerity. The "honest" gentleman's partner lies in a different and more ingenuous fashion. He deceives his author as he deceives his wife, with tricks from the vaudeville stage. The sub-editor, a crude, straightforward man, lies quite simply, like an architect who promises that your house will be ready at a date when it will not have been begun. The editor, an angelic soul, flutters from one to another of the three, and without knowing what the matter is, gives them, out of brotherly scruple and affectionate solidarity, the precious support of an unimpeachable word. These four persons live in a state of perpetual dissension to which the arrival of the author puts a stop. Over and above their private quarrels, each of them remembers the paramount military duty of rallying to the support of the threatened "corps." Without realising it, I had long been playing the part of this author in relation to the little band. If Gisèle had been thinking, when she used the word "happen," of one of Albertine's friends who was prepared to go away with her as soon as my mistress should have found some pretext or other for leaving me, and had meant to warn Albertine that the hour had now come or would shortly strike, she, Gisèle, would have let herself be torn to pieces rather than tell me so; it was quite useless therefore to ply her with questions.

Meetings such as this one with Gisèle were not alone in reinforcing my doubts. For instance, I admired Albertine's paintings. The touching pastimes of a captive, they moved me so that I congratulated her upon them. "No, they're dreadfully bad, but I've never had a drawing lesson in my life." "But one evening at Balbec you sent word to me that you had stayed at home to have a drawing lesson." I reminded her of the day and told her that I had realised at the time that people did not have drawing lessons at that hour in the evening. Albertine blushed. "It's true," she said, "I wasn't having drawing lessons. I told you a great many lies at the beginning, that I admit. But I never lie to you now." How I should have loved to know what were the many lies that she had told me at the beginning! But I knew beforehand that her answers would be fresh lies. And so I contented myself with kissing her. I asked her to tell me one only of those lies. She replied: "Oh, well; for instance when I said that the sea air was bad for me." I ceased to insist in the face of this unwillingness to oblige.

Every person we love, indeed to a certain extent every person, is to us like Janus, presenting to us a face that pleases us if the person leaves us, a dreary face if we know him or her to be at our perpetual disposal. In the case of Albertine, the prospect of her continued society was painful to me in another way which I cannot explain in this narrative. It is terrible to have the life of another person attached to one's own like a bomb which one holds in one's hands, unable to get rid of it without committing a crime. But one has only to compare this with the ups and downs, the dangers, the anxieties, the fear that false but probable things will come to be believed when we will no longer be able to explain them—feelings that one experiences if one lives on intimate terms with a madman. For instance, I pitied M. de Charlus for living with Morel (immediately the memory of the scene that afternoon made me feel that the left side of my chest was heavier than the other); leaving aside the relations that may or may not have existed between them, M. de Charlus must have been unaware at the outset that Morel was mad. Morel's beauty, his stupidity, his pride must have deterred the Baron from exploring so deeply, until the days of melancholia when Morel accused M. de Charlus of responsibility for his sorrows, without being able to furnish any explanation, abused him for his want of trust with the help of false but extremely subtle arguments, threatened him with desperate resolutions in the midst of which there persisted the most cunning regard for his own most immediate interests. But all this is only a comparison. Albertine was not mad.

To make her chains appear lighter, the clever thing seemed to me to be to make her believe that I myself was about to break them. But I could not confide this mendacious plan to her at that moment, since she had returned so sweetly from the Trocadéro that afternoon; the most I could do, far from distressing her with the threat of a

rupture, was to keep to myself those dreams of a perpetual life together which my grateful heart had formed. As I
looked at her, I found it hard to restrain myself from
pouring them out to her, and she may perhaps have noticed this. Unfortunately the expression of such feelings is
not contagious. The case of an affected old woman like
M. de Charlus who, by dint of never seeing in his imagination anything but a proud young man, thinks that he
has himself become a proud young man, all the more so
the more affected and ridiculous he becomes—this case is
more general, and it is the misfortune of an impassioned
lover not to realise that while he sees in front of him a
beautiful face, his mistress is seeing his face, which is not
made any more beautiful, far from it, when it is distorted
by the pleasure that is aroused in it by the sight of
beauty. Nor indeed does love exhaust the generality of
this case; we do not see our own bodies, which other people see, and we "follow" our own train of thought, the
object, invisible to other people, which is before our eyes.
At times the artist reveals this object in his work. Whence
it arises that the admirers of that work are disappointed in
its author, on whose face that inner beauty is imperfectly
reflected.

Retaining from my dream of Venice only what could
concern Albertine and sweeten the time she spent in my
house, I mentioned a Fortuny gown which we ought to go
and order one of these days. I was looking for new
pleasures with which to distract her. I would have liked to
surprise her with a gift of old French silver, had it been
possible to find any. As a matter of fact, when we had
planned to acquire a yacht, a plan judged unrealisable by
Albertine—and by me whenever I thought her virtuous

and life with her began to appear as financially ruinous as marriage to her seemed impossible—we had, though without her believing I would buy one, asked advice from Elstir.

I learned that a death had occurred that day which distressed me greatly—that of Bergotte. It was known that he had been ill for a long time past. Not, of course, with the illness from which he had suffered originally and which was natural. Nature scarcely seems capable of giving us any but quite short illnesses. But medicine has developed the art of prolonging them. Remedies, the respite that they procure, the relapses that a temporary cessation of them provokes, produce a simulacrum of illness to which the patient grows so accustomed that he ends by stabilising it, stylising it, just as children have regular fits of coughing long after they have been cured of the whooping cough. Then the remedies begin to have less effect, the doses are increased, they cease to do any good, but they have begun to do harm thanks to this lasting indisposition. Nature would not have offered them so long a tenure. It is a great wonder that medicine can almost rival nature in forcing a man to remain in bed, to continue taking some drug on pain of death. From then on, the artificially grafted illness has taken root, has become a secondary but a genuine illness, with this difference only, that natural illnesses are cured, but never those which medicine creates, for it does not know the secret of their cure.

For years past Bergotte had ceased to go out of doors. In any case he had never cared for society, or had cared for it for a day only, to despise it as he despised everything else, and in the same fashion, which was his own, namely to despise a thing not because it was beyond his reach but as soon as he had attained it. He lived so simply that nobody suspected how rich he was, and anyone who had known would still have been mistaken, having thought him a miser whereas no one was ever more generous. He was generous above all towards women—girls, one ought rather to say—who were ashamed to receive so much in return for so little. He excused himself in his own eyes because he knew that he could never produce such good work as in an atmosphere of amorous feelings. Love is too strong a word, but pleasure that is at all rooted in the flesh is helpful to literary work because it cancels all other pleasures, for instance the pleasures of society, those which are the same for everyone. And even if this love leads to disillusionment, it does at least stir, even by so doing, the surface of the soul which otherwise would be in danger of becoming stagnant. Desire is therefore not without its value to the writer in detaching him first of all from his fellow men and from conforming to their standards, and afterwards in restoring some degree of movement to a spiritual machine which, after a certain age, tends to come to a standstill. We do not achieve happiness but we gain some insights into the reasons which prevent us from being happy and which would have remained invisible to us but for these sudden revelations of disappointment. Dreams, we know, are not realisable; we might not form any, perhaps, were it not for desire, and it is useful to us to form them in order to see them fail and to learn from their failure. And so Bergotte said to himself: "I spend more than a multimillionaire on girls, but the pleasures or disappointments that they give me make

me write a book which brings me in money." Economi-
cally, this argument was absurd, but no doubt he found
some charm in thus transmuting gold into caresses and
caresses into gold. We saw, at the time of my grandmother's death, how a weary old age loves repose. Now in
society there is nothing but conversation. Vapid though it
is, it has the capacity to eliminate women, who become
nothing more than questions and answers. Removed from
society, women become once more what is so reposeful to
a weary old man, an object of contemplation. In any case,
now there was no longer any question of all this. I have
said that Bergotte never went out of doors, and when he
got out of bed for an hour in his room, he would be
smothered in shawls, rugs, all the things with which a
person covers himself before exposing himself to intense
cold or going on a railway journey. He would apologise
for them to the few friends whom he allowed to penetrate
to his sanctuary; pointing to his tartan plaids, his travel-
ling-rugs, he would say merrily: "After all, my dear fellow, life, as Anaxagoras has said, is a journey." Thus he
went on growing steadily colder, a tiny planet offering a
prophetic image of the greater, when gradually heat will
withdraw from the earth, then life itself. Then the resurrection will have come to an end, for, however far forward
into future generations the works of men may shine, there
must none the less be men. If certain species hold out
longer against the invading cold, when there are no longer
any men, and if we suppose Bergotte's fame to have lasted
until then, suddenly it will be extinguished for all time. It
will not be the last animals that will read him, for it is
scarcely probable that, like the Apostles at Pentecost, they

will be able to understand the speech of the various races of mankind without having learned it.

In the months that preceded his death, Bergotte suffered from insomnia, and what was worse, whenever he did fall asleep, from nightmares which, if he awoke, made him reluctant to go to sleep again. He had long been a lover of dreams, even bad dreams, because thanks to them, thanks to the contradiction they present to the reality which we have before us in our waking state, they give us, at the moment of waking if not before, the profound sensation of having slept. But Bergotte's nightmares were not like that. When he spoke of nightmares, he used in the past to mean unpleasant things that happened in his brain. Latterly, it was as though from somewhere outside himself that he would see a hand armed with a damp cloth which, rubbed over his face by an evil woman, kept trying to wake him; or an intolerable itching in his thighs; or the rage—because Bergotte had murmured in his sleep that he was driving badly—of a raving lunatic of a cabman who flung himself upon the writer, biting and gnawing his fingers. Finally, as soon as it had grown sufficiently dark in his sleep, nature would arrange a sort of undress rehearsal of the apoplectic stroke that was to carry him off. Bergotte would arrive in a carriage beneath the porch of Swann's new house, and would try to get out. A shattering attack of dizziness would pin him to his seat; the concierge would try to help him out; he would remain seated, unable to lift himself up or straighten his legs. He would cling to the stone pillar in front of him, but could not find sufficient support to enable him to stand.

He consulted doctors who, flattered to be summoned by him, saw in his virtues as an incessant worker (he had done nothing for twenty years), in overwork, the cause of his ailments. They advised him not to read frightening stories (he never read anything), to take more advantage of the sunshine, which was "indispensable to life" (he had owed a few years of comparative health only to his rigorous confinement at home), to take more nourishment (which made him thinner, and nourished nothing but his nightmares). One of his doctors was blessed with an argumentative and contrary spirit, and whenever Bergotte saw him in the absence of the others and, in order not to offend him, suggested to him as his own ideas what the others had advised, this doctor, thinking that Bergotte was trying to get him to prescribe something that he liked, would at once forbid it, often for reasons invented so hurriedly to meet the case that, in face of the material objections which Bergotte raised, the doctor, contradicting him, was obliged in the same sentence to contradict himself, but, for fresh reasons, repeated the original prohibition. Bergotte would return to one of the previous doctors, a man who prided himself on his wit, especially in the presence of one of the masters of the pen, and who, if Bergotte insinuated: "I seem to remember, though, that Dr X—— told me—long ago, of course—that that might affect my kidneys and my brain . . . ," would smile mischievously, raise his finger and announce: "I said use, I did not say abuse. Naturally every drug, if one takes it in excess, becomes a double-edged weapon." There is in the human body a certain instinct for what is beneficial to us, as there is in the heart for what is our moral duty, an instinct which no authorisation by a doctor of medicine or divinity can replace. We know that cold baths are bad for us, but we like them: we can always find a doctor to recommend them, not to prevent them from doing us harm. From each of these doctors Bergotte took something which, in his own wisdom, he had forbidden himself for years past. After a few weeks, his old troubles had reappeared and the new ones had become worse. Maddened by uninterrupted pain, to which was added insomnia broken only by brief spells of nightmare, Bergotte called in no more doctors and tried with success, but to excess, different narcotics, trustingly reading the prospectus that accompanied each of them, a prospectus which proclaimed the necessity of sleep but hinted that all the preparations which induce it (except the one contained in the bottle round which the prospectus was wrapped, which never produced any toxic effect) were toxic, and therefore made the remedy worse than the disease. Bergotte tried them all. Some of these drugs may be of a different family from those to which one is accustomed, by-products, for instance, of amyl and ethyl. When one absorbs a new drug, entirely different in composition, it is always with a delicious expectancy of the unknown. One's heart beats as at a first assignation. To what unknown forms of sleep, of dreams, is the newcomer going to lead one? It is inside one now, it is in control of one's thoughts. In what way is one going to fall asleep? And, once asleep, by what strange paths, up to what peaks, into what unfathomed gulfs will this all-powerful master lead one? What new group of sensations will one meet with on this journey? Will it lead to illness? To blissful happiness? To death?

Bergotte's death came to him the day after he had thus entrusted himself to one of these friends (a friend? an enemy?) who proved too strong.

The circumstances of his death were as follows. A fairly mild attack of uraemia had led to his being ordered to rest. But, an art critic having written somewhere that in Vermeer's *View of Delft* (lent by the Gallery at The Hague for an exhibition of Dutch painting), a picture which he adored and imagined that he knew by heart, a little patch of yellow wall (which he could not remember) was so well painted that it was, if one looked at it by itself, like some priceless specimen of Chinese art, of a beauty that was sufficient in itself, Bergotte ate a few potatoes, left the house, and went to the exhibition. At the first few steps he had to climb, he was overcome by an attack of dizziness. He walked past several pictures and was struck by the aridity and pointlessness of such an artificial kind of art, which was greatly inferior to the sunshine of a windswept Venetian palazzo, or of an ordinary house by the sea. At last he came to the Vermeer which he remembered as more striking, more different from anything else he knew, but in which, thanks to the critic's article, he noticed for the first time some small figures in blue, that the sand was pink, and, finally, the precious substance of the tiny patch of yellow wall. His dizziness increased; he fixed his gaze, like a child upon a yellow butterfly that it wants to catch, on the precious little patch of wall. "That's how I ought to have written," he said. "My last books are too dry, I ought to have gone over them with a few layers of colour, made my language precious in itself, like this little patch of yellow wall." Meanwhile he was not unconscious of the gravity of his

condition. In a celestial pair of scales there appeared to
him, weighing down one of the pans, his own life, while
the other contained the little patch of wall so beautifully
painted in yellow. He felt that he had rashly sacrificed the
former for the latter. "All the same," he said to himself,
"I shouldn't like to be the headline news of this exhibition
for the evening papers."

He repeated to himself: "Little patch of yellow wall,
with a sloping roof, little patch of yellow wall." Meanwhile he sank down on to a circular settee; whereupon he
suddenly ceased to think that his life was in jeopardy and,
reverting to his natural optimism, told himself: "It's nothing, merely a touch of indigestion from those potatoes,
which were under-cooked." A fresh attack struck him
down; he rolled from the settee to the floor, as visitors
and attendants came hurrying to his assistance. He was
dead. Dead for ever? Who can say? Certainly, experiments in spiritualism offer us no more proof than the
dogmas of religion that the soul survives death. All that
we can say is that everything is arranged in this life as
though we entered it carrying a burden of obligations contracted in a former life; there is no reason inherent in the
conditions of life on this earth that can make us consider
ourselves obliged to do good, to be kind and thoughtful,
even to be polite, nor for an atheist artist to consider himself obliged to begin over again a score of times a piece of
work the admiration aroused by which will matter little to
his worm-eaten body, like the patch of yellow wall
painted with so much skill and refinement by an artist
destined to be for ever unknown and barely identified under the name Vermeer. All these obligations, which have
no sanction in our present life, seem to belong to a differ-

ent world, a world based on kindness, scrupulousness, self-sacrifice, a world entirely different from this one and which we leave in order to be born on this earth, before perhaps returning there to live once again beneath the sway of those unknown laws which we obeyed because we bore their precepts in our hearts, not knowing whose hand had traced them there—those laws to which every profound work of the intellect brings us nearer and which are invisible only—if then!—to fools. So that the idea that Bergotte was not dead for ever is by no means improbable.

They buried him, but all through that night of mourning, in the lighted shop-windows, his books, arranged three by three, kept vigil like angels with outspread wings and seemed, for him who was no more, the symbol of his resurrection.

I learned, as I have said, that Bergotte had died that day. And I was amazed at the inaccuracy of the newspapers which—each of them reproducing the same paragraph—stated that he had died the day before. For Albertine had met him the day before, as she informed me that very evening, and indeed she had been a little late in coming home, for he had chatted to her for some time. She was probably the last person to whom he had spoken. She knew him through me, for although I had long ceased to see him, as she had been anxious to be introduced to him I had written a year earlier to ask the old master whether I might bring her to see him. He had granted my request, though he was a trifle hurt, I fancy, that I should be visiting him only to give pleasure to another person, which was a confirmation of my indifference to him.

These cases are frequent: sometimes the man or woman whom we approach not for the pleasure of conversing with them again, but on behalf of a third person, refuses so obstinately that our protégé concludes that we have boasted of an influence which we do not possess; more often the man of genius or the famous beauty consents, but, humiliated in their glory, wounded in their affection, they feel for us afterwards only a diminished, sorrowful, slightly contemptuous regard. It was not until long afterwards that I discovered that I had wrongly accused the newspapers of inaccuracy, since on the day in question Albertine had not in fact met Bergotte. At the time I had never suspected this for a single instant, so artlessly had she described the meeting to me, and it was not until much later that I discovered her charming skill in lying naturally. What she said, what she admitted, had to such a degree the same characteristics as the formal evidence of the case—what we see with our own eyes or learn from irrefutable sources—that she sowed thus in the gaps of her life episodes of another life the falsity of which I did not then suspect. I have added "what she admitted" for the following reason. Sometimes odd coincidences would give me jealous suspicions about her in which another person figured by her side in the past, or alas in the future. In order to appear certain of my facts, I would mention the person's name, and Albertine would say: "Yes, I met her a week ago, just outside the house. I acknowledged her greeting out of politeness. I walked a little way with her. But there's never been anything between us. There never will be." Now Albertine had not even met this person, for the simple reason that the person had not been in Paris for the last ten months. But my mistress felt that a complete denial would not sound very probable. Whence this imaginary brief encounter, related so simply that I could see the lady stop, greet her, and walk a little way with her. The evidence of my senses, if I had been in the street at that moment, would perhaps have informed me that the lady had not been with Albertine. But if I had known this to be the case, it was by one of those chains of reasoning in which the words of people in whom we have confidence insert strong links, and not by the evidence of my senses. To invoke this evidence by the senses I should have had to be in the street at that particular moment, and I had not been. One can imagine, however, that such a hypothesis is not improbable: I might have gone out, and have been passing along the street at the time at which Albertine was to tell me in the evening (not having seen me there) that she had walked a few steps with the lady, and I should then have known that Albertine was lying. But is this absolutely certain even then? A strange darkness would have clouded my mind, I should have begun to doubt whether I had seen her alone, I should hardly even have sought to understand by what optical illusion I had failed to perceive the lady, and I should not have been greatly surprised to find myself mistaken, for the stellar universe is not so difficult of comprehension as the real actions of other people, especially of the people we love, fortified as they are against our doubts by fables devised for their protection. For how many years on end can they not allow our apathetic love to believe that they have in some foreign country a sister, a brother, a sister-in-law who have never existed!

The evidence of the senses is also an operation of the mind in which conviction creates the facts. We have often seen her sense of hearing convey to Françoise not the word that was uttered but what she thought to be its correct form, which was enough to prevent her from hearing the implicit correction in a superior pronunciation. Our butler was cast in a similar mould. M. de Charlus was in the habit of wearing at this time—for he was constantly changing—very light trousers which were recognisable a mile off. Now our butler, who thought that the word *pissotière* (the word denoting what M. de Rambuteau[8] had been so annoyed to hear the Duc de Guermantes call a Rambuteau convenience) was really *pistière*, never once in the whole of his life heard a single person say *pissotière*, albeit the word was frequently pronounced thus in his hearing. But error is more obstinate than faith and does not examine the grounds of its belief. Constantly the butler would say: "I'm sure M. le Baron de Charlus must have caught a disease to stand about as long as he does in a *pistière*. That's what comes of chasing the ladies at his age. You can tell what he is by his trousers. This morning, Madame sent me with a message to Neuilly. As I passed the *pistière* in the Rue de Bourgogne I saw M. le Baron de Charlus go in. When I came back from Neuilly, a good hour later, I saw his yellow trousers in the same *pistière*, in the same place, in the middle stall where he always stands so that people shan't see him." I can think of no one more beautiful, more noble or more youthful than a certain niece of Mme de Guermantes. But I once heard the commissionaire of a restaurant where I used sometimes to dine say as she went by: "Just look at that old trollop, what a fright! And she must be eighty if she's a day." As far as age went, I find it difficult to believe that he meant what he said. But the pages clustered round him, who sniggered whenever she went past the hotel on her way to visit her charming great-aunts, Mmes de Fezensac and de Balleroy, who lived not far from there, saw upon the face of the young beauty the four-score years with which, in jest or otherwise, the commissionaire had endowed the "old trollop." You would have made them shriek with laughter had you told them that she was more distinguished than one of the two cashiers of the hotel, who, devoured by eczema, ridiculously fat, seemed to them a fine-looking woman. Perhaps sexual desire alone, if it had been let loose in the wake of the alleged old trollop, and if the pages had suddenly begun to covet the young goddess, would have been capable of preventing their error from taking shape. But for reasons unknown, which were most probably of a social nature, this desire had not come into play. The point is however highly debatable. The universe is real for us all and dissimilar to each one of us. If we were not obliged, in the interests of narrative tidiness, to confine ourselves to frivolous reasons, how many more serious reasons would enable us to demonstrate the mendacious flimsiness of the opening pages of this volume in which, from my bed, I hear the world awake, now to one sort of weather, now to another! Yes, I have been forced to whittle down the facts, and to be a liar, but it is not one universe, but millions, almost as many as the number of human eyes and brains in existence, that awake every morning.

To return to Albertine, I have never known any woman more amply endowed than herself with the happy aptitude for a lie that is animated, coloured with the very hues of life, unless it be one of her friends—one of my blossoming girls also, rose-pink as Albertine, but one whose irregular profile, concave in one place, then convex again, was exactly like certain clusters of pink flowers the name of which I have forgotten, but which have long and sinuous recesses. This girl was, from the point of view of story-telling, superior to Albertine, for her narrative was never interspersed with those painful moments, those furious innuendoes, which were frequent with my mistress. The latter was however charming, as I have said, when she invented a story which left no room for doubt, for one saw then in front of one the thing—albeit imaginary—which she was describing, through the eyes, as it were, of her words. Verisimilitude alone inspired Albertine, never the desire to make me jealous. For Albertine, not perhaps from motives of self-interest, liked people to be nice to her. And if in the course of this work I have had and shall have many occasions to show how jealousy intensifies love, it is from the lover's point of view that I write. But if that lover has a little pride, and even though he would die of a separation, he will not respond to a supposed betrayal with kind words or favours, but will turn away or, without withdrawing, will force himself to assume a mask of coldness. And so it is entirely to her own disadvantage that his mistress makes him suffer so acutely. If, on the contrary, she dispels with a tactful word, with loving caresses, the suspicions that have been torturing him for all his show of indifference, no doubt the lover does not feel that despairing increase of love to which jealousy drives him, but ceasing there and then to suffer, happy, mollified, relaxed as one is after a storm when the rain has stopped and one hears only at long intervals under the tall chestnut-trees the splash of the suspended raindrops which already the reappearing sun has dyed with colour, he does not know how to express his gratitude to her who has cured him. Albertine knew that I liked to reward her for being nice to me, and this perhaps explained why she used to invent, in order to exculpate herself, confessions as natural as these stories which I never doubted and one of which was her meeting with Bergotte when he was already dead. Previously I had never known any of Albertine's lies save those, for instance, which Françoise used to report to me at Balbec and which I have omitted from these pages although they caused me so much pain: "As she didn't want to come, she said to me: 'Couldn't you say to Monsieur that you couldn't find me, that I had gone out?'" But "inferiors" who love us, as Françoise loved me, take pleasure in wounding us in our self-esteem.

After dinner, I told Albertine that I wanted to take advantage of the fact that I was up to go and see some of my friends, Mme de Villeparisis, Mme de Guermantes, the Cambremers, anyone, in short, whom I might find at home. I omitted to mention only the people whom I did intend to visit, the Verdurins. I asked her if she would like to come with me. She pleaded that she had no suitable clothes. "Besides, my hair is so awful. Do you really want me to go on doing it like this?" And by way of farewell she held out her hand to me in that brusque fashion, the arm outstretched, the shoulders thrust back, which she used to adopt on the beach at Balbec and had since entirely abandoned. This forgotten gesture transformed the body which it animated into that of the Albertine who as yet scarcely knew me. It restored to Albertine, ceremonious beneath an air of brusqueness, her initial novelty, her mystery, even her setting. I saw the sea behind this girl whom I had never seen shake hands with me in this way since I was at the seaside. "My aunt thinks it ages me," she added glumly. "Would that her aunt were right!" thought I. "That Albertine by looking like a child should make Mme Bontemps appear younger than she is, is all that her aunt would ask, and also that Albertine should cost her nothing between now and the day when, by marrying me, she will bring her in money." But that Albertine should appear less young, less pretty, should turn fewer heads in the street, that is what I, on the contrary, hoped. For the agedness of a duenna is less reassuring to a jealous lover than that of the face of the woman he loves. I regretted only that the style in which I had asked her to do her hair should appear to Albertine an additional bolt on the door of her prison. And it was again this new domestic feeling that never ceased, even when I was away from Albertine, to bind me to her.

I said to Albertine, who was disinclined, as she had told me, to accompany me to the Guermantes' or the Cambremers', that I was not quite sure where I might go, and set off for the Verdurins'. At the moment when, on leaving the house, the thought of the concert that I was going to hear brought back to my mind the scene that afternoon: "*grand pied de grue, grand pied de grue*"—a scene of disappointed love, of jealous love perhaps, but if so as bestial as the scene to which (minus the words) a woman might be subjected by an orang-outang that was, if one may so say, enamoured of her—at the moment when, having reached the street, I was about to hail a cab, I heard the sound of sobs which a man who was sitting upon a curbstone was endeavouring to stifle. I came nearer; the man, whose face was buried in his hands, appeared to be quite young, and I was surprised to see, from the gleam of white in the opening of his cloak, that he was wearing evening clothes and a white tie. On hearing me he uncovered a face bathed in tears, but at once, having recognised me, turned away. It was Morel. He saw that I had recognised him and, checking his tears with an effort, told me that he had stopped for a moment because he was in such anguish.

"I have grossly insulted, this very day," he said, "a person for whom I had the strongest feelings. It was a vile thing to do, for she loves me."

"She will forget perhaps, in time," I replied, without realising that by speaking thus I made it apparent that I had overheard the scene that afternoon. But he was so absorbed in his grief that it never even occurred to him that I might know something about the affair.

"She may forget, perhaps," he said. "But I myself can never forget. I feel such a sense of shame, I'm so disgusted with myself! However, what I have said I have said, and nothing can unsay it. When people make me lose my temper, I don't know what I'm doing. And it's so bad for me, my nerves are all tied up in knots"—for, like all neurotics, he was keenly interested in his own health. If, during the afternoon, I had witnessed the amorous rage of an infuriated animal, this evening, within a few hours, centuries had elapsed and a new sentiment, a sentiment of shame, regret, grief, showed that an important stage had been reached in the evolution of the beast destined to be transformed into a human being. Nevertheless, I still heard ringing in my ears his "grand pied de grue" and feared an imminent return to the savage state. I had only

a very vague idea, however, of what had happened, and
this was all the more natural in that M. de Charlus himself was totally unaware that for some days past, and especially that day, even before the shameful episode which
had no direct connexion with the violinist's condition,
Morel had been suffering from a recurrence of his neurasthenia. He had, in the previous month, proceeded as
rapidly as he had been able, which was a great deal less
rapidly than he would have liked, towards the seduction
of Jupien's niece, with whom he was at liberty, now that
they were engaged, to go out whenever he chose. But as
soon as he had gone a little too far in his attempts at rape,
and especially when he suggested to his betrothed that she
might make friends with other girls whom she would then
procure for him, he had met with a resistance that had
enraged him. All at once (either because she had proved
too chaste, or on the contrary had finally given herself) his
desire had subsided. He had decided to break with her,
but feeling that the Baron, depraved though he might be,
was far more moral than himself, he was afraid lest, in the
event of a rupture, M. de Charlus might throw him out.
And so he had decided, a fortnight ago, that he would not
see the girl again, would leave M. de Charlus and Jupien
to clean up the mess (he employed a more scatological
term) by themselves, and, before announcing the rupture,
to "bugger off" to an unknown destination.

This outcome had left him a little sad, and it is therefore probable that although his conduct towards Jupien's
niece coincided exactly, down to the minutest details, with
the plan of conduct which he had outlined to the Baron as
they were dining together at Saint-Mars-le-Vétu, in reality
it had been somewhat different, and that sentiments of a

less heinous nature, which he had not foreseen in his the-
oretical conduct, had embellished and softened it in practice. The sole point in which the reality was worse than
the theory was this, that in the original plan it had not
appeared to him possible that he could remain in Paris after such an act of betrayal. Now, on the contrary, actually
to "bugger off" for so small a matter seemed to him excessive. It meant leaving the Baron, who would probably
be furious, and forfeiting his position. He would lose all
the money that the Baron was now giving him. The
thought that this was inevitable made him hysterical; he
whimpered for hours on end, and to take his mind off the
subject dosed himself cautiously with morphine. Then
suddenly he hit upon an idea which no doubt had gradually been taking shape in his mind and gaining strength
there for some time, and this was that a rupture with the
girl would not inevitably mean a complete break with
M. de Charlus. To lose all the Baron's money was a serious thing. Morel in his uncertainty remained for some
days a prey to black thoughts, such as came to him at the
sight of Bloch. Then he decided that Jupien and his niece
had been trying to set a trap for him, that they might
consider themselves lucky to be rid of him so cheaply. He
found in short that the girl had been in the wrong in having been so maladroit in failing to keep him attached to
her through the senses. Not only did the sacrifice of his
position with M. de Charlus seem to him absurd, but he
even regretted the expensive dinners he had given the girl
since they had become engaged, the exact cost of which
he knew by heart, being a true son of the valet who used
to bring his "book" every month for my uncle's inspec-
tion. For the word book, in the singular, which means a

printed volume to humanity in general, loses that meaning among royalty and servants. To the latter it means their account-book, to the former the register in which we inscribe our names. (At Balbec one day when the Princesse de Luxembourg told me that she had not brought a book with her, I was about to offer her *Le Pêcheur d'Islande* and *Tartarin de Tarascon*, when I realised that she had meant not that she would pass the time less agreeably, but that it would be more difficult for me to get on to her list.)

Notwithstanding the change in Morel's point of view with regard to the consequences of his behaviour, although that behaviour would have seemed to him abominable two months earlier when he was passionately in love with Jupien's niece, whereas during the last fortnight he had never ceased to assure himself that the same behaviour was natural and praiseworthy, it could not fail to intensify the state of nervous tension in which, finally, he had served notice of the rupture that afternoon. And he was quite prepared to vent his rage, if not (except in a momentary outburst) upon the girl, for whom he still felt that lingering fear which is the last trace of love, at any rate upon the Baron. He took care, however, not to say anything to him before dinner, for, valuing his own professional virtuosity above everything, whenever he had any difficult music to play (as this evening at the Verdurins') he avoided (as far as possible, and the scene that afternoon was already more than ample) anything that might make his movements at all jerky. Similarly, a surgeon who is an enthusiastic motorist does not drive when he has an operation to perform. This explained to me why, as he was speaking to me, he kept bending his fingers gently one after another to see whether they had re-

gained their suppleness. A slight frown seemed to indicate
that there was still a trace of nervous stiffness. But in order not to aggravate it, he relaxed his features, as we try
to prevent ourselves from getting agitated about not being
able to sleep or to persuade a woman to give herself, for
fear lest our phobia itself may retard the moment of sleep
or of pleasure. And so, anxious to regain his serenity in
order to be able to concentrate, as usual, on what he was
going to play at the Verdurins', and anxious, so long as I
was watching him, to let me see how unhappy he was, he
decided that the simplest course was to entreat me to
leave him immediately. The entreaty was superfluous, for
it was a relief to me to get away from him. I had trembled
lest, as we were due at the same house within a few minutes of one another, he might ask me to take him with
me, my memory of the scene that afternoon being too
vivid not to give me a certain distaste for the idea of having Morel by my side during the drive. It is quite possible
that the love, and afterwards the indifference or hatred,
felt by Morel for Jupien's niece had been sincere. Unfortunately, it was not the first time (nor would it be the
last) that he had behaved thus, that he had suddenly
"ditched" a girl to whom he had sworn undying love, going so far as to produce a loaded revolver and telling her
that he would blow out his brains if ever he was vile
enough to desert her. He would nevertheless desert her in
time, and feel, instead of remorse, a sort of rancour
against her. It was not the first time that he had behaved
thus, and it was not to be the last, with the result that
many young girls—girls less forgetful of him than he was
of them—suffered—as Jupien's niece, continuing to love

Morel while despising him, was to suffer for a long time—their heads ready to burst with the stabbing of an inner pain, because in each of them, like a fragment of a Greek sculpture, an aspect of Morel's face, hard as marble and beautiful as the art of antiquity, was embedded in the brain, with his blossoming hair, his fine eyes, his straight nose—forming a protuberance in a cranium not shaped to receive it, and on which no one could operate. But in the fullness of time these stony fragments end by slipping into a place where they cause no undue laceration, from which they never stir again; their presence is no longer felt: the pain has been forgotten, or is remembered with indifference.

Meanwhile I had gained two things in the course of the day. On the one hand, thanks to the calm induced by Albertine's docility, there was the possibility, and in consequence the resolve, to break with her; on the other—the fruit of my reflexions during the interval that I had spent waiting for her, seated at the piano—the idea that Art, to which I would try to devote my reconquered liberty, was not something that was worth a sacrifice, something above and beyond life, that did not share in its fatuity and futility; the appearance of genuine individuality achieved in works of art being due merely to the illusion produced by technical skill. If my afternoon had left behind it other deposits, possibly more profound, they were not to impinge upon my consciousness until much later. As for the two which I was able thus to ponder, they were not to be long-lived; for, from that very evening, my ideas about art were to recover from the diminution that they had suffered in the afternoon, while on the other hand my calm, and consequently the freedom that would enable me to devote myself to it, was once again to be withdrawn from me.

As my cab, driving along the riverside, was approaching the Verdurins' house, I made the driver pull up. I had just seen Brichot alighting from a tram at the corner of the Rue Bonaparte, after which he dusted his shoes with an old newspaper and put on a pair of pearl-grey gloves. I went up to him on foot. For some time past, his sight having grown steadily worse, he had been equipped—as richly as an observatory—with new spectacles of a powerful and complicated kind, which, like astronomical instruments, seemed to be screwed into his eyes; he focused their exaggerated beams upon myself and recognised me. They—the spectacles—were in marvellous condition. But behind them I could see, minute, pallid convulsive, expiring, a remote gaze placed under this powerful apparatus, as, in a laboratory too richly endowed for the work that is done in it, you may watch the last throes of some tiny insignificant beast under the latest and most advanced type of microscope. I offered the purblind man my arm to steady his steps. "This time it is not by great Cherbourg that we meet," he said to me, "but by little Dunkirk," a remark which I found extremely tiresome, as I did not understand what it meant; and yet I dared not ask Brichot, dreading not so much his scorn as his explanations. I replied that I was longing to see the drawing-room in which Swann used to meet Odette every evening. "What, so you know that old story, do you?" he said.

Swann's death had deeply distressed me at the time. Swann's death! Swann's, in this phrase, is something more than a mere genitive. I mean thereby his own particular death, the death assigned by destiny to the service of Swann. For we talk of "death" for convenience, but there are almost as many deaths as there are people. We do not possess a sense that would enable us to see, moving at full speed in every direction, these deaths, the active deaths aimed by destiny at this person or that. Often they are deaths that will not be entirely relieved of their duties until two or even three years later. They come in haste to plant a tumour in the side of a Swann, then depart to attend to other tasks, returning only when, the surgeons having performed their operations, it is necessary to plant the tumour there afresh. Then comes the moment when we read in the *Gaulois* that Swann's health has been causing anxiety but that he is now making an excellent recovery. Then, a few minutes before the last gasp, death, like a sister of charity who has come to nurse rather than to destroy us, enters to preside over our last moments, and crowns with a final aureole the cold and stiffening creature whose heart has ceased to beat. And it is this diversity of deaths, the mystery of their circuits, the colour of their fatal badge, that makes so moving a paragraph in the newspapers such as this:

"We learn with deep regret that M. Charles Swann passed away yesterday at his residence in Paris after a long and painful illness. A Parisian whose wit was widely appreciated, a discriminating but steadfastly loyal friend, he will be universally mourned, not only in those literary and artistic circles where the rare discernment of his taste made him a willing and a welcome guest, but also at the Jockey Club of which he was one of the oldest and most respected members. He belonged also to the Union and the Agricole. He had recently resigned his membership of the Rue Royale. His witty and striking personality never failed to arouse the interest of the public at all the great events of the musical and artistic seasons, notably at private views, where he was a regular attendant until the last few years, when he rarely left his house. The funeral will take place, etc."

From this standpoint, if one is not "somebody," the absence of a well-known title makes the process of decomposition even more rapid. No doubt it is more or less anonymously, without any individual identity, that a dead man remains the Duc d'Uzès. But the ducal coronet does for some time hold the elements of him together, as their moulds held together those artistically designed ices which Albertine admired, whereas the names of ultra-fashionable commoners, as soon as they are dead, melt and disintegrate, "turned out" of their moulds. We have seen Mme de Guermantes speak of Cartier as the most intimate friend of the Duc de La Trémoïlle, as a man highly sought after in aristocratic circles. To a later generation, Cartier has become something so amorphous that it would almost be aggrandising him to link him with the jeweller Cartier, with whom he would have smiled to think that anybody could be so ignorant as to confuse him! Swann on the contrary was a remarkable intellectual and artistic personality, and although he had "produced" nothing, still he was lucky enough to survive a little longer. And yet, my dear Charles Swann, whom I used to know when I was still so young and you were nearing your grave, it is because he whom you must have regarded as a young idiot has made you the hero of one of his novels that people are beginning to speak of you again and that your name will perhaps live. If, in Tissot's picture representing the balcony of the Rue Royale club, where you figure with Galliffet, Edmond de Polignac and Saint-Maurice, people are always drawing attention to you, it is because they see that there are some traces of you in the character of Swann.

To return to more general realities, it was of this death of his, foretold and yet unforeseen, that I had heard Swann speak himself to the Duchesse de Guermantes, on the evening of her cousin's party. It was the same death whose striking and specific strangeness had recurred to me one evening when, as I ran my eye over the newspaper, my attention was suddenly arrested by the announcement of it, as though traced in mysterious lines inopportunely interpolated there. They had sufficed to make of a living man someone who could never again respond to what one said to him, to reduce him to a mere name, a written name, that had suddenly passed from the real world to the realm of silence. It was they that even now gave me a desire to get to know the house in which the Verdurins had formerly lived, and where Swann, who at that time was not merely a row of letters printed in a newspaper, had dined so often with Odette. I must also add (and this is what for a long time made Swann's death more painful than any other, although these reasons bore no relation to the individual strangeness of *his* death) that I had never gone to see Gilberte as I promised him at the Princesse de Guermantes's; that he had never told me what the "other reason" was, to which he had alluded that evening, for his choosing me as the recipient of his conversation with the Prince; that countless questions occurred to me (as bubbles rise from the bottom of a pond) which I longed to ask him about the most disparate subjects: Vermeer,

M. de Mouchy, Swann himself, a Boucher tapestry, Combray—questions which were doubtless not very urgent since I had put off asking them from day to day, but which seemed to me of cardinal importance now that, his lips being sealed, no answer would ever come. The death of others is like a journey one might oneself make, when, already sixty miles out of Paris, one remembers that one has left two dozen handkerchiefs behind, forgotten to leave a key with the cook, to say good-bye to one's uncle, to ask the name of the town where the old fountain is that you want to see. While all these oversights which assail you, and which you relate aloud and purely for form's sake to your travelling companion, are getting as sole response a blank disregard from the seat opposite, the name of the station, called out by the guard, only takes you further away from henceforth impossible realisations, so much so that you cease to think about irremediable omissions, and you unpack your lunch and exchange papers and magazines.

"No," Brichot went on, "it wasn't here that Swann used to meet his future wife, or rather it was here only in the very latest period, after the fire that partially destroyed Mme Verdurin's former home."

Unfortunately, in my fear of displaying before the eyes of Brichot a luxury which seemed to me out of place, since the professor had no share in it, I had alighted too hastily from the carriage and the driver had not understood the words I had flung at him over my shoulder in order that I might be well clear of the carriage before Brichot caught sight of me. The consequence was that the driver drew alongside us and asked me whether he was to call for me later. I answered hurriedly in the affirmative and intensified all the more my respectful attentions to the professor who had come by omnibus.

"Ah! so you were in a carriage," he said gravely.

"Only by the purest accident. I never take one as a rule. I always travel by omnibus or on foot. However, it may perhaps earn me the great honour of taking you home tonight if you will oblige me by consenting to travel in that rattle-trap. We shall be packed rather tight. But you are always so kind to me."

Alas, in making him this offer, I am depriving myself of nothing, I reflected, since in any case I shall be obliged to go home because of Albertine. Her presence in my house, at an hour when nobody could possibly call to see her, allowed me to dispose as freely of my time as I had that afternoon, when I knew that she was on her way back from the Trocadéro and I was in no hurry to see her again. But at the same time, as also that afternoon, I felt that I had a woman in the house and that on returning home I would not taste the fortifying thrill of solitude.

"I heartily accept," replied Brichot. "At the period to which you allude, our friends occupied a magnificent ground-floor apartment in the Rue Montalivet with an entresol and a garden behind, less sumptuous of course, and yet to my mind preferable to the old Venetian Embassy."

Brichot informed me that this evening there was to be at the "Quai Conti" (thus it was that the faithful spoke of the Verdurin salon since it had been transferred to that address) a great musical "jamboree" organised by M. de Charlus. He went on to say that in the old days to which I had referred, the little nucleus had been different and its tone not at all the same, not only because the faithful had then been younger. He told me of elaborate practical jokes played by Elstir (what he called "pure buffooneries"), as for instance one day when the painter, having pretended to "defect" at the last moment, had come disguised as an extra waiter and, as he handed round the dishes, murmured ribald remarks in the ear of the extremely prudish Baroness Putbus, who was crimson with anger and alarm; then, disappearing before the end of dinner, he had had a hip-bath carried into the drawing-room, out of which, when the party left the dinner-table, he had emerged stark naked uttering fearful oaths; and also of supper parties to which the guests came in paper costumes designed, cut out and painted by Elstir, which were veritable masterpieces, Brichot having worn on one occasion that of a nobleman of the court of Charles VII, with long pointed shoes, and another time that of Napoleon I, for which Elstir had fashioned a Grand Cordon of the Legion of Honour out of sealing-wax. In short Brichot, seeing again with the eyes of memory the salon of those days, the drawing-room with its high windows, its low settees bleached by the midday sun which had had to be replaced, declared that he preferred it to the drawing-room of today. Of course, I quite understood that by "salon" Brichot meant—as the word church implies not merely the religious edifice but the congregation of worshippers—not merely the apartment, but the people who frequented it, and the special pleasures that they came to enjoy there, and that were symbolised in his memory by those settees upon which, when you called to see Mme Verdurin in the afternoon, you waited until she was ready, while the blossom on the chestnut-trees outside, and the carnations in vases on the mantelpiece, seemed to offer a graceful and kindly thought for the visitor, expressed in the smiling welcome of their rosy hues, as they watched unblinkingly for the tardy appearance of the lady of the house. But if that salon seemed to him superior to the present one, it was perhaps because one's mind is an old Proteus who cannot remain the slave of any one shape and, even in the social world, suddenly transfers its allegiance from a salon which has slowly and arduously climbed to a pitch of perfection to another that is less brilliant, just as the "touched-up" photographs which Odette had had taken at Otto's, in which she queened it in a "princess" gown, her hair waved by Lenthéric, appealed less to Swann than a little snapshot taken at Nice, in which, in a plain cloth cape, her loosely dressed hair protruding beneath a straw hat trimmed with pansies and a black velvet bow, though a woman of fashion twenty years younger, she looked (for the earlier a photograph the older a woman looks in it) like a little maidservant twenty years older. Perhaps too Brichot derived some pleasure from praising to me what I myself had never known, from showing me that he had enjoyed pleasures that I could never have. He succeeded, moreover, merely by citing the names of two or three people who were no longer alive and whom he invested with a kind of mysterious charm by the way he spoke of them. I felt that everything that had been told me about the Verdurins was far too crude; and indeed in the case of Swann, whom I had known, I reproached myself for not having paid sufficient attention to him, for not having paid attention to him in a sufficiently disinterested spirit, for not having listened to him properly when he used to entertain me while we waited for his wife to come home for lunch and he showed me his treasures, now that I knew that he was to be classed with the most brilliant talkers of the past.

Just as we were coming to Mme Verdurin's doorstep, I caught sight of M. de Charlus, steering towards us the bulk of his huge body, drawing unwillingly in his wake one of those ruffians or beggars who nowadays when he passed sprang out without fail from even the most apparently deserted corners, and by whom this powerful monster was, despite himself, invariably escorted, although at a certain distance, as a shark is by its pilot—in short, contrasting so markedly with the haughty stranger of my first visit to Balbec, with his stern aspect, his affectation of virility, that I seemed to be discovering, accompanied by its satellite, a planet at a wholly different period of its revolution, when one begins to see it full, or a sick man devoured by the malady that a few years ago was but a tiny spot which was easily concealed and the gravity of which was never suspected. Although an operation that Brichot had undergone had restored to some small extent the sight which he had thought to be lost for ever, I do not know whether he had observed the ruffian following in the Baron's footsteps. Not that this mattered much, for since La Raspelière, and notwithstanding the professor's friendly regard for M. de Charlus, the sight of the latter always made him feel somehow uneasy. No doubt to every man the life of every other extends along shadowy paths of which he has no inkling. Lying, though it is so often deceptive and is the basis of all conversation, conceals less thoroughly a feeling of hostility, or of self-interest, or a visit which one wants to appear not to have paid, or a short-lived escapade with a mistress which one is anxious to keep from one's wife, than a good reputation covers up—to the extent of not letting its existence be guessed—sexual depravity. It may remain unsuspected for a lifetime; an accidental encounter on a pier, at night, discloses it; even then this accidental discovery is frequently misunderstood and a third person who is in the know must supply the elusive clue of which everyone is unaware. But, once known, it scares one by making one feel that that way madness lies, far more than by its immorality. Mme de Surgis le Duc could not be said to have a highly developed moral sense, and would have tolerated in her sons anything, however base, that could be explained by material interest, which is comprehensible to all mankind. But she forbade them to go on visiting M. de Charlus when she learned that, by a sort of internal clockwork, he was inevitably drawn upon each of their visits to pinch their chins and to make each of them pinch his brother's. She felt that uneasy sense of a physical mystery which makes us wonder whether the neighbour with whom we have been on friendly terms is not tainted with cannibalism, and to the Baron's repeated inquiry: "When am I going to see the young men?" she would reply, conscious of the wrath she was bringing down on herself, that they were very busy working for examinations, preparing to go abroad, and so forth. Irresponsibility aggravates faults, and even crimes, whatever may be said. Landru (assuming that he really did kill his women) may be pardoned if he did so from financial motives, which it is possible to resist, but not if it was from irresistible sadism.

The coarse pleasantries in which Brichot had indulged in the early days of his friendship with the Baron had given place, as soon as it was a question not of uttering commonplaces but of trying to understand, to an awkward

feeling which was cloaked by gaiety. He reassured himself
by recalling pages of Plato, lines of Virgil, because, being
mentally as well as physically blind, he did not understand that in their day to love a young man was the
equivalent (Socrates's jokes reveal this more clearly than
Plato's theories) of keeping a dancing girl before getting
engaged to be married in ours. M. de Charlus himself
would not have understood, he who confused his ruling
passion with friendship, which does not resemble it in the
least, and the athletes of Praxiteles with obliging boxers.
He refused to see that for nineteen hundred years ("a pious courtier under a pious prince would have been an
atheist under an atheist prince," as La Bruyère reminds
us) all conventional homosexuality—that of Plato's young
friends as well as that of Virgil's shepherds—has disappeared, that what survives and increases is only the involuntary, the neurotic kind, which one conceals from other
people and misrepresents to oneself. And M. de Charlus
would have been wrong in not disowning frankly the pagan genealogy. In exchange for a little plastic beauty, how
vast the moral superiority! The shepherd in Theocritus
who sighs for love of a boy will have no reason later on to
be less hard of heart, less dull of wit than the other shepherd whose flute sounds for Amaryllis. For the former is
not suffering from a disease; he is conforming to the customs of his time. It is the homosexuality that survives in
spite of obstacles, shameful, execrated, that is the only
true form, the only form that corresponds in one and the
same person to an intensification of the intellectual qualities. One is dismayed at the relationship that can exist between these and a person's bodily attributes when one
thinks of the tiny dislocation of a purely physical taste,

the slight blemish in one of the senses, that explains why the world of poets and musicians, so firmly barred against the Duc de Guermantes, opens its portals to M. de Charlus. That the latter should show taste in the furnishing of his home, which is that of a housewife with a taste for curios, need not surprise us; but the narrow loophole that opens upon Beethoven and Veronese! But this does not exempt the sane from a feeling of alarm when a madman who has composed a sublime poem, after explaining to them in the most logical fashion that he has been shut up by mistake through his wife's machinations, imploring them to intercede for him with the governor of the asylum, complaining of the promiscuous company that is forced upon him, concludes as follows: "You see that man in the courtyard, who I'm obliged to put up with; he thinks he's Jesus Christ. That should give you an idea of the sort of lunatics I've been shut up with; he *can't* be Jesus Christ, because *I'm* Jesus Christ!" A moment earlier, you were on the point of going to assure the psychiatrist that a mistake had been made. On hearing these words, even if you bear in mind the admirable poem at which this same man is working every day, you shrink from him, as Mme de Surgis's sons shrank from M. de Charlus, not because he had done them any harm, but because of the ceaseless invitations which ended up with his pinching their chins. The poet is to be pitied who must, with no Virgil to guide him, pass through the circles of an inferno of sulphur and brimstone, who must cast himself into the fire that falls from heaven in order to rescue a few of the inhabitants of Sodom! No charm in his work; the same severity in his life as in those of the unfrocked priests who follow the strictest rule of celibacy so that no one may be able to ascribe to anything but loss of faith their discarding of the cassock. Even then, it is not always so with these writers. What asylum doctor has not had his own attack of madness by dint of continual association with madmen? He is lucky if he is able to affirm that it is not a previous latent madness that had predestined him to look after them. The subject of a psychiatrist's study often rebounds on him. But before that, what obscure inclination, what dreadful fascination had made him choose that subject?

Pretending not to see the shady individual who was gliding in his wake (whenever the Baron ventured on to the boulevards or crossed the main hall of the Gare Saint-Lazare, these hangers-on who dogged his heels in the hope of touching him for a few francs could be counted by the dozen), and fearful lest the man might be bold enough to accost him, the Baron had devoutly lowered his mascara'ed eyelids which, contrasting with his powdered cheeks, gave him the appearance of a Grand Inquisitor painted by El Greco. But this priest was frightening and looked like an excommunicate, the various compromises to which he had been driven by the need to indulge his taste and to keep it secret having had the effect of bringing to the surface of his face precisely what the Baron sought to conceal, a debauched life betrayed by moral degeneration. This last, indeed, whatever be its cause, is easily detected, for it is never slow to materialise and proliferates upon a face, especially on the cheeks and round the eyes, as physically as the ochreous yellows of jaundice or the repulsive reds of a skin disease. Nor was it merely in the cheeks, or rather the chaps, of this painted face, in the mammiferous chest, the fleshy rump of this body abandoned to self-indulgence and invaded by obesity, that there now lingered, spreading like a film of oil, the vice at one time so jealously confined by M. de Charlus in the most secret recesses of his being. Now it overflowed into his speech.

"So this is how you prowl the streets at night, Brichot, with a good-looking young man," he said on joining us, while the disappointed ruffian made off. "A fine example. We must tell your young pupils at the Sorbonne that this is how you behave. But I must say the society of youth seems to agree with you, Monsieur le Professeur, you're as fresh as a rosebud. I've interrupted you though: you looked as though you were enjoying yourselves like a pair of giddy girls, and had no need of an old Granny Killjoy like me. But I shan't go to confession for it, since you were almost at your destination." The Baron's mood was all the more blithe since he was totally ignorant of the scene that afternoon, Jupien having decided that he would be better advised to protect his niece against a renewed onslaught than to go and inform M. de Charlus. And so the Baron still looked forward to the marriage and was delighted at the thought of it. One may suppose that it is a consolation to these great solitaries to alleviate their tragic celibacy with a fictitious fatherhood.

"But, upon my word, Brichot," he went on, turning towards us with a laugh, "I feel quite embarrassed to see you in such gallant company. You looked like a pair of lovers, going along arm in arm. I say, Brichot, you do go the pace!" Ought these remarks to have been ascribed to the ageing of a mind less master of its reflexes than in the past, which in moments of automatism lets out a secret that has been so carefully hidden for forty years? Or rather to that contempt for the opinion of commoners which all the Guermantes felt in their hearts, and which M. de Charlus's brother, the Duke, displayed in a different form when, heedless of the fact that my mother could see him, he used to shave by his bedroom window in his unbuttoned nightshirt? Had M. de Charlus contracted, during those stimulating journeys between Doncières and Douville, the dangerous habit of putting himself at his ease and, just as he would push back his straw hat in order to cool his huge forehead, of loosening—for a few moments only at first—the mask that for too long had been rigorously imposed upon his true face? His conjugal attitude towards Morel might well have astonished anyone who was aware that he no longer loved him. But M. de Charlus had reached the stage when the monotony of the pleasures that his vice has to offer had become wearying. He had instinctively sought after new exploits, and tiring of the strangers whom he picked up, had gone to the opposite extreme, to what he used to imagine that he would always loathe, the imitation of "a household" or of "fatherhood." Sometimes even this did not suffice him; he required novelty, and would go and spend the night with a woman, just as a normal man may once in his life have wished to go to bed with a boy, from a similar though inverse curiosity, in either case equally unhealthy. The Baron's existence as one of the "faithful," living, for Charlie's sake, exclusively among the little clan, by undermining the efforts he had made for years to keep up lying appearances, had had the same influence as a voyage of exploration or residence in the colonies has upon certain Europeans who discard the ruling principles by which they were guided at home. And yet, the internal revolution of a mind ignorant at first of the anomaly it carried within it, then—having recognised it—horrified by it, and finally becoming so accustomed to it as to fail to perceive that one cannot with impunity confess to other people what one has come round to confessing without shame to oneself, had been even more effective in liberating M. de Charlus from the last vestiges of social constraint than the time that he spent at the Verdurins'. No banishment, indeed, to the South Pole, or to the summit of Mont Blanc, can separate us so entirely from our fellow creatures as a prolonged sojourn in the bosom of an inner vice, that is to say of a way of thinking different from theirs. A vice (so M. de Charlus used at one time to style it) to which the Baron now gave the genial aspect of a mere failing, extremely common, attractive on the whole and almost amusing, like laziness, absent-mindedness or greed. Conscious of the curiosity that his peculiar characteristics aroused, M. de Charlus derived a certain pleasure from satisfying, whetting, sustaining it. Just as a Jewish journalist will come forward day after day as the champion of Catholicism, probably not with any hope of being taken seriously, but simply in order not to thwart the expectation of a good-natured laugh, M. de Charlus would jokingly denounce sexual depravity in the company of the little clan, as he might have mimicked an English accent or imitated Mounet-Sully,[9] without waiting to be asked, simply to do his bit with good grace, by displaying an amateur talent in society; so that when he now threatened Brichot that he would report to the Sorbonne that he was in the habit of walking about with young men, it was in exactly the same way as the circumcised scribe keeps referring in and out of season to the "Eldest Daughter of

the Church" and the "Sacred Heart of Jesus," that is to
say without the least trace of hypocrisy, but with more
than a hint of play-acting. It was not only the change in
the words themselves, so different from those that he allowed himself to use in the past, that seemed to require
some explanation, there was also the change that had occurred in his intonation and his gestures, which now singularly resembled what M. de Charlus used most fiercely
to castigate; he would now utter involuntarily almost the
same little squeaks (involuntary in his case and all the
more deep-rooted) as are uttered voluntarily by those inverts who hail one another as "my dear!"—as though this
deliberate "camping," against which M. de Charlus had
for so long set his face, were after all merely a brilliant
and faithful imitation of the manner that men of the
Charlus type, whatever they may say, are compelled to
adopt when they have reached a certain stage in their malady, just as sufferers from general paralysis or locomotor
ataxia inevitably end by displaying certain symptoms. As
a matter of fact—and this is what this purely unconscious
"camping" revealed—the difference between the stern,
black-clad Charlus with his hair *en brosse* whom I had
known, and the painted and bejewelled young men, was
no more than the purely apparent difference that exists
between an excited person who talks fast and keeps fid-
geting all the time, and a neurotic who talks slowly, preserves a perpetual phlegm, but is tainted with the same
neurasthenia in the eyes of the physician who knows that
each of the two is devoured by the same anxieties and
marred by the same defects. At the same time one could
tell that M. de Charlus had aged from wholly different
signs, such as the extraordinary frequency in his conversa-

tion of certain expressions that had taken root in it and used now to crop up at every moment (for instance: "the concatenation of circumstances") and upon which the Baron's speech leaned in sentence after sentence as upon a necessary prop.

"Is Charlie already here?" Brichot asked M. de Charlus as we were about to ring the door-bell.

"Ah! I really don't know," said the Baron, raising his arms and half-shutting his eyes with the air of a person who does not wish to be accused of indiscretion, all the more so as he had probably been reproached by Morel for things which he had said and which the other, as cowardly as he was vain, and as ready to disown M. de Charlus as he was to boast of his friendship, had considered serious although they were quite trivial. "You know, I've no idea what he does."

If the conversations of two people bound by a tie of intimacy are full of lies, these crop up no less spontaneously in the conversations that a third person holds with a lover about the person with whom the latter is in love, whatever the sex of that person.

"Have you seen him lately?" I asked M. de Charlus, in order to appear at the same time not to be afraid of mentioning Morel to him and not to believe that they were actually living together.

"He came in, as it happened, for five minutes this morning while I was still half asleep, and sat down on the side of my bed, as though he wanted to ravish me."

I guessed at once that M. de Charlus had seen Charlie within the last hour, for if one asks a woman when she last saw the man whom one knows to be—and whom she may perhaps suppose that one suspects of being—her lover, if she has just had tea with him she replies: "I saw him for a minute before lunch." Between these two facts the only difference is that one is false and the other true. But both are equally innocent, or, if you prefer it, equally guilty. Hence one would be unable to understand why the mistress (and in this case, M. de Charlus) always chooses the false version, were one not aware that such replies are determined, unbeknown to the person who makes them, by a number of factors which appear so out of proportion to the triviality of the incident that one does not bother to raise them. But to a physicist the space occupied by the tiniest ball of pith is explained by the clash or the equilibrium of laws of attraction or repulsion which govern far bigger worlds. Here we need merely record, as a matter of interest, the desire to appear natural and fearless, the instinctive impulse to conceal a secret assignation, a blend of modesty and ostentation, the need to confess what one finds so delightful and to show that one is loved, a divination of what one's interlocutor knows or guesses—but does not say—a divination which, exceeding or falling short of his, makes one now exaggerate, now underestimate it, the unwitting desire to play with fire and the determination to rescue something from the blaze. Just as many different laws acting in opposite directions dictate the more general responses with regard to the innocence, the "platonic" nature, or on the contrary the carnal reality, of one's relations with the person whom one says one saw in the morning when one has seen him or her in the evening. However, on the whole it must be said that M. de Charlus, notwithstanding the aggravation of his malady which perpetually urged him to reveal, to insinuate, sometimes quite simply to invent compromising details, sought, during this period in his life, to maintain that Charlie was not a man of the same kind as himself and that they were friends and nothing more. This (though it may quite possibly have been true) did not prevent him from contradicting himself at times (as with regard to the hour at which they had last met), either because he forgot himself at such moments and told the truth, or proffered a lie out of boastfulness or a sentimental affectation or because he thought it amusing to mislead his interlocutor.

"You know that he is to me," the Baron went on, "a nice little friend, for whom I have the greatest affection, as I am sure" (did he doubt it, then, if he felt the need to say that he was sure?) "he has for me, but there's nothing else between us, nothing of that sort, you understand, nothing of that sort," said the Baron, as naturally as though he had been speaking of a woman. "Yes, he came in this morning to pull me out of bed. Though he knows that I hate being seen first thing in the morning, don't you? Oh, it's horrible, it flusters one so, one looks so perfectly hideous. Of course I'm no longer five-and-twenty, they won't choose me to be Queen of the May, but still one does like to feel that one's looking one's best."

It is possible that the Baron was sincere when he spoke of Morel as a nice little friend, and that he was being even more truthful than he supposed when he said: "I've no idea what he does; I know nothing about his life."

Indeed we may mention (to anticipate by a few weeks before resuming our narrative at the point where M. de Charlus, Brichot and myself are arriving at Mme Verdurin's front door), we may mention that shortly after this evening the Baron was plunged into a state of grief and stupefaction by a letter addressed to Morel which he had opened by mistake. This letter, which was also indirectly to cause me acute distress, was written by the actress Léa, notorious for her exclusive taste for women. And yet her letter to Morel (whom M. de Charlus had never even suspected of knowing her) was written in the most passionate terms. Its indelicacy prevents us from reproducing it here, but we may mention that Léa addressed him throughout in the feminine gender, with such expressions as "Go on with you, naughty girl!" or "Of course you're one of us, you pretty sweetheart." And in this letter reference was made to various other women who seemed to be no less Morel's friends than Léa's. At the same time, Morel's sarcasm at the Baron's expense and Léa's at that of an officer who was keeping her, and of whom she said: "He keeps writing me letters begging me to be good! You bet! eh, my little white puss," revealed to M. de Charlus a state of things no less unsuspected by him than were Morel's peculiar and intimate relations with Léa. What most disturbed the Baron was the phrase "one of us." Ignorant at first of its application, he had eventually, now many moons ago, learned that he himself was "one of them." And now this notion that he had acquired was thrown back into question. When he had discovered that he was "one of them," he had supposed this to mean that his tastes, as Saint-Simon says, did not lie in the direction of women. And here was this expression taking on, for Morel, an extension of meaning of which M. de Charlus was unaware, so much so that Morel gave proof, according to this letter, of being "one of them" by having the same taste as certain women for other women. From then on the Baron's jealousy could no longer confine itself to the men of Morel's acquaintance, but would have to extend to the women also. So, to be "one of them" meant not simply what he had hitherto assumed, but to belong to a whole vast section of the inhabitants of the planet, consisting of women as well as of men, of men loving not merely men but women also, and the Baron, in the face of this novel meaning of a phrase that was so familiar to him, felt himself tormented by an anxiety of the mind as well as of the heart, born of this twofold mystery which combined an enlargement of the field of his jealousy with the sudden inadequacy of a definition.

M. de Charlus had never in his life been anything but an amateur. That is to say that incidents of this sort could never be of any use to him. He worked off the painful impression that they might make upon him in violent scenes in which he was a past-master of eloquence, or in crafty intrigues. But to a person endowed with the qualities of a Bergotte, for instance, they might have been of inestimable value. This may indeed explain to a certain extent (since we act blindly, but choose, like the lower animals, the plant that is good for us) why men like Bergotte generally surround themselves with women who are inferior, false and ill-natured. Their beauty is sufficient for the writer's imagination, and excites his generosity, but does not in any way alter the nature of his mistresses, whose lives, situated thousands of feet below the level of his own, whose improbable connexions, whose lies, carried further and moreover in a different direction from what might have been expected, appear in occasional flashes. The lie, the perfect lie, about people we know, about the relations we have had with them, about our motive for some action, formulated in totally different terms, the lie as to what we are, whom we love, what we feel with regard to people who love us and believe that they have fashioned us in their own image because they keep on kissing us morning, noon and night—that lie is one of the few things in the world that can open windows for us on to what is new and unknown, that can awaken in us sleeping senses for the contemplation of universes that otherwise we should never have known. As far as M. de Charlus is concerned, it must be said that if he was stupefied to learn with regard to Morel a certain number of things which the latter had carefully concealed from him, he was not justified in concluding from this that it is a mistake to make friends with the lower orders. Indeed, in the concluding section of this work, we shall see M. de Charlus himself engaged in doing things which would have stupefied the members of his family and his friends far more than he could possibly have been stupefied by Léa's revelations. (The revelation that he had found most painful had been that of a trip which Morel had made with Léa at a time when he had assured M. de Charlus that he was studying music in Germany. To build up his alibi he had made use of some obliging people to whom he had sent his letters in Germany, whence they were forwarded to M. de Charlus who, as it happened, was so positive that Morel was there that he had not even looked at the postmark.)

But it is time to rejoin the Baron as he advances with Brichot and myself towards the Verdurins' door.

"And what," he went on, turning to me, "has become of your young Hebrew friend whom we met at Douville? It occurred to me that, if you liked, one might perhaps invite him to the house one evening." For M. de Charlus, who did not shrink from employing a private detective agency to spy on Morel's every movement, for all the world like a husband or a lover, had not ceased to pay attention to other young men. The surveillance which he instructed one of his old servants to arrange for the agency to maintain over Morel was so indiscreet that his footmen thought they were being shadowed, and one of the housemaids lived in terror, no longer daring to go out into the street for fear of finding a detective at her heels. "She can do whatever she likes! Who'd waste time and money tailing her? As if her doings were of the slightest interest to us!" the old servant ironically exclaimed, for he was so passionately devoted to his master that although he in no way shared the Baron's tastes, he had come in time, with such ardour did he employ himself in their service, to speak of them as though they were his own. "He is the very best of good fellows," M. de Charlus would say of this old servant, for there is no one we appreciate more than a person who combines with other great virtues that of placing those virtues wholeheartedly at the service of our vices. It was of men alone that M. de Charlus was capable of feeling any jealousy so far as Morel was concerned. Women inspired in him none whatever. This is indeed an almost universal rule with the Charluses of this world. The love of the man they love for a woman is something else, which occurs in another animal species (a lion leaves tigers in peace), does not bother them, and if anything reassures them. Sometimes, it is true, in the case of those who exalt their inversion to the level of a priesthood, this love arouses disgust. These men resent their friends' having succumbed to it, not as a betrayal but as a

fall from grace. A Charlus of a different variety from the
Baron would have been as indignant to find Morel having
relations with a woman as to read in a newspaper that he,
the interpreter of Bach and Handel, was going to play
Puccini. This is in fact why the young men who acquiesce
in the love of Charluses for mercenary reasons assure
them that women inspire them only with disgust, just as
they would tell a doctor that they never touch alcohol and
care only for spring water. But M. de Charlus, in this respect, departed to some extent from the general rule.
Since he admired everything about Morel, the latter's successes with women, causing him no offence, gave him the
same joy as his successes on the concert platform or at
cards. "But do you know, my dear fellow, he has
women," he would say, with an air of revelation, of scandal, possibly of envy, above all of admiration. "He's extraordinary," he would continue. "Wherever he goes, the
most prominent whores have eyes for him alone. One notices it everywhere, whether it's on the underground or in
the theatre. It's becoming such a bore! I can't go out with
him to a restaurant without the waiter bringing him notes
from at least three women. And always pretty women too.
Not that it's anything to be wondered at. I was looking at
him only yesterday, and I can quite understand them.
He's become so beautiful, he looks like a sort of Bronzino;
he's really marvellous." But M. de Charlus liked to show
that he loved Morel, and to persuade other people, possibly to persuade himself, that Morel loved him. He took a
sort of pride in having Morel always with him, in spite of
the damage the young man might do to his social position. For (and this is often the case with men of some social standing and snobbish to boot, who, in their vanity,

sever all their social ties in order to be seen everywhere with a mistress, a *demi-mondaine* or a lady of tarnished reputation who is no longer received in society but with whom nevertheless it seems to them flattering to be associated) he had arrived at the stage at which self-esteem devotes all its energy to destroying the goals to which it has attained, whether because, under the influence of love, a man sees a sort of glamour, which he is alone in perceiving, in ostentatious relations with the beloved object, or because, by the waning of social ambitions that have been gratified, and the rising tide of ancillary curiosities that are all the more absorbing for being platonic, the latter have not only reached but have passed the level at which the former found it difficult to sustain themselves.

As for other young men, M. de Charlus found that the existence of Morel was no obstacle to his taste for them, and that indeed his brilliant reputation as a violinist or his growing fame as a composer and journalist might in certain instances provide a bait. If a young composer of pleasing appearance was introduced to the Baron, it was in Morel's talents that he sought an opportunity of doing the newcomer a favour. "You must," he would tell him, "bring me some of your work so that Morel can play it at a concert or on tour. There's so little decent music written for the violin. It's a godsend to find something new. And abroad they appreciate that sort of thing enormously. Even in the provinces there are little musical societies where they love music with a fervour and intelligence that are quite admirable." Without any greater sincerity (for all this served only as bait and it was seldom that Morel condescended to fulfil these promises), Bloch having confessed that he was something of a poet ("in my idle mo-

ments," he had added with the sarcastic laugh with which
he would accompany a trite remark when he could think
of nothing original), M. de Charlus said to me: "You
must tell your young Hebrew, since he writes verse, that
he really must bring me some for Morel. For a composer
that's always the stumbling-block, finding something decent to set to music. One might even consider a libretto.
It mightn't be uninteresting, and would acquire a certain
value from the distinction of the poet, from my patronage,
from a whole concatenation of auxiliary circumstances,
among which Morel's talent would take the chief place.
For he's composing a lot just now, and writing too, and
very nicely—I must talk to you about it. As for his talent
as an executant (there, as you know, he's already a real
master), you shall see this evening how well the lad plays
Vinteuil's music. He staggers me; at his age, to have such
understanding while remaining such a schoolboy, such an
urchin! Oh, this evening is only to be a little rehearsal.
The big affair is to come off in two or three days. But it
will be much more distinguished this evening. And so
we're delighted that you've come," he went on, using the
royal plural. "The programme is so magnificent that I've
advised Mme Verdurin to give two parties: one in a few
days' time, at which she will have all her own acquain-
tances, the other tonight at which the hostess is, as they
say in legal parlance, 'disseized.' It is I who have issued
the invitations, and I have collected a few people from another sphere, who may be useful to Charlie and whom it
will be nice for the Verdurins to meet. It's all very well,
don't you agree, to have the finest music played by the
greatest artists, but the effect of the performance remains
muffled, as though in cotton-wool, if the audience is com-

posed of the milliner from across the way and the grocer from round the corner. You know what I think of the intellectual level of society people, but there are certain quite important roles which they can perform, among others the role which in public events devolves upon the press, and which is that of being an organ of dissemination. You understand what I mean: I have for instance invited my sister-in-law Oriane; it is not certain that she will come, but it is on the other hand certain that, if she does come, she will understand absolutely nothing. But one doesn't ask her to understand, which is beyond her capacity, but to talk, a task for which she is admirably suited, and which she never fails to perform. The result? Tomorrow as ever is, instead of the silence of the milliner and the grocer, an animated conversation at the Mortemarts' with Oriane telling everyone that she has heard the most marvellous music, that a certain Morel, and so forth, and indescribable rage among the people not invited, who will say: 'Palamède obviously thought we were not worth asking; but in any case, who are these people in whose house it happened?'—a counterblast quite as useful as Oriane's praises, because Morel's name keeps cropping up all the time and is finally engraved in the memory like a lesson one has read over a dozen times. All this forms a concatenation of circumstances which may be of value to the artist, and to the hostess, may serve as a sort of megaphone for an event which will thus be made audible to a wide public. It really is worth the trouble; you shall see what progress Charlie has made. And what is more, we've discovered a new talent in him, my dear fellow: he writes like an angel. Like an angel, I tell you."

M. de Charlus omitted to say that for some time past he had been employing Morel, like those great noblemen of the seventeenth century who scorned to sign and even to write their own lampoons, to compose certain vilely calumnious little paragraphs at the expense of Comtesse Molé. Their effrontery being apparent even to those who merely glanced at them, how much more cruel were they to the young woman herself, who found in them, so slyly introduced that nobody but herself saw the point, certain passages from her own letters, quoted verbatim but twisted in a way that made them as deadly as the cruellest revenge. They killed the young woman. But there is published every day in Paris, Balzac would tell us, a sort of spoken newspaper, more terrible than its printed rivals. We shall see later on that this oral press reduced to nothing the power of a Charlus who had fallen out of fashion, and exalted far above him a Morel who was not worth the millionth part of his former patron. But at least this intellectual fashion is naïve and genuinely believes in the nullity of a gifted Charlus and in the incontestable authority of a crass Morel. The Baron was not so innocent in his implacable vindictiveness. Whence, no doubt, that bitter venom on his tongue the irruption of which seemed to dye his cheeks with jaundice when he was in a rage.

"Since you know Bergotte,"[10] M. de Charlus went on, "I thought that you might perhaps, by refreshing his memory with regard to the stripling's writings, as it were collaborate with me, help me to create a concatenation of circumstances capable of fostering a twofold talent, that of a musician and a writer, which might one day acquire the prestige of that of Berlioz. As you know, the illustrious have often other things to think about, they are smothered in flattery, they take little interest except in themselves. But Bergotte, who is genuinely unpretentious and obliging, promised me that he would arrange for the *Gaulois*, or some such paper, to publish these little articles, a blend of the humorist and the musician, which are really very nicely done, and I should be so pleased if Charlie could combine with his violin this extra little hobby. I know I'm prone to exaggeration where he is concerned, like all the old sugar-mammies of the Conservatoire. What, my dear fellow, didn't you know that? You've clearly never noticed my gullible side. I pace up and down for hours on end outside the examination hall. I'm as happy as a queen. As for Charlie's prose, Bergotte assured me that it was really very good indeed."

M. de Charlus, who had long been acquainted with Bergotte through Swann, had indeed gone to see him to ask him to find an opening on some newspaper for a sort of half-humorous column by Morel about music. In doing so, M. de Charlus had felt some remorse, for, a great admirer of Bergotte, he was conscious that he never went to see him for his own sake, but in order—thanks to the respect, partly intellectual, partly social, that Bergotte had for him—to be able to do Morel or Mme Molé or others of his friends a good turn. That he no longer made use of the social world except for such purposes did not shock him, but to treat Bergotte thus seemed to him more reprehensible, because he felt that Bergotte was not at all calculating like society people, and deserved better. But his life was fully occupied and he could never find the time to spare unless he wanted something very badly, for instance when it affected Morel. Moreover, though he was himself extremely intelligent, the conversation of an intel-

ligent man left him comparatively cold, especially that of
Bergotte who was too much the man of letters for his liking, belonged to another clan and did not see things from
his point of view. Bergotte for his part was well aware of
the utilitarian motive for M. de Charlus's visits, but bore
him no grudge; for though he was incapable of sustained
kindness, he was anxious to give pleasure, tolerant, and
impervious to the pleasure of administering a snub. As for
M. de Charlus's vice, he had never to the smallest degree
shared it, but found in it rather an element of colour in
the person affected, *fas et nefas*, for an artist, consisting
not in moral examples but in memories of Plato or of Il
Sodoma.

"I should have very much liked him to come this
evening, for he would have heard Charlie in the things he
plays best. But I gather he doesn't go out, that he doesn't
want to be bothered, and he's quite right. But you, fair
youth, we never see you at the Quai Conti. You don't
abuse their hospitality!"

I explained that I went out as a rule with my cousin.

"Do you hear that! He goes out with his cousin!
What a most particularly pure young man!" said M. de
Charlus to Brichot. Then, turning again to me: "But we
are not asking you to give an account of your life, my
boy. You are free to do anything that amuses you. We
merely regret that we have no share in it. You have very
good taste, by the way: your cousin is charming. Ask Brichot, she quite turned his head at Douville. Shall we be
seeing her this evening? She really is extremely pretty.
And she would be even prettier if she cultivated a little
more the rare art, which she possesses naturally, of dressing well."

Here I must remark that M. de Charlus "possessed"—and this made him the exact opposite, the antithesis of me—the gift of observing minutely and distinguishing the details of a woman's clothes as much as of a painting. As regards dresses and hats, certain scandalmongers or certain over-dogmatic theorists will aver that, in a man, a fondness for male attractions is balanced by an innate taste, a knowledge and feeling for female dress. And this is indeed sometimes the case, as though, men having monopolised all the physical desire, all the deep tenderness of a Charlus, the other sex were to be favoured with what comes under the heading of "platonic" (a highly inappropriate adjective) taste, or quite simply everything that comes under the heading of taste, with the most subtle and assured discrimination. In this respect M. de Charlus merited the nickname which was given to him later on, "the dressmaker." But his taste and his gift for observation extended to many other things. The reader will have seen how, on the evening I went to see him after a dinner-party at the Duchesse de Guermantes's, I had not noticed the masterpieces he had in his house until he pointed them out to me one by one. He recognised immediately things to which no one would ever have paid any attention, and this not only in works of art but in the dishes at a dinner-party (and everything else between painting and cooking). I always regretted that M. de Charlus, instead of restricting his artistic talents to the painting of a fan as a present for his sister-in-law (we have seen the Duchesse de Guermantes holding it in her hand and spreading it out not so much to fan herself with it as to show it off and parade Palamède's friendship for her) and to the improvement of his pianistic technique in order to accompany Morel's violin flourishes without playing wrong notes—I always regretted, as I say, and I still regret, that M. de Charlus never wrote anything. Of course one cannot draw from the eloquence of his conversation or even of his correspondence the conclusion that he would have been a talented writer. Those merits are not on the same plane. One has come across purveyors of conversational banality who have written masterpieces, and supreme talkers who have proved inferior to the most mediocre hack as soon as they turned to writing. Nevertheless I believe that if M. de Charlus had tried his hand at prose, to begin with on those artistic subjects about which he knew so much, the fire would have blazed, the lightning would have flashed, and the society dilettante would have become a master of the pen. I often told him so, but he never wished to try his hand, perhaps simply from laziness, or because his time was taken up with dazzling entertainments and sordid diversions, or from a Guermantes need to go on gossiping indefinitely. I regret it all the more because in his most brilliant conversation the wit was never divorced from the character, the inspired invention of the one from the arrogance of the other. If he had written books, instead of being admired and hated as he was in drawing-rooms where, in his most remarkable moments of inventive intelligence, he at the same time trampled down the weak, took revenge on people who had not insulted him, basely sought to sow discord between friends—if he had written books, one would have had his spiritual qualities in isolation, drained of evil, the admiration would have been unalloyed, and friendship kindled by many a trait.

In any case, even if I am mistaken about what he

might have achieved with the merest page of prose, he would have performed a rare service by writing, for, while he observed and distinguished everything, he also knew the name of everything he distinguished. Certain it is that by talking to him, if I did not learn to see (the natural tendency of my mind and sensibility lying elsewhere), at least I glimpsed things that without him would have remained invisible to me, though their names, which would have helped me to recall their design or their colour, I always forgot fairly quickly. If he had written books, even bad ones (though I do not believe they would have been bad), what a delightful dictionary, what an inexhaustible inventory they would have been! But after all, who knows? Instead of bringing to the task his knowledge and his taste, perhaps, through that daemon that so often thwarts our destinies, he would have written insipid romances or pointless books of travel and adventure.

"Yes, she knows how to dress, or more precisely how to wear clothes," M. de Charlus went on apropos of Albertine. "My only doubt is whether she dresses in conformity with her particular style of beauty, and I am in fact to some extent responsible for this, as a result of some rather ill-considered advice I gave her. What I often used to tell her on the way to La Raspelière, which was perhaps dictated—I regret to say—by the nature of the countryside, the proximity of the beaches, rather than by your cousin's distinctive type of looks, has made her err slightly on the side of flimsiness. I have seen her, I admit, in some very pretty muslins, some charming gauze scarves, and a certain pink toque by no means disfigured by a little pink feather. But I feel that her beauty, which is real and solid, demands more than dainty chiffons.

Does a toque really suit that enormous head of hair which a kakochnyk would set off to full advantage? Very few women are suited by old-fashioned dresses which give an impression of theatre or fancy dress. But the beauty of this young girl who is already a woman is an exception, worthy of some old dress in Genoese velvet" (I thought at once of Elstir and of Fortuny's dresses) "which I would not be afraid of weighing down even more with incrustations or pendants of stones, marvellous and outmoded— I can think of no higher praise—such as the peridot, the marcasite and the incomparable labradorite. Moreover she herself seems to have an instinct for the counter-balance that a somewhat heavy beauty calls for. Remember, on the way to dinner at La Raspelière, all that accompaniment of pretty cases and weighty bags, into which, when she is married, she will be able to put more than the whiteness of face-powder or the crimson of cosmetics but—in a casket of lapis lazuli not too tinged with indigo—those of pearls and rubies, not imitation ones, I suspect, for she may well marry into money."

"Well, well, Baron," interrupted Brichot, fearing that I might be distressed by these last words, for he had some doubts as to the purity of my relations and the authenticity of my cousinage with Albertine, "you *do* take an interest in young ladies!"

"Will you please hold your tongue in front of this child, you nasty thing," M. de Charlus replied with a giggle, raising and lowering, in the gesture of imposing silence on Brichot, a hand which he did not fail to let fall on my shoulder. "We shall regret your cousin's absence this evening. But you did just as well, perhaps, not to bring her with you. Vinteuil's music is admirable. But I

heard from Charlie this morning that there'll be the composer's daughter and her friend, who both have a terrible
reputation. That sort of thing is always awkward for a
young girl. I'm even a trifle worried about my guests. But
since they're practically all of advanced years it's of no
consequence to them. They'll be there, unless the two
young ladies haven't been able to come, because they were
to have been present without fail all afternoon at a rehearsal Mme Verdurin was giving earlier and to which she
had invited only the bores, the family, the people who
were not to be invited this evening. But just before dinner, Charlie told me that the Misses Vinteuil, as we call
them, though positively expected, had failed to turn up."

In spite of the intense pain I felt at this sudden association (as of the cause, at last discovered, with the effect,
which I had already known) of Albertine's desire to be
there that afternoon with the expected presence (unknown
to me) of Mlle Vinteuil and her friend, I still had the
presence of mind to notice that M. de Charlus, who had
told us a few minutes earlier that he had not seen Charlie
since the morning, was now brazenly admitting that he
had seen him before dinner. But my anguish was becoming visible.

"Why, what's the matter with you?" said the Baron,
"you've turned quite green. Come, let's go in; you'll catch
cold, you don't look at all well."

It was not my first doubt as to Albertine's virtue that
M. de Charlus's words had awakened in me. Many others
had penetrated my mind already. Each new doubt makes
us feel that the limit has been reached, that we cannot
cope with it; then we manage to find room for it all the
same, and once it is introduced into the fabric of our lives

it enters into competition there with so many longings to believe, so many reasons to forget, that we speedily become accustomed to it, and end by ceasing to pay attention to it. It lies there dormant like a half-healed pain, a mere threat of suffering which, the reverse side of desire, a feeling of the same order that has become, like it, the focus of our thoughts, irradiates them from infinite distances with wisps of sadness, as desire irradiates them with unidentifiable pleasures, wherever anything can be associated with the person we love. But the pain revives as soon as a new doubt enters our mind intact; even if we assure ourselves almost at once: "I shall deal with this, there'll be some way of avoiding suffering, it can't be true," nevertheless there has been a first moment in which we suffered as though we believed it. If we had merely limbs, such as legs and arms, life would be endurable. Unfortunately we carry inside us that little organ which we call the heart, which is subject to certain maladies in the course of which it is infinitely impressionable as regards everything that concerns the life of a certain person, so that a lie—that most harmless of things, in the midst of which we live so unconcernedly, whether the lie be told by ourselves or by others—coming from that person, causes that little heart, which we ought to be able to have surgically removed, intolerable spasms. Let us not speak of the brain, for our mind may go on reasoning interminably in the course of these spasms, but it does no more to mitigate them than by taking thought we can soothe an aching tooth. It is true that this person is blameworthy for having lied to us, for she had sworn to us that she would always tell us the truth. But we know, from our own shortcomings towards other people, how little such vows are worth. And we wanted to give credence to them when they came from her, the very person in whose interest it has always been to lie to us, and whom, moreover, we did not choose for her virtues. It is true that, later on, she would almost cease to have any need to lie to us—precisely when our heart will have grown indifferent to her lying—because then we shall no longer take an interest in her life. We know this, and, notwithstanding, we deliberately sacrifice our own life, either by killing ourselves for her sake, or by getting ourselves sentenced to death for having murdered her, or simply by spending our whole fortune on her in a few years and then being obliged to commit suicide because we have nothing left in the world. Moreover, however easy in one's mind one may imagine oneself to be when one loves, one always has love in one's heart in a state of precarious balance. The smallest thing is enough to place it in the position of happiness; one glows with it, one smothers with affection not her whom we love but those who have raised one in her esteem, who have protected her from every evil temptation; one feels easy in one's mind, and a single word is enough—"Gilberte is not coming," "Mademoiselle Vinteuil is expected"—for all the preconceived happiness towards which we were reaching out to collapse, for the sun to hide its face, for the compass card to revolve and let loose the inner tempest which one day we shall be incapable of resisting. On that day, the day on which the heart has become so fragile, friends who admire us will grieve that such trifles, that certain persons, can so affect us, can bring us to death's door. But what can they do? If a poet is dying of septic pneumonia, can one imagine his friends explaining to the pneumococcus that the poet is a

man of talent and that it ought to let him recover? My
doubt, in so far as it referred to Mlle Vinteuil, was not
entirely new. But even to that extent, my jealousy of the
afternoon, inspired by Léa and her friends, had abolished
it. The danger of the Trocadéro once removed, I had felt,
I had believed that I had recaptured for ever complete
peace of mind. But what was entirely new to me was a
certain excursion as to which Andrée had told me: "We
went to this place and that, and we didn't meet anyone,"
but during which, on the contrary, Mlle Vinteuil had evidently arranged to meet Albertine at Mme Verdurin's. At
this moment I would gladly have allowed Albertine to go
out by herself, to go wherever she might choose, provided
that I might lock up Mlle Vinteuil and her friend somewhere and be certain that Albertine would not meet them.
The fact is that jealousy is as a rule partial, intermittent
and localised, whether because it is the painful extension
of an anxiety which is provoked now by one person, now
by another of whom one's mistress may be enamoured, or
because of the exiguity of one's thought which is able to
realise only what it can represent to itself and leaves everything else in a vague penumbra from which one can
suffer relatively little.

Just as we were about to enter the courtyard we were
overtaken by Saniette, who had not at first recognised us.
"And yet I contemplated you for some time," he told us
breathlessly. "Is not it curious that I should have hesitated?"

To say "Is it not curious" would have seemed to him
wrong, and he had acquired a familiarity with obsolete
forms of speech that was becoming exasperating. "Albeit
you are people whom one may acknowledge as friends."

His grey complexion seemed to be illuminated by the livid glow of a storm. His breathlessness, which had been noticeable, as recently as last summer, only when M. Verdurin "jumped down his throat," was now continuous.

"I understand that an unknown work of Vinteuil is to be performed by excellent artists, and singularly by Morel."

"Why singularly?" inquired the Baron, who detected a criticism in the adverb.

"Our friend Saniette," Brichot made haste to explain, playing the part of interpreter, "is prone to speak, like the excellent scholar that he is, the language of an age in which 'singularly' was equivalent to our 'in particular.' "

As we entered the Verdurins' hall, M. de Charlus asked me whether I was engaged upon any work, and as I told him that I was not, but that I was greatly interested at the moment in old dinner-services of silver and porcelain, he assured me that I could not see any finer than those that the Verdurins had; that indeed I might have seen them at La Raspelière, since, on the pretext that one's possessions are also one's friends, they were foolish enough to take everything down there with them; that it would be less convenient to bring everything out for my benefit on the evening of a party, but that he would nevertheless ask them to show me anything I wished to see. I begged him not to do anything of the sort. M. de Charlus unbuttoned his overcoat and took off his hat, and I saw that the top of his head had now turned silver in patches. But like a precious shrub which is not only coloured with autumn tints but certain leaves of which are protected with cotton-wool or incrustations of plaster, M. de Charlus received from these few white hairs at his crest only a

further variegation added to those of his face. And yet,
even beneath the layers of different expressions, of paint
and of hypocrisy which formed such a bad "make-up,"
his face continued to hide from almost everyone the secret
that it seemed to me to be crying aloud. I was almost embarrassed by his eyes, for I was afraid of his surprising me
in the act of reading it therein as in an open book, and by
his voice which seemed to me to repeat it in every con-
ceivable key, with unrelenting indecency. But secrets are
well kept by such people, for everyone who comes in contact with them is deaf and blind. The people who learned
the truth from someone else, from the Verdurins for instance, believed it, but only for so long as they had not
met M. de Charlus. His face, so far from disseminating,
dispelled every scandalous rumour. For we have so ex-
travagant a notion of certain entities that we cannot identify it with the familiar features of a person of our
acquaintance. And we find it difficult to believe in such a
person's vices, just as we can never believe in the genius
of a person with whom we went to the Opera only last
night.

M. de Charlus was engaged in handing over his overcoat with the instructions of a familiar guest. But the footman to whom he was handing it was a newcomer, and
quite young. Now M. de Charlus was inclined these days
sometimes to "lose his bearings," as they say, and did not
always remember what was or was not "done." The
praiseworthy desire that he had had at Balbec to show
that certain topics did not alarm him, that he was not
afraid to say of someone or other: "He's a nice-looking
boy," to say, in a word, the same things as might have

been said by somebody who was not like himself, this desire he had now begun to express by saying on the contrary things which nobody who was not like him could
ever have said, things upon which his mind was so constantly fixed that he forgot that they do not form part of
the habitual preoccupation of people in general. And so,
looking at the new footman, he raised his forefinger in the
air in a menacing fashion and, thinking that he was making an excellent joke, said: "You are not to make eyes at
me like that, do you hear?" and, turning to Brichot: "He
has a quaint little face, that boy, his nose is rather fun";
then, rounding off his pleasantry, or yielding to a desire,
he lowered his forefinger horizontally, hesitated for an instant, and, unable to control himself any longer, thrust it
irresistibly towards the footman and touched the tip of his
nose, saying "Pif!", then walked into the drawing-room
followed by Brichot, myself and Saniette, who told us that
Princess Sherbatoff had died at six o'clock. "That's a rum
card," the footman said to himself, and inquired of his
companions whether the Baron was a joker or a madman.
"It's just a way he has," said the butler (who regarded the
Baron as slightly "touched," "a bit barmy"), "but he's one
of Madame's friends for whom I've always had the greatest respect, he has a good heart."

"Will you be returning to Incarville this year?" Brichot asked me. "I believe that our hostess has taken La
Raspelière again, although she had some trouble with her
landlords. But that's nothing, a mere passing cloud," he
added in the optimistic tone of the newspapers that say:
"Mistakes have been made, it is true, but who does not
make mistakes at times?" But I remembered the state of

anguish in which I had left Balbec, and felt no desire to return there. I kept putting off to the morrow my plans for Albertine.

"Why, of course he's coming back, we need him, he's indispensable to us," declared M. de Charlus with the dictatorial and uncomprehending egoism of benevolence.

M. Verdurin, to whom we expressed our sympathy over Princess Sherbatoff, said: "Yes, I believe she is rather ill."

"No, no, she died at six o'clock," exclaimed Saniette.

"Oh you, you exaggerate everything," was M. Verdurin's brutal retort, for, the evening not having been cancelled, he preferred the hypothesis of illness, thereby unconsciously imitating the Duc de Guermantes.

Saniette, fearful of catching cold, for the outer door was continually being opened, stood waiting resignedly for someone to take his hat and coat.

"What are you hanging about there for like a whipped dog?" M. Verdurin asked him.

"I am waiting until one of the persons who are charged with the cloakroom can take my coat and give me a number."

"What's that you say?" demanded M. Verdurin with a stern expression. "'Charged with the cloakroom'? Are you going gaga? 'In charge of the cloakroom' is what we say. Have we got to teach you to speak your own language, like someone who's had a stroke?"

"'Charged with a thing is the correct form," murmured Saniette in a wheezy tone; "the abbé Le Batteux . . ."

"You madden me, you do," cried M. Verdurin in a

voice of thunder. "How you do wheeze! Have you just walked up six flights of stairs?"

The effect of M. Verdurin's rudeness was that the servants in the cloakroom allowed other guests to take precedence over Saniette and, when he tried to hand over his things, said to him: "Wait for your turn, Sir, don't be in such a hurry."

"There's system for you, there's competence. That's right, my lads," said M. Verdurin with an approving smile, in order to encourage them in their inclination to keep Saniette waiting till last. "Come along," he said to us, "the creature wants us all to catch our death hanging about in his beloved draught. Come and warm up in the drawing-room. 'Charged with the cloakroom,' indeed. What an idiot!"

"He *is* inclined to be a little precious, but he's not a bad fellow," said Brichot.

"I never said he was a bad fellow, I said he was an idiot," M. Verdurin retorted sourly.

Meanwhile Mme Verdurin was in deep conclave with Cottard and Ski. Morel had just declined (because M. de Charlus could not be present) an invitation from some friends of hers to whom she had promised the services of the violinist. The reason for Morel's refusal, which we shall presently see reinforced by others of a far more serious kind, might have found its justification in a habit peculiar to the leisured classes in general but more particularly to the little nucleus. To be sure, if Mme Verdurin intercepted between a newcomer and one of the faithful a whispered remark which might let it be supposed that they knew each other or wished to become better acquainted ("On Friday, then, at So-and-so's," or "Come to the studio any day you like. I'm always there until five o'clock, I shall look forward to seeing you"), she would become restless and excited, assuming that the newcomer occupied a "position" which would make him a brilliant recruit to the little clan, and while pretending not to have heard anything, and preserving in her fine eyes, ringed with dark shadows by addiction to Debussy more than they would have been by addiction to cocaine, the exhausted look induced by musical intoxication alone, would revolve nevertheless behind her splendid brow, bulging with all those quartets and the resultant headaches, thoughts which were not exclusively polyphonic; and unable to contain herself any longer, unable to postpone the injection for another instant, would fling herself upon the speakers, draw them apart, and say to the newcomer, pointing to the "faithful" one: "You wouldn't care to come and dine with *him*, next Saturday, shall we say, or any day you like, with some really nice people? Don't speak too loud, as I don't want to invite all this mob" (a term used to designate for five minutes the little nucleus, disdained for the moment in favour of the newcomer in whom so many hopes were placed).

But this need for new enthusiasms, and also for bringing people together, had its reverse side. Assiduous attendance at their Wednesdays aroused in the Verdurins an opposite tendency. This was the desire to set people at odds, to estrange them from one another. It had been strengthened, had almost been carried to a frenzy during the months spent at La Raspelière, where they were all together morning, noon and night. M. Verdurin would go out of his way to catch someone out, to spin webs in

which he might hand over to his spider mate some innocent fly. Failing a grievance, he would try ridicule. As
soon as one of the faithful had been out of the house for
half an hour, the Verdurins would make fun of him in
front of the others, would feign surprise that their guests
had not noticed how his teeth were never clean, or how
on the contrary he had a mania for brushing them twenty
times a day. If anyone took the liberty of opening a window, this want of breeding would cause host and hostess
to exchange a glance of disgust. A moment later Mme
Verdurin would ask for a shawl, which gave M. Verdurin
an excuse for saying in a tone of fury: "No, I shall close
the window. I wonder who had the impertinence to open
it," in the hearing of the guilty wretch who blushed to the
roots of his hair. You were rebuked indirectly for the
quantity of wine you had drunk. "Doesn't it make you ill?
It's all right for navvies!" If two of the faithful went for
walks together without first obtaining permission from the
Mistress, these walks were the subject of endless comment, however innocent they might be. Those of M. de
Charlus with Morel were not innocent. It was only the
fact that M. de Charlus was not staying at La Raspelière
(because of Morel's garrison life) that retarded the hour of
satiety, disgust, nausea. That hour was, however, about to
strike.

Mme Verdurin was furious and determined to "enlighten" Morel as to the ridiculous and detestable role
that M. de Charlus was making him play. "I must add,"
she went on (for when she felt that she owed someone a
debt of gratitude which would weigh upon her, and was
unable to rid herself of it by killing him, she would discover a serious defect in him which would honourably

dispense her from showing her gratitude), "I must add
that he gives himself airs in my house which I do not at
all like." The truth was that Mme Verdurin had another
reason more serious than Morel's refusal to play at her
friends' party for resentment against M. de Charlus. The
latter, highly conscious of the honour he was doing the
Mistress by bringing to the Quai Conti people who after
all would never have come there for her sake, had, on
hearing the first few names put forward by Mme Verdurin of people who ought to be invited, pronounced the
most categorical veto on them in a peremptory tone which
blended the rancorous arrogance of a crotchety nobleman
with the dogmatism of the artist who is an expert in questions of entertainment and who would withdraw his piece
and withhold his collaboration sooner than agree to con-
cessions which in his opinion would ruin the overall effect. M. de Charlus had given his approval, hedging it
round with reservations, to Saintine alone, with whom, in
order not to be lumbered with his wife, Mme de Guermantes had passed from a daily intimacy to a complete
severance of relations, but whom M. de Charlus, finding
him intelligent, continued to see. True, it was in a middle-class circle cross-bred with minor nobility, where people are merely very rich and connected by marriage with
an aristocracy which the higher aristocracy does not know,
that Saintine, at one time the flower of the Guermantes
set, had gone to seek his fortune and, he imagined, a social foothold. But Mme Verdurin, knowing the blue-
blooded pretensions of the wife's circle, and unaware of
the husband's position (for it is what is immediately
above our head that gives us the impression of altitude
and not what is almost invisible to us, so far is it lost in

the clouds), thought to justify an invitation for Saintine by pointing out that he knew a great many people, "having married Mlle——." The ignorance which this assertion, the direct opposite of the truth, revealed in Mme Verdurin caused the Baron's painted lips to part in a smile of indulgent scorn and generous understanding. He did not deign to reply directly, but as he was always ready, in social matters, to elaborate theories in which his fertile intelligence and lordly pride were combined with the hereditary frivolity of his preoccupations, "Saintine ought to have consulted me before marrying," he said. "There's such a thing as social as well as physiological eugenics, in which I am perhaps the only specialist in existence. There could be no argument about Saintine's case: it was clear that, in marrying as he did, he was tying a stone round his neck, and hiding his light under a bushel. His social career was at an end. I should have explained this to him, and he would have understood me, for he is intelligent. Conversely, there was a certain person who had everything that he required to make his position exalted, predominant, world-wide, only a terrible cable bound him to the earth. I helped him, partly by pressure, partly by force, to break his moorings and now he has won, with a triumphant joy, the freedom, the omnipotence that he owes to me. It required, perhaps, a little determination on his part, but what a reward! Thus a man can himself, when he has the sense to listen to me, become the artificer of his destiny." (It was only too clear that M. de Charlus had not been able to influence his own; action is a different thing from words, however eloquent, and from thought, however ingenious.) "But, so far as I am concerned, I live the life of a philosopher who looks on with interest at the social reactions which he has foretold, but does not assist them. And so I have continued to see Saintine, who has always shown me the cordial deference which is my due. I have even dined with him in his new abode, where one is as heavily bored, in the midst of the most sumptuous splendour, as one used to be amused in the old days when, living from hand to mouth, he used to assemble the best society in a little attic. Him, therefore, you may invite; I authorise it. But I must impose a veto on all the other names that you have proposed. And you will thank me for it, for if I am an expert in the matter of marriages, I am no less an expert in the matter of festivities. I know the rising personalities who can lift a gathering, give it tone and distinction; and I know also the names that will bring it down to the ground, make it fall flat."

These exclusions of the Baron's were not always based on the resentments of a crackpot or the subtleties of an artist, but on the wiles of an actor. When he brought off, at the expense of somebody or something, an entirely successful tirade, he was anxious to let it be heard by the largest possible audience, but took care not to admit to the second performance the audience of the first who could have borne witness that the piece had not changed. He reconstituted his audience precisely because he did not alter his programme, and, when he had scored a success in conversation, would willingly have organised a tour and given performances in the provinces. Whatever the various motives for these exclusions, they did not merely annoy Mme Verdurin, who felt her authority as a hostess impaired; they also did her great damage socially, and for two reasons. The first was that M. de Charlus, even more

touchy than Jupien, used to quarrel for no apparent reason with the people who were most suited to be his
friends. Naturally, one of the first punishments that he
could inflict upon them was that of not allowing them to
be invited to a reception which he was organising at the
Verdurins'. Now these pariahs were often people who
ruled the roost, as the saying is, but who in M. de Charlus's eyes had ceased to rule it from the day on which he
had quarrelled with them. For his imagination, in addition
to manufacturing faults in people in order to quarrel with
them, was no less ingenious in stripping them of all importance as soon as they ceased to be his friends. If, for
instance, the guilty person came of an extremely old family whose dukedom, however, dates only from the nineteenth century—the Montesquious for instance—from
that moment all that counted for M. de Charlus was the
seniority of the dukedom, the family becoming nothing.
"They're not even dukes," he would exclaim. "It's the title of the Abbé de Montesquiou which passed most irreg-
ularly to a collateral, less than eighty years ago. The
present duke, if duke he can be called, is the third. You
may talk to me if you like of people like the Uzès, the La
Trémoïlles, the Luynes, who are tenth or fourteenth
dukes, or my brother who is twelfth Duc de Guermantes
and seventeenth Prince de Condom. Even if the Montesquious are descended from an old family, what would
that prove, supposing that it *were* proved? They have descended so far that they've reached the fourteenth storey
below stairs." Had he on the contrary quarrelled with a
gentleman who possessed an ancient dukedom, who
boasted the most magnificent connexions, was related to
ruling princes, but to whose line this distinction had come

quite suddenly without any great length of pedigree, a
Luynes for instance, the case was altered, pedigree alone
counted. "I ask you—Monsieur Alberti, who does not
emerge from the mire until Louis XIII! Why should we
be impressed because court favour allowed them to pick
up dukedoms to which they had no right?" What was
more, with M. de Charlus the fall followed close upon the
high favour because of that tendency peculiar to the
Guermantes family to expect from conversation, from
friendship, something that these are incapable of giving,
as well as the symptomatic fear of becoming the object of
slander. And the fall was all the greater the higher the
favour had been. Now nobody had ever found such
favour with the Baron as he had ostentatiously shown to
Comtesse Molé. By what sign of indifference did she
prove one fine day that she had been unworthy of it? The
Countess herself always declared that she had never been
able to discover. The fact remains that the mere sound of
her name aroused in the Baron the most violent rage, provoked the most eloquent but the most terrible philippics.
Mme Verdurin, to whom Mme Molé had been extremely
amiable and who, as we shall see, was founding great
hopes upon her, had rejoiced in anticipation at the
thought that the Countess would meet in her house all the
noblest names, as the Mistress said, "of France and of
Navarre": she at once proposed inviting "Madame de
Molé." "Goodness gracious me! I suppose it takes all sorts
to make a world," M. de Charlus had replied, "and if
you, Madame, feel a desire to converse with Mme Pipelet,
Mme Gibout and Mme Joseph Prudhomme,[11] I'm only
too delighted, but let it be on an evening when I am not
present. I could see as soon as you opened your mouth

that we don't speak the same language, since I was talking of aristocratic names and you come up with the most obscure names of lawyers, of crooked little commoners, evil-minded tittle-tattles, and of little ladies who imagine themselves patronesses of the arts because they echo an octave lower the manners of my Guermantes sister-in-law, like a jay trying to imitate a peacock. I must add that it would be positively indecent to admit to a celebration which I am pleased to give at Mme Verdurin's a person whom I have with good reason excluded from my society, a goose of a woman devoid of birth, loyalty or wit who is foolish enough to suppose that she is capable of playing the Duchesse de Guermantes and the Princesse de Guermantes, a combination which is in itself idiotic, since the Duchesse de Guermantes and the Princesse de Guermantes are poles apart. It is as though a person should pretend to be at once Reichenberg and Sarah Bernhardt. In any case, even if it were not wholly incompatible, it would be extremely ridiculous. Even though I myself may smile at times at the exaggerations of the one and regret the limitations of the other, that is my right. But that little middle-class toad trying to inflate herself to the magnitude of two great ladies who at least always exhibit the incomparable distinction of blood, it's enough, as the saying is, to make a cat laugh. The Molé! That is a name which must not be uttered in my hearing, or I shall be obliged to withdraw," he concluded with a smile, in the tone of a doctor who, having the good of his patient at heart in spite of the patient himself, lets it be understood that he will not tolerate the collaboration of a homoeopath.

In addition to this, certain persons whom M. de

Charlus regarded as negligible might indeed be so for him but not for Mme Verdurin. M. de Charlus, from the height of his exalted birth, could afford to dispense with the most elegant people, the assemblage of whom would have made Mme Verdurin's drawing-room one of the first in Paris. But Mme Verdurin was beginning to feel that she had already on more than one occasion missed the bus, not to mention the enormous setback that the social error of the Dreyfus case had inflicted upon her—though it had not been an unmixed bane. "I forget whether I've told you," I might ask the reader, as one might ask a friend with regard to whom one has forgotten, after so many conversations, whether one has remembered or had a chance to tell him something, "how disapproving the Duchesse de Guermantes had been of certain persons of her world who, subordinating everything else to the Affair, excluded fashionable women from their drawing-rooms and admitted others who were not fashionable, because they were in favour of a retrial or against it, and had then been criticised in her turn by those same ladies as being lukewarm, unsound in her views, and guilty of placing social formalities above the national interest?" Whether I have done so or not, the attitude of the Duchesse de Guermantes at that time can easily be imagined, and indeed if we look at it in the light of subsequent history may appear, from the social point of view, perfectly correct. M. de Cambremer regarded the Dreyfus case as a foreign machination intended to destroy the Intelligence Service, to undermine discipline, to weaken the army, to divide the French people, to pave the way for invasion. Literature being, apart from a few of La Fontaine's fables, a closed book to the Marquis, he left it to his wife to show that the cruelly probing literature of the day had, by creating a spirit of disrespect, brought about a parallel upheaval. "M. Reinach and M. Hervieu are in league," she would say. Nobody will accuse the Dreyfus case of having premeditated such dark designs upon Society. But there it certainly broke down barriers. Society people who refuse to allow politics into their world are as far-sighted as soldiers who refuse to allow politics to permeate the army. Society is like sexual behaviour, in that no one knows what perversions it may develop once aesthetic considerations are allowed to dictate its choices. The reason that they were nationalists gave the Faubourg Saint-Germain the habit of entertaining ladies from another class of society; the reason vanished with nationalism, but the habit remained. Mme Verdurin, thanks to Dreyfusism, had attracted to her house certain writers of distinction who for the moment were of no use to her socially, because they were Dreyfusards. But political passions are like all the rest, they do not last. New generations arise which no longer understand them; even the generation that experienced them changes, experiences new political passions which, not being modelled exactly upon their predecessors, rehabilitate some of the excluded, the reason for exclusion having altered. Monarchists no longer cared, at the time of the Dreyfus case, whether a man had been republican, or even radical, or even indeed anti-clerical, provided he was anti-semitic and nationalist. Should a war ever come, patriotism would assume another form and if a writer was chauvinistic enough nobody would stop to think whether he had or had not been a Dreyfusard.

It was thus that, from each political crisis, from each

artistic revival, Mme Verdurin had picked up one by one, like a bird building its nest, the several scraps, temporarily unusable, of what would one day be her salon. The Dreyfus case had passed, Anatole France remained. Mme Verdurin's strength lay in her genuine love of art, the trouble she took for her faithful, the marvellous dinners that she gave for them alone, without inviting anyone from fashionable society. Each of the faithful was treated at her table as Bergotte had been treated at Mme Swann's. When a familiar guest of this sort becomes one fine day a famous man whom everyone wants to come and see, his presence in the house of a Mme Verdurin has none of the artificial, adulterated quality of an official banquet or a college feast with a menu by Potel and Chabot,[12] but is like a delicious everyday meal which you would have found there in the same perfection on a day when there was no party at all. At Mme Verdurin's, the cast was trained to perfection, the repertory most select; all that was lacking was an audience. And now that the public taste had begun to turn from the rational Gallic art of Bergotte and was developing a taste for exotic forms of music, Mme Verdurin, a sort of accredited representative in Paris of all foreign artists, would soon be making her appearance, by the side of the exquisite Princess Yourbeletieff, as an aged Fairy Godmother, grim but all-powerful, to the Russian dancers. This charming invasion, against whose seductions only the stupidest of critics protested, infected Paris, as we know, with a fever of curiosity less agonising, more purely aesthetic, but quite as intense perhaps as that aroused by the Dreyfus case. There too Mme Verdurin, but with a very different result socially, was to be in the vanguard. Just as she had been

seen by the side of Mme Zola, immediately below the
judges' bench, during the trial in the Assize Court, so
when the new generation, in their enthusiasm for the Russian ballet, thronged to the Opéra, they invariably saw in
a stage box Mme Verdurin, crowned with fantastic ai-
grettes, by the side of Princess Yourbeletieff. And just as,
after the excitements of the law courts, people used to go
in the evening to Mme Verdurin's to meet Picquart or
Labori in the flesh, and above all to hear the latest news,
to learn what hopes might be placed in Zurlinden, Lou-
bet, Colonel Jouaust, so years later, little inclined for sleep
after the enthusiasm aroused by *Sheherazade* or the dances
from *Prince Igor*, they would again repair to Mme Verdurin's, where, under the auspices of Princess Yourbeletieff and their hostess, an exquisite supper brought together
every night the dancers themselves, who had abstained
from dinner in order to remain more elastic, their director,
their designers, the great composers Igor Stravinsky and
Richard Strauss, a permanent little nucleus around which,
as round the supper-table of M. and Mme Helvétius, the
greatest ladies in Paris and foreign royalty were not too
proud to gather. Even those society people who professed
to be endowed with taste and drew otiose distinctions between the various Russian ballets, regarding the production of *Les Sylphides* as somehow more "delicate" than
that of *Sheherazade*, which they were almost prepared to
attribute to the inspiration of Negro art, were enchanted
to meet face to face these great theatrical innovators who,
in an art that is perhaps a little more artificial than painting, had created a revolution as profound as Impressionism itself.

     To revert to M. de Charlus, Mme Verdurin would

not have minded so much if he had placed on his Index only Mme Bontemps, whom she had picked out at Odette's on the strength of her love of the arts, and who during the Dreyfus case had come to dinner occasionally with her husband, whom Mme Verdurin called "luke-warm" because he was not making any move for a fresh trial but who, being extremely intelligent, and glad to form relations in every camp, was delighted to show his independence by dining at the same table as Labori, to whom he listened without uttering a word that might compromise himself, but slipping in at the right moment a tribute to the honesty, recognised by all parties, of Jaurès. But the Baron had similarly proscribed several ladies of the aristocracy with whom Mme Verdurin, on the occasion of some musical festivity or fashion show, had recently formed an acquaintanceship and who, whatever M. de Charlus might think of them, would have been, far more than himself, essential ingredients in the formation of a fresh nucleus, this time aristocratic. Mme Verdurin had indeed been counting on this party to mingle her new friends with ladies of the same set whom M. de Charlus would be bringing, and had been relishing in advance the surprise of the former on meeting at the Quai Conti their own friends or relations invited there by the Baron. She was disappointed and furious at his veto. It remained to be seen whether, in these circumstances, the evening would result in profit or loss to herself. The loss would not be too serious if, at least, M. de Charlus's guests proved so well-disposed towards her that they would be-come her friends in the future. In this case no great harm would be done, and sooner or later these two sections of the fashionable world, which the Baron had insisted upon keeping apart, could be brought together even if it meant excluding him on the evening in question. And so Mme Verdurin was awaiting the Baron's guests with a certain trepidation. It would not be long before she discovered the frame of mind in which they were coming and could judge what sort of relationship she could hope to have with them. In the meantime she was taking counsel with the faithful, but, on seeing M. de Charlus enter the room with Brichot and myself, stopped short.

Greatly to our astonishment, when Brichot told her how sorry he was to learn that her dear friend was so seriously ill, Mme Verdurin replied: "You know, I'm bound to confess that I feel no regret at all. It's no use feigning emotions one doesn't feel . . ." No doubt she spoke thus from want of energy, because she shrank from the idea of wearing a long face throughout her reception; from pride, in order not to appear to be seeking excuses for not having cancelled it; yet also from fear of what people might think of her and from social shrewdness, because the absence of grief which she displayed was more honourable if it could be attributed to a particular antipathy, suddenly revealed, for the Princess, rather than to a general insensitivity, and because her hearers could not fail to be disarmed by a sincerity as to which there could be no doubt: for if Mme Verdurin had not been genuinely indifferent to the death of the Princess, would she, in order to explain why she was entertaining, have gone so far as to accuse herself of a far more serious fault? This was to forget that Mme Verdurin would have had to admit, at the same time as confessing her grief, that she had not had the strength of mind to forgo a pleasure; whereas the indifference of the friend was something more shocking, more immoral, but less humiliating and consequently easier to confess than the frivolity of the hostess. In matters of crime, where there is danger for the culprit, it is self-interest that dictates confessions; where the offence incurs no penalty, it is self-esteem. Whether it was that, doubtless finding rather hackneyed the excuse of people who, in order not to allow a bereavement to interrupt their life of pleasure, go about saying that it seems to them futile to wear on their sleeves a grief which they feel in their hearts, she preferred to imitate those intelligent culprits who are repelled by the clichés of innocence and whose defence—a partial admission, though they do not know it—consists in saying that they would see no harm in doing what they are accused of doing, although, as it happens, they have had no occasion to do it, or whether, having adopted the theory of indifference in order to explain her conduct, she found, once she had started on the downward slope of her unnatural feeling, that there was some originality in having felt it, a rare perspicacity in having managed to diagnose it, and a certain "nerve" in proclaiming it, Mme Verdurin kept dwelling upon her want of grief, not without something of the complacent pride of a paradoxical psychologist and daring dramatist.

"Yes, it's very odd," she said, "it made scarcely any impression on me. Of course, I don't mean to say that I wouldn't rather she were still alive, she wasn't a bad person."

"Yes she was," put in M. Verdurin.

"Ah! he doesn't approve of her because he thought I was doing myself harm by having her here, but he's rather pig-headed about that."

"Do me the justice to admit," said M. Verdurin,

"that I never approved of the association. I always told you that she had a bad reputation."

"But I've never heard a thing against her," protested Saniette.

"What!" exclaimed Mme. Verdurin, "everybody knew; bad isn't the word, it was shameful, degrading. No, but it has nothing to do with that. I couldn't myself explain what I feel. I didn't dislike her, but she meant so little to me that when we heard that she was seriously ill my husband himself was quite surprised and said: 'Anyone would think you didn't mind.' Why, earlier this evening he offered to put off the rehearsal, and I insisted upon having it because I should have thought it a farce to show a grief which I don't feel."

She said this because she felt that it had an intriguing smack of the "independent theatre," and was at the same time singularly convenient; for avowed insensitivity or immorality simplifies life as much as does easy virtue; it converts reprehensible actions, for which one no longer need seek excuses, into a duty imposed by sincerity. And the faithful listened to Mme Verdurin's words with the mixture of admiration and uneasiness which certain cruelly realistic and painfully observant plays used at one time to cause; and while they marvelled to see their beloved Mistress display her rectitude and independence in a new form, more than one of them, although he assured himself that after all it would not be the same thing, thought of his own death, and wondered whether, on the day it occurred, they would drop a tear or give a party at the Quai Conti.

"I'm very glad for my guests' sake that the evening hasn't been cancelled," said M. de Charlus, not realising that in expressing himself thus he was offending Mme Verdurin.

Meanwhile I was struck, as was everybody who approached Mme Verdurin that evening, by a far from pleasant odour of rhino-gomenol. This was how it came about. We know that Mme Verdurin never expressed her artistic emotions in a mental but always in a physical way, so that they might appear more inescapable and more profound. Now, if one spoke to her of Vinteuil's music, her favourite, she would remain unmoved, as though she expected to derive no emotion from it. But after looking at you for a few moments with a fixed, almost abstracted gaze, she would answer you in a sharp, matter of fact, scarcely civil tone (as though she had said to you: "I don't in the least mind your smoking, but it's because of the carpet; it's a very fine one—not that that matters either—but it's highly inflammable, I'm dreadfully afraid of fire, and I shouldn't like to see you all roasted because someone had carelessly dropped a lighted cigarette end on it"), not professing any admiration, but coldly expressing her regret that something of his was being played that evening: "I have nothing against Vinteuil; to my mind, he's the greatest composer of the age. Only, I can never listen to that sort of stuff without weeping all the time" (there was not the slightest suggestion of pathos in the way she said "weeping"; she would have used precisely the same tone for "sleeping"; certain slandermongers used indeed to insist that the latter verb would have been more applicable, though no one could ever be certain, for she listened to the music with her face buried in her hands, and certain snoring sounds might after all have been sobs). "I don't mind weeping, not in the least; only I get the most appalling sniffles afterwards. It stuffs up my mucous membrane, and forty-eight hours later I look like an old drunk. I have to inhale for days on end to get my vocal cords functioning. However, one of Cottard's pupils . . ." "Oh, by the way, I never offered you my condolences: he was carried off very quickly, poor fellow!" "Ah, yes, there we are, he died, as everyone has to. He'd killed enough people for it to be his turn to have a bit of his own medicine.[13] Anyhow, I was saying that one of his pupils, a delightful creature, has been treating me for it. He goes by quite an original rule: 'Prevention is better than cure.' And he greases my nose before the music begins. The effect is radical. I can weep like all the mothers who ever lost a child, and not a trace of a cold. Sometimes a little conjunctivitis, that's all. It's completely efficacious. Otherwise I could never have gone on listening to Vinteuil. I was just going from one bronchial attack to another."

I could not refrain from mentioning Mlle Vinteuil. "Isn't the composer's daughter to be here," I asked Mme Verdurin, "with one of her friends?"

"No, I've just had a telegram," Mme Verdurin said evasively, "they were obliged to remain in the country."

I had a momentary hope that there might never have been any question of their coming and that Mme Verdurin had announced the presence of these representatives of the composer only in order to make a favourable impression on the performers and their audience.

"What, so they didn't even come to the rehearsal this afternoon?" said the Baron with feigned curiosity, anxious to appear not to have seen Charlie.

The latter came up to greet me. I whispered a question in his ear about Mlle Vinteuil's non-appearance; he seemed to me to know little or nothing about the matter. I signed to him to keep his voice down and told him we would talk again later. He bowed, and assured me that he would be entirely at my disposal. I observed that he was far more polite, far more respectful, than he had been in the past. I spoke warmly of him—since he might perhaps be able to help me to clear up my suspicions—to M. de Charlus who replied: "He only does what he should: there would be no point in his living among respectable people if he didn't learn good manners." These, according to M. de Charlus, were the old manners of France, without a hint of British stiffness. Thus when Charlie, returning from a tour in the provinces or abroad, arrived in his travelling suit at the Baron's, the latter, if there were not too many people present, would kiss him without ceremony on both cheeks, perhaps a little in order to banish by so ostentatious a display of his affection any idea of its being criminal, perhaps because he could not deny himself a pleasure, but still more, no doubt, for literary reasons, as upholding and illustrating the traditional manners of France, and, just as he would have protested against the Munich or modern style of furniture by keeping old armchairs that had come to him from a great-grandmother, countering British phlegm with the affection of a warmhearted eighteenth-century father who does not conceal his joy at seeing his son again. Was there indeed a trace of incest in this paternal affection? It is more probable that the way in which M. de Charlus habitually appeased his vice—as to which we shall learn something in due course—did not meet his emotional needs, which had remained unsatisfied since the death of his wife; certain it is that after having thought more than once of remarrying, he was now devoured by a maniacal desire to adopt an heir, and certain persons close to him feared that it might be fulfilled in favour of Morel. And there is nothing extraordinary in this. The invert who has been able to feed his passion only on a literature written for women-loving men, who used to think of men when he read Musset's *Nuits*, feels the need to enter in the same way into all the social activities of the man who is not an invert, to keep a lover, as the old frequenter of the Opéra keeps ballet-girls, to settle down, to marry or form a permanent tie, to become a father.

M. de Charlus took Morel aside, on the pretext of getting him to explain what was going to be played, but above all taking a sweet delight, while Charlie showed him his music, in displaying thus publicly their secret intimacy. In the meantime I was surrounded by enchantment. For although the little clan included few girls, a fair number were invited on big occasions. There were several present, very pretty ones, whom I knew. They sent smiles of greeting to me across the room. The air was thus continually embellished with charming girlish smiles. They are the multifarious scattered adornment of evenings as of days. One remembers an atmosphere because girls were smiling in it.

On the other hand, people might have been greatly surprised had they overheard the furtive remarks which M. de Charlus exchanged with a number of important men at this party. These were two dukes, a distinguished general, a celebrated author, an eminent physician and a great lawyer. And the remarks in question were: "By the way, did you notice that footman, no, I mean the little fellow they take on the carriage . . . And at your cousin Guermantes's, you don't know of anyone?" "At the moment, no." "I say, though, outside the door, where the carriages stop, there was a little blonde person in short breeches, who seemed to me most attractive. She called my carriage most charmingly. I'd gladly have prolonged the conversation." "Yes, but I believe she's altogether hostile, and besides, she makes such a fuss! Since you like to get down to business at once, you'd be fed up. Anyhow, I know there's nothing doing, a friend of mine tried." "That's a pity, I thought the profile very fine, and the hair superb." "Really, you found her as nice as that? I think if you'd seen a little more of her you would have been disillusioned. No, in the supper-room only two months ago you would have seen a real marvel, a big strapping fellow over six feet tall, with a perfect skin, and loves it, too. But he's gone off to Poland." "Ah, that's a bit far." "You never know, he may come back. One always meets again somewhere." There is no great social function that does not, if one takes a cross-section of it and cuts sufficiently deep, resemble those parties to which doctors invite their patients, who utter the most intelligent remarks, have perfect manners, and would never show that they were mad if they did not whisper in your ear, pointing to some old gentleman going past: "That's Joan of Arc."

"I feel it's our duty to enlighten him," Mme Verdurin said to Brichot. "I don't mean any harm to Charlus, far from it. He's an agreeable man, and as for his reputation, I may say that it isn't of the kind that can do me any harm! You know how much, in the interests of our little clan and our table talk, I detest flirting, men talking non-

sense to a woman in a corner instead of discussing interesting topics, but with Charlus I've never been afraid of
what happened to me with Swann, and Elstir, and lots of
others. With him I felt no need to worry; he would come
to my dinners, all the women in the world might be there,
yet you could be certain that the general conversation
wouldn't be disturbed by flirting and whispering. Charlus
is a special case, one doesn't have to worry, it's like having a priest. But he simply can't be allowed to take charge
of the young men he meets here and cause trouble in our
little nucleus, otherwise it will be even worse than having
a womaniser." And Mme Verdurin was sincere in thus
proclaiming her tolerance of Charlusism. Like every ecclesiastical power, she regarded human frailties as less dangerous than anything that might undermine the principle
of authority, impair the orthodoxy, modify the ancient
creed of her little Church. "Otherwise," she went on, "I
shall bare my teeth. What do you say to a gentleman who
prevents Charlie from coming to a recital because he himself hasn't been invited? So he's going to be taught a lesson, and I hope he'll profit by it, otherwise he can simply
take his hat and go. Upon my word, he keeps the boy
cooped up!" And, using exactly the same expressions that
almost anyone else might have used, for there are certain
phrases not in common currency which some particular
subject, some given circumstance, will recall almost infallibly to the mind of the talker who imagines he is speaking his mind freely when he is merely repeating
mechanically the universal version, she continued: "It's
impossible to see Morel nowadays without that great spin-
dle-shanks hanging round him like a bodyguard."

M. Verdurin offered to take Charlie out of the room

for a minute to talk to him, on the pretext of asking him something. Mme Verdurin was afraid that this might upset him, and that he would play badly in consequence. "It would be better to postpone this performance until after the other. Perhaps even until a later occasion." For however much Mme Verdurin might look forward to the delicious emotion that she would feel when she knew that her husband was engaged in enlightening Charlie in the next room, she was afraid, if the plan misfired, that he would lose his temper and fail to appear on the 16th.

What caused M. de Charlus's downfall that evening was the ill-breeding—so common in those circles—of the people whom he had invited and who were now beginning to arrive. Having come there partly out of friendship for M. de Charlus and also out of curiosity to explore these novel surroundings, each duchess made straight for the Baron as though it were he who was giving the party, and then said to me, within a yard of the Verdurins, who could hear every word: "Show me which is Mother Verdurin. Do you think I really need to get myself introduced to her? I do hope, at least, that she won't put my name in the paper tomorrow; nobody in my family would ever speak to me again. What, that woman with the white hair? But she looks quite presentable." Hearing some mention of Mlle Vinteuil, who, however, was not in the room, several of them said: "Ah! the sonata-man's daughter? Show me her." And, each of them finding a number of her friends, they formed a group by themselves, watched, bubbling over with ironical curiosity, the arrival of the faithful, but were able at the most to point a finger at the somewhat peculiar hair-style of a person who, a few years later, was to make this the fashion in the highest society, and, in short, regretted that they did not find this salon as different from the salons they knew as they had hoped to find it, feeling the same disappointment that they might have felt if, having gone to Bruant's nightclub in the hope that the *chansonnier* would make a butt of them, they found themselves greeted on their arrival with a polite bow instead of the expected refrain: "Ah! look at that mug, look at that phizog. There's a sight for sore eyes."

M. de Charlus had, at Balbec, given me a perspicacious criticism of Mme de Vaugoubert who, in spite of her considerable intelligence, and after her husband's unexpected success, had brought about his irremediable disgrace. The rulers to whose court M. de Vaugoubert was accredited, King Theodosius and Queen Eudoxia, having returned to Paris, but this time for a prolonged visit, daily festivities had been held in their honour in the course of which the Queen, on friendly terms with Mme de Vaugoubert whom she had seen for the last ten years in her own capital, and knowing neither the wife of the President of the Republic nor the wives of his ministers, had neglected these ladies and kept entirely aloof with the Ambassadress. The latter, believing her own position to be unassailable—M. de Vaugoubert having been responsible for the alliance between King Theodosius and France— had derived from the preference that the Queen showed for her society a self-satisfied pride but no anxiety at the danger which threatened her and which took shape a few months later in M. de Vaugoubert's brutal retirement from the service, an event wrongly considered impossible by the over-confident couple. M. de Charlus, remarking in the "twister" upon the downfall of his childhood

friend, expressed his astonishment that an intelligent
woman had not in such circumstances used all her influence with the King and Queen to persuade them to behave as though she had none, and to transfer their civility
to the wives of the President and his ministers who would
have been all the more flattered by it, that is to say all the
more inclined in their self-contentedness to be grateful to
the Vaugouberts, inasmuch as they would have supposed
that civility to be spontaneous and not dictated by them.
But the man who can see other people's errors often suc-
cumbs to them himself if sufficiently intoxicated by circumstances. And M. de Charlus, while his guests elbowed
their way towards him to congratulate him and thank him
as though he were the master of the house, never thought
of asking them to say a few words to Mme Verdurin.
Only the Queen of Naples, in whom survived the same
noble blood that had flowed in the veins of her sisters the
Empress Elisabeth and the Duchesse d'Alençon, made a
point of talking to Mme Verdurin as though she had
come for the pleasure of meeting her rather than for the
music and for M. de Charlus, made endless gracious
speeches to her hostess, never stopped telling her how
much she had always wanted to make her acquaintance,
complimented her on her house and spoke to her on all
manner of subjects as though she were paying a call. She
would so much have liked to bring her niece Elisabeth,
she said (the niece who shortly afterwards was to marry
Prince Albert of Belgium), who would be so disappointed!
She stopped talking when she saw the musicians mount
the platform, and asked which of them was Morel. She
could scarcely have been under any illusion as to the motives that led M. de Charlus to desire that the young vir-

tuoso should be surrounded with so much glory. But the venerable wisdom of a sovereign in whose veins flowed the blood of one of the noblest families in history, one of the richest in experience, scepticism and pride, made her merely regard the inevitable blemishes of the people whom she loved best, such as her cousin Charlus (whose mother had been a Duchess of Bavaria like herself), as misfortunes that rendered more precious to them the support that they might find in her and consequently gave her all the more pleasure in providing it. She knew that M. de Charlus would be doubly touched by her having taken the trouble to come in these circumstances. Only, being as kind as she had long ago shown herself brave, this heroic woman who, a soldier-queen, had herself fired her musket from the ramparts of Gaeta, always ready to place herself chivalrously on the side of the weak, seeing Mme Verdurin alone and abandoned, and moreover unaware that she ought not to leave the Queen, had sought to pretend that for her, the Queen of Naples, the centre of the evening, the focal point of attraction that had brought her there, was Mme Verdurin. She apologised endlessly for not being able to stay until the end, since, although she never went anywhere, she had to go on to another reception, and begged that by no means, when she had to go, should any fuss be made on her account, thus discharging Mme Verdurin from the honours which the latter did not even know that she ought to render her.

It must however be said in fairness to M. de Charlus that if he entirely forgot Mme Verdurin and allowed her to be ignored to a scandalous degree by the people "of his own world" whom he had invited, he did, on the other hand, realise that he must not allow them to display, during the "musical presentation" itself, the bad manners they were exhibiting towards the Mistress. Morel had already mounted the platform, and the musicians were assembling, but one could still hear conversations, not to say laughter, and remarks such as "Apparently you have to be initiated in order to understand it." Immediately M. de Charlus, drawing himself erect as though he had entered a different body from the one I had seen, a short while before, dragging itself towards Mme Verdurin's door, assumed a prophetic expression and glared at the assembly with a severity which signified that this was no time for laughter, thus bringing a sudden blush to the cheeks of more than one lady caught out like a schoolgirl by her teacher in front of the whole class. To my mind, M. de Charlus's attitude, so noble in other respects, was somehow slightly comic; for at one moment he withered the guests with his blazing eyes, and at the next, in order to indicate to them with a sort of vade-mecum the religious silence it was proper to observe, the detachment from any worldly preoccupation, he himself presented, raising his white-gloved hands to his handsome forehead, a model (to which they were expected to conform) of gravity, already almost of ecstasy, ignoring the greetings of latecomers so indelicate as not to realise that it was now the time for High Art. They were all hypnotised; no one dared to utter another sound, to move a chair; respect for music—by virtue of Palamède's prestige—had been instantaneously inculcated in a crowd as ill-bred as it was elegant.

When I saw not only Morel and a pianist but other instrumentalists too line up on the little platform, I supposed that the programme was to begin with works of

composers other than Vinteuil. For I imagined that the
only work of his in existence was his sonata for piano and
violin.

Mme Verdurin sat alone, the twin hemispheres of her
pale, slightly roseate brow magnificently bulging, her hair
drawn back, partly in imitation of an eighteenth-century
portrait, partly from the need for coolness of a feverish
person reluctant to reveal her condition, aloof, a deity pre-
siding over the musical rites, goddess of Wagnerism and
sick-headaches, a sort of almost tragic Norn, conjured up
by the spell of genius in the midst of all these "bores," in
whose presence she would scorn even more than usual to
express her feelings upon hearing a piece of music which
she knew better than they. The concert began; I did not
know what was being played; I found myself in a strange
land. Where was I to place it? Who was the composer? I
longed to know, and, seeing nobody near me whom I
could ask, I should have liked to be a character in those
Arabian Nights which I never tired of reading and in
which, in moments of uncertainty, there appears a genie,
or a maiden of ravishing beauty, invisible to everyone else
but not to the perplexed hero to whom she reveals exactly
what he wishes to learn. And indeed at that very moment
I was favoured with just such a magical apparition. As
when, in a stretch of country which one thinks one does
not know and which in fact one has approached from a
new direction, after turning a corner one finds oneself
suddenly emerging on to a road every inch of which is familiar, but one had simply not been in the habit of approaching it that way, one suddenly says to oneself:
"Why, this is the lane that leads to the garden gate of my
friends the X——s; I'm only two minutes from their

house," and there, indeed, is their daughter who has come out to greet one as one goes by; so, all of a sudden, I found myself, in the midst of this music that was new to me, right in the heart of Vinteuil's sonata; and, more marvellous than any girl, the little phrase, sheathed, harnessed in silver, glittering with brilliant sonorities, as light and soft as silken scarves, came to me, recognisable in this new guise. My joy at having rediscovered it was enhanced by the tone, so friendly and familiar, which it adopted in addressing me, so persuasive, so simple, and yet without subduing the shimmering beauty with which it glowed. Its intention, however, this time was merely to show me the way, which was not the way of the sonata, for this was an unpublished work of Vinteuil in which he had merely amused himself, by an allusion that was explained at this point by a sentence in the programme which one ought to have been reading simultaneously, by reintroducing the little phrase for a moment. No sooner was it thus recalled than it vanished, and I found myself once more in an unknown world, but I knew now, and everything that followed only confirmed my knowledge, that this world was one of those which I had never even been capable of imagining that Vinteuil could have created, for when, weary of the sonata which was to me a universe thoroughly explored, I tried to imagine others equally beautiful but different, I was merely doing what those poets do who fill their artificial paradise with meadows, flowers and streams which duplicate those existing already upon earth. What was now before me made me feel as keen a joy as the sonata would have given me if I had not already known it, and consequently, while no less beautiful, was different. Whereas the sonata opened upon a lily-

white pastoral dawn, dividing its fragile purity only to
hover in the delicate yet compact entanglement of a rustic
bower of honeysuckle against white geraniums, it was
upon flat, unbroken surfaces like those of the sea on a
morning that threatens storm, in the midst of an eerie silence, in an infinite void, that this new work began, and it
was into a rose-red daybreak that this unknown universe
was drawn from the silence and the night to build up
gradually before me. This redness, so new, so absent from
the tender, pastoral, unadorned sonata, tinged all the sky,
as dawn does, with a mysterious hope. And a song already pierced the air, a song on seven notes, but the
strangest, the most remote from anything I had ever
imagined, at once ineffable and strident, no longer the
cooing of a dove as in the sonata, but rending the air, as
vivid as the scarlet tint in which the opening bars had
been bathed, something like a mystical cock-crow, the
ineffable but ear-piercing call of eternal morning. The
atmosphere, cold, rain-washed, electric—of a quality
so different, subject to quite other pressures, in a world
so remote from the virginal, plant-strewn world of the
sonata—changed continually, eclipsing the crimson promise of the dawn. At noon, however, in a burst of scorching but transitory sunlight, it seemed to reach fulfilment
in a heavy, rustic, almost cloddish gaiety in which the
lurching, riotous clangour of bells (like those which set
the church square of Combray aglow and which Vinteuil, who must often have heard them, had perhaps discovered at that moment in his memory like a colour
which a painter has at hand on his palette) seemed the
material representation of the coarsest joy. Truth to tell,
this joyous motif did not appeal to me aesthetically; I

found it almost ugly, its rhythm was so laboriously earth-
bound that one could have imitated almost all its essen-
tials simply with the noises made by rapping on a table
with drumsticks in a particular way. It seemed to me that
Vinteuil had been lacking, here, in inspiration, and consequently I was a little lacking also in the power of attention.

I looked at the Mistress, whose fierce immobility
seemed to be a protest against the rhythmic noddings of
the ignorant heads of the ladies of the Faubourg. She did
not say: "You realise, of course, that I know a thing or
two about this music! If I were to express all that I feel,
you'd never hear the end of it!" She did not say this. But
her upright, motionless body, her expressionless eyes, her
straying locks said it for her. They spoke also of her
courage, said that the musicians could carry on, that they
need not spare her nerves, that she would not flinch at the
andante, would not cry out at the allegro. I looked at the
musicians. The cellist was hunched over the instrument
which he clutched between his knees, his head bowed forward, his coarse features assuming an involuntary expression of disgust at the more mannerist moments; another
leaned over his double bass, fingering it with the same
domestic patience with which he might have peeled a cab-
bage, while by his side the harpist, a mere child in a short
skirt, framed behind the diagonal rays of her golden
quadrilateral, recalling those which, in the magic chamber
of a sibyl, arbitrarily denote the ether according to the traditional forms, seemed to be picking out exquisite sounds
here and there at designated points, just as though, a tiny
allegorical goddess poised before the golden trellis of the
heavenly vault, she were gathering, one by one, its stars.

As for Morel, a lock, hitherto invisible and submerged in the rest of his hair, had fallen loose and formed a curl on his forehead.

I turned my head slightly towards the audience to discover what M. de Charlus might be feeling at the sight of this curl. But my eyes encountered only Mme Verdurin's face, or rather the hands, for the former was entirely buried in the latter. Did the Mistress wish to indicate by this meditative attitude that she considered herself as though in church, and regarded this music as no different from the most sublime of prayers? Did she wish, as some people do in church, to hide from prying eyes, out of modesty or shame, their presumed fervour or their culpable inattention or an irresistible sleepiness? A regular noise which was not musical gave me momentarily to think that this last hypothesis was the correct one, but I realised later that it was produced by the snores, not of Mme Verdurin, but of her dog.

But very soon, the triumphant motif of the bells having been banished, dispersed by others, I succumbed once again to the music; and I began to realise that if, in the body of this septet, different elements presented themselves one after another to combine at the close, so also Vinteuil's sonata and, as I later discovered, his other works as well, had been no more than timid essays, exquisite but very slight, beside the triumphal and consummate masterpiece now being revealed to me. And I could not help recalling by comparison that, in the same way too, I had thought of the other worlds that Vinteuil had created as being self-enclosed as each of my loves had been; whereas in reality I was obliged to admit that just as, within the context of the last of these—my love for

Albertine—my first faint stirrings of love for her (at Balbec at the very beginning, then after the game of ferret,
then on the night when she slept at the hotel, then in
Paris on the foggy Sunday, then on the night of the Guermantes party, then at Balbec again, and finally in Paris
where my life was now closely linked to hers) had been,
so, if I now considered not my love for Albertine but my
whole life, my other loves too had been no more than
slight and timid essays that were paving the way, appeals
that were unconsciously clamouring, for this vaster love:
my love for Albertine. And I ceased to follow the music,
in order to ask myself once again whether Albertine had
or had not seen Mlle Vinteuil during the last few days, as
one interrogates anew an inner pain from which one has
been distracted for a moment. For it was in myself that
Albertine's possible actions were performed. Of every person we know we possess a double; but, being habitually
situated on the horizon of our imagination, of our memory, it remains more or less extraneous to us, and what it
has done or may have done has no greater capacity to
cause us pain than an object situated at a certain distance
which provides us with only the painless sensations of vision. The things that affect these people we perceive in a
contemplative fashion; we are able to deplore them in appropriate language which gives other people a sense of our
kindness of heart, but we do not feel them. But ever since
the wound I had received at Balbec, it was deep in my
heart, and very difficult to extricate, that Albertine's double was lodged. What I saw of her hurt me, as a sick man
would be hurt whose senses were so seriously deranged
that the sight of a colour would be felt by him internally
like an incision in his living flesh. It was fortunate that I

had not already yielded to the temptation to break with Albertine; the tedium of having to rejoin her presently, when I went home, was a trifling matter compared with the anxiety that I should have felt if the separation had occurred when I still had a doubt about her and before I had had time to grow indifferent to her. And at the moment when I thus pictured her waiting for me at home like a beloved wife, finding the time of waiting long, perhaps having fallen asleep for a while in her room, my ears were caressed by a passing phrase, tender, homely and domestic, of the septet. Perhaps—everything being so interwoven and superimposed in our inner life—it had been inspired in Vinteuil by his daughter's sleep (that daughter who was today the cause of all my distress) when it enveloped the composer's work on peaceful evenings with its quiet sweetness, this phrase which had so much power to calm me by virtue of the same soft background of silence that gives a hushed serenity to certain of Schumann's reveries, during which, even when "the Poet speaks," one can tell that "the child sleeps." Asleep or awake, I should find her again this evening, Albertine, my little child, when I chose to return home. And yet, I said to myself, something more mysterious than Albertine's love seemed to be promised at the outset of this work, in those first cries of dawn. I tried to banish the thought of my mistress and to think only of the musician. Indeed, he seemed to be present. It was as though, reincarnate, the composer lived for all time in his music; one could feel the joy with which he chose the colour of some timbre, harmonising it with the others. For with other and more profound gifts Vinteuil combined that which few composers, and indeed few painters, have possessed, of using colours not merely so lasting but so personal that, just as time has been powerless to spoil their freshness, so the disciples who imitate their discoverer, and even the masters who surpass him, do not dim their originality. The revolution that their apparition has effected does not see its results merge unacknowledged in the work of subsequent generations; it is unleashed, it explodes anew, when, and only when, the works of the once-for-all-time innovator are performed again. Each tone was identified by a colour which all the rules in the world could not have taught the most learned composers to imitate, with the result that Vinteuil, although he had appeared at his appointed hour and had his appointed place in the evolution of music, would always leave that place to stand in the forefront whenever any of his compositions was performed, compositions which would owe their appearance of having originated after the works of more recent composers to this apparently paradoxical and indeed deceptive quality of permanent novelty. A page of symphonic music by Vinteuil, familiar already on the piano, revealed, when one heard it played by an orchestra—like a ray of summer sunlight which the prism of the window decomposes before it enters a dark dining-room—all the jewels of the *Arabian Nights* in unsuspected, multicoloured splendour. But how could one compare to that motionless dazzle of light what was life, perpetual and blissful motion? This Vinteuil, whom I had known so timid and sad, had been capable—when he had to choose a timbre and to blend another with it—of an audacity, and in the full sense of the word a felicity, as to which the hearing of any of his works left one in no doubt. The joy that certain sonorities had caused him, the increase of strength they had given him wherewith to discover others, led the listener on too from one discovery to another, or rather it was the creator himself who guided him, deriving, from the colours he had just hit upon, a wild joy which gave him the strength to discover, to fling himself upon others which they seemed to call for, enraptured, quivering as though from the shock of an electric spark when the sublime came spontaneously to life at the clang of the brass, panting, in-toxicated, unbridled, vertiginous, while he painted his great musical fresco, like Michelangelo strapped to his scaffold and from his upside-down position hurling tu-multuous brush-strokes on to the ceiling of the Sistine Chapel. Vinteuil had been dead for a number of years; but in the sound of these instruments which he had loved, it had been given him to go on living, for an unlimited time, a part at least of his life. Of his life as a man solely? If art was indeed but a prolongation of life, was it worth while to sacrifice anything to it? Was it not as unreal as life itself? The more I listened to this septet, the less I could believe this to be so. No doubt the glowing septet differed singularly from the lily-white sonata; the timid question to which the little phrase replied, from the breathless supplication to find the fulfilment of the strange promise that had resounded, so harsh, so super-natural, so brief, causing the still inert crimson of the morning sky above the sea to vibrate. And yet these very different phrases were composed of the same elements; for, just as there was a certain world, perceptible to us in those fragments scattered here and there, in private houses, in public galleries, which was Elstir's world, the world he saw, the world in which he lived, so too the mu-sic of Vinteuil extended, note by note, stroke by stroke, the unknown, incalculable colourings of an unsuspected world, fragmented by the gaps between the different occasions of hearing his work performed; those two very dissimilar questions that governed the very different movement of the sonata and the septet, the former interrupting a pure, continuous line with brief calls, the latter welding together into an indivisible structure a medley of scattered fragments—one so calm and shy, almost detached and as if philosophical, the other so urgent, anxious, imploring—were nevertheless the same prayer, bursting forth like different inner sunrises, and merely refracted through the different mediums of other thoughts, of artistic researches carried on through the years in which he had sought to create something new. A prayer, a hope which was at heart the same, distinguishable beneath these disguises in the various works of Vinteuil, and at the same time not to be found elsewhere than in his works. For those phrases, historians of music could no doubt find affinities and pedigrees in the works of other great composers, but only for secondary reasons, external resemblances, analogies ingeniously discovered by reasoning rather than felt as the result of a direct impression. The impression conveyed by these Vinteuil phrases was different from any other, as though, in spite of the conclusions which seem to emerge from science, the individual did exist. And it was precisely when he was striving with all his might to create something new that one recognised, beneath the apparent differences, the profound similarities and the deliberate resemblances that existed in the body of a work; when Vinteuil took up the same phrase again and again, diversified it, amused himself by altering its rhythm, by making it reappear in its original form, those deliberate resemblances, the work of his intellect, necessarily superficial, never succeeded in being as striking as the disguised, involuntary resemblances, which broke out in different colours, between the two separate masterpieces; for then Vinteuil, striving to do something new, interrogated himself, with all the power of his creative energy, reached down to his essential self at those depths where, whatever the question asked, it is in the same accent, that is to say its own, that it replies. Such an accent, the accent of Vinteuil, is separated from the accents of other composers by a difference far greater than that which we perceive between the voices of two people, even between the bellowings and the squeals of two animal species; by the real difference that exists between the thought of this or that other composer and the eternal investigations of Vinteuil, the question that he put to himself in so many forms, his habitual speculation, but as free from analytical forms of reasoning as if it were being carried out in the world of the angels, so that we can gauge its depth, but no more translate it into human speech than can disembodied spirits when, evoked by a medium, they are questioned by him about the secrets of death. And even when I bore in mind that acquired originality which had struck me that afternoon, that kinship, too, which musicologists might discover between composers, it is indeed a unique accent, an unmistakable voice, to which in spite of themselves those great singers that original composers are rise and return, and which is a proof of the irreducibly individual existence of the soul. Though Vinteuil might try to make more solemn, more grandiose, or to make more sprightly and gay, to re-create what he saw reflected in the mind of the public, in spite of himself he submerged it all beneath a ground-swell which makes his song eternal and at once recognisable. Where had he learned this song, different from those of other singers, similar to all his own, where had he heard it? Each artist seems thus to be the native of an unknown country, which he himself has forgotten, and which is different from that whence another great artist, setting sail for the earth, will eventually emerge. Certain it was that Vinteuil, in his latest works, seemed to have drawn nearer to that unknown country. The atmosphere was no longer the same as in the sonata, the questioning phrases had become more pressing, more unquiet, the answers more mysterious; the washed-out air of morning and evening seemed to affect the very strings of the instruments. Marvellously though Morel played, the sounds that came from his violin seemed to me singularly piercing, almost shrill. This harshness was pleasing, and, as in certain voices, one felt in it a sort of moral quality and intellectual superiority. But it could shock. When his vision of the universe is modified, purified, becomes more adapted to his memory of his inner homeland, it is only natural that this should be expressed by a musician in a general alteration of sonorities, as of colours by a painter. In any case, the more intelligent section of the public is not misled, since Vinteuil's last compositions were ultimately declared to be his most profound. And yet no programme, no subject matter, supplied any intellectual basis for judgment. One simply sensed that it was a question of the transposition of profundity into terms of sound.

Composers do not remember this lost fatherland, but each of them remains all his life unconsciously attuned to it; he is delirious with joy when he sings in harmony with

his native land, betrays it at times in his thirst for fame,
but then, in seeking fame, turns his back on it, and it is
only by scorning fame that he finds it when he breaks out
into that distinctive strain the sameness of which—for
whatever its subject it remains identical with itself—
proves the permanence of the elements that compose his
soul. But in that case is it not true that those elements—
all the residuum of reality which we are obliged to keep
to ourselves, which cannot be transmitted in talk, even
from friend to friend, from master to disciple, from lover
to mistress, that ineffable something which differentiates
qualitatively what each of us has felt and what he is
obliged to leave behind at the threshold of the phrases in
which he can communicate with others only by limiting
himself to externals, common to all and of no interest—
are brought out by art, the art of a Vinteuil like that of an
Elstir, which exteriorises in the colours of the spectrum
the intimate composition of those worlds which we call
individuals and which, but for art, we should never know?
A pair of wings, a different respiratory system, which enabled us to travel through space, would in no way help
us, for if we visited Mars or Venus while keeping the
same senses, they would clothe everything we could see in
the same aspect as the things of Earth. The only true voyage, the only bath in the Fountain of Youth, would be not
to visit strange lands but to possess other eyes, to see the
universe through the eyes of another, of a hundred others,
to see the hundred universes that each of them sees, that
each of them is; and this we can do with an Elstir, with a
Vinteuil; with men like these we do really fly from star to
star.

The andante had just ended on a phrase filled with a

tenderness to which I had entirely surrendered. There followed, before the next movement, a short interval during
which the performers laid down their instruments and the
audience exchanged impressions. A duke, in order to
show that he knew what he was talking about, declared:
"It's a difficult thing to play well." Other more agreeable
people chatted for a moment with me. But what were
their words, which like every human and external word
left me so indifferent, compared with the heavenly phrase
of music with which I had just been communing? I was
truly like an angel who, fallen from the inebriating bliss of
paradise, subsides into the most humdrum reality. And,
just as certain creatures are the last surviving testimony to
a form of life which nature has discarded, I wondered
whether music might not be the unique example of what
might have been—if the invention of language, the formation of words, the analysis of ideas had not intervened—the means of communication between souls. It is
like a possibility that has come to nothing; humanity has
developed along other lines, those of spoken and written
language. But this return to the unanalysed was so intoxicating that, on emerging from that paradise, contact with
more or less intelligent people seemed to me of an extraordinary insignificance. I had been able, while the music was playing, to remember people, to associate them
with it; or rather I had associated with the music scarcely
more than the memory of one person only, which was Albertine. And the phrase that ended the andante seemed to
me so sublime that I told myself that it was a pity that
Albertine did not know, and if she had known had not
understood, what an honour it was to be associated with
something so great as this which reunited us, and the

heartbreaking voice of which she seemed to have assumed. But once the music was interrupted, the people who were there seemed too insipid. Refreshments were handed round. M. de Charlus hailed a footman now and then with: "How are you? Did you get my note? Can you come?" No doubt there was in these salutations the freedom of the great nobleman who thinks he is flattering his interlocutor and is more one of the people than the bourgeois, but there was also the cunning of the delinquent who imagines that anything one flaunts is on that account considered innocent. And he added, in the Guermantes tone of Mme de Villeparisis: "He's a good boy, a friendly soul, I often employ him at home." But his adroitness turned against the Baron, for people thought his intimate courtesies and correspondence with footmen extraordinary. The footmen themselves were not so much flattered as embarrassed in the presence of their comrades.

Meanwhile the septet, which had begun again, was moving towards its close; again and again one phrase or another from the sonata recurred, but altered each time, its rhythm and harmony different, the same and yet something else, as things recur in life; and they were phrases of the sort which, without our being able to understand what affinity assigns to them as their sole and necessary abode the past of a certain composer, are to be found only in his work, and appear constantly in his work, of which they are the spirits, the dryads, the familiar deities; I had at first distinguished in the septet two or three which reminded me of the sonata. Presently—bathed in the violet mist which was wont to rise particularly in Vinteuil's later work, so much so that, even when he introduced a dance measure, it remained captive in the heart of an opal—I caught a hint of another phrase from the sonata, still so distant that I scarcely recognised it; hesitantly it approached, vanished as though in alarm, then returned, intertwined with others that had come, as I later learned, from other works, summoned yet others which became in their turn seductive and persuasive as soon as they were tamed, and took their places in the round, the divine round that yet remained invisible to the bulk of the audience, who, having before their eyes only a dim veil through which they saw nothing, punctuated arbitrarily with admiring exclamations a continuous boredom of which they thought they would die. Then the phrases withdrew, save one which I saw reappear five times or six without being able to distinguish its features, but so caressing, so different—as no doubt the little phrase from the sonata had been for Swann—from anything that any woman had ever made me desire, that this phrase—this invisible creature whose language I did not know but whom I understood so well—which offered me in so sweet a voice a happiness that it would really have been worth the struggle to obtain, is perhaps the only Unknown Woman that it has ever been my good fortune to meet. Then this phrase broke up, was transformed, like the little phrase in the sonata, and became the mysterious call of the start. A phrase of a plaintive kind rose in answer to it, but so profound, so vague, so internal, almost so organic and visceral, that one could not tell at each of its re-entries whether it was a theme or an attack of neuralgia. Presently these two motifs were wrestling together in a close embrace in which at times one of them would disappear entirely, and then only a fragment of the other could be glimpsed. A wrestling match of disembodied en-

ergies only, to tell the truth; for if these creatures confronted one another, they did so stripped of their physical
bodies, of their appearance, of their names, finding in me
an inward spectator—himself indifferent, too, to names
and particulars—to appreciate their immaterial and dynamic combat and follow passionately its sonorous vicissitudes. In the end the joyous motif was left triumphant; it
was no longer an almost anxious appeal addressed to an
empty sky, it was an ineffable joy which seemed to come
from paradise, a joy as different from that of the sonata as
some scarlet-clad Mantegna archangel sounding a trumpet
from a grave and gentle Bellini seraph strumming a the-
orbo. I knew that this new tone of joy, this summons to a
supraterrestrial joy, was a thing that I would never forget.
But would it ever be attainable to me? This question
seemed to me all the more important inasmuch as this
phrase was what might have seemed most eloquently to
characterise—as contrasting so sharply with all the rest of
my life, with the visible world—those impressions which
at remote intervals I experienced in my life as starting-
points, foundation-stones for the construction of a true
life: the impression I had felt at the sight of the steeples
of Martinville, or of a line of trees near Balbec. In any
case, to return to the particular accent of this phrase, how
strange it was that the presentiment most different from
what life assigns to us on earth, the boldest approximation
to the bliss of the Beyond, should have materialised precisely in the melancholy, respectable little bourgeois
whom we used to meet in the Month of Mary at Combray! But above all, how was it possible that this revelation, the strangest that I had yet received, of an unknown
type of joy, should have come to me from him, since, it

was said, when he died he had left nothing but his sonata, everything else existing only as indecipherable scribblings. Indecipherable they may have been, but they had nevertheless been in the end deciphered, by dint of patience, intelligence and respect, by the only person who had been sufficiently close to Vinteuil to understand his method of working, to interpret his orchestral indications: Mlle Vinteuil's friend. Even in the lifetime of the great composer, she had acquired from his daughter the veneration that the latter felt for her father. It was because of this veneration that, in those moments in which people run counter to their true inclinations, the two girls had been able to take an insane pleasure in the profanations which have already been narrated. (Her adoration of her father was the very condition of his daughter's sacrilege. And no doubt they ought to have forgone the voluptuous pleasure of that sacrilege, but it did not express the whole of their natures.) And, moreover, the profanations had become rarer until they disappeared altogether, as those morbidly carnal relations, that troubled, smouldering conflagration, had gradually given way to the flame of a pure and lofty friendship. Mlle Vinteuil's friend was sometimes tormented by the nagging thought that she might have hastened Vinteuil's death. At any rate, by spending years unravelling the scribblings left by him, by establishing the correct reading of those secret hieroglyphs, she had the consolation of ensuring an immortal and compensatory glory for the composer over whose last years she had cast such a shadow. Relations which are not sanctioned by the law establish bonds of kinship as manifold, as complex, and even more solid, than those which spring from marriage. Indeed, without pausing to consider relations of so special a nature, do we not find every day that adultery, when it is based on genuine love, does not weaken family feelings and the duties of kinship, but rather revivifies them? Adultery then brings the spirit into what marriage would often have left a dead letter. A good daughter who will wear mourning for her mother's second husband for reasons of propriety has not tears enough to shed for the man whom her mother singled out as her lover. In any case Mlle Vinteuil had acted only out of sadism, which did not excuse her, though it gave me a certain consolation to think so later on. No doubt she must have realised, I told myself, at the moment when she and her friend had profaned her father's photograph, that what they were doing was merely morbidity, silliness, and not the true and joyous wickedness which she would have liked to feel. This idea that it was merely a pretence of wickedness spoiled her pleasure. But if this idea recurred to her later on, since it had spoiled her pleasure so it must have diminished her grief. "It wasn't me," she must have told herself, "I was out of my mind. I can still pray for my father's soul, and not despair of his forgiveness." Only it is possible that this idea, which had certainly occurred to her in her pleasure, may not have occurred to her in her grief. I would have liked to be able to put it into her mind. I am sure that I would have done her good and that I could have re-established between her and the memory of her father a more comforting relationship.

As in the illegible note-books in which a chemist of genius, who does not know that death is at hand, jots down discoveries which will perhaps remain for ever unknown, Mlle Vinteuil's friend had disentangled, from papers more illegible than strips of papyrus dotted with a cuneiform script, the formula, eternally true and for ever fertile, of this unknown joy, the mystic hope of the crimson Angel of the Dawn. And I for whom, albeit not so much, perhaps, as for Vinteuil, she had also been, had just been once more this very evening by reawakening my jealousy of Albertine, was to be above all in the future, the cause of so many sufferings, it was thanks to her, in compensation, that I had been able to apprehend the strange summons which I should henceforth never cease to hear, as the promise and proof that there existed something other, realisable no doubt through art, than the nullity that I had found in all my pleasures and in love itself, and that if my life seemed to me so futile, at least it had not yet accomplished everything.

What she had enabled us, thanks to her labour, to know of Vinteuil was to all intents and purposes the whole of Vinteuil's work. Compared with this septet, certain phrases from the sonata which were all that the public knew appeared so commonplace that it was difficult to understand how they could have aroused so much admiration. Similarly we are surprised that, for years past, pieces as trivial as the *Song to the Evening Star* or *Elisabeth's Prayer* can have aroused in the concert-hall fanatical worshippers who wore themselves out applauding and shouting *encore* at the end of what after all seems poor and trite to us who know *Tristan*, the *Rhinegold* and the *Mastersingers*. One must assume that those featureless melodies nevertheless already contained, in infinitesimal and for that reason perhaps more easily assimilable quantities, something of the originality of the masterpieces which alone matter to us in retrospect, but whose very perfection might perhaps have prevented them from being understood; those earlier melodies may have prepared the way for them in people's hearts. But the fact remains that, if they gave a vague presentiment of the beauties to come, they left these in complete obscurity. The same was true of Vinteuil; if at his death he had left behind him—excepting certain parts of the sonata—only what he had been able to complete, what we should have known of him would have been, in relation to his true greatness, as inconsiderable as in the case of, say, Victor Hugo if he had died after the *Pas d'Armes du Roi Jean*, the *Fiancée du Timbalier* and *Sarah la Baigneuse*, without having written a line of the *Légende des Siècles* or the *Contemplations*: what is to us his real achievement would have remained purely potential, as unknown as those universes to which our perception does not reach, of which we shall never have any idea.

Moreover this apparent contrast and profound union between genius (talent too and even virtue) and the sheath of vices in which, as had happened in the case of Vinteuil, it is so frequently contained and preserved, was detectable, as in a popular allegory, in the very assembly of the guests among whom I found myself once again when the music had come to an end. This assembly, albeit limited this time to Mme Verdurin's salon, resembled many others, the ingredients of which are unknown to the general public, and which journalist-philosophers, if they are at all well-informed, call Parisian, or Panamist, or Dreyfusard, never suspecting that they may equally well be found in Petersburg, Berlin, Madrid, and in every epoch; if as a matter of fact the Under Secretary of State for Fine Arts, an artist to his fingertips, well-born and snobby, several duchesses and three ambassadors with their wives were present this evening at Mme Verdurin's, the proximate, immediate cause of their presence lay in the relations that existed between M. de Charlus and Morel, relations which made the Baron anxious to give as wide a celebrity as possible to the artistic triumphs of his young idol, and to obtain for him the cross of the Legion of Honour; the remoter cause which had made this assembly possible was that a girl who enjoyed a relationship with Mlle Vinteuil analogous to that of Charlie and the Baron had brought to light a whole series of works of genius which had been such a revelation that before long a subscription was to be opened under the patronage of the Minister of Education, with the object of erecting a statue to Vinteuil. Moreover, these works had been assisted, no less than by Mlle Vinteuil's relations with her friend, by the Baron's relations with Charlie, a sort of short cut, as it were, thanks to which the world was enabled to catch up with these works without the detour, if not of an incomprehension which would long persist, at least of a complete ignorance which might have lasted for years. Whenever an event occurs which is within the range of the vulgar mind of the journalist-philosopher, a political event as a rule, the journalist-philosophers are convinced that there has been some great change in France, that we shall never see such evenings again, that no one will ever again admire Ibsen, Renan, Dostoievsky, D'Annunzio, Tolstoy, Wagner, Strauss. For the journalist-philosophers take their cue from the equivocal undercurrents of these official manifestations, in order to find something decadent in the art which is there celebrated and which as often as not is more austere than any other. There is not a name, among those most revered by these journalist-philosophers, which has not quite naturally given rise to some such strange gathering, although its strangeness may have been less flagrant and better concealed. In the case of this gathering, the impure elements that came together therein struck me from another aspect; true, I was as well able as anyone to dissociate them, having learned to know them separately; but those which concerned Mlle Vinteuil and her friend, speaking to me of Combray, spoke to me also of Albertine, that is to say of Balbec, since it was because I had long ago seen Mlle Vinteuil at Montjouvain and had learned of her friend's intimacy with Albertine that I was presently, when I returned home, to find, instead of solitude, Albertine awaiting me; and those which concerned Morel and M. de Charlus, speaking to me of Balbec, where I had seen, on the platform at Doncières, their intimacy begin, spoke to me of Combray and of its two "ways," for M. de Charlus was one of those Guermantes, Counts of Combray, inhabiting Combray without having any dwelling there, suspended in mid-air, like Gilbert the Bad in his window, while Morel was the son of that old valet who had introduced me to the lady in pink and enabled me, years after, to identify her as Mme Swann.*

At the moment when, the music having come to an end, his guests came to take leave of him, M. de Charlus committed the same error as on their arrival. He did not ask them to shake hands with their hostess, to include her and her husband in the gratitude that was being showered on himself. There was a long procession, a procession which led to the Baron alone, and of which he was clearly aware, for as he said to me a little later: "The form of the artistic celebration ended in a 'few-words-in-the-vestry'

touch that was quite amusing." The guests even prolonged their expressions of gratitude with various remarks
which enabled them to remain for a moment longer in the
Baron's presence, while those who had not yet congratulated him on the success of his party hung around impatiently in the rear. (Several husbands wanted to go; but
their wives, snobs even though duchesses, protested: "No,
no, even if we have to wait for an hour, we can't go away
without thanking Palamède, who has gone to so much
trouble. There's nobody else these days who can give entertainments like this." Nobody would have thought of
asking to be introduced to Mme Verdurin any more than
to the attendant in a theatre to which some great lady has
for one evening brought the entire aristocracy.)

"Were you at Eliane de Montmorency's yesterday,
cousin?" asked Mme de Mortemart, seeking an excuse to
prolong their conversation.

"As a matter of fact, no; I'm fond of Eliane, but I
never can understand her invitations. I must be very
dense, I'm afraid," he went on with a beaming smile,
while Mme de Mortemart realised that she was to be
made the first recipient of "one of Palamède's" as she had
often been of "one of Oriane's." "I did indeed receive a
card a fortnight ago from the charming Eliane. Above the
questionably authentic name of 'Montmorency' was the
following kind invitation: 'My dear cousin, will you do
me the honour of thinking of me next Friday at halfpast
nine.' Underneath were written the two less gracious
words: 'Czech Quartet.' These seemed to me to be unintelligible, and in any case to have no more connexion with
the sentence above than in those letters on the back of
which one sees that the writer had begun another with the

words 'My dear—' and nothing else, and failed to take a fresh sheet, either from absentmindedness or in order to save paper. I'm fond of Eliane, and so I bore her no ill-will; I merely ignored the strange and inappropriate allusion to a Czech Quartet, and, as I am a methodical man, I placed on my chimney-piece the invitation to think of Madame de Montmorency on Friday at half past nine. Although renowned for my obedient, punctual and meek nature, as Buffon says of the camel"—at this, laughter seemed to radiate from M. de Charlus, who knew that on the contrary he was regarded as the most impossibly difficult man—"I was a few minutes late (the time that it took me to change my clothes), though without feeling undue remorse, thinking that half past nine meant ten. At the stroke of ten, in a comfortable dressing-gown, with warm slippers on my feet, I sat down in my chimney corner to think of Eliane as she had requested me, and with an intensity which did not begin to falter until half past ten. Do tell her, if you will, that I complied strictly with her audacious request. I am sure she will be gratified."

Mme de Mortemart swooned with laughter, in which M. de Charlus joined. "And tomorrow," she went on, oblivious of the fact that she had already long exceeded the time that could reasonably be allotted to her, "are you going to our La Rochefoucauld cousins?"

"Oh, that, now, is quite impossible. They have invited me, and you too, I see, to a thing it is utterly impossible to imagine, which is called, if I am to believe the invitation card, a 'thé dansant.' I used to be considered pretty nimble when I was young, but I doubt whether I could ever decently have drunk a cup of tea while dancing. And I have never cared to eat or drink in an unseemly fashion. You will remind me that my dancing days are done. But even sitting down comfortably drinking my tea—of the quality of which I am in any case suspicious since it is called 'dancing'—I should be afraid lest other guests younger than myself, and less nimble possibly than I was at their age, might spill their cups over my tails and thus interfere with my pleasure in draining my own."

Nor was M. de Charlus content with leaving Mme Verdurin out of the conversation while he spoke of all manner of subjects (which he seemed to take a delight in developing and varying, for the cruel pleasure which he had always enjoyed of keeping indefinitely "queuing up" on their feet the friends who were waiting with excruciating patience for their turn to come); he even criticised all that part of the entertainment for which Mme Verdurin was responsible. "But, talking of cups, what in the world are those strange little bowls which remind me of the vessels in which, when I was a young man, people used to get sorbets from Poiré Blanche? Somebody said to me just now that they were for 'iced coffee.' But I have seen neither coffee nor ice. What curious little objects, with so ill-defined a purpose!"

While saying this M. de Charlus had placed his white-gloved hands vertically over his lips and cautiously swivelled his eyes with a meaning look as though he were afraid of being heard and even seen by his host and hostess. But this was only a pretence, for in a few minutes he would be offering the same criticisms to the Mistress herself, and a little later would be insolently enjoining her: "No more iced-coffee cups, remember! Give them to one of your friends whose house you wish to disfigure. But warn her not to have them in the drawing-room, or people might think that they had come into the wrong room, the things are so exactly like chamberpots."

"But, cousin," said the guest, lowering her voice too and casting a questioning glance at M. de Charlus, for fear of offending not Mme Verdurin but the Baron himself, "perhaps she doesn't yet quite know these things . . ."

"She shall be taught."

"Oh!" laughed the guest, "she couldn't have a better teacher! She *is* lucky! If you're in charge one can be sure there won't be a false note."

"There wasn't one, if it comes to that, in the music."

"Oh! it was sublime. One of those pleasures which can never be forgotten. Talking of that marvellous violinist," she went on, imagining in her innocence that M. de Charlus was interested in the violin for its own sake, "do you happen to know one whom I heard the other day playing a Fauré sonata wonderfully well. He's called Frank . . ."

"Oh, he's ghastly," replied M. de Charlus, oblivious of the rudeness of a contradiction which implied that his cousin was lacking in taste. "As far as violinists are concerned, I advise you to confine yourself to mine."

This led to a fresh exchange of glances, at once furtive and watchful, between M. de Charlus and his cousin, for, blushing and seeking by her zeal to repair her blunder, Mme de Mortemart was about to suggest to M. de Charlus that she might organise an evening to hear Morel play. Now, for her the object of the evening was not to bring an unknown talent into prominence, though this was the object which she would pretend to have in mind and which was indeed that of M. de Charlus. She

regarded it simply as an opportunity for giving a particularly elegant reception and was calculating already whom
she would invite and whom she would leave out. This
process of selection, the chief preoccupation of people who
give parties (the people whom "society" journalists have
the nerve or the stupidity to call "the élite"), alters at
once the expression—and the handwriting—of a hostess
more profoundly than any hypnotic suggestion. Before she
had even thought of what Morel was to play (which she
rightly regarded as a secondary consideration, for even if
everybody observed a polite silence during the music,
from fear of M. de Charlus, nobody would even think of
listening to it), Mme de Mortemart, having decided that
Mme de Valcourt was not to be one of the "chosen," had
automatically assumed that secretive, conspiratorial air
which so degrades even those society women who can
most easily afford to ignore what "people will say."

"Might it be possible for me to give a party for people to hear your friend play?" murmured Mme de
Mortemart, who, while addressing herself exclusively to
M. de Charlus, could not refrain, as though mesmerised,
from casting a glance at Mme de Valcourt (the excluded
one) in order to make certain that she was sufficiently far
away not to hear her. "No, she can't possibly hear what
I'm saying," Mme de Mortemart concluded inwardly, reassured by her own glance which in fact had had a totally
different effect upon Mme de Valcourt from that intended: "Why," Mme de Valcourt had said to herself
when she caught this glance, "Marie-Thérèse is arranging
something with Palamède to which I'm not to be invited."

"You mean my protégé," M. de Charlus corrected, as
merciless to his cousin's choice of words as he was to her

musical endowments. Then, without paying the slightest attention to her mute entreaties, for which she herself apologised with a smile, "Why, yes . . ." he said in a voice loud enough to be heard throughout the room, "although there is always a risk in that sort of exportation of a fascinating personality into surroundings that must inevitably diminish his transcendent gifts and would in any case have to be adapted to them."

Mme de Mortemart told herself that the mezza voce, the pianissimo of her question had been a waste of effort, after the megaphone through which the answer had issued. She was mistaken: Mme de Valcourt heard nothing, for the simple reason that she did not understand a single word. Her anxiety subsided, and would quickly have evaporated entirely, had not Mme de Mortemart, afraid that she might have been given away and might have to invite Mme de Valcourt, with whom she was on too intimate terms to be able to leave her out if the other knew about her party beforehand, raised her eyelids once again in Edith's direction, as though not to lose sight of a threatening peril, lowering them again briskly so as not to commit herself too far. She intended, on the morning after the party, to write her one of those letters, the complement of the revealing glance, letters which are meant to be subtle but are tantamount to a full and signed confession. For instance: "Dear Edith, I've been missing you. I did not really expect you last night" ("How could she have expected me," Edith would say to herself, "since she never invited me?") "as I know that you're not very fond of gatherings of that sort which rather bore you. We should have been greatly honoured, all the same, by your company" (Mme de Mortemart never used the word "honoured," except in letters in which she attempted to cloak a lie in the semblance of truth). "You know that you are always welcome in our house. In any case you were quite right, as it was a complete failure, like everything that is got up at a moment's notice." But already the second furtive glance darted at her had enabled Edith to grasp everything that was concealed by the complicated language of M. de Charlus. This glance was indeed so potent that, after it had struck Mme de Valcourt, the obvious secrecy and intention to conceal that it betrayed rebounded upon a young Peruvian whom Mme de Mortemart intended, on the contrary, to invite. But being of a suspicious nature, seeing all too plainly the mystery that was being made without realising that it was not intended to mystify him, he at once conceived a violent hatred for Mme de Mortemart and vowed to play all sorts of disagreeable hoaxes on her, such as ordering fifty iced coffees to be sent to her house on a day when she was not entertaining, or, on a day when she was, inserting a notice in the papers to the effect that the party was postponed, and publishing mendacious accounts of subsequent parties in which would appear the notorious names of all the people whom for various reasons a hostess does not invite or even allow to be introduced to her.

Mme de Mortemart need not have bothered herself about Mme de Valcourt. M. de Charlus was about to take it upon himself to denature the projected entertainment far more than that lady's presence would have done. "But, my dear cousin," she said in response to the remark about "adapting the surroundings," the meaning of which her momentary state of hyperaesthesia had enabled her to discern, "we shall spare you the least trouble. I undertake to ask Gilbert to arrange everything."

"Not on any account, and moreover he will not be invited. Nothing will be done except through me. The first thing is to exclude all those who have ears and hear not."

M. de Charlus's cousin, who had been reckoning on Morel as an attraction in order to give a party at which she could say that, unlike so many of her kinswomen, she had "had Palamède," abruptly switched her thoughts from this prestige of M. de Charlus's to all the people with whom he would get her into trouble if he took it upon himself to do the inviting and excluding. The thought that the Prince de Guermantes (on whose account, partly, she was anxious to exclude Mme de Valcourt, whom he declined to meet) was not to be invited alarmed her. Her eyes assumed an uneasy expression.

"Is this rather bright light bothering you?" inquired M. de Charlus with an apparent seriousness the underlying irony of which she failed to perceive.

"No, not at all. I was thinking of the difficulty, not because of me of course, but because of my family, if Gilbert were to hear that I had given a party without inviting him, when he never has half a dozen people in without . . ."

"But precisely, we must begin by eliminating the half-dozen people, who would only jabber. I'm afraid that the din of talk has prevented you from realising that it was a question not of doing the honours as a hostess but of conducting the rites appropriate to every true celebration."

Then, having decided, not that the next person had

been kept waiting too long, but that it did not do to exaggerate the favours shown to one who had in mind not so much Morel as her own visiting-list, M. de Charlus, like a doctor cutting short a consultation when he considers that it has lasted long enough, served notice on his cousin to withdraw, not by bidding her good-night but by turning to the person immediately behind her.

"Good evening, Madame de Montesquiou. It was marvellous, wasn't it? I didn't see Hélène. Tell her that any policy of general abstention, even the most noble, that is to say hers, must allow exceptions, if they are dazzling enough, as has been the case tonight. To show that one is rare is good, but to subordinate one's rarity, which is only negative, to what is precious is better still. In your sister's case—and I value more than anyone her systematic *absence* from places where what is in store for her is not worthy of her—here tonight, on the contrary, her presence at so memorable an occasion as this would have been a precedence, and would have given your sister, already so prestigious, an additional prestige."

Then he turned to a third lady.

I was greatly astonished to see there, as friendly and flattering towards M. de Charlus as he had been curt with him in the past, insisting on being introduced to Charlie and telling him that he hoped he would come and see him, M. d'Argencourt, that terrible scourge of the species of men to which M. de Charlus belonged. At the moment he was living in the thick of them. It was certainly not because he had become one of them himself. But for some time past he had more or less deserted his wife for a young society woman whom he adored. Being intelligent herself, she made him share her taste for intelligent people, and was most anxious to have M. de Charlus to her house. But above all M. d'Argencourt, extremely jealous and somewhat impotent, feeling that he was failing to satisfy his conquest and anxious to keep her amused, could do so without risk to himself only by surrounding her with innocuous men, whom he thus cast in the role of guardians of his seraglio. The latter found that he had become quite pleasant and declared that he was a great deal more intelligent than they had supposed, a discovery that delighted him and his mistress.

The remainder of M. de Charlus's guests drifted away fairly rapidly. Several of them said: "I don't want to go to the sacristy" (the little room in which the Baron, with Charlie by his side, was receiving congratulations), "but I must let Palamède see me so that he knows that I stayed to the end." Nobody paid the slightest attention to Mme Verdurin. Some pretended not to recognise her and deliberately said good-night to Mme Cottard, appealing to me for confirmation with a "That *is* Mme Verdurin, isn't it?" Mme d'Arpajon asked me in our hostess's hearing: "Tell me, has there ever been a Monsieur Verdurin?" The duchesses who still lingered, finding none of the oddities they had expected in this place which they had hoped to find more different from what they were used to, made the best of a bad job by going into fits of laughter in front of Elstir's paintings; for everything else, which they found more in keeping than they had expected with what they were already familiar with, they gave the credit to M. de Charlus, saying: "How clever Palamède is at arranging things! If he were to stage a pantomime in a shed or a bathroom, it would still be perfectly ravishing." The most noble ladies were those who showed most fervour in congratulating M. de Charlus upon the success of a party of the secret motive for which some of them were not unaware, without however being embarrassed by the knowledge, this class of society—remembering perhaps certain epochs in history when their own families had already arrived in full consciousness at a similar effrontery—carrying their contempt for scruples almost as far as their respect for etiquette. Several of them engaged Charlie on the spot for different evenings on which he was to come and play them Vinteuil's septet, but it never occurred to any of them to invite Mme Verdurin.

The latter was already blind with fury when M. de Charlus who, his head in the clouds, was incapable of noticing her state, decided that it was only seemly to invite the Mistress to share his joy. And it was perhaps to indulge his taste for literature rather than from an overflow of pride that this specialist in artistic entertainments said to Mme Verdurin: "Well, are you satisfied? I think you have reason to be. You see that when I take it upon myself to organise a festivity there are no half-measures. I don't know whether your heraldic notions enable you to gauge the precise importance of the event, the weight that I have lifted, the volume of air that I have displaced for you. You have had the Queen of Naples, the brother of the King of Bavaria, the three premier peers. If Vinteuil is Muhammad, we may say that we have brought to him some of the least movable of mountains. Bear in mind that to attend your party the Queen of Naples came up from Neuilly, which is a great deal more difficult for her than it was to leave the Two Sicilies," he added with malicious intent, notwithstanding his admiration for the Queen. "It's a historic event. Just think that it's perhaps the first time she has gone anywhere since the fall of Gaeta. It may well be that the history books will record as climactic dates the day of the fall of Gaeta and that of the Verdurin reception. The fan that she laid down the better to applaud Vinteuil deserves to become more famous than the fan that Mme de Metternich broke because the audience hissed Wagner."

"In fact she left it here," said Mme Verdurin, momentarily appeased by the memory of the Queen's kindness to her, and she showed M. de Charlus the fan which was lying on a chair.

"Oh, how moving!" exclaimed M. de Charlus, approaching the relic with veneration. "It is all the more touching for being so hideous; the little violet is incredible!" And spasms of emotion and irony ran through him by turns. "Oh dear, I don't know whether you feel these things as I do. Swann would positively have died of convulsions if he had seen it. I know that whatever price it fetches, I shall buy that fan at the sale of the Queen's belongings, for she's bound to be sold up, she hasn't a penny," he went on, for he never ceased to intersperse the cruellest gossip with the most sincere veneration, although they sprang from two opposing natures, which, however, were combined in him. (They might even be brought to bear alternately on the same fact. For the M. de Charlus who from his comfortable position as a rich man jeered at the poverty of the Queen was the same who was often to be heard extolling that poverty and who, when anyone spoke of Princess Murat, Queen of the Two Sicilies, would reply: "I don't know who you mean. There is only one Queen of Naples, a sublime person who does not keep a carriage. But from her omnibus she annihilates

every carriage in the street and one could kneel down in
the dust on seeing her drive past.") "I shall bequeath it to
a museum. In the meantime, it must be sent back to her,
so that she need not hire a cab to come and fetch it. The
wisest thing, in view of the historical interest of such
an object, would be to steal the fan. But that would be
awkward for her—since it is probable that she does not
possess another!" he added with a shout of laughter.
"Anyhow, you see that for my sake she came. And that
is not the only miracle I have performed. I don't believe
that anyone at the present day has the power to shift the
people whom I persuaded to come. However, everyone
must be given his due. Charlie and the rest of the musicians played divinely. And, my dear hostess," he added
condescendingly, "you yourself have played your part on
this occasion. Your name will not go unrecorded. History
has preserved that of the page who armed Joan of Arc
when she set out for battle. In sum, you served as a
connecting link, you made possible the fusion between
Vinteuil's music and its inspired interpreter, you had the
intelligence to appreciate the cardinal importance of the
whole concatenation of circumstances which would enable
the interpreter to benefit from the whole weight of a considerable—if I were not referring to myself I might almost say providential—personage, whom you had the
good sense to ask to ensure the success of the gathering,
to bring before Morel's violin the ears directly attached to
the tongues that have the widest hearing; no, no, it's by
no means negligible. Nothing is negligible in so complete
a realisation. Everything has its part. The Duras was marvellous. In fact, everything; that is why," he concluded,
for he could not resist admonishing people, "I set my face

against your inviting those human divisors who, among
the superior people whom I brought you, would have
played the part of the decimal points in a sum, reducing
the others to a merely fractional value. I have a very exact
appreciation of that sort of thing. You realise that we
must avoid social blunders when we are giving a party
which is to be worthy of Vinteuil, of his inspired interpreter, of yourself, and, I venture to say, of me. If you
had invited the Molé woman, everything would have been
spoiled. It would have been the tiny counteracting, neu-
tralising drop which deprives a potion of its virtue. The
electric lights would have fused, the pastries would not
have arrived in time, the orangeade would have given
everybody a stomach-ache. She was the one person not to
have here. At the mere sound of her name, as in a fairy-
tale, not a note would have issued from the brass; the
flute and the oboe would have suddenly lost their voices.
Morel himself, even if he had succeeded in playing a few
bars, would not have been in tune, and instead of Vinteuil's septet you would have had a parody of it by
Beckmesser, ending amid catcalls. I who believe strongly
in the influence of personalities could feel quite plainly in
the blossoming of a certain largo, which opened out like a
flower, and in the supreme fulfilment of the finale, which
was not merely allegro but incomparably lively,[14] that the
absence of the Molé was inspiring the musicians and
causing the very instruments to swell with joy. In any
case, when one is at home to queens one does not invite
one's concierge."

In calling her "the Molé" (as for that matter he said
quite affectionately "the Duras") M. de Charlus was doing the lady justice. For all these women were the ac-

tresses of society, and it is true that, even regarding her
from this point of view, the Comtesse Molé did not live
up to the extraordinary reputation for intelligence that she
had acquired, which reminded one of those mediocre actors or novelists who at certain periods are hailed as men
of genius, either because of the mediocrity of their com-
petitors, among whom there is no supreme artist capable
of showing what is meant by true talent, or because of the
mediocrity of the public, which, if any extraordinary individuality existed, would be incapable of understanding it.
In Mme Molé's case it is preferable, if not entirely accurate, to settle for the former explanation. The social world
being the realm of nullity, there exist between the merits
of different society women only the most insignificant degrees, which can however be crazily exaggerated by the
rancours or the imagination of a M. de Charlus. And certainly, if he spoke as he had just been speaking in this
language which was an affected mixture of artistic and social elements, it was because his old-womanly rages and
his culture as a man of society provided the genuine eloquence that he possessed with only the most trivial
themes. Since the world of differentials does not exist on
the surface of the earth among all the countries which our
perception renders uniform, all the more reason why it
should not exist in the social "world." But does it exist
anywhere? Vinteuil's septet had seemed to tell me that it
did. But where?

Since M. de Charlus also enjoyed repeating what one
person had said of another, seeking to stir up trouble, to
divide and rule, he added: "You have, by not inviting her,
deprived Mme Molé of the opportunity of saying: 'I can't
think why this Mme Verdurin should have invited me. I

can't imagine who these people are, I don't know them.'
She was already saying a year ago that you were wearying
her with your advances. She's a fool; never invite her
again. After all, she's nothing so very wonderful. She can
perfectly well come to your house without making a fuss
about it, seeing that I come here. In short," he concluded,
"it seems to me that you have every reason to thank me,
for, as far as it went, the whole thing was perfect. The
Duchesse de Guermantes didn't come, but one never
knows, perhaps it was better that she didn't. We shan't
hold it against her, we'll think of her all the same another
time, not that one can help remembering her, her very
eyes say to us 'Forget me not!', for they remind one of
those flowers" (here I thought to myself how strong the
Guermantes spirit—the decision to go to one house and
not to another—must be, to have outweighed in the
Duchess's mind her fear of Palamède). "Faced with so
complete a success, one is tempted like Bernardin de
Saint-Pierre to see everywhere the hand of Providence.
The Duchesse de Duras was enchanted. She even asked
me to tell you so," added M. de Charlus, dwelling upon
the words as though Mme Verdurin must regard this as a
sufficient honour. Sufficient and indeed scarcely credible,
for he thought it necessary, in order to be believed, to add
"Yes, indeed," completely carried away by the madness of
those whom Jupiter has decided to destroy. "She has engaged Morel to come to her house, where the same programme will be repeated, and I'm even thinking of asking
her for an invitation for M. Verdurin." This civility to the
husband alone was, although no such idea even occurred
to M. de Charlus, the most cruel insult to the wife, who,
believing herself to possess with regard to the violinist, by

virtue of a sort of ukase which prevailed in the little clan, the right to forbid him to perform elsewhere without her express authorisation, was absolutely determined to forbid his appearance at Mme de Duras's party.

The Baron's volubility was in itself an irritation to Mme Verdurin, who did not like people to form separate conversational groups within the little clan. How often, even at La Raspelière, hearing M. de Charlus talking incessantly to Charlie instead of being content with taking his part in the concerted ensemble of the clan, had she not pointed to him and exclaimed: "What a windbag he is! What a windbag! He really is the most colossal windbag!"?[15] But this time it was far worse. Intoxicated by the sound of his own voice, M. de Charlus failed to realise that by acknowledging Mme Verdurin's role and confining it within narrow limits, he was unleashing that feeling of hatred which was in her only a special, social form of jealousy. Mme Verdurin was genuinely fond of her regular visitors, the faithful of the little clan, but wished them to be entirely devoted to their Mistress. Cutting her losses, like those jealous lovers who will tolerate unfaithfulness, but only under their own roof and even in front of their eyes, that is to say when it scarcely counts as unfaithfulness, she would allow the men to have mistresses or male lovers, on condition that the affair had no social consequence outside her own house, that the tie was formed and perpetuated in the shelter of her Wednesdays. In the old days, every furtive giggle that came from Odette when she was with Swann had gnawed at Mme Verdurin, and so of late had every aside exchanged by Morel and the Baron; she found one consolation alone for her vexations, which was to destroy the happiness of others. She would have been unable to endure the Baron's for long. And here was that rash individual precipitating the catastrophe by appearing to restrict the Mistress's position in her little clan. Already she could see Morel going into society, without her, under the Baron's aegis. There was only one remedy, to make Morel choose between the Baron and herself, and, taking advantage of the ascendancy that she had acquired over Morel by giving him proof of her extraordinary perspicacity thanks to reports which she commissioned and lies which she herself concocted, all of which served to corroborate what he himself was inclined to believe, and what would in time be made plain to him thanks to the booby-traps which she was preparing and into which her unsuspecting victims would fall—taking advantage of this ascendancy, to make him choose herself in preference to the Baron. As for the society ladies who had been present and had not even asked to be introduced to her, as soon as she grasped their hesitations or indifference, she had said: "Ah! I see what they are, the sort of old frumps that don't fit in with us. It's the last time they'll set foot in this house." For she would have died rather than admit that anyone had been less civil to her than she had hoped.

"Ah! my dear General," M. de Charlus suddenly exclaimed, abandoning Mme Verdurin on catching sight of General Deltour, Secretary to the Presidency of the Republic, who might be of great value in securing Charlie his medal, and who, after asking Cottard for a piece of advice, was slipping away. "Good evening, my dear, delightful friend. Trying to get away without saying goodbye to me, eh?" said the Baron with a genial, self-satisfied smile, for he knew quite well that people were always glad to stay a little longer to talk to him. And as, in his present state of exhilaration, he would answer his own questions in a shrill tone: "Well, did you enjoy it? Wasn't it really beautiful? The andante, what? It's the most touching thing that was ever written. I defy anyone to listen to the end without tears in his eyes. Charming of you to have come. By the way, I had the most excellent telegram this morning from Froberville, who tells me that as far as the Chancellery of the Legion goes the difficulties have been smoothed over, as they say." M. de Charlus's voice continued to rise, as piercing, as different from his normal voice, as that of a barrister grandiloquently addressing the court: a phenomenon of vocal amplification through over-excitement and nervous euphoria analogous to that which, at her own dinner-parties, raised to so high a pitch the voice and gaze alike of Mme de Guermantes.

"I intended to send you a note tomorrow by messenger to tell you of my enthusiasm, until I could find an opportunity to speak to you, but you were so popular! Froberville's support is not to be despised, but for my own part, I have the Minister's promise," said the General.

"Ah! excellent. Anyhow you've seen for yourself that it's no more than what such talent deserves. Hoyos was delighted. I didn't manage to see the Ambassadress. Was she pleased? Who would not have been, except those that have ears and hear not, which doesn't matter so long as they have tongues and can speak."

Taking advantage of the Baron's having moved away to speak to the General, Mme Verdurin beckoned to Brichot. The latter, who did not know what she was about to say, sought to amuse her, and without suspecting the anguish that he was causing me, said to the Mistress: "The Baron is delighted that Mlle Vinteuil and her friend didn't come. They shock him terribly. He declares that their morals are appalling. You can't imagine how prudish and severe the Baron is on moral questions." Contrary to Brichot's expectation, Mme Verdurin was not amused: "He's unspeakable," was her answer. "Suggest to him that he should come and smoke a cigarette with you, so that my husband can get hold of his Dulcinea without his noticing and warn him of the abyss at his feet."

Brichot seemed to hesitate.

"I don't mind telling you," Mme Verdurin went on, to remove his final scruples, "that I don't feel at all safe with a man like that in the house. I know he's been involved in some nasty business and the police have their eye on him." And, as she had a certain talent for improvisation when inspired by malice, Mme Verdurin did not stop at this: "Apparently he's been in prison. Yes, yes, I've been told by people who knew all about it. In any case I know from a person who lives in his street that you can't imagine the ruffians he brings to his house." And as Brichot, who often went to the Baron's, began to protest, Mme Verdurin, growing more and more animated, exclaimed: "But I assure you! You can take my word for it," an expression with which she habitually sought to give weight to an assertion flung out more or less at random. "He'll be found murdered in his bed one of these days, as those people always are. It may not quite come to that, perhaps, because he's in the clutches of that Jupien whom he had the impudence to send to me and who's an ex-convict—yes, really, I know it for a positive fact. He has a hold on him because of some letters which are perfectly dreadful, it seems. I got it from somebody who has seen them and who told me: 'You'd be sick on the spot if you saw them.' That's how Jupien gets him to toe the line and makes him cough up all the money he wants. I'd sooner die than live in the state of terror Charlus lives in. In any case, if Morel's family decides to bring an action against him, I've no desire to be dragged in as an accessory. If he goes on, it will be at his own risk, but I shall have done my duty. What is one to do? It's no joke, I can tell you."

And, already agreeably excited at the thought of her husband's impending conversation with the violinist, Mme Verdurin said to me: "Ask Brichot whether I'm not a courageous friend, and whether I'm not capable of sacrificing myself to save my comrades." (She was alluding to the circumstances in which she had forced him in the nick of time to break first of all with his laundress and then with Mme de Cambremer, as a result of which Brichot had gone almost completely blind and, people said, had taken to morphine.)

"An incomparable friend, farsighted and valiant," replied the Professor with ingenuous fervour.

"Mme Verdurin prevented me from doing something extremely foolish," Brichot told me when she had left us. "She doesn't hesitate to strike at the roots. She's an interventionist, as our friend Cottard would say. I admit, however, that the thought that the poor Baron is still unconscious of the blow that is about to fall upon him distresses me deeply. He's completely mad about that boy. If Mme Verdurin succeeds, there's a man who is going to be very miserable. However, I'm not at all sure she won't fail. I fear that she may only succeed in sowing discord between them, which in the end, without separating them, will only make them break with her."

It was often thus with Mme Verdurin and her faithful. But it was evident that the need she felt to preserve their friendship was more and more dominated by the requirement that this friendship should never be thwarted by the friendship they might feel for one another. She had no objection to homosexuality so long as it did not tamper with the orthodoxy of the little clan, but, like the Church, she preferred any sacrifice rather than a concession on orthodoxy. I was beginning to be afraid that her irritation with myself might be due to her having heard that I had prevented Albertine from going to her that day, and that she might presently set to work, if she had not already begun, upon the same task of separating her from me which her husband, in the case of Charlus, was now going to attempt with the violinist.

"Come along, get hold of Charlus, find some excuse, there's no time to lose," said Mme Verdurin, "and whatever you do, don't let him come back here until I send for you. Ah! what an evening," she added, revealing the true cause of her rage. "Performing a masterpiece in front of those nitwits. I don't include the Queen of Naples, she's intelligent, she's a nice woman" (which meant: "She was nice to me"). "But the others. Ah! it's enough to drive you mad. After all, I'm no longer a schoolgirl. When I was young, people used to tell me that one had to put up with a bit of boredom, so I made an effort; but now, ah! no, I just can't help it, I'm old enough to do as I please, life's too short. Allow myself to be bored stiff, listen to idiots, smile, pretend to think them intelligent—no, I simply can't do it. Go along, Brichot, there's no time to lose."

"I'm going, Madame, I'm going," said Brichot, as General Deltour moved away. But first of all the Professor took me aside for a moment: "Moral Duty," he said, "is less clearly imperative than our Ethics teach us. Whatever the theosophical coffee-houses and the Kantian beer-cellars may say, we are deplorably ignorant of the nature of the Good. I myself who, without wishing to boast, have lectured to my pupils, in all innocence, on the philosophy of the aforesaid Immanuel Kant, can see no precise directive for the case of social casuistry with which I am now confronted in that *Critique of Practical Reason* in which the great unfrocked priest of Protestantism platonised in the Teutonic manner for a prehistorically sentimental and aulic Germany, in the obscure interests of a Pomeranian mysticism. It's the *Symposium* once again, but held this time at Königsberg, in the local style, indigestible and sanitised, with sauerkraut and without gigolos. It is obvious on the one hand that I cannot refuse our excellent hostess the small service that she asks of me, in fully orthodox conformity with traditional Morality. One must avoid above all else—for there are few things that engender more inanities than that one—letting oneself be duped by words. But after all, one cannot but admit that if mothers were entitled to vote, the Baron would run the risk of being lamentably blackballed for the Chair of Virtue. It is unfortunately with the temperament of a rake that he pursues the vocation of a pedagogue. Mind you, I don't wish to speak ill of the Baron. He can be as amusing as a superior clown, whereas with the average colleague of mine, Academician though he be, I am bored, as Xenophon would say, at a hundred drachmas to the hour. Moreover this gentle man, who can carve a joint like nobody else, combines with a genius for anathema a wealth of kindness. But I fear that he is expending upon Morel rather more than a wholesome morality would enjoin, and without knowing to what extent the young penitent shows himself docile or recalcitrant to the special exercises which his catechist imposes upon him by way of mortification, one does not need to be a mastermind to be aware that we should be erring, as they say, on the side of mansuetude with regard to this Rosicrucian who seems to have come down to us from Petronius by way of Saint-Simon, if we granted him with our eyes shut, duly signed and sealed, a licence to satanise. And yet, in keeping this man occupied while Mme Verdurin, for the sinner's good and indeed justly tempted by such a cure of souls, proceeds—by speaking unequivocally to the young harum-scarum—to remove from him all that he loves, to deal him perhaps a fatal blow, it seems to me that I am leading him into what might be termed an ambush, and I recoil from it as though from an act of treachery."

This said, he did not hesitate to commit it, but, taking me by the arm, approached M. de Charlus: "Shall we go and smoke a cigarette, Baron. This young man hasn't yet seen all the marvels of the house." I made the excuse that I was obliged to go home. "Wait just another minute," said Brichot. "You know you're supposed to be giving me a lift, and I haven't forgotten your promise." "Are you sure you wouldn't like me to get them to show you the silver plate? Nothing could be simpler," said M. de Charlus. "You promised me, remember, not a word about Morel's decoration. I mean to give him a surprise by announcing it presently when people have begun to leave, although he says that it is of no importance to an artist, but that his uncle would like him to have it" (I blushed, for the Verdurins knew through my grandfather who Morel's uncle was). "Then you wouldn't like me to get them to bring out the best pieces?" said M. de Charlus. "But you know them already, you've seen them a dozen times at La Raspelière."

I did not venture to tell him that what might have interested me was not the mediocre glitter of even the most opulent bourgeois silver, but some specimen, were it only reproduced in a fine engraving, of Mme du Barry's. I was far too preoccupied and—even without this revelation as to Mlle Vinteuil's expected presence—always, in society, far too distracted and agitated to fasten my attention on objects, however beautiful. It could have been arrested only by the appeal of some reality that addressed itself to my imagination, as might have done, this evening, a picture of that Venice of which I had thought so much during the afternoon, or some general element, common to several aspects and truer than they, which, of its own accord, never failed to awake in me an inner spirit, habitually dormant, the ascent of which to the surface of my consciousness filled me with joy. Now, as I emerged from the room known as the concert-room and crossed the other drawing-rooms with Brichot and M. de Charlus, on discovering, transposed among others, certain pieces of furniture which I had seen at La Raspelière and to which I had paid no attention, I perceived, between the arrangement of the town house and that of the country house, a certain family resemblance, a permanent identity, and I understood what Brichot meant when he said to me with a smile: "There, look at this room, it may perhaps give you an idea of what things were like in the Rue Mon-

talivet, twenty-five years ago, *grande mortalis aevi spa-
tium.*" From his smile, a tribute to the defunct salon
which he saw with his mind's eye, I understood that what
Brichot, perhaps without realising it, preferred in the old
drawing-room, more than the large windows, more than
the gay youth of his hosts and their faithful, was that unreal aspect (which I myself could discern from certain
similarities between La Raspelière and the Quai Conti) of
which, in a drawing-room as in everything else, the actual, external aspect, verifiable by everyone, is but the
prolongation, the aspect which has detached itself from
the outer world to take refuge in our soul, to which it
gives as it were a surplus-value, in which it is absorbed
into its habitual substance, transforming itself—houses
that have been pulled down, people long dead, bowls of
fruit at suppers which we recall—into that translucent al-
abaster of our memories of which we are incapable of conveying the colour which we alone can see, so that we can
truthfully say to other people, when speaking of these
things of the past, that they can have no conception of
them, that they are unlike anything they have seen, and
that we ourselves cannot inwardly contemplate without a
certain emotion, reflecting that it is on the existence of
our thoughts that their survival for a little longer depends,
the gleam of lamps that have been extinguished and the
fragrance of arbours that will never bloom again. And
doubtless for this reason, the drawing-room in the Rue
Montalivet diminished, for Brichot, the Verdurins' present
home. But on the other hand it added to this home, in the
Professor's eyes, a beauty which it could not have in those
of a newcomer. Those pieces of the original furniture that
had been transplanted here, and sometimes arranged in

the same groups, and which I myself remembered from
La Raspelière, introduced into the new drawing-room
fragments of the old which recalled it at moments to the
point of hallucination and then seemed themselves scarcely
real from having evoked in the midst of the surrounding
reality fragments of a vanished world which one seemed
to see elsewhere. A sofa that had risen up from dream-
land between a pair of new and thoroughly substantial armchairs, little chairs upholstered in pink silk, the brocaded
covering of a card-table raised to the dignity of a person
since, like a person, it had a past, a memory, retaining
in the chill and gloom of the Quai Conti the tan of its
sun-warming through the windows of the Rue Montalivet
(where it could tell the time of day as accurately as Mme
Verdurin herself) and through the glass doors at La
Raspelière, where they had taken it and where it used to
gaze out all day long over the flower-beds of the garden at
the valley below, until it was time for Cottard and the violinist to sit down to their game; a bouquet of violets and
pansies in pastel, the gift of a painter friend, now dead,
the sole surviving fragment of a life that had vanished
without leaving any trace, epitomising a great talent and a
long friendship, recalling his gentle, searching eyes, his
shapely, plump and melancholy hand as he painted it; the
attractively disordered clutter of the presents from the
faithful which had followed the lady of the house from
place to place and had come in time to assume the fixity
of a trait of character, of a line of destiny; the profusion of
cut flowers, of chocolate-boxes, which here as in the
country systematised their efflorescence in accordance
with an identical mode of blossoming; the curious inter-

polation of those singular and superfluous objects which still appear to have just been taken from the box in which they were offered and remain for ever what they were at first, New Year presents; all those things, in short, which one could not have isolated from the rest but which for Brichot, an old habitué of Verdurin festivities, had that patina, that velvety bloom of things to which, giving them a sort of depth, a spiritual *Doppelgänger* has come to be attached—all this sent echoing round him so many scattered chords, as it were, awakening in his heart cherished resemblances, confused reminiscences which, here in this actual drawing-room that was speckled with them, cut out, defined, delimited—as on a fine day a shaft of sunlight cuts a section in the atmosphere—the furniture and carpets, pursued, from a cushion to a flower-stand, from a footstool to a lingering scent, from a lighting arrangement to a colour scheme, sculpted, evoked, spiritualised, called to life, a form which was as it were the idealisation, immanent in each of their successive homes, of the Verdurin drawing-room.

"We must try," Brichot whispered in my ear, "to get the Baron on to his favourite topic. He's prodigious." Now on the one hand I was glad of an opportunity to try to obtain from M. de Charlus information as to the movements of Mlle Vinteuil and her friend, information for which I had decided to leave Albertine that evening. On the other hand, I did not wish to leave the latter too long alone, not that she could (being uncertain of the moment of my return, not to mention that, at so late an hour, she could not have received a visitor or left the house herself without being noticed) make any nefarious use of my ab-

sence, but simply so that she might not find it too prolonged. And so I told Brichot and M. de Charlus that I
must shortly leave them.

"Come with us all the same," said the Baron, whose
social excitement was beginning to flag, but feeling that
need to prolong, to spin out a conversation, which I had
already observed in the Duchesse de Guermantes as well
as in himself, and which, while peculiarly characteristic of
their family, extends in a more general fashion to all those
who, offering their minds no other fulfilment than talk,
that is to say an imperfect fulfilment, remain unsatisfied
even after hours in company and attach themselves more
and more hungrily to their exhausted interlocutor, from
whom they mistakenly expect a satiety which social pleasures are incapable of giving. "Come, won't you," he repeated. "This is the pleasant moment at a party, the
moment when all the guests have gone, the hour of Doña
Sol; let us hope that it will end less tragically.[16] Unfortunately you're in a hurry, in a hurry, no doubt, to go and
do things which you would much better leave undone.
People are always in a hurry, and leave at the moment
when they ought to be arriving. We're like Couture's
philosophers,[17] this is the time to go over the events of the
evening, to carry out what is called in military parlance a
review of operations. We might ask Mme Verdurin to
send us in a little supper to which we should take care not
to invite her, and we might request Charlie—still
Hernani—to play for us alone the sublime adagio. Isn't it
simply beautiful, that adagio? But where *is* the young violinist, I should like to congratulate him; this is the moment for tender words and embraces. Do admit, Brichot,
that they played like gods, Morel especially. Did you no-

tice the moment when that lock of hair came loose? Ah, my dear fellow, then you saw nothing at all. There was an F sharp which was enough to make Enesco, Capet and Thibaud die of jealousy. Calm though I am, I don't mind telling you that at the sound of it I had such a lump in the throat I could scarcely control my tears. The whole room sat breathless. Brichot, my dear fellow," cried the Baron, gripping the other's arm and shaking it violently, "it was sublime. Only young Charlie preserved a stony immobility, you couldn't even see him breathe, he looked like one of those objects of the inanimate world of which Théodore Rousseau speaks, which make us think but do not think themselves. And then all of a sudden," cried M. de Charlus with a grandiloquent gesture as though miming a *coup de théâtre*, "then, the Forelock! And meanwhile, the graceful little quadrille of the allegro vivace. You know, that lock was a revelatory sign even for the most obtuse. The Princess of Taormina, deaf until then, for there are none so deaf as those that have ears and hear not, the Princess of Taormina, confronted by the message of the miraculous forelock, suddenly realised that it was music they were playing and not poker. Oh, that was indeed a solemn moment."

"Forgive me for interrupting you, Monsieur," I said to M. de Charlus, to bring him to the subject in which I was interested, "you told me that the composer's daughter was to be present. I should have been most interested to meet her. Are you certain she was expected?"

"Oh, that I couldn't say."

M. de Charlus thus complied, perhaps involuntarily, with that universal rule by which one withholds information from a jealous lover, whether with the absurd intention of proving oneself a "good pal"—as a point of hon-our, and even if one hates her—to the woman who has excited his jealousy, or out of malice towards her because one guesses that jealousy would only intensify his love, or from that need to be disagreeable to other people which consists in telling the truth to the rest of the world but concealing it from the jealous, ignorance increasing their torment, or so at least they suppose—and in order to cause people pain one is guided by what they themselves believe, wrongly perhaps, to be most painful.

"You know," he went on, "in this house they're a tri-fle prone to exaggerate. They're charming people, but still they do like to entice celebrities of one sort or another. But you're not looking well, and you'll catch cold in this damp room," he said, pushing a chair towards me. "Since you haven't been well, you must take care of yourself. Let me go and fetch your coat. No, don't go for it yourself, you'll lose your way and catch cold. How careless people are; you might be an infant in arms, you want an old nanny like me to look after you." "Don't worry, Baron, I'll go," said Brichot, and went off at once: not being pre-cisely aware perhaps of the very warm affection that M. de Charlus had for me and of the charming lapses into simplicity and devotedness that alternated with his fren-zied outbursts of arrogance and persecution mania, he was afraid lest the Baron, whom Mme Verdurin had entrusted like a prisoner to his vigilance, might simply be seeking, under the pretext of asking for my overcoat, to return to Morel, and thus upset the Mistress's plan.

Meanwhile Ski had sat down, uninvited, at the piano, and assuming—with a playful knitting of his brows, a distant gaze and a slight twist of his lips—what he imagined to be an artistic air, was insisting that Morel should play something by Bizet. "What, you don't like it, that boyish side to Bizet's music? Why, my dearr fellow," he said, with that rolling of the *r* which was one of his peculiarities, "it's rravishing." Morel, who did not like Bizet, said so in exaggerated terms and (as he had the reputation in the little clan of being, though it seems incredible, a wit) Ski, pretending to take the violinist's diatribes as paradoxes, burst out laughing. His laugh was not, like M. Verdurin's, the choking fit of a smoker. Ski first of all assumed a subtle air, then let out, as though in spite of himself, a single note of laughter, like the first clang from a belfry, followed by a silence in which the subtle look seemed to be judiciously examining the comic quality of what was said; then a second peal of laughter shook the air, followed presently by a merry angelus.

I expressed to M. de Charlus my regret that M. Brichot should have put himself out. "Not at all, he's delighted. He's very fond of you, everyone's fond of you. Somebody was saying only the other day: 'But we never see him now, he's cut himself off.' Besides, he's such a good fellow, Brichot," M. de Charlus went on, doubtless never suspecting, in view of the frank and affectionate manner in which the Professor of Moral Philosophy conversed with him, that he had no hesitation in pulling him to pieces behind his back. "He is a man of great merit, immensely learned, and his learning hasn't shrivelled him up, hasn't turned him into a pedantic bookworm like so many others, who smell of ink. He has retained a breadth of outlook, a tolerance, rare in his kind. Sometimes, when one sees how well he understands life, with what a natural grace he renders everyone his due, one wonders where a humble little Sorbonne professor, a former school-master, can have picked it all up. I'm astonished at it myself."

I was even more astonished to see the conversation of this Brichot, which the least discriminating of Mme de Guermantes's guests would have found so dull and heavy, impressing the most critical of them all, M. de Charlus. Among the influences that had contributed towards this result were those, in other respects different, by virtue of which Swann had on the one hand so long enjoyed the company of the little clan, when he was in love with Odette, and on the other hand, after he married, seen an attraction in Mme Bontemps who, pretending to adore the Swanns, came constantly to call on the wife, revelled in the husband's stories, and spoke of them with scorn. Like a writer who gives the palm for intelligence, not to the most intelligent man, but to the worldling who utters a bold and tolerant comment on the passion of a man for a woman, a comment which makes the writer's blue-stocking mistress agree with him in deciding that of all the people who come to her house the least stupid is after all this old beau who is experienced in matters of love, so M. de Charlus found Brichot more intelligent than the rest of his friends, Brichot who was not merely kind to Morel, but would cull from the Greek philosophers, the Latin poets, the oriental storytellers, appropriate texts which decorated the Baron's propensity with a strange and charming florilegium. M. de Charlus had reached the age at which a Victor Hugo chooses to surround himself mainly with Vacqueries and Meurices.[18] He preferred to all others those men who tolerated his outlook upon life. "I see a great deal of him," he went on in a measured squeak, allowing no movement save of his lips to disturb the grave, powdered mask of his face, over which his ecclesiastical eyelids were deliberately lowered. "I attend his lectures: that Latin Quarter atmosphere refreshes me: there's a studious, thoughtful breed of young bourgeois, more intelligent, better read than were, in a different milieu, my own contemporaries. It's another world, which you know probably better than I do: they're young *bourgeois*," he said, detaching the last word to which he prefixed a string of *b*s, and emphasising it from a sort of elocutionary habit, itself corresponding to a taste for fine shades of meaning that was peculiar to him, but perhaps also from inability to resist the pleasure of giving me a flick of his insolence. This did not in any way diminish the great and affectionate pity that M. de Charlus inspired in me (after Mme Verdurin had revealed her plan in my hearing); it merely amused me, and, even in circumstances when I did not feel so kindly disposed towards him, would not have offended me. I derived from my grandmother such a want of self-importance as could easily make me seem lacking in dignity. Doubtless I was little aware of this, and by dint of having seen and heard, from my schooldays onwards, my most highly regarded companions refuse to tolerate an affront, refuse to overlook disloyal behaviour, I had come in time to exhibit in my speech and actions a second nature which was tolerably proud. It was indeed considered to be extremely proud, because, being not in the least timorous, I was easily provoked into duels, the moral prestige of which, however, I diminished by making little of them, which easily persuaded other people that they were absurd. But the true nature which we repress continues nevertheless to abide within us. Thus it is that at times, if we read the latest masterpiece of a man of genius, we are delighted to find in it all those of our own reflexions which we have despised, joys and sorrows which we have repressed, a whole world of feelings we have scorned, and whose value the book in which we discover them afresh suddenly teaches us. I had come to learn from my experience of life that it was a mistake to smile a friendly smile when somebody made fun of me, instead of getting angry. But this absence of self-importance and resentment, if I had so far ceased to express it as to have become almost entirely unaware that it existed in me, was nevertheless the primordial vital element in which I was steeped. Anger and spite came to me only in a wholly different manner, in fits of rage. What was more, the notion of justice, to the extent of a complete absence of moral sense, was unknown to me. I was in my heart of hearts entirely on the side of the weaker party, and of anyone who was in trouble. I had no opinion as to the proportion in which good and evil might be blended in the relations between Morel and M. de Charlus, but the thought of the sufferings that were in store for M. de Charlus was intolerable to me. I would have liked to warn him, but did not know how to do so.

"The spectacle of that industrious little world is very pleasing to an old stick like myself. I do not know them," he went on, raising his hand with a depreciatory air, in order not to appear to be boasting, to testify to his own purity and not to allow any suspicion to hover over that of the students—"but they are most polite, they often go so far as to keep a place for me, since I'm a very old gentleman. Yes indeed, my dear boy, do not protest, I'm past forty," said the Baron, who was past sixty. "It's a trifle stuffy in the hall in which Brichot lectures, but it's always an interesting experience."

Although the Baron preferred to mingle with the scholarly young and indeed to be jostled by them, sometimes, to save him a long wait in the lecture-room, Brichot took him in by his own door. For all that Brichot was at home in the Sorbonne, at the moment when the beadle, loaded with his chains of office, stepped out before him, and the master so admired by his young students followed, he could not overcome a certain shyness, and much as he desired to profit by that moment in which he felt himself so important to display his affability towards Charlus, he was nevertheless slightly embarrassed; so that the beadle should allow him in, he said to him in an artificial tone and with a busy air: "Follow me, Baron, they'll find a place for you," then, without paying any further attention to him, to make his own entry he advanced briskly and alone down the aisle. On either side, a double hedge of young lecturers bowed to him; Brichot, anxious not to appear to be posing in front of these young men, in whose eyes he knew that he was a great pundit, bestowed on them countless winks, countless little nods of complicity, to which his desire to remain martial and thoroughly French gave the effect of a sort of cordial encouragement, the *sursum corda* of an old soldier saying: "We'll fight them, God damn it!" Then the applause of the students broke out. Brichot sometimes extracted from this attendance by M. de Charlus at his lectures an opportunity for giving pleasure, almost for returning hospitality. He would say to some parent, or to one of his bourgeois friends: "If it would interest your wife or daughter, I may tell you that the Baron de Charlus, Prince d'Agrigente, a scion of the House of Condé, will be attending my lecture. For a young person, to have seen one of the last descendants of our aristocracy who preserves the type will be a memory to cherish. If they care to come, they will recognise him from the fact that he'll be seated next to my rostrum. Besides, he'll be the only one, a stout man, with white hair and black moustaches, wearing the military medal." "Oh, thank you," the father would say; and although his wife had other things to do, in order not to offend Brichot he would force her to attend the lecture, while the daughter, troubled by the heat and the crowd, nevertheless gazed intently at the descendant of Condé, surprised that he was not wearing a ruff and that he looked just like a man of the present day. He, meanwhile, had no eyes for her, but more than one student, who did not know who he was, would be astonished at his friendly glances and become self-conscious and stiff, and the Baron would depart full of dreams and melancholy.

"Forgive me if I return to the subject," I said quickly to M. de Charlus, for I could hear Brichot returning, "but could you let me know by wire if you should hear that Mlle Vinteuil or her friend is expected in Paris, letting me know exactly how long they will be staying and without telling anybody that I asked you."

I had almost ceased to believe that she had been expected, but I wanted thus to be forewarned for the future.

"Yes, I will do that for you. First of all because I owe you a great debt of gratitude. By not accepting what I proposed to you long ago, you rendered me, to your own loss, an immense service: you left me my liberty. It is true that I have abdicated it in another fashion," he added in a melancholy tone which betrayed a desire to confide in me. "But it's something that I continue to regard as a major factor, a whole combination of circumstances which you failed to turn to your own account, possibly because fate warned you at that precise minute not to obstruct my path. For always man proposes and God disposes. If, that day when we came away together from Mme de Villeparisis's, you had accepted, perhaps—who knows?—many things that have since happened would never have occurred."

In some embarrassment, I turned the conversation by seizing on the name of Mme de Villeparisis, and saying how sad I had been to hear of her death.[19] "Ah, yes," M. de Charlus muttered drily and insolently, taking note of my condolences without appearing to believe in their sincerity for a moment. Seeing that in any case the subject of Mme de Villeparisis was not painful to him, I sought to find out from him, since he was so well qualified in every respect, for what reasons she had been held at arm's length by the aristocratic world. Not only did he not give me the solution to this little social problem, he did not even appear to be aware of it. I then realised that the position of Mme de Villeparisis, which was in later years to appear great to posterity, and even in the Marquise's lifetime to the ignorant commonalty, had appeared no less great—at the opposite extremity of society, that which touched Mme de Villeparisis—to the Guermantes family. She was their aunt; they saw first and foremost birth, connexions by marriage, the opportunity of impressing this or that sister-in-law with the importance of their family. They saw it all less from the social than from the family point of view. Now this was more lustrous in the case of Mme de Villeparisis than I had supposed. I had been struck when I heard that the title Villeparisis was falsely assumed. But there are other examples of great ladies who have married beneath them and preserved a leading position in society. M. de Charlus began by informing me that Mme de Villeparisis was a niece of the famous Duchesse de——, the most celebrated member of the higher aristocracy during the July Monarchy, who had nevertheless refused to associate with the Citizen King and his family. I had so longed to hear stories about this duchess! And Mme de Villeparisis, the kind Mme de Villeparisis, with those cheeks that for me had represented the cheeks of a middle-class lady, Mme de Villeparisis who sent me so many presents and whom I could so easily have seen every day, Mme de Villeparisis was her niece, brought up by her, in her very home, in the Hôtel de——.

"She asked the Duc de Doudeauville," M. de Charlus told me, "speaking of the three sisters, 'Which of the sisters do you prefer?' And when Doudeauville said: 'Mme de Villeparisis,' the Duchesse de —— replied 'Pig!' For the Duchess was extremely *witty*," said M. de Charlus, giving the word the importance and the special emphasis that was customary among the Guermantes. That he should find the expression so "witty" did not moreover surprise me, for I had on many other occasions remarked the centrifugal, objective tendency which leads men to abjure, when they are relishing the wit of others, the severity with which they would judge their own, and to observe and treasure what they would have scorned to create.

"But what on earth is he doing? That's my overcoat

he's bringing," he said, on seeing that Brichot had made so long a search to no better effect. "I would have done better to go myself. However, you can put it over your shoulders. Are you aware that it's highly compromising, my dear boy, it's like drinking out of the same glass: I shall be able to read your thoughts. No, not like that, come, let me do it," and arranging his overcoat round me, he smoothed it over my shoulders, fastened it round my throat, and brushed my chin with his hand apologetically. "At his age, he doesn't know how to put on a coat, one has to cosset him. I've missed my vocation, Brichot, I was born to be a nanny."

I wanted to leave, but M. de Charlus having expressed his intention of going in search of Morel, Brichot detained us both. Moreover, the certainty that when I went home I should find Albertine there, a certainty as absolute as that which I had felt in the afternoon that she would return home from the Trocadéro, made me at this moment as little impatient to see her as I had been then, while sitting at the piano after Françoise had telephoned me. And it was this sense of security that enabled me, whenever, in the course of this conversation, I attempted to rise, to obey the injunctions of Brichot who was afraid that my departure might prevent Charlus from remaining until Mme Verdurin came to fetch us.

"Come," he said to the Baron, "stay with us a little longer, you shall give him the accolade presently." Brichot focused upon me as he spoke his almost sightless eyes, to which the many operations that he had undergone had restored some degree of life, but which no longer had the mobility necessary to the sidelong expression of malice.

"The accolade, how absurd!" cried the Baron, in a

shrill and rapturous tone. "I tell you, dear boy, he always imagines he's at a prize-giving, he day-dreams about his young pupils. I often wonder whether he doesn't sleep with them."

"You wish to meet Mlle Vinteuil," said Brichot, who had overheard the last words of our conversation. "I promise to let you know if she comes. I shall hear of it from Mme Verdurin." For he doubtless foresaw that the Baron was in grave danger of imminent expulsion from the little clan.

"I see, so you think that I have less claim than yourself upon Mme Verdurin," said M. de Charlus, "to be informed of the arrival of these terribly disreputable persons. They're quite notorious, you know. Mme Verdurin is wrong to allow them to come here, they're only fit for low company. They're friends with a terrible gang, and they must meet in the most appalling places."

At each of these words, my anguish was augmented by a new anguish, and its aspect constantly changed. And, suddenly remembering certain gestures of impatience which Albertine instantly repressed, I was terrified that she had already conceived a plan to leave me. This suspicion made it all the more necessary for me to prolong our life together until such time as I should have recovered my serenity. And in order to rid Albertine of the idea, if she entertained it, of forestalling my plan to break with her, in order to make her chains seem lighter until I could put my intention into practice without too much pain, the shrewd thing to do (perhaps I was infected by the presence of M. de Charlus, by the unconscious memory of the play-acting he liked to indulge in), the shrewd thing to do seemed to be to give Albertine to understand that I myself intended to leave her. As soon as I returned home, I would simulate farewells, a final rupture.

"Of course I don't think I have more influence with Mme Verdurin than you do," Brichot emphatically declared, afraid that he might have aroused the Baron's suspicions. And seeing that I was anxious to leave, he sought to detain me with the bait of the promised entertainment: "There is one thing which the Baron seems to me not to have taken into account when he speaks of the reputation of these two ladies, namely that a person's reputation may be at the same time appalling and undeserved. Thus for instance, in the more notorious of these groups which I may venture to call unofficial, it is certain that miscarriages of justice are many and that history has recorded convictions for sodomy against illustrious men who were wholly innocent of the charge. The recent discovery of Michelangelo's passionate love for a woman is a fresh fact which should entitle the friend of Leo X to the benefit of a posthumous retrial. The Michelangelo case seems to me to be eminently calculated to excite the snobs and mobilise the underworld when another case, in which anarchy was all the rage and became the fashionable sin of our worthy dilettantes, but which must not even be mentioned now for fear of stirring up quarrels, shall have run its course."

From the moment Brichot had begun to speak of masculine reputations, M. de Charlus had betrayed all over his features that special sort of impatience which one sees on the face of a medical or military expert when society people who know nothing about the subject begin to talk nonsense about points of therapeutics or strategy.

"You don't know the first thing about these matters,"

he finally said to Brichot. "Give me a single example of an undeserved reputation. Mention a few names . . . Yes, I know it all," he retorted vehemently to a timid interruption by Brichot, "the people who tried it once long ago out of curiosity, or out of affection for a dead friend, and the person who's afraid he has gone too far, and if you speak to him of the beauty of a man, replies that it's all Greek to him, that he can no more distinguish between a beautiful man and an ugly one than between the engines of two motor-cars, mechanics not being in his line. That's all stuff and nonsense. Mind you, I don't mean to say that a bad (or what is conventionally so called) and yet undeserved reputation is absolutely impossible. But it's so exceptional, so rare, that for practical purposes it doesn't exist. At the same time, I who am by nature inquisitive and enjoy ferreting things out, have known cases which were not mythical. Yes, in the course of my life I have verified (I mean scientifically verified—I'm not talking hot air) two unjustified reputations. They generally arise from a similarity of names, or from certain outward signs, a profusion of rings, for instance, which persons who are not qualified to judge imagine to be characteristic of what you were mentioning, just as they think that a peasant never utters a sentence without adding *jarniguié*, 'I d'ny God,' or an Englishman 'Goddam.' It's the conventionalism of the boulevard theatre."

M. de Charlus surprised me greatly when he cited among the inverts the "friend of the actress" whom I had seen at Balbec and who was the leader of the little society of the four friends.

"But this actress, then?"

"She serves him as a cover, and besides he has relations with her, perhaps more than with men, with whom he has hardly any."

"Does he have relations with the other three?"

"No, not at all! They're not at all friends in that way! Two are entirely for women. One of them is, but isn't sure about his friend, and in any case they hide their doings from each other. What will surprise you is that the unjustified reputations are those most firmly established in the eyes of the public. You yourself, Brichot, who would stake your life on the virtue of some man or other who comes to this house and whom the initiated would recognise a mile away, you feel obliged to believe like everyone else what is said about someone in the public eye who is the incarnation of those propensities to the common herd, when as a matter of fact he doesn't care a sou for that sort of thing. I say a sou, because if we were to offer twenty-five louis, we should see the number of plaster saints dwindle down to nothing. As things are, the average rate of sanctity, if you see any sanctity in that sort of thing, is somewhere between three and four out of ten."

If Brichot had transferred to the male sex the question of bad reputations, in my case, conversely, it was to the female sex that, thinking of Albertine, I applied the Baron's words. I was appalled at his statistic, even when I bore in mind that he probably inflated his figures in accordance with what he himself would have wished, and based them moreover on the reports of persons who were scandalmongers and possibly liars, and had in any case been led astray by their own desire, which, added to that of M. de Charlus himself, doubtless falsified his calculations.

"Three out of ten!" exclaimed Brichot. "Why, even if
the proportions were reversed I should still have to multi-
ply the guilty a hundredfold. If it is as you say, Baron,
and you are not mistaken, then we must confess that you
are one of those rare visionaries who discern a truth which
nobody round them has ever suspected. Just as Barrès
made discoveries as to parliamentary corruption the truth
of which was afterwards established, like the existence of
Leverrier's planet. Mme Verdurin would cite for preference men whom I would rather not name who detected in
the Intelligence Bureau, in the General Staff, activities inspired, I'm sure, by patriotic zeal but which I had never
imagined. On freemasonry, German espionage, drug addiction, Léon Daudet concocts day by day a fantastic
fairy-tale which turns out to be the barest truth. Three
out of ten!" Brichot repeated in stupefaction. And it is
true to say that M. de Charlus taxed the great majority of
his contemporaries with inversion, excepting, however, the
men with whom he himself had had relations, their case,
provided there had been some element of romance in
those relations, appearing to him more complex. So it is
that we see Lotharios who refuse to believe in women's
honour making an exception in the case of one who has
been their mistress and of whom they protest sincerely
and with an air of mystery: "No, no, you're mistaken, she
isn't a whore." This unlooked-for tribute is dictated partly
by their own vanity for which it is more flattering that
such favours should have been reserved for them alone,
partly by their gullibility which all too easily swallows
everything that their mistress has led them to believe,
partly from that sense of the complexity of life whereby,
as soon as one gets close to other people, other lives, ready-

made labels and classifications appear unduly crude. "Three out of ten! But have a care, Baron: less fortunate than the historians whose conclusions the future will justify, if you were to present to posterity the statistics that you offer us, it might find them erroneous. Posterity judges only on documentary evidence, and will insist on being shown your files. But as no document would be forthcoming to authenticate this sort of collective phenomenon which the initiated are only too concerned to leave in obscurity, the tender-hearted would be moved to indignation, and you would be regarded as nothing more than a slanderer or a lunatic. After having won top marks and unquestioned supremacy in the social examinations on this earth, you would taste the sorrows of being blackballed beyond the grave. The game is not worth the candle, to quote—may God forgive me—our friend Bossuet."

"I'm not interested in history," replied M. de Charlus, "this life is sufficient for me, it's quite interesting enough, as poor Swann used to say."

"What, you knew Swann, Baron? I didn't know that. Tell me, was he that way inclined?" Brichot inquired with an air of misgiving.

"What a mind the man has! So you think I only know men of that sort? No, I don't think so," said Charlus, looking at the ground and trying to weigh the pros and cons. And deciding that, since he was dealing with Swann whose contrary tendencies had always been so notorious, a half-admission could only be harmless to him who was its object and flattering to him who let it out in an insinuation: "I don't deny that long ago in our schooldays, once in a while," said the Baron, as though in spite of himself and thinking aloud; then pulling himself up:

"But that was centuries ago. How do you expect me to re-member? You're embarrassing me," he concluded with a laugh.

"In any case he was never what you'd call a beauty!" said Brichot who, himself hideous, thought himself good-looking and was always ready to pronounce other men ugly.

"Hold your tongue," said the Baron, "you don't know what you're talking about. In those days he had a peaches-and-cream complexion, and," he added, finding a fresh note for each syllable, "he was as pretty as a cherub. Besides he was always charming. The women were madly in love with him."

"But did you ever know his wife?"

"Why, it was through me that he came to know her. I had thought her charming in her boyish get-up one evening when she played Miss Sacripant; I was with some club-mates, and each of us took a woman home with him, and although all I wanted was to go to sleep, slanderous tongues alleged—it's terrible how malicious people are— that I went to bed with Odette. In any case she took ad-vantage of the slanders to come and bother me, and I thought I might get rid of her by introducing her to Swann. From that moment on she never let me go. She couldn't spell the simplest word, it was I who wrote all her letters for her. And it was I who, later on, was re-sponsible for taking her out. That, my boy, is what comes of having a good reputation, you see. Though I only half deserved it. She used to force me to get up the most dreadful orgies for her, with five or six men."

And the lovers whom Odette had had in succession (she had been with this, that and the other man, not one of whose names had ever been guessed by poor Swann, blinded by jealousy and by love, by turns weighing up the chances and believing in oaths, more affirmative than a contradiction which the guilty woman lets slip, a contradiction far more elusive and yet far more significant, of which the jealous lover might take advantage more logically than of the information which he falsely pretends to have received, in the hope of alarming his mistress), these lovers M. de Charlus began to enumerate with as absolute a certainty as if he had been reciting the list of the Kings of France. And indeed the jealous lover, like the contemporaries of a historical event, is too close, he knows nothing, and it is for strangers that the chronicle of adultery assumes the precision of history, and prolongs itself in lists which are a matter of indifference to them and become painful only to another jealous lover, such as I was, who cannot help comparing his own case with that which he hears spoken of and wonders whether the woman he suspects cannot boast an equally illustrious list. But he can never find out; it is a sort of universal conspiracy, a "blind man's buff" in which everyone cruelly participates, and which consists, while his mistress flits from one to another, in holding over his eyes a bandage which he is perpetually trying to tear off without success, for everyone keeps him blindfold, poor wretch, the kind out of kindness, the cruel out of cruelty, the coarse-minded out of their love of coarse jokes, the well-bred out of politeness and good-breeding, and all alike respecting one of those conventions which are called principles.

"But did Swann ever know that you had enjoyed her favours?"

"What an idea! Confess such a thing to Charles! It's

enough to make one's hair stand on end. Why, my dear fellow, he would have killed me on the spot, he was as jealous as a tiger. Any more than I ever confessed to Odette, not that she would have minded in the least, that . . . But you mustn't make my tongue run away with me. And the joke of it is that it was she who fired a revolver at him, and nearly hit me. Oh! I used to have a fine time with that couple; and naturally it was I who was obliged to act as his second against d'Osmond, who never forgave me. D'Osmond had carried off Odette, and Swann, to console himself, had taken as his mistress, or make-believe mistress, Odette's sister. But really you mustn't start making me tell you Swann's story, or we should be here all night—nobody knows more about it than I do. It was I who used to take Odette out when she didn't want to see Charles. It was all the more awkward for me as I have a very close kinsman who bears the name Crécy, without of course having any sort of right to it, but still he was none too well pleased. For she went by the name of Odette de Crécy, as she perfectly well could, being merely separated from a Crécy whose wife she still was—an extremely authentic one, he, a most estimable gentleman out of whom she had drained his last farthing. But why should I have to tell you about this Crécy? I've seen you with him on the twister, you used to have him to dinner at Balbec. He must have needed it, poor fellow, for he lived on a tiny allowance that Swann made him, and I'm very much afraid that, since my friend's death, that income must have stopped altogether. What I do not understand," M. de Charlus said to me, "is that, since you used often to go to Charles's, you didn't ask me this evening to present you to the Queen of Naples. In fact I can see that you're not interested in *people* as curiosities, and that always surprises me in someone who knew Swann, in whom that sort of interest was so highly developed that it's impossible to say whether it was I who initiated him in these matters or he me. It surprises me as much as if I met a person who had known Whistler and remained ignorant of what is meant by taste. However, it was chiefly important for Morel to meet her. He was passionately keen to as well, for he's nothing if not intelligent. It's a nuisance that she's gone. However, I shall effect the conjunction one of these days. It's inevitable that he'll get to know her. The only possible obstacle would be if she were to die in the night. Well, it's to be hoped that that won't happen."

All of a sudden Brichot, who was still suffering from the shock of the proportion "three out of ten" which M. de Charlus had revealed to him, and had continued to pursue the idea all this time, burst out with an abruptness which was reminiscent of an examining magistrate seeking to make a prisoner confess but which was in reality the result of the Professor's desire to appear perspicacious and of the misgivings that he felt about launching so grave an accusation: "Isn't Ski like that?" he inquired of M. de Charlus with a sombre air. He had chosen Ski in order to show off his alleged intuitive powers, telling himself that since there were only three innocents in every ten, he ran little risk of being mistaken if he named Ski, who seemed to him a trifle odd, suffered from insomnia, used scent, in short was not entirely normal.

"But not in the *least*!" exclaimed the Baron with bitter, dogmatic, exasperated irony. "What you say is so wrong, so absurd, so wide of the mark! Ski is like that precisely to the people who know nothing about it. If he was, he wouldn't look so like it, be it said without any intention to criticise, for he has a certain charm, indeed I find there's something very engaging about him."

"But give us a few names, then," Brichot persisted. M. de Charlus drew himself up with a haughty air.

"Ah! my dear Sir, I, as you know, live in the world of the abstract; all this interests me only from a transcendental point of view," he replied with the querulous touchiness peculiar to men of his kind, and the affectation of grandiloquence that characterised his conversation. "To me, you understand, it's only general principles that are of any interest. I speak to you of this as I might of the law of gravity." But these moments of irritable retraction in which the Baron sought to conceal his true life lasted but a short time compared with the hours of continual progression in which he allowed it to betray itself, flaunted it with an irritating complacency, the need to confide being stronger in him than the fear of disclosure. "What I meant to say," he went on, "is that for one bad reputation that is unjustified there are hundreds of good ones which are no less so. Obviously, the number of those who don't deserve their reputations varies according to whether you rely on what is said by their own kind or by others. And it is true that if the malevolence of the latter is limited by the extreme difficulty they would find in believing that a vice as horrible to them as robbery or murder can be practised by people whom they know to be sensitive and kind, the malevolence of the former is stimulated to excess by the desire to regard as—how shall I put it?—accessible, men who attract them, on the strength of information given them by people who have been led astray by a similar desire, in fact by the very aloofness with which they are generally regarded. I've heard a man who was somewhat ill thought of on account of these tastes say that he supposed that a certain society figure shared them. And his sole reason for believing it was that this society figure had been polite to him! All the more reason for *optimism*," said the Baron artlessly, "in the computation of the number. But the true reason for the enormous disparity between the number calculated by the layman and the number calculated by the initiated arises from the mystery with which the latter surround their actions, in order to conceal them from the rest, who, lacking any means of knowing, would be literally stupefied if they were to learn merely a quarter of the truth."

"So in our day things are as they were among the Greeks," said Brichot.

"What do you mean, among the Greeks? Do you suppose that it hasn't been going on ever since? Take the reign of Louis XIV. You have Monsieur, young Vermandois, Molière, Prince Louis of Baden, Brunswick, Charolais, Boufflers, the Great Condé, the Duc de Brissac."

"Stop a moment. I knew about Monsieur, I knew about Brissac from Saint-Simon, Vendôme of course, and many others as well. But that old pest Saint-Simon often refers to the Great Condé and Prince Louis of Baden and never mentions it."

"It seems rather deplorable, I must say, that I should have to teach a Professor of the Sorbonne his history. But, my dear fellow, you're as ignorant as a carp."

"You are harsh, Baron, but just. But wait a moment, now this will please you: I've just remembered a song of the period composed in macaronic verse about a storm in

which the Great Condé was caught as he was going down
the Rhône in the company of his friend the Marquis de
La Moussaye. Condé says:

> *Carus Amicus Mussaeus,*
> *Ah! Deus bonus, quod tempus!*
>   *Landerirette,*
> *Imbre sumus perituri.*

And La Moussaye reassures him with:

> *Securae sunt nostrae vitae,*
> *Sumus enim Sodomitae,*
> *Igne tantum perituri,*
> *Landeriri."* [20]

"I take back what I said," said Charlus in a shrill and
mannered tone, "you are a well of learning. You'll write it
down for me, won't you? I must preserve it in my family
archives, since my great-great-great-grandmother was a
sister of M. le Prince."

"Yes, but, Baron, with regard to Prince Louis of
Baden I can think of nothing. However, I suppose that
generally speaking the art of war . . ."

"What nonsense! In that period alone you have
Vendôme, Villars, Prince Eugène, the Prince de Conti,
and if I were to tell you of all our heroes of Tonkin, of
Morocco—and I'm thinking of the ones who are truly
sublime, and pious, and 'new generation'—you'd be
amazed. Ah! I could teach them a thing or two, the people who conduct inquiries into the new generation, which
has rejected the futile complications of its elders,
M. Bourget tells us! I have a young friend out there,
who's highly spoken of, who has done great things . . .

However, I'm not going to tell tales out of school; let's get back to the seventeenth century. You know that Saint-Simon says of the Maréchal d'Huxelles—one among many: 'Voluptuous in Grecian debaucheries which he made no attempt to conceal, he would hook young officers whom he trained to his purpose, not to mention stalwart young valets, and this openly, in the army and at Strasbourg.' You've probably read Madame's *Letters*: all his men called him 'Putana.' She's fairly explicit about it."

"And she was in a good position to judge, with her husband."

"Such an interesting character, Madame," said M. de Charlus. "One might take her as model for the definitive portrait, the lyrical synthesis of the 'Wife of an Auntie.' First of all, the masculine type; generally the wife of an Auntie is a man—that's what makes it so easy for him to give her children. Then Madame doesn't talk about Monsieur's vices, but she does talk incessantly about the same vice in other men, writing as someone in the know and from that habit which makes us enjoy finding in other people's families the same defects as afflict us in our own, in order to prove to ourselves that there's nothing exceptional or degrading in them. I was saying that things have been much the same in every age. Nevertheless, our own is especially remarkable in that respect. And notwithstanding the instances I've borrowed from the seventeenth century, if my great ancestor François de La Rochefoucauld were alive in our day, he might say of it with even more justification than of his own—come, Brichot, help me out: 'Vices are common to every age; but if certain persons whom everyone knows had appeared in the first centuries of our era, would anyone speak today of the prostitutions of Heliogabalus?' *'Whom everyone knows'* appeals to me immensely. I see that my sagacious kinsman understood the tricks of his most illustrious contemporaries as I understand those of my own. But men of that sort are not only far more numerous today. There's also something special about them."

I could see that M. de Charlus was about to tell us in what fashion these habits had evolved. And not for a moment while he was speaking, or while Brichot was speaking, was the semi-conscious image of my home, where Albertine awaited me—an image associated with the intimate and caressing motif of Vinteuil—absent from my mind. I kept coming back to Albertine, just as I would be obliged in fact to go back to her presently as to a sort of ball and chain to which I was somehow attached, which prevented me from leaving Paris and which at this moment, while from the Verdurin salon I pictured my home, made me think of it not as an empty space, exalting to the personality if a little melancholy, but as being filled— alike in this to the hotel in Balbec on a certain evening— with that immutable presence, which lingered there for me and which I was sure to find there whenever I chose. The insistence with which M. de Charlus kept reverting to this topic—into which his mind, constantly exercised in the same direction, had indeed acquired a certain penetration—was in a rather complex way distinctly trying. He was as boring as a specialist who can see nothing outside his own subject, as irritating as an initiate who prides himself on the secrets which he possesses and is burning to divulge, as repellent as those people who, whenever their own weaknesses are in question, blossom and expatiate without noticing that they are giving offence, as obsessed as a maniac and as uncontrollably imprudent as a criminal. These characteristics, which at certain moments became as striking as those that stamp a madman or a felon, brought me, as it happened, a certain consolation. For, subjecting them to the necessary transposition in order to be able to draw from them deductions with regard to Albertine, and remembering her attitude towards Saint-Loup and towards me, I said to myself, painful as one of these memories and melancholy as the other was to me, I said to myself that they seemed to preclude the kind of deformation, so distinctive and pronounced, the kind of specialisation, inevitably exclusive it seemed, that emanated so powerfully from the conversation as from the person of M. de Charlus. But the latter, unfortunately, made haste to destroy these grounds for hope in the same way as he had furnished me with them, that is to say unwittingly.

"Yes," he said, "I'm no longer a stripling, and I've already seen many things change round about me. I no longer recognise either society, in which all the barriers have been broken down, in which a mob devoid of elegance or decency dance the tango even in my own family, or fashion, or politics, or the arts, or religion, or anything. But I must admit that the thing that has changed most of all is what the Germans call homosexuality. Good heavens, in my day, leaving aside the men who loathed women, and those who, caring only for women, did the other thing merely with an eye to profit, homosexuals were sound family men and never kept mistresses except as a cover. Had I had a daughter to give away, it's among them that I should have looked for my son-in-law if I'd

wanted to be certain that she wouldn't be unhappy. Alas!
things have changed. Nowadays they're also recruited
from among the most rabid womanisers. I thought I had a
certain flair, and that when I said to myself: 'Certainly
not,' I couldn't have been mistaken. Well, now I give up.
One of my friends who is well-known for it had a coachman whom my sister-in-law Oriane found for him, a lad
from Combray who had dabbled in all sorts of trades but
particularly that of chasing skirts, and who, I would have
sworn, was as hostile as possible to that sort of thing. He
broke his mistress's heart by deceiving her with two
women whom he adored, not to mention the others, an
actress and a barmaid. My cousin the Prince de Guermantes, who has the irritating mind of people who are too
ready to believe anything, said to me one day: 'But why
in the world doesn't X——sleep with his coachman? It
might give pleasure to Théodore' (which is the coachman's name) 'and he may even be rather hurt that his
master doesn't make advances to him.' I couldn't help
telling Gilbert to hold his tongue; I was irritated by that
would-be perspicacity which, when exercised indiscriminately, is a want of perspicacity, and also by the blatant
guile of my cousin who would have liked X——to test
the ground so that he himself could follow if the going
was good."

"Then the Prince de Guermantes has those tastes
too?" asked Brichot with a mixture of astonishment and
dismay.

"Good lord," replied M. de Charlus, highly delighted,
"it's so notorious that I don't think I'm being guilty of an
indiscretion if I tell you that he does. Well, the following
year I went to Balbec, where I heard from a sailor who

used to take me out fishing occasionally that my
Théodore, whose sister, I may mention, is the maid of a
friend of Mme Verdurin, Baroness Putbus, used to come
down to the harbour to pick up this or that sailor, with
the most infernal cheek, to go for a boat-trip 'with
extras.' "

It was now my turn to inquire whether the coachman's employer, whom I had identified as the gentleman
who at Balbec used to play cards all day long with his
mistress, was like the Prince de Guermantes.

"Why, of course, everyone knows. He doesn't even
make any attempt to conceal it."

"But he had his mistress there with him."

"Well, and what difference does that make? How innocent these children are," he said to me in a fatherly
tone, little suspecting the grief that I extracted from his
words when I thought of Albertine. "She's charming, his
mistress."

"So then his three friends are like himself?"

"Not at all," he cried, stopping his ears as though, in
playing some instrument, I had struck a wrong note.

"Now he's gone to the other extreme. So a man no
longer has the right to have friends? Ah! youth; it gets
everything wrong. We shall have to begin your education
over again, my boy. Now," he went on, "I admit that this
case—and I know of many others—however open a mind
I may try to keep for every form of effrontery, does embarrass me. I may be very old-fashioned, but I fail to understand," he said in the tone of an old Gallican speaking
of certain forms of Ultramontanism, of a liberal royalist
speaking of the *Action Française* or of a disciple of Claude
Monet speaking of the Cubists. "I don't condemn these

innovators. I envy them if anything. I try to understand them, but I simply can't. If they're so passionately fond of women, why, and especially in this working-class world where it's frowned upon, where they conceal it from a sense of shame, have they any need of what they call 'a bit of brown'? It's because it represents something else to them. What?"

"What else can a woman represent to Albertine," I thought, and there indeed lay the cause of my anguish.

"Decidedly, Baron," said Brichot, "should the University Council ever think of founding a Chair of Homosexuality, I shall see that your name is the first to be submitted. Or rather, no; an Institute of Special Psychophysiology would suit you better. And I can see you, best of all, provided with a Chair in the Collège de France, which would enable you to devote yourself to personal researches the results of which you would deliver, like the Professor of Tamil or Sanskrit, to the handful of people who are interested in them. You would have an audience of two, with your beadle, not that I mean to cast the slightest aspersion upon our corps of ushers, whom I believe to be above suspicion."

"You know nothing about it," the Baron retorted in a harsh and cutting tone. "Besides you're wrong in thinking that so few people are interested in the subject. It's just the opposite." And without stopping to consider the incompatibility between the invariable trend of his own conversation and the reproaches he was about to level at others, "It is, on the contrary, most alarming," said the Baron with a shocked and contrite air, "people talk about nothing else. It's a disgrace, but I'm not exaggerating, my dear fellow! It appears that the day before yesterday, at the Duchesse d'Ayen's, they talked about nothing else for two hours on end. Just imagine, if women have taken to discussing that sort of thing, it's a positive scandal! The most revolting thing about it," he went on with extraordinary fire and vigour, "is that they get their information from pests, real scoundrels like young Châtellerault, about whom there's more to be told than anyone, who tell them stories about other men. I gather he's been vilifying me, but I don't care; I'm convinced that the mud and filth flung by an individual who barely escaped being turned out of the Jockey for cheating at cards can only rebound on him. I know that if I were Jane d'Ayen, I should have sufficient respect for my salon not to allow such subjects to be discussed there, nor to allow my own flesh and blood to be dragged through the mire in my house. But society's finished, there are no longer any rules, any proprieties, in conversation any more than in dress. Ah, my dear fellow, it's the end of the world. Everyone has become so malicious. People vie with one another in speaking ill of their fellows. It's appalling!"

As cowardly still as I had been long ago in my boyhood at Combray when I used to run away in order not to see my grandfather tempted with brandy and the vain efforts of my grandmother imploring him not to drink it, I had but one thought, which was to leave the Verdurins' house before the execution of M. de Charlus occurred.

"I simply must go," I said to Brichot.

"I'm coming with you," he replied, "but we can't just slip away, English fashion. Come and say good-bye to Mme Verdurin," the Professor concluded, as he made his way to the drawing-room with the air of a man who, in a parlour game, goes to find out whether he may "come back."

While we had been talking, M. Verdurin, at a signal from his wife, had taken Morel aside. Even if Mme Verdurin had decided on reflexion that it was wiser to postpone Morel's enlightenment, she was powerless now to prevent it. There are certain desires, sometimes confined to the mouth, which, as soon as we have allowed them to grow, insist upon being gratified, whatever the consequences may be; one can no longer resist the temptation to kiss a bare shoulder at which one has been gazing for too long and on which one's lips pounce like a snake upon a bird, or to bury one's sweet tooth in a tempting cake; nor can one deny oneself the satisfaction of seeing the amazement, anxiety, grief or mirth to which one can move another person by some unexpected communication. So, drunk with melodrama, Mme Verdurin had ordered her husband to take Morel out of the room and at all costs to explain matters to him. The violinist had begun by deploring the departure of the Queen of Naples before he had had a chance of being presented to her. M. de Charlus had told him so often that she was the sister of the Empress Elizabeth and of the Duchesse d'Alençon that the sovereign had assumed an extraordinary importance in his eyes. But the Master explained to him that they were not there to talk about the Queen of Naples, and then went straight to the point. "Listen," he had concluded after a long explanation, "if you like, we can go and ask my wife what she thinks. I give you my word of honour, I've said nothing to her about it. We'll see what she thinks of it all. My advice may not be right, but you know how sound her judgment is, and besides, she has an immense affection for you; let's go and submit the case to her." And as Mme Verdurin, impatiently looking forward to the excitement that she would presently be relishing when she talked to the musician, and then, after he had gone, when she made her husband give her a full report of their conversation, went on repeating to herself: "But what in the world can they be doing? I do hope that Gustave, in keeping him all this time, has managed to give him his cue," M. Verdurin reappeared with Morel, who seemed extremely agitated.

"He'd like to ask your advice," M. Verdurin said to his wife, in the tone of a man who does not know whether his request will be granted. Instead of replying to M. Verdurin, it was to Morel that, in the heat of her passion, Mme Verdurin addressed herself.

"I agree entirely with my husband. I consider that you cannot put up with it any longer," she exclaimed vehemently, discarding as a useless fiction her agreement with her husband that she was supposed to know nothing of what he had been saying to the violinist.

"How do you mean? Put up with what?" stammered M. Verdurin, endeavouring to feign astonishment and seeking, with an awkwardness that was explained by his dismay, to defend his falsehood.

"I guessed what you'd been saying to him," replied Mme Verdurin, undisturbed by the improbability of this explanation, and caring little what the violinist might think of her veracity when he recalled this scene. "No," Mme Verdurin continued, "I feel that you cannot possibly persist in this degrading promiscuity with a tainted person whom nobody will have in their house," she went on, regardless of the fact that this was untrue and forgetting that she herself entertained him almost daily. "You're the talk of the Conservatoire," she added, feeling that this was the argument that would carry most weight. "Another month of this life and your artistic future will be shattered, whereas without Charlus you ought to be making at least a hundred thousand francs a year."

"But I'd never heard a thing, I'm astounded, I'm very grateful to you," Morel murmured, the tears starting to his eyes. But, being obliged at once to feign astonishment and to conceal his shame, he had turned redder and was sweating more abundantly than if he had played all Beethoven's sonatas in succession, and tears welled from his eyes which the Bonn Master would certainly not have drawn from him.

"If you've never heard anything, you're unique in that respect. He is a gentleman with a vile reputation and has been mixed up in some very nasty doings. I know that the police have their eye on him and that is perhaps the best thing for him if he's not to end up like all such men, murdered by ruffians," she went on, for as she thought of Charlus the memory of Mme de Duras recurred to her, and in the intoxication of her rage she sought to aggravate still further the wounds that she was inflicting on the unfortunate Charlie, and to avenge those that she herself had received in the course of the evening. "Anyhow, even financially he can be of no use to you; he's completely ruined since he has become the prey of people who are blackmailing him, and who can't even extract from him the price of the tune they call, any more than you can extract the price for yours, because everything's mortgaged up to the hilt, town house, country house, everything."

Morel was all the more inclined to believe this lie since M. de Charlus liked to confide in him his relations with ruffians, a race for which the son of a valet, however villainous himself, professes a feeling of horror as strong as his attachment to Bonapartist principles.

Already, in his cunning mind, a scheme had begun to take shape analogous to what was called in the eighteenth century a reversal of alliances. Resolving never to speak to M. de Charlus again, he would return on the following evening to Jupien's niece, and see that everything was put right with her. Unfortunately for him this plan was doomed to failure, M. de Charlus having made an appointment for that same evening with Jupien, which the ex-tailor dared not fail to keep in spite of recent events. Other events, as we shall see, having occurred as regards Morel, when Jupien in tears told his tale of woe to the Baron, the latter, no less woeful, assured him that he would adopt the forsaken girl, that she could take one of the titles that were at his disposal, probably that of Mlle d'Oloron, that he would see that she received a thorough finishing and married a rich husband. Promises which filled Jupien with joy but left his niece unmoved, for she still loved Morel, who, from stupidity or cynicism, would come into the shop and tease her in Jupien's absence. "What's the matter with you," he would say with a laugh, "with those big circles under your eyes? A broken heart? Dammit, time passes and things change. After all, a man has a right to try on a shoe, and all the more so a woman, and if she doesn't fit him . . ." He lost his temper once only, because she cried, which he considered cowardly, unworthy of her. People are not always very tolerant of the tears which they themselves have provoked.

But we have looked too far ahead, for all this did not happen until after the Verdurin reception which we interrupted, and which we must take up again at the point where we left off.

"I'd never have suspected," Morel groaned, in answer to Mme Verdurin.

"Naturally people don't say it to your face, but that doesn't prevent your being the talk of the Conservatoire," Mme Verdurin went on spitefully, seeking to make it plain to Morel that it was not only M. de Charlus who was being criticised, but himself too. "I'm quite prepared to believe that you know nothing about it; all the same, people are talking freely. Ask Ski what they were saying the other day at Chevillard's concert within a few feet of us when you came into my box. In other words, people are pointing a finger at you. Personally I don't pay the slightest attention, but what I do feel is that it makes a man supremely ridiculous and that he becomes a public laughing-stock for the rest of his life."

"I don't know how to thank you," said Charlie in the tone in which one speaks to a dentist who has just caused one the most excruciating pain without one's daring to show it, or to a too bloodthirsty second who has forced one into a duel on account of some casual remark of which he has said: "You can't swallow that."

"I believe that you have plenty of character, that you're a man," replied Mme Verdurin, "and that you will be capable of speaking out boldly, although he tells everybody that you'd never dare, that he's got you under his thumb."

Charlie, seeking a borrowed dignity in which to cloak the tatters of his own, found in his memory something that he had read or, more probably, heard quoted, and at once proclaimed: "I wasn't brought up to stomach such an affront. This very evening I shall break with M. de Charlus. The Queen of Naples has gone, hasn't she? Otherwise, before breaking with him, I'd have asked him . . ."

"It isn't necessary to break with him altogether," said Mme Verdurin, anxious to avoid a disruption of the little nucleus. "There's no harm in your seeing him here, among our little group, where you are appreciated, where no one speaks ill of you. But you must insist upon your freedom, and not let him drag you about among all those silly women who are friendly to your face; I wish you could have heard what they were saying behind your back. Anyhow, you need feel no regret. Not only are you getting rid of a stain which would have marked you for the rest of your life, but from the artistic point of view, even without this scandalous presentation by Charlus, I don't mind telling you that debasing yourself like this in these sham society circles would give the impression that you aren't serious, would earn you the reputation of being an amateur, a mere salon performer, which is a terrible thing at your age. I can understand that to all those fine ladies it's highly convenient to be able to return their friends' hospitality by making you come and play for nothing, but it's your future as an artist that would foot the bill. I don't say that there aren't one or two. You

mentioned the Queen of Naples—who has left, for she
had to go on to another party—now she's a nice woman,
and I may tell you that I think she has a poor opinion of
Charlus. I'm sure she came here chiefly to please me. Yes,
yes, I know she was longing to meet M. Verdurin and
myself. That is a house in which you might play. And
then of course if I take you—because the artists all know
me, you understand, they've always been very sweet to
me, and regard me almost as one of themselves, as their
Mistress—that's quite a different matter. But whatever
you do, you must never go near Mme de Duras! Don't go
and make a bloomer like that! I know several artists who
have come here and told me all about her. They know
they can trust me," she said, in the sweet and simple tone
which she knew how to adopt instantaneously, imparting
an appropriate air of modesty to her features, an appropriate charm to her eyes, "they come here, just like that, to
tell me all their little troubles; the ones who are said to be
most taciturn go on chatting to me sometimes for hours
on end, and I can't tell you how interesting they are. Poor
Chabrier always used to say: 'There's nobody like Mme
Verdurin for getting them to talk.' Well, do you know,
I've seen them all, every one of them without exception,
literally in tears after having gone to play for Mme de
Duras. It's not only the way she enjoys making her servants humiliate them, but they could never get an engagement anywhere else again. The agents would say: 'Oh
yes, the fellow who plays at Mme de Duras's.' That settled it. There's nothing like that for ruining a man's future. You see, with society people it doesn't seem serious;
you may have all the talent in the world, it's a sad thing
to have to say, but one Mme de Duras is enough to give

you the reputation of an amateur. And artists, you realise—and after all I know them, I've been moving among them for forty years, launching them, taking an interest in them—well, when they say that somebody's an amateur, that's the end of it. And people were beginning to say it of you. Indeed, the number of times I've been obliged to take up the cudgels on your behalf, to assure them that you wouldn't play in some absurd drawing-room! Do you know what the answer was: 'But he'll be forced to. Charlus won't even consult him, he never asks him for his opinion.' Somebody wanted to pay him a compliment by saying: 'We greatly admire your friend Morel.' Do you know the answer he gave, with that insolent air which you know so well? 'But what do you mean by calling him my friend. We're not of the same class. Say rather that he is my creature, my protégé.'"

At this moment there stirred beneath the domed forehead of the musical goddess the one thing that certain people cannot keep to themselves, a word which it is not merely abject but imprudent to repeat. But the need to repeat it is stronger than honour or prudence. It was to this need that, after a few convulsive twitches of her spherical and sorrowful brow, the Mistress succumbed: "Someone actually told my husband that he had said 'my servant,' but for that I cannot vouch," she added. It was a similar need that had impelled M. de Charlus, shortly after he had sworn to Morel that nobody should ever know the story of his birth, to say to Mme Verdurin: "His father was a valet." A similar need again, now that the word had been said, would make it circulate from one person to another, each of whom would confide it under the seal of a secrecy which would be promised and not kept by the hearer, as by the informant himself. These words would end, as in the game called hunt-the-thimble, by being traced back to Mme Verdurin, bringing down upon her the wrath of the person concerned, who would finally have heard them. She knew this, but could not repress the word that was burning her tongue. "Servant" could not but offend Morel. She said "servant" nevertheless, and if she added that she could not vouch for the word, this was so as to appear certain of the rest, thanks to this hint of uncertainty, and to show her impartiality. She herself found this impartiality so touching that she began to speak tenderly to Charlie: "Because, don't you see, I don't blame him. He's dragging you down into his abyss, it is true, but it's not his fault since he wallows in it himself, since he wallows in it," she repeated in a louder tone, having been struck by the aptness of the image which had taken shape so quickly that her attention only now caught up with it and sought to make the most of it. "No, what I do reproach him for," she went on in a melting tone— like a woman drunk with her own success—"is a want of delicacy towards you. There are certain things that one doesn't say in public. For instance, this evening he was betting that he would make you blush with joy by telling you (stuff and nonsense, of course, for his recommenda-tion would be enough to prevent your getting it) that you were to have the Cross of the Legion of Honour. Even that I could overlook, although I've never much liked," she went on with a delicate and dignified air, "seeing someone make a fool of his friends, but, don't you know, there are certain little things that do stick in one's gullet. Such as when he told us, with screams of laughter, that if you want the Cross it's to please your uncle and that your uncle was a flunkey."

"He told you that!" cried Charlie, believing, on the strength of this adroitly interpolated remark, in the truth of everything that Mme Verdurin had said. Mme Verdurin was overwhelmed with the joy of an old mistress who, just as her young lover is on the point of deserting her, succeeds in breaking up his marriage. And perhaps the lie had not been a calculated one, perhaps she had not even consciously lied. A sort of sentimental logic, or perhaps, more elementary still, a sort of nervous reflex, that impelled her, in order to brighten up her life and preserve her happiness, to sow discord in the little clan, may have brought impulsively to her lips, without giving her time to check their veracity, these assertions that were so diabolically effective if not strictly accurate.

"If he had only said it to us it wouldn't matter," the Mistress went on, "we know better than to pay any attention to what he says, and besides, what does a man's origin matter, you have your worth, you're what you make yourself, but that he should use it to make Mme de Portefin laugh" (Mme Verdurin named this lady on purpose because she knew that Charlie admired her) "that's what makes us sick. My husband said to me when he heard him: 'I'd sooner he had struck me in the face.' For he's as fond of you as I am, you know, is Gustave" (it was thus that one learned that M. Verdurin's name was Gustave). "He's really very sensitive."

"But I never told you I was fond of him," muttered M. Verdurin, acting the kind-hearted curmudgeon. "It's Charlus who's fond of him."

"Oh, no! Now I realise the difference. I was betrayed by a wretch and you, you're good," Charlie fervently exclaimed.

"No, no," murmured Mme Verdurin, seeking to safeguard her victory (for she felt that her Wednesdays were safe) but not to abuse it, "wretch is too strong; he does harm, a great deal of harm, unwittingly; you know that tale about the Legion of Honour was only a momentary squib. And it would be painful to me to repeat all that he said about your family," she added, although she would have been greatly embarrassed had she been asked to do so.

"Oh, even if it *was* only momentary, it proves that he's a traitor," cried Morel.

It was at this moment that we returned to the drawing-room. "Ah!" exclaimed M. de Charlus when he saw that Morel was in the room, and, advancing upon the musician with the alacrity of a man who has skilfully organised a whole evening's entertainment for the purpose of an assignation with a woman, and in his excitement never imagines that he has with his own hands set the snare in which he will be caught and publicly thrashed by bravoes stationed in readiness by her husband, "so here you are at last. Well, are you pleased, young hero, and presently young knight of the Legion of Honour? For very soon you will be able to sport your Cross," he said to Morel with a tender and triumphant air, but by the very mention of the decoration endorsing Mme Verdurin's lies, which appeared to Morel to be indisputable truth.

"Leave me alone. I forbid you to come near me," Morel shouted at the Baron. "You know what I mean all right. I'm not the first person you've tried to pervert!"

My sole consolation lay in the thought that I was about to see Morel and the Verdurins pulverised by M. de Charlus. For a thousand times less than that I had been visited with his furious rage; no one was safe from it; a king would not have intimidated him. Instead of which, an extraordinary thing happened. M. de Charlus stood speechless, dumbfounded, measuring the depths of his misery without understanding its cause, unable to think of a word to say, raising his eyes to gaze at each of the company in turn, with a questioning, outraged, suppliant air, which seemed to be asking them not so much what had happened as what answer he ought to make. And yet M. de Charlus possessed all the resources, not merely of eloquence but of audacity, when, seized by a rage which had been simmering for a long time, he reduced someone to despair with the most cruel words in front of a shocked society group which had never imagined that anyone could go so far. M. de Charlus, on these occasions, almost foamed at the mouth, working himself up into a veritable frenzy which left everyone trembling. But in these instances he had the initiative, he was on the attack, he said whatever came into his head (just as Bloch was able to make fun of the Jews yet blushed if the word Jew was uttered in his hearing). These people whom he hated, he hated because he thought they looked down on him. Had they been civil to him, instead of flying into a furious rage with them he would have taken them to his bosom. Perhaps what now struck him speechless was— when he saw that M. and Mme Verdurin turned their eyes away from him and that no one was coming to his rescue—his present anguish and, still more, his dread of greater anguish to come; or else the fact that, not having worked himself up and concocted an imaginary rage in advance, having no ready-made thunderbolt at hand, he had been seized and struck down suddenly at a moment when he was unarmed (for, sensitive, neurotic, hysterical, he was genuinely impulsive but pseudo-brave—indeed, as I had always thought, and it was something that had rather endeared him to me, pseudo-cruel—and did not have the normal reactions of an outraged man of honour); or else that, in a milieu that was not his own, he felt less at ease and less courageous than he would in the Faubourg. The fact remains that, in this salon which he despised, this great nobleman (in whom superiority over commoners was no more essentially inherent than it had been in this or that ancestor of his trembling before the revolutionary tribunal) could do nothing, in the paralysis of his every limb as well as his tongue, but cast around him terror-stricken, suppliant, bewildered glances, outraged by the violence that was being done to him. In a situation so cruelly unforeseen, this great talker could do no more than stammer: "What does it all mean? What's wrong?" His question was not even heard. And the eternal pantomime of panic terror has so little changed that this elderly gentleman to whom a disagreeable incident had occurred in a Parisian drawing-room unconsciously re-enacted the basic formal attitudes in which the Greek sculptors of the earliest times symbolised the terror of nymphs pursued by the god Pan.

The disgraced ambassador, the under-secretary placed suddenly on the retired list, the man about town who finds himself cold-shouldered, the lover who has been shown the door, examine, sometimes for months on end, the event that has shattered their hopes; they turn it over and over like a projectile fired at them they know not from whence or by whom, almost as though it were a meteorite. They long to know the constituent elements of this strange missile which has burst upon them, to learn what animosities may be detected therein. Chemists have at least the means of analysis; sick men suffering from a disease the origin of which they do not know can send for the doctor; criminal mysteries are more or less unravelled by the examining magistrate. But for the disconcerting actions of our fellow-men we rarely discover the motives. Thus M. de Charlus—to anticipate the days that followed this evening to which we shall presently return—could see in Charlie's attitude one thing alone that was self-evident. Charlie, who had often threatened the Baron that he would tell people of the passion that he inspired in him, must have seized the opportunity to do so when he considered that he had now sufficiently "arrived" to be able to stand on his own feet. And he must, out of sheer ingratitude, have told Mme Verdurin everything. But how had she allowed herself to be taken in (for the Baron, having made up his mind to deny the story, had already persuaded himself that the sentiments of which he would be accused were imaginary)? Friends of Mme Verdurin's, themselves perhaps with a passion for Charlie, must have prepared the ground. Accordingly, during the next few days M. de Charlus wrote ferocious letters to a number of the faithful, who were entirely innocent and concluded that he must be mad; then he went to Mme Verdurin with a long and affecting tale, which had not at all the effect that he had hoped. For in the first place Mme Verdurin simply said to him: "All you need do is pay no more attention to him, treat him with scorn, he's a mere boy." Now the Baron longed only for a reconciliation, and to bring this about by depriving Charlie of everything he had felt assured of, he asked Mme Verdurin not to invite him again; a request which she met with a refusal that brought her angry and sarcastic letters from M. de Charlus. Flitting from one supposition to another, the Baron never hit upon the truth, which was that the blow had not come from Morel. It is true that he could have learned this by asking him if they could have a few minutes' talk. But he felt that this would be prejudicial to his dignity and to the interests of his love. He had been insulted; he awaited an explanation. In any case, almost invariably, attached to the idea of a talk which might clear up a misunderstanding, there is another idea which, for whatever reason, prevents us from agreeing to that talk. The man who has abased himself and shown his weakness on a score of occasions will make a show of pride on the twenty-first, the only occasion on which it would be advisable not to persist in an arrogant attitude but to dispel an error which is taking root in his adversary failing a denial. As for the social side of the incident, the rumour spread abroad that M. de Charlus had been turned out of the Verdurins' house when he had attempted to rape a young musician. The effect of this rumour was that nobody was surprised when M. de Charlus did not appear again at the Verdurins', and whenever he chanced to meet somewhere else one of the faithful whom he had suspected and insulted, as this person bore a grudge against the Baron who himself abstained from greeting him, people were not surprised, realising that no member of the little clan would ever wish to speak to the Baron again.

While M. de Charlus, momentarily stunned by

Morel's words and by the attitude of the Mistress, stood there in the pose of a nymph seized with Panic terror, M. and Mme Verdurin had retired to the outer drawing-room, as a sign of diplomatic rupture, leaving M. de Charlus by himself, while on the platform Morel was putting his violin in its case: "Now you must tell us exactly what happened," Mme Verdurin exclaimed avidly to her husband.

"I don't know what you can have said to him," said Ski. "He looked quite upset; there were tears in his eyes."

Pretending not to have understood, "I'm sure nothing that I said could have affected him," said Mme Verdurin, employing one of those stratagems which deceive no one, so as to force the sculptor to repeat that Charlie was in tears, tears which excited the Mistress's pride too much for her to be willing to run the risk that one or other of the faithful, who might have misheard, remained in ignorance of them.

"Oh, but it must have: I saw big tears glistening in his eyes," said the sculptor in a low voice with a smile of malicious connivance and a sidelong glance to make sure that Morel was still on the platform and could not overhear the conversation. But there was somebody who did overhear and whose presence, as soon as it was observed, would restore to Morel one of the hopes that he had forfeited. This was the Queen of Naples, who, having left her fan behind, had thought it more polite, on coming away from another party to which she had gone on, to call back for it in person. She had entered the room quietly, as though she were a little embarrassed, prepared to make apologies for her presence, and not to outstay her welcome now that the other guests had gone. But no one had heard her enter in the heat of the incident, the meaning of which she had at once gathered and which set her ablaze with indignation.

"Ski says he had tears in his eyes. Did you notice that?" said Mme Verdurin. "I didn't see any tears. Ah, yes, I remember now," she corrected herself, afraid that her denial might be believed. "As for Charlus, he's almost done in, he ought to take a chair, he's tottering on his feet, he'll be on the floor in another minute," she said with a pitiless laugh.

At that moment Morel hastened towards her: "Isn't that lady the Queen of Naples?" he asked (although he knew quite well that she was), pointing to the sovereign who was making her way towards Charlus. "After what has just happened, I can no longer, I'm afraid, ask the Baron to introduce me."

"Wait, I shall take you to her myself," said Mme Verdurin, and, followed by a few of the faithful, but not by myself and Brichot who made haste to go and collect our hats and coats, she advanced upon the Queen who was chatting to M. de Charlus. The latter had imagined that the fulfilment of his great desire that Morel should be presented to the Queen of Naples could be prevented only by the improbable demise of that lady. But we picture the future as a reflexion of the present projected into an empty space, whereas it is the result, often almost immediate, of causes which for the most part escape our notice. Not an hour had passed, and now M. de Charlus would have given anything to prevent Morel from being presented to the Queen. Mme Verdurin made the Queen a curtsey. Seeing that the other appeared not to recognise her, "I am Mme Verdurin," she said. "Your Majesty doesn't remember me."

"Quite well," said the Queen, continuing to talk to M. de Charlus so naturally and with such a casual air that Mme Verdurin doubted whether it was to herself that this "Quite well" was addressed, uttered as it was in a marvellously off-hand tone, which wrung from M. de Charlus, despite his lover's anguish, the grateful and epicurean smile of an expert in the art of rudeness. Morel, who had watched from the distance the preparations for his presentation, now approached. The Queen offered her arm to M. de Charlus. With him, too, she was vexed, but only because he did not make a more energetic stand against vile detractors. She was crimson with shame on his behalf that the Verdurins should dare to treat him in this fashion. The unaffected civility which she had shown them a few hours earlier, and the arrogant pride with which she now confronted them, had their source in the same region of her heart. The Queen was a woman of great kindness, but she conceived of kindness first and foremost in the form of an unshakeable attachment to the people she loved, to her own family, to all the princes of her race, among whom was M. de Charlus, and, after them, to all the people of the middle classes or of the humblest populace who knew how to respect those whom she loved and were well-disposed towards them. It was as to a woman endowed with these sound instincts that she had shown kindness to Mme Verdurin. And no doubt this is a narrow conception of kindness, somewhat Tory and increasingly obsolete. But this does not mean that her kindness was any less genuine or ardent. The ancients were no less strongly attached to the human group to which they devoted themselves because it did not go beyond the limits of their city, nor are the men of today to their country, than those who in the future will love the United States of the World. In my own immediate surroundings, I had the example of my mother, whom Mme de Cambremer and Mme de Guermantes could never persuade to take part in any philanthropic undertaking, to join any patriotic ladies' work party, to sell raffle tickets or sponsor charity shows. I do not say that she was right in acting only when her heart had first spoken, and in reserving for her own family, for her servants, for the unfortunate whom chance brought in her way, the riches of her love and generosity, but I do know that these, like those of my grandmother, were inexhaustible and exceeded by far anything that Mme de Guermantes or Mme de Cambremer ever could have done or did. The case of the Queen of Naples was altogether different, but it must be admitted that lovable people were conceived of by her not at all as in those novels of Dostoievsky which Albertine had taken from my shelves and hoarded, that is to say in the guise of wheedling parasites, thieves, drunkards, obsequious one minute, insolent the next, debauchees, even murderers. Extremes, however, meet, since the noble man, the close relative, the outraged kinsman whom the Queen sought to defend was M. de Charlus, that is to say, notwithstanding his birth and all the family ties that bound him to the Queen, a man whose virtue was hedged round by many vices. "You don't look at all well, my dear cousin," she said to M. de Charlus. "Lean on my arm. You may be sure that it will always support you. It is strong enough for that." Then, raising her eyes proudly in front of her (where, Ski later told me, Mme Verdurin and Morel were standing): "You know how in the past, at Gaeta, it held the mob at bay. It will be a shield to you." And it was thus, taking the Baron on her arm and without having allowed Morel to be presented to her, that the glorious sister of the Empress Elisabeth left the house.

It might have been assumed, in view of M. de Charlus's ferocious temper and the persecutions with which he terrorised even his own family, that after the events of this evening he would have unleashed his fury and taken reprisals upon the Verdurins. Nothing of the sort happened, and the principle reason was certainly that the Baron, having caught cold a few days later, and contracted the septic pneumonia which was very rife that winter, was for long regarded by his doctors, and regarded himself, as being at the point of death, and lay for many months suspended between it and life. Was there simply a physical metastasis, and the substitution of a different malady for the neurosis that had previously made him lose all control of himself in veritable orgies of rage? For it is too simple to suppose that, never having taken the Verdurins seriously from the social point of view, he was unable to feel the same resentment against them as he would have felt against his equals; too simple also to recall that neurotics, irritated at the slightest provocation by imaginary and inoffensive enemies, become on the contrary inoffensive as soon as anyone takes the offensive against them, and that they are more easily calmed by flinging cold water in their faces than by attempting to prove to them the inanity of their grievances. But it is probably not in a metastasis that we ought to seek the explanation of this absence of rancour, but far more in the disease itself. It exhausted the

Baron so completely that he had little leisure left in which to think about the Verdurins. He was almost moribund. We mentioned offensives; even those that will have only a posthumous effect require, if they are to be properly "staged," the sacrifice of a part of one's strength. M. de Charlus had too little strength left for the activity of preparation required. We hear often of mortal enemies who open their eyes to gaze on one another in the hour of death and close them again, satisfied. This must be a rare occurrence, except when death surprises us in the midst of life. It is, on the contrary, when we have nothing left to lose that we do not embark upon the risks which, when full of life, we would have undertaken lightly. The spirit of vengeance forms part of life; it deserts us as a rule—in spite of exceptions which, in one and the same character, as we shall see, are human contradictions—on the threshold of death. After having thought for a moment about the Verdurins, M. de Charlus felt that he was too weak, turned his face to the wall, and ceased to think about anything. It was not that he had lost his eloquence, which demanded little effort. It still flowed freely, but it had changed. Detached from the violence which it had so often adorned, it was now a quasi-mystical eloquence, embellished with words of meekness, parables from the Gospel, an apparent resignation to death. He talked especially on the days when he thought that he would live. A relapse made him silent. This Christian meekness into which his splendid violence had been transposed (as into *Esther* the so different genius of *Andromaque*) provoked the admiration of those who came to his bedside. It would have provoked that of the Verdurins themselves, who

could not have helped adoring a man whose weaknesses
had made them hate him. It is true that thoughts which
were Christian only in appearance rose to the surface. He
would implore the Archangel Gabriel to appear and announce to him, as to the Prophet, precisely when the
Messiah would come. And, breaking off with a sweet and
sorrowful smile, he would add: "But the Archangel
mustn't ask me, as he asked Daniel, to have patience for
'seven weeks, and threescore and two weeks,' for I should
be dead before then." The person whom he awaited thus
was Morel. And so he asked the Archangel Raphael to
bring him to him, as he had brought the young Tobias.
And, introducing more human measures (like sick Popes
who, while ordering masses to be said, do not neglect to
send for their doctors), he insinuated to his visitors that if
Brichot were to bring him without delay his young Tobias, perhaps the Archangel Raphael would consent to restore Brichot's sight, as he had done to the father of
Tobias, or as had happened in the purifying waters of
Bethesda. But, notwithstanding these human lapses, the
moral purity of M. de Charlus's conversation had none
the less become charming. Vanity, slander, the madness of
malevolence and pride, had alike disappeared. Morally
M. de Charlus had risen far above the level at which he
had lived in the past. But this moral improvement, as to
the reality of which, it must be said, his oratorical skill
was capable of deceiving somewhat his impressionable audience, vanished with the malady which had laboured on
its behalf. M. de Charlus redescended the downward
slope with a speed which, as we shall see, continued
steadily to increase. But the Verdurins' attitude towards

him was by that time no more than a somewhat distant memory which more immediate outbursts prevented from reviving.

To turn back to the Verdurin reception, when the host and hostess were alone, M. Verdurin said to his wife: "You know why Cottard didn't come? He's with Saniette, whose attempt to recover his losses on the Stock Exchange has failed. Learning that he hadn't a penny in the world and nearly a million francs of debts, Saniette had a stroke."

"But then why did he gamble? It's idiotic, he was the last person in the world to succeed at that game. Cleverer men than he get plucked at it, and he was born to let himself be swindled by every Tom, Dick and Harry."

"But of course, we've always known he was an idiot," said M. Verdurin. "Anyhow, this is the result. Here you have a man who will be turned out of house and home to-morrow by his landlord, and who's going to find himself in utter penury; his relations don't like him, Forcheville is the last man in the world who would do anything for him. And so it occurred to me—I don't wish to do anything that doesn't meet with your approval, but we might perhaps be able to scrape up a small income for him so that he shan't be too conscious of his ruin, so that he can keep a roof over his head."

"I entirely agree with you, it's very good of you to have thought of it. But you say 'a roof'; the fool has kept on an apartment beyond his means, he can't remain in it, we shall have to find him a couple of rooms somewhere. I understand that at present he's still paying six or seven thousand francs."

"Six thousand five hundred. But he's greatly attached

to his home. And after all, he's had a first stroke, he can scarcely live more than two or three years. Suppose we were to spend ten thousand francs on his behalf for three years. It seems to me that we should be able to afford that. We might for instance this year, instead of renting La Raspelière again, take somewhere more modest. With our income, it seems to me that to write off ten thousand francs for three years isn't out of the question."

"So be it. The only trouble is that people will get to know about it, and we'll be expected to do it for others."

"You can imagine that I thought of that. I shall do it only on the express condition that nobody knows about it. I've no wish for us to become the benefactors of the human race, thank you very much. No philanthropy! What we might do is to tell him that the money has been left to him by Princess Sherbatoff."

"But will he believe it? She consulted Cottard about her will."

"If the worst comes to the worst, we might take Cottard into our confidence. He's used to professional secrecy, he makes an enormous amount of money, he won't be like one of those busybodies for whom one's obliged to cough up. He may even perhaps be willing to say that the Princess appointed him as her executor. In that way we wouldn't even appear. That would avoid all the nuisance of scenes of gratitude, effusions and speeches."

M. Verdurin added an expression which made quite plain the kind of touching scenes and speeches which they were anxious to avoid. But it could not be reported to me precisely, for it was not a French expression, but one of those terms that are employed in certain families to denote certain things, annoying things especially, probably because people wish to be able to refer to them in the hearing of the persons concerned without being understood. An expression of this sort is generally a survival from an earlier condition of the family. In a Jewish family, for instance, it will be a ritual term diverted from its true meaning, and perhaps the only Hebrew word with which the family, now thoroughly Gallicised, is still acquainted. In a family that is strongly provincial, it will be a term of local dialect, albeit the family no longer speaks or even understands that dialect. In a family that has come from South America and no longer speaks anything but French, it will be a Spanish word. And, in the next generation, the word will no longer exist save as a childhood memory. It will be remembered perfectly well that the parents used to allude to the servants who were waiting at table by employing some such word, but the children have no idea what the word meant, whether it was Spanish, Hebrew, German, dialect, if indeed it ever belonged to any language and was not a proper name or a word entirely made up. The uncertainty can be cleared up only if they have a great-uncle or an old cousin still alive who must have used the same expression. As I never knew any relations of the Verdurins, I was never able to reconstruct the word. All I know is that it certainly drew a smile from Mme Verdurin, for the use of such a vocabulary, less general, more personal, more secret, than everyday speech, inspires in those who use it among themselves an egocentric feeling which is always accompanied by a certain self-satisfaction. After this moment of mirth, "But if Cottard talks," Mme Verdurin objected. "He won't talk." He did talk, to myself at least, for it was from him that I learned the story a few years later, actually at Saniette's funeral. I was sorry that I had not known of it earlier. For one thing the knowledge would have brought me more rapidly to the idea that we ought never to bear a grudge against people, ought never to judge them by some memory of an unkind action, for we do not know all the good that, at other moments, their hearts may have sincerely desired and realised. And thus, even simply from the point of view of prediction, one is mistaken. For doubtless the evil aspect which we have noted once and for all will recur; but the heart is richer than that, has many other aspects which will recur also in the same person and which we refuse to acknowledge because of his earlier bad behaviour. But from a more personal point of view, this revelation of Cottard's, if it had been made to me earlier, would have dispelled the suspicions I had formed as to the part that the Verdurins might be playing between Albertine and myself—would have dispelled them wrongly perhaps as it happened, for if M. Verdurin had virtues, he nevertheless teased and bullied to the point of the most savage persecution, and was so jealous of his position of dominance in the little clan as not to shrink from the basest falsehoods, from the fomentation of the most unjustified hatreds, in order to sever any ties among the faithful which had not as their sole object the strengthening of the little group. He was a man capable of disinterestedness, of unostentatious generosity, but that does not necessarily mean a man of feeling, or a likeable man, or a scrupulous or a truthful or always a kind man. A partial kindness—in which there subsisted, perhaps, a trace of the family whom my great-aunt had known—probably existed in him before I discovered it through this fact, as America or the North Pole existed before Columbus or Peary. Nevertheless, at the moment of my discovery, M. Verdurin's nature offered me a new and unsuspected facet; and I concluded that it is as difficult to present a fixed image of a character as of societies and passions. For a character alters no less than they do, and if one tries to take a snapshot of what is relatively immutable in it, one finds it presenting a succession of different aspects (implying that it is incapable of keeping still but keeps moving) to the disconcerted lens.

Seeing how late it was, and fearing that Albertine might be growing impatient, I asked Brichot, as we left the Verdurins' party, to be so kind as to drop me home first, and my carriage would then take him on. He commended me for going straight home like this (unaware that a girl was waiting for me in the house) and for ending the evening so early and so wisely, when in fact all I had done was postpone its real beginning. Then he spoke to me about M. de Charlus. The latter would doubtless have been amazed had he heard the Professor, who was so amiable to him, the Professor who always assured him: "I never repeat anything," speaking of him and of his life without the slightest reticence. And Brichot's indignant amazement would perhaps have been no less sincere if M. de Charlus had said to him: "I'm told you've been speaking ill of me." Brichot did indeed have an affection for M. de Charlus, and if he had had to call to mind some conversation that had turned upon him, would have been far more likely to remember the friendly feelings he had had for the Baron, while saying the same things about him as everyone else, than those things themselves. He would not have thought that he was lying if he had said: "I who speak of you with such friendliness," since he did feel friendly when he was speaking about M. de Charlus. The Baron had for Brichot the charm which he demanded above all else from the world of society—that of offering him real specimens of what he had long supposed to be an invention of the poets. Brichot, who had often expounded the second *Eclogue* of Virgil without really knowing whether its fiction had any basis in reality, belatedly found, in conversing with Charlus, some of the pleasure which he knew that his masters, M. Mérimée and M. Renan, and his colleague M. Maspéro, had felt when travelling in Spain, Palestine and Egypt on recognising in the landscapes and the present inhabitants of Spain, Palestine and Egypt the settings and the selfsame actors of the ancient scenes which they themselves had expounded in their books.

"Be it said without offence to that knight of noble lineage," Brichot declared to me in the carriage that was taking us home, "he is quite simply prodigious when he illustrates his satanic catechism with a dash of Bedlamite verve and the obsessiveness, I was going to say the candour, of a *blanc d'Espagne*[21] or an émigré. I can assure you, if I dare express myself like Mgr d'Hulst, I am by no means bored on the days when I receive a visit from that feudal lord who, seeking to defend Adonis against our age of miscreants, has followed the instincts of his race, and, in all sodomist innocence, has gone crusading."

I listened to Brichot, and I was not alone with him. As, for that matter, I had never ceased to feel since I left home that evening, I felt myself, in however obscure a fashion, tied fast to the girl who was at that moment in her bedroom. Even when I was talking to someone or other at the Verdurins', I had somehow felt that she was by my side, I had that vague impression of her that we have of our own limbs, and if I happened to think of her it was as we think, with annoyance at being bound to it in complete subjection, of our own body.

"And what a fund of scandal," Brichot went on, "enough to supply all the appendixes of the *Causeries du Lundi*, is the conversation of that apostle! Just imagine, I learned from him that the treatise on ethics which I had always admired as the most splendid moral edifice of our age was inspired in our venerable colleague X by a young telegraph messenger. Needless to say, my eminent friend omitted to give us the name of this ephebe in the course of his demonstrations. In this he showed more circumspection, or, if you prefer, less gratitude, than Phidias, who inscribed the name of the athlete whom he loved upon the ring of his Olympian Zeus. The Baron had not heard this last story. Needless to say, it appealed to his orthodoxy. You can readily imagine that whenever I have to discuss with my colleague a candidate's thesis, I find in his dialectic, which for that matter is extremely subtle, the additional savour which spicy revelations added, for Sainte-Beuve, to the insufficiently confidential writings of Chateaubriand. From our colleague, whose wisdom is golden but who had little money, the telegraph-boy passed into the hands of the Baron, 'with the most honourable intentions' (you should have heard his voice when he said it). And as this Satan is the most obliging of men, he found his protégé a post in the Colonies, from which the young man, who has a sense of gratitude, sends him from time to time the most excellent fruit. The Baron offers these to his distinguished friends; some of the young

man's pineapples appeared quite recently on the table at
the Quai Conti, causing Mme Verdurin to remark, with
no malicious intent: 'You must have an uncle or a nephew
in America, M. de Charlus, to get pineapples like these!' I
admit that I ate them with a certain gaiety, reciting to
myself the opening lines of a Horatian ode which Diderot
loved to recall. In fact, like my colleague Boissier, strolling
from the Palatine to Tibur, I derive from the Baron's conversation a singularly more vivid and more savoury idea
of the writers of the Augustan age, without mentioning
those of the Decadence, or harking back to the Greeks, although I once said to the excellent Baron that in his company I felt like Plato in the house of Aspasia. To tell the
truth, I had considerably enlarged the scale of the two
characters and, as La Fontaine says, my example was
taken 'from smaller animals.' However that may be, you
do not, I imagine, suppose that the Baron took offence.
Never have I seen him so ingenuously delighted. A childish excitement caused him to depart from his aristocratic
phlegm. 'What flatterers all these Sorbonnards are!' he exclaimed with rapture. 'To think that I should have had to
wait until my age before being compared to Aspasia! An
old fright like me! Oh, my youth!' I should have loved
you to see him as he said this, outrageously powdered as
he always is, and, at his age, scented like a young fop. All
the same, beneath his genealogical obsessions, the best fellow in the world. For all these reasons, I should be distressed were this evening's rupture to prove final. What
did surprise me was the way in which the young man
turned on him. His manner towards the Baron has been,
for some time past, that of a henchman, of a feudal vassal,
which scarcely betokened such an insurrection. I hope

that, in any event, even if (*quod di omen avertant*) the
Baron were never to return to the Quai Conti, this schism
will not extend to me. Each of us derives too much benefit from the exchange that we make of my feeble stock of
learning with his experience." (We shall see that if M. de
Charlus showed no violent rancour towards Brichot, at
any rate his affection for the Professor vanished so completely as to allow him to judge him without indulgence.)
"And I swear to you that the exchange is so much in my
favour that when the Baron yields up to me what his life
has taught him, I am unable to endorse the opinion of
Sylvestre Bonnard that a library is still the best place in
which to ponder the dream of life."

We had now reached my door. I got out of the carriage to give the driver Brichot's address. From the pavement, I could see the window of Albertine's room, that
window, formerly quite black at night when she had not
been staying in the house, which the electric light from
inside, segmented by the slats of the shutters, striped
from top to bottom with parallel bars of gold. This magic
scroll, clear as it was to myself, tracing before my tranquil
mind precise images, near at hand, of which I should
presently be taking possession, was invisible to Brichot
who had remained in the carriage and was almost blind,
and would in any case have been incomprehensible to him
since, like the friends who called on me before dinner,
when Albertine had returned from her drive, the Professor
was unaware that a girl who was all my own was waiting
for me in a bedroom adjoining mine. The carriage drove
off. I remained for a moment alone on the pavement. It
was true that I endowed those luminous streaks which I
could see from below, and which to anyone else would

have seemed quite superficial, with the utmost plenitude, solidity and volume, because of all the significance that I placed behind them, in a treasure unsuspected by the rest of the world which I had hidden there and from which those horizontal rays emanated, but a treasure in exchange for which I had forfeited my freedom, my solitude, my thought. If Albertine had not been up there, and indeed if I had merely been in search of pleasure, I would have gone to demand it of unknown women, into whose life I should have attempted to penetrate, in Venice perhaps, or at least in some corner of nocturnal Paris. But now what I had to do when the time came for love-making was not to set out on a journey, was not even to leave my own house, but to return there. And to return there not to find myself alone and, after taking leave of the friends who provide one from the outside with food for one's thoughts, to find myself at any rate compelled to seek it in myself, but to be on the contrary less alone than when I was at the Verdurins', welcomed as I was about to be by the person to whom I had abdicated, to whom I had handed over most completely my own person, without having for an instant the leisure to think of myself nor even requiring the effort, since she would be by my side, to think of her. So that, as I raised my eyes for one last look from the outside at the window of the room in which I should presently find myself, I seemed to behold the luminous gates which were about to close behind me and of which I myself had forged, for an eternal slavery, the inflexible bars of gold.

Albertine had never told me that she suspected me of being jealous of her, preoccupied with everything that she did. The only words we had exchanged—fairly long ago, it must be said—on the subject of jealousy seemed to prove the opposite. I remembered that, on a fine moonlight evening towards the beginning of our relationship, on one of the first occasions when I had accompanied her home and would have been just as glad not to do so and to leave her in order to run after other girls, I had said to her: "You know, if I'm offering to take you home, it's not from jealousy; if you have anything else to do, I shall slip discreetly away." And she had replied: "Oh, I know quite well that you aren't jealous and that you don't care a fig, but I've nothing else to do except to stay with you." Another occasion was at La Raspelière, when M. de Charlus, not without casting a covert glance at Morel, had made a display of friendly gallantry towards Albertine; I had said to her: "Well, he gave you a good hug, I hope." And as I had added half ironically: "I suffered all the torments of jealousy," Albertine, employing the language proper either to the vulgar background from which she sprang or to that other, more vulgar still, which she frequented, replied: "What a kidder you are! I know quite well you're not jealous. For one thing, you told me so, and besides, it's perfectly obvious, get along with you!" She had never told me since then that she had changed her mind; but she must have formed a number of fresh ideas on the subject, which she concealed from me but which an accident might betray willy-nilly, for that evening when, on reaching home, after going to fetch her from her own room and taking her to mine, I said to her (with a certain awkwardness which I did not myself understand, for I had indeed told Albertine that I was going to pay a call and had said that I did not know where, perhaps on Mme de Villeparisis, perhaps on Mme de Guermantes, perhaps on Mme de Cambremer; it is true that I had not actually mentioned the Verdurins): "Guess where I've been—at the Verdurins'," I had barely had time to utter the words before Albertine, a look of utter consternation on her face, had answered me in words which seemed to explode of their own accord with a force which she was unable to contain: "I thought as much."

"I didn't know that you'd be annoyed by my going to see the Verdurins." (It is true that she had not told me that she was annoyed, but it was obvious. It is true also that I had not said to myself that she would be annoyed. And yet, faced with the explosion of her wrath, as with one of those events which a sort of retrospective second sight makes us imagine that we have already experienced in the past, it seemed to me that I could never have expected anything else.)

"Annoyed? What difference does it make to me? I couldn't care less. Wasn't Mlle Vinteuil to be there?"

Beside myself at these words, "You never told me you'd met her the other day," I said to her, to show her that I was better informed than she knew.

Believing that the person whom I reproached her for having met without telling me was Mme Verdurin and not, as I meant to imply, Mlle Vinteuil, "Did I meet her?" she inquired with a pensive air, addressing both herself, as though she were seeking to collect her fugitive memories, and me, as though it was I who could have enlightened her; and no doubt in order that I might indeed say what I knew, and perhaps also in order to gain time before making a difficult reply. But I was far less preoccupied with the thought of Mlle Vinteuil than with a fear which had already crossed my mind but which now gripped me more forcibly. Indeed I imagined that Mme Verdurin had purely and simply invented the story of having expected Mlle Vinteuil and her friend, in order to enhance her own prestige, so that I was quite calm on arriving home. Only Albertine, by saying: "Wasn't Mlle Vinteuil to be there?" had shown me that I had not been mistaken in my original suspicion; but anyhow my mind was at rest in that quarter as far as the future was concerned, since by giving up her plan of visiting the Verdurins' Albertine had sacrificed Mlle Vinteuil for my sake.

"Besides," I said to her angrily, "there are plenty of other things which you hide from me, even the most trivial things, such as for instance when you went for three days to Balbec—I mention it by the way." I had added the words "I mention it by the way" as a complement to "even the most trivial things" so that if Albertine said to me "What was there wrong about my trip to Balbec?" I might be able to answer: "Why, I've quite forgotten. The things people tell me get muddled up in my mind, I attach so little importance to them." And indeed if I referred to that three-day excursion she had made with the chauffeur to Balbec, from where her postcards had reached me after so long a delay, I did so purely at random, and regretted that I had chosen so bad an example, for in fact, as they had barely had time to go there and return, it was certainly the one excursion in which there had not even been time for the interpolation of a meeting that was at all protracted with anybody. But Albertine supposed, from what I had just said, that I knew the real truth and had merely concealed my knowledge from her.

She had in any case been convinced, for some time past, that in one way or another, by having her followed, or in some such fashion, I was, as she had said the week before to Andrée, better informed about her life than she was herself. And so she interrupted me with a wholly unnecessary admission, for certainly I suspected nothing of what she now told me, and I was on the other hand shattered by it, so vast can the disparity be between the truth which a liar has travestied and the idea which, from her lies, the man who is in love with the said liar has formed of that truth. Scarcely had I uttered the words: "When you went for three days to Balbec, I mention it by the way," than Albertine, cutting me short, declared to me as something quite natural: "You mean I never went to Balbec at all? Of course I didn't! And I've always wondered why you pretended to believe that I did. All the same, there was no harm in it. The driver had some business of his own for three days. He didn't dare to mention it to you. And so out of kindness to him (it's typical of me, and I'm the one who always gets the blame), I invented a trip to Balbec. He simply put me down at Auteuil, at the house of a girlfriend of mine in the Rue de l'Assomption, where I spent the three days bored to tears. You see it's not very serious, no great harm done. I did begin to think that you perhaps knew all about it, when I saw how you laughed when the postcards began to arrive, a week late. I quite see that it was absurd, and that it would have been better not to send any cards at all. But that wasn't my fault. I'd bought them in advance and given them to the driver before he dropped me at Auteuil, and then the fat-head put them in his pocket and forgot about them instead of sending them on in an envelope to a friend of his near Balbec who was to forward them to you. I kept on imagining they were about to arrive. He only remembered them after five days, and instead of telling me, the idiot sent them on at once to Balbec. When he did tell me, I really let him have it, I can tell you! To go and worry you unnecessarily, the great fool, as a reward for my shutting myself up for three whole days, so that he could go and look after his family affairs! I didn't even venture out into Auteuil for fear of being seen. The only time I did go out, I was dressed as a man, just for a joke, really. And it was just my luck that the first person I came across was your Yid friend Bloch. But I don't believe it was from him that you learned that my trip to Balbec never existed except in my imagination, for he seemed not to recognise me."

I did not know what to say, not wishing to appear surprised, and shattered by all these lies. A feeling of horror, which gave me no desire to turn Albertine out of the house, far from it, was combined with a strong inclination to burst into tears. This last was caused not by the lie itself and by the annihilation of everything that I had so firmly believed to be true that I felt as though I were in a town that had been razed to the ground, where not a house remained standing, where the bare soil was merely heaped with rubble—but by the melancholy thought that, during those three days when she had been bored to tears in her friend's house at Auteuil, Albertine had never once felt the desire, that the idea had perhaps not even occurred to her, to come and pay me a visit one day on the quiet, or to send a message asking me to go and see her at Auteuil. But I had no time to give myself up to these reflexions. Whatever happened, I did not wish to appear surprised. I smiled with the air of man who knows far more than he is prepared to say: "But that's only one thing out of hundreds. For instance, only this evening, at the Verdurins', I learned that what you had told me about Mlle Vinteuil . . ."

Albertine gazed at me fixedly with a tormented air, seeking to read in my eyes how much I knew. Now, what I knew and what I was about to tell her was the truth about Mlle Vinteuil. It is true that it was not at the Verdurins' that I had learned it, but at Montjouvain long ago. But since I had always refrained, deliberately, from mentioning it to Albertine, I could now appear to have learned it only this evening. And I had a feeling almost of joy—after having felt such anguish in the little train—at possessing this memory of Montjouvain, which I would postdate, but which would nevertheless be the unanswerable proof, a crushing blow to Albertine. This time at least, I had no need to "seem to know" and to "make Albertine talk": I *knew*, I had *seen* through the lighted window at Montjouvain. It had been all very well for Albertine to tell me that her relations with Mlle Vinteuil and her friend had been perfectly pure, but how could she, when I swore to her (and swore without lying) that I knew the habits of these two women, how could she maintain any longer that, having lived in daily intimacy with them, calling them "my big sisters," she had not been the object of approaches on their part which would have made her break with them, if on the contrary she had not acquiesced in them? But I had no time to tell her what I knew. Albertine, imagining, as in the case of the pretended excursion to Balbec, that I had learned the truth either from Mlle Vinteuil, if she had been at the Verdurins', or simply from Mme Verdurin herself, who might have mentioned her to Mlle Vinteuil, did not allow me the chance to speak but made a confession, precisely contrary to what I should have imagined, which nevertheless, by showing me that she had never ceased to lie to me, caused me perhaps just as much pain (especially since I was no longer, as I said a moment ago, jealous of Mlle Vinteuil). Taking the initiative, she spoke as follows: "You mean that you found out this evening that I lied to you when I pretended that I had been more or less brought up by Mlle Vinteuil's friend. It's true that I did lie to you a little. But I felt so looked down on by you, and I saw that you were so keen on that man Vinteuil's music, that as one of my schoolfriends—this is true, I swear to you—had been a friend of Mlle Vinteuil's friend, I stupidly thought that I might make myself seem interesting to you by inventing the story that I had known the girls quite well. I felt that I bored you, that you thought me a goose; I thought that if I told you that those people used to see a lot of me, that I could easily tell you all sorts of things about Vinteuil's work, you'd think more highly of me, that it would bring us closer together. When I lie to you, it's always out of affection for you. And it needed this fatal Verdurin party to open your eyes to the truth, which perhaps they exaggerated a bit, incidentally. I bet Mlle Vinteuil's friend told you that she didn't know me. She met me at least twice at my friend's house. But of course, I'm not smart enough for people who've become so famous. They prefer to say that they've never met me."

Poor Albertine, when she had thought that to tell me that she had been on such intimate terms with Mlle Vinteuil's friend would postpone her being "ditched," would bring her closer to me, she had, as so often happens, reached the truth by a different road from that which she had intended to take. Her showing herself better informed about music than I had supposed would never have prevented me from breaking with her that evening in the little train; and yet it was indeed that speech, which she had made with that object, that had immediately brought about far more than the impossibility of a rupture. Only she made an error of interpretation, not about the effect which that speech was to have, but about the cause by virtue of which it was to produce that effect—that cause being my discovery not of her musical culture but of her disreputable associations. What had abruptly drawn me closer to her—far more, fused indissolubly with her—was not the expectation of a pleasure—and pleasure is too strong a word, a mildly agreeable interest—but the grip of an agonising pain.

Once again I had to be careful not to keep too long a silence which might have led her to suppose that I was surprised. And so, touched by the discovery that she was so modest and had thought herself despised in the Verdurin circle, I said to her tenderly: "But, my darling, I'd gladly give you several hundred francs to let you go and play the fashionable lady wherever you please and invite M. and Mme Verdurin to a grand dinner."

Alas! Albertine was several persons in one. The most mysterious, most simple, most loathsome of these revealed herself in the answer which she made me with an air of disgust, and the exact words of which, to tell the truth, I could not quite make out (even the opening words, for she did not finish her sentence). I did not succeed in reconstituting them until some time later when I had guessed what was in her mind. We hear things retrospectively when we have understood them.

"Thank you for nothing! Spend money on them! I'd a great deal rather you left me free for once in a way to go and get myself b . . . (*me faire casser*) . . ."

At once her face flushed crimson, she looked appalled, and she put her hand over her mouth as though she could have thrust back the words which she had just uttered and which I had quite failed to catch.

"What did you say, Albertine?"

"Nothing, I was half asleep and talking to myself."

"Not a bit of it, you were wide awake."

"I was thinking about asking the Verdurins to dinner, it's very good of you."

"No, I mean what you said just now."

She gave me endless versions, none of which tallied in the least, not simply with her words which, having been interrupted, remained obscure to me, but with the interruption itself and the sudden flush that had accompanied it.

"Come, my darling, that's not what you were going to say, otherwise why did you stop short?"

"Because I felt that my request was presumptuous."

"What request?"

"To be allowed to give a dinner-party."

"No, no, that's not it, there's no need for ceremony between you and me."

"Indeed there is, we ought never to take advantage of the people we love. In any case, I swear to you that that was all."

On the one hand it was still impossible for me to doubt her sworn word; on the other hand her explanations did not satisfy my reason. I continued to press her. "Anyhow, you might at least have the courage to finish what you were saying, you stopped short at *casser*."

"No, leave me alone!"

"But why?"

"Because it's dreadfully vulgar, I'd be ashamed to say such a thing in front of you. I don't know what I was thinking of. The words—I don't even know what they mean, I heard them used in the street one day by some very low people—just came into my head without rhyme or reason. It had nothing to do with me or anybody else, I was simply dreaming aloud."

I felt that I would extract nothing more from Albertine. She had lied to me when she had sworn a moment ago that what had cut her short had been a social fear of being over-presumptuous, since it had now become the shame of using a vulgar expression in front of me. Now this was certainly another lie. For when we were alone together there was no expression too perverse, no word too coarse for us to utter during our embraces. However, it was useless to insist at that moment. But my memory remained obsessed by the word *casser*. Albertine often used expressions such as *casser du bois* or *casser du sucre*, meaning "to run someone down," or would say *Ah! ce que je lui en ai cassé!*, meaning "I fairly gave it to him!" But she would say this quite freely in my presence, and if it was this that she had meant to say, why had she suddenly stopped short, why had she blushed so deeply, placed her hands over her mouth, tried to refashion her sentence, and, when she saw that I had heard the word *casser*, offered a false explanation? Meanwhile, abandoning the pursuit of an interrogation from which I would get no response, the best thing to do was to appear to have lost interest in the matter, and, retracing my thoughts to Albertine's reproaches to me for having gone to the Mistress's, I said to her, somewhat clumsily, making indeed a sort of stupid excuse for my conduct: "Actually I'd been meaning to ask you to come to the Verdurins' party this evening," a remark that was doubly maladroit, for if I meant it, since I saw her all the time, why wouldn't I have suggested it? Furious at my lie and emboldened by my timidity: "You could have gone on asking me for a thousand years," she said, "and I'd never have consented. Those people have always been against me, they've done everything they could to mortify me. There was nothing I didn't do for Mme Verdurin at Balbec, and look at the thanks I get. If she summoned me to her deathbed, I wouldn't go. There are some things it's impossible to forgive. As for you, it's the first time you've behaved badly to me. When Françoise told me you'd gone out (and she enjoyed telling me all right), I'd sooner have had my skull split down the middle. I tried not to show any sign, but never in my life have I felt so grossly insulted."

But while she was speaking there continued within me, in that curiously alive and creative sleep of the unconscious (a sleep in which the things that have barely touched us succeed in carving an impression, in which our sleeping hands take hold of the key that turns the lock, the key for which we have sought in vain), the quest for what it was that she had meant by that interrupted sentence, the missing end of which I was so anxious to know. And all of a sudden an appalling word, of which I had never dreamed, burst upon me: *le pot*.[22] I cannot say that it came to me in a single flash, as when, in a long passive submission to an incomplete recollection, while one tries gently and cautiously to unfold it, one remains ravelled in it, glued to it. No, in contrast to my habitual method of recall, there were, I think, two parallel lines of search: the first took into account not merely Albertine's words, but her look of exasperation when I had offered her a sum of money with which to give a grand dinner, a look which seemed to say: "Thank you, the idea of spending money upon things that bore me, when without money I could do things that I enjoy doing!" And it was perhaps the memory of the look she had given me that made me alter my method in order to discover the end of her unfinished sentence. Until then I had been hypnotised by the last word, *casser*. What was it she meant by *break*? *Casser du bois*? No. *Du sucre*? No. Break, break, break. And all at once her look, and her shrug, when I had suggested that she should give a dinner-party sent me back to the words that had preceded. And immediately I saw that she had not simply said *casser* but *me faire casser*. Horror! It was this that she would have preferred. Twofold horror! For even the vilest of prostitutes, who consents to such a thing, or even desires it, does not use that hideous expression to the man who indulges in it. She would feel it too degrading. To a woman alone, if she loves women, she might say it, to excuse herself for giving herself presently to a man. Albertine had not been lying when she told me that she was half dreaming. Her mind elsewhere, forgetting that she was with me, impulsively she had shrugged her shoulders and begun to speak as she would have spoken to one of those women, perhaps to one of my budding girls. And abruptly recalled to reality, crimson with shame, pushing back into her mouth what she was about to say, desperately ashamed, she had refused to utter another word. I had not a moment to lose if I was not to let her see the despair I was in. But already, after my first impulse of rage, the tears were coming to my eyes. As at Balbec, on the night that followed her revelation of her friendship with the Vinteuil pair, I must immediately invent a plausible reason for my grief, and one that was at the same time capable of having so profound an effect on Albertine as to give me a few days' respite before coming to a decision. And so, just as she was telling me that she had never felt so affronted as when she had heard that I had gone out alone, that she would sooner have died than be told this by Françoise, and just as, irritated by her absurd susceptibility, I was on the point of telling her that what I had done was trivial, that there was nothing wounding to her in my having gone out, my unconscious parallel search for what she had meant to say had come to fruition, and the despair into which my discovery plunged me could not be completely hidden, so that instead of defending, I accused myself. "My little Albertine," I said to her in a gentle voice which was drowned in my first tears, "I could tell you that you're mistaken, that what I did this evening was nothing, but I should be lying; it's you who are right, you have realised the truth, my poor sweet, which is that six months ago, three months ago, when I was still so fond of you, I should never have done such a thing. It's a mere nothing, and yet it's enormous, because of the immense change in my heart of which it is the sign. And since you have detected this change which I hoped to conceal from you, I feel impelled to say this to you: My little Albertine" (I went on in a tone of profound gentleness and sorrow), "don't you see that the life you're leading here is boring for you. It is better that we should part, and as the best partings are those that are effected most swiftly, I ask you, to cut short the great sorrow that I am bound to feel, to say good-bye to me tonight and to leave in the morning without my seeing you again, while I'm asleep."

She appeared stunned, incredulous and desolate: "Tomorrow? You really mean it?"

And in spite of the anguish that I felt in speaking of our parting as though it were already in the past—partly perhaps because of that very anguish—I began to give Albertine the most precise instructions as to certain things which she would have to do after she left the house. And passing from one request to another, I soon found myself entering into the minutest details.

"Be so kind," I said with infinite sadness, "as to send me back that book of Bergotte's which is at your aunt's. There's no hurry about it, in three days, in a week, whenever you like, but remember that I don't want to have to write and ask you for it: that would be too painful. We have been happy together, but now we feel that we should be unhappy."

"Don't say that we feel that we'd be unhappy," Albertine interrupted me, "don't say 'we,' it's only you who feel that."

"Yes, very well, you or I, as you like, for one reason or another. But it's absurdly late, you must go to bed—we've decided to part tonight."

"Excuse me, *you*'ve decided, and I obey you because I don't want to upset you."

"Very well, it's I who have decided, but that doesn't make it any less painful for me. I don't say that it will be painful for long, you know that I'm not capable of remembering things for long, but for the first few days I shall be so miserable without you. And so I feel that it's no use stirring up the memory with letters, we must end everything at once."

"Yes, you're right," she said to me with a crushed air, which was enhanced by the signs of fatigue on her features due to the lateness of the hour, "rather than have one finger chopped off and then another, I prefer to lay my head on the block at once."

"Heavens, I'm appalled when I think how late I'm keeping you out of bed, it's madness. However, it's the last night! You'll have plenty of time to sleep for the rest of your life."

And thus while telling her that it was time to say good-night I sought to postpone the moment when she would have said it: "Would you like me, in order to take your mind off things during the first few days, to ask Bloch to send his cousin Esther to the place where you'll be staying? He'll do that for me."

"I don't know why you say that" (I had said it in an attempt to wrest a confession from Albertine), "there's only one person I care about, and that's you," Albertine said to me, and her words were infinitely sweet to me. But, the next moment, what a blow she dealt me! "I remember, of course, that I did give this Esther my photograph because she kept on asking me for it and I saw that it would give her pleasure, but as for having any great liking for her or wanting to see her again, never!" And yet Albertine was of so frivolous a nature that she went on: "If she wants to see me, it's all the same to me. She's very nice, but I don't care in the least either way."

Thus, when I had spoken to her of the photograph of Esther which Bloch had sent me (and which I had not even received when I mentioned it to her) Albertine had gathered that Bloch had shown me a photograph of herself which she had given to Esther. In my worst suppositions, I had never imagined that any such intimacy could have existed between Albertine and Esther. Albertine had been at a loss for words when I mentioned the photograph. And now, wrongly, supposing me to be in the know, she thought it advisable to confess. I was shattered.

"And, Albertine, let me ask you to do me one more favour: never attempt to see me again. If at any time, as may happen in a year, in two years, in three years, we should find ourselves in the same town, avoid me." And seeing that she did not answer my request in the affirmative, I went on: "My Albertine, don't do it, don't ever see me again in this life. It would hurt me too much. For I was really fond of you, you know. Of course, when I told you the other day that I wanted to see the friend I mentioned to you at Balbec again, you thought it was all settled. Not at all, I assure you, it was quite immaterial to me. You're convinced that I had long made up my mind to leave you, that my affection was all make-believe."

"Not at all, you're crazy, I never thought so," she said sadly.

"You're right, you must never think so, I did genuinely feel for you, not love perhaps, but a great, a very great affection, more than you can imagine."

"Of course I can imagine. And do you suppose that I don't love you!"

"It hurts me terribly to have to leave you."

"It hurts me a thousand times more," replied Albertine.

Already for some little time I had felt that I could no longer hold back the tears that came welling up in my eyes. And these tears did not spring from at all the same sort of misery which I had felt long ago when I said to Gilberte: "It is better that we should not see one another again; life is dividing us." No doubt when I wrote this to Gilberte, I said to myself that when I was in love not with her but with another, the excess of my love would diminish that which I might perhaps have been able to inspire, as though two people must inevitably have only a certain quantity of love at their disposal, of which the surplus taken by one is subtracted from the other, and that from her too, as from Gilberte, I should be doomed to part. But the situation was entirely different for several reasons, the first of which (and it had, in its turn, given rise to the others) was that the lack of will-power which my grandmother and my mother had observed in me with alarm, at Combray, and before which each of them, so great is the energy with which an invalid imposes his weakness upon others, had capitulated in turn, this lack of will-power had gone on increasing at an ever accelerated pace. When I felt that my presence bored Gilberte, I had still enough strength left to give her up; I had no longer the same strength when I had made a similar discovery with regard to Albertine, and could think only of keeping her by force. With the result that, whereas I wrote to Gilberte saying that I would not see her again and really meant it, I said this to Albertine quite untruthfully and in the hope of bringing about a reconciliation. Thus we presented each to the other an appearance which was very different from the reality. And no doubt it is always so when two people are face to face, since each of them is ignorant of a part of what exists in the other (even what he knows, he can understand only in part) and both of them reveal what is least personal to them, either because they have themselves not properly untangled and regard as negligible what is most personal or because insignificant advantages which do not belong to them particularly seem more important and more flattering to themselves, and at the same time they pretend not to care about certain things they admire, in order not to be despised for not having them, and these are precisely the things that they appear to scorn above all else and even to abhor. But in love this misunderstanding is carried to its supreme pitch because, except perhaps in childhood, we try to see to it that the appearance we assume, instead of reflecting exactly what is in our thoughts, is what is best calculated to enable us to obtain what we desire, and this, in my case, since I had come in, was to be able to keep Albertine as docile as she had been in the past, and to ensure that she did not in her irritation ask me for greater freedom, which I wanted to grant her some day but which at this moment, when I was afraid of her hankerings after independence, would have made me too jealous. After a certain age, from self-esteem and from sagacity, it is to the things we most desire that we pretend to attach no importance. But in love,

mere sagacity—which in any case is probably not true
wisdom—drives us all too quickly to this kind of duplicity. What I had dreamed of, as a child, as being the
sweetest thing in love, what had seemed to me to be the
very essence of love, was to pour out freely, to the one I
loved, my tenderness, my gratitude for her kindness, my
longing for an everlasting life together. But I had become
only too well aware, from my own experience and from
that of my friends, that the expression of such sentiments
is far from being contagious. The case of an affected old
woman like M. de Charlus who, as a result of seeing in
his mind's eye only a handsome young man, thinks he
himself has become a handsome young man, and betrays
more and more effeminacy in his risible affectations of
virility—such a case falls under a law which applies far
more widely than to the Charluses alone, a law so gener-
alised that not even love itself exhausts it entirely; we do
not see our bodies, though others do, and we "follow" our
thoughts, the object that is in front of us, invisible to others (made visible at times in a work of art, whence the
frequent disillusionment of its admirers when they are admitted into the presence of the artist, whose inner beauty
is so imperfectly reflected in his face). Once one has noticed this, one no longer "lets oneself go"; I had taken
good care that afternoon not to tell Albertine how grateful
I was to her that she had not remained at the Trocadéro.
And tonight, having been afraid that she might leave me,
I had feigned a desire to leave her, a pretence which
moreover, as we shall see presently, had not been dictated
solely by the experience I believed myself to have gained
from my former loves and was seeking to turn to the
profit of this one.

The fear that Albertine was perhaps going to say to me: "I want to be allowed to go out by myself at certain hours, I want to be able to stay away for twenty-four hours," or some such request for freedom which I did not attempt to define, but which alarmed me, this fear had crossed my mind for a moment during the Verdurin reception. But it had been dispelled, contradicted moreover by the memory of Albertine's constant assurances of how happy she was with me. The intention to leave me, if it existed in Albertine, manifested itself only in an obscure fashion, in certain mournful glances, certain gestures of impatience, remarks which meant nothing of the sort but which, if one analysed them (and there was not even any need for analysis, for one understands at once this language of passion, even the most uneducated understand these remarks which can be explained only by vanity, rancour, jealousy, unexpressed as it happens, but detectable at once by the interlocutor through an intuitive faculty which, like the "good sense" of which Descartes speaks, is "the most evenly distributed thing in the world"), could only be explained by the presence in her of a sentiment which she concealed and which might lead her to form plans for another life without me. Just as this intention did not express itself in her speech in a logical fashion, so the presentiment of this intention, which I had felt tonight, remained just as vague in me. I continued to live by the hypothesis which accepted as true everything that Albertine told me. But it may be that during this time a wholly contrary hypothesis, of which I refused to think, never left me; this is all the more probable since otherwise I should not have felt uncomfortable about telling Albertine that I had been to the Verdurins', and my lack of astonishment at her anger would not have been comprehensible. So that what probably existed in me was an idea of Albertine entirely contrary to that which my reason formed of her, and also to that which her own words suggested, an Albertine who was none the less not wholly invented, since she was like an internal mirror of certain impulses that occurred in her, such as her ill-humour at my having gone to the Verdurins'. Besides, for a long time past, my constant anxieties, my fear of telling Albertine that I loved her, all this corresponded to another hypothesis which explained far more things and had also this to be said for it, that if one adopted the first hypothesis the second became more probable, for by allowing myself to give way to effusions of tenderness for Albertine, I obtained from her nothing but irritation (to which moreover she assigned a different cause).

I may say that what had seemed to me most serious and had struck me most forcibly as a symptom of the fact that she anticipated my accusation was that she had said to me: "I believe Mlle Vinteuil was to be there," to which I had replied in the cruellest possible way: "You didn't tell me you'd met her." As soon as I found Albertine less than nice, instead of telling her I was sad, I became nasty.

Analysing my feelings on the basis of this, on the basis of the unvarying system of ripostes expressing the opposite of what I felt, I can be quite certain that if, that night, I told her that I was going to leave her, it was because—even before I had realised it—I was afraid that she might desire some freedom (I should have been hard put to it to say what this freedom was that made me tremble, but anyhow a freedom which might have given her an opportunity of being unfaithful to me, or at least which was such that I should no longer have been able to be certain that she was not) and because I wanted to show her, from pride and from cunning, that I was very far from fearing anything of the sort, as I had already shown at Balbec, when I was anxious that she should have a good opinion of me, and later on, when I was anxious that she should not have time to feel bored with me.

Finally, the objection that might be offered to this second, unformulated hypothesis, that everything that Albertine said to me indicated on the contrary that the life which she preferred was the life she led in my house, rest, quiet, reading, solitude, a loathing for Sapphic loves, and so forth, need not be considered seriously. For if on her part Albertine had wanted to gauge what I felt from what I said to her, she would have learned the exact opposite of the truth, since I never expressed a desire to part from her except when I was unable to do without her, and at Balbec I had twice confessed to her that I was in love with another woman, first Andrée, then a mysterious stranger, on the two occasions when jealousy had revived my love for her. My words, therefore, did not in the least reflect my feelings. If the reader has no more than a faint impression of these, that is because, as narrator, I expose my feelings to him at the same time as I repeat my words. But if I concealed the former and he were acquainted only with the latter, my actions, so little in keeping with them, would so often give him the impression of strange reversals that he would think me more or less mad. A procedure which would not, for that matter, be much more false than the one I adopted, for the images which prompted me to action, so opposed to those which were portrayed in my words, were at that moment extremely obscure; I was but imperfectly aware of the nature which guided my actions; today, I have a clear conception of its subjective truth. As for its objective truth, that is to say whether the intuitions of that nature grasped more exactly than my reason Albertine's true intentions, whether I was right to trust to that nature or whether on the contrary it did not alter Albertine's intentions instead of making them plain—that I find difficult to say.

That vague fear which I had felt at the Verdurins' that Albertine might leave me had at first subsided. When I returned home, it had been with the feeling that I myself was a captive, not with that of finding a captive in the house. But the fear that had subsided had gripped me even more violently when, as soon as I informed Albertine that I had been to the Verdurins', I saw her face veiled with a look of enigmatic irritation which moreover was not making itself visible for the first time. I knew perfectly well that it was only the crystallisation in the flesh of reasoned grievances, of ideas clear to the person who forms but does not express them, a synthesis rendered visible but not therefore rational, which he who gathers its precious residue from the face of the beloved endeavours in his turn, so that he may understand what is occurring in her, to reduce by analysis to its intellectual elements. The approximate equation of that unknown quantity which Albertine's thoughts were to me had given me, more or less, the following: "I knew his suspicions, I was sure that he would attempt to verify them, and so that I might not hinder him, he has worked out his little plan in secret." But if this was the state of mind (which she had never expressed to me) in which Albertine was living, must she not regard with horror, no longer have

the strength to lead, might she not at any moment decide
to terminate, a life in which, if she was, in desire at any
rate, guilty, she must feel herself suspected, hunted, prevented from ever yielding to her desires, without thereby
disarming my jealousy, and in which, if she was innocent
in intention and fact, she had had every right, for some
time past, to feel discouraged, seeing that, ever since Balbec, where she had shown so much perseverance in avoiding the risk of ever being alone with Andrée, until this
very day when she had given up the idea of going to the
Verdurins' and of staying at the Trocadéro, she had not
succeeded in regaining my trust? All the more so because
I could not say that her behaviour was not exemplary. If
at Balbec, when anyone mentioned girls who behaved
scandalously, she used often to copy their laughter, their
wrigglings, their general manner, which was a torture to
me because of what I supposed it must mean to her girlfriends, now that she knew my opinion on the subject she
ceased, as soon as anyone made an allusion to things of
that sort, to take part in the conversation, not only orally
but with her facial expression. Whether it was in order
not to contribute her share to the slanders that were being
uttered about some woman or other, or for a quite different reason, the only thing that was noticeable then, upon
those so mobile features, was that as soon as the topic was
broached they had made their inattention evident, while
preserving exactly the same expression as they had worn
a moment earlier. And this immobility of even a light
expression was as heavy as a silence. It would have been
impossible to say whether she blamed, whether she approved, whether she knew or did not know about these
things. Her features no longer bore any relation to any-

thing except one another. Her nose, her mouth, her eyes formed a perfect harmony, isolated from everything else; she looked like a pastel, and seemed to have no more heard what had just been said than if it had been uttered in front of a portrait by La Tour.

My servitude, which had again been brought home to me when, as I gave the driver Brichot's address, I had seen her lighted window, had ceased to weigh upon me shortly afterwards, when I saw that Albertine appeared so cruelly conscious of her own. And in order that it might seem to her less burdensome, that she might not decide to break her bonds of her own accord, I had felt that the most effective plan was to give her the impression that it would not be permanent and that I myself was looking forward to its termination. Seeing that my feint had proved successful, I might well have felt happy, in the first place because what I had so dreaded, Albertine's supposed wish to leave me, seemed to be ruled out, and secondly because, quite apart from the object that I had had in mind, the very success of my feint, by proving that I was something more to Albertine than a scorned lover, whose jealousy is flouted, all of his ruses detected in advance, restored to our love a sort of virginity, revived for it the days in which she could still, at Balbec, so readily believe that I was in love with another woman. Doubtless she would no longer have believed that, but she gave credence to my feigned determination to part from her now and for ever.

She appeared to suspect that the cause of it might lie at the Verdurins'. I told her that I had seen a dramatist (Bloch), who was a great friend of Léa's and to whom Léa had said some strange things (I hoped by telling her this to make her think that I knew a great deal more than I cared to say about Bloch's cousins). But feeling a need to calm the agitation induced in me by my pretence of a rupture, I said to her: "Albertine, can you swear that you have never lied to me?"

She gazed fixedly into space before replying: "Yes . . . that's to say no. I was wrong to tell you that Andrée was greatly taken with Bloch. We never met him."

"Then why did you say so?"

"Because I was afraid that you believed other stories about her."

"That's all?"

She stared once again into space and then said: "I ought not to have kept from you a three weeks' trip I went on with Léa. But I knew you so slightly in those days!"

"It was before Balbec?"

"Before the second time, yes."

And that very morning, she had told me that she did not know Léa! I watched a tongue of flame seize and devour in an instant a novel which I had spent millions of minutes in writing. To what end? To what end? Of course I realised that Albertine had revealed these two facts to me because she thought that I had learned them indirectly from Léa; and that there was no reason why a hundred similar facts should not exist. I realised too that Albertine's words, when one interrogated her, never contained an atom of truth, that the truth was something she let slip only in spite of herself, as a result of a sudden mixing together in her mind of the facts which she had previously been determined to conceal with the belief that one had got wind of them.

"But two things are nothing," I said to Albertine, "let's have as many as four, so that you may leave me with some memories. What other revelations have you got for me?"

Once again she stared into space. To what belief in a future life was she adapting her falsehood, with what gods less accommodating than she had supposed was she seeking to make a deal? It cannot have been an easy matter, for her silence and the fixity of her gaze continued for some time.

"No, nothing else," she said at length. And, notwithstanding my persistence, she adhered, easily now, to "nothing else." And what a lie! For, from the moment she had acquired those tastes until the day when she had been shut up in my house, how many times, in how many places, on how many excursions must she have gratified them! The daughters of Gomorrah are at once rare enough and numerous enough for one not to pass unnoticed by another in any given crowd. Thenceforward, a rendezvous is an easy matter.

I remembered with horror an evening which at the time had struck me as merely absurd. One of my friends had invited me to dine at a restaurant with his mistress and another of his friends who had also brought his. The two women were not long in coming to an understanding, but were so impatient to enjoy one another that already at the soup stage their feet were searching for one another, often finding mine. Presently their legs were intertwined. My two friends noticed nothing; I was in agonies. One of the women, who could contain herself no longer, stooped under the table, saying that she had dropped something. Then one of them complained of a headache and asked to go upstairs to the lavatory. The other remembered that it was time for her to go and meet a woman friend at the theatre. Finally I was left alone with my two friends, who suspected nothing. The lady with the headache reappeared, but begged to be allowed to go home by herself to wait for her lover at his house, so that she might take a febrifuge. The two women became great friends and used to go about together, one of them, dressed as a man, picking up little girls and taking them home to the other to be initiated. This other had a little boy with whom she would pretend to be displeased and would hand him over for correction to her friend, who went to it with a will. One may say that there was no place, however public, in which they did not do what is most secret.

"But Léa behaved perfectly properly with me throughout the trip," Albertine told me. "In fact she was a great deal more reserved than plenty of society women."

"Are there any society women who have shown a lack of reserve with you, Albertine?"

"Never."

"Then what do you mean?"

"Oh, well, she was less free in her speech."

"For instance?"

"She would never, like many of the women you meet, have used the expression 'rotten,' or say: 'I don't care a damn for anybody.'"

It seemed to me that a part of the novel which the flames had so far spared had finally crumbled into ashes.

My discouragement might have persisted. Albertine's words, when I thought of them, made it give way to a furious rage. This subsided into a sort of tenderness. I too, since I had come home and declared that I wished to break with her, had been lying. And this desire to separate, which I simulated perseveringly, brought for me little by little something of the sadness I would have felt had I truly wanted to leave Albertine.

Besides, even when I thought in fits and starts, in twinges, as we say of other bodily pains, of that orgiastic life which Albertine had led before she met me, I wondered all the more at the docility of my captive and ceased to feel any resentment. Never, in the course of our life together, had I ceased to make it clear to Albertine that that life would in all probability be merely temporary, so that she might continue to find some charm in it. But tonight I had gone further, having feared that vague threats of separation were no longer sufficient, contradicted as they would doubtless be, in Albertine's mind, by her idea of a great and jealous love of her, which must have made me, she seemed to imply, go and investigate at the Verdurins'. That night I thought that, among the other reasons which might have made me suddenly decide to put on this comedy of rupture, without even realising what I was doing except as I went on, there was above all the fact that when, in one of those impulses to which my father was prone, I threatened another person's safety, since unlike him I did not have the courage to put a threat into practice, in order not to give the impression that it had been nothing but empty words, I would go to considerable lengths in pretending to carry out my threat and would recoil only when my adversary, genuinely convinced of my sincerity, had begun seriously to tremble.

Besides, we feel that in these lies there is indeed a grain of truth, that, if life does not bring about any changes in our loves, it is we ourselves who will seek to bring about or to feign them, so strongly do we feel that all love, and everything else in life, evolves rapidly towards a farewell. We want to shed the tears that it will bring long before it comes. No doubt there was, on this occasion, a practical reason for the scene that I had enacted. I had suddenly wanted to keep Albertine because I felt that she was scattered about among other people with whom I could not prevent her from mixing. But even if she had renounced them all for ever for my sake, I might perhaps have been still more firmly resolved never to leave her, for separation is made painful by jealousy but impossible by gratitude. I felt that in any case I was fighting the decisive battle in which I must conquer or succumb. I would have offered Albertine in an hour all that I possessed, because I said to myself: "Everything depends upon this battle." But such battles are less like those of old, which lasted for a few hours, than like those of today which do not end the next day, or the day after, or the following week. We give all our strength, because we steadfastly believe that we shall never need it again. And more than a year goes by without producing a "decision."

Perhaps an unconscious reminiscence of lying scenes enacted by M. de Charlus, in whose company I had been when the fear of Albertine's leaving me had seized hold of me, had contributed thereto. But later on I heard my mother tell a story, of which I then knew nothing, which leads me to believe that I had found all the elements of this scene in myself, in one of those obscure reserves of heredity which certain emotions, acting in this as drugs such as alcohol or coffee act upon the residue of our stored-up strength, place at our disposal. When my aunt Léonie learned from Eulalie that Françoise, convinced that her mistress would never again leave the house, had secretly planned an outing of which my aunt was to know nothing, she pretended, the day before, to have suddenly decided to go for a drive next day. The incredulous Françoise was ordered not only to prepare my aunt's clothes beforehand, and to air those that had been put away for too long, but even to order the carriage and arrange all the details of the excursion down to the last quarter of an hour. It was only when Françoise, convinced or at any rate shaken, had been forced to confess to my aunt the plan that she herself had made, that my aunt publicly abandoned her own, so as not, she said, to interfere with Françoise's arrangements. Similarly, in order that Albertine should not think that I was exaggerating and in order to make her proceed as far as possible in the idea that we were to part, myself drawing the obvious inferences from the proposal I had advanced, I had begun to anticipate the time which was to begin next day and was to last for ever, the time when we should be separated, addressing to Albertine the same requests as if we were not presently to be reconciled. Like a general who considers that if a feint is to succeed in deceiving the enemy it must be pushed to the limit, I had used up almost as much of my store of sensibility as if it had been genuine. This fictitious parting scene ended by causing me almost as much grief as if it had been real, possibly because one of the actors, Albertine, by believing it to be real, had heightened the illusion for the other. We lived a day-to-day life which, however tedious, was still endurable, held down to earth by the ballast of habit and by that certainty that the next day, even if it should prove painful, would contain the presence of the other. And here was I foolishly destroying all that heavy life. I was destroying it, it is true, only in a fictitious fashion, but this was enough to make me wretched; perhaps because the sad words which we utter, even mendaciously, carry in themselves their sorrow and inject it deeply into us; perhaps because we realise that, by feigning farewells, we anticipate an hour which must inevitably come sooner or later; then we cannot be certain that we have not triggered off the mechanism which will make it strike. In every bluff there is an element of uncertainty, however small, as to what the person whom we are deceiving is going to do. What if this make-believe parting should lead to a real parting! One cannot consider the possibility, however unlikely it may seem, without a pang of anguish. One is doubly anxious, because the parting would then occur at the moment when it would be most intolerable, when one has been made to suffer by the woman who would be leaving us before having healed, or at least soothed, one's pain. Finally, one no longer has the solid ground of habit upon which to rest, even in one's sorrow. One has deliberately deprived oneself of it, one has given the present day an exceptional importance, detached it from the days before and after it; it floats without roots like a day of departure; one's imagination, ceasing to be paralysed by habit, has awakened, one has suddenly added to one's everyday love sentimental dreams which enormously enhance it, making indispensable to one a presence upon which in fact one is no longer certain that one can rely. No doubt it is precisely in order to assure oneself of that presence for the future that one has indulged in the make-believe of being able to dispense with it. But one has oneself been taken in by the game, one has begun to suffer

anew because one has created something new and unfamiliar which thus resembles those cures that are destined
in time to heal the malady from which one is suffering,
but the first effects of which are to aggravate it.

I had tears in my eyes, like those people who, alone
in their rooms, imagining, in the wayward course of their
meditations, the death of someone they love, conjure up
so precise a picture of the grief that they would feel that
they end by feeling it. So, multiplying my injunctions as
to how Albertine should behave towards me after we had
parted, I seemed to feel almost as much distress as though
we had not been on the verge of a reconciliation. Besides,
was I so certain that I could bring about this reconciliation, bring Albertine back to the idea of a shared life, and,
if I succeeded for the time being, that, in her, the state of
mind which this scene had dispelled would not revive? I
felt that I was in control of the future but I did not quite
believe it because I realised that this feeling was due
merely to the fact that the future did not yet exist, and
that thus I was not crushed by its inevitability. And while
I lied, I was perhaps putting into my words more truth
than I supposed. I had just had an example of this, when
I told Albertine that I would quickly forget her; this was
what had indeed happened to me in the case of Gilberte,
whom I now refrained from going to see in order to avoid,
not suffering, but an irksome duty. And certainly I had
suffered when I wrote to Gilberte to tell her that I would
not see her any more. Yet I saw Gilberte only from time
to time. Whereas the whole of Albertine's time belonged
to me. And in love, it is easier to relinquish a feeling
than to give up a habit. But all these painful words about
our parting, if the strength to utter them had been given

me because I knew them to be untrue, were on the other hand sincere on Albertine's lips when I heard her exclaim: "Ah! I promise I shall never see you again. Anything sooner than see you cry like that, my darling. I don't want to cause you pain. Since it must be, we'll never meet again." They were sincere, as they could not have been coming from me, because, since Albertine felt nothing stronger for me than friendship, on the one hand the renunciation that they promised cost her less, and on the other hand because my tears, which would have been so small a matter in a great love, seemed to her almost extraordinary and distressed her, transposed into the domain of that state of friendship in which she dwelt, a friendship greater than mine for her, to judge by what she had just said—what she had just said, because when two people part it is the one who is not in love who makes the tender speeches, since love does not express itself directly—what she had just said and what was perhaps not altogether untrue, for the countless kindnesses of love may end by arousing, in the person who inspires without feeling it, an affection and a gratitude less selfish than the sentiment that provoked them, which, perhaps, after years of separation, when nothing of that sentiment remains in the former lover, will still persist in the beloved.

There was only one moment when I felt a kind of hatred for her, which merely sharpened my need to hold on to her. Since, being exclusively jealous of Mlle Vinteuil that night, I thought of the Trocadéro with the greatest indifference (not only because I had sent her there to avoid the Verdurins, but even when I thought of Léa's presence there, on account of which I had brought her back so that she should not meet her), I mentioned Léa's name without thinking, and Albertine, at once on her guard, supposing that I had perhaps heard something more, took the initiative and exclaimed volubly, but without looking me straight in the face: "I know her very well. Some of my friends and I went to see her act last year, and after the performance we went behind to her dressing-room. She changed in front of us. It was most interesting." Then my mind was compelled to relinquish Mlle Vinteuil and, in a despairing effort, in that fruitless hunt through the abysses of possible reconstructions, attached itself to the actress, to that evening when Albertine had gone to see her in her dressing-room. On the one hand, after all the oaths she had sworn to me, and in so truthful a tone, after her complete sacrifice of her freedom, how could I possibly believe that there was anything wrong in it? And yet, on the other hand, were not my suspicions antennae pointing in the direction of the truth, since if she had given up the Verdurins for my sake in order to go to the Trocadéro, nevertheless at the Verdurins' Mlle Vinteuil had been expected, and at the Trocadéro, which she had moreover given up in order to go for a drive with me, there had been this Léa, who seemed to me to be disturbing me without cause and yet whom, in a remark which I had not extracted from her, she admitted having known on a larger scale than my fears had ever envisaged, in circumstances that were indeed dubious: for what could have induced her to go behind like that to her dressing-room? If I ceased to suffer on account of Mlle Vinteuil when I suffered because of Léa, those two tormentors of my day, it was either because of the inability of my mind to picture too many scenes at one time, or because of the intrusion of my nervous emotions of which my jealousy was but the echo. I could deduce from them only that she had no more belonged to Léa than to Mlle Vinteuil and that I believed in the Léa hypothesis only because she was now uppermost in my mind. But the fact that my jealousies subsided— to revive from time to time one after another—did not mean, either, that they did not correspond each to some truth of which I had had a foreboding, that of these various women I must not say to myself none, but all. I say a foreboding, for I could not project myself to all the points of time and space which I should have had to occupy; and besides, what instinct would have given me the sequence and the co-ordinates to enable me to surprise Albertine at such and such a time with Léa, or with the Balbec girls, or with that friend of Mme Bontemps whom she had brushed against, or with the girl on the tennis-court who had nudged her with her elbow, or with Mlle Vinteuil?

"My little Albertine," I replied, "it is very good of you to make me this promise. Anyhow, for the first few years at least, I shall avoid the places where I might meet you. You don't know whether you'll be going to Balbec this summer? Because in that case I should arrange not to go there myself." Now, if I went on in this way, anticipating the future in my lying inventions, it was less with the object of frightening Albertine than that of distressing myself. As a man who at first has had no serious reason for losing his temper becomes completely intoxicated by the sound of his own voice and lets himself be carried away by a fury engendered not by his grievance but by his anger itself as it steadily grows, so I was sliding faster and faster down the slope of my wretchedness, towards an ever more profound despair, with the inertia of a man who feels the cold grip him, makes no effort to struggle against it, and even finds a sort of pleasure in shivering. And if, presently, I had the strength at last to pull myself together, to react, to go into reverse, as I had every intention of doing, it was not so much for the pain that Albertine had caused me by greeting me with such hostility on my return, as for the pain I had felt in imagining, in order to pretend to be settling them, the formalities of an imaginary separation, in foreseeing its consequences, that Albertine's kiss, when the time came for her to bid me good-night, would have to console me now. In any case, it was important that this leave-taking should not come of its own accord from her, for that would have made more difficult the reversal whereby I would propose to her to abandon the idea of our parting. I therefore continued to remind her that the time to say good-night had long since come and gone, and this, by leaving the initiative to me, enabled me to put it off for a moment longer. And thus I interspersed the questions which I continued to put to Albertine with allusions to our exhaustion and the lateness of the hour.

"I don't know where I shall be going," she replied to the last of these questions with a preoccupied air. "Perhaps I shall go to Touraine, to my aunt's." And this first plan that she suggested froze me as though it were beginning actually to put our final separation into effect. She looked round the room, at the pianola, the blue satin armchairs. "I still can't get used to the idea that I shan't see all this again, tomorrow, or the next day, or ever. Poor little room. It seems to me quite impossible; I can't get it into my head."

"It had to be; you were unhappy here."

"No, I wasn't at all unhappy, it's now that I shall be unhappy."

"No, I assure you, it's better for you."

"For you, perhaps!"

I began to stare into space as though, tormented by a great uncertainty, I was struggling with an idea that had just occurred to me. Then, all of a sudden: "Listen, Albertine, you say that you're happier here, that you're now going to be unhappy."

"Why, of course."

"That appals me. Would you like us to try to carry on for a few weeks? Who knows, week by week, we may perhaps go on for a long time. You know that there are temporary arrangements which end by becoming permanent."

"Oh, it would be sweet of you!"

"Only in that case it's ridiculous of us to have made ourselves wretched like this over nothing for hours on end. It's like making all the preparations for a long journey and then staying at home. I'm absolutely dead beat."

I sat her on my knee, took Bergotte's manuscript which she so longed to have, and wrote on the cover: "To my little Albertine, in memory of a new lease of life."

"Now," I said to her, "go and sleep until tomorrow, my darling, for you must be worn out."

"Most of all I'm very happy."

"Do you love me a bit?"

"A hundred times more than ever."

I should have been wrong to be pleased with this little piece of play-acting. Even if it had stopped short of the sort of full-scale production I had given it, even if we had done no more than simply discuss a separation, it would have been serious enough. In conversations of this sort, we imagine that we are speaking not just insincerely, which is true, but freely. Whereas they are generally the first faint murmur of an unsuspected storm, whispered to us without our knowing it. In reality, what we express at such times is the opposite of our desire (which is to live for ever with the one we love), but also the impossibility of living together which is the cause of our daily suffering, a suffering preferred by us to that of a separation, which will, however, end by separating us in spite of ourselves. But not, as a rule, at once. More often than not it happens—this was not, as we shall see, my case with Albertine—that, some time after the words in which we did not believe, we put into action a vague attempt at a deliberate separation, not painful, temporary. We ask the woman, so that afterwards she may be happier in our company, so that we at the same time may momentarily escape from continual bouts of gloom and exhaustion, to go away without us, or to let us go away without her, for a few days—the first that we have spent away from her for a long time past, and something that we should have thought inconceivable. Very soon she returns to take her place by our fireside. Only this separation, short but effectuated, is not so arbitrarily decided upon, not so certainly the only one that we have in mind. The same bouts of gloom begin again, the same difficulty in living together makes itself felt, only a parting is no longer so difficult as before; we have begun by talking about it, and have then put it into practice amicably. But these are only premonitory symptoms which we have failed to recognise. Presently, the temporary and benign separation will be succeeded by the terrible and final separation for which, without knowing it, we have paved the way.

"Come to my room in five minutes and let me see something of you, my darling one. It would so nice if you would. But afterwards I shall fall asleep at once, for I'm almost dead."

It was indeed a dead woman that I saw when, presently, I entered her room. She had fallen asleep as soon as she lay down; her sheets, wrapped round her body like a shroud, had assumed, with their elegant folds, the rigidity of stone. It was as though, reminiscent of certain mediaeval Last Judgments, the head alone was emerging from the tomb, awaiting in its sleep the Archangel's trumpet. This head had been surprised by sleep almost upside down, the hair dishevelled. Seeing that expressionless body lying there, I asked myself what logarithmic table it constituted, that all the actions in which it might have been involved, from the nudge of an elbow to the brushing of a skirt, should be capable of causing me, stretched out to the infinity of all the points that it had occupied in space and time, and from time to time sharply reawakened in my memory, so intense an anguish, even though I knew that it was determined by impulses and desires of hers which in another person, in herself five years earlier or five years later, would have left me quite indifferent. It was all a lie, but a lie for which I had not the courage to seek any solution other than my own death. And so I remained, in the fur-lined coat which I had not taken off since my return from the Verdurins', beside that twisted body, that allegorical figure. Allegorising what? My death? My love? Soon I began to hear her regular breathing. I went and sat down on the edge of her bed to take that soothing cure of breeze and contemplation. Then I withdrew very quietly so as not to wake her.

It was so late that, in the morning, I warned Françoise to tread very softly when she had to pass by the door of Albertine's room. And so Françoise, convinced that we had spent the night in what she used to call orgies, sarcastically warned the other servants not to "wake the Princess." And this was one of the things that I dreaded, that Françoise might one day be unable to contain herself any longer, might treat Albertine with insolence, and that this might introduce complications into our life. Françoise was now no longer, as at the time when it distressed her to see Eulalie treated generously by my aunt, of an age to endure her jealousy with fortitude. It distorted, paralysed our old servant's face to such an extent that at times I wondered, after some outburst of rage, whether she had not had a slight stroke. Having thus asked that Albertine's sleep should be respected, I was unable to sleep myself. I tried to understand Albertine's true state of mind. Was it a real peril that I had averted by that wretched farce which I had played, and notwithstanding her assurance that she was so happy living with me, had she really felt at certain moments a longing for freedom, or on the contrary was I to believe what she said? Which of these two hypotheses was the truth? If it often happened to me, especially later on, to extend an incident in my past life to the dimensions of history when I wished to understand some political event, conversely, that morning, in trying to understand the significance of our overnight scene, I could not help identifying it, in spite of all the differences, with a diplomatic incident that had just occurred. I had perhaps the right to reason thus. For it was highly probable that the example of M. de Charlus had guided me unwittingly in the sort of lying scene which I had so often seen him enact with such authority; and what else was this on his part than an unconscious importation into the domain of his private life of the innate tendency of his German blood, guilefully provocative and arrogantly bellicose at need?

Various persons, among them the Prince of Monaco, having suggested the idea to the French Government that, if it did not dispense with M. Delcassé, a menacing Germany would definitely declare war, the Minister for Foreign Affairs had been asked to resign. Thus the French Government had admitted the hypothesis of an intention to make war upon us if we did not yield. But others thought that it was all a mere "bluff" and that if France had stood firm Germany would not have drawn the sword. No doubt in this case the scenario was not merely different but almost the reverse, since the threat of a rupture had never been put forward by Albertine; but a series of impressions had led me to believe that she was thinking of it, as France had been led to believe it of Germany. On the other hand, if Germany desired peace, to have provoked in the French Government the idea that she was anxious for war was a questionable and dangerous trick. True, my conduct had been adroit enough, if it was the thought that I would never make up my mind to break with her that provoked in Albertine sudden longings for independence. And was it not difficult to believe that she did not have such longings, to shut one's eyes to a whole secret existence, directed towards the satisfaction of her vice, simply on the strength of the anger with which, on learning that I had gone to see the Verdurins, she had exclaimed: "I thought as much," and then gone on to reveal everything by saying: "Wasn't Mlle Vinteuil to be there?" All this was corroborated by Albertine's meeting with Mme Verdurin of which Andrée had informed me. And yet, perhaps, I told myself, when I tried to go against my own instinct, these sudden longings for independence were caused—supposing them to exist—or would eventually be caused by the opposite theory, to wit, that I had never had any intention of marrying her, that it was when I made, as though involuntarily, an allusion to our approaching separation that I was telling the truth, that I would leave her sooner or later whatever happened—a belief which the scene I had fabricated that night could then only have reinforced and which might end by engendering in her the resolution: "If it's bound to happen sooner or later, we might as well get it over with at once." Preparations for war, which are recommended by the most misleading of adages as the best way of ensuring peace, on the contrary create first of all the belief in each of the adversaries that the other desires a rupture, a belief which brings the rupture about, and then, when it has occurred, the further belief in each of the two that it is the other that has sought it. Even if the threat was not sincere, its success encourages a repetition. But the exact point up to which a bluff may succeed is difficult to determine; if one party goes too far, the other, which has yielded hitherto, advances in its turn; the first party, no longer capable of changing its methods, accustomed to the idea that to seem not to fear a rupture is the best way of avoiding one (which is what I had done that night with

Albertine), and moreover driven by pride to prefer death to surrender, perseveres in its threat until the moment when neither can draw back. The bluff may also be blended with sincerity, may alternate with it, and what was yesterday a game may become a reality tomorrow. Finally it may also happen that one of the adversaries is really determined upon war—that Albertine, for instance, had the intention of sooner or later not continuing this life any longer, or on the contrary that the idea had never even entered her head and that my imagination had invented the whole thing from start to finish.

Such were the different hypotheses which I considered while she lay asleep that morning. And yet as to the last I can say that never, in the period that followed, did I threaten to leave Albertine unless in response to a hankering for a baleful freedom on her part, a hankering which she did not express to me, but which seemed to me to be implied by certain mysterious dissatisfactions, certain words, certain gestures, for which it could be the only possible explanation and for which she refused to give me any other. Even then, quite often, I noted them without making any allusion to a possible separation, hoping that they were the result of a bad mood which would end that same day. But sometimes that mood would continue without remission for weeks on end, during which Albertine seemed anxious to provoke a conflict, as though she knew of pleasures which were available at that moment in some more or less remote place and which would continue to influence her until they came to an end, like those atmospheric changes which, right by our own fireside, affect our nerves even when they are occurring as far away as the Balearic islands.

That morning, while Albertine lay asleep and I was trying to guess what was concealed in her, I received a letter from my mother in which she expressed her anxiety at having heard nothing of what I had decided in these words from Mme de Sévigné: "As for me, I am convinced that he will not marry; but then, why trouble this girl whom he will never marry? Why risk making her refuse suitors whom she will henceforth regard only with scorn? Why disturb the mind of a person whom it would be so easy to avoid?" This letter from my mother brought me back to earth. "Why do I go on seeking after a mysterious soul, interpreting a face, and feeling myself surrounded by presentiments which I dare not explore?" I asked myself. "I've been dreaming, the matter is quite simple. I am an indecisive young man, and it is a case of one of those marriages as to which it takes time to find out whether they will happen or not. There is nothing in this peculiar to Albertine." This thought brought me immense but short-lived relief. Very soon I said to myself: "One can of course reduce everything, if one regards it in its social aspect, to the most commonplace item of newspaper gossip. From outside, it is perhaps thus that I myself would look at it. But I know very well that what is true, what at least is also true, is everything that I have thought, what I have read in Albertine's eyes, the fears that torment me, the problem that I continually put to myself with regard to Albertine. The story of the hesitant suitor and the broken engagement may correspond to this, as the report of a theatrical performance made by an intelligent reporter may give us the subject of one of Ibsen's plays. But there is something beyond those facts that are reported. It is

true that this other thing exists perhaps, were we capable
of seeing it, in all hesitant suitors and in all engagements
that drag on, because there is perhaps an element of mystery in everyday life." It was possible for me to neglect it
in the lives of other people, but Albertine's life and my
own I was living from within.

Albertine did not say to me after this midnight scene,
any more than she had said before it: "I know you don't
trust me, and I'm going to try to dispel your suspicions."
But this idea, which she never expressed in words, might
have served as an explanation of even her most trivial actions. Not only did she take care never to be alone for a
moment, so that I could not help but know what she had
been doing if I did not believe her own statements, but
even when she had to telephone to Andrée, or to the
garage, or to the livery stable or elsewhere, she pretended
that it was too boring to stand about by herself waiting to
telephone, what with the time the girls took to give you
your number, and was careful that I should be with her at
such times, or, failing me, Françoise, as though she were
afraid that I might imagine reprehensible telephone conversations in which she would make mysterious assignations.

Alas, all this did not set my mind at rest. Aimé had
sent me back Esther's photograph, saying that she was not
the person. So there were yet others? Who? I sent this
photograph back to Bloch. The one I should have liked to
see was the one Albertine had given to Esther. How was
she dressed in it? Perhaps in a low-cut dress. Who knew
whether they had not been photographed together? But I
dared not mention it to Albertine (for it would then have

appeared that I had not seen the photograph), or to Bloch, since I did not wish him to think that I was interested in Albertine.

And this life, which anyone who knew of my suspicions and her bondage would have seen to be agonising both to myself and to Albertine, was regarded from without, by Françoise, as a life of unmerited pleasures of which full advantage was cunningly taken by that "wheedler" and (as Françoise said, using the feminine form far more often than the masculine, for she was more envious of women) "charlatante." Indeed, as Françoise, by contact with myself, had enriched her vocabulary with new expressions, but adapted them to her own style, she said of Albertine that she had never known a person of such "perfidity," who was so skilful at "drawing my money" by play-acting (which Françoise, who was as prone to mistake the particular for the general as the general for the particular and who had but a very vague idea of the various forms of dramatic art, called "acting a pantomime"). Perhaps I was myself to some extent responsible for this misconception as to the true nature of the life led by Albertine and myself, owing to the vague confirmations of it which, when I was talking to Françoise, I cunningly let fall, from a desire either to tease her or to appear, if not loved, at any rate happy. And yet it did not take her long to detect my jealousy and the watch I kept over Albertine (which I would have given anything for Françoise not to be aware of), guided, like a thought-reader who finds a hidden object while blindfolded, by that intuition which she possessed for anything that might be painful to me, which would not allow itself to be turned aside by any lies that I might tell in the hope of putting her off the scent, and also by that clairvoyant hatred which drove her—even more than it drove her to believe her enemies more prosperous, more cunning play-actresses than they really were—to uncover what might prove their undoing and precipitate their downfall. Françoise certainly never made any scenes with Albertine. But I knew her skill in the art of insinuation, the way she knew how to make the most of the implications of a particular situation, and I cannot believe that she resisted the temptation to let Albertine know, day after day, what a humiliating role she was playing in the household, to madden her by a slyly exaggerated portrayal of the confinement to which she was subjected. On one occasion I found Françoise, armed with a huge pair of spectacles, rummaging through my papers and replacing among them a sheet on which I had jotted down a story about Swann and his inability to do without Odette. Had she maliciously left it lying in Albertine's room? Besides, above all Françoise's innuendoes, which had merely been the muttering and perfidious accompaniment of it in the bass, it is probable that there must have risen, louder, clearer, more insistent, the accusing and calumnious voice of the Verdurins, irritated to see that Albertine was involuntarily keeping me and that I was voluntarily keeping her away from the little clan.

As for the money that I spent on Albertine, it was almost impossible for me to conceal it from Françoise, since I was unable to conceal any of my expenditure from her. Françoise had few faults, but those faults had created in her, for their own purposes, positive talents which she often lacked apart from the exercise of those faults. The principal one was her curiosity as to all money spent by us upon people other than herself. If I had a bill to pay or a tip to give, it was useless my going into a corner, she would find a plate to be put in the right place, a napkin to be picked up, which would give her an excuse for approaching. And however short a time I allowed her before dismissing her with fury, this woman who had almost lost her sight, who could scarcely count, guided by the same expert sense whereby a tailor, on catching sight of you, instinctively calculates the price of the stuff of which your coat is made, and indeed cannot resist fingering it, or a painter is immediately responsive to a colour effect, Françoise furtively glimpsed and instantaneously calculated the amount that I was giving. If, in order that she should not tell Albertine that I was corrupting her chauffeur, I tried to forestall her and, apologising for the tip, said: "I wanted to be generous to the chauffeur, so I gave him ten francs," Françoise, for whom the merciless glance of an old and almost blind eagle had sufficed, would reply: "No no, Monsieur gave him a tip of 43 francs. He told Monsieur that the charge was 45 francs, Monsieur gave him 100 francs, and he handed back only 12 francs." She had had time to see and to reckon the amount of the gratuity which I myself did not know.

I wondered whether Albertine, feeling herself watched, would not herself put into effect the separation with which I had threatened her, for life in its changing course makes realities of our fables. Whenever I heard a door open, I gave a start, as my grandmother used to start in her last moments whenever I rang the bell. I did not believe that she would have left the house without telling me, but my unconscious thought so, as my grandmother's unconscious quivered at the sound of the bell when she was no longer conscious. One morning, indeed, I had a sudden anxious fear that she had not only left the house but gone for good: I had just heard the sound of a door which seemed to me to be that of her room. I tiptoed towards the room, opened the door, and stood on the threshold. In the dim light the bedclothes bulged in a semicircle. It had to be Albertine, lying in a curve, sleeping with her head and her feet nearest the wall. The hair on that head, abundant and dark, which alone showed above the bedclothes, made me realise that it was she, that she had not opened her door, had not stirred, and I sensed this motionless and living semicircle, in which a whole human life was contained and which was the only thing to which I attached any value; I sensed that it was there, in my despotic possession.

If Albertine's object was to restore my peace of mind, she was partly successful; my reason moreover asked nothing better than to prove to me that I had been mistaken as to her evil plans, as I had perhaps been mistaken as to her vicious instincts. No doubt I took into account, in assessing the value of the arguments with which my reason furnished me, my desire to find them sound. But in order to be really impartial and to have a chance of perceiving the truth, short of acknowledging that it can never be known save by presentiment, by a telepathic emanation, ought I not to tell myself that if my reason, in seeking to bring about my cure, let itself be guided by my desire, on the other hand, as regards Mlle Vinteuil, Albertine's vices, her intention to lead a different life, her plan of separation, which were the corollaries of her vices, my instinct, in trying to make me ill, might have allowed itself to be led astray by my jealousy? Besides, her seclusion, which Albertine herself contrived so ingeniously to render absolute, in eradicating my suffering gradually eradicated my suspicion and I could begin again, when evening revived my anxieties, to find in Albertine's presence the consolation of earlier days. Seated beside my bed, she would talk to me about one of those dresses or one of those objects which I was constantly giving her in order to make her life more agreeable and her prison more beautiful.

If I had questioned M. de Charlus about old French silver, this was because, when we had been planning to have a yacht, we had asked Elstir's advice on the off chance, even though Albertine did not believe that we would ever have one. Now, no less than in matters of women's dress, the painter's taste in the furnishing of yachts was refined and severe. He would allow only English furniture and old silver. This had led Albertine, who had at first thought only of clothes and furniture, to become interested in silver, and since our return from Balbec she had read books on the silversmith's art and on the hallmarks of the old craftsmen. But old French silver—having been melted down twice, at the time of the Treaty of Utrecht when the King himself, setting the example to his great nobles, sacrificed his silver plate, and again in 1789—is now extremely rare. At the same time, although modern silversmiths have managed to copy all this old plate from the Pont-aux-Choux designs, Elstir considered this reproduction work unworthy to enter the dwelling of a woman of taste, even a floating one. I knew that Albertine had read the description of the marvels that Roettiers had made for Mme du Barry. If any of these pieces remained, she longed to see them, and I to give them to her. She had even begun to form a neat collection which she installed with charming taste in a glass case and which I could not contemplate without affectionate dismay, for the art with which she arranged them was that, born of patience, ingenuity, homesickness, the need to forget, which prisoners practise.

In the matter of dress, what appealed to her most at this time was everything made by Fortuny. These Fortuny gowns, one of which I had seen Mme de Guermantes wearing, were those of which Elstir, when he told us about the magnificent garments of the women of Carpaccio's and Titian's day, had prophesied the imminent return, rising from their ashes, as magnificent as of old, for everything must return in time, as it is written beneath the vaults of St Mark's, and proclaimed, as they drink from the urns of marble and jasper of the Byzantine capitals, by the birds which symbolise at once death and resurrection. As soon as women had begun to wear them, Albertine had remembered Elstir's prophecy, had coveted them, and we were shortly to go and choose one. Now even if these gowns were not those genuine antiques in which women today seem a little too got up in fancy dress and which it is preferable to keep as collector's items (I was looking for some of these also, as it happens, for Albertine), neither did they have the coldness of the artificial, the sham antique. Like the theatrical designs of Sert, Bakst and Benois, who at that moment were re-creating in the Russian ballet the most cherished periods of art with the aid of works of art impregnated with their spirit and yet original, these Fortuny gowns, faithfully antique but markedly original, brought before the eye like a stage decor, and with an even greater evocative power since the decor was left to the imagination, that Venice saturated with oriental splendour where they would have been worn and of which they constituted, even more than a relic in the shrine of St Mark, evocative as they were of the sunlight and the surrounding turbans, the fragmented, mysterious and complementary colour. Everything of those days had perished, but everything was being reborn, evoked and linked together by the splendour and the swarming life of the city, in the piecemeal reappearance of the still-surviving fabrics worn by the Doges' ladies. I had tried once or twice to obtain advice on this subject from Mme de Guermantes. But the Duchess did not care for clothes that gave the effect of fancy dress. She herself, though she possessed several, never looked so well as in black velvet with diamonds. And with regard to gowns like Fortuny's, she had little useful advice to give. Besides, I had scruples about asking her advice lest I might give the impression that I called on her only when I happened to need her help, whereas for a long time past I had been declining several invitations a week from her. It was not only from her, moreover, that I received them in such profusion. Certainly, she and many other women had always been extremely friendly to me. But my seclusion had undoubtedly multiplied their friendliness tenfold. It seems that in our social life, a minor echo of what occurs in love, the best way to get oneself sought after is to withhold oneself. A man may think up everything that he can possibly cite to his credit, in order to find favour with a woman; he may wear different clothes every day, look after his appearance; yet she will not offer him a single one of the attentions and favours which he receives from another woman to whom, by being unfaithful to her, and in spite

of his appearing before her ill-dressed and without any artifice to attract, he has endeared himself for ever. Similarly, if a man were to regret that he was not sufficiently
courted in society, I should not advise him to pay more
calls, to keep an even finer carriage; I should tell him not
to accept any invitation, to live shut up in his room, to
admit nobody, and that then there would be a queue outside his door. Or rather I should not tell him so. For it is
a sure way to become sought-after which succeeds only
like the way to be loved, that is to say if you have not
adopted it with that object in view, if, for instance, you
confine yourself to your room because you are seriously
ill, or think you are, or are keeping a mistress shut up
with you whom you prefer to society (or for all these reasons at once), in the eyes of which, even if it is unaware
of the woman's existence, and simply because you resist
its overtures, it will simply be a reason to prefer you to all
those who offer themselves, and to attach itself to you.

"We shall have to begin to think soon about your
Fortuny dressing-gown," I said to Albertine one evening.
Surely, for her, who had long desired them, who would
choose them with me after long deliberation, who had a
place reserved for them in advance, not only in her
wardrobe but in her imagination, the possession of these
gowns, every detail of which, before deciding among so
many others, she would carefully examine, was something
more than it would have been to a woman with too much
money who has more dresses than she knows what to do
with and never even looks at them. And yet, notwithstanding the smile with which Albertine thanked me, saying: "It's so sweet of you," I noticed how weary and even
sad she was looking.

From time to time, while we were waiting for these gowns to be finished, I used to borrow others of the kind, sometimes merely the stuffs, and would dress Albertine in them, drape them over her; she walked about my room with the majesty of a Doge's wife and the grace of a mannequin. But my captivity in Paris was made more burdensome to me by the sight of these garments which reminded me of Venice. True, Albertine was far more of a prisoner than I. And it was curious to remark how fate, which transforms persons, had contrived to penetrate the walls of her prison, to change her in her very essence, and turn the girl I had known at Balbec into a dreary, docile captive. Yes, the walls of her prison had not prevented that influence from reaching her; perhaps indeed it was they that had produced it. It was no longer the same Albertine, because she was not, as at Balbec, incessantly in flight upon her bicycle, impossible to find owing to the number of little watering-places where she would go to spend the night with friends and where moreover her lies made it more difficult to lay hands on her; because, shut up in my house, docile and alone, she was no longer what at Balbec, even when I had succeeded in finding her, she used to be upon the beach, that fugitive, cautious, deceitful creature, whose presence was expanded by the thought of all those assignations which she was skilled in concealing, which made one love her because they made one suffer and because, beneath her coldness to other people and her casual answers, I could sense yesterday's assignation and tomorrow's, and for myself a sly, disdainful thought; because the sea breeze no longer puffed out her skirts; because, above all, I had clipped her wings, and she had ceased to be a winged Victory and become a burdensome slave of whom I would have liked to rid myself.

Then, to change the course of my thoughts, rather than begin a game of cards or draughts with Albertine, I would ask her to give me a little music. I remained in bed, and she would go and sit down at the end of the room before the pianola, between the two bookcases. She chose pieces which were either quite new or which she had played to me only once or twice, for, beginning to know me better, she was aware that I liked to fix my thoughts only upon what was still obscure to me, and to be able, in the course of these successive renderings, thanks to the increasing but, alas, distorting and alien light of my intellect, to link to one another the fragmentary and interrupted lines of the structure which at first had been almost hidden in mist. She knew and, I think, understood the joy that my mind derived, at these first hearings, from this task of modelling a still shapeless nebula. And as she played, of all Albertine's multiple tresses I could see but a single heart-shaped loop of black hair clinging to the side of her ear like the bow of a Velasquez Infanta. Just as the volume of that angel musician was constituted by the multiple journeys between the different points in the past which the memory of her occupied within me and the different signs, from the purely visual to the innermost sensations of my being, which helped me to descend into the intimacy of hers, so the music that she played had also a volume, produced by the unequal visibility of the different phrases, according as I had more or less succeeded in throwing light on them and joining up the lines of the seemingly nebulous structure. She guessed that at the third or fourth repetition my intellect, having grasped, having consequently placed at the same distance, all the parts, and no longer having to exert any effort on them, had conversely projected and immobilised them on a uniform plane. She did not, however, yet move on to another piece, for, without perhaps having any clear idea of the process that was going on inside me, she knew that at the moment when the exertions of my intelligence had succeeded in dispelling the mystery of a work, it was very rarely that, in compensation, it had not, in the course of its baleful task, picked up some profitable reflexion. And when in time Albertine said: "We might give this roll to Françoise and get her to change it for something else," often there was for me a piece of music the less in the world, perhaps, but a truth the more.

I was so convinced that it would be absurd to be jealous of Mlle Vinteuil and her friend, inasmuch as Albertine gave not the least sign of wanting to see them again, and among all the plans for a holiday in the country which we had formed had herself rejected Combray, so near to Montjouvain, that often I would ask her to play to me some of Vinteuil's music, without its causing me pain. Once only this music had been an indirect cause of jealousy. This was when Albertine, who knew that I had heard it performed at Mme Verdurin's by Morel, spoke to me one evening about him, expressing a keen desire to go and hear him play and to make his acquaintance. This, as it happened, was shortly after I had learned of the letter, unintentionally intercepted by M. de Charlus, from Léa to Morel. I wondered whether Léa might not have mentioned him to Albertine. The words "you naughty girl," "you vicious thing," came back to my horrified mind. But precisely because Vinteuil's music was in this way painfully associated with Léa—and not with Mlle Vinteuil and her friend—when the anguish caused by Léa had subsided, I could listen to this music without pain; one malady had cured me of the possibility of the others. In the music I had heard at Mme Verdurin's, phrases I had not noticed, obscure larvae that were then indistinct, turned into dazzling architectural structures; and some of them became friends, that I had scarcely distinguished, that at best had appeared to me to be ugly, so that I could never have supposed that they were like those people, antipathetic at first sight, whom we discover to be what they really are only after we have come to know them well. Between the two states there was a real transmutation. At the same time, phrases which had been quite distinct the first time but which I had not then recognised, I identified now with phrases from other works, such as that phrase from the Sacred Variation for Organ which, at Mme Verdurin's, had passed unperceived by me in the septet, where nevertheless, like a saint that had stepped down from the sanctuary, it found itself consorting with the composer's familiar sprites. Moreover, the phrase evoking the joyful clanging of the bells at noon, which had seemed to me too unmelodious, too mechanical in its rhythm, had now become my favourite, either because I had grown accustomed to its ugliness or because I had discovered its beauty. This reaction from the disappointment which great works of art cause at first may in fact be attributed to a weakening of the initial impression or to the effort necessary to lay bare the truth—two hypotheses which recur in all important questions, questions about the truth of Art, of Reality, of the Immortality of the

Soul; we must choose between them; and, in the case of Vinteuil's music, this choice was constantly presenting itself under a variety of forms. For instance, this music seemed to me something truer than all known books. At moments I thought that this was due to the fact that, what we feel about life not being felt in the form of ideas, its literary, that is to say intellectual expression describes it, explains it, analyses it, but does not recompose it as does music, in which the sounds seem to follow the very movement of our being, to reproduce that extreme inner point of our sensations which is the part that gives us that peculiar exhilaration which we experience from time to time and which, when we say "What a fine day! What glorious sunshine!" we do not in the least communicate to others, in whom the same sun and the same weather evoke quite different vibrations. In Vinteuil's music, there were thus some of those visions which it is impossible to express and almost forbidden to contemplate, since, when at the moment of falling asleep we receive the caress of their unreal enchantment, at that very moment in which reason has already deserted us, our eyes seal up and before we have had time to know not only the ineffable but the invisible, we are asleep. It seemed to me, when I abandoned myself to this hypothesis that art might be real, that it was something even more than the merely nerve-tingling joy of a fine day or an opiate night that music can give; a more real, more fruitful exhilaration, to judge at least by what I felt. It is inconceivable that a piece of sculpture or a piece of music which gives us an emotion that we feel to be more exalted, more pure, more true, does not correspond to some definite spiritual reality, or life would be meaningless. Thus nothing resembled more closely than some such phrase of Vinteuil the peculiar pleasure which I had felt at certain moments in my life, when gazing, for instance, at the steeples of Martinville, or at certain trees along a road near Balbec, or, more simply, at the beginning of this book, when I tasted a certain cup of tea. Like that cup of tea, all those sensations of light, the bright clamour, the boisterous colours that Vinteuil sent to us from the world in which he composed, paraded before my imagination, insistently but too rapidly for me to be able to apprehend it, something that I might compare to the perfumed silkiness of a geranium. But whereas in memory this vagueness may be, if not fathomed, at any rate identified, thanks to a pinpointing of circumstances which explain why a certain taste has been able to recall to us luminous sensations, the vague sensations given by Vinteuil coming not from a memory but from an impression (like that of the steeples of Martinville), one would have had to find, for the geranium scent of his music, not a material explanation, but the profound equivalent, the unknown, colourful festival (of which his works seemed to be the disconnected fragments, the scarlet-flashing splinters), the mode by which he "heard" the universe and projected it far beyond himself. Perhaps it was in this, I said to Albertine, this unknown quality of a unique world which no other composer had ever yet revealed, that the most authentic proof of genius lies, even more than in the content of the work itself. "Even in literature?" Albertine inquired. "Even in literature." And thinking again of the sameness of Vinteuil's works, I explained to Albertine that the great men of letters have never created more than a single work, or rather have never done more than refract through various media an identical beauty which they bring into the world. "If it were not so late, my sweet," I said to her, "I would show you this quality in all the writers whose works you read while I'm asleep, I would show you the same identity as in Vinteuil. These key-phrases, which you are beginning to recognise as I do, my little Albertine, the same in the sonata, in the septet, in the other works, would be, say for instance in Barbey d'Aurevilly, a hidden reality revealed by a physical sign, the physiological blush of the Bewitched, of Aimée de Spens, of old Clotte, the hand in the *Rideau cramoisi*, the old manners and customs, the old words, the ancient and peculiar trades behind which there is the Past, the oral history made by the herdsmen with their mirror, the noble Norman cities redolent of England and charming as a Scottish village, the hurler of curses against which one can do nothing, la Vellini, the Shepherd, a similar sensation of anxiety in a passage, whether it be the wife seeking her husband in *Une vieille maîtresse*, or the husband in *L'Ensorcelée* scouring the plain and the Bewitched herself coming out from mass. Another example of Vinteuil's key-phrases is that stonemason's geometry in the novels of Thomas Hardy."

Vinteuil's phrases made me think of the "little phrase" and I told Albertine that it had been as it were the national anthem of the love of Swann and Odette, "the parents of Gilberte, whom I believe you know. You told me she was a bad girl. Didn't she try to have relations with you? She spoke to me about you."

"Yes, you see, her parents used to send a carriage to fetch her from school when the weather was bad, and I seem to remember she took me home once and kissed me," she said, after a momentary pause, laughing as though it were an amusing revelation. "She asked me all of a sudden whether I was fond of women." (But if she only "seemed to remember" that Gilberte had taken her home, how could she say with such precision that Gilberte had asked her this odd question?) "In fact, I don't know what weird idea came into my head to fool her, but I told her that I was." (It was as though Albertine was afraid that Gilberte had told me this and did not want me to see that she was lying to me.) "But we did nothing at all." (It was strange, if they had exchanged these confidences, that they should have done nothing, especially as, before this, they had kissed, according to Albertine.) "She took me home like that four or five times, perhaps more, and that's all."

It cost me a great effort not to ply her with questions, but, mastering myself so as to appear not to be attaching any importance to all this, I returned to Thomas Hardy. "Do you remember the stonemasons in *Jude the Obscure*, and in *The Well-Beloved* the blocks of stone which the father hews out of the island coming in boats to be piled up in the son's work-shop where they are turned into statues; and in *A Pair of Blue Eyes* the parallelism of the tombs, and also the parallel line of the boat and the nearby railway coaches containing the lovers and the dead woman; and the parallel between *The Well-Beloved*, where the man loves three women, and *A Pair of Blue Eyes*, where the woman loves three men, and in short all those novels which can be superimposed on one another like the houses piled up vertically on the rocky soil of the island. I can't sum up the greatest writers like this in a few moments, but you'll see in Stendhal a certain sense of altitude symbolising the life of the spirit: the lofty place in which Julien Sorel is imprisoned, the tower at the top of which Fabrice is incarcerated, the belfry in which the Abbé Blanès pores over his astrology and from which Fabrice has such a magnificent bird's-eye view. You told me you had seen some of Vermeer's pictures: you must have realised that they're fragments of an identical world, that it's always, however great the genius with which they have been re-created, the same table, the same carpet, the same woman, the same novel and unique beauty, an enigma at that period in which nothing resembles or explains it, if one doesn't try to relate it all through subject matter but to isolate the distinctive impression produced by the colour. Well, this novel beauty remains identical in all Dostoievsky's works. Isn't the Dostoievsky woman (as distinctive as a Rembrandt woman) with her mysterious face, whose engaging beauty changes abruptly, as though her apparent good nature was only play-acting, into terrible insolence (although at heart it seems that she is more good than bad), isn't she always the same, whether it's Nastasia Philipovna writing love letters to Aglaya and telling her that she hates her, or in a visit that's absolutely identical with this—as also the one where Nastasia Philipovna insults Gania's family—Grushenka, as charming in Katerina Ivanovna's house as the latter had supposed her to be terrible, then suddenly revealing her malevolence by insulting Katerina Ivanovna (although Grushenka is good at heart)? Grushenka, Nastasia—figures as original, as mysterious, not merely as Carpaccio's courtesans but as Rembrandt's Bathsheba. Mind you, he certainly didn't only know how to depict that striking dual face, with its sudden explosions of furious pride, which makes the woman seem other than she is ('You are

not like that,' says Myshkin to Nastasia during the visit to
Gania's family, and Alyosha might have said the same to
Grushenka during the visit to Katerina Ivanovna). But on
the other hand when he wants 'ideas for paintings' they're
always stupid and would at best result in the pictures
where Munkacsy wanted to see a condemned man represented at the moment when . . . etc., or the Virgin Mary
at the moment when . . . etc. But to return to the new
kind of beauty that Dostoievsky brought to the world,
just as, in Vermeer, there's the creation of a certain soul,
of a certain colour of fabrics and places, so in Dostoievsky
there's the creation not only of people but of their homes,
and the house of the Murder in *Crime and Punishment*,
with its janitor, isn't it as marvellous as the masterpiece of
the house of Murder in *The Idiot*, that sombre house of
Rogozhin's, so long, and so high, and so vast, in which he
kills Nastasia Philipovna. That new and terrible beauty of
a house, that new and two-sided beauty of a woman's
face, that is the unique thing that Dostoievsky has given
to the world, and the comparisons that literary critics may
make, between him and Gogol, or between him and Paul
de Kock, are of no interest, being external to this secret
beauty. Besides, if I've said to you that from one novel
to another it's the same scene, it's in the compass of a
single novel that the same scenes, the same characters
reappear if the novel is at all long. I could illustrate this
to you easily in *War and Peace*, and a certain scene in a
carriage . . ."

"I didn't want to interrupt you, but now that I see
that you're leaving Dostoievsky, I'm afraid I might forget.
My sweet, what was it you meant the other day when you
said: 'It's like the Dostoievsky side of Mme de Sévigné.' I

must confess that I didn't understand. It seems to me so different."

"Come, little girl, let me give you a kiss to thank you for remembering so well what I say. You shall go back to the pianola afterwards. And I must admit that what I said was rather stupid. But I said it for two reasons. The first is a special reason. What I meant was that Mme de Sévigné, like Elstir, like Dostoievsky, instead of presenting things in their logical sequence, that is to say beginning with the cause, shows us first of all the effect, the illusion that strikes us. That is how Dostoievsky presents his characters. Their actions seem to us as deceptive as those effects in Elstir's pictures where the sea appears to be in the sky. We're quite surprised to find later on that some sly-looking individual is really the best of men, or vice versa."

"Yes, but give me an example in Mme de Sévigné."

"I admit," I answered her with a laugh, "that it's very far-fetched, but still I could find examples. For instance . . ."[23]

"But did he ever murder anyone, Dostoievsky? The novels of his that I know might all be called The Story of a Crime. It's an obsession with him, it isn't natural that he should always be talking about it."

"I don't think so, dear Albertine. I know little about his life. It's certain that, like everyone else, he was acquainted with sin, in one form or another, and probably in a form which the laws condemn. In that sense he must have been a bit criminal, like his heroes—who in any case are not entirely criminal, who are found guilty with extenuating circumstances. And perhaps it wasn't necessary for him to be criminal himself. I'm not a novelist; it's possible that creative writers are tempted by certain forms of life of which they have no personal experience. If I come with you to Versailles as we arranged, I shall show you the portrait of an ultra-respectable man, the best of husbands, Choderlos de Laclos, who wrote the most appallingly perverse book, and just opposite it the portrait of Mme de Genlis who wrote moral tales and, not content with betraying the Duchesse d'Orléans, tortured her by turning her children against her. I admit all the same that in Dostoievsky this preoccupation with murder is something extraordinary which makes him very alien to me. I'm amazed enough when I hear Baudelaire say:

> If not yet poison, arson, rape, and stabbing . . .
> It is because our soul, alas! lacks daring.

But I can at least assume that Baudelaire is not sincere. Whereas Dostoievsky . . . All that sort of thing seems to me as remote from myself as possible, unless there are parts of myself of which I know nothing, for we realise our own nature only in the course of time. In Dostoievsky I find the deepest wells of insight but only into certain isolated regions of the human soul. But he is a great creator. For one thing, the world which he describes does really appear to have been created by him. All those buffoons who keep on reappearing, like Lebedev, Karamazov, Ivolgin, Segrev, that incredible procession, are human types even more fantastic than those that people Rembrandt's *Night Watch*. And yet perhaps they're fantastic only in the same way, by the effect of lighting and costume, and are quite normal really. In any case the whole thing is full of profound and unique truths, which belong only to Dostoievsky. They almost suggest, those buffoons, some trade or calling that no longer exists, like certain characters in the old drama, and yet how they reveal true aspects of the human soul! What I find so tedious is the solemn manner in which people talk and write about Dostoievsky. Have you ever noticed the part that self-esteem and pride play in his characters? It's as though, for him, love and the most passionate hatred, goodness and treachery, timidity and insolence, are merely two aspects of a single nature, their self-esteem, their pride preventing Aglaya, Nastasia, the Captain whose beard Mitya pulls, Krassotkin, Alyosha's enemy-friend, from showing themselves in their true colours. But there are many other great qualities as well. I know very few of his books. But what a simple, sculptural notion it is, worthy of the most classical art, a frieze interrupted and resumed in which the theme of vengeance and expiation is unfolded in the crime of old Karamazov getting the poor simpleton with child, the mysterious, animal, unexplained impulse whereby the mother, herself unconsciously the instrument of an avenging destiny, obeying also obscurely her maternal instinct, feeling perhaps a combination of resentment and physical gratitude towards her violator, comes to give birth to her child in old Karamazov's garden. This is the first episode, mysterious, grandiose, august, like the Creation of Woman in one of the sculptures at Orvieto. And as counterpart, the second episode more than twenty years later, the murder of old Karamazov, the infamy committed against the Karamazov family by the madwoman's son, Smerdiakov, followed shortly afterwards by another act as mysteriously sculpturesque and unexplained, of a beauty as obscure and natural as the childbirth in old Karamazov's garden, Smerdiakov hanging himself, his crime ac-

complished. Actually I wasn't straying as far from Dostoievsky as you thought when I mentioned Tolstoy, who
imitated him a great deal. In Dostoievsky there's concentrated, still tense and peevish, a great deal of what was to
blossom later on in Tolstoy. There's that proleptic gloom
of the primitives which the disciples will brighten and dispel."

"What a bore it is that you're so lazy, my sweet. Just
look at your view of literature, so much more interesting
than the way we were made to study it; the essays that
they used to make us write about *Esther*: 'Monsieur,' —
you remember," she said with a laugh, less from a desire
to make fun of her masters and herself than from the
pleasure of finding in her memory, in our common memory, a recollection that was already quite venerable.

But while she was speaking, and I thought once more
of Vinteuil, it was the other, the materialist hypothesis,
that of there being nothing, that in turn presented itself to
my mind. I began to doubt again; I told myself that after
all it might be the case that, if Vinteuil's phrases seemed
to be the expression of certain states of soul analogous to
that which I had experienced when I tasted the madeleine
soaked in tea, there was nothing to assure me that the
vagueness of such states was a sign of their profundity
rather than of our not having yet learned to analyse them,
so that there might be nothing more real in them than in
other states. And yet that happiness, that sense of certainty in happiness while I was drinking the cup of tea, or
when I smelt in the Champs-Elysées a smell of moulder-
ing wood, was not an illusion. In any case, whispered the
spirit of doubt, even if these states are more profound
than others that occur in life, and defy analysis for that

very reason, because they bring into play too many forces of which we have hitherto been unaware, the charm of certain phrases of Vinteuil's music makes us think of them because it too defies analysis, but this does not prove that it has the same profundity; the beauty of a phrase of pure music can easily appear to be the image of or at least akin to an unintellectual impression which we have received, but simply because it is unintellectual. And why then do we suppose to be specially profound those mysterious phrases which haunt certain quartets and this septet by Vinteuil?

It was not, however, his music alone that Albertine played me; the pianola was to us at times like a scientific magic lantern (historical and geographical), and on the walls of this room in Paris, supplied with inventions more modern than my room at Combray, I would see extending before me, according to whether Albertine played me Rameau or Borodin, now an eighteenth-century tapestry sprinkled with cupids and roses, now the Eastern steppe in which sounds are muffled by the boundless distances and the soft carpet of snow. And these fleeting decorations were as it happened the only ones in my room, for although, at the time of inheriting my aunt Léonie's fortune, I had resolved to become a collector like Swann, to buy pictures and statues, all my money went on horses, a motor-car, dresses for Albertine. But did not my room contain a work of art more precious than all these—Albertine herself? I looked at her. It was strange to me to think that it was she, she whom I had for so long thought it impossible even to know, who now, a wild beast tamed, a rosebush to which I had acted as the prop, the framework, the trellis of its life, was seated thus, day by day, at

home, by my side, before the pianola, with her back to
my bookcase. Her shoulders, which I had seen drooping
sullenly when she was carrying her golf-clubs, now leaned
against my books. Her shapely legs, which on the first
day I had with good reason imagined as having manipu-
lated throughout her girlhood the pedals of a bicycle, now
rose and fell alternately upon those of the pianola, upon
which Albertine, who had acquired an elegance which
made me feel her more my own, because it was from myself that it came, pressed her shoes of cloth of gold. Her
fingers, at one time accustomed to handlebars, now rested
upon the keys like those of a St Cecilia. Her throat, the
curve of which, seen from my bed, was strong and full, at
that distance and in the lamplight appeared pinker, less
pink however than her face, bent forward in profile, which
my gaze, issuing from the innermost depths of myself,
charged with memories and burning with desire, invested
with such a brilliancy, such an intensity of life that its relief seemed to stand out and turn with the same almost
magic power as on the day, in the hotel at Balbec, when
my vision was clouded by my overpowering desire to kiss
her; and I prolonged each of its surfaces beyond what I
was able to see and beneath what concealed it from me
and made me feel all the more strongly—eyelids which
half hid her eyes, hair that covered the upper part of her
cheeks—the relief of those superimposed planes; her eyes
(like two facets that alone have yet been polished in the
matrix in which an opal is still embedded), become more
resistant than metal while remaining more brilliant than
light, disclosed, in the midst of the blind matter over-
hanging them, as it were the mauve, silken wings of a
butterfly placed under glass; and her dark, curling hair,

presenting different conformations whenever she turned to ask me what she was to play next, now a splendid wing, sharp at the tip, broad at the base, black, feathered and triangular, now massing the contours of its curls in a powerful and varied chain, full of crests, of watersheds, of precipices, with its soft, creamy texture, so rich and so multiple, seeming to exceed the variety that nature habitually achieves and to correspond rather to the desire of a sculptor who accumulates difficulties in order to emphasise the suppleness, the vibrancy, the fullness, the vitality of his creation, brought out more strongly, but interrupting in order to cover it, the animated curve and, as it were, the rotation of the smooth, roseate face, with its glazed matt texture as of painted wood. And, by contrast with all this relief, by the harmony also which united them with her, who had adapted her attitude to their form and purpose, the pianola which half concealed her like an organ-case, the bookcase, the whole of that corner of the room, seemed to be reduced to the dimensions of a lighted sanctuary, the shrine of this angel musician, a work of art which, presently, by a charming magic, was to detach itself from its niche and offer to my kisses its precious, rose-pink substance. But no, Albertine was for me not at all a work of art. I knew what it meant to admire a woman in an artistic fashion, having known Swann. For my own part, however, no matter who the woman might be, I was incapable of doing so, having no sort of power of detached observation, never knowing what it was that I saw, and I had been amazed when Swann added retrospectively an artistic dignity—by comparing her to me, as he liked to do gallantly to her face, to some portrait by Luini, by recalling in her attire the gown or the jewels of a picture by Giorgione—to a woman who had seemed to me to be devoid of interest. Nothing of that sort with me. Indeed, to tell the truth, when I began to regard Albertine as an angel musician glazed with a marvellous patina whom I congratulated myself upon possessing, it was not long before I found her uninteresting; I soon became bored in her company; but these moments were of brief duration: one only loves that in which one pursues the inaccessible, one only loves what one does not possess, and very soon I began to realise once more that I did not possess Albertine. I saw flitting across her eyes, now the hope, now the memory, perhaps the regret, of joys which I could not guess at, which in that case she preferred to renounce rather than reveal to me, and which, glimpsing no more of them than that gleam in her pupils, I no more perceived than does the spectator who has been refused admission to the theatre, and who, his face glued to the glass panes of the door, can take in nothing of what is happening on the stage. (I do not know whether this was the case with her, but it is a strange thing—like evidence of a belief in good in the most incredulous—this perseverance in falsehood shown by all those who deceive us. It would be no good our telling them that their lies hurt us more than a confession, it would be no good their realising it for themselves, they would start lying again a moment later, to remain consistent with what they had always told us that they were, or with what they had told us that we were to them. Similarly, an atheist who values his life will let himself be burned alive rather than give the lie to the view that is generally held of his bravery.) During these hours, I used sometimes to see hover over her face, in her expression, in her pout, in her smile, the reflexion of those inner visions the contemplation of which made her on these evenings unlike her usual self, remote from me to whom they were denied. "What are you thinking about, my darling?" "Why, nothing." Sometimes, in answer to the reproaches I made to her that she told me nothing, she would at one moment tell me things which she was not unaware that I knew as well as anyone (like those statesmen who will never give you the least bit of news, but speak to you instead of what you could have read for yourself in the papers the day before), at another would describe without any precise details, in the manner of false confidences, bicycle rides that she had had at Balbec, the year before our first meeting. And as though I had guessed aright long ago, when I inferred therefrom that she must be a girl who was allowed a great deal of freedom, who went on long jaunts, the mention of those rides insinuated between Albertine's lips the same mysterious smile that had captivated me in those first days on the front at Balbec. She spoke to me also of the excursions she had made with some girlfriends through the Dutch countryside, of returning to Amsterdam in the evening, at a late hour, when a dense and happy crowd of people, almost all of whom she knew, thronged the streets and the towpaths of the canals, of which I felt that I could see reflected in Albertine's brilliant eyes, as in the glancing windows of a fast-moving carriage, the innumerable, flickering lights. How much more deserving of the name indifference is so-called aesthetic curiosity compared with the painful, unwearying curiosity I felt as to the places in which Albertine had stayed, as to what she might have been doing on a particular evening, her smiles, the expressions in her eyes, the words that she had uttered, the

kisses that she had received! No, never would the jealousy
that I had felt one day of Saint-Loup, if it had persisted,
have caused me this immense uneasiness. This love between women was something too unfamiliar; there was
nothing to enable me to form a precise and accurate idea
of its pleasures, its quality. How many people, how many
places (even places which did not concern her directly,
vague haunts of pleasure where she might have enjoyed
some pleasure, places where there are a great many people, where people brush against one) had Albertine—like
a person who, shepherding all her escort, a whole crowd,
past the barrier in front of her, secures their admission to
the theatre—from the threshold of my imagination or of
my memory, where I paid no attention to them, introduced into my heart! Now, the knowledge that I had of
them was internal, immediate, spasmodic, painful. Love is
space and time made perceptible to the heart.

And yet perhaps, had I myself been entirely faithful,
I might not have suffered because of infidelities which I
would have been incapable of conceiving; whereas what it
tortured me to imagine in Albertine was my own perpetual desire to find favour with new women, to start up new
romances, was to suppose her guilty of the glance which I
had been unable to resist casting, the other day, even
while I was by her side, at the young bicyclists seated at
tables in the Bois de Boulogne. As there is no knowledge,
one might almost say that there is no jealousy, except of
oneself. Observation counts for little. It is only from the
pleasure that we ourselves have felt that we can derive
knowledge and pain.

At moments, in Albertine's eyes, in the sudden in-
flammation of her cheeks, I felt as it were a gust of

warmth pass furtively through regions more inaccessible
to me than the sky, in which Albertine's memories, unknown to me, lived and moved. Then this beauty which,
when I thought of the successive years in which I had
known Albertine, whether on the beach at Balbec or in
Paris, I found that I had but recently discovered in her,
and which consisted in the fact that she existed on so
many planes and embodied so many days that had passed,
this beauty became almost heart-rending. Then beneath
that rose-pink face I felt that there yawned like a gulf the
inexhaustible expanse of the evenings when I had not
known Albertine. I could, if I chose, take Albertine on my
knee, hold her head in my hands, I could caress her, run
my hands slowly over her, but, just as if I had been handling a stone which encloses the salt of immemorial
oceans or the light of a star, I felt that I was touching no
more than the sealed envelope of a person who inwardly
reached to infinity. How I suffered from that position to
which we are reduced by the obliviousness of nature
which, when instituting the division of bodies, never
thought of making possible the interpenetration of souls!
And I realised that Albertine was not even for me (for if
her body was in the power of mine, her thoughts eluded
the grasp of my thoughts) the marvellous captive with
whom I had thought to enrich my home, while concealing
her presence there as completely, even from the friends
who came to see me and never suspected that she was at
the end of the corridor, in the room next to my own, as
did that person of whom nobody knew that he kept the
Princess of China sealed in a bottle; urging me with cruel
and fruitless insistence in quest of the past, she resembled, if anything, a mighty goddess of Time. And if I had

to waste years of my life and much of my fortune for her sake—and provided that I can tell myself, which is by no means certain, alas, that she herself lost nothing—I have nothing to regret. No doubt solitude would have been better, more fruitful, less painful. But if I had led the collector's life which Swann counselled, and the joys of which M. de Charlus reproached me with not knowing, when, with a blend of wit, insolence and good taste, he complained to me how ugly my rooms were, what statues, what pictures long pursued, at length possessed, or even, to put it in the best light, contemplated with detachment, would—like the little wound which healed quickly enough, but which the unconscious tactlessness of Albertine, or of people generally, or of my own thoughts, was never long in reopening—have given me access to that way out of oneself, that connecting road which, though private, opens on to the highway along which passes what we learn to know only from the day when it has made us suffer: the life of other people?

Sometimes there was such a beautiful moonlight that, an hour after Albertine had gone to bed, I would go to her bedside to tell her to look out of the window. I am certain that it was for this reason that I went to her room, and not to assure myself that she was really there. What likelihood was there of her being able to escape, even if she had wished? It would have required an improbable collusion with Françoise. In the dim room, I could see nothing except, against the whiteness of the pillow, a slender diadem of dark hair. But I could hear Albertine's breathing. Her sleep was so deep that I hesitated at first to go as far as the bed. Then I sat down on the edge of it. Her sleep continued to flow with the same murmur.

What I find it impossible to express is how gay her awakenings were. I would kiss her and shake her. At once she would cease to sleep, without even a moment's interval, would break out in a laugh, saying as she twined her arms round my neck: "I was just beginning to wonder whether you were coming," and then laugh even more blithely and tenderly. It was as though her charming head, when she slept, was filled with nothing but gaiety, affection and laughter. And in waking her I had merely, as when we cut open a fruit, released the gushing juice which quenches thirst.

Meanwhile winter was at an end; the fine weather returned, and often when Albertine had just bidden me good-night, my curtains and the wall above the curtains being still quite dark, in the nuns' garden next door I could hear, rich and mellow in the silence like a harmonium in church, the modulation of an unknown bird which, in the Lydian mode, was already chanting matins, and into the midst of my darkness flung the rich dazzling note of the sun that it could see. Soon the nights grew shorter still, and before what had been the hour of daybreak, I could see already stealing above my window-curtains the daily increasing whiteness of the dawn. If I resigned myself to allowing Albertine to continue to lead this life in which, notwithstanding her denials, I felt that she had the impression of being a prisoner, it was only because each day I was sure that on the morrow I should be able to set to work from time to time, to get up, to go out, to prepare our departure for some country place which we should buy and where Albertine would be able to lead, more freely and without anxiety on my account, the open-air life of the country or the seaside, of boating or hunting, which appealed to her.

Only, the next day, from that past which I loved and detested by turns in Albertine (since, when it is the present, everyone, from calculation, or politeness, or pity, sets to work to weave, between himself and us, a curtain of falsehood which we mistake for the truth) it would happen that, retrospectively, one of the hours which composed it, even of those which I thought I knew, presented to me all of a sudden an aspect which she no longer made any attempt to conceal from me and which was then quite different from the aspect in which it had previously appeared to me. Behind some look in her eyes, in place of the benign thought which I had formerly supposed that I could read in it, a hitherto unsuspected desire would reveal itself, alienating from me a fresh region of Albertine's heart which I had believed to be assimilated to my own. For instance, when Andrée had left Balbec in the month of July, Albertine had never told me that she was to see her again shortly, and I imagined that she had seen her even sooner than she expected since, because of the great unhappiness that I had suffered at Balbec, on that night of the fourteenth of September, she had made me the sacrifice of not remaining there and of returning at once to Paris. When she had arrived there on the fifteenth, I had asked her to go and see Andrée and had said to her: "Was she pleased to see you again?" Now one day Mme Bontemps called round to bring something for Albertine. I saw her for a moment and told her that Albertine had gone out with Andrée: "They've gone for a drive in the country."

"Yes," replied Mme Bontemps, "Albertine is always ready to go to the country. Three years ago, for instance, she simply had to go every day to the Buttes-Chaumont." At the name Buttes-Chaumont, a place where Albertine had told me that she had never been, my breath stopped for a moment. The truth is the most cunning of enemies. It delivers its attacks at the point in one's heart where one was least expecting them and where one has prepared no defence. Had Albertine been lying, to her aunt then, when she said that she went every day to the Buttes-Chaumont, or to myself since, when she told me that she did not know the place? "Fortunately," Mme Bontemps went on, "that poor Andrée will soon be leaving for a more bracing countryside, for the real countryside. She needs it badly, she's not looking at all well. It's true that she didn't get all the fresh air she needs last summer. You see, she left Balbec at the end of July, expecting to go back there in September, and then her brother put his knee out, and she was unable to go back."

So Albertine was expecting her at Balbec and had concealed this from me! It is true that it was all the more kind of her to have offered to return to Paris with me. Unless . . .

"Yes, I remember Albertine's mentioning it to me" (this was untrue). "When did the accident occur, again? I'm a bit muddled about it all."

"Actually, in a way it happened just at the right moment, because a day later the lease of the villa would have begun, and Andrée's grandmother would have had to pay a month's rent for nothing. He damaged his leg on the fourteenth of September, and she had time to cable Albertine on the morning of the fifteenth that she wasn't coming and Albertine was in time to warn the agency. A day later, and the lease would have run on to the middle of October."

And so, no doubt, when Albertine, changing her mind, had said to me: "Let's go this evening," what she saw with her mind's eye was an apartment unknown to me, that of Andrée's grandmother, where, as soon as we returned, she would be able to see the friend whom, without my suspecting it, she had hoped to see again shortly at Balbec. The kind words with which she had expressed her willingness to return to Paris with me, in contrast to her stubborn refusal a little earlier, I had sought to attribute to a genuine change of heart. In fact they were simply the reflexion of one of those changes in a situation of which we do not know, and which are the whole secret of the variations in the conduct of women who do not love us. They obstinately refuse to meet us the following evening, because they are tired, because their grandfather insists on their dining with him: "But come later," we insist. "He keeps me very late. He may want to see me home." The simple truth is that they have a rendezvous with some man whom they like. Suddenly he is no longer free. And they come to tell us how sorry they are to have hurt us, that the grandfather has been given the brush-off, and that there is nothing in the world that could keep them from remaining with us. I ought to have recognised these phrases in what Albertine had said to me on the day of my departure from Balbec. But to interpret her words I should have needed not only to recognise those phrases but to remember two traits peculiar to Albertine's character.

The two traits now recurred to my mind, one to con-

sole me, the other to make me wretched, for we find a little of everything in our memory; it is a sort of pharmacy,
a sort of chemical laboratory, in which our groping hand
may come to rest now on a sedative drug, now on a dangerous poison. The first trait, the consoling one, was that
habit of making a single action serve the pleasure of several persons, that multiple utilisation of whatever she did,
which was characteristic of Albertine. It was quite in
keeping with her character that, returning to Paris (the
fact that Andrée was not coming back might have made it
inconvenient for her to remain at Balbec without this
meaning that she could not do without Andrée), she
should use that single journey as an opportunity for pleasing two people of whom she was genuinely fond: myself
by making me believe that it was in order not to leave me
on my own, in order that I should not be unhappy, out of
devotion to me, and Andrée by persuading her that, since
she was not coming to Balbec, she herself did not wish to
remain there a moment longer, that she had prolonged her
stay there only in the hope of seeing Andrée and was now
hurrying back to join her. Now, Albertine's departure
with me was such an immediate sequel, on the one hand
to my access of grief and my desire to return to Paris, and
on the other hand to Andrée's telegram, that it was quite
natural that Andrée and I, respectively unaware, she of
my grief, I of her telegram, should both have supposed
that Albertine's departure from Balbec was the effect of
the one cause that each of us knew, which indeed it followed at so short an interval and so unexpectedly. And in
this case, it was still possible for me to believe that the
thought of keeping me company had been Albertine's real

object, though she had not wanted to neglect an opportunity of thereby establishing a claim to Andrée's gratitude.

But unfortunately I remembered almost at once another of Albertine's characteristics, which was the swiftness with which she was seized by the irresistible temptation of a pleasure. And I recalled how, when she had decided to leave, she had been so impatient to get to the train, how she had pushed past the hotel manager who in trying to detain us might have made us miss the omnibus, the shrug of complicity which she had given me and by which I had been so touched when, on the twister, M. de Cambremer had asked us whether we could not "postpone it by a sennight." Yes, what she saw in front of her eyes at that moment, what made her so feverishly anxious to leave, what she was so impatient to get to, was an uninhabited apartment I had once visited, belonging to Andrée's grandmother, a luxurious apartment looked after by an old manservant, facing south, but so empty, so silent, that the sun appeared to spread dust-sheets over the sofa and the armchairs of the room in which Albertine and Andrée would ask the respectful caretaker, perhaps unsuspecting, perhaps conniving, to allow them to rest for a while. I saw it constantly now, empty, with a bed or a sofa, and a maid who was either a dupe or an accomplice, that apartment to which, whenever Albertine seemed serious and in a hurry, she set off to meet her friend, who had doubtless arrived there before her since her time was more her own. Until then I had never given a thought to that apartment, which now possessed for me a horrible beauty. The unknown element in the lives of other people is like that of nature, which each fresh scientific discovery merely reduces but does not abolish. A jealous lover exasperates the woman he loves by depriving her of a thousand unimportant pleasures, but those pleasures which are the keystone of her life she conceals in a place where, even at moments when he thinks that he is showing the most intelligent perspicacity and third parties are keeping him most closely informed, he never dreams of looking. However, at least Andrée was going to leave Paris. But I did not want Albertine to be in a position to despise me as having been the dupe of herself and Andrée. One of these days I would tell her. And thus I would force her perhaps to speak to me more frankly, by showing her that I was after all informed of the things that she concealed from me. But I did not wish to mention it to her for the moment, first of all because, so soon after her aunt's visit, she would guess where my information came from, would block that source and would not be worried about other, unknown ones; and then because I did not want to run the risk, so long as I was not absolutely certain of keeping Albertine for as long as I chose, of provoking her irritation to the extent of making her decide to leave me. It is true that if I reasoned, sought the truth, prognosticated the future on the basis of her words, which always approved of all my plans, assuring me how much she loved this life, how little her seclusion deprived her of, I had no doubt that she would remain with me always. I was in fact dismayed by the thought; I felt that life and the world, whose fruits I had never really tasted, were passing me by, bartered for a woman in whom I could no longer find anything new. I could not even go to Venice, where, while I lay in bed, I should be too tormented by the fear of the advances that might be made to her by the gondolier, the people in the hotel, the Venetian women. But if on the contrary I reasoned on the basis of the other hypothesis, that which rested not upon Albertine's words but upon silences, looks, blushes, sulks, and even fits of anger, which I could quite easily have shown her to be unfounded and which I preferred to appear not to notice, then I told myself that she was finding this life unbearable, that she felt constantly deprived of what she loved, and that inevitably she would leave me one day. All that I wished, if she did so, was that I might choose the moment, a moment when it would not be too painful to me, and also at a time of the year when she could not go to any of the places in which I imagined her debaucheries, neither to Amsterdam, nor to Andrée's, nor to Mlle Vinteuil's, though she would see them again, it was true, a few months later. But in the meantime I should have become calmer and it would no longer matter to me. In any case, before even thinking of it I must wait until I was cured of the slight relapse that had been caused by my discovery of the reasons on account of which Albertine, at a few hours' interval, had been determined not to leave, and then to leave Balbec immediately; I must allow time for the symptoms to disappear, since they could only go on diminishing if I learned nothing new, but were still too acute not to render more painful, more difficult, a process of separation now recognised as inevitable, but in no sense urgent, and one that would be better performed in "cold blood." I could control the choice of moment, for if she decided to leave me before I had made up my mind, as soon as she informed me that she had had enough of this life, there would always be time enough for me to think up some way of countering her arguments, to offer her a larger freedom, to promise her some great pleasure in the near future which she herself would be anxious not to miss, and at worst, if I could find no other recourse but to appeal to her heart, to confess my anguish to her. My mind was therefore at rest from this point of view though I was not being very logical with myself. For, though the basis of this hypothesis was that I precisely disregarded what she said or intimated, I was assuming that, when the question of her leaving arose, she would give me her reasons beforehand, would allow me to resist and overcome them.

I felt that my life with Albertine was on the one hand, when I was not jealous, nothing but boredom, and on the other hand, when I was jealous, nothing but pain. If there had been any happiness in it, it could not last. In the same spirit of wisdom which had inspired me at Balbec, on the evening when we had been happy together after Mme de Cambremer's visit, I wanted to leave her, because I knew that by carrying on I should gain nothing. Only, even now, I imagined that the memory that I retained of her would be like a sort of vibration, prolonged by a pedal, of the last moment of our parting. Hence I was anxious to choose a moment of sweetness, so that it might be it that continued to vibrate in me. I must not be too particular, and wait too long, I must be sensible. And yet, having waited so long, it would be madness not to wait a few days longer, until an acceptable moment should offer itself, rather than risk seeing her depart with that same sense of revolt which I had felt in the past when Mamma left my bedside without bidding me goodnight, or when she said good-bye to me at the station. To be on the safe side, I heaped more and more presents on

her. As regards the Fortuny gowns, we had at length decided upon one in blue and gold lined with pink which
was just ready. And I had ordered all the same the other
five which she had relinquished with regret in favour of
this one.

Yet with the coming of spring, two months after her
aunt's conversation with me, I lost my temper with her
one evening. It was the very evening on which Albertine
had put on for the first time the indoor gown in gold and
blue by Fortuny which, by reminding me of Venice, made
me feel all the more strongly what I was sacrificing for
her, who showed no corresponding gratitude towards me.
If I had never seen Venice, I had dreamed of it incessantly since those Easter holidays which, when still a boy,
I had been going to spend there, and earlier still, since the
Titian prints and Giotto photographs which Swann had
given me long ago at Combray. The Fortuny gown which
Albertine was wearing that evening seemed to me the
tempting phantom of that invisible Venice. It was overrun
by Arab ornamentation, like Venice, like the Venetian
palaces hidden like sultan's wives behind a screen of per-
forated stone, like the bindings in the Ambrosian Library,
like the columns from which the oriental birds that symbolised alternatively life and death were repeated in the
shimmering fabric, of an intense blue which, as my eyes
drew nearer, turned into a malleable gold by those same
transmutations which, before an advancing gondola,
change into gleaming metal the azure of the Grand Canal.
And the sleeves were lined with a cherry pink which is so
peculiarly Venetian that it is called Tiepolo pink.

In the course of the day, Françoise had let fall in my
hearing that Albertine was satisfied with nothing, that

when I sent word to her that I would be going out with her, or that I would not be going out, that the car would or would not come to fetch her, she almost shrugged her shoulders and would barely give a polite answer. That evening when I felt that she was in a bad mood, and when the first heat of summer had wrought upon my nerves, I could not restrain my anger and reproached her for her ingratitude. "Yes, you can ask anybody," I shouted at the top of my voice, quite beside myself, "you can ask Françoise, it's common knowledge." But immediately I remembered how Albertine had once told me how terrifying she found me when I was angry, and had applied to me the lines from *Esther*:

> Judge how, incensed against me, that great forehead
> Must then have cast into my troubled soul such dread.
> Alas! where is the heart audacious that defies
> Unmoved those lightnings starting from your eyes?

I felt ashamed of my violence. And, to make amends for what I had done, without however acknowledging defeat, so that my peace might be an armed and formidable peace, while at the same time I thought it as well to show her once again that I was not afraid of a rupture so that she might not feel tempted to provoke it: "Forgive me, my little Albertine, I'm ashamed of my violence, I don't know how to apologise. If we can't get on together, if we're to be obliged to part, it mustn't be like this, it wouldn't be worthy of us. We will part, if part we must, but first of all I wish to beg your pardon most humbly and from the bottom of my heart." I decided that, to atone for my outburst and also to make certain of her intention to remain with me for some time to come, at any rate until Andrée should have left Paris, which would be in three weeks' time, it would be as well, next day, to think of some pleasure greater than any that she had yet had, but fairly far ahead; and since I was going to wipe out the offence that I had given her, perhaps it would be as well to take advantage of this moment to show her that I knew more about her life than she supposed. The resentment that she would feel would be removed next day by my generosity, but the warning would remain in her mind. "Yes, my little Albertine, forgive me if I was violent. But I'm not quite as much to blame as you think. There are wicked people in the world who are trying to make us quarrel; I've always refrained from mentioning it, as I didn't want to torment you. But sometimes I'm driven out of my mind by these accusations." And wishing to make the most of the fact that I was going to be able to show her that I was in the know as regards the departure from Balbec, I went on: "For instance, you knew that Mlle Vinteuil was expected at Mme Verdurin's that afternoon when you went to the Trocadéro."

She blushed: "Yes, I knew that."

"Can you swear to me that it was not in order to renew your relations with her that you wanted to go to the Verdurins'."

"Why, of course I can swear it. Why do you say *renew*, I never had any relations with her, I swear it."

I was deeply grieved to hear Albertine lie to me like this, deny the facts which her blush had made all too evident. Her mendacity appalled me. And yet, as it contained a protestation of innocence which, almost unconsciously, I was prepared to accept, it hurt me less than her sincerity when, after I had asked her: "Can you at least

swear to me that the pleasure of seeing Mlle Vinteuil
again had nothing to do with your anxiety to go to the
Verdurins' that afternoon?" she replied: "No, that I cannot swear. It would have been a great pleasure to see Mlle
Vinteuil again."

A moment earlier, I had been angry with her because
she concealed her relations with Mlle Vinteuil, and now
her admission of the pleasure she would have felt at seeing her again turned my bones to water. True, when Albertine had said to me, on my return from the Verdurins':
"Wasn't Mlle Vinteuil to be there?" she had revived all
my anguish by proving that she knew of her coming. But
doubtless in the meantime I had reasoned thus: "She
knew of her coming, which gave her no pleasure in the
least, but since she must have realised, after the event,
that it was the revelation that she knew someone with
such a bad reputation as Mlle Vinteuil that had distressed
me at Balbec to the point of thinking of suicide, she
didn't want to mention it." And now here she was being
obliged to admit that the prospect of seeing Mlle Vinteuil
gave her pleasure. Besides, the mystery in which she had
cloaked her intention of going to see the Verdurins ought
to have been a sufficient proof. But I had not given the
matter enough thought. And so, while saying to myself
now: "Why does she only half confess? It's even more
stupid than wicked and sad," I was so crushed that I did
not have the heart to pursue the question, as to which I
was not in a strong position, having no damning evidence
to produce, and to recover my ascendancy I hurriedly
turned to the subject of Andrée which would enable me
to put Albertine to rout by means of the overwhelming
revelation of Andrée's telegram. "Anyhow," I said to her,

"now I'm being tormented and persecuted again with reports of your relations, this time with Andrée."

"With Andrée?" she cried. Her face was ablaze with fury. And astonishment or the desire to appear astonished made her open her eyes wide. "How charming! And may one know who has been telling you these pretty tales? May I be allowed to speak to these persons, to learn from them what basis they have for their slanders?"

"My little Albertine, I don't know, the letters are anonymous, but from people whom you would perhaps have no difficulty in finding" (this to show her that I did not believe that she would try) "for they must know you quite well. The last one, I must admit (and I mention it because it deals with a trivial thing and there's nothing at all unpleasant in it), made me furious all the same. It informed me that if, on the day when we left Balbec, you first of all wished to remain there and then decided to go, that was because in the meantime you had received a letter from Andrée telling you that she wasn't coming."

"I know quite well that Andrée wrote to tell me that she wasn't coming, in fact she telegraphed; I can't show you the telegram because I didn't keep it, but it wasn't that day. Besides, even if it had been that day, what difference do you suppose it could make to me whether Andrée came or not?"

The words "what difference do you suppose it could make to me" were a proof of anger and that it did make some difference, but were not necessarily a proof that Albertine had returned to Paris solely from a desire to see Andrée. Whenever Albertine saw one of the real or alleged motives of one of her actions discovered by a person to whom she had pleaded a different motive, she became angry, even if the person was someone for whose sake she had really performed the action. That Albertine believed that this information about what she had been doing did not come to me from anonymous letters which I had received willy-nilly but was eagerly solicited by me could never have been deduced from the words which she next uttered, in which she appeared to accept my story of the anonymous letters, but rather from her look of fury with me, a fury which appeared to be merely the explosion of her previous ill-humour, just as the espionage in which, on this hypothesis, she must suppose that I had been indulging would have been only the culmination of a surveillance of all her actions which she had suspected for a long time past. Her anger extended even to Andrée herself, and deciding no doubt that from now on I should no longer be unworried even when she went out with Andrée, she went on: "Besides, Andrée exasperates me. She's a deadly bore. I never want to go anywhere with her again. You can tell that to the people who informed you that I came back to Paris for her sake. Suppose I were to tell you that after all the years I've known Andrée I couldn't even describe her face to you, so little have I ever looked at it!"

But at Balbec, that first year, she had said to me: "Andrée is lovely." It is true that this did not mean that she had had amorous relations with her, and indeed I had never heard her speak at that time except with indignation of any relations of that sort. But was it not possible that she had changed, even without being aware that she had changed, not thinking that her amusements with a girl-friend were the same thing as the immoral relations, not very clearly defined in her own mind, which she condemned in other women? Was this not possible, since this same change, and this same unawareness of change, had occurred in her relations with myself, whose kisses she had repulsed at Balbec with such indignation, kisses which afterwards she was to give me of her own accord every day, which, I hoped, she would give me for a long time to come, which she was going to give me in a moment?

"But, my darling, how do you expect me to tell them when I don't know who they are?"

This answer was so forceful that it ought to have dissolved the objections and doubts which I saw crystallised in Albertine's pupils. But it left them intact. I was now silent, and yet she continued to gaze at me with that persistent attention which we give to someone who has not finished speaking. I asked her forgiveness once more. She replied that she had nothing to forgive me. She had become very gentle again. But, beneath her sad and troubled features, it seemed to me that a secret plan had taken shape. I knew quite well that she could not leave me without warning me; in fact she could neither want to leave me (it was in a week's time that she was to try on the new Fortuny gowns), nor decently do so, as my mother was returning to Paris at the end of the week and her aunt also. Why, since it was impossible for her to leave, did I repeat to her several times that we should be going out together next day to look at some Venetian glass which I wished to give her, and why was I comforted when I heard her say that that was agreed? When it was time for her to say good-night and I kissed her, she did not behave as usual, but turned her face away—it was barely a minute or two since I had been thinking how pleasing it was that she now gave me every evening what she had refused me at Balbec—and did not return my kiss. It was as though, having quarrelled with me, she was not prepared to give me a token of affection which might later on have appeared to me an act of duplicity that belied the quarrel. It was as though she was attuning her actions to that quarrel, and yet with moderation, whether so as not to announce it, or because, while breaking off carnal relations with me, she wished nevertheless to remain my friend. I kissed her then a second time, pressing to my heart the shimmering golden azure of the Grand Canal and the mating birds, symbols of death and resurrection. But for the second time, instead of returning my kiss, she drew away with the sort of instinctive and baleful obstinacy of animals that feel the hand of death. This presentiment which she seemed to be expressing overcame me too, and filled me with such anxious dread that when she had reached the door I could not bear to let her go, and called her back.

"Albertine," I said to her, "I'm not at all sleepy. If you don't want to go to sleep yourself, you might stay here a little longer, if you like, but I don't really mind, and I don't on any account want to tire you." I felt that if I had been able to make her undress, and to have her there in her white nightdress, in which she seemed pinker and warmer, in which she excited my senses more keenly, the reconciliation would have been more complete. But I hesitated for an instant, for the sky-blue border of her dress added to her face a beauty, a luminosity, without which she would have seemed to me harder.

She came back slowly and said to me very sweetly, and still with the same downcast, sorrowful expression: "I

can stay as long as you like, I'm not sleepy." Her reply
calmed me, for, so long as she was in the room, I felt that
I could prepare for the future, and it also reflected friendliness and obedience, but of a certain sort, which seemed
to me to be limited by that secret which I sensed behind
her sorrowful gaze, her altered manner, altered partly in
spite of herself, partly no doubt to attune it in advance to
something which I did not know. I felt that, all the same,
I needed only to have her all in white, with her throat
bare, in front of me, as I had seen her at Balbec in bed, to
find the courage which would oblige her to yield.

"Since you're being kind enough to stay here a moment to console me, you ought to take off your gown, it's
too hot, too stiff, I dare not approach you for fear of
crumpling that fine stuff, and there are those fateful birds
between us. Undress, my darling."

"No, I couldn't possibly take off this dress here. I
shall undress in my own room presently."

"Then you won't even come and sit down on my
bed?"

"Why, of course."

She remained, however, some way away from me, by
my feet. We talked. Suddenly we heard the regular
rhythm of a plaintive call. It was the pigeons beginning to
coo. "That proves that day has come already," said Albertine; and, her brows almost knitted, as though she missed,
by living with me, the joys of the fine weather, "Spring
has begun, if the pigeons have returned." The resemblance between their cooing and the crow of the cock was
as profound and as obscure as, in Vinteuil's septet, the resemblance between the theme of the adagio and that of
the opening and closing passages, it being built on the

same key-theme but so transformed by differences of
tonality, tempo, etc. that the lay listener who opens a
book on Vinteuil is astonished to find that they are all
three based on the same four notes, four notes which for
that matter he may pick out with one finger upon the piano without recognising any of the three passages. Likewise, this melancholy refrain performed by the pigeons
was a sort of cockcrow in the minor key, which did not
soar up into the sky, did not rise vertically, but, regular as
the braying of a donkey, enveloped in sweetness, went
from one pigeon to another along a single horizontal line,
and never raised itself, never changed its lateral plaint into
that joyous appeal which had been uttered so often in the
allegro of the introduction and the finale. I know that I
then uttered the word "death," as though Albertine were
about to die. It seems that events are larger than the moment in which they occur and cannot be entirely contained in it. Certainly they overflow into the future
through the memory that we retain of them, but they demand a place also in the time that precedes them. One
may say that we do not then see them as they are to be,
but in memory are they not modified too?

When I saw that she deliberately refrained from kissing me, realising that I was merely wasting my time, that
it was only after a kiss that the really soothing moments
would begin, I said to her: "Good-night, it's too late," because that would make her kiss me and we would go on
kissing afterwards. But after saying to me, "Good-night,
try and sleep well," she contented herself with letting me
kiss her on the cheek, exactly as she had done twice before. This time I dared not call her back. But my heart
beat so violently that I could not lie down again. Like a

bird flying from one end of its cage to the other I alternated between anxiety lest Albertine should leave me and
a state of comparative calm. This calm was produced by
the argument which I kept repeating several times a
minute: "She cannot go without warning me, and she
never said anything about going," and I was more or less
calmed. But at once I said to myself: "But what if tomorrow I find her gone! My very anxiety must be founded on
something. Why didn't she kiss me?" At this my heart
ached horribly. Then it was slightly soothed by the argument which I advanced once more, but I ended with a
headache, so incessant and monotonous was this fluctua-
tion of my thoughts. There are thus certain mental states,
and especially anxiety, which, offering us only two alter-
natives, are somehow as atrociously circumscribed as a
simple physical pain. I perpetually repeated both the argument which justified my anxiety and the one which
proved it false and reassured me, within as narrow a space
as the sick man who explores without ceasing, on an internal impulse, the organ that is causing his suffering and
withdraws for an instant from the painful spot only to return to it a moment later. Suddenly, in the silence of the
night, I was startled by a noise which, though apparently
insignificant, filled me with terror, the noise of Albertine's
window being violently opened. When I heard nothing
more, I wondered why this noise had caused me such
alarm. In itself there was nothing so extraordinary about
it, but I probably gave it two interpretations which
alarmed me equally. In the first place it was one of the
conventions of our life together that, since I was afraid of
draughts, nobody must ever open a window at night. This
had been explained to Albertine when she came to stay in

the house, and although she was convinced that this was a fad on my part and thoroughly unhealthy, she had promised me that she would never infringe the rule. And she was so timorous about everything that she knew to be my wish, even if she disapproved of it, that she would have gone to sleep amid the fumes of a smouldering fire rather than open her window, just as, however important the circumstances, she would not have had me woken up in the morning. It was only one of the minor conventions of our life, but if she was prepared to violate this one without consulting me, might it not mean that she no longer needed to behave with circumspection, that she would violate them all just as easily? Besides, the noise had been violent, almost rude, as though she had flung the window open, crimson with rage, saying to herself: "This life is stifling me. I don't care, I must have air!" I did not exactly say all this to myself, but I continued to think, as of an omen more mysterious and more funereal than the hoot of an owl, of that sound of the window which Albertine had opened. Filled with an agitation such as I had not perhaps felt since the evening at Combray when Swann had been dining downstairs, I paced the corridor all night long, hoping, by the noise that I made, to attract Albertine's attention, hoping that she would take pity on me and would call me to her, but I heard no sound from her room. At Combray, I had asked my mother to come. But with my mother I feared only her anger; I knew that I would not diminish her affection by displaying mine. This made me hesitate to call out to Albertine. Gradually I began to feel that it was too late. She must long have been asleep. I went back to bed. In the morning, as soon as I awoke, since no one ever came to

my room, whatever happened, without a summons, I rang
for Françoise. And at the same time I thought: "I must
speak to Albertine about a yacht which I mean to have
built for her." As I took my letters I said to Françoise
without looking at her: "I shall have something to say to
Mlle Albertine presently. Is she up yet?" "Yes, she got up
early." I felt untold anxieties which I could scarcely contain rise up in me as in a gust of wind. The tumult in my
chest was so great that I was quite out of breath, as
though buffeted by a storm. "Ah! but where is she just
now?" "I expect she's in her room." "Ah! good! Well, I
shall see her presently." I breathed again; my agitation
subsided; Albertine was here; it was almost a matter of
indifference to me whether she was or not. Besides, had it
not been absurd of me to suppose that she could possibly
not be there? I fell asleep, but, in spite of my certainty
that she would not leave me, it was a light sleep and its
lightness related to her alone. For the sounds that were
obviously connected with work in the courtyard, while I
heard them vaguely in my sleep, left me untroubled,
whereas the slightest rustle that came from her room,
when she left it, or noiselessly returned, pressing the bell
so gently, made me start, ran through my whole body, left
me with a palpitating heart, although I had heard it in a
deep drowse, just as my grandmother in the last days before her death, when she was plunged in a motionless torpor which nothing could disturb and which the doctors
called coma, would begin, I was told, to tremble for a moment like a leaf when she heard the three rings with
which I was in the habit of summoning Françoise, and
which, even when I made them softer, during that week,
so as not to disturb the silence of the death-chamber, no-

body, Françoise assured me, could mistake for anyone else's ring because of a way that I had, and was quite unconscious of having, of pressing the bell. Had I then myself entered into my last agony? Was this the approach of death?

That day and the next we went out together, since Albertine refused to go out again with Andrée. I did not even mention the yacht to her. These outings had completely restored my peace of mind. But in the evening she had continued to embrace me in the same new way, which left me furious. I could interpret it now in no other way than as a means of showing me that she was sulking, which seemed to me perfectly absurd after the kindnesses I continued to heap upon her. And so, no longer receiving from her even those carnal satisfactions on which I depended, finding her ugly in her ill humour, I felt all the more keenly my deprivation of all the women and of the travels for which these first warm days reawakened my desire. Thanks no doubt to scattered memories of forgotten assignations that I had had, while still a schoolboy, with women, beneath trees already in full leaf, this springtime region in which the journey of our dwelling-place through the seasons had halted three days since beneath a clement sky, and in which all the roads sped away towards picnics in the country, boating parties, pleasure trips, seemed to me to be the land of women just as much as it was the land of trees, and the land in which the pleasure that was everywhere on offer became permissible to my convalescent strength. Resigning myself to idleness, resigning myself to chastity, to tasting pleasure only with a woman whom I did not love, resigning myself to remaining shut up in my room, to not travelling, all this was possible in the old world where we had been only yesterday, the empty world of winter, but not any longer in this new leafy world, in which I had awoken like a young Adam faced for the first time with the problem of existence, of happiness, and not bowed down beneath the accumulation of previous negative solutions. Albertine's presence weighed upon me. I looked at her, grim-faced and sullen, and felt it was a pity we had not broken with each other. I wanted to go to Venice, I wanted in the meantime to go to the Louvre to look at Venetian pictures and to the Luxembourg to see the two Elstirs which, as I had just heard, the Princesse de Guermantes had recently sold to that gallery, those that I had so greatly admired at the Duchesse de Guermantes's, the *Pleasures of the Dance* and the *Portrait of the X Family*. But I was afraid that, in the former, certain lascivious poses might give Albertine a desire, a nostalgic longing for popular rejoicings, might make her think that perhaps a certain life which she had never led, a life of fireworks and suburban pleasure-grounds, had something to recommend it. Already, in anticipation, I was afraid lest, on the Fourteenth of July, she would ask me to take her to a popular ball and I longed for some impossible event which would do away with the national holiday. And besides, there were also in those Elstirs nude female figures in verdant southern landscapes which might make Albertine think of certain pleasures, albeit Elstir himself (but would she not degrade his work?) had seen in them no more than sculptural beauty, or rather the beauty of white monuments, which women's bodies seated amidst verdure assume.

And so I resigned myself to abandoning that pleasure and decided instead to go to Versailles. Not wanting to go out with Andrée, Albertine had remained in her room, reading, in her Fortuny dressing-gown. I asked her if she would like to go with me to Versailles. She had the charming quality of being always ready for anything, perhaps because she had been accustomed in the past to spend half her time as the guest of other people, and, just as she had made up her mind to come to Paris in two minutes, she said to me: "I can come as I am if we don't get out of the car." She hesitated for a moment between two Fortuny coats beneath which to conceal her dressing-gown—as she might have hesitated between two friends in choosing an escort—chose a beautiful dark-blue one, and stuck a pin into a hat. In a minute, she was ready, before I had put on my overcoat, and we went to Versailles. This very promptitude, this absolute docility left me more reassured, as though, without having any precise reason for anxiety, I had indeed been in need of reassurance. "After all I have nothing to fear. She does everything that I ask, in spite of the noise of her window the other night. The moment I spoke of going out, she flung that blue coat over her gown and out she came. That's not what a rebel would have done, a person who was no longer on friendly terms with me," I said to myself as we went to Versailles. We stayed there a long time. The sky consisted entirely of that radiant and slightly pale blue which the wayfarer lying in a field sees at times above his head, but so uniform and so deep that one feels that the pigment of which it is composed has been applied without the least alloy and with such an inexhaustible richness that one might delve more and more deeply into its substance without encountering an atom of anything but the same blue. I thought of my grandmother who—in human art as in nature—loved grandeur, and who used to enjoy gazing at the steeple of Saint-Hilaire soaring into that same blue. Suddenly I felt once again a longing for my lost freedom on hearing a noise which I did not at first recognise and which my grandmother would also have loved. It was like the buzz of a wasp. "Look," said Albertine, "there's an aeroplane, high up there, very very high." I looked all over the sky but could see only, unmarred by any black spot, the unbroken pallor of the unalloyed blue. I continued nevertheless to hear the humming of the wings, which suddenly entered my field of vision. Up there, a pair of tiny wings, dark and flashing, punctured the continuous blue of the unalterable sky. I had at last been able to attach the buzzing to its cause, to that little insect throbbing up there in the sky, probably six thousand feet above me; I could see it hum. Perhaps at a time when distances by land had not yet been habitually shortened by speed as they are today, the whistle of a passing train two thousand yards away was endowed with that beauty which now and for some time to come will stir our emotions in the drone of an aeroplane six thousand feet up, at the thought that the distances traversed in this vertical journey are the same as those on the ground, and that in this other direction, where measurements appear different to us because the reach seemed impossible, an aeroplane at six thousand feet is no further away than a train at two thousand yards, is nearer even, the identical trajectory occurring in a purer medium, with no obstacle between the traveller and his starting point, just as on the sea or across the plains, in calm weather, the wake of a ship that is already far away or the breath of a single zephyr will furrow the ocean of water or of corn.

I wanted something to eat. We stopped at a big pastry-cook's, situated almost outside the town, which at the time enjoyed a certain vogue. A lady was leaving the place, and asked the proprietress for her things. And after the lady had gone, Albertine cast repeated glances at the proprietress as though she wished to attract her attention while she was putting away cups, plates, cakes, for it was already late. She approached us only if I asked for something. And it happened then that, as the woman, who incidentally was extremely tall, was standing up while she waited on us and Albertine was seated beside me, Albertine, each time, in an attempt to attract her attention, raised vertically towards her a sunny gaze which compelled her to elevate her pupils to an inordinate height since, the woman being close up against us, Albertine had no possibility of tempering the angle with a sidelong glance. She was obliged, without raising her head unduly, to make her eyes ascend to that disproportionate height at which the woman's eyes were situated. Out of consideration for me, Albertine would quickly lower her eyes and then, the woman having paid no attention to her, would begin again. This led to a series of vain imploring elevations before an inaccessible deity. Then the proprietress moved away to clear a large table next to ours. Now Albertine could look sideways. But never once did the woman's eyes come to rest upon my mistress. This did not surprise me, for I knew that this woman, with whom I was slightly acquainted, had lovers, although she was married, but managed skilfully to conceal her intrigues,

which astonished me vastly in view of her prodigious stupidity. I studied the woman while we finished our meal.
Engrossed in her task, she carried her disregard for Albertine's glances (which incidentally were in no way improper) almost to the point of rudeness. She went on
clearing away and arranging things without letting anything distract her. The putting away of the coffee-spoons,
the fruit-knives, might have been entrusted not to this
large and handsome woman, but, by a labour-saving de-
vice, to a mere machine, and you would not have seen so
complete an isolation from Albertine's attention; and yet
she did not lower her eyes, did not appear self-absorbed,
allowed her eyes, her charms to shine in an undivided attention to her work. It is true that if this woman had not
been a particularly stupid person (not only was this her
reputation, but I knew it from experience), this detachment might have been a supreme proof of guile. And I
know very well that the stupidest person, if his desire or
his pocket is involved, can, in that sole instance, emerging
from the nullity of his stupid life, adapt himself immediately to the workings of the most complicated machinery;
all the same, this would have been too subtle a supposition in the case of a woman as brainless as this. Her
stupidity even took her to improbable lengths of impolite-
ness. Not once did she look at Albertine whom, after all,
she could not help seeing. It was not very flattering for
my mistress, but, when all was said, I was delighted that
Albertine should receive this little lesson and should see
that frequently women paid no attention to her. We left
the pastry-cook's, got into our carriage and were already
on our way home when I was seized by a sudden regret
that I had not taken the proprietress aside and begged her

on no account to tell the lady who had come out of the shop as we were going in my name and address, which she must know perfectly well because of the orders I had constantly left with her. It was undesirable that the lady should be enabled thus to learn, indirectly, Albertine's address. But I felt that it was not worth while turning back for so small a matter, and that I should appear to be attaching too great an importance to it in the eyes of the idiotic and deceitful proprietress. I decided, however, that I should have to return there, in a week's time, to make this request, and that it is a great bore, since one always forgets half the things one has to say, to have to do even the simplest things in instalments.

We returned home very late, in a half-light through which here and there, by the roadside, a pair of red breeches pressed against a skirt revealed an amorous couple. Our carriage passed in through the Porte Maillot. For the monuments of Paris had been substituted, pure, linear, two-dimensional, a drawing of the monuments of Paris, as though in an attempt to recapture the appearance of a city that had been destroyed. But, at the edges of this picture, there rose so delicately the pale-blue mounting in which it was framed that one's thirsty eyes sought everywhere for a little more of that delicious hue which was too sparingly meted out to them: the moon was shining. Albertine admired the moonlight. I dared not tell her that I would have admired it more if I had been alone, or in quest of an unknown woman. I recited to her some lines of verse or passages of prose about moonlight, pointing out to her how from "silvery" which it had been at one time, it had turned "blue" in Chateaubriand, and in the

Victor Hugo of *Eviradnus* and *La Fête chez Thérèse*, to become in turn yellow and metallic in Baudelaire and Leconte de Lisle. Then, reminding her of the image that is used for the crescent moon at the end of *Booz endormi*, I talked to her about the whole poem.

Looking back, I find it difficult to describe how densely her life was covered in a network of alternating, fugitive, often contradictory desires. No doubt falsehood complicated this still further, for, as she retained no accurate memory of our conversations, if, for example, she had said to me: "Ah! that was a pretty girl, if you like, and a good golfer," and, when I had asked the girl's name, had answered with that detached, universal, superior air of which no doubt there is always enough and to spare, for all liars of this category borrow it for a moment when they do not wish to answer a question, and it never fails them: "Ah, I'm afraid I don't know" (with regret at her inability to enlighten me), "I never knew her name, I used to see her on the golf course, but I didn't know what she was called"—if, a month later, I said to her: "Albertine, you remember that pretty girl you mentioned to me, who used to play golf so well," "Ah, yes," she would answer without thinking, "Emilie Daltier, I don't know what's become of her." And the lie, like a line of earthworks, was carried back from the defence of the name, now captured, to the possibilities of meeting her again. "Oh, I couldn't say, I never knew her address. I can't think of anyone who could give it to you. Oh, no! Andrée never knew her. She wasn't one of our little band, now so scattered."

At other times the lie took the form of a base admission: "Ah! if I had three hundred thousand francs a

year . . ." She bit her lip. "Well? what would you do
then?" "I should ask your permission," she said, kissing
me, "to stay with you always. Where else could I be so
happy?"

But, even allowing for her lies, it was incredible how
spasmodic her life was, how fugitive her strongest desires.
She would be mad about a person whom, three days later,
she would refuse to see. She could not wait for an hour
while I sent out for canvas and colours, for she wished to
start painting again. For two whole days she would be impatient, almost shed the tears, quickly dried, of an infant
that has just been weaned from its nurse. And this instability of her feelings with regard to people, things, occupations, arts, places, was in fact so universal that, if she
did love money, which I do not believe, she cannot have
loved it for longer than anything else. When she said:
"Ah! if I had three hundred thousand francs a year!" or
even if she expressed a nefarious but short-lived thought,
she could not have held on to it any longer than to the
idea of going to Les Rochers, of which she had seen an
engraving in my grandmother's edition of Mme de Sévigné, of meeting an old friend from the golf course, of going up in an aeroplane, of going to spend Christmas with
her aunt, or of taking up painting again.

"By the way, since neither of us is really hungry, we
might look in at the Verdurins'," Albertine said to me.
"This is their day and their hour."

"But I thought you were cross with them?"

"Oh! there are all sorts of stories about them, but really they're not so bad as all that. Madame Verdurin has
always been very nice to me. Besides, one can't keep on

quarrelling all the time with everybody. They have their faults, but who hasn't?"

"You're not properly dressed, you would have to go home and dress, and that would make us very late."

"Yes, you're right, let's just go home," replied Albertine with that marvellous docility which never ceased to amaze me.

The fine weather, that night, made a leap forward as the mercury in a thermometer darts upwards in the heat. On those early-risen spring mornings I could hear from my bed the tramcars rumbling through a cloud of perfumes, in an atmosphere which became more and more saturated by the warmth until it reached the solidification and density of noon. In my bedroom, where on the contrary it was cooler, when the unctuous air had succeeded in glazing and isolating the smell of the wash-stand, the smell of the wardrobe, the smell of the sofa, simply by the sharpness with which they stood out, vertical and erect, in adjacent but distinct slices, in a pearly chiaroscuro which added a softer glaze to the shimmer of the curtains and the blue satin armchairs, I saw myself, not by a mere caprice of my imagination but because it was physically possible, following, in some new suburban quarter like that in which Bloch's house at Balbec was situated, the streets blinded by the sun, and finding in them not the dull butchers' shops and the white freestone facings, but the country dining-room which I could reach in no time, and the smells that I would find there on my arrival, the smell of the bowl of cherries and apricots, the smell of cider, the smell of gruyère cheese, held in suspense in the luminous coagulation of shadow which they delicately vein like the heart of an agate, while the knife-rests of prismatic glass scatter rainbows athwart the room or paint the oilcloth here and there with peacock-eyes.

Like a wind that swells in a steady roar, I heard with joy a car beneath the window. I sniffed its smell of petrol. The latter may seem regrettable to the oversensitive (who are always materialists and for whom it spoils the country), and to certain thinkers (materialists after their own fashion also) who, believing in the importance of facts, imagine that man would be happier, capable of higher flights of poetry, if his eyes were able to perceive more colours and his nostrils to distinguish more scents, a philosophical misrepresentation of the naïve idea of those who believe that life was finer when men wore sumptuous costumes instead of black coats. But to me (just as an aroma, unpleasing perhaps in itself, of naphthalene and vetiver would have thrilled me by bringing back to me the blue purity of the sea on the day of my arrival at Balbec), this smell of petrol which, together with the smoke from the exhaust of the car, had so often melted into the pale azure on those scorching days when I used to drive from Saint-Jean-de-la-Haise to Gourville, since it had accompanied me on my excursions during those summer afternoons when I left Albertine painting, called into blossom now on either side of me, for all that I was lying in my darkened bedroom, corn-flowers, poppies and red clover, intoxicated me like a country scent, not circumscribed and fixed like that of the hawthorns which, held in by its dense, oleaginous elements, hangs with a certain stability about the hedge, but like a scent before which the roads sped away, the landscape changed, stately houses came hurrying to meet me, the sky turned pale, forces were in-

creased tenfold, a scent which was like a symbol of elastic
motion and power and which revived the desire that I had
felt at Balbec to climb into the cage of steel and crystal,
but this time no longer to pay visits to familiar houses
with a woman I knew too well, but to make love in new
places with a woman unknown. A scent that was accompanied incessantly by the horns of passing motors, which
I set to words like a military summons: "Parisian, get up,
get up, come out and picnic in the country, and take a
boat on the river, under the trees, with a pretty girl; get
up, get up!" And all these day-dreams were so agreeable
that I congratulated myself upon the "stern decree" which
prescribed that until I had rung my bell no "timid mortal," whether Françoise or Albertine, should dare come in
and disturb me "within this palace" where a majesty so
terrible

Means that to my subjects I remain invisible.[24]

But all of a sudden the scene changed; it was the
memory, no longer of old impressions but of an old desire, only recently reawakened by the Fortuny gown in
blue and gold, that spread before me another spring, a
spring not leafy at all but on the contrary suddenly
stripped of its trees and flowers by the name that I had
just murmured to myself: "Venice"; a decanted springtime, which is reduced to its own essence and expresses
the lengthening, the warming, the gradual unfolding of its
days in the progressive fermentation, no longer, now, of
an impure soil, but of a blue and virginal water, springlike
without bud or blossom, which could answer the call of
May only by gleaming facets fashioned and polished by

May, harmonising exactly with it in the radiant, unalterable nakedness of its dusky sapphire. Likewise, too, no more than the seasons to its flowerless creeks, do modern times bring any change to the Gothic city; I knew it, even if I could not imagine it, or rather, imagining it, this was what I longed for with the same desire which long ago, when I was a boy, in the very ardour of departure, had broken and robbed me of the strength to make the journey: to find myself face to face with my Venetian imaginings, to observe how that divided sea enclosed in its meanderings, like the sinuosities of the ocean stream, an urbane and refined civilisation, but one that, isolated by their azure girdle, had evolved independently, had had its own schools of painting and architecture, to admire that fabulous garden of fruits and birds in coloured stone, flowering in the midst of the sea which kept it refreshed, lapped the base of the columns with its tide, and, like a sombre azure gaze watching in the shadows, kept patches of light perpetually flickering on the bold relief of the capitals.

Yes, I must go, the time had come. Now that Albertine no longer appeared to be angry with me, the possession of her no longer seemed to me a treasure in exchange for which one is prepared to sacrifice every other. For perhaps one would have done so only to rid oneself of a grief, an anxiety, which are now appeased. One has succeeded in jumping through the calico hoop through which one thought for a moment that one would never be able to pass. One has dispersed the storm, returned to a smiling serenity. The agonising mystery of a hatred with no known cause, and perhaps no end, is dispelled. Henceforward one finds oneself once more face to face with the problem, momentarily thrust aside, of a happiness which one knows to be impossible.

It might well occur to us, were we better able to analyse our loves, to see that women often attract us only because of the counterpoise of all the men with whom we have to compete for them, although we suffer agonies from having thus to compete; this counterpoise removed, the charm of the woman declines. We have a painful and cautionary example of this in the predilection men have for women who have strayed before they came to know them, for those women whom they feel to be sinking in perilous quicksands and whom they must spend the whole period of their love in rescuing; a posthumous example, on the other hand, and one that is not in the least tragic, in the man who, conscious of a decline in his affection for the woman he loves, spontaneously applies the rules that he has deduced, and, to make sure that he does not cease to love the woman, places her in a dangerous environment where he is obliged to protect her daily. (The opposite of the men who insist on a woman's retiring from the stage even though it was because she was on the stage that they fell in love with her.)

Now that life with Albertine had become possible once again, I felt that I could derive nothing from it but misery, since she did not love me; better to part from her in the gentle solace of her acquiescence, which I would prolong in memory. Yes, this was the moment; I must make quite certain of the date on which Andrée was leaving Paris, use all my influence with Mme Bontemps to make sure that at that moment Albertine should not be able to go either to Holland or to Montjouvain; and when in this way there were no immediate drawbacks to Albertine's departure, choose a fine day like this—and there would be plenty of them before long—when she had ceased to matter to me, when I was tempted by countless desires. I should have to let her leave the house without my seeing her, then, getting up and preparing myself in haste, leave a note for her, taking advantage of the fact that as she could not for the time being go anywhere that would upset me, I might be spared, during my travels, from imagining the wicked things which she might do—and which in any case for the moment seemed quite unimportant—and, without seeing her again, set off for Venice.

I rang for Françoise to ask her to buy me a guidebook and a timetable, as I had done as a boy when already I wanted to prepare in advance a journey to Venice, the fulfilment of a desire as violent as that which I felt at this moment. I forgot that, in the meantime, there was a desire which I had attained without any satisfaction—the desire for Balbec—and that Venice, being also a visible phenomenon, was probably no more able than Balbec to fulfil an ineffable dream, that of the Gothic age made actual by a springtime sea, that now teased my mind from moment to moment with an enchanted, caressing, elusive, mysterious, confused image. Françoise, having heard my ring, came into the room, rather uneasy as to how I would take what she had to say and what she had done. "I was very worried," she said to me, "that Monsieur should be so late in ringing this morning. I didn't know what I ought to do. This morning at eight o'clock Mademoiselle Albertine asked me for her boxes. I dared not refuse her, and I was afraid that Monsieur might scold me if I came and waked him. It was no use lecturing her, telling her to wait an hour because I expected all the time that Monsieur would ring; she wouldn't have it, she left this letter with me for Monsieur, and at nine o'clock off she went." Then—so ignorant can we be of what is inside us, since I was convinced of my indifference to Albertine—my breath was cut short, I gripped my heart in my hands, which were suddenly moistened by a perspiration I had not experienced since the revelation she had made to me on the little train with regard to Mlle Vinteuil's friend, and I was incapable of saying anything else but: "Ah! very good, Françoise, you were of course quite right not to wake me. Leave me now for a moment, I shall ring for you presently."

THE FUGITIVE

Chapter One

GRIEVING AND FORGETTING

"Mademoiselle Albertine has gone!" How much further does anguish penetrate in psychology than psychology itself! A moment before, in the process of analysing myself, I had believed that this separation without having seen each other again was precisely what I wished, and, comparing the mediocrity of the pleasures that Albertine afforded me with the richness of the desires which she prevented me from realising, I had felt that I was being subtle, had concluded that I no longer wished to see her, that I no longer loved her. But now these words: "Mademoiselle Albertine has gone," had produced in my heart an anguish such that I felt I could not endure it much longer. So what I had believed to be nothing to me was simply my entire life. How ignorant one is of oneself. My anguish must be made to end at once; tender towards myself as my mother had been towards my dying grandmother, I said to myself with that genuine wish that one has to relieve the suffering of a person one loves: "Be patient for a moment, we shall find something to take the pain away, don't fret, we're not going to allow you to suffer like this." It was in this category of ideas that my instinct of self-preservation sought for the first balms to lay upon my open wound: "None of this is of the slightest importance, because I'm going to bring her back at once. I shall have to think how, but in any case she will be here this evening. Therefore it's useless to torment myself." "None of this is of the slightest importance"—I had not been content merely with giving myself this assurance, but had tried to convey the same impression to Françoise by not allowing her to see my suffering, because, even at the moment when I was feeling it so acutely, my love did not forget how important it was that it should appear a happy love, a mutual love, especially in the eyes of Françoise, who disliked Albertine and had always doubted her sincerity.

Yes, a moment ago, before Françoise came into the room, I had believed that I no longer loved Albertine, I had believed that I was leaving nothing out of account, like a rigorous analyst; I had believed that I knew the state of my own heart. But our intelligence, however lucid, cannot perceive the elements that compose it and remain unsuspected so long as, from the volatile state in which they generally exist, a phenomenon capable of isolating them has not subjected them to the first stages of solidification. I had been mistaken in thinking that I could see clearly into my own heart. But this knowledge, which the shrewdest perceptions of the mind would not have given me, had now been brought to me, hard, glittering, strange, like a crystallised salt, by the abrupt reaction of pain. I was so much in the habit of having Albertine with me, and now I suddenly saw a new aspect of Habit. Hitherto I had regarded it chiefly as an annihilating force which suppresses the originality and even the awareness of one's perceptions; now I saw it as a dread deity, so riveted to one's being, its insignificant face so incrusted in one's heart, that if it detaches itself, if it turns away from one, this deity that one had barely distinguished inflicts on one sufferings more terrible than any other and is then as cruel as death itself.

The first thing to be done was to read Albertine's letter, since I was anxious to think of some way of bringing her back. I felt that this lay in my power, because, as the future is what exists as yet only in the mind, it seems to us to be still alterable by the intervention, at the eleventh hour, of the will. But at the same time, I remembered that I had seen forces other than my own act upon it, forces against which, even if I had had more time, I could never have prevailed. Of what use is it that the hour has not yet struck if we can do nothing to influence what will happen when it does? When Albertine was living in the house I had been quite determined to retain the initiative in our parting. And then she had gone. I opened her letter. It ran as follows:

"MY DEAR FRIEND,

Forgive me for not having dared to say to you in person what I am now writing, but I am such a coward, and have always been so afraid in your presence, that however much I tried to force myself I could not find the courage to do so. This is what I should have said to you: Our life together has become impossible; indeed you must have realised, from your outburst the other evening, that there had been a change in our relations. What we were able to patch up that night would become irreparable in a few days' time. It is better for us, therefore, since we have had the good fortune to be reconciled, to part as friends. That is why, my darling, I am sending you this line, and I beg you to be kind enough to forgive me if I am causing you a little grief when you think of the immensity of mine. Dearest one, I do not want to become your enemy; it will be bad enough to become by degrees, and all too soon, a stranger to you; and so, as I have absolutely made up my mind, before sending you this letter by Françoise I shall have asked her to let me have my boxes. Good-bye: I leave you the best of myself.

ALBERTINE"

"All this means nothing," I told myself, "it's even better than I thought, for as she doesn't mean a word of what she says, she obviously wrote it only in order to give me a shock, to frighten me, to stop me behaving unbearably towards her. I must think of something to do as soon as possible, so that Albertine will be back here this evening. It's sad to think that the Bontemps are unscrupulous people who make use of their niece to extort money from me. But what does that matter? Even if, to have Albertine here this evening, I must give half my fortune to Mme Bontemps, we shall still have enough left, Albertine and I, to live in comfort." And at the same time I calculated whether I had time to go out that morning and order the yacht and the Rolls-Royce which she coveted, quite forgetting, all my doubts having vanished, that I had decided that it would be unwise to give them to her. "Even if Mme Bontemps's agreement isn't enough, if Albertine refuses to obey her aunt and makes it a condition of her return that she shall enjoy complete independence, well, however much it may distress me, I shall let her have it; she shall go out by herself, as and when she likes. One must be prepared to make sacrifices, however painful they may be, for the thing to which one attaches most importance, which is, in spite of everything I decided this morning on the strength of my precise and absurd arguments, that Albertine shall continue to live here." Can I say moreover that to grant her that freedom would have been altogether painful to me? I should be lying if I did. Already I had often felt that the anguish of leaving her free to misbehave far away from me was perhaps less acute even than the sort of misery which I used to feel when I sensed that she was bored in my company, under my roof. No doubt at the actual moment of her asking me to let her go somewhere, allowing her to do so, with my mind obsessed by the idea of organised orgies, would have been agonising for me. But to say to her: "Take our yacht, or the train, and go away for a month, to some place which I have never seen, where I shall know nothing of what you're doing"—this had often appealed to me, because of the thought that, by force of contrast, when she was far away from me, she would hanker after my society, and would be happy when she returned. "Besides, it's certainly what she herself wants; she doesn't in the least demand that freedom on which moreover, by offering her every day some new pleasure, I could easily succeed in imposing day by day some further restriction. No, what Albertine wanted was for me not to go on behaving insufferably to her, and above all—like Odette with Swann—for me to make up my mind to marry her. Once she is married, her independence will cease to matter to her; we shall stay here together, in perfect happiness." No doubt this meant giving up any thought of Venice. But the cities for which we have most longed (and *a fortiori* the most agreeable hostesses, the most pleasurable diversions—even more than Venice, the Duchesse de Guermantes or the theatre), how pale, insignificant, dead they become when we are tied to another's heart by a bond so painful that it prevents us from tearing ourselves away! "Besides, Albertine is perfectly right about our marriage. Mamma herself was saying that all this procrastination was ridiculous. Marry her, that's what I ought to have done long ago, that's what I must do now, that's what made her write her letter without meaning a word of it; it's only to bring about our marriage that she has postponed for a few hours what she must desire as keenly as I do: her return to this house. Yes, that's what she wanted, that was the purpose of her action," my compassionate reason assured me; but I felt that, in doing so, my reason was still basing itself on the same hypothesis which it had adopted from the start. Whereas I was well aware that it was the other hypothesis which had invariably proved correct. No doubt this second hypothesis would never have been so bold as to formulate in so many words the notion that Albertine could have been on intimate terms with Mlle Vinteuil and her friend. And yet, when I had been overwhelmed by the impact of that terrible revelation, as the train slowed down before stopping at Incarville station, it was the second hypothesis that had been confirmed. This hypothesis had subsequently never conceived the idea that Albertine might leave me of her own accord, in this fashion, without warning me and giving me time to prevent her departure. But all the same, if, after the immense new leap which life had just caused me to make, the reality that confronted me was as novel as that which is presented to us by the discovery of a scientist, by the inquiries of an examining magistrate or the researches of a historian into the hidden aspects of a crime or a revolution, this reality, while exceeding the puny predictions of my second hypothesis, nevertheless fulfilled them. This second hypothesis was not an intellectual one, and the panic fear that had gripped me on the evening when Albertine had refused to kiss me, or the night when I had heard the sound of her window being opened, was not based upon reason. But—and what follows will show it even more clearly, as many episodes must have indicated it already—the fact that our intelligence is not the subtlest, most powerful, most appropriate instrument for grasping the truth is only one reason the more for beginning with the intelligence, and not with an unconscious intuition, a ready-made faith in presentiments. It is life that, little by little, case by case, enables us to observe that what is most important to our hearts or to our minds is taught us not by reasoning but by other powers. And then it is the intelligence itself which, acknowledging their superiority, abdicates to them through reasoning and consents to become their collaborator and their servant. Experimental faith. It seemed to me that the unforeseen calamity with which I found myself grappling was also something that I had already known (as I had known of Albertine's friendship with a pair of lesbians), from having read it in so many signs in which (notwithstanding the contrary affirmations of my reason, based upon Albertine's own statements) I had discerned the weariness, the loathing that she felt at having to live in that state of slavery, signs that had so often seemed to me to be written as though in invisible ink behind her sad, submissive eyes, upon her cheeks suddenly inflamed with an unaccountable blush, in the sound of the window that had suddenly been flung open. Doubtless I had not dared to explore them fully or to form explicitly the idea of her sudden departure. I had thought, with a mind kept in equilibrium by Albertine's presence, only of a departure arranged by myself at an undetermined date, that is to say a date situated in a non-existent time; consequently I had had merely the illusion of thinking of a departure, just as people imagine that they are not afraid of death when they think of it while they are in good health and are actually doing no more than introduce a purely nega-tive idea into a healthy state which the approach of death would of course precisely alter. Besides, the idea of Alber-tine's departure on her own initiative might have occurred to my mind a thousand times over, in the clearest, the most sharply defined form, without my suspecting any the more what, in relation to myself, that is to say in reality, that departure would be, what an unprecedented, ap-palling, unknown thing, how entirely novel a calamity. I might have gone on thinking of that departure (had I foreseen it) unceasingly for years on end, without all those thoughts, placed end to end, having the faintest connex-ion, not merely in intensity but in kind, with the unimag-inable hell the curtain of which Françoise had raised for me when she said: "Mademoiselle Albertine has gone." In order to picture to itself an unknown situation the imagi-nation borrows elements that are already familiar and, for that reason, cannot picture it. But the sensibility, even in its most physical form, receives, like the wake of a thun-derbolt, the original and for long indelible imprint of the novel event. And I hardly dared say to myself that, if I had foreseen this departure, I would perhaps have been incapable of picturing it to myself in all its horror, or in-deed, with Albertine informing me of it, and myself threatening, imploring her, of preventing it. How far re-moved from me now was the desire to go to Venice! Just as, long ago at Combray, had been the desire to know Mme de Guermantes when the moment came at which I longed for one thing only, to have Mamma in my room. And it was indeed all the anxieties I had felt ever since my childhood which, at the bidding of this new anguish, had come hastening to reinforce it, to amalgamate themselves with it in a homogeneous mass that suffocated me.

To be sure, the physical blow which such a parting administers to the heart, and which, because of that terrible capacity for registering things with which the body is endowed, makes the pain somehow contemporaneous with all the epochs in our life in which we have suffered—to be sure, this blow to the heart which—so little compunction do we feel for the sufferings of others—she who wishes to give the maximum intensity to the regret she causes, whether because, her departure being only a sham, she merely wants to demand better terms, or because, leaving us for ever—for ever!—she desires to wound us, or in order to avenge herself, or to continue to be loved, or (with an eye to the quality of the memory that she will leave behind her) to destroy the web of lassitude and indifference which she has felt being woven about her—to be sure, this blow to the heart is something we had vowed that we would avoid, assuring ourselves that we would part on good terms. But it is seldom indeed that one does part on good terms, because if one were on good terms one would not part. And then the woman to whom we show the utmost indifference nevertheless obscurely feels that in growing tired of her, by virtue of an identical force of habit, we have grown more and more attached to her, and she reflects that one of the essential elements in parting on good terms is to warn the other person before one goes. But she is afraid, by warning, of preventing. Every woman feels that the greater her power over a man, the

more impossible it is to leave him except by sudden
flight: a fugitive precisely because a queen. True, there is
an extraordinary discrepancy between the boredom which
she inspired a moment ago and, because she has gone,
this furious desire to have her back again. But for this—
over and above those which have been given in the course
of this work and others which will be given later on—
there are reasons. For one thing, her departure occurs as
often as not at the moment when her companion's indifference—real or imagined—is greatest, at the extreme
point of the swing of the pendulum. The woman says to
herself: "No, this can't go on any longer," precisely because the man speaks of nothing but leaving her, or thinks
of nothing else; and it is she who leaves him. Then, the
pendulum swinging back to the other extreme, the distance is all the greater. In an instant it returns to this
point; once more, apart from all the reasons that have
been given, it is so natural! The heart still beats; and besides, the woman who has gone is no longer the same as
the woman who was with us. Her life under our roof, all
too well known, is suddenly enlarged by the addition of
the lives with which she is inevitably to be associated, and
it is perhaps to associate herself with them that she has
left us. So that this new richness of the life of the woman
who has gone retroacts upon the woman who was with us
and was perhaps premeditating her departure. To the sequence of psychological facts which we are able to deduce
and which form part of her life with us, our too evident
boredom in her company, our jealousy too (and the effect
of which is that men who have been left by a number of
women have been left almost always in the same way because of their character and of certain always identical re-

actions which can be calculated: everyone has his own way of being betrayed, as he has his own way of catching cold), to this sequence that is not too mysterious for us there doubtless corresponded a sequence of facts of which we were unaware. She must for some time past have been keeping up relations, written, or verbal, or through messengers, with some man, or some woman, have been awaiting some signal which we may perhaps have given her unwittingly ourselves when we said: "X called yesterday to see me," if she had arranged with X that on the eve of the day when she was to join him he was to call on me. How many possible hypotheses! Possible only. I constructed the truth so well, but in the realm of possibility only, that, having one day opened by mistake a letter addressed to one of my mistresses, a letter written in a prearranged code which said: "Still awaiting signal to go to the Marquis de Saint-Loup's; please inform tomorrow by telephone," I reconstructed a sort of projected flight; the name of the Marquis de Saint-Loup was there only as a substitute for some other name, for my mistress did not know Saint-Loup, but had heard me speak of him, and moreover the signature was some sort of nickname, without any intelligible form. As it happened, the letter was addressed not to my mistress but to another person in the building who bore a different name which had been misread. The letter was written not in a code but in bad French because it was from an American woman, who was indeed a friend of Saint-Loup, as he himself told me. And the odd way in which this American woman formed certain letters had given the appearance of a nickname to a name which was quite genuine, only foreign. And so I had on that occasion been utterly mistaken in my suspi-

cions. But the intellectual structure which had linked
these facts, all of them false, together in my mind was itself so strict and accurate a model of the truth that when,
three months later, my mistress (who had at that time
been meaning to spend the rest of her life with me) left
me, it was in a fashion absolutely identical with that
which I had imagined on the former occasion. A letter arrived, containing the same peculiarities which I had
wrongly attributed to the former letter, but this time it
was indeed meant as a signal.

The present calamity was the worst that I had experienced in my life. And yet the suffering that it caused me
was perhaps even exceeded by my curiosity to learn the
causes of this calamity: who Albertine had desired and
gone to join. But the sources of great events are like those
of rivers; in vain do we explore the earth's surface, we can
never find them. Had Albertine been planning her flight
for a long time past? I have not mentioned the fact (because at the time it had seemed to me simply affectation
and ill-humour, what in the case of Françoise we called "a
fit of the sulks") that, from the day when she had ceased
to kiss me, she had gone about as though tormented by a
devil, stiffly erect, unbending, saying the simplest things
in a mournful voice, slow in her movements, never smiling. I cannot say that there was any concrete proof of
conspiracy with the outer world. True, Françoise told me
later that, having gone into Albertine's room two days before her departure, she had found it empty, with the curtains drawn, but had sensed from the atmosphere of the
room and from the noise that the window was open. And
indeed she had found Albertine on the balcony. But it is
difficult to see with whom she could have been communi-

cating from there, and moreover the drawn curtains screening the open window could doubtless be explained by the fact that she knew I was afraid of draughts, and that even if the curtains afforded me little protection they would prevent Françoise from seeing from the passage that the shutters had been opened so early. No, I can see nothing apart from one trifling fact which proves merely that on the day before her departure she knew that she was going. For during that day she took from my room without my noticing it a large quantity of wrapping paper and packing cloth which was kept there, and in which she spent the whole night packing her innumerable negligées and dressing-gowns so that she might leave the house in the morning. This is the only fact; that was all. I cannot attach any importance to her having repaid that evening, practically by force, a thousand francs which she owed me; there is nothing extraordinary in that, for she was extremely scrupulous about money.

Yes, she took the wrapping paper the night before, but it was not only then that she knew that she was going to leave me! For it was not resentment that made her leave but the decision, already taken, to leave me, to abandon the life of which she had dreamed, that gave her that air of resentment. A resentful air, almost solemnly cold towards myself, except on the last evening when, after staying in my room longer than she had intended, she said—a remark which surprised me, coming from her who had always sought to postpone the moment of parting—she said to me from the door: "Good-bye, little one, good-bye." But I did not take any notice of this at the time. Françoise told me that next morning when Albertine informed her that she was going (but this may be explained also by exhaustion, for she had not undressed and had spent the whole night packing everything except the things she had to ask Françoise for, as they were not in her bedroom or her dressing-room), she was still so sad, so much more erect, so much stiffer than during the previous days that Françoise thought, when Albertine said to her: "Good-bye, Françoise," that she was about to fall. When one is told a thing like that one realises that the woman who appealed to us so much less than any of the women whom one meets so easily in the course of the briefest outing, the woman who makes us resent having to sacrifice them to her, is on the contrary the one we would a thousand times prefer. For the choice lies no longer between a certain pleasure—which has become by force of habit, and perhaps by the mediocrity of its object, almost null and void—and other pleasures which tempt and thrill us, but between these latter pleasures and something that is far stronger than they, compassion for suffering.

When I vowed to myself that Albertine would be back in the house before night, I had proceeded as quickly as possible to cover with a fresh belief the open wound from which I had torn the belief I had lived with until then. But swiftly though my instinct of self-preservation had acted, I had, when Françoise spoke to me, been left helpless for an instant, and for all that I now knew that Albertine would be back that same evening, the pain I had felt during the instant in which I had not yet assured myself of her return (the instant that had followed the words: "Mademoiselle Albertine has asked for her boxes; Mademoiselle Albertine has gone"), this pain reawoke in me of its own accord, as sharp as it had been before, that is to say as if I had still been unaware of Albertine's imminent return. However, it was essential that she should return, but of her own accord. On any assumption, to appear to be taking the first step, to be begging her to return, would be to defeat my own object. True, I lacked the strength to give her up as I had given up Gilberte. Even more than to see Albertine again, what I wanted was to put an end to the physical anguish which my heart, less robust than of old, could endure no longer. Then, by dint of accustoming myself not to use my will-power, whether it was a question of work or of anything else, I had become more cowardly. But above all, this anguish was incomparably more intense for a number of reasons of which the most important was perhaps not that I had never tasted any sensual pleasure with Mme de Guermantes or with Gilberte, but that, not seeing them every day, and at every hour of the day, having no opportunity and consequently no need to see them, there had been lacking, in my love for them, the immense force of Habit. Perhaps, now that my heart, incapable of willing and of voluntarily enduring suffering, could think of only one possible solution, that Albertine should return at all costs, perhaps the opposite solution (a deliberate renunciation, a gradual resignation) would have seemed to me a novelist's solution, improbable in real life, had I not myself opted for it in the case of Gilberte. I knew therefore that this other solution might be accepted also, and by one and the same man, for I had remained more or less the same. But time had played its part, time which had aged me, time which moreover had kept Albertine perpetually in my company while we were living together. But at least, without giving her up, what survived in me of all that I had felt for Gilberte was the pride which made me

refuse to be to Albertine a despicable plaything by begging her to return; I wanted her to come back without my
appearing to care whether she did or not. I got up, in order to lose no more time, but my anguish made me pause;
this was the first time that I had got out of bed since Albertine had left me. Yet I must dress at once in order to
go and make inquiries of Albertine's concierge.

Suffering, the prolongation of a spiritual shock that
has come from without, keeps aspiring to change its form;
one hopes to be able to dispel it by making plans, by
seeking information; one wants it to pass through its
countless metamorphoses, for this requires less courage
than keeping our suffering intact; the bed on which we lie
down with our grief appears so narrow, hard and cold. I
therefore put my feet to the ground, and I stepped across
the room with infinite care, placing myself in such a way
as not to see Albertine's chair, the pianola on the pedals
of which she used to press her golden slippers, or a single
one of the things which she had used and all of which, in
the secret language that my memories had taught them,
seemed to be seeking to give me a translation, a different
version, for a second time to tell me, of her departure. But
even without looking at them I could see them: my
strength left me; I sank down on one of those blue satin
armchairs, the glossy surface of which an hour earlier, in
the dimness of my bedroom anaesthetised by a ray of
morning light, had made me dream dreams which then I
had passionately caressed but which were infinitely remote
from me now. Alas, I had never sat in one of them until
this minute except when Albertine was still with me. And
so I could not remain sitting there, and stood up again;
and thus, at every moment, there was one more of those

innumerable and humble "selves" that compose our personality which was still unaware of Albertine's departure and must be informed of it; I was obliged—and this was more cruel than if they had been strangers and did not share my susceptibility to suffering—to announce to all these beings, to all these "selves" who did not yet know of it, the calamity that had just occurred; each of them in turn must hear for the first time the words: "Albertine has asked for her boxes"—those coffin-shaped boxes which I had seen loaded on to the train at Balbec with my mother's—"Albertine has gone." Each of them had to be told of my grief, the grief which is in no way a pessimistic conclusion freely drawn from an accumulation of baneful circumstances, but is the intermittent and involuntary reviviscence of a specific impression that has come to us from without and was not chosen by us. There were some of these "selves" which I had not encountered for a long time past. For instance (I had not remembered that it was the day on which the barber called) the "self" that I was when I was having my hair cut. I had forgotten this "self," and his arrival made me burst into tears, as, at a funeral, does the appearance of an old retired servant who has not forgotten the deceased. Then all of a sudden I remembered that, during the past week, I had from time to time been seized by panic fears which I had not confessed to myself. At those moments, however, I had debated the question, saying to myself: "No need, of course, to consider the hypothesis of her suddenly leaving me. It's absurd. If I were to confide it to a sensible, intelligent man" (and I would have done so to set my mind at rest, had not jealousy prevented me from confiding in anyone) "he would be sure to say to me: 'Why, you're mad. It's impossible.' (And, as a matter of fact, during these last days we had not quarrelled once.) People leave you for a reason. They tell you the reason. They give you a chance to reply. They don't run away like that. No, it's perfectly childish. It's the only really absurd hypothesis." And yet, every day, on finding her still there in the morning when I rang my bell, I had heaved an immense sigh of relief. And when Françoise handed me Albertine's letter, I had at once been certain that it referred to the one thing that could not happen, to this departure which I had somehow perceived several days in advance, in spite of the logical reasons for feeling reassured. I had told myself this, almost with self-satisfaction at my perspicacity in my despair, like a murderer who knows that he cannot be found out but is nevertheless afraid and all of a sudden sees his victim's name written at the top of a document on the table of the examining magistrate who has sent for him.

My only hope was that Albertine had gone to Touraine, to her aunt's house, where after all she would be under some sort of surveillance and could not do anything very serious before I brought her back. My worst fear was that she might have stayed in Paris, or have gone to Amsterdam or to Montjouvain, in other words that she had escaped in order to pursue some intrigue the preliminaries of which I had failed to observe. But in reality, when I said to myself Paris, Amsterdam, Montjouvain, that is to say several places, I was thinking of places that were merely potential. And so, when Albertine's concierge informed me that she had gone to Touraine, that place of residence which I had thought desirable seemed to me the most dreadful of all, because it was real, and because for the first time, tortured by the certainty of the present and

the uncertainty of the future, I pictured Albertine starting
on a life which she had deliberately chosen to lead apart
from me, perhaps for a long time, perhaps for ever, a life
in which she would realise that unknown element which
in the past had so often troubled me, even though I enjoyed the good fortune of possessing, of caressing what
was its outer shell, that charming face, impenetrable and
captive. It was this unknown element that formed the core
of my love. As for Albertine herself, she scarcely existed
in me save under the form of her name, which, but for
certain rare moments of respite when I awoke, came and
engraved itself upon my brain and continued incessantly
to do so. If I had thought aloud, I should have kept on
repeating it, and my speech would have been as monotonous, as limited, as if I had been transformed into a
bird, a bird like the one in the fable whose song repeated
incessantly the name of her whom it had loved when a
man. One says the name to oneself, and since one remains
silent it is as though one were inscribing it inside oneself,
as though it were leaving its trace on one's brain, which
must end up, like a wall on which somebody has amused
himself scribbling, by being entirely covered with the
name, written a thousand times over, of the woman one
loves. One rewrites it all the time in one's mind when
one is happy, and even more when one is unhappy. And
one feels a constantly recurring need to repeat this name
which brings one nothing more than what one already
knows, until, in course of time, it wearies us. I did not
even give a thought to carnal pleasure at this moment; I
did not even see in my mind's eye the image of that Albertine who had been the cause of such an upheaval of
my being, I did not perceive her body, and if I had tried

to isolate the idea—for there is always one—that was
bound up with my suffering, it would have been, alternately, on the one hand my doubt as to the intention with
which she had left me, with or without any thought of returning, and on the other hand the means of bringing her
back. Perhaps there is something symbolical and true in
the infinitesimal place occupied in our anxiety by the one
who is its cause. The fact is that her person itself counts
for little or nothing; what is almost everything is the series of emotions and anxieties which chance occurrences
have made us feel in the past in connexion with her and
which habit has associated with her. What proves this
clearly is (even more than the boredom which we feel in
moments of happiness) the extent to which seeing or not
seeing the person in question, being or not being admired
by her, having or not having her at our disposal, will
seem to us utterly irrelevant when we no longer have to
pose ourselves the problem (so otiose that we shall no
longer take the trouble to consider it) save in relation to
the person herself—the series of emotions and anxieties
being forgotten, at least so far as she is concerned, for it
may have developed anew, but transferred to another. Before this, when it was still attached to her, we supposed
that our happiness was dependent upon her person; it depended merely upon the cessation of our anxiety. Our unconscious was therefore more clairvoyant than ourselves at
that moment, when it made the figure of the beloved so
minute, a figure which we had even perhaps forgotten,
which we might have been comparatively unfamiliar with
and thought mediocre, in the terrible drama in which seeing her again in order to cease waiting for her could be a
matter of life and death for us. Minuscule proportions of

the woman's form; logical and necessary effect of the manner in which love develops; clear allegory of the subjective nature of that love.

Outside the door of Albertine's house I found a little poor girl who gazed at me with huge eyes and who looked so sweet-natured that I asked her whether she would care to come home with me, as I might have taken home a dog with faithful eyes. She seemed pleased at the suggestion. When I got home, I held her for some time on my knee, but very soon her presence, by making me feel too keenly Albertine's absence, became intolerable. And I asked her to go away, after giving her a five-hundred franc note. And yet, soon afterwards, the thought of having some other little girl in the house with me, of never being alone without the comfort of an innocent presence, was the only thing that enabled me to endure the idea that Albertine might perhaps remain away for some time. The spirit in which Albertine had left me was similar no doubt to that of nations who pave the way by a demonstration of their armed force for the exercise of their diplomacy. She must have left me only in order to obtain from me better terms, greater freedom, more luxury. In that case, of the two of us, the one who prevailed would have been myself, had I had the strength to await the moment when, seeing that she could gain nothing, she would return of her own accord. But if at cards, or in war, where victory alone matters, we can hold out against bluff, the conditions are not the same as those created by love and jealousy, not to mention suffering. If, in order to wait, to "hold out," I allowed Albertine to remain away from me for several days, for several weeks perhaps, I was ruining what had been my sole purpose for more than a year: never to leave her

by herself for a single hour. All my precautions would be
rendered fruitless if I allowed her the time and the opportunity to be unfaithful to me to her heart's content; and if
in the end she capitulated, I should never be able to forget the time when she had been alone, and even though
victorious in the end, nevertheless in the past, that is to
say irreparably, I should be the vanquished one.

As for the means of bringing Albertine back, they
had all the more chance of success the more plausible the
hypothesis appeared that she had left me only in the hope
of being summoned back on more favourable terms. And
of course to the people who did not believe in Albertine's
sincerity, certainly to Françoise for instance, it was indeed
plausible. But my reason, to which, before I knew anything, the only explanation of certain bouts of ill-humour,
of certain attitudes, had appeared to be that she had
planned to leave for good, found it difficult to believe
that, now that her departure had occurred, it was a mere
feint. I say my reason, not myself. The hypothesis of a
feint became all the more necessary to me the more improbable it was, and gained in strength what it lost in
probability. When we find ourselves on the verge of despair and it seems as though God has forsaken us, we no
longer hesitate to expect a miracle of him.

I realise that in all this I was the most apathetic, albeit the most anxious of detectives. But Albertine's flight
had not restored to me the faculties of which the habit of
having her watched by other people had deprived me. I
could think of one thing only: employing another person
to search for her. This other person was Saint-Loup, who
agreed. The transference of the anxiety of so many days
to another person filled me with joy and I jigged about,

certain of success, my hands becoming suddenly dry again as in the past, and no longer moist with the sweat in which Françoise had soaked me when she said: "Mademoiselle Albertine has gone."

It will be remembered that when I decided to live with Albertine, and even to marry her, it was in order to guard her, to know what she was doing, to prevent her from returning to her old habits with Mlle Vinteuil. It had been in the appalling anguish caused by her revelation at Balbec, when she had told me, as a thing which was quite natural, and which I succeeded, although it was the greatest sorrow I had ever experienced in my life, in appearing to find quite natural, the thing which in my worst suppositions I should never have been bold enough to imagine. (It is astonishing what a want of imagination jealousy, which spends its time making petty suppositions that are false, shows when it comes to discovering what is true.) Now this love, born first and foremost of a need to prevent Albertine from doing wrong, this love had thereafter preserved the traces of its origin. Being with her mattered little to me so long as I could prevent the fugitive creature from going to this place or to that. In order to prevent her, I had had recourse to the vigilance, to the company, of the people who escorted her, and they had only to give me at the end of the day a report that was fairly reassuring for my anxieties to dissolve into good humour.

Having given myself the assurance that, whatever steps I might have to take, Albertine would be back in the house that same evening, I had granted a respite to the pain which Françoise had caused me when she told me that Albertine had gone (because at that moment my mind, caught unawares, had believed for an instant that her departure was final). But after an interruption, when under the momentum of its own independent life the initial pain revived spontaneously in me, it was just as agonising as before, because it pre-existed the consoling promise that I had given myself to bring Albertine back that evening. My suffering was oblivious of this promise which would have calmed it. To set in motion the means of bringing about her return, once again I was condemned—not that such an attitude had ever proved very successful, but because I had always adopted it since I had been in love with Albertine—to behave as though I did not love her, as though I was not hurt by her departure; I was condemned to continue to lie to her. I could be all the more energetic in my efforts to bring her back in that personally I should appear to have given her up for good. I proposed to write Albertine a farewell letter in which I would regard her departure as final, while at the same time I would send Saint-Loup down, as though without my knowledge, to put the most brutal pressure on Mme Bontemps to make Albertine return as soon as possible. No doubt I had had experience with Gilberte of the danger of letters expressing an indifference which, feigned at first, ends by becoming genuine. And this experience ought to have restrained me from writing to Albertine letters of the same sort as those I had written to Gilberte. But what we call experience is merely the revelation to our own eyes of a trait in our character which naturally reappears, and reappears all the more markedly because we have already once brought it to light, so that the spontaneous impulse which guided us on the first occasion finds itself reinforced by all the suggestions of memory.

The human plagiarism which is most difficult to avoid, for individuals (and even for nations which persevere in their faults and indeed intensify them), is self-plagiarism.

Knowing that Saint-Loup was in Paris, I summoned him there and then; he hastened round at once, swift and efficient as he had been long ago at Doncières, and agreed to set off at once for Touraine. I suggested to him the following arrangement. He was to take the train to Châtellerault, find out where Mme Bontemps lived, and wait until Albertine had left the house, since there was a risk of her recognising him. "But does the girl in question know me, then?" he asked. I told him that I did not think so. This plan of action filled me with indescribable joy. It was nevertheless diametrically opposed to my original intention: to arrange things so that I should not appear to be seeking Albertine's return; whereas by so acting I must inevitably appear to be seeking it. But this plan had the inestimable advantage over "the proper thing to do" that it enabled me to say to myself that someone sent by me was going to see Albertine, and would doubtless bring her back with him. And if I had been able to see clearly into my own heart at the outset, I might have foreseen that it was this solution, which was hidden in the shadows and which I thought deplorable, that would ultimately prevail over the alternative course of patience which I had decided to adopt, from lack of will-power. As Saint-Loup already appeared slightly surprised to learn that a girl had been living with me through the whole winter without my having said a word to him about her, as moreover he had often spoken to me of the girl he had seen at Balbec and I had never said in reply: "But she's living here," he might have been offended by my lack of trust. It was true that

Mme Bontemps might talk to him about Balbec. But I was too impatient for his departure, and for his arrival at the other end, to be willing or able to think of the possible consequences of his journey. As for the risk of his recognising Albertine (whom in any case he had resolutely refrained from looking at when he had met her at Doncières), she had, everyone said, so changed and put on weight that it was hardly likely. He asked me whether I had a picture of Albertine. I replied at first that I had not, so that he might not have a chance of recognising Albertine from her photograph, taken at about the time of our stay at Balbec, though he had had no more than a glimpse of her in the railway carriage. But then I realised that in the photograph she would be already as different from the Albertine of Balbec as the living Albertine now was, and that he would recognise her no better from her photograph than in the flesh. While I was looking for it, he laid his hand gently on my forehead, by way of consoling me. I was touched by the distress which the grief that he guessed me to be feeling was causing him. In the first place, however final his breach with Rachel, what he had felt at that time was not yet so remote for him not to have a special sympathy, a special pity for sufferings of that kind, as one feels closer to a person who is afflicted with the same illness as oneself. Besides, he had so strong an affection for me that the thought of my suffering was intolerable to him. Hence he conceived a mixture of rancour and admiration for the girl who was the cause of it. He regarded me as so superior a being that he felt that for me to be in thrall to another creature she must be quite out of the ordinary. I quite expected that he would think Albertine pretty in her photograph, but since at the same time I did not imagine that it would produce upon him the impression that Helen made upon the Trojan elders, as I continued to look for it I said modestly: "Oh, you know, you mustn't get ideas into your head. For one thing it's a bad photograph, and besides there's nothing startling about her, she's not a beauty, she's merely very nice."

"Oh, but she must be wonderful," he said with a naïve, sincere enthusiasm as he sought to form a mental picture of the person who was capable of plunging me into such despair and agitation. "I'm angry with her for hurting you, but at the same time one can't help seeing that someone who's an artist to his fingertips as you are, someone who loves beauty in all its forms and with so passionate a love, that you were predestined to suffer more than an ordinary person when you found it in a woman."

At last I had found the photograph. "She's bound to be wonderful," Robert was still saying, not yet having seen that I was holding out the photograph to him. All at once he caught sight of it, and held it for a moment between his hands. His face expressed a stupefaction which amounted to stupidity. "Is this the girl you love?" he said at length in a tone in which astonishment was curbed by his fear of offending me. He made no comment, but he had assumed the reasonable, prudent, unavoidably somewhat disdainful air which one assumes in front of a sick person—even if he is a man of outstanding gifts, and your friend—who is now nothing of the sort, for, raving mad, he speaks to you of a celestial being who has appeared to him, and continues to behold this being where you, being sane, can see nothing but a quilt on the bed. I at once understood Robert's astonishment, realising that it was the same as that which the sight of his mistress had provoked in me, the only difference being that I had recognised in her a woman whom I already knew, where he imagined that he had never seen Albertine. But no doubt the difference between our respective impressions of the same person was equally great. The time was long past when I had all too tentatively begun at Balbec by adding to my visual sensations when I gazed at Albertine sensations of taste, of smell, of touch. Since then, other more profound, more tender, more indefinable sensations had been added to them, and afterwards painful sensations. In short, Albertine was merely, like a stone round which snow has gathered, the generating centre of an immense structure which rose above the plane of my heart. Robert, to whom all this stratification of sensations was invisible, grasped only a residue which it prevented me, on the contrary, from perceiving. What had struck Robert when his eyes fell upon Albertine's photograph was not the thrill of wonderment that overcame the Trojan elders seeing Helen go by and saying:

One single glance from her eclipses all our ills[25]

but precisely the opposite impression which may be expressed by: "What, it's for this that he has worked himself into such a state, has grieved himself so, has done so many idiotic things!" It must indeed be admitted that this sort of reaction at the sight of the person who has caused the suffering, upset the life, sometimes brought about the death of someone we love, is infinitely more frequent than that of the Trojan elders, indeed to all intents and purposes the habitual one. This is not merely because love is individual, nor because, when we ourselves do not feel it, finding it avoidable and philosophising about the folly of others comes naturally to us. No, it is because, when it has reached the stage at which it causes such misery, the edifice of the sensations interposed between the face of the woman and the eyes of her lover—the huge egg of pain which encases it and conceals it as a mantle of snow conceals a fountain—is already raised so high that the point at which the lover's gaze comes to rest, the point at which he finds his pleasure and his sufferings, is as far from the point which other people see as is the real sun from the place in which its refracted light enables us to see it in the sky. And what is more, during this time, beneath the chrysalis of grief and tenderness which renders the worst metamorphoses of the beloved object invisible to the lover, her face has had time to grow old and to change. With the result that, if the face which the lover saw for the first time is very far removed from that which he has seen since he has loved and suffered, it is, in the opposite sense, equally far from the face which may now be seen by the indifferent onlooker. (What would have happened if, instead of the photograph of one who was still a girl, Robert had seen the photograph of an elderly mistress?) And indeed, in order to feel this astonishment, we have no need to see for the first time the woman who has caused such ravages. Often we know her already, as my great-uncle knew Odette. So the difference in optics extends not only to people's physical appearance but to their character, and to their individual importance. It is more likely than not that the woman who is causing the man who loves her to suffer has always behaved good-

naturedly towards someone who was indifferent to her, as
Odette, who was so cruel to Swann, had been the kind,
attentive "lady in pink" to my great-uncle, or indeed that
the person whose every decision is computed in advance
by the man who loves her, with as much dread as that of
a deity, appears as a person of no consequence, only too
glad to do anything he asks, in the eyes of the man who
does not love her, as Saint-Loup's mistress had appeared
to me who saw in her merely that "Rachel when from the
Lord" who had so repeatedly been offered to me. I recalled my own amazement, the first time I met her with
Saint-Loup, at the thought that anybody could be tormented by not knowing what such a woman had been doing one evening, what she might have whispered to
someone, why she had desired a rupture. And I felt that
all this past existence—but, in this case, Albertine's—towards which every fibre of my heart, of my life, was directed with a throbbing and importunate pain, must
appear just as insignificant to Saint-Loup, and would one
day, perhaps, appear so to me; I felt that I might gradually pass, so far as the insignificance or gravity of Albertine's past was concerned, from the state of mind in which
I was at the moment to that of Saint-Loup, for I was under no illusion as to what Saint-Loup might be thinking,
as to what anyone else than the lover himself may think.
And I was not unduly distressed. Let us leave pretty
women to men with no imagination. I recalled that tragic
explanation of so many lives which is furnished by an inspired but not lifelike portrait such as Elstir's portrait of
Odette, which is a portrait not so much of a mistress as of
the distortions of love. All that it lacked was—what so
many portraits have—the fact of coming at once from a

great painter and from a lover (and even then it was said that Elstir had been Odette's). The whole life of a lover, of a lover whose folly nobody understands—the whole life of a Swann—goes to prove this disparity. But let the lover be embodied in a painter like Elstir and then we have the clue to the enigma, we have at last before our eyes those lips which the common herd have never perceived, that nose which nobody has ever seen, that unsuspected carriage. The portrait says: "What I have loved, what has made me suffer, what I have never ceased to behold, is this." By an inverse gymnastic, I who had made a mental effort to add to Rachel all that Saint-Loup had added to her of himself, I now attempted to subtract the contribution of my heart and mind from the composition of Albertine and to picture her to myself as she must appear to Saint-Loup, as Rachel had appeared to me. But how much importance does all this have? Would we give credence to these differences, even if we could see them ourselves? When, in the summer at Balbec, Albertine used to wait for me beneath the arcades of Incarville and jump into my carriage, not only had she not yet "thickened," but, as a result of too much exercise, she had lost weight; thin, made plainer by an ugly hat which left visible only the tip of an ugly nose and, at a side-view, pale cheeks like white slugs, there was very little of her that I recognised, enough, however, to know, when she sprang into the carriage, that it was she, that she had been punctual in keeping our appointment and had not gone somewhere else; and this was enough; what we love is too much in the past, consists too much in the time that we have wasted together for us to require the whole woman; we wish only to be sure that it is she, not to be mistaken

as to her identity, a thing far more important than beauty
to those who love; her cheeks may grow hollow, her body
thin, even to those who were originally proudest, in the
eyes of the world, of their domination over a beauty, and
yet that little tip of nose, that sign which epitomises the
permanent personality of a woman, that algebraical formula, that constant factor, is sufficient to prevent a man
who is courted in the highest society, and was once fond
of it, from having a single evening free because he spends
his time combing and uncombing, until it is time to go to
sleep, the hair of the woman he loves, or simply sitting by
her side, in order to be with her, or in order that she may
be with him, or merely in order that she may not be with
other men.

"Are you sure," Robert asked me, "that I can offer
this woman thirty thousand francs just like that for her
husband's election committee? She's as dishonest as all
that? If you're right, three thousand francs would be
enough."

"No, I beg of you, don't be cheeseparing about a
thing that matters so much to me. This is what you're to
say to her (and it's to some extent true): 'My friend had
borrowed these thirty thousand francs from a relative for
the election expenses of the uncle of the girl he was engaged to marry. It was because of this engagement that
the money was given him. And he had asked me to bring
it to you so that Albertine should know nothing about it.
And now Albertine has left him. He doesn't know what
to do. He's obliged to pay back the thirty thousand francs
if he doesn't marry Albertine. And if he *is* going to marry
her, then if only to keep up appearances she ought to re-

turn immediately, because it will make a very bad impression if she stays away for long.' You think I've deliberately made all this up?"

"Not at all," Saint-Loup assured me out of kindness, out of tact, and also because he knew that circumstances are often stranger than one supposes.

After all, it was by no means impossible that in this tale of the thirty thousand francs there might be, as I assured him, a large element of truth. It was possible, but it was not true, and this element of truth was in fact a lie. But we lied to each other, Robert and I, as in every conversation when one friend is genuinely anxious to help another who is unhappy in love. The friend who is being counsellor, prop, comforter, may pity the other's distress but cannot share it, and the kinder he is to him the more he lies. And the other confesses to him as much as is necessary in order to secure his help, but, precisely in order to secure that help, perhaps, conceals many things from him. And the happy one of the two is, when all is said, he who takes trouble, goes on a journey, carries out a mission, but has no inner anguish. I was at this moment the person Robert had been at Doncières when he thought that Rachel had left him.

"Very well, just as you like; if I get a snub, I accept it in advance for your sake. And even if it does seem a bit queer to make such an undisguised bargain, I know that in our world there are plenty of duchesses, even the stuffiest of them, who if you offered them thirty thousand francs would do things far more difficult than telling their nieces not to stay in Touraine. Anyhow, I'm doubly glad to be doing you a service, since it's the only thing that will make you agree to see me. If I marry," he went on, "don't you think we might see more of one another, won't you regard my house as your own? . . ."

He suddenly stopped short, the thought having occurred to him (as I supposed at the time) that, if I too were to marry, Albertine might not be a suitable friend for his wife. And I remembered what the Cambremers had said to me about the probability of his marrying a niece of the Prince de Guermantes.

He consulted the timetable, and found that he could not leave Paris until the evening. Françoise inquired: "Am I to take Mlle Albertine's bed out of the study?" "On the contrary," I said, "you must make it for her." I hoped that she would return any day and did not wish Françoise to suppose that there could be any doubt of this. Albertine's departure must appear to have been agreed between ourselves, and not in any way to imply that she loved me less than before. But Françoise looked at me with an air, if not of incredulity, at any rate of doubt. She too had her alternative hypotheses. Her nostrils flared, she scented a quarrel, she must have felt it in the air for a long time past. And if she was not absolutely sure of it, this was perhaps only because, like myself, she hesitated to believe unconditionally what would have given her too much pleasure. Now the weight of the affair no longer rested on my overtaxed mind but on Saint-Loup. I was buoyed up with gladness because I had made a decision, because I told myself: "I have answered quick as a flash."

Saint-Loup could scarcely have been in the train when I ran into Bloch in my hall. I had not heard his ring, and was obliged to let him stay with me for a while. He had met me recently with Albertine (whom he had known at Balbec) on a day when she was in a bad mood. "I met M. Bontemps at dinner," he told me, "and as I have a certain influence over him, I told him that I was grieved that his niece was not nicer to you, and that he ought to have a word with her about it." I choked with rage; these remonstrations and complaints would destroy the whole effect of Saint-Loup's intervention and involve me directly in the eyes of Albertine, whom I now seemed to be imploring to return. To make matters worse, Françoise, who was lingering in the hall, could hear every word. I heaped every imaginable reproach upon Bloch, telling him that I had never authorised him to do anything of the sort and that, besides, the whole thing was nonsense. From then on, Bloch never left off smiling, less, I think, from joy than from embarrassment at having annoyed me. He laughingly expressed his surprise at having provoked such anger. Perhaps he said this in the hope of minimising in my eyes the importance of his indiscreet intervention, perhaps because he was of a cowardly nature and lived gaily and idly in an atmosphere of falsehood, as jellyfish float upon the surface of the sea, perhaps because, even if he had been a man of a different kind, other people can never see things from our point of view and therefore do not realise the magnitude of the injury that words uttered at random can do us. I had barely shown him out, unable to think of any remedy for the mischief he had done, when the bell rang again and Françoise brought me a summons from the head of the Sûreté. The parents of the little girl whom I had brought into the house for an hour had decided to bring a charge against me for abduction of a minor. There are moments in life when a sort of beauty is born of the multiplicity of the troubles that assail us, intertwined like Wagnerian leitmotifs, and also from the notion, which then emerges, that events are not situated in the sum of the reflexions portrayed in the wretched little mirror which the mind holds in front of it and which it calls the future, that they are somewhere outside and spring up as suddenly as a person who comes to catch us in the act. Even when left to itself, an event becomes modified, whether frustration amplifies it for us or satisfaction reduces it. But it is rarely unaccompanied. The feelings aroused by each one of them contradict one another, and fear, to a certain extent, as I felt on my way to see the head of the Sûreté, is an at least temporary and fairly efficacious counter-irritant for sentimental miseries.

At the Sûreté, I found the girl's parents, who insulted me and with the words "We'd rather starve" handed me back the five hundred francs which I did not want to take, and the head of the Sûreté who, setting himself the inimitable example of the judicial facility in repartee, seized upon a word in each sentence that I uttered for the purpose of concocting a witty and crushing retort. My innocence of the alleged crime was never taken into consideration, for that was the sole hypothesis which nobody was willing to accept for an instant. Nevertheless the difficulty of proving the charge enabled me to escape with this castigation, which was extremely violent for as long as the parents were in the room. But as soon as they had gone, the head of the Sûreté, who had a weakness for little girls, changed his tone and admonished me as man to man: "Next time, you must be more careful. Good God, you can't pick them up as easily as that, or you'll get into trouble. Anyhow, you'll find dozens of little girls who are better-looking than that one, and far cheaper. It was a perfectly ridiculous amount to pay." I was so certain that he would fail to understand me if I attempted to tell him the truth that without saying a word I took advantage of his permission to withdraw. Every passer-by, until I was safely at home, seemed to me an inspector appointed to spy on my every movement. But this leitmotif, like that of my anger with Bloch, died away, leaving the field clear for that of Albertine's departure.

The latter resumed on an almost joyous note now that Saint-Loup had set out. Since he had undertaken to go and see Mme Bontemps, my sufferings had been dispelled. I believed that this was because I had acted, and I believed it sincerely, for we never know what is concealed in our hearts of hearts. But what really made me happy was not, as I supposed, that I had unburdened my indecisions on to Saint-Loup. I was not in fact entirely mistaken; the specific for curing an unfortunate event (and three events out of four are unfortunate) is a decision; for it has the effect, by a sudden reversal of our thoughts, of interrupting the flow of those that come from the past event and prolong its vibration, and breaking it with a counter-flow of thoughts from the outside, from the future. But these new thoughts are most of all beneficial to us (and this was the case with the thoughts that assailed me at this moment) when from the depths of that future it is a hope that they bring us. What really made me so happy was the secret certainty that Saint-Loup's mission could not fail and that Albertine was bound to return. I realised this; for not having received any word from Saint-Loup on the following day, I began to suffer anew. My decision, my transference to him of plenipotentiary powers, was not, therefore, the cause of my joy, which in that case would have persisted; its cause was rather the "Success is certain" which had been in my mind when I said "Come what may." And the thought, aroused by his delay, that after all his mission might not prove successful, was so hateful to me that all my gaiety evaporated. It is in reality our anticipation, our hope of happy events that fills us with a joy which we ascribe to other causes and which ceases, plunging us once more into misery, if we are no longer so certain that what we desire will come to pass. It is always an invisible belief that sustains the edifice of our sensory world and deprived of which it totters. We have seen that it created for us the merit or the nullity of other people, our excitement or boredom at seeing them. It similarly creates the possibility of enduring a grief which seems to us trivial simply because we are convinced that it will presently be brought to an end, or its sudden intensification to the point where a person's presence matters to us as much as, sometimes even more than, life itself.

One thing finally succeeded in making my heartache as acute as it had been in the first instant and (I am bound to admit) no longer was. This was when I re-read a sentence in Albertine's letter. However much we love people, the pain of losing them—when in our isolation we are confronted with it alone, to which our mind to a certain extent gives whatever form it chooses—is endurable and different from that other pain, less human, less our own—as unforeseen and unusual as an accident in the moral world and in the region of the heart—which is caused not so much by the people themselves as by the manner in which we have learned that we will never see them again. I could think of Albertine while weeping gently and accepting the fact that I should not be seeing her tonight any more than I had yesterday; but to re-read "my decision is irrevocable" was another matter; it was like taking a dangerous drug which had given me a heart attack from which I might never recover. There is in inanimate objects, in events, in farewell letters, a special danger which amplifies and alters the very nature of the grief that people are capable of causing us. But this pain did not last long. I was, when all was said, so sure of Saint-Loup's skill, of his eventual success, Albertine's return seemed to me so certain, that I wondered whether I had been right to wish for it. Nevertheless, I rejoiced at the thought. Unfortunately, although I had assumed that the business with the Sûreté was over and done with, Françoise came in to tell me that an inspector had called to inquire whether I was in the habit of having girls in the house, that the concierge, supposing him to be referring to Albertine, had replied in the affirmative, and that since then it seemed as though the house was being watched. Henceforth it would be impossible for me ever to bring a little girl into the house to console me in my grief, without risking the shame of an inspector suddenly appearing and of her taking me for a criminal. And in the same instant I realised how much more important certain longings are to us than we suppose, for this impossibility of my ever taking a little girl on my knee again seemed to me to strip life of all its value but what was more, I realised how understandable it is that people will readily refuse wealth and risk death, whereas we imagine that pecuniary interest and the fear of dying rule the world. For, rather than think that even an unknown little girl might be given a bad impression of me by the arrival of a policeman, I should have preferred to kill myself! Indeed there was no possible comparison between the two degrees of suffering. Yet in everyday life people never bear in mind that those to whom they offer money, or whom they threaten to kill, may have mistresses, or merely friends, whose respect they value even if they do not value their own. But all of a sudden, by a confusion of which I was not aware (for it did not occur to me that Albertine, being of age, was free to live under my roof and even to be my mistress), it seemed to me that the charge of corrupting minors might apply to Albertine also. Thereupon my life appeared to me to be hedged in on every side. And reflecting that I had not lived chastely with her, I saw, in the punishment that had been inflicted upon me for having dandled an unknown little girl on my knee, that relation which almost always exists in human sanctions, whereby there is hardly ever either a just sentence or a judicial error, but a sort of compromise between the false idea that the judge forms of an innocent act and the culpable deeds of which he is unaware. But then when I thought that Albertine's return might involve me in an ignominious charge which would degrade me in her eyes and might perhaps even do her some damage for which she would not forgive me, I ceased to look forward to her return, it terrified me. I wanted to cable her to tell her not to come back. And immediately, a passionate desire for her return overwhelmed me, drowning everything else. The fact was that, having envisaged for a moment the possibility of telling her not to return and of living without her, all of a sudden I felt on the contrary ready to abandon all travel, all pleasure, all work, if only Albertine would return!

Ah, how my love for Albertine, the course of which I had imagined that I could foretell on the basis of my love for Gilberte, had developed differently from the latter, indeed in perfect contrast with it! How impossible it was for me to live without seeing her! And with each of my actions, even the most trivial, since they had all been steeped beforehand in the blissful atmosphere which was Albertine's presence, I was obliged time after time, at renewed cost, with the same pain, to relive the first experience of separation. Then the competition of other forms of life thrust this new pain into the background, and during those days which were the first days of spring, as I waited until Saint-Loup had managed to see Mme Bontemps, I even enjoyed a few moments of agreeable calm in imagining Venice and beautiful, unknown women. As soon as I was conscious of this, I felt within me a panic terror. This calm which I had just enjoyed was the first apparition of that great intermittent force which was to wage war in me against grief, against love, and would ultimately get the better of them. This state of which I had just had a foretaste and had received the warning was for a moment only what would in time to come be my permanent state, a life in which I should no longer be able to suffer on account of Albertine, in which I should no longer love her. And my love, which had just seen and recognised the one enemy by whom it could be conquered, forgetfulness, began to tremble, like a lion which in the cage in which it has been confined has suddenly caught sight of the python that will devour it.

I thought of Albertine all the time, and Françoise, when she came into my room, never said to me "There are no letters" quickly enough to curtail my anguish.

From time to time I succeeded, by letting some current or other of ideas flow through my grief, in freshening, in airing to some slight extent the vitiated atmosphere of my heart; but at night, if I succeeded in going to sleep, then it was as though the memory of Albertine had been the drug that had procured my sleep and the cessation of whose influence would awaken me. I thought all the time of Albertine while I was asleep. It was a special sleep of her own that she gave me, and one in which, moreover, I was no longer at liberty, as when awake, to think of other things. Sleep and the memory of her were like two substances which one must mix together and take at one draught in order to sleep. When I was awake, meanwhile, my suffering went on increasing day by day instead of diminishing. Not that oblivion was not performing its task, but by that very fact it encouraged the idealisation of the lamented image and thereby the assimilation of my initial suffering to other analogous sufferings which intensified it. At least that image was endurable. But if all of a sudden I thought of her room, of her room in which the bed stood empty, of her piano, of her motor-car, all my strength left me, I shut my eyes and let my head droop on my shoulder like someone who is about to faint. The sound of doors being opened hurt me almost as much because it was not she that was opening them. When it was possible that a telegram might have come from Saint-Loup, I dared not ask: "Is there a telegram?" At length one did come, but brought with it only a postponement, with the message: "The ladies have gone away for three days."

No doubt, if I had endured the four days that had already elapsed since her departure, it was because I said to

myself: "It's only a matter of time. By the end of the
week she will be here." But this consideration did not alter the fact that for my heart, for my body, the action to
be performed was the same: living without her, returning
home and not finding her in the house, passing the door
of her room (as for opening it, I did not yet have the
courage to do that) knowing that she was not inside, going
to bed without having said good-night to her—such were
the tasks that my heart had been obliged to perform in
their terrible entirety, and for all the world as though I
was not going to see Albertine again. But the fact that my
heart had already performed this daily task four times
proved that it was now capable of continuing to perform
it. And soon, perhaps, the consideration that was helping
me thus to go on living—the prospect of Albertine's return—would cease to be necessary to me; I should be
able to say to myself: "She will never come back," and go
on living all the same as I had already done for the last
four days, like a cripple who has recovered the use of his
legs and can dispense with his crutches. No doubt when I
came home at night I still found, taking my breath away,
suffocating me in the vacuum of solitude, the memories,
placed end to end in an interminable series, of all the
evenings on which Albertine had been waiting for me; but
already I also found the memory of last night, of the night
before and of the two previous nights, that is to say the
memory of the four nights that had passed since Albertine's departure, during which I had remained without
her, alone, through which none the less I had lived, four
nights already forming a strip of memories which was
very slender compared with the other, but which would
be filled out, perhaps, by every day that went by.

I shall say nothing of the letter conveying a declaration of affection which I received at this time from a niece of Mme de Guermantes who was considered to be the prettiest girl in Paris, or of the overtures made to me by the Duc de Guermantes on behalf of her parents, resigned, in their anxiety to secure their daughter's happiness, to the inequality of the match, to an apparent misalliance. Such incidents which might prove gratifying to one's self-esteem are too painful when one is in love. One might have the desire but not the indelicacy to communicate them to her who has a less flattering opinion of one, an opinion which moreover would not be modified by the knowledge that one is capable of inspiring a quite different one. What the Duke's niece wrote to me could only have irritated Albertine.

From the moment of waking, when I picked up my grief again at the point where I had left it before going to sleep, like a book which had been shut for a while but which I would keep before my eyes until night, it was invariably to some thought concerning Albertine that I related every sensation, whether it came to me from without or from within. The bell would ring: it must be a letter from her, or she herself perhaps! If I felt well and not too miserable, I was no longer jealous, I no longer had any grievance against her, I wanted to see her at once, to kiss her, to live happily with her ever after. The act of telegraphing to her "Come at once" seemed to me to have become a perfectly simple thing, as though my new mood had changed not merely my attitude, but things external to myself, had made them easier. If I was in a sombre mood, all my anger with her revived, I no longer felt any desire to kiss her, I felt how impossible it was that she could ever make me happy, I sought only to harm her and to prevent her from belonging to other people. But the outcome of these two opposite moods was identical: it was essential that she should return as soon as possible. And yet, whatever joy I might feel at the moment of her return, I sensed that very soon the same difficulties would recur and that to seek happiness in the satisfaction of a desire of the mind was as naïve as to attempt to reach the horizon by walking straight ahead. The further the desire advances, the further does real possession recede. So that if happiness, or at least the absence of suffering, can be found, it is not the satisfaction, but the gradual reduction and the eventual extinction of desire that one should seek. One seeks to see the beloved object, but one ought to seek not to: forgetfulness alone brings about the ultimate extinction of desire. And I imagine that if an author were to publish truths of this sort he would dedicate the book that contained them to a woman with whom he would thus take pleasure in striking up a relationship, saying to her: "This book is yours." And thus, while telling the truth in his book, he would be lying in his dedication, for he will attach to the book's being hers only the importance that he attaches to the stone which came to him from her and which will remain precious to him only so long as he is in love with her. The bonds between ourselves and another person exist only in our minds. Memory as it grows fainter loosens them, and notwithstanding the illusion by which we want to be duped and with which, out of love, friendship, politeness, deference, duty, we dupe other people, we exist alone. Man is the creature who cannot escape from himself, who knows other people only in himself, and when he asserts the contrary, he is lying. And I should have been so afraid of being robbed (had anyone been capable of so robbing me) of this need of her, this love for her, that I convinced myself that it was a precious necessity in my life. To be able to hear, without being charmed and pained by them, the names of the stations through which the train passed on its way to Touraine would have seemed to me a diminution of myself (for no other reason really than that it would have proved that I was becoming indifferent to Albertine). It was right, I told myself, that by incessantly asking myself what she could be doing, thinking, wishing, at every moment, whether she intended, whether she was going to return, I should keep open that communicating door which love had opened up in me, and feel another person's life flooding through open sluices to fill the reservoir which must not again become stagnant.

Presently, as Saint-Loup's silence persisted, a subordinate anxiety—my expectation of a further telegram or a telephone call from him—masked the first, my uncertainty as to the result, whether Albertine was going to return. Listening for every sound in expectation of the telegram became so intolerable that I felt that, whatever its contents might be, the arrival of the telegram, which was the only thing I could think of at the moment, would put an end to my sufferings. But when at last I received a telegram from Robert in which he informed me that he had seen Mme Bontemps but that in spite of all his precautions Albertine had seen him, and that this had upset everything, I burst out in a torrent of fury and despair, for this was what I had wanted at all costs to avoid. Once it came to Albertine's knowledge, Saint-Loup's mission gave me an appearance of needing her which could only dissuade her from returning and my horror of which was moreover all that I had retained of the pride that my love had boasted in Gilberte's day and had since lost. I cursed Robert, then told myself that, if this scheme had failed, I would try another. Since man is capable of influencing the external world, how could I fail, by bringing into play cunning, intelligence, money, affection, to abolish this terrible fact: Albertine's absence? We believe that we can change the things around us in accordance with our desires—we believe it because otherwise we can see no favourable outcome. We do not think of the outcome which generally comes to pass and is also favourable: we do not succeed in changing things in accordance with our desires, but gradually our desires change. The situation that we hoped to change because it was intolerable becomes unimportant to us. We have failed to surmount the obstacle, as we were absolutely determined to do, but life has taken us round it, led us beyond it, and then if we turn round to gaze into the distance of the past, we can barely see it, so imperceptible has it become.

From the floor above I could hear one of the neighbours playing some tunes from *Manon*. I applied their words, which I knew, to Albertine and myself, and was stirred so deeply that I began to cry. The words were:

> Alas, most often at night
> The bird that flees from what it felt was bondage
> Returns to beat at the glass in desperate flight,

and the death of Manon:

> Then, Manon, answer me!—The one love of my soul,
> Never till now did I know the goodness of your heart.

Since Manon returned to Des Grieux, it seemed to me that I was to Albertine the one and only love of her life. Alas, it is probable that, if she had been listening at that moment to the same tune, it would not have been me that she cherished under the name of Des Grieux, and, even if the idea had occurred to her at all, the memory of me would have prevented her from being moved by this music which, though subtler and better-written, was very much of the kind that she admired. As for me, I had not the heart to abandon myself to the comforting thought of Albertine calling me her "soul's one love" and realising that she had been mistaken over what she had "felt was bondage." I knew that one can never read a novel without giving its heroine the form and features of the woman one loves. But however happy the book's ending may be, our love has not advanced an inch and, when we have shut it, she whom we love and who has come to us at last in its pages, loves us no better in real life.

In a fit of fury, I telegraphed to Saint-Loup to return as quickly as possible to Paris, in order to avoid at least the appearance of an aggravating persistence in a mission which I had been so anxious to keep secret. But even before he had returned in obedience to my instructions, it was from Albertine herself that I received the following message:

"My dear, you have sent your friend Saint-Loup to my aunt, which was foolish. My dearest, if you needed me, why did you not write to me direct? I should have been only too delighted to come back. Do not let us have any more of these absurd approaches."

"I should have been only too delighted to come back"! If she said this, it must mean that she regretted her departure, and was only waiting for an excuse to return. I had only to do what she said, to write to her that I needed her, and she would return. So I was going to see her again, her, the Albertine of Balbec (for since her departure this was what she had once more become for me; like a sea-shell to which one ceases to pay any attention when it is always there on one's chest of drawers, and once one has parted with it, either by giving it away or by losing it, one begins to think about again, she recalled to me all the joyous beauty of the blue mountains of the sea). And it was not only she that had become a creature of the imagination, that is to say desirable, but life with her had become an imaginary life, that is to say a life freed from all difficulties, so that I said to myself: "How happy we are going to be!" But, now that I was assured of her return, I must not appear to be seeking to hasten it, but must on the contrary efface the bad impression left by Saint-Loup's intervention, which I could always disavow later on by saying that he had acted on his own initiative, because he had always been in favour of our marriage.

Meanwhile, I read her letter again, and was after all disappointed to be reminded of how little there is of a person in a letter. Doubtless the characters traced on the paper express our thoughts, as do also our features; it is still a thought of some kind that we are confronted with. But even so, in the person, the thought is not apparent to us until it has been diffused through the corolla of the face opened up like a water lily. This modifies it considerably, after all. And it is perhaps one of the causes of our perpetual disappointments in love, this perpetual displacement whereby, in response to our expectation of the ideal person whom we love, each meeting provides us with a person in flesh and blood who yet contains so little trace of our dream. And then, when we demand something of this person, we receive from her a letter in which even of the person very little remains, as in the letters of an algebraical formula there no longer remains the precise value of the arithmetical figures, which themselves do not contain the qualities of the fruit or flowers that they enumerate. And yet "love," the "beloved," her letters, are perhaps nevertheless translations (unsatisfying though it may be to pass from one to the other) of the same reality, since the letter seems to us inadequate only while we are reading it, but we sweat blood until its arrival, and it is sufficient to calm our anguish, if not to appease, with its tiny black symbols, our desire which knows that it contains after all only the equivalent of a word, a smile, a kiss, not those things themselves.

I wrote to Albertine:

"Dear friend, I was just about to write to you. Thank you for saying that if I had been in need of you you would have come at once; it is good of you to have so exalted a sense of loyalty to an old friend, and my regard for you can only be increased thereby. But no, I did not ask and I shall not ask you to return; our seeing each other again—for a long time to come—might not perhaps be painful to you, a heartless girl. To me, whom at times you have thought so cold, it would be most painful. Life has driven us apart. You have made a decision which I consider very wise, and which you made at the right moment, with wonderful prescience, for you left me on the day when I had just received my mother's consent to my asking for your hand. I would have told you this when I awoke, when I received her letter (at the same time as yours). Perhaps you would have been afraid of hurting me by leaving there and then. And we might perhaps have linked our lives together in what (who knows?) could have been unhappiness. If that was what was in store for us, then I bless you for your wisdom. We should lose all the fruit of it were we to meet again. This is not to say that I should not find it a temptation. But I claim no great credit for resisting it. You know what an inconstant person I am and how quickly I forget. Therefore I am not greatly to be pitied. As you have told me often, I am first and foremost a man of habit. The habits which I am beginning to form in your absence are not as yet very strong. Naturally, for the moment, the habits which I shared with you and which your departure has disturbed are still the stronger. They will not remain so for very long. For that reason, indeed, I had thought of taking advantage of these last few days in which our meeting would not yet be for me what it will be in a fortnight's time, perhaps even sooner, a . . . (forgive my frankness) an inconvenience—I had thought of taking advantage of them, before oblivion finally comes, in order to settle certain little material questions with you, in which you might, as a kind and charming friend, have rendered a service to him who for five minutes imagined himself your future husband. Since I never doubted my mother's approval, and since moreover I desired that we should each of us enjoy all that liberty of which you had too generously and abundantly made a sacrifice which was acceptable for a few weeks' living together but would have become as hateful to you as to myself now that we were to spend the rest of our lives together (it almost pains me as I write to you to think that this nearly happened, that we came within a few seconds of it), I had thought of organising our existence in the most independent manner possible, and to begin with I wished you to have that yacht in which you could go cruising while I, not being well enough to accompany you, would wait for you in port (I had written to Elstir to ask for his advice, since you admire his taste); and on land I wished you to have a motor-car to yourself, for your very own, in which you could go out, could travel wherever you chose. The yacht was almost ready, it is named, after a wish that you expressed at Balbec, the *Swan*. And remembering that you preferred Rolls-Royces to any other cars, I had ordered one. But now that we are never to meet again, as I have no hope of persuading you to accept either the boat or the car (to me they would be quite useless), I had thought—as I had ordered them through a middleman, in your name—that you might perhaps by countermanding them yourself save me the expense of the yacht and the car which are no longer required. But this, and many other matters, would have needed to be discussed. And I find that so long as I am capable of falling in love with you again, which will not be for long, it would be madness, for the sake of a sailing boat and a Rolls-Royce, to meet again and to jeopardise your life's happiness since you have decided that it lies in your living apart from me. No, I prefer to keep the Rolls and even the yacht. And as I shall make no use of them and they are likely to remain for ever, one in its dock, dismantled, the other in its garage, I shall have engraved on the . . . of the yacht (Heavens, I'm afraid of calling it the wrong thing and committing a heresy which would shock you) those lines of Mallarmé which you used to like:

> A swan of olden times recalls that he,
> Splendid yet void of hope to free himself,
> Had left unsung the realm of life itself
> When sterile winter glittered with ennui.

You remember—it's the poem that begins: "The lively, lovely, virginal today." Alas, today is no longer either virginal or lovely. But those who, like me, know that they will very soon make of it an endurable "tomorrow" are seldom *endurable* themselves. As for the Rolls, it would deserve rather those other lines of the same poet which you said you could not understand:

> Say then if I am not joyful
> Thunder and rubies at the axle
> To see in the air pierced by this fire
>
> With every scattered palatine
> Dying as though in purple of Tyre
> The wheel of my chariot vespertine.

Farewell for ever, my little Albertine, and thank you once again for the enjoyable drive which we went for together on the eve of our separation. I retain a very pleasant memory of it.

PS. I make no reference to what you tell me of the alleged suggestions which Saint-Loup (whom I do not for a moment believe to be in Touraine) may have made to your aunt. It's pure Sherlock Holmes. What do you take me for?"

No doubt, just as I had said in the past to Albertine: "I don't love you," in order that she should love me, "I forget people when I don't see them," in order that she might see me often, "I have decided to leave you," in order to forestall any idea of separation, now it was because I was absolutely determined that she must return within a week that I said to her: "Farewell for ever"; it was because I wished to see her again that I said to her: "I think it would be dangerous to see you"; it was because living apart from her seemed to me worse than death that I wrote to her: "You were right, we would be unhappy together." Alas, in writing this sham letter in order to appear not to need her (the only vestige of pride that survived from my former love for Gilberte in my love for Albertine), and also to enjoy the pleasure of saying certain things which were only capable of moving me and not her, I ought to have foreseen from the start that it was possible that it would invite a negative response, that is to say, one which substantiated what I had said; that this was indeed probable, for even had Albertine been less intelligent than she was, she would never have doubted for an instant that what I said to her was untrue. Indeed, without pausing to consider the intentions that I expressed in this letter, the mere fact of my writing it, even if it had not been preceded by Saint-Loup's intervention, was enough to prove to her that I desired her return and to prompt her to let me become more and more inextricably ensnared. Then, having foreseen the possibility of a negative reply, I ought also to have foreseen that this reply would at once revive in its fullest intensity my love for Albertine. And I ought, still before posting my letter, to have asked myself whether, in the event of Albertine's replying in the same tone and refusing to return, I should have sufficient control over my grief to force myself to remain silent, not to telegraph to her "Come back," not to send her some other emissary—all of which, after I had written to her to say that we would never meet again, would make it perfectly obvious that I could not do without her, and would lead to her refusing more emphatically than ever, whereupon, unable to endure my anguish for another moment, I would go down to her myself and might, for all I knew, be refused admission. And doubtless this would have been, after three enormous blunders, the worst of all, after which there would be nothing left but to kill myself in front of her house. But the disastrous way in which the psychopathological universe is constructed has decreed that the clumsy act, the act which we ought most sedulously to avoid, is precisely the act that will calm us, the act that, opening before us, until we discover its outcome, fresh avenues of hope, momentarily relieves us of the intolerable pain which a refusal has aroused in us. So that, when the pain is too acute, we dash headlong into the blunder that consists in writing to, in sending somebody to intercede with, in going in person to see, in proving that we cannot do without, the woman we love.

But I foresaw none of all this. The probable outcome of my letter seemed to me on the contrary to be to make Albertine return to me at once. And so, with this outcome in mind, I had felt a sweet pleasure in writing the letter. But at the same time I had not ceased to shed tears while writing it; partly, first of all, in the same way as on the day when I had acted a pretence of separation, because, as the words represented for me the idea which they expressed to me although they were addressed to a different end (uttered mendaciously because my pride forbade me to admit that I loved), they carried their own load of sorrow, but also because I felt that the idea contained a grain of truth.

As this letter seemed to me to be certain of its effect, I began to regret that I had sent it. For when I pictured to myself Albertine's return and what an easy matter it was after all, suddenly all the reasons which made our marriage a thing disastrous to myself returned in their fullest force. I hoped that she would refuse to come back. I was in the process of calculating that my liberty, my whole future depended upon her refusal, that I had been mad to write to her, that I ought to have retrieved my letter which, alas, had gone, when Françoise brought it back to me (at the same time handing me the newspaper which she had just brought upstairs). She was not certain how many stamps it required. But immediately I changed my mind; I hoped that Albertine would not return, but I wanted the decision to come from her, so as to put an end to my anxiety, and I handed the letter back to Françoise. I opened the newspaper. It announced a performance by Berma. Then I remembered the two different ways in which I had listened to *Phèdre*, and it was now in a third way that I thought of the declaration scene. It seemed to me that what I had so often recited to myself, and had seen and heard in the theatre, was the statement of the laws which I was to experience in my life. There are things in our hearts to which we do not realise how strongly we are attached. Or else, if we live without them, it is because day after day, from fear of failure, or of being made to suffer, we put off entering into possession of them. This was what had happened to me in the case of Gilberte, when I thought that I was giving her up. If before the time comes when we are entirely detached from these things—a time long subsequent to that in which we believe ourselves to be detached from them—the girl we love becomes, for instance, engaged to someone else, we are driven mad, we can no longer endure the life which appeared to us to be so mournfully calm. Or else, if the thing is already in our possession, we feel that it is a burden, that we should be only too glad to be rid of it; and this was what had happened to me in the case of Albertine. But let a sudden departure remove the unwanted person from us, and we can no longer bear to live. Now, did not the "argument" of *Phèdre* combine these two cases? Hippolyte is about to leave. Phèdre, who until then has gone out of her way to court his enmity, from qualms of conscience, she says (or rather the poet makes her say), but really because she does not see that it can lead anywhere and feels that she is not loved, Phèdre can endure the situation no longer. She comes to him to confess her love, and this was the scene which I had so often recited to myself:

They say a prompt departure takes you from us.

Doubtless Hippolyte's departure is a secondary reason, one may feel, compared to the death of Thésée. And sim-

ilarly when, a few lines further on, Phèdre pretends for a
moment that she has been misunderstood:

> Would I have cast off all care for my honour?

we may suppose that it is because Hippolyte has repulsed
her declaration:

> Do you not remember,
> Lady, Theseus is your husband, and my father?

But if he had evinced no indignation, Phèdre, her happiness achieved, might have had the same feeling that it did
not amount to much. Whereas, as soon as she sees that it
still eludes her grasp, that Hippolyte thinks he has misunderstood her and makes apologies, then, like myself when
I decided to give my letter back to Françoise, she decides
that the refusal must come from him, decides to stake everything on one last throw of the dice:

> Ah, cruel! You have understood me all too well.

And even the very harshness with which, I had been told,
Swann had treated Odette, or with which I myself had
treated Albertine, a harshness which substituted for the
original love a new love composed of pity, tenderness, the
need for an outpouring of emotion which was merely a
variant of the first, is to be found also in this scene:

> You hated me the more, I did not love you less.
> Your misfortunes lent you further and fresh charms.

What proves that it is not to the "care for her honour"
that Phèdre attaches most importance is that she would

have forgiven Hippolyte and turned a deaf ear to Oenone's advice had she not learned that Hippolyte was in love with Aricie. For jealousy, which in love is equivalent to the loss of all happiness, outweighs mere loss of reputation. It is then that she allows Oenone (who is merely a name for the baser side of herself) to slander Hippolyte without taking upon herself the "burden of his defence" and thus sends the man who will have none of her to a fate the calamities of which are moreover no consolation to herself, since her own suicide follows immediately upon the death of Hippolyte. Thus at least it was that, reducing the part played by all the "Jansenist" scruples, as Bergotte would have put it, which Racine ascribed to Phèdre to make her appear less guilty, I saw this scene, as a sort of prophecy of the amorous episodes in my own life. These reflexions had, however, in no way altered my resolve, and I handed my letter to Françoise so that she might post it after all, in order to carry into effect that approach to Albertine which seemed to me to be essential now that I had learned that my former attempt had failed. And no doubt we are wrong when we suppose that the fulfilment of our desire is a small matter, since as soon as we believe that it cannot be realised we become intent upon it once again, and decide that it was not worth our while to pursue it only when we are quite certain that our attempt will not fail. And yet we are right also. For if that fulfilment, if the achievement of happiness, appears of small account only in the light of certainty, nevertheless it is an unstable element from which only sorrows can arise. And those sorrows will be all the greater the more completely our desire will have been fulfilled, all the more impossible to endure when our happiness has been, in defiance of the law of nature, prolonged for a certain time, when it has received the consecration of habit. In another sense, too, these two tendencies, in this particular case that which made me anxious that my letter should be posted, and, when I thought that it had gone, that which made me regret the fact, have each of them a certain element of truth. As regards the first tendency, it is only too understandable that we should go in pursuit of our happiness—or misery—and that at the same time we should hope to keep before us, by this latest action which is about to involve us in its consequences, a state of expectancy which does not leave us in absolute despair, in a word that we should seek to convert into other forms which, we imagine, must be less painful to us, the malady from which we are suffering. But the other tendency is no less important, for, born of our belief in the success of our enterprise, it is simply an anticipation of the disillusionment which we should very soon feel in the presence of a satisfied desire, our regret at having fixed for ourselves, at the expense of others which are necessarily excluded, this particular form of happiness.

I gave the letter back to Françoise and asked her to go out at once and post it. As soon as it had gone, I began once more to think of Albertine's return as imminent. The thought did not fail to introduce into my mind certain pleasing images which neutralised to some extent the dangers I foresaw in her return. The pleasure, so long lost, of having her with me was intoxicating.

Time passes, and little by little everything that we have spoken in falsehood becomes true; I had learned this only too well with Gilberte; the indifference I had feigned while never ceasing to weep had eventually become a fact; gradually life, as I told Gilberte in a lying formula which retrospectively had come true, life had driven us apart. I remembered this, saying to myself: "If Albertine allows a few months to go by, my lies will become the truth. And now that the worst moments are over, isn't it to be wished that she will allow this month to elapse? If she returns, I shall have to renounce the true life which certainly I am not in a fit state to enjoy as yet, but which as time goes on may begin to offer me attractions while my memory of Albertine grows fainter."

I do not say that the process of forgetting was not beginning to operate. But one of the effects of forgetting was precisely—since it meant that many of Albertine's less pleasing aspects, of the boring hours that I had spent with her, no longer figured in my memory, ceased therefore to be reasons for my wanting her not to be there as I used to when she was—that it gave me a more concise impression of her enhanced by all the love that I had ever felt for other women. In this particular form, forgetfulness, although it was working towards inuring me to separation from her, nevertheless, by showing me a sweeter and more beautiful Albertine, made me long all the more for her return.

Often, since her departure, when I was confident that I showed no trace of tears, I had rung for Françoise and said to her: "We must make sure that Mademoiselle Albertine hasn't forgotten anything. See that you do her room so that it's nice and tidy for her when she comes." Or simply: "Only the other day Mademoiselle Albertine was saying to me, let me think now, it was the day before she left . . ." I wanted to diminish Françoise's detestable pleasure at Albertine's departure by giving her the impression that it was not to be prolonged. I wanted, too, to show Françoise that I was not afraid to speak of this departure, to proclaim it—like certain generals who describe a forced retreat as a strategic withdrawal in conformity with a prearranged plan—as deliberate, as constituting an episode the true meaning of which I was concealing for the moment, but in no way implying the end of my friendship with Albertine. I wanted, finally, by repeating her name incessantly, to introduce, like a breath of air, something of her into that room in which her departure had left a vacuum, in which I could no longer breathe. Besides, one seeks to reduce the dimensions of one's grief by fitting it into one's everyday talk between ordering a suit of clothes and ordering dinner.

While she was doing Albertine's room, Françoise, out of curiosity, opened the drawer of a little rosewood table in which my mistress used to put away the ornaments which she discarded when she went to bed. "Oh! Monsieur, Mademoiselle Albertine has forgotten to take her rings, they're still in the drawer."

My first impulse was to say: "We must send them after her." But this would make me appear uncertain of her return. "Oh well," I replied after a moment's silence, "it's hardly worth while sending them to her as she's coming back so soon. Give them to me, I shall see about them."

Françoise handed me the rings with some misgiving. She loathed Albertine, but, judging me by her own standards, she reckoned that one could not give me a letter in my mistress's handwriting without the risk of my opening it. I took the rings.

"Monsieur must take care not to lose them," said

Françoise. "They're real beauties, they are! I don't know who gave them to her, whether it was Monsieur or some-one else, but I can tell it was someone rich, who had good taste!"

"It wasn't me," I assured her, "and besides, they don't both come from the same person. One was given her by her aunt and the other she bought for herself."

"Not from the same person!" Françoise exclaimed. "Monsieur must be joking, they're exactly the same, ex-cept for the ruby that's been added to one of them, there's the same eagle on both, the same initials inside . . ."

I do not know whether Françoise was conscious of the pain she was causing me, but a smile began to flicker across her lips and thereafter never left them.

"What do you mean, the same eagle? You're talking nonsense. It's true that the one without the ruby has an eagle on it, but the other has a sort of man's head carved on it."

"A man's head? Where did Monsieur see that? I had only to put on my specs to see at once that it was one of the eagle's wings. If Monsieur takes his magnifying glass, he'll see the other wing on the other side, and the head and the beak in the middle. You can count every feather. Oh, it's a fine piece of work."

My intense anxiety to know whether Albertine had lied to me made me forget that I ought to maintain a cer-tain dignity in Françoise's presence and deny her the wicked pleasure that she felt, if not in torturing me, at least in harming Albertine. I almost gasped for breath as Françoise went to fetch my magnifying glass. I took it from her, and asked her to show me the eagle on the ring with the ruby. She had no difficulty in making me pick out the wings, stylised in the same way as on the other ring, the relief of the feathers, the head. She also pointed out to me the similar inscriptions, to which, it is true, others were added on the ring with the ruby. And on the inside of both was Albertine's monogram.

"But I'm surprised that it should need all this to make Monsieur see that the rings are the same," said Françoise. "Even without examining them, you can see that it's the same style, the same way of turning the gold, the same shape. As soon as I looked at them I could have sworn they came from the same place. You can tell straight away, just as you can tell the dishes of a good cook."

And indeed, to the curiosity of a servant fanned by hatred and trained to observe details with terrifying precision, there had been added, to assist her in this expert criticism, her natural taste, that same taste, in fact, which she showed in her cookery and which was sharpened perhaps, as I had noticed on the way to Balbec in the way she dressed, by the coquetry of a woman who has once been pretty and has studied the jewellery and dresses of other women. I might have picked up the wrong bottle of pills and, instead of swallowing a few veronal tablets on a day when I felt that I had drunk too many cups of tea, might have swallowed as many caffeine tablets, and my heart would not have pounded more violently. I asked Françoise to leave the room. I would have liked to see Albertine immediately. My horror at her lie, my jealousy of the unknown donor, was combined with pain at the thought that she should have allowed herself to accept presents. I gave her even more, it is true, but a woman whom we are keeping does not seem to us to be a kept woman as long as we are unaware that she is being kept by other men. And yet, since I had never ceased to spend a great deal of money on her, I had taken her in spite of this moral baseness; I had encouraged this baseness of hers, I had perhaps increased, perhaps even created it. Then, just as we have the faculty of making up stories to soothe our anguish, just as we manage, when we are dying of hunger, to persuade ourselves that a stranger is going to leave us a fortune of a hundred million, I imagined Albertine in my arms, explaining to me without the slightest hesitation that it was because of the similarity of its workmanship that she had bought the second ring, that it was she who had had her initials engraved on it. But this explanation was still fragile, it had not yet had time to thrust into my mind its beneficent roots, and my pain could not be so quickly assuaged. And I reflected that many men who tell their friends that their mistress is very sweet to them must suffer similar torments. Thus it is that they lie to others and to themselves. They do not altogether lie; they do spend in her company hours that are genuinely delightful; but the sweetness which she shows her lover in front of his friends and which enables him to preen himself, and the sweetness which she shows him when they are alone together and which enables him to bless her, conceal all too many unrecorded hours in which the lover has suffered, doubted, sought everywhere in vain to discover the truth! Such sufferings are inseparable from the pleasure of loving, of delighting in a woman's most trivial remarks, remarks which we know to be trivial but which we perfume with her fragrance. At that moment, I was no longer capable of delighting, through memory, in

the fragrance of Albertine. Shattered, holding the two
rings in my hand, I stared at that pitiless eagle whose
beak was rending my heart, whose wings, chiselled in
high relief, had borne away the trust that I still retained
in my mistress, in whose claws my tortured mind was unable to escape for an instant from the incessantly recurring questions concerning the stranger whose name the
eagle doubtless symbolised though without allowing me to
decipher it, whom she had doubtless loved in the past,
and whom she had doubtless seen again not so long ago,
since it was on the day, so peaceful, so loving and so intimate, of our drive together through the Bois that I had
seen, for the first time, the second ring, the one in which
the eagle appeared to be dipping its beak in the bright
blood of the ruby.

If, however, from morning till night, I never ceased to
grieve over Albertine's departure, this did not mean that I
thought only of her. For one thing, her charm having for
a long time past spread gradually over things which had
since become quite remote from her, but were none the
less electrified by the same emotion as she gave me, if
something made me think of Incarville, or of the Verdurins, or of some new part that Léa was playing, a sudden flux of pain would overwhelm me. For another thing,
what I myself called thinking of Albertine meant thinking
of how I might get her back, how I might join her, how I
might discover what she was doing. With the result that
if, during those hours of incessant torment, a pictogram
could have represented the images that accompanied my
sufferings, it would have shown pictures of the Gare
d'Orsay, of the banknotes offered to Mme Bontemps, of
Saint-Loup stooping over the sloping desk of a telegraph

office filling in a telegram form to me, never the picture of Albertine. Just as, throughout the whole course of one's life, one's egoism sees before it all the time the objects that are of concern to the self, but never takes in that "I" itself which is perpetually observing them, so the desire which directs our actions descends towards them, but does not reach back to itself, whether because, being unduly utilitarian, it plunges into the action and disdains all knowledge of it, or because it looks to the future to compensate for the disappointments of the present, or because the inertia of the mind urges it to slide down the easy slope of imagination, rather than to climb the steep slope of introspection. In reality, during those hours of crisis in which we would stake our whole life, in proportion as the woman upon whom it depends reveals more and more clearly the immensity of the place that she occupies for us, leaving nothing in the world that is not disrupted by her, so the image of that woman diminishes until it is no longer perceptible. We find in everything the effect of her presence in the emotion that we feel; herself, the cause, we find nowhere. I was so incapable during those days of forming any picture of Albertine that I could almost have believed that I did not love her, just as my mother, in the moments of despair when she was incapable of ever picturing my grandmother (except once in the chance encounter of a dream, the importance of which she felt so strongly, although asleep, that she strove with all the strength that remained to her in her sleep to make it last), might have accused and did in fact accuse herself of not missing her mother, whose death had been a mortal blow to her but whose features eluded her memory.*

Why should I have supposed that Albertine did not

care for women? Because she had said, especially of late, that she did not care for them: but did not our life rest upon a perpetual lie? Never once had she said to me: "Why can't I go out as and when I choose? Why do you always ask other people what I have been doing?" And yet, after all, the conditions of her life were so unusual that she must have asked me this had she not herself guessed the reason. And was it not understandable that my silence as to the causes of her confinement should be matched by a similar and constant silence on her part as to her perpetual desires, her innumerable memories, her countless hopes and longings? Françoise looked as though she knew that I was lying when I alluded to the imminence of Albertine's return. And her belief seemed to be founded upon something more than that truth which generally guided our old housekeeper, to the effect that masters do not like to be humiliated in front of their servants, and allow them to know only so much of the truth as does not depart too far from a flattering fiction calculated to maintain respect for themselves. This time, Françoise's belief seemed to be founded upon something else, as though she had herself aroused and fostered distrust in Albertine's mind, stimulated her anger, driven her, in short, to the point at which she could predict her departure as inevitable. If this was true, my version of a temporary absence, of which I had known and approved, could be received with nothing but incredulity by Françoise. But the idea that she had formed of Albertine's venal nature, the exasperation with which, in her hatred, she magnified the "profit" that Albertine was supposed to be making out of me, might to some extent belie that certainty. And so when in her hearing I made an allusion, as if to something perfectly natural, to Albertine's imminent return, Françoise would look at my face to see whether I was making it up, in the same way as, when the butler teased her by pretending to read out some political news which she hesitated to believe, as for instance the closing of churches and the expulsion of the clergy, even from the other end of the kitchen, and without being able to read it, she would stare instinctively and greedily at the paper, as though she were capable of seeing whether the report was really written there.

But when Françoise saw that after writing a long letter I added the exact address of Mme Bontemps, her alarm that Albertine might return, hitherto quite vague, began to increase. It grew to the point of consternation when one morning she had to bring me with the rest of my mail a letter on the envelope of which she had recognised Albertine's handwriting. She wondered whether Albertine's departure had not been a mere sham, a supposition which distressed her twice over as finally ensuring Albertine's future presence in the house, and as constituting for me, and thereby, as I was her employer, for herself, the humiliation of having been tricked by Albertine. Impatient though I was to read the letter, I could not refrain from studying for a moment Françoise's eyes from which all hope had fled, inferring from this omen the imminence of Albertine's return, as a lover of winter sports concludes with joy that the cold weather is at hand when he sees the swallows fly south. At length Françoise left me, and when I had made sure that she had shut the door behind her, I opened, noiselessly so as not to appear anxious, the letter which ran as follows:

"Dear friend, thank you for all the nice things you wrote to me. I am at your disposal for the countermanding of the Rolls, if you think that I can help in any way, as I am sure I can. You have only to let me know the name of the agents. You would let yourself be taken for a ride by these people who are only interested in selling, and what would you do with a motor-car, you who never stir out of the house? I am deeply touched that you have kept a happy memory of our last outing. You may be sure that for my part I shall never forget that drive in a double twilight (since night was falling and we were about to part) and that it will be effaced from my thoughts only when the darkness is complete."

I felt that this last sentence was merely phrase-making and that Albertine could not possibly retain until death any such sweet memory of this drive from which she had certainly derived no pleasure since she had been impatient to leave me. But I was impressed also, when I thought of the cyclist, the golfer of Balbec, who had read nothing but *Esther* before she came to know me, to see how gifted she was and how right I had been in thinking that she had enriched herself in my house with new qualities which made her different and more complete. And thus, the words that I had said to her at Balbec: "I feel that my friendship would be of value to you, that I am just the person who could give you what you lack" (I had written by way of dedication on a photograph I gave her: "with the certainty of being providential"), words which I uttered without believing them and simply that she might derive some benefit from my society which would outweigh any possible boredom, these words turned out to have been true as well; as, for that matter, had been my remark to her that I did not wish to see her for fear of falling in love with her. I had said this because on the contrary I knew that in constant proximity my love became deadened and that separation kindled it, but in reality constant proximity had given rise to a need of her that was infinitely stronger than my love in the first weeks at Balbec, so that that remark too had proved true.

But Albertine's letter in no way advanced matters. She spoke to me only of writing to the agents. It was essential to break out of this situation, to hasten things on, and I had the following idea. I sent a letter at once to Andrée in which I told her that Albertine was at her aunt's, that I felt very lonely, that she would give me immense pleasure if she came and stayed with me for a few days and that, as I did not wish to make any mystery of it, I begged her to inform Albertine. And at the same time I wrote to Albertine as though I had not yet received her letter:

"Dear friend, forgive me for what I am sure you will understand. I have such a hatred of secrecy that I wanted you to be informed both by her and by myself. I have acquired, from having you staying so charmingly in the house with me, the bad habit of not being able to be alone. Since we have decided that you will not come back, it occurred to me that the person who would best fill your place, because she would make least change in my life, would remind me most of you, is Andrée, and I have asked her to come. So that all this should not appear too sudden, I have spoken to her only of a short visit, but between ourselves I am pretty certain that this time it will be a permanent thing. Don't you agree that I'm right? You know that your little group of girls at Balbec has always been the social unit that exerted the greatest influence upon me, in which I was most happy to be eventually included. No doubt this influence is still making itself felt. Since the fatal incompatibility of our characters and the mischances of life have decreed that my little Albertine can never be my wife, I believe that I shall nevertheless find

a wife—less charming than herself but one whom greater natural affinities will enable perhaps to be happier with me—in Andrée."

But after I had sent off this letter, the suspicion occurred to me suddenly that, when Albertine had written
to me to say: "I should have been only too glad to come
back if you had written to me direct," she had said this
only because I had not written to her, and that had I done
so she would still not have come back, that she would be
happy to know that Andrée was with me, and was to be
my wife, provided that she herself remained free, because
she could now, as already for a week past, stultifying the
hourly precautions which I had taken during more than
six months in Paris, abandon herself to her vices and do
what, minute by minute, I had prevented her from doing.
I told myself that she was probably making an improper
use of her freedom down there, and no doubt this idea
which I formed seemed to me sad but remained general,
showing me no specific details, and, by the indefinite
number of possible mistresses which it allowed me to
imagine, prevented me from stopping to consider any one
of them, drew my mind on in a sort of perpetual motion
not untinged with pain, but with a pain which the absence of any concrete image rendered endurable. It ceased,
however, to be endurable and became atrocious when
Saint-Loup arrived.

Before I explain why the information that he gave me
made me so unhappy, I must relate an incident which occurred immediately before his visit and the memory of
which so disturbed me afterwards that it weakened, if not
the painful impression made on me by my conversation

with Saint-Loup, at any rate the practical effect of that conversation. This incident was as follows. Burning with impatience to see Saint-Loup, I was waiting for him on the staircase (a thing which I could not have done had my mother been at home, for it was what she most abominated, next to "talking out of the window") when I heard the following words: "What! you mean to say you don't know how to get a fellow you don't like sacked? It's not difficult. For instance, you need only hide the things he has to take in. Then, when they're in a hurry and ring for him, he can't find anything, he loses his head. My aunt will be furious with him, and will say to you: 'But what's the man doing?' When he does show his face, everybody will be raging, and he won't have what's wanted. After this has happened four or five times you may be sure that he'll be sacked, especially if you take care to dirty the things that he's supposed to bring in clean, and a dozen other tricks of that kind."

I remained speechless with astonishment, for these cruel, Machiavellian words were uttered by the voice of Saint-Loup. Now I had always regarded him as so kind, so tender-hearted a person that these words had the same effect on me as if he had been rehearsing the role of Satan for a play: it could not be in his own name that he was speaking.

"But, after all, a man has to earn his living," said the other person, of whom I then caught sight and who was one of the Duchesse de Guermantes's footmen.

"What the hell does that matter to you so long as you're all right?" Saint-Loup replied callously. "It will be all the more fun for you, having a whipping-boy. You can easily spill ink over his livery just when he has to go and wait at a big dinner-party, and never leave him in peace for a moment until he's only too glad to give notice. Anyhow, I can put a spoke in his wheel. I shall tell my aunt that I admire your patience in working with a great lout like that, and so dirty too."

I showed myself, and Saint-Loup came to greet me, but my confidence in him was shaken since I had heard him speak in a manner so different from anything that I knew. And I wondered whether a person who was capable of acting so cruelly towards some poor wretch might not have played the part of a traitor towards me on his mission to Mme Bontemps. This reflexion served mainly, after he had left, to help me not to regard his failure as a proof that I myself might not succeed. But while he was with me, it was still of the Saint-Loup of old, and especially of the friend who had just come from Mme Bontemps, that I thought. He began by saying: "You feel that I ought to have telephoned to you more often, but I was always told that you were engaged." But the point at which my pain became unendurable was when he said: "To begin where my last telegram left you, after going through a sort of shed, I went into the house and at the end of a long passage was shown into a drawing-room."

At these words, shed, passage, drawing-room, and before he had even finished uttering them, my heart was convulsed more instantaneously than by an electric current, for the force that circles the earth most times in a second is not electricity but pain. How I repeated to myself these words, shed, passage, drawing-room, renewing the shock at will, after Saint-Loup had left me! In a shed one girl can hide with another. And in that drawing-room, who knew what Albertine did when her aunt was not there? Had I then imagined the house in which she was living as incapable of possessing either a shed or a drawing-room? No, I had not imagined it at all, except as a vague dwelling. I had suffered first of all when the place where Albertine was had acquired a geographical identity, when I had learned that, instead of being in two or three possible places, she was in Touraine; those words uttered by her concierge had marked in my heart as upon a map the place where I must suffer. But once I had grown accustomed to the idea that she was in a house in Touraine, I had still not seen the house; never had there occurred to my imagination this appalling idea of a drawing-room, a shed, a passage, which struck me now, facing me in the retina of Saint-Loup's eyes which had seen them, as the rooms in which Albertine came and went, lived her life, as those rooms in particular and not an infinity of possible rooms which had cancelled one another out. With the words shed, passage, drawing-room, I became aware of my folly in having left Albertine for a week in that accursed place whose *existence* (instead of its mere possibility) had just been revealed to me. Alas! when Saint-Loup told me also that in this drawing-room he had heard someone singing at the top of her voice in an adjoining room and that it was Albertine who was singing, I realised with despair that, rid of me at last, she was happy! She had regained her freedom. And I had been thinking that she would come to take the place of Andrée! My grief turned to anger with Saint-Loup.

"That's the one thing in the world I asked you to avoid, that she should know of your coming."

"Do you think it was easy! They assured me that she wasn't in the house. Oh, I know very well that you're not pleased with me, I could tell that from your telegrams. But you're not being fair; I did what I could."

Set free once more, released from the cage in which, here at home, I used to leave her for days on end without letting her come to my room, Albertine had regained all her attraction in my eyes; she had become once more the girl whom everyone pursued, the marvellous bird of the earliest days.

"Anyhow, to sum up—as regards the money, I don't know what to say to you. I found myself addressing a woman who seemed to me to be so scrupulous that I was afraid of offending her. However, she didn't say a word when I mentioned the money. In fact, a little later she told me that she was touched to find that we understood one another so well. And yet everything that she said afterwards was so delicate, so refined, that it seemed to me impossible that she could have been referring to my offer of money when she said: 'We understand one another so well,' for after all I was behaving like a cad."

"But perhaps she didn't understand what you meant, perhaps she didn't hear. You ought to have repeated the offer, because then it would certainly have worked."

"But how could she possibly not have heard? I spoke to her as I'm speaking to you, and she's neither deaf nor mad."

"And she made no comment?"

"None."

"You ought to have repeated the offer."

"How do you mean, repeat it? As soon as we met I saw what sort of person she was. I said to myself that you'd been mistaken, that you were making me commit the most awful gaffe, and that it would be terribly difficult to offer her the money like that. I did it, however, to oblige you, convinced that she'd turn me out of the house."

"But she didn't. Therefore, either she hadn't heard you and you should have started afresh, or you could have pursued the subject."

"You say: 'She hadn't heard,' because you were here in Paris, but, I repeat, if you'd been present at our conversation, there wasn't a sound to interrupt us, I said it quite plainly, it's not possible that she failed to understand."

"But anyhow she's quite convinced that I've always wished to marry her niece?"

"No, as to that, if you want my opinion, she didn't believe that you had any intention of marrying the girl. She told me that you yourself had informed her niece that you wished to leave her. I'm not really sure that she's convinced even now that you want to marry."

This reassured me slightly by showing me that I was in a less humiliating position, and therefore more capable of being still loved, more free to take some decisive action. Nevertheless I was tormented.

"I'm sorry, because I can see you're not pleased," Saint-Loup went on.

"Well, I'm touched by your kindness, and I'm grateful to you, but it seems to me that you might have . . ."

"I did my best. No one else could have done more or even as much. Try sending someone else."

"No, no, as a matter of fact, if I had known I wouldn't have sent you, but the failure of your attempt prevents me from making another."

I heaped reproaches on him: he had tried to do me a service and had not succeeded.

On leaving the Bontemps' house he had met some girls arriving. I had already conjectured often enough that Albertine knew other girls in the neighbourhood; but this was the first time that I felt the pain of that conjecture. It would seem that nature has endowed the mind with the means of secreting a natural antidote which destroys the suppositions that we form unremittingly but without danger to ourselves; but nothing could immunise me against these girls whom Saint-Loup had met. But were not all these details precisely what I had sought to learn from everyone with regard to Albertine? Was it not I who, in order to learn them more fully, had begged Saint-Loup, summoned back to Paris by his colonel, to come and see me at all costs? Was it not I, therefore, who had desired them, or rather my famished grief, longing to feed and to wax fat upon them? Finally Saint-Loup told me that he had had the pleasant surprise of meeting down there—the only familiar face that had reminded him of the past—a former friend of Rachel, a pretty actress who was taking a holiday in the neighbourhood. And the name of this actress was enough to make me say to myself: "Perhaps it's with her"; was enough to make me see, in the very arms of a woman whom I did not know, Albertine smiling and flushed with pleasure. And, after all, why should this not have been so? Had I myself refrained from thinking of other women since I had known Albertine? On the evening of my first visit to the Princesse de Guermantes, when I returned home, had I not been thinking far less of her than of the girl of whom Saint-Loup had told me,

who frequented houses of assignation, and of Mme Putbus's maid? Was it not for the latter that I had returned
to Balbec? More recently, had I not longed to go to
Venice? Why then might Albertine not have longed to go
to Touraine? Only, when it came to the point, as I now
realised, I would not have left her, I would not have gone
to Venice. Indeed, in my heart of hearts, when I said to
myself: "I shall leave her soon," I knew that I would
never leave her, just as I knew that I would never settle
down to work, or live a healthy life, or do any of the
things which, day after day, I vowed to do on the morrow. Only, whatever I might feel in my heart, I had
thought it more adroit to let her live under the perpetual
threat of a separation. And no doubt, thanks to my detestable adroitness, I had convinced her only too well. In
any case, things could not now go on like this; I could not
leave her in Touraine with those girls, with that actress; I
could not endure the thought of that life which eluded
me. I would await her reply to my letter: if she was doing
wrong, alas! a day more or less made no difference (and
perhaps I said this to myself because, being no longer in
the habit of taking note of every minute of her life, a single one of which wherein she was unobserved would formerly have thrown me into a panic, my jealousy no longer
observed the same time-scale). But as soon as I received
her answer, if she was not coming back I would go and
fetch her; willy-nilly, I would tear her away from her
women friends. Besides, was it not better for me to go
down in person, now that I had discovered Saint-Loup's
hitherto unsuspected duplicity? Might he not, for all I
knew, have organised a plot to separate me from Albertine? Was it because I had changed, or because I had

been incapable of imagining then that natural causes would bring me one day to this unprecedented pass? At all events, how I should have lied now had I written to her, as I had said to her in Paris, that I hoped that no accident might befall her! Ah! if some accident had happened to her, my life, instead of being poisoned for ever by this incessant jealousy, would at once regain, if not happiness, at least a state of calm through the suppression of suffering.

The suppression of suffering? Can I really have believed it, have believed that death merely strikes out what exists, and leaves everything else in its place, that it removes the pain from the heart of him for whom the other's existence has ceased to be anything but a source of pain, that it removes the pain and puts nothing in its place? The suppression of pain! As I glanced at the news items in the papers, I regretted that I had not had the courage to form the same wish as Swann. If Albertine could have been the victim of an accident, were she alive I should have had a pretext for hastening to her bedside, were she dead I should have recovered, as Swann said, my freedom to live. Did I believe this? He had believed it, that subtlest of men who thought that he knew himself well. How little do we know of what we have in our hearts! How clearly, a little later, had he been still alive, I could have proved to him that his wish was not only criminal but absurd, that the death of the woman he loved would have delivered him from nothing!

I forsook all pride with regard to Albertine, and sent her a despairing telegram begging her to return on any terms, telling her that she could do whatever she liked, that I asked only to be allowed to take her in my arms for a minute three times a week, before she went to bed. And if she had said once a week only, I would have accepted the restriction.

She never came back. My telegram had just gone off to her when I myself received one. It was from Mme Bontemps. The world is not created once and for all for each of us individually. There are added to it in the course of our lives things of which we have never had any suspicion. Alas! it was not a suppression of suffering that the first two lines of the telegram produced in me: "My poor friend, our little Albertine is no more. Forgive me for breaking this terrible news to you who were so fond of her. She was thrown by her horse against a tree while she was out riding. All our efforts to restore her to life were unavailing. If only I had died in her stead!" No, not the suppression of suffering, but a suffering until then unimagined, that of realising that she would not come back. But had I not told myself many times that she might not come back? I had indeed done so, but now I saw that I had never believed it for a moment. As I needed her presence, her kisses, to enable me to endure the pain that my suspicions caused me, I had formed, since Balbec, the habit of being always with her. Even when she had gone out, when I was alone, I was kissing her still. I had continued to do so since her departure for Touraine. I had less need of her fidelity than of her return. And if my reason might with impunity cast doubt upon it now and again, my imagination never ceased for an instant to picture it for me. Instinctively I drew my hand over my throat, over my lips, which felt themselves kissed by her lips still after she had gone away, and would never be kissed by them again; I drew my hand over them, as Mamma had caressed me at the time of my grandmother's death, saying to me: "My poor boy, your grandmother who was so fond of you will never kiss you again." All my life to come seemed to have been wrenched from my heart. My life to come? Had I not, then, thought at times of living it without Albertine? Of course not! Had I then for a long time past pledged her every minute of my life until my death? I had indeed! This future indissolubly blended with hers was something I had never had the vision to perceive, but now that it had just been demolished, I could feel the place that it occupied in my gaping heart. Françoise, who still knew nothing, came into my room. In a sudden fury I shouted at her: "What do you want?" Then (sometimes there are words that set a different reality in the same place as that which confronts us; they bewilder us in the same way as a fit of dizziness) she said to me: "Monsieur has no need to look cross. On the contrary he's going to be pleased. Here are two letters from Mademoiselle Albertine."

I felt, afterwards, that I must have stared at her with the eyes of a man whose mind has become unhinged. I was not even glad, nor was I incredulous. I was like a person who sees the same place in his room occupied by a sofa and by a grotto: nothing seeming real to him any more, he collapses on the floor. Albertine's two letters must have been written shortly before the fatal ride. The first said:

"My dear, I must thank you for the proof of your confidence which you give me when you tell me of your intention to bring Andrée to live with you. I am sure that she will be delighted to accept, and I think that it will be a very good thing for her. Gifted as she is, she will know how to make the most of the companionship of a man like yourself, and of the admirable influence which you manage to exert over other people. I feel that you have had an idea from which as much good may spring for her as for yourself. And so, if she should make the slightest difficulty (which I do not believe she will), telegraph to me and I will undertake to bring pressure to bear upon her."

The second was dated the following day. (In fact she must have written them both within a few minutes of one another, perhaps at the same time, and must have predated the first. For, all the time, I had been forming absurd ideas of her intentions, which had simply been to return to me, and which anyone not directly interested in the matter, a man without imagination, the negotiator of a peace treaty, the merchant who has to examine a transaction, would have judged more accurately than myself.) It contained only these words:

"Is it too late for me to return to you? If you have not yet written to Andrée, would you be prepared to take me back? I shall abide by your decision, but I beg you not to be long in making it known to me; you can imagine how impatiently I shall be waiting. If it is to tell me to return, I shall take the train at once. Yours with all my heart, Albertine."

For the death of Albertine to have been able to eliminate my suffering, the shock of the fall would have had to kill her not only in Touraine but in myself. There, she had never been more alive. In order to enter into us, another person must first have assumed the form, have adapted himself to the framework of time; appearing to us only in a succession of momentary flashes, he has never been able to reveal to us more than one aspect of himself at a time, to present us with more than a single photograph of himself. A great weakness no doubt for a person, to consist merely of a collection of moments; a great strength also: he is a product of memory, and our memory of a moment is not informed of everything that has happened since; this moment which it has recorded endures still, lives still, and with it the person whose form is outlined in it. And moreover, this disintegration does not only make the dead one live, it multiplies him or her. In order to be consoled I would have to forget, not one, but innumerable Albertines. When I had succeeded in bearing the grief of losing this Albertine, I must begin again with another, with a hundred others.

So then my life was entirely altered. What had constituted its sweetness—not because of Albertine, but concurrently with her, when I was alone—was precisely the perpetual resurgence, at the bidding of identical moments, of moments from the past. From the sound of pattering raindrops I recaptured the scent of the lilacs at Combray; from the shifting of the sun's rays on the balcony the pigeons in the Champs-Elysées; from the muffling of sounds in the heat of the morning hours, the cool taste of cherries; the longing for Brittany or Venice from the noise of the wind and the return of Easter. Summer was at hand, the days were long, the weather was warm. It was the season when, early in the morning, pupils and teachers repair to the public gardens to prepare for the final examinations under the trees, seeking to extract the sole drop of coolness vouchsafed by a sky less ardent than in the midday heat but already as sterilely pure. From my darkened room, with a power of evocation equal to that of former days but capable now of evoking only pain, I felt that outside, in the heaviness of the atmosphere, the setting sun was plastering the vertical fronts of houses and churches with a tawny distemper. And if Françoise, when she came in, accidentally disturbed the folds of the big curtains, I stifled a cry of pain at the rent that had just been made in my heart by that ray of long-ago sunlight which had made beautiful in my eyes the modern façade of Marcouville-l'Orgueilleuse when Albertine had said to me: "It's restored." Not knowing how to account to Françoise for my groan, I said to her: "Oh, I'm so thirsty." She left the room, then returned, but I turned sharply away under the impact of the painful discharge of one of the thousand invisible memories which incessantly exploded around me in the darkness: I had noticed that she had brought me cider and cherries, things which a farm-lad had brought out to us in the carriage, at Balbec, "kinds" in which I should have made the most perfect communion, in those days, with the prismatic gleam in shuttered dining-rooms on days of scorching heat. Then I thought for the first time of the farm called Les Ecorres, and said to myself that on certain days when Albertine had told me, at Balbec, that she would not be free, that she was obliged to go somewhere with her aunt, she had perhaps been with one or another of her girlfriends at some farm to which she knew that I was not in the habit of going, and, while I waited desperately for her at Marie-Antoinette where they told me: "No, we haven't seen her today," had been saying to her friend the same words as she used to say to me when we went out together: "He'll never think of looking for us here, so there's no fear of our being disturbed." I told Françoise to draw the cur-

tains together, so that I would no longer see that ray of
sunlight. But it continued to filter through, just as corro-
sively, into my memory. "It doesn't appeal to me, it's
been restored, but tomorrow we'll go to Saint-Mars-le-
Vêtu, and the day after to . . ." Tomorrow, the day after, it was a prospect of life together, perhaps for ever,
that was opening up; my heart leapt towards it, but it was
no longer there, Albertine was dead.

I asked Françoise the time. Six o'clock. At last, thank
God, that oppressive heat, of which in the past I used to
complain to Albertine and which we so enjoyed, was
about to die down. The day was drawing to its close. But
what did that profit me? The cool evening air was rising;
it was sunset; in my memory, at the end of a road which
we had taken, she and I, on our way home, I saw it now,
beyond the furthest village, like some distant place, inaccessible that evening, which we would spend at Balbec,
still together. Together then; now I must stop short on
the brink of that same abyss; she was dead. It was not
enough now to draw the curtains; I tried to stop the eyes
and ears of my memory in order not to see that band of
orange in the western sky, in order not to hear those invisible birds responding from one tree to the next on either side of me who was then so tenderly embraced by
her who was now dead. I tried to avoid those sensations
that are produced by the dampness of leaves in the
evening air, the rise and fall of humpback roads. But already those sensations had gripped me once more, carrying me far enough back from the present moment to give
the necessary recoil, the necessary momentum to strike me
anew, to the idea that Albertine was dead. Ah! never
again would I enter a forest, never again would I stroll be-

neath the trees. But would the broad plains be less painful to me? How often had I crossed, on the way to fetch Albertine, how often had I retrodden, on the way back with her, the great plain of Cricqueville, sometimes in foggy weather when the swirling mists gave us the illusion of being surrounded by a vast lake, sometimes on limpid evenings when the moonlight, dematerialising the earth, making it appear from a few feet away as celestial as it is, in the daytime, in the distance only, enclosed the fields and the woods with the firmament to which it had assimilated them in the moss-agate of a universal blue!

Françoise must have been pleased by Albertine's death, and in fairness to her it should be said that by a sort of tact and decorum she made no pretence of sorrow. But the unwritten laws of her immemorial code and the tradition of the mediaeval peasant woman who weeps as in the romances of chivalry were older than her hatred of Albertine and even of Eulalie. Thus, on one of these late afternoons, as I was not quick enough in concealing my distress, she caught sight of my tears, prompted by her instinct as a former peasant girl which at one time had led her to catch and maltreat animals, to feel nothing but merriment in wringing the necks of chickens and in boiling lobsters alive, and, when I was ill, in observing, as it might be the wounds that she had inflicted on an owl, my suffering expression which she afterwards proclaimed in a sepulchral tone as a presage of coming disaster. But her Combray "unwritten law" did not permit her to treat tears and sorrow lightly—things which in her judgment were as fatal as shedding one's flannel vest or toying with one's food. "Oh, no, Monsieur, it doesn't do to cry like that, it isn't good for you." And in trying to stem my tears she looked as anxious as if they had been torrents of blood. Unfortunately I adopted a chilly air that cut short the effusions in which she was hoping to indulge and which might well have been sincere. Her attitude towards Albertine was perhaps akin to her attitude towards Eulalie, and, now that my mistress could no longer derive any profit from me, Françoise had ceased to hate her. She felt bound, however, to let me see that she was perfectly well aware that I was crying, and that, following the deplorable example set by my family, I did not wish to "show it." "You mustn't cry, Monsieur," she adjured me, in a calmer tone this time, and with the intention of proving her perspicacity rather than displaying her pity. And she added: "It was bound to happen; she was too happy, poor creature, she never knew how happy she was."

How slow the day is in dying on these interminable summer evenings! A pale ghost of the house opposite continued indefinitely to tinge the sky with its persistent whiteness. At last it was dark in the apartment; I stumbled against the furniture in the hall, but in the door that opened on to the staircase, in the midst of the darkness I had thought to be complete, the glazed panel was translucent and blue, with the blueness of a flower, the blueness of an insect's wing, a blueness that would have seemed to me beautiful had I not felt it to be a last glint, sharp as a steel blade, a final blow that was being dealt me, in its indefatigable cruelty, by the day. Finally, however, complete darkness came, but then a glimpse of a star behind the tree in the courtyard was enough to remind me of the times when we used to set out in a carriage, after dinner, for the woods of Chantepie, carpeted with moonlight. And even in the streets I might chance to isolate upon the back of a bench, to glean the natural purity of a moon-beam in the midst of the artificial lights of Paris—of Paris over which, by restoring the city for a moment, in my imagination, to a state of nature, with the infinite silence of the fields thus evoked, it enthroned the heart-rending memory of the walks that I had taken there with Albertine. Ah! when would the night end? But at the first coolness of dawn I shivered, for it had brought back to me the sweetness of that summer when, from Balbec to Incarville, from Incarville to Balbec, we had so many times escorted each other home until daybreak. I had now only one hope left for the future—a hope far more poignant than any fear—and that was that I might forget Albertine. I knew that I should forget her one day; I had forgotten Gilberte and Mme de Guermantes; I had forgotten my grandmother. And it is our most just and cruel punishment for that forgetfulness, as total and as tranquil as the oblivion of the graveyard, through which we have detached ourselves from those we no longer love, that we should recognise it to be inevitable in the case of those we love still. In reality, we know that it is not a painful state but a state of indifference. But not being able to think at one and the same time of what I was and of what I would be, I thought with despair of all that integument of ca-resses, of kisses, of friendly slumber, of which I must presently let myself be stripped for ever. The influx of these tender memories, breaking against the idea that Al-bertine was dead, oppressed me with such a clash of war-ring currents that I could not remain still; I rose, but all of a sudden I stopped, overwhelmed; the same faint day-break that I used to see when I had just left Albertine, still radiant and warm from her kisses, had just drawn above the curtains its now sinister blade whose whiteness, cold, implacable and compact, glinted like a dagger thrust into my heart.

Presently the sounds from the street would begin, enabling me to tell from the qualitative scale of their sonorities the degree of the steadily increasing heat in which they resounded. But in this heat which a few hours later would become saturated with the fragrance of cherries, what I found (as in a medicine which the substitution of one ingredient for another is sufficient to transform from the stimulant and tonic that it was into a depressant) was no longer the desire for women but the anguish of Albertine's departure. Besides, the memory of all my desires was as much impregnated with her, and with suffering, as the memory of my pleasures. Venice, where I had thought that her company would be irksome (doubtless because I had felt in a confused way that it would be necessary to me), no longer attracted me now that Albertine was no more. Albertine had seemed to me to be an obstacle interposed between me and all other things, because she was for me their container, and it was from her alone, as from a vase, that I could receive them. Now that this vase was shattered, I no longer felt that I had the courage to grasp things, and there was not one of them from which I did not now turn away, despondent, preferring not to taste it. So that my separation from her did not in the least throw open to me the field of possible pleasures which I had imagined to be closed to me by her presence. Besides, the obstacle which her presence had perhaps indeed been in the way of my travelling and enjoying life had merely (as always happens) concealed from me other obstacles which reappeared intact now that this one had been removed.

Likewise, in the past, when some friendly call had prevented me from working, if on the following day I was left undisturbed I did not work any better. Let an illness, a duel, a runaway horse make us see death face to face, and how richly we should have enjoyed the life of pleasure, the travels in unknown lands, which are about to be snatched from us! And no sooner is the danger past than we resume once more the same dull life in which none of those delights existed for us.

No doubt these short summer nights last only for a brief season. Winter would at length return, when I should no longer have to dread the memory of drives with her until the too early dawn. But would not the first frosts bring back to me, preserved in their ice, the germ of my first desires, when at midnight I used to send for her, when the time seemed so long until I heard her ring at the door, a sound for which I might now wait everlastingly in vain? Would they not bring back to me the germ of my first anxieties, when twice I thought she would not come? At that time I saw her only rarely, but even those intervals between her visits which made her suddenly appear, after many weeks, from the heart of an unknown life which I made no attempt to possess, ensured my peace of mind by preventing the first inklings, constantly interrupted, of my jealousy from coagulating, from forming a solid mass in my heart. Soothing though they may have been at the time, in retrospect those intervals were stamped with pain since the unknown things she might have done in the course of them had ceased to be a matter of indifference to me, and especially now that no visit from her would ever occur again; so that those January evenings on which she used to come, and which for that reason had been so dear to me, would inject into me now with their biting winds an anxiety which was unknown to me then, and would bring back to me (but now grown pernicious) the first germ of my love. And when I thought how I would see the return of that cold season which, since the time of Gilberte and our games in the Champs-Elysées, had always seemed to me so melancholy, when I thought how evenings would come back like that snowy evening when I had waited in vain for Albertine far into the night, then, like an invalid—in his case physically, fearing for his chest, in my case mentally—what at such moments I still dreaded most, for my grief, for my heart, was the return of the intense cold, and I said to myself that what it would be hardest to live through was perhaps the winter.

Linked as it was to each of the seasons, in order for me to discard the memory of Albertine I should have had to forget them all, even if it meant having to get to know them all over again, like an old man learning to read again after a stroke; I should have had to renounce the entire universe. Nothing, I told myself, but a veritable extinction of myself would be capable (but that is impossible) of consoling me for hers. It did not occur to me that the death of oneself is neither impossible nor extraordinary; it is effected without our knowledge, even against our will, every day of our lives. And I should have to suffer from the recurrence of all sorts of days which not only nature, but adventitious circumstances, a purely conventional order, introduce into a season. Soon the date would return on which I had gone to Balbec, that last summer, and when my love, which was not yet inseparable from jealousy and did not concern itself with what Albertine was doing all day, was to undergo so many evolutions, before becoming that very different love of recent months, that this final year, in which Albertine's destiny had begun to change and had come to an end, appeared to me as full, as diverse and as vast as a whole century. Then it would be the memory of days more dilatory but dating from still earlier years, the rainy Sundays on which nevertheless everyone else had gone out, in the emptiness of the afternoon, when the sound of wind and rain would in the past have bidden me stay at home, to "philosophise in my garret"; with what anxiety would I see the hour approach at which Albertine, so little expected, had come to visit me, had caressed me for the first time, breaking off when Françoise had brought in the lamp, in that time now doubly dead when it had been Albertine who was curious about me, when my tenderness for her could legitimately cherish so many hopes! And even, later in the season, those glorious evenings when offices and girls' schools, half open like chapels, bathed in a golden dust, enable the street to crown itself with those demi-goddesses who, conversing not far from us with others of their kind, fill us with a feverish longing to penetrate into their mythological existence, now reminded me only of the tenderness of Albertine, whose presence by my side had been an obstacle to my approaching them.

Moreover, to the memory even of hours that were purely natural would inevitably be added the psychological background that makes each of them a thing apart. When, later on, I should hear the goatherd's horn, on a first fine almost Italian morning, that same day would blend alternately with its sunshine the anxiety of knowing that Albertine was at the Trocadéro, possibly with Léa

and the two girls, then the homely, familial sweetness, almost that of a wife who seemed to me then an embarrassment and whom Françoise was bringing home to me.
That telephone message from Françoise which had conveyed to me the dutiful homage of an Albertine returning
with her had seemed to me then to be a matter for pride.
I was mistaken. If it had exhilarated me, it was because it
had made me feel that she whom I loved was really mine,
lived only for me, and even at a distance, without my
needing to occupy my mind with her, regarded me as her
lord and master, returning home at a sign from me. And
thus that telephone message had been a fragment of
sweetness, coming to me from afar, sent out from that
Trocadéro district where there happened to be, for me,
sources of happiness directing towards me molecules of
comfort, healing balms, restoring to me at length so precious an equanimity of mind that I need do no more—
surrendering myself without the slightest qualm or
reservation to Wagner's music—than await the certain
arrival of Albertine, without anxiety, with an entire absence of impatience in which I had not had the perspicacity to recognise happiness. And the cause of this
happiness at the knowledge of her returning home, of her
obeying me and belonging to me, lay in love and not in
pride. It would have been quite immaterial to me now to
have at my behest fifty women returning, at a sign from
me, not from the Trocadéro but from the Indies. But that
day, thinking of Albertine coming dutifully home to me
as I sat alone in my room making music, I had breathed
in one of those substances, scattered like motes in a sun-
beam, which, just as others are salutary to the body, do
good to the soul. Then there had been, half an hour later,

the arrival of Albertine, then the drive with Albertine, both of which had seemed to me boring because they were accompanied for me by certainty, but which, because of that very certainty, had, from the moment of Françoise's telephoning to me that she was bringing Albertine home, poured a golden calm over the hours that followed, had made of them as it were a second day, wholly unlike the first, because it had a very different emotional basis, an emotional basis which made it a uniquely original day, one to be added to the variety of the days that I had previously known, a day which I should never have been able to imagine—any more than we could imagine the delicious idleness of a summer day if such days did not exist in the calendar of those through which we have lived—a day of which I could not say absolutely that I recalled it, for to this calm I added now an anguish which I had not felt at the time. But much later, when I went back gradually, in reverse order, over the times through which I had passed before I had come to love Albertine so much, when my healed heart could detach itself without suffering from Albertine dead, then I was able to recall at length without suffering that day on which Albertine had gone shopping with Françoise instead of remaining at the Trocadéro; I recalled it with pleasure as belonging to an emotional season which I had not known until then; I recalled it at last exactly, no longer injecting it with suffering, but rather, on the contrary, as we recall certain days in summer which we found too hot while they lasted, and from which only after they have passed do we extract their unalloyed essence of pure gold and indestructible azure.

So that these few years imposed upon my memory of

Albertine, which made them so painful, successive colourings, the different modulations, the embers, not only of
their seasons or of their hours, from late afternoons in
June to winter evenings, from moonlight on the sea to
daybreak on the way home, from snow in Paris to fallen
leaves at Saint-Cloud, but also of each of the particular
ideas of Albertine that I successively formed, of the physical aspect in which I pictured her at each of those moments, the degree of frequency with which I had seen her
during that season, which itself appeared consequently
more or less dispersed or compact, the anxieties which she
might have caused me by keeping me waiting, the desire
which I had for her at such and such a moment, the
hopes formed and then shattered—all this modified the
character of my retrospective sadness fully as much as
the impressions of light or of perfume which were associated with it, and complemented each of the solar years
through which I had lived and which, simply with their
springs, their autumns, their winters, were already so sad
because of the inseparable memory of her, endowed it
with a sort of sentimental counterpart in which the hours
were defined not by the sun's position, but by the time
spent waiting for a rendezvous, in which the length of the
days or the changes in the temperature were measured by
the soaring of my hopes, the progress of our intimacy, the
gradual transformation of her face, the journeys she had
made, the frequency and style of the letters she had written me during her absence, her eagerness, greater or
lesser, to see me on her return. And lastly, if these
changes of weather, these variegated days, each brought
me back a different Albertine, it was not only through the
evocation of similar moments. It will be remembered that

always, even before I began to love, each season had made me a different person, having other desires because he had other perceptions, a person who, having dreamed only of cliffs and storms overnight, if the indiscreet spring daybreak had insinuated a scent of roses through the gaps in the ill-fitting enclosure of his sleep, would wake up on the way to Italy. Even in the course of my love, had not the volatile state of my emotional climate, the varying pressure of my beliefs, had they not one day reduced the visibility of the love that I was feeling, and the next day indefinitely extended it, one day embellished it to a smile, another day condensed it to a storm? We exist only by virtue of what we possess, we possess only what is really present to us, and many of our memories, our moods, our ideas sail away on a voyage of their own until they are lost to sight! Then we can no longer take them into account in the total which is our personality. But they know of secret paths by which to return to us. And on certain nights, having gone to sleep almost without missing Albertine any more—we can only miss what we remember—on awakening I found a whole fleet of memories which had come to cruise upon the surface of my clearest consciousness and which I could distinguish perfectly. Then I wept over what I could see so plainly, though the night before it had been non-existent to me. In an instant, Albertine's name, her death, had changed their meaning; her betrayals had suddenly resumed their old importance.

How could she have seemed dead to me when now, in order to think of her, I had at my disposal only those same images one or other of which I used to recall when she was alive? Either swift-moving and bent over the mythological wheel of her bicycle, strapped on rainy days inside the warrior tunic of her waterproof which moulded her breasts, her head turbaned and dressed with snakes, when she spread terror through the streets of Balbec; or else on the evenings when we had taken champagne into the woods of Chantepie, her voice provocative and altered, her face suffused with warm pallor, reddened only on the cheekbones, and when, unable to make it out in the darkness of the carriage, I drew her into the moonlight in order to see it more clearly, the face I was now trying in vain to recapture, to see again in a darkness that would never end. A little statuette on the drive to the island in the Bois, a still and plump face with coarse-grained skin at the pianola, she was thus by turns rain-soaked and swift, provoking and diaphanous, motionless and smiling, an angel of music. In this way each one was attached to a moment, to the date of which I found myself carried back when I saw again that particular Albertine. And these moments of the past do not remain still; they retain in our memory the motion which drew them towards the future—towards a future which has itself become the past—drawing us along in their train. Never had I caressed the waterproofed Albertine of the rainy days; I wanted to ask her to take off that armour, in order to experience with her the love of the tented field, the fraternity of travel. But this was no longer possible, for she was dead. Neither, for fear of corrupting her, had I ever shown any sign of comprehension on the evenings when she seemed to be offering me pleasures which, but for my self-restraint, she might not perhaps have sought from others, and which aroused in me now a frantic desire. I should not have found them the same in any other woman, but I might scour the whole world now without encountering the woman who was prepared to give them to me, for Albertine was dead. It seemed that I had to choose between two facts, to decide which of them was true, to such an extent was the fact of Albertine's death—arising for me from a reality which I had not known, her life in Touraine—in contradiction with all my thoughts of her, my desires, my regrets, my tenderness, my rage, my jealousy. So great a wealth of memories borrowed from the treasury of her life, such a profusion of feelings evoking, implicating her life, seemed to make it incredible that Albertine should be dead. Such a profusion of feelings, for my memory, in preserving my affection, left it all its variety. It was not Albertine alone who was a succession of moments, it was also myself. My love for her was not simple: to a curiosity about the unknown had been added a sensual desire, and to a feeling of almost conjugal sweetness, at one moment indifference, at another a furious jealousy. I was not one man only, but as it were the march-past of a composite army in which there were passionate men, indifferent men, jealous men—jealous men not one of whom was jealous of the same woman. And no doubt it would be from this that one day would come the cure for which I had no wish. In a composite mass, the elements may one by one, without our noticing it, be replaced by others, which others again eliminate, until in the end a change has been brought about which it would be impossible to conceive if we were a single person. The complexity of my love, of my person, multiplied and diversified my sufferings. And yet they could still be ranged in the two categories whose alternation had made up the whole life of my love for Albertine, swayed alternately by trust and by jealous suspicion.

If I found it difficult to imagine that Albertine, so alive in me (wearing as I did the double harness of the present and the past), was dead, perhaps it was equally paradoxical in me that this suspicion of the misdeeds which Albertine, stripped now of the flesh that had enjoyed them, of the mind that had conceived the desire for them, was no longer either capable of or responsible for, should excite in me such suffering, which I should only have blessed could I have seen it as the token of the spiritual reality of a person materially non-existent, instead of the reflexion, destined itself to fade, of impressions that she had made on me in the past. A woman who could no longer experience pleasures with others ought no longer to have excited my jealousy, if only my tenderness had been able to come to the surface. But it was precisely this that was impossible, since it could not find its object, Albertine, except among memories in which she was still alive. Since, merely by thinking of her, I brought her back to life, her infidelities could never be those of a dead woman, the moment at which she had committed them becoming the present moment, not only for Albertine, but for that one of my various selves thus suddenly evoked who happened to be thinking of her. So that no anachronism could ever separate the indissoluble couple, in which each new culprit was immediately mated with a jealous lover, pitiable and always contemporaneous. I had, during the last months, kept her shut up in my own house. But in my imagination now, Albertine was free; she was abusing her freedom, was prostituting herself to this person or that. Formerly, I used constantly to think of the uncertainty of the future that stretched before us, and endeavour to read its message. And now, what lay ahead of me, like a counterpart of the future—as worrying as the future because it was equally uncertain, equally difficult to decipher, equally mysterious, and crueller still because I did not have, as with the future, the possibility, or the illusion, of influencing it, and also because it would go on unfolding throughout the whole length of my life without my companion's being present to soothe the anguish that it caused me—was no longer Albertine's future, it was her past. Her past? That is the wrong word, since for jealousy there can be neither past nor future, and what it imagines is invariably the present.

Atmospheric changes, provoking other changes in the inner man, awaken forgotten selves, counteract the torpor of habit, restore their old force to certain memories, to certain sufferings. How much more so with me if this change of weather recalled to me the weather in which Albertine, at Balbec, in the lashing rain, had set out, heaven knows why, on long rides, in the clinging tunic of her waterproof! If she had lived, no doubt today, in this so similar weather, she would be setting out on a comparable expedition in Touraine. Since she could do so no longer, I ought not to have suffered from the thought; but, as with people who have lost a limb, the slightest change in the weather revived the pain I felt in the limb that no longer existed.

Then a recollection that had not come back to me for a long time—for it had remained dissolved in the fluid and invisible expanse of my memory—suddenly crystallised. Many years ago, when somebody mentioned her bath-wrap, Albertine had blushed. At that time I was not jealous of her. But since then I had intended to ask her if she could remember that conversation, and why she had blushed. It had preoccupied me all the more because I had been told that the two girls who were friends of Léa's frequented the bathing establishment of the hotel, and, it was said, not merely for the purpose of taking showers. But, for fear of annoying Albertine, or else pending some more opportune moment, I had always put off mentioning it to her and in time had ceased to think about it. And all of a sudden, some time after Albertine's death, I recalled this memory, stamped with the character, at once tormenting and solemn, of puzzles left for ever insoluble by the death of the one person who could have explained them. Might I not at least try to find out whether Albertine had ever done anything wrong or even behaved suspiciously in that bathing establishment? By sending someone to Balbec, I might perhaps succeed in doing so. Had she been alive, I should doubtless have been unable to learn anything. But tongues become strangely loosened and will readily talk about a misdeed when the culprit's resentment need no longer be feared. As the constitution of our imagination, which has remained rudimentary and over-simplified (not having undergone the countless transformations which improve upon the primitive models of human inventions, whether it be the barometer, the balloon, the telephone, or anything else, which become barely recognisable in their ultimate perfection), allows us to see only a very few things at one time, the memory of the bathing establishment occupied the whole field of my inner vision. It was as though nothing else had ever happened in the whole of Albertine's life.

Sometimes I came into collision in the dark lanes of sleep with one of those bad dreams which are not very serious because for one thing the sadness they engender lasts for barely an hour after we awake, like the faintness caused by an artificial soporific, and for another we encounter them only very rarely, no more than once in two or three years. And, moreover, it remains uncertain whether we have encountered them before, whether they have not rather that aspect of not being seen for the first time which is projected on to them by an illusion, a subdivision (for duplication would not be a strong enough term). Of course, since I entertained doubts as to the life and the death of Albertine, I ought long since to have begun to make inquiries, but the same lassitude, the same cowardice which had made me give way to Albertine when she was with me prevented me from undertaking anything since I had ceased to see her. And yet, from a weakness that has dragged on for years, a flash of energy sometimes emerges. I decided to make this investigation at least, partial though it was.

I wondered who I could best send down to make inquiries on the spot, at Balbec. Aimé seemed to me to be a suitable person. Apart from his thorough knowledge of the place, he belonged to that category of working-class people who have a keen eye to their own advantage, are loyal to those they serve and indifferent to any form of morality, and of whom—because, if we pay them well, they prove themselves, in their obedience to our will, as incapable of indiscretion, lethargy or dishonesty as they are devoid of scruples—we say: "They are excellent people." In such we can have absolute confidence. When Aimé had gone, I thought how much more to the point it

would have been if I could now interrogate Albertine herself about what he was going to try to find out down
there. And at once the thought of this question which I
would have liked to put, which it seemed to me that I was
about to put to her, having brought Albertine to my side,
not by dint of a conscious effort of resuscitation but as
though by one of those chance encounters which, as is the
case with photographs that are not posed, with snapshots,
always make the person appear more alive, at the same
time as I imagined our conversation I became aware of its
impossibility; I had just approached from a new angle the
idea that Albertine was dead, Albertine who inspired in
me that tenderness we feel for absent ones the sight of
whom does not come to correct the embellished image, inspiring also sorrow at the thought that this absence was
eternal and that the poor child had been deprived for ever
of the joys of life. And immediately, by an abrupt transposition, from the torments of jealousy I passed to the despair of separation.

What filled my heart now, instead of odious suspicions, was the affectionate memory of hours of confiding
tenderness spent with the sister that her death had really
deprived me of, since my grief was related not to what
Albertine had been to me, but to what my heart, anxious
to participate in the most general emotions of love, had
gradually persuaded me that she was; then I became
aware that the life that had bored me so (or so I thought)
had been on the contrary delightful; the briefest moments
spent in talking to her about even the most trivial things
were now augmented, blended with a pleasure which at
the time—it is true—had not been perceived by me, but
which was already the cause of my having sought those

moments so persistently to the exclusion of any others; the most trivial incidents which I recalled, a movement she had made in the carriage by my side, or when sitting down to dinner facing me in her room, sent through my heart a surge of sweet sadness which gradually overwhelmed it altogether.

That room in which we used to dine had never seemed to me attractive; I had told Albertine that it was, merely in order that she should be content to live in it. Now, the curtains, the chairs, the books, had ceased to be a matter of indifference to me. Art is not alone in imparting charm and mystery to the most insignificant things; pain is endowed with the same power to bring them into intimate relation with ourselves. At the time I had paid no attention to the dinner which we had eaten together after our return from the Bois, before I went to the Verdurins', and towards the beauty, the solemn sweetness of which I now turned with my eyes full of tears. An impression of love is out of proportion to the other impressions of life, but when it is lost in their midst we are incapable of appreciating it. It is not from immediately below, in the tumult of the street and amid the thronging houses nearby, but when we have moved away, that, from the slope of a neighbouring hill, at a distance from which the whole town seems to have vanished or forms only a confused heap at ground level, we can appreciate, in the calm detachment of solitude and dusk, the towering splendour of a cathedral, unique, enduring and pure. I tried to embrace the image of Albertine through my tears as I thought of all the serious and sensible things that she had said that evening.

One morning, I thought I saw the oblong shape of a

hill swathed in mist, and sniffed the warm odour of a cup of chocolate, while my heart was horribly wrung by the memory of the afternoon on which Albertine had come to see me and I had kissed her for the first time: the fact was that I had heard the hiccuping of the hot-water system which had just been turned on. And I flung angrily away an invitation which Françoise brought me from Mme Verdurin. How much more forcibly the impression I had felt when I went to dine for the first time at La Raspelière, that death does not strike us all at the same age, overcame me now that Albertine had died so young, while Brichot continued to dine with Mme Verdurin who was still entertaining and would perhaps continue to entertain for many years to come! At once the name of Brichot recalled to me the close of that same evening when he had accompanied me home, when I had seen from the street below the light of Albertine's lamp. I had already thought of it many times, but I had not approached this memory from the same angle. For, if our memories do indeed belong to us, they do so after the fashion of those country properties which have little hidden gates of which we ourselves are often unaware, and which someone in the neighbourhood opens for us, so that from one direction at least which is new to us, we find ourselves back in our own house. Then, when I thought of the void which I should now find on returning home, when I realised that never again would I see Albertine's window from below, that its light was extinguished for ever, I remembered how that evening, on leaving Brichot, I had felt irritated and regretful at my inability to roam the streets and make love elsewhere, and I saw how greatly I had been mistaken, that it was only because the treasure whose reflexions came down to me from above had seemed to be entirely in my possession that I had failed to appreciate its value, so that it appeared necessarily inferior to pleasures, however slight, whose value I estimated in seeking to imagine them. I understood how much this light, which seemed to me to issue from a prison, contained for me a plenitude of life and sweetness, this light which had intoxicated me for a moment, and then on the evening when Albertine had slept under the same roof as me, at Balbec, had appeared for ever impossible. I was perceiving that this life I had led in Paris, in a home of mine which was also a home of hers, was precisely the realisation of that profound peace I had dreamt of.

Remembering the conversation I had had with Albertine after our return from the Bois before that last party at the Verdurins', I would have been inconsolable had I felt that it had never occurred, that conversation which had to some extent involved Albertine in my intellectual life and in certain respects had made us one. For no doubt, if I returned with tender emotion to her intelligence and her sweetness to me, it was not because they had been any greater than those of other persons whom I had known; had not Mme de Cambremer said to me at Balbec: "What! you could be spending your days with Elstir, who is a genius, and you spend them with your cousin!" Albertine's intelligence pleased me because, by association, it reminded me of what I called her sweetness, as we call the sweetness of a fruit a certain sensation which exists only in our palate. And in fact, when I thought of Albertine's intelligence, my lips instinctively protruded and savoured a memory of which I preferred that the reality should remain external to me and should consist in the objective superiority of a person. There could be no denying that I had known people whose intelligence was greater. But the infinitude of love, or its egoism, brings it about that the people whom we love are those whose intellectual and moral physiognomy is least objectively defined in our eyes; we alter them incessantly to suit our desires and fears, we do not separate them from ourselves, they are simply a vast, vague arena in which to exteriorise our emotions. We do not have as clear an outline of our own body, into which so many sensations of pain and pleasure perpetually flow, as we have of a tree or a house or a passer-by. And where I had been wrong was perhaps in not making a greater effort to know Albertine in herself. Just as, from the point of view of her charm, I had long considered only the different positions that she occupied in my memory on the plane of the years, and had been surprised to see that she had become spontaneously enriched with modifications which were not due merely to the difference of perspective, so I ought to have sought to understand her character as that of an ordinary person, and thus perhaps, grasping the reason for her persistence in keeping her secret from me, might have avoided prolonging between us, through that strange tenacity, the conflict which had led to her death. And I then felt, together with an intense pity for her, a shame at having survived her. It seemed to me indeed, in the hours when I suffered least, that I had somehow benefited from her death, for a woman is of greater utility to our life if, instead of being an element of happiness in it, she is an instrument of suffering, and there is not a woman in the world the possession of whom is as precious as that of the truths which she reveals to us by causing us to suffer. In these moments, juxtaposing the deaths of my grand-mother and of Albertine, I felt that my life was defiled by a double murder from which only the cowardice of the world could absolve me. I had dreamed of being under-stood by Albertine, of not being misjudged by her, think-ing that it was for the great happiness of being understood, of not being misjudged, when so many other people could have done it better. One wants to be under-stood because one wants to be loved, and one wants to be loved because one loves. The understanding of others is a matter of indifference to us and their love importunate. My joy at having possessed a little of Albertine's intelli-gence and of her heart arose not from their intrinsic worth, but from the fact that this possession was a stage further towards the complete possession of Albertine, a possession which had been my goal and my chimera ever since the day when I had first set eyes on her. When we speak of the "niceness" of a woman, we are doing no more perhaps than project outside ourselves the pleasure that we feel in seeing her, like children when they say: "My dear little bed, my dear little pillow, my dear little hawthorns." Which explains, incidentally, why men never say of a woman who is not unfaithful to them: "She is so nice," and say it so often of a woman by whom they are betrayed.

Mme de Cambremer was right in thinking that El-stir's intellectual charm was greater. But one cannot judge in the same way the charm of a person who is external to oneself like every other person, painted upon the horizon of one's mind, and that of a person who, as a result of an error in localisation consequent upon certain accidents but nevertheless tenacious, has lodged herself in one's own body to the point where wondering retrospectively whether or not she looked at a woman on a particular day in the corridor of a little seaside railway-train causes one the same pain as would a surgeon probing for a bullet in one's heart. A simple slice of bread, but one that we eat, gives us more pleasure than all the ortolans, leverets and rock-partridges that were set before Louis XV, and the blade of grass quivering a few inches in front of our eyes as we lie on the hillside may conceal from us the vertiginous summit of a mountain if the latter is several miles away.

Moreover, our error does not lie in prizing the intelligence and amiability of a woman whom we love, however slight they may be. Our error is to remain indifferent to the amiability and intelligence of others. Falsehood begins to cause us the indignation, and kindness the gratitude, which they ought always to arouse in us, only if they come from a woman whom we love, and physical desire has the marvellous faculty of giving intelligence its true value and providing solid foundations for the moral life. Never should I find again that divine thing, a person with whom I could talk freely of everything, in whom I could confide. Confide? But did not others offer me greater confidence than Albertine? With others, did I not have more extensive conversations? The fact is that confidence and conversation are ordinary things in themselves, and what does it matter if they are less than perfect if only there enters into them love, which alone is divine. I could see Albertine now, seated at her pianola, pink-faced beneath her dark hair; I could feel against my lips, which she would try to part, her tongue, her maternal, incomestible, nutritious, hallowed tongue, whose secret dewy flame, even when she merely ran it over the surface of my neck or my stomach, gave to those caresses of hers, superficial but somehow imparted by the inside of her flesh, externalised like a piece of material reversed to show its lining, as it were the mysterious sweetness of a penetration.

I cannot even say that what I felt at the loss of all those moments of sweetness which nothing could ever restore to me was despair. To feel despair, we must still be attached to that life which can no longer be anything but unhappy. I had been in despair at Balbec when I saw the day break and realised that none of the days to come could ever be a happy one for me. I had remained just as selfish since then, but the self to which I was now attached, the self which constituted those vital reserves that bring the instinct of self-preservation into play, this self was no longer alive; when I thought of my inner strength, of my vital force, of what was best in me, I thought of a certain treasure which I had possessed (which I had been alone in possessing since others could not know exactly the feeling, hidden within myself, that it had inspired in me) and which no one could ever again take from me since I possessed it no longer. And in fact I had only ever possessed it because I had wanted to imagine myself as possessing it. I had not merely committed the imprudence, in looking at Albertine with my lips and lodging the treasure in my heart, of making it live within me, and that other imprudence of combining a domestic love with the pleasure of the senses. I had sought also to persuade myself that our relations were love, that we were mutually practising the relations that are called love, because she obediently returned the kisses that I gave her. And through having acquired the habit of believing this, I had lost not merely a woman whom I loved but a woman who loved me, my sister, my child, my tender mistress. And on the whole I had had a happiness and a misfortune which Swann had not experienced, for, after all, during the whole of the time in which he had loved Odette and had been so jealous of her, he had barely seen her, having found it so difficult, on certain days when she put him off at the last moment, to gain admission to her. But afterwards he had had her to himself, as his wife, and until the day of his death. I, on the contrary, while I was so jealous of Albertine, more fortunate than Swann, had had her with me in my own house. I had experienced in actuality what Swann had so often dreamed of and had experienced only when he had become indifferent to it. But, after all, I had not managed to keep Albertine as he had kept Odette. She had gone, she was dead. For nothing ever repeats itself exactly, and the most analogous lives which, thanks to kinship of character and similarity of circumstances, we may select in order to represent them as symmetrical, remain in many respects opposed. By losing my life I should not have lost very much; I should have lost only an empty form, the empty frame of a work of art. Indifferent as to what I might henceforth put into it, but happy and proud to think of what it had contained, I dwelt upon the memory of those hours of sweetness, and this moral support gave me a feeling of well-being which the approach of death itself would not have disturbed.

How she used to hasten to see me at Balbec when I sent for her, lingering only to sprinkle scent on her hair to please me! These images of Balbec and Paris which I loved thus to see again were the pages, still so recent, and so quickly turned, of her short life. All this, which for me

was only memory, had been for her action, action speeding headlong, as in a tragedy, towards a swift death. For
people develop in one way inside us, but in another way
outside us (I had felt this strongly on those evenings when
I remarked in Albertine an enrichment of qualities which
was due not only to my memory), and these two ways inevitably react upon each other. Although, in seeking to
know Albertine, then to possess her entirely, I had merely
obeyed the need to reduce by experiment to elements
meanly akin to those of our own ego the mystery of every
being, I had been unable to do so without in my turn influencing Albertine's life. Perhaps my wealth, the
prospect of a brilliant marriage, had attracted her; my
jealousy had kept her; her kindness, or her intelligence, or
her sense of guilt, or her shrewd cunning, had made her
accept, and had led me on to make harsher and harsher, a
captivity in chains forged simply by the internal development of my mental toil, but which had none the less had
repercussions on Albertine's life, themselves destined, by
a natural backlash, to pose new and ever more painful
problems to my psychology, since from my prison she
had escaped to go and kill herself on a horse which but
for me she would not have owned, leaving me, even after
she was dead, with suspicions the verification of which, if
it was to come, would perhaps be more painful to me
than the discovery at Balbec that Albertine had known
Mlle Vinteuil, since Albertine would no longer be there to
soothe me. So that the long plaint of the soul which
thinks that it is living shut up within itself is a monologue
in appearance only, since the echoes of reality alter its
course, and a given life is like an essay in subjective psychology spontaneously pursued, but providing from a dis-

tance the "plot" for the purely realistic novel of another reality, another existence, the vicissitudes of which come in their turn to inflect the curve and change the direction of the psychological essay. How highly geared had been the mechanism, how rapid had been the evolution of our love, and, notwithstanding a few delays, interruptions and hesitations at the start, as in certain of Balzac's tales or Schumann's ballads, how sudden the dénouement! It was in the course of this last year, as long as a century to me—so often had Albertine changed position in relation to my thoughts between Balbec and her departure from Paris, and also, independently of me and often without my knowing it, changed in herself—that I must place the whole of that happy life of tenderness which had lasted so short a while and which yet appeared to me with an amplitude, almost an immensity, which now was for ever impossible and yet was indispensable to me. Indispensable without perhaps having been in itself and at the outset something necessary, since I should not have known Albertine had I not read in an archaeological treatise a description of the church at Balbec, had not Swann, by telling me that this church was almost Persian, directed my taste to the Byzantine Norman, had not a financial syndicate, by erecting at Balbec a hygienic and comfortable hotel, made my parents decide to grant my wish and send me to Balbec. To be sure, in that Balbec so long desired, I had not found the Persian church of my dreams, nor the eternal mists. Even the famous 1.22 train had not corresponded to my mental picture of it. But in exchange for what our imagination leads us to expect and we give ourselves so much futile trouble trying to find, life gives us something which we were very far from imagining.

Who would have told me at Combray, when I lay waiting for my mother's good-night with so heavy a heart, that those anxieties would be healed, and would then break out again one day, not for my mother, but for a girl who would at first be no more, against the horizon of the sea, than a flower upon which my eyes would daily be invited to gaze, but a thinking flower in whose mind I was so childishly anxious to occupy a prominent place that I was distressed by her not being aware that I knew Mme de Villeparisis? Yes, it was for the good-night kiss of such an unknown girl that, in years to come, I was to suffer as intensely as I had suffered as a child when my mother did not come up to my room. And yet if Swann had not spoken to me of Balbec, I should never have known this Albertine who had become so necessary, of love for whom my soul was now almost exclusively composed. Her life would perhaps have been longer, mine would have been devoid of what was now making it a martyrdom. And thus it seemed to me that, by my entirely selfish love, I had allowed Albertine to die just as I had murdered my grandmother. Even later, even after I had already got to know her at Balbec, it is possible that I might not have loved her as I eventually did. For, when I gave up Gilberte and knew that I might love another woman some day, I hardly dared entertain a doubt as to whether, at any rate as regards the past, I could have loved anyone else but Gilberte. Whereas in the case of Albertine I no longer even had any doubt, I was sure that it might well not have been her that I loved, that it might have been someone else. It would have been enough that Mlle de Stermaria, on the evening when I was to dine with her on the island in the Bois, should not have cancelled the appointment. There was still time then, and it would have been upon Mlle de Stermaria that I would have directed that activity of the imagination which makes us extract from a woman so special a notion of individuality that she appears to us unique in herself and predestined and necessary for us. At the most, adopting an almost physiological point of view, I could say that I might have been able to feel that same exclusive love for another woman but not for *any* other woman. For Albertine, plump and dark, did not resemble Gilberte, slim and fair, and yet they were fashioned of the same healthy stuff, and above the same sensual cheeks there was a look in the eyes of both whose meaning was difficult to grasp. They were women of a sort that would not attract the attention of men who for their part would go mad about other women who "meant nothing" to me. A man has almost always the same way of catching cold, of falling ill; that is to say, he requires for it to happen a particular combination of circumstances; it is natural that when he falls in love he should love a certain type of woman, a type which for that matter is very widespread. The first glances from Albertine which had set me dreaming were not absolutely different from Gilberte's first glances. I could almost believe that the obscure personality, the sensuality, the wilful, cunning nature of Gilberte had returned to tempt me, incarnate this time in Albertine's body, a body quite different and yet not without analogies. In Albertine's case, thanks to a wholly different life shared with me where no fissure of distraction or obliviousness had been able to penetrate a block of thoughts in which a painful preoccupation maintained a permanent cohesion, her living body had not, like Gilberte's, ceased one day to be that in

which I found what I subsequently recognised as being to
me (what they would not have been to other men) the attributes of feminine charm. But she was dead. I would
forget her. Who could say whether the same qualities of
rich blood, of uneasy brooding would then return one day
to create turmoil in me? But in what feminine form they
would be embodied I could not foretell. The example of
Gilberte would as little have enabled me to form an idea
of Albertine and guess that I should fall in love with her,
as the memory of Vinteuil's sonata would have enabled
me to imagine his septet. Indeed, what was more, the first
few times I had seen Albertine, I had even managed to
believe that it was others I would love. Moreover, she
might even have appeared to me, had I met her a year
earlier, as dull as a grey sky in which dawn has not yet
broken. If I had changed in relation to her, she herself
had changed too, and the girl who had come and sat on
my bed on the day of my letter to Mlle de Stermaria was
no longer the same girl I had known at Balbec, whether
by virtue of the explosion of womanhood which occurs at
the age of puberty, or as a result of circumstances which I
was never able to discover. In any case, even if the
woman I was one day to love must to a certain extent resemble her, that is to say if my choice of a woman was
not entirely free, this nevertheless meant that, directed in
a manner that was perhaps predetermined, it was directed
towards something more considerable than an individual,
towards a type of woman, and this removed all necessi-
tude from my love for Albertine.

We are well aware that the woman whose face we
have before our eyes more constantly than light itself,
since even with our eyes shut we never cease for an in-

stant to adore her beautiful eyes, her beautiful nose, to arrange opportunities of seeing them again—that this
woman who to us is unique might well have been another
if we had been in a different town from the one in which
we met her, if we had explored other quarters of the
town, if we had frequented a different salon. Unique, we
suppose? She is legion. And yet she is compact and indestructible in our loving eyes, irreplaceable for a long time
to come by any other. The truth is that this woman has
only raised to life by a sort of magic countless elements of
tenderness existing in us already in a fragmentary state,
which she has assembled, joined together, effacing every
gap between them, and it is we ourselves who by giving
her her features have supplied all the solid matter of the
beloved object. Whence it arises that even if we are only
one among a thousand to her and perhaps the last of them
all, to us she is the only one, the one towards whom our
whole life gravitates. It was, indeed, true that I had been
quite well aware that this love was not inevitable, not only
because it might have crystallised round Mlle de Stermaria, but even apart from that, through knowing the
feeling itself, finding it to be only too like what it had
been for others, and also sensing it to be vaster than Albertine, enveloping her, unconscious of her, like a tide
swirling round a tiny rock. But gradually, by dint of living with Albertine, I was no longer able to fling off the
chains which I myself had forged; the habit of associating
Albertine's person with the sentiment which she had not
inspired made me none the less believe that it was peculiar to her, as habit gives to the mere association of ideas
between two phenomena, according to a certain school of
philosophy, the illusory force and necessity of a law of

causation. I had thought that my connexions, my wealth, would dispense me from suffering, and only too effectively perhaps, since it seemed to dispense me from feeling, loving, imagining; I envied a poor country girl whom the absence of connexions, even by telegraph, allows to day-dream for months on end about a sorrow which she cannot artificially put to sleep. And now I began to realise that if, in the case of Mme de Guermantes, endowed with everything that must make the gulf between her and myself infinite, I had seen that gulf suddenly bridged by abstract opinion, for which social advantages are no more than inert and transmutable matter, so, in a similar albeit converse fashion, my social relations, my wealth, all the material means by which not only my own position but the civilisation of my age enabled me to profit, had done no more than postpone the day of reckoning in my hand-to-hand struggle against the contrary, inflexible will of Albertine, upon which no pressure had had any effect. True, I had been able to exchange telegrams and telephone messages with Saint-Loup, to remain in constant communication with the post office at Tours, but had not the delay in waiting for them proved useless, the result nil? And country girls without social advantages or connexions, or human beings in general before these improvements of civilisation—do they not suffer less, because one desires less, because one regrets less what one has always known to be inaccessible, what for that reason has continued to seem unreal? One desires more the woman who has yet to give herself to us; hope anticipates possession; regret is an amplifier of desire. Mlle de Stermaria's refusal to come and dine with me on the island in the Bois was what had prevented her from becoming the object of my love. It

might also have sufficed to make me love her if afterwards
I had seen her again in time. As soon as I knew that she
would not come, entertaining the improbable hypothesis
—which had been proved correct—that perhaps she had
a jealous lover who kept her away from other men and
that therefore I should never see her again, I had suffered
so intensely that I would have given anything in the
world to see her, and it was one of the most desolating
agonies that I had ever felt that Saint-Loup's arrival had
assuaged. But after we have reached a certain age our
loves, our mistresses, are begotten of our anguish; our
past, and the physical lesions in which it is recorded, determine our future. In the case of Albertine in particular,
the fact that it was not necessarily she that I was predestined to love was inscribed, even without those circumam-
bient loves, in the history of my love for her, that is to
say for herself and her friends. For it was not even a love
like my love for Gilberte, but was created by division
among a number of girls. Conceivably it was because of
her and because they appeared to me more or less similar
to her that I had been attracted to her friends. The fact
remains that for a long time it was possible for me to wa-
ver between them all, for my choice to stray from one to
another, and when I thought that I preferred one, it was
enough that another should keep me waiting, should
refuse to see me, to make me feel the first premonitions of
love for her. Often it might have happened that when
Andrée was coming to see me at Balbec, a little before her
visit, if Albertine had let me down, my heart would beat
without ceasing, I felt that I would never see her again
and that it was she whom I loved. And when Andrée
came it was quite truthfully that I said to her (as I said to

her in Paris after I had learned that Albertine had known Mlle Vinteuil) what she might suppose me to be saying with an ulterior motive, insincerely, what I would indeed have said and in the same words had I been happy with Albertine the day before: "Alas! if you had only come sooner, now I love someone else." Even then, in this case of Andrée being replaced by Albertine after I learned that the latter had known Mlle Vinteuil, my love had alternated between them, so that after all there had been only one love at a time. But there had been previous cases where I had fallen out with two of the girls. The one who took the first step towards a reconciliation would restore my peace of mind, but it was the other that I would love if she remained hostile, which does not mean that it was not with the former that I would form a definitive tie, for she would console me—however ineffectually—for the harshness of the other, whom I would end by forgetting if she did not return to me. Now, it sometimes happened that, convinced though I was that one or the other at least would come back to me, for some time neither of them did so. My anguish was therefore twofold, and twofold my love; pending the likelihood of my ceasing to love the one who came back, in the meantime I continued to suffer on account of them both. It is our fate at a certain stage in life, which may come to us quite early, to be made less enamoured by a person than by a desertion, in which event we end by knowing one thing and one thing only about the person, her face being dim, her soul non-existent, our preference quite recent and unexplained: namely that what we need to make our suffering cease is a message from her: "May I come and see you?" My separation from Albertine on the day when Françoise had said to me: "Mademoiselle Albertine has gone" was like an allegory of countless other separations. For very often, in order that we may discover that we are in love, perhaps indeed in order that we may fall in love, the day of separation must first have come.

In these cases, when it is an unkept appointment, a letter of refusal, that dictates one's choice, one's imagination, goaded by suffering, sets about its work so swiftly, fashions with so frenzied a rapidity a love that had scarcely begun and remained inchoate, destined, for months past, to remain a rough sketch, that there are times when one's intelligence, which has been unable to keep pace with one's heart, cries out in astonishment: "But you must be mad. What are these strange thoughts that are making you so miserable? None of this is real life." And indeed at that moment, had one not been roused to action by the unfaithful one, a few healthy distractions that would calm one's heart physically would be sufficient to nip one's infatuation in the bud. In any case, if this life with Albertine was not in its essence necessary, it had become indispensable to me. I had trembled when I was in love with Mme de Guermantes because I said to myself that, with her too abundant means of seduction, not only beauty but position and wealth, she would be too much at liberty to belong to too many people, that I should have too little hold over her. Albertine, being penniless and obscure, must have been anxious to marry me. And yet I had not been able to possess her exclusively. Whatever our social position, however wise our precautions, when the truth is confessed we have no hold over the life of another person. Why had she not said to me: "I have those tastes"? I would have yielded, would have allowed her to gratify them. In a novel I had read there was a woman whom no objurgation from the man who was in love with her could induce to speak. When I read the book, I had thought this situation absurd; had I been the hero, I assured myself, I would first of all have forced the woman to speak, then we could have come to an understanding. What was the good of all those futile miseries? But I saw now that we are not free to refrain from forging the chains of our own misery, and that however well we may know our own will, other people do not obey it.

And yet how often we had expressed them, those painful, those ineluctable truths which dominated us and to which we were blind, the truth of our feelings, the truth of our destiny, how often we had expressed them without knowing it, without meaning it, in words which doubtless we ourselves thought mendacious but the prophetic force of which had been established by subsequent events. I remembered many words that each of us had uttered without knowing at the time the truth that they contained, which indeed we had said thinking that we were play-acting and yet the falseness of which was very slight, very uninteresting, wholly confined within our pitiable insincerity, compared with what they contained unbeknown to us—lies and errors falling short of the profound reality which neither of us perceived, truth extending beyond it, the truth of our natures, the essential laws of which escape us and require Time before they reveal themselves, the truth of our destinies also. I had believed myself to be lying when I said to her at Balbec: "The more I see you, the more I shall love you" (and yet it was that constant intimacy which, through the medium of jealousy, had attached me so strongly to her), "I feel that I could be of use to you intellectually"; and in Paris: "Do be careful. Remember that if you met with an accident, it would break my heart" (and she: "But I may meet with an accident"); in Paris too, on the evening when I had pretended that I wished to leave her: "Let me look at you once again since presently I shall not be seeing you again, and it will be for ever!" and she, when that same evening she had looked round the room: "To think that I shall never see this room again, those books, that pianola, the whole house, I cannot believe it and yet it's true." In her last letters again, when she had written (probably saying to herself that it was eyewash): "I leave you the best of myself" (and was it not now indeed to the fidelity, to the strength—also too frail, alas—of my memory that her intelligence, her kindness, her beauty were entrusted?) and: "That moment of double twilight, since night was falling and we were about to part, will be effaced from my thoughts only when the darkness is complete" (that sentence written on the eve of the day when her mind had indeed been plunged into complete darkness, and when, in those last brief glimmers which the anguish of the moment subdivides ad infinitum, she had indeed perhaps recalled our last drive together and in that instant when everything forsakes us and we create a faith for ourselves, as atheists turn Christian on the battlefield, she had perhaps summoned to her aid the friend whom she had so often cursed but had so deeply respected, who himself— for all religions are alike—was cruel enough to hope that she had also had time to see herself as she was, to give her last thought to him, to confess her sins at length to him, to die in him).

But to what purpose, since even if, at that moment, she had had time to see herself as she was, we had both of us understood where our happiness lay, what we ought to do, only when, only because, that happiness was no longer possible, when and because we could no longer do it— whether it is that, so long as things are possible, we postpone them, or that they cannot assume that force of attraction, that apparent ease of realisation except when, projected on to the ideal void of the imagination, they are removed from their deadening and degrading submersion in physical being. The idea that one will die is more painful than dying, but less painful than the idea that another person is dead, that, becoming once more a still, plane surface after having engulfed a person, a reality extends, without even a ripple at the point of disappearance, from which that person is excluded, in which there no longer exists any will, any knowledge, and from which it is as difficult to reascend to the idea that that person has lived as, from the still recent memory of his life, it is to think that he is comparable with the insubstantial images, the memories, left us by the characters in a novel we have been reading.

At any rate I was glad that before she died she had written me that letter, and above all had sent me that final message which proved to me that she would have returned had she lived. It seemed to me that it was not merely more soothing, but more beautiful also, that the event would have been incomplete without that message, would not have had so markedly the form of art and destiny. In reality it would have been just as markedly so had it been different; for every event is like a mould of a particular shape, and, whatever it may be, it imposes, upon the series of incidents which it has interrupted and seems to conclude, a pattern which we believe to be the only possible one, because we do not know the other which might have been substituted for it.

Why, I repeated to myself, had she not said to me: "I have those tastes"? I would have yielded, would have allowed her to gratify them; at this moment I would be kissing her still. How sad it was to have to remind myself that she had lied to me thus when she swore to me, three days before she left me, that she had never had with Mlle Vinteuil's friend those relations which at the moment when she swore it her blush had confessed! Poor child, she had at least had the honesty to be reluctant to swear that the pleasure of seeing Mlle Vinteuil again had no part in her desire to go that day to the Verdurins'. Why had she not made her admission complete? Perhaps, however, it was partly my fault that she had never, despite all my entreaties which were powerless against her denial, been willing to say to me: "I have those tastes." It was perhaps partly my fault because at Balbec, on the day when, after Mme de Cambremer's visit, I had had things out with Albertine for the first time, and when I was so far from imagining that she could possibly have had anything more than a rather too passionate friendship with Andrée, I had expressed with undue violence my disgust at those proclivities, had condemned them too categorically. I could not recall whether Albertine had blushed when I had naïvely expressed my horror of that sort of thing, for it is often only long afterwards that we long to know what attitude a person adopted at a moment when we were paying no attention to it, an attitude which, later on, when we think again of our conversation, would elucidate an agonising problem. But in our memory there is a blank, there is no trace of it. And very often we have not paid sufficient attention, at the actual moment, to the things which might even then have seemed to us important, we have not properly heard a sentence, have not noticed a gesture, or else we have forgotten them. And when later on, eager to discover a truth, we work back from deduction to deduction, leafing through our memory like a sheaf of written evidence, when we arrive at that sentence, at that gesture, we find it impossible to remember, and we repeat the process a score of times, in vain: the road goes no further. Had she blushed? I do not know whether she had blushed, but she could not have failed to hear, and the memory of my words had pulled her up later on when perhaps she had been on the point of confessing to me. And now she no longer existed anywhere; I could have scoured the earth from pole to pole without finding Albertine; the reality which had closed over her was once more unbroken, had obliterated every trace of the being who had sunk without trace. She was now no more than a name, like that Mme de Charlus of whom people who had known her said with indifference: "She was charming." But I could not conceive for more than an instant the existence of this reality of which Albertine had no knowledge, for in me she existed only too vividly, in me whose every feeling, every thought, related to her life. Perhaps, if she had known, she would have been touched to see that her lover had not forgotten her, now that her own life was finished, and would have been sensitive to things which in the past had left her indifferent. But as we would choose to abstain from infidelities, however secret, so fearful are we that she whom we love is not abstaining from them, I was terrified by the thought that if the dead do exist somewhere, my grandmother was as well aware of my forgetfulness as Albertine of my remembrance. And when all is said, even in the case of a single dead person, can we be sure that the joy we should feel in learning that she knows certain things would compensate for our alarm at the thought that she knows them *all*; and, however agonising the sacrifice, would we not sometimes forbear to keep those we have loved as friends after their death, for fear of having them also as judges?

My jealous curiosity as to what Albertine might have done was unbounded. I suborned any number of women from whom I learned nothing. If this curiosity was so tenacious, it was because people do not die for us immediately, but remain bathed in a sort of aura of life which bears no relation to true immortality but through which they continue to occupy our thoughts in the same way as when they were alive. It is as though they were travelling abroad. This is a thoroughly pagan survival. Conversely, when we have ceased to love, the curiosity which people arouse dies before they themselves are dead. Thus I would no longer have taken a single step to find out with whom Gilberte had been strolling on a certain evening in the Champs-Elysées. Now, I was well aware that these two forms of curiosity were absolutely identical, had no value in themselves, were incapable of lasting. But I continued to sacrifice everything to the cruel satisfaction of this transient curiosity, although I knew in advance that my enforced separation from Albertine, by the fact of her death, would lead me to the same indifference as had resulted from my voluntary separation from Gilberte.

If she could have known what was going to happen,

she would have stayed with me. But this simply amounted to saying that, once she saw herself dead, she would have preferred to remain alive with me. Because of the very contradiction that it implied, such a supposition was absurd. But it was not innocuous, for in imagining how glad Albertine would be, if she could know, if she could retrospectively understand, to come back to me, I saw her before me, I wanted to kiss her, and alas, it was impossible, she would never come back, she was dead.

My imagination sought for her in the sky, at nightfall when, still together, we had gazed at it; beyond that moonlight which she loved, I tried to raise up to her my tenderness so that it might be a consolation to her for being no longer alive, and this love for a being who was now so remote was like a religion; my thoughts rose towards her like prayers. Desire is powerful indeed: it engenders belief; I had believed that Albertine would not leave me because I desired that she should not do so. Because I desired it, I began to believe that she was not dead; I took to reading books about table-turning; I began to believe in the possibility of the immortality of the soul. But that did not suffice me. I required that, after my own death, I should find her again in her body, as though eternity were like life. Life, did I say? I was more exacting still. I should have liked not to be for ever deprived by death of the pleasures of which in any case it is not alone in robbing us. For without it they would eventually have lost their edge; indeed they had already begun to do so through the effect of long-established habit, of fresh curiosities. Besides, had she been alive, Albertine, even physically, would gradually have changed; day by day I would have adapted myself to that change. But my mem-

ory, calling up only detached moments of her life, demanded to see her again as she would already have ceased
to be had she lived; what it wanted was a miracle that
would satisfy the natural and arbitrary limitations of
memory, which cannot escape from the past. And yet,
with the naïvety of the old theologians, I imagined this
living creature vouchsafing me not simply the explanations which she might possibly have given me but, by a
final contradiction, those that she had always refused me
during her life. And thus, her death being a sort of
dream, my love would seem to her an unlooked-for happiness; all I retained of death was the comfort and the optimism of a dénouement which simplifies, which settles
everything.

Sometimes it was not so far off, it was not in another
world, that I imagined our reunion. Just as, in the past,
when I knew Gilberte only from playing with her in the
Champs-Elysées, at home in the evening I used to imagine that I was about to receive a letter from her in which
she would confess her love for me, that she was about to
come into the room, so a similar force of desire, no more
troubled by the laws of nature which inhibited it than on
the former occasion, in the case of Gilberte (when after all
it had not been mistaken since it had had the last word),
made me think now that I was about to receive a message
from Albertine, informing me that she had indeed had a
riding accident but that for romantic reasons (and as, after
all, has sometimes happened with people whom we have
long believed to be dead) she had not wished me to hear
of her recovery and now, repentant, asked to be allowed
to come and live with me for ever. And—giving me an
insight into the nature of certain mild lunacies in people

who otherwise appear sane—I felt co-existing in me the certainty that she was dead and the constant hope that I might see her come into the room.

I had not yet received news from Aimé, although he must by now have reached Balbec. No doubt my inquiry turned upon a secondary point, and one quite arbitrarily chosen. If Albertine's life had been really culpable, it must have contained many other things of far greater importance, which chance had not allowed me to consider as it had in the case of the conversation about the bathing-wrap and Albertine's blushes. But those things precisely did not exist for me since I had not seen them. But it was quite arbitrarily that I had hit upon that particular day and, several years later, was trying to reconstruct it. If Albertine had been a lover of women, there were thousands of other days in her life which I did not know how she had spent and about which it might be just as interesting for me to learn; I might have sent Aimé to many other places in Balbec, to many other towns besides Balbec. But these other days, precisely because I did not know how she had spent them, did not present themselves to my imagination, had no existence for it. Things and people did not begin to exist for me until they assumed in my imagination an individual existence. If there were thousands of others like them, they became for me representative of all the rest. If I had long felt a desire to know, in the matter of my suspicions with regard to Albertine, what exactly had happened in the baths, it was in the same manner in which, in the matter of my desires for women, and although I knew that there were any number of young girls and lady's-maids who could satisfy them

and whom chance might just as easily have brought to my
notice, I wished to know—since it was they whom Saint-
Loup had mentioned to me, they who existed individually
for me—the girl who frequented houses of ill fame and
Mme Putbus's maid. The difficulties which my health,
my indecision, my "procrastination," as M. de Charlus
called it, placed in the way of my carrying anything
through, had made me put off from day to day, from
month to month, from year to year, the elucidation of certain suspicions as well as the accomplishment of certain
desires. But I retained them in my memory, promising
myself that I would not forget to learn the truth of them,
because they alone obsessed me (since the others had no
form in my eyes, did not exist), and also because the very
accident that had chosen them out of the surrounding reality gave me a guarantee that it was indeed in them that
I should come in contact with a trace of the reality, of the
true and coveted life. Besides, is not a single small fact, if
it is well chosen, sufficient to enable the experimenter to
deduce a general law which will reveal the truth about
thousands of analogous facts? Although Albertine might
exist in my memory only as she had successively appeared
to me in the course of her life, that is, subdivided in accordance with a series of fractions of time, my mind, re-
establishing unity in her, made her a single person, and it
was on this person that I wished to arrive at a general
judgment, to know whether she had lied to me, whether
she loved women, whether it was in order to associate
with them freely that she had left me. What the woman
in the baths would have to say might perhaps put an end
for ever to my doubts as to Albertine's proclivities.

My doubts! Alas, I had supposed that it would be immaterial to me, even agreeable, not to see Albertine again, until her departure had revealed to me my error. Similarly her death had shown me how greatly I had been mistaken in believing that I sometimes wished for her death and supposed that it would be my deliverance. So it was that, when I received Aimé's letter, I realised that if I had not until then suffered too painfully from my doubts as to Albertine's virtue it was because in reality they were not doubts at all. My happiness, my life required that Albertine should be virtuous; they had laid it down once and for all that she was. Armed with this self-protective belief, I could with impunity allow my mind to play sadly with suppositions to which it gave a form but lent no credence. I said to myself, "She is perhaps a woman-lover," as we say "I may die tonight"; we say it, but we do not believe it, we make plans for the following day. This explains why, believing mistakenly that I was uncertain whether Albertine did or did not love women, and believing in consequence that a proof of Albertine's guilt would not tell me anything that I had not often envisaged, I experienced, in the face of the images, insignificant to anyone else, which Aimé's letter evoked for me, an unexpected anguish, the most painful that I had ever yet felt, and one that formed with those images, with the image, alas! of Albertine herself, a sort of precipitate, as they say in chemistry, in which everything was indivisible and of which the text of Aimé's letter, which I isolate in a purely conventional fashion, can give no idea whatsoever, since each of the words that compose it was immediately transformed, coloured for ever by the suffering it had just aroused.

"MONSIEUR,

Monsieur will kindly forgive me for not having written sooner to Monsieur. The person whom Monsieur instructed me to see had gone away for a few days, and, anxious to justify the confidence which Monsieur had placed in me, I did not wish to return empty-handed. I have just spoken at last to this person who remembers (Mlle A.) very well." (Aimé, who possessed certain rudiments of culture, meant to put "Mlle A." in italics or between inverted commas. But when he meant to put inverted commas he put brackets, and when he meant to put something in brackets he put it between inverted commas. In the same way Françoise would say that someone *stayed* in my street meaning that he *dwelt* there, and that one could *dwell* for a few minutes, meaning *stay*, the mistakes of popular speech consisting merely, as often as not, in interchanging—as for that matter the French language has done—terms which in the course of centuries have replaced one another.) "According to her the thing that Monsieur supposed is absolutely certain. For one thing, it was she who looked after (Mlle A.) whenever she came to the baths. (Mlle A.) came very often to take her shower with a tall woman older than herself, always dressed in grey, whom the shower-attendant without knowing her name recognised from having often seen her going after girls. But she took no notice of any of them after she met (Mlle A.). She and (Mlle A.) always shut themselves up in the cabin, remained there a very long time, and the lady in grey used to give at least 10 francs as a tip to the person I spoke to. As this person said to me, you can imagine that if they were just stringing beads they wouldn't have given a ten-franc tip. (Mlle A.) also used to come sometimes with a woman with a very dark skin and a lorgnette. But (Mlle A.) came most often with girls younger than herself, especially one with very red hair. Apart from the lady in grey, the people (Mlle A.) was in the habit of bringing were not from Balbec and must even quite often have come from quite a distance. They never went in together, but (Mlle A.) would come in, and ask for the door of her cabin to be left unlocked—as she was expecting a friend, and the person I spoke to knew what that meant. This person could not give me any other details as she did not remember very well, 'which is easy to understand after such a long time.' Besides, this person did not try to find out, because she is very discreet and it was to her advantage because (Mlle A.) brought her in a lot of money. She was quite sincerely touched to hear that she was dead. It is true that so young it is a great calamity for her and for her family. I await Monsieur's orders to know whether I may leave Balbec where I do not think that I can learn anything more. I thank Monsieur again for the little holiday that he has procured me, and which has been very pleasant especially as the weather is as fine as could be. The season promises well for this year. Everyone hopes that Monsieur will come and put in a little apparition.

"I can think of nothing else to say that will interest Monsieur," etc.

To understand how deeply these words penetrated my being, it must be remembered that the questions which I had been asking myself with regard to Albertine were not secondary, insignificant questions, questions of detail, the only questions in fact that one asks about anyone who is not oneself, whereby one is enabled to carry on, wrapped in the imperviousness of one's thoughts, through the midst of suffering, falsehood, vice and death. No, in Albertine's case they were essential questions: In her heart of hearts what was she? What were her thoughts? What were her loves? Did she lie to me? Had my life with her been as lamentable as Swann's life with Odette? Hence Aimé's reply, although it was not a general but a particular reply—indeed precisely because of that—struck home, in Albertine and in myself, to the very depths.

At last I saw before my eyes, in that arrival of Albertine at the baths along the narrow lane with the lady in grey, a fragment of that past which seemed to me no less mysterious, no less horrifying than I had feared when I imagined it enclosed in the memory, in the look in the eyes of Albertine. No doubt anyone but myself might have dismissed as insignificant these details on which, now that Albertine was dead, my inability to secure a denial of them from her conferred the equivalent of a sort of probability. It is indeed probable that for Albertine, even if they had been true, even if she had admitted them, her own misdeeds (whether her conscience had thought them innocent or reprehensible, whether her sensuality had found them exquisite or somewhat insipid) would not have been accompanied by that inexpressible sense of horror from which I was unable to detach them. I myself, with the help of my own love of women, and although they could not have meant the same thing to Albertine, could imagine a little of what she felt. And indeed there was already an initial pain in my picturing her to myself desiring as I had so often desired, lying to me as I had so often lied to her, preoccupied with this or that girl, putting herself out for her, as I had done for Mlle de Stermaria and so many others, for the peasant girls I met on country roads. Yes, all my own desires helped me to a certain extent to understand hers; it was by this time an immense anguish in which all desires were transformed into torments that were all the more cruel the more intense they had been; as though in this algebra of sensibility they reappeared with the same coefficient but with a minus instead of a plus sign. To Albertine, so far as I was capable of judging her by my own standard, her misdeeds—however anxious she might have been to conceal them from me (which made me suppose that she considered herself guilty or was afraid of hurting me)—because she had planned them to suit her own taste in the clear light of the imagination in which desire operates, must after all have appeared as things of the same kind as the rest of life, pleasures for herself which she had not had the strength to deny herself, griefs for me which she had sought to avoid causing me by concealing them from me, but pleasures and griefs which might be numbered among the other pleasures and griefs of life. But for me, it was from the outside, without my having been forewarned, without my having been able myself to elaborate them, it was from Aimé's letter that there had come to me the visions of Albertine arriving at the baths and preparing her tip.

No doubt it was because in that silent and deliberate arrival of Albertine with the woman in grey I read the assignation they had made, that convention of going to make love in a shower-cabin, which implied an experience of corruption, the well-concealed organisation of a double life, it was because these images brought me the terrible tidings of Albertine's guilt, that they had immediately caused me a physical grief from which they would never be detached. But at once my grief had reacted upon them: an objective fact, an image, differs according to the internal state in which we approach it. And grief is as powerful a modifier of reality as intoxication. Combined with these images, my suffering had at once made of them something absolutely different from what might be for anyone else a lady in grey, a tip, a shower, the street where the purposeful arrival of Albertine with the lady in grey had taken place. All those images—a vista of a life of lies and iniquities such as I had never conceived—my suffering had immediately altered them in their very essence; I did not see them in the light that illuminates earthly spectacles, they were a fragment of another world, of an unknown and accursed planet, a glimpse of Hell. My Hell was the whole region of Balbec, all those neighbouring villages from which, according to Aimé's letter, she frequently collected girls younger than herself whom she took to the baths. That mystery which I had long ago imagined in the country around Balbec and which had been dispelled after I had lived there, which I had then hoped to grasp again when I knew Albertine because, when I saw her pass by on the beach, when I was mad enough to hope that she was not virtuous, I thought that she must be its incarnation—how fearfully now everything that related to Balbec was impregnated with it! The names of those watering-places, Toutainville, Epreville, Incarville, that had become so familiar, so soothing, when I heard them shouted at night as I returned from the Verdurins', now that I thought how Albertine had been staying at one, had gone from there to another, must often have ridden on her bicycle to a third, aroused in me an anxiety more cruel than on the first occasion, when I had observed them with such misgivings from the little local train with my grandmother before arriving at a Balbec which I did not yet know.

It is one of the faculties of jealousy to reveal to us the extent to which the reality of external facts and the sentiments of the heart are an unknown element which lends itself to endless suppositions. We imagine that we know exactly what things are and what people think, for the simple reason that we do not care about them. But as soon as we have a desire to know, as the jealous man has, then it becomes a dizzy kaleidoscope in which we can no

longer distinguish anything. Had Albertine been unfaithful to me? With whom? In what house? On what day?
On the day when she had said this or that to me, when I
remembered that I had in the course of it said this or
that? I could not tell. Nor did I know what her feelings
were for me, whether they were inspired by self-interest
or by affection. And all of a sudden I remembered some
trivial incident, for instance that Albertine had wished to
go to Saint-Mars-le-Vêtu, saying that the name interested
her, and perhaps simply because she had made the acquaintance of some peasant girl who lived there. But it
was useless that Aimé should have informed me of what
he had learned from the woman at the baths, since Albertine must remain eternally unaware that he had informed
me, the need to know having always been exceeded, in my
love for Albertine, by the need to show her that I knew;
for this broke down the partition of different illusions that
stood between us, without having ever had the result of
making her love me more, far from it. And now, since she
was dead, the second of these needs had been amalga-
mated with the effect of the first: the need to picture to
myself the conversation in which I would have informed
her of what I had learned, as vividly as the conversation
in which I would have asked her to tell me what I did not
know; that is to say, to see her by my side, to hear her
answering me kindly, to see her cheeks become plump
again, her eyes shed their malice and assume an air of
melancholy; that is to say, to love her still and to forget
the fury of my jealousy in the despair of my loneliness.
The painful mystery of this impossibility of ever making
known to her what I had learned and of establishing our
relations upon the truth of what I had only just discov-

ered (and would not have been able, perhaps, to discover but for her death) substituted its sadness for the more painful mystery of her conduct. What? To have so desperately desired that Albertine—who no longer existed—should know that I had heard the story of the baths! This again was one of the consequences of our inability, when we have to consider the fact of death, to picture to ourselves anything but life. Albertine no longer existed; but to me she was the person who had concealed from me that she had assignations with women at Balbec, who imagined that she had succeeded in keeping me in ignorance of them. When we try to consider what will happen to us after our own death, is it not still our living self which we mistakenly project at that moment? And is it much more absurd, when all is said, to regret that a woman who no longer exists is unaware that we have learned what she was doing six years ago than to desire that of ourselves, who will be dead, the public shall still speak with approval a century hence? If there is more real foundation in the latter than in the former case, the regrets of my retrospective jealousy proceeded none the less from the same optical error as in other men the desire for posthumous fame. And yet, if this impression of the solemn finality of my separation from Albertine had momentarily supplanted my idea of her misdeeds, it only succeeded in aggravating them by bestowing upon them an irremediable character. I saw myself astray in life as on an endless beach where I was alone and where, in whatever direction I might turn, I would never meet her.

Fortunately, I found most opportunely in my memory—as there are always all sorts of things, some noxious, others salutary, in that jumble from which recollections

come to light only one by one—I discovered, as a craftsman discovers the object that will serve for what he
wishes to make, a remark of my grandmother's. She had
said to me, with reference to an improbable story which
the bath-attendant had told Mme de Villeparisis: "She is a
woman who must suffer from a disease of mendacity."
This memory was a great comfort to me. What significance could there be in the story she had told Aimé? Especially as, after all, she had seen nothing. A girl can
come and take a shower with her friends without necessarily meaning any harm. Perhaps the woman had exaggerated the size of the tip in order to boast. I had indeed
heard Françoise maintain once that my aunt Léonie had
said in her hearing that she had "a million a month to
spend," which was utter nonsense; another time that she
had seen my aunt Léonie give Eulalie four thousand-franc
notes, whereas a fifty-franc note folded in four seemed to
me scarcely probable. And thus I sought to rid myself—
and gradually succeeded in ridding myself—of the
painful certainty which I had taken such trouble to acquire, tossed to and fro as I still was between the desire to
know and the fear of suffering. Then my tenderness could
revive anew, but, simultaneously with it, a sorrow at being parted from Albertine which made me perhaps even
more wretched than I had been during the recent hours
when it had been jealousy that tormented me. But the latter suddenly revived at the thought of Balbec, because of
the vision which all at once reappeared (and which until
then had never made me suffer and indeed appeared one
of the most innocuous in my memory) of the dining-room
at Balbec in the evening, with all that populace crowded
together in the dark on the other side of the window, as in

front of the luminous wall of an aquarium, watching the strange creatures moving around in the light but (and this I had never thought of) in its conglomeration causing the fisher-girls and other daughters of the people to brush against girls of the bourgeoisie envious of that luxury, new to Balbec, from which, if not their means, at any rate parsimony and tradition excluded their parents, girls among whom there had certainly been almost every evening Albertine whom I did not know and who doubtless used to pick up some little girl whom she would meet a few minutes later in the dark, upon the sands, or else in a deserted bathing hut at the foot of the cliff. Then my sadness would return as I heard like a sentence of banishment the sound of the lift, which instead of stopping at my floor went on higher. And yet the only person from whom I could have hoped for a visit would never come again, for she was dead. And in spite of this, when the lift did stop at my floor, my heart leapt, and for an instant I said to myself: "What if it was only a dream after all! Perhaps it's her—she's going to ring the bell, she has come back, Françoise will come in and say with more alarm than anger—for she's even more superstitious than vindictive, and would be less afraid of the living girl than of what she will perhaps take for a ghost—'Monsieur will never guess who's here.'" I tried not to think of anything, to take up a newspaper. But I found it impossible to read all those articles written by men who felt no real grief. Of a trivial song, one of them said: "It moves one to *tears*," whereas I myself would have listened to it with joy had Albertine been alive. Another, albeit a great writer, having been greeted with applause when he alighted from a train, said that he had received "an *unforgettable* welcome," whereas I, if it had been I who received that welcome, would not have given it even a moment's thought. And a third assured his readers that but for tiresome politics life in Paris would be "altogether delightful," whereas I knew well that even without politics that life could not but be odious to me, and would have seemed to me delightful, even with politics, if I had found Albertine again. The field sports correspondent said (we were in the month of May): "This season of the year is truly distressing, nay, catastrophic, to the true sportsman, for there is nothing, absolutely nothing in the way of game," and the art critic said of the Salon: "Faced with this method of arranging an exhibition one is overcome by an immense discouragement, by an infinite gloom . . ." If the strength of my feelings made me regard as untruthful and colourless the expressions of men who had no true happiness or sorrow in their lives, on the other hand the most insignificant lines which could, however remotely, be related either to Normandy, or to Touraine, or to hydrotherapeutic establishments, or to Léa, or to the Princesse de Guermantes, or to love, or to absence, or to infidelity, at once brought back before my eyes the image of Albertine, without my having the time to turn away from it, and my tears started afresh. In any case, usually I could not even read these newspapers, for the mere act of opening one of them reminded me at once that I used to open them when Albertine was alive, and that she was alive no longer; and I let it drop without having the strength to unfold its pages. Each impression called up an impression that was identical but marred, because Albertine's existence had been excised from it, so that I never had the heart to live these mutilated minutes to the end. Even when she gradually ceased to be present in my thoughts and all-powerful over my heart, I felt a sudden pang if I had occasion, as in the time when she was there, to go into her room, to grope for the light, to sit down by the pianola. Divided into a number of little household gods, she dwelt for a long time in the flame of the candle, the doorknob, the back of a chair, and other domains more immaterial such as a night of insomnia or the emotion that was caused me by the first visit of a woman who had attracted me. In spite of this the few sentences which I read in the course of a day, or which my mind recalled that I had read, often aroused in me a cruel jealousy. To do this, they required not so much to supply me with a valid proof of the immorality of women as to revive an old impression connected with the life of Albertine. Transported then to a forgotten moment the force of which had not been blunted by the habit of thinking of it, and in which Albertine still lived, her misdeeds became more immediate, more painful, more agonising. Then I asked myself whether I could be certain that the bath-attendant's revelations were false. A good way of finding out the truth would be to send Aimé to Touraine, to spend a few days in the neighbourhood of Mme Bontemps's villa. If Albertine enjoyed the pleasures which one woman takes with others, if it was in order not to be deprived of them any longer that she had left me, she must, as soon as she was free, have sought to indulge in them and have succeeded, in a neighbourhood which she knew and to which she would not have chosen to withdraw had she not expected to find greater facilities there than with me. No doubt there was nothing extraordinary in the fact that Albertine's death had so little altered my preoccupations. When one's mistress is alive, a large proportion of the thoughts which form what one calls one's love comes to one during the hours when she is not by one's side. Thus one acquires the habit of having as the object of one's musings an absent person, and one who, even if she remains absent for a few hours only, during those hours is no more than a memory. Hence death does not make any great difference. When Aimé returned, I asked him to go down to Châtellerault, and thus by virtue not only of my thoughts, my sorrows, the emotion caused me by a name connected, however remotely, with a certain person, but also of all my actions, the inquiries that I undertook, the use that I made of my money, all of which was devoted to the discovery of Albertine's actions, I may say that throughout the whole of that year my life remained fully occupied with a love affair, a veritable liaison. And she who was its object was dead. It is often said that something may survive of a person after his death, if that person was an artist and put a little of himself into his work. It is perhaps in the same way that a sort of cutting taken from one person and grafted on to the heart of another continues to carry on its existence even when the person from whom it had been detached has perished.

Aimé took lodgings close to Mme Bontemps's villa; he made the acquaintance of a maidservant, and of a livery-stable keeper from whom Albertine had often hired a carriage by the day. These people had noticed nothing. In a second letter, Aimé informed me that he had learned from a young laundry-girl in the town that Albertine had a peculiar way of gripping her arm when she brought back the washing. "But," she said, "the young lady never did anything more." I sent Aimé the money to pay for his

journey, to pay for the pain he had caused me by his letter, and meanwhile I was doing my best to heal it by
telling myself that what he had described was a familiarity
which gave no proof of any vicious desire, when I received a telegram from him: "Have learned most interesting things. Have heaps of news for Monsieur. Letter
follows." On the following day came a letter the envelope
of which was enough to make me tremble; I had recognised that it was from Aimé, for every person, even the
humblest, has under his control those little familiar creatures, at once alive and reclining in a sort of torpor upon
the paper: the characters of his handwriting which he
alone possesses.

"At first the young laundry-girl refused to tell me anything,
she assured me that Mlle Albertine had never done anything
more than pinch her arm. But to get her to talk, I took her out
to dinner and gave her plenty to drink. Then she told me that
Mlle Albertine often used to meet her on the bank of the Loire,
when she went to bathe, that Mlle Albertine, who was in the
habit of getting up very early to go and bathe, was in the habit
of meeting her by the water's edge, at a spot where the trees are
so thick that nobody can see you, and besides there is nobody
who can see you at that hour in the morning. Then the laundry-
girl brought her girlfriends and they bathed and afterwards, as it
is already very hot down there and the sun beats down on you
even through the trees, they used to lie about on the grass dry-
ing themselves and playing and stroking and tickling one another. The young laundry-girl confessed to me that she enjoyed
playing around with her girlfriends and that seeing that Mlle
Albertine was always rubbing up against her in her bathing-
wrap she made her take it off and used to caress her with her
tongue along the throat and arms, even on the soles of her feet
which Mlle Albertine held out to her. The laundry-girl undressed too, and they played at pushing each other into the wa-

ter. After that she told me nothing more, but being always at your service and ready to do anything to oblige you, I took the young laundry-girl to bed with me. She asked me if I would like her to do to me what she used to do to Mlle Albertine when she took off her bathing-dress. And she said to me: (If you could have seen how she used to wriggle, that young lady, she said to me (oh, it's too heavenly) and she got so excited that she could not keep from biting me.) I could still see the marks on the laundry-girl's arms. And I can understand Mlle Albertine's pleasure, for that young wench is really a very good performer."

I had suffered indeed at Balbec when Albertine told me of her friendship with Mlle Vinteuil. But Albertine was there to console me. Then, when by my excessive curiosity as to her actions I had succeeded in making Albertine leave me, when Françoise informed me that she was no longer in the house and I found myself alone, I had suffered even more. But at least the Albertine whom I had loved remained in my heart. Now, in her place—to punish me for having pushed even further a curiosity to which, contrary to what I had supposed, death had not put an end—what I found was a different girl, heaping up lies and deceit there where the other had so sweetly re-assured me by swearing that she had never tasted those pleasures, which in the intoxication of her recaptured liberty she had set out to enjoy to the point of fainting, to the point of biting that young laundress whom she used to meet at sunrise, on the bank of the Loire, and to whom she used to say "Oh, it's too heavenly." A different Albertine, not only in the sense in which we understand the word different when we apply it to other people. If people are different from what we have supposed, as this differ-ence does not affect us deeply, and the pendulum of intuition cannot swing outward with a greater oscillation than that of its inward swing, it is only in superficial areas of their being that we situate these differences. Formerly, when I learned that a woman loved other women, she did not seem to me on that account to be a quintessentially different woman. But in the case of a woman one loves, in order to rid oneself of the pain one feels at the thought that such a thing is possible, one wants to know not only what she has done, but what she felt while she was doing it, what she thought of what she was doing; then, probing ever more deeply, through the intensity of one's pain one arrives at the mystery, the quintessence. I suffered to the very depths of my being, in my body and in my heart, far more than the pain of losing my life would have made me suffer, from this curiosity to which all the force of my intelligence and my unconscious contributed; and thus it was into the core of Albertine's own being that I now projected everything that I learned about her. And the pain that the revelation of her vice had thus driven into me to such a depth was to render me, much later, a final service. Like the harm that I had done my grandmother, the harm that Albertine had done me was a last bond between her and myself which outlived memory even, for with the conservation of energy which belongs to everything that is physical, suffering has no need of the lessons of memory. Thus a man who has forgotten the glorious nights spent by moonlight in the woods, suffers still from the rheumatism which he then contracted.

Those tastes which she had denied but which were hers, those tastes the discovery of which had come to me not by a cold process of reasoning but in the burning anguish I had felt on reading the words "Oh, it's too heavenly," an anguish that gave them a qualitative distinction, those tastes were not merely added to the image of Albertine as the new shell which it drags after it is affixed to the hermit crab, but rather as a salt which, coming in contact with another salt, alters not only its colour but its nature. When the laundry-girl must have said to her friends, "Just fancy, I'd never have believed it, but the young lady is one too," to me it was not merely a vice hitherto unsuspected by them that they added to Albertine's person, but the discovery that she was another person, a person like themselves, speaking the same language, and this, by making her the compatriot of others, made her even more alien to myself, proved that what I had possessed of her, what I carried in my heart, was only quite a small part of her, and that the rest, which was made so extensive by not being merely that thing which is already mysteriously important enough, an individual desire, but being shared with others, she had always concealed from me, had kept me away from, as a woman might conceal from me that she was a native of an enemy country and a spy, and far more treacherously even than a spy, for the latter deceives us only as to her nationality, whereas Albertine had deceived me as to her profoundest humanity, the fact that she did not belong to ordinary humankind, but to an alien race which moves among it, hides itself among it and never merges with it. I had as it happened seen two paintings by Elstir showing naked women in a thickly wooded landscape. In one of them, a girl is raising her foot as Albertine must have raised hers when she offered it to the laundress. With her other foot she is pushing into the water another girl who gaily resists, her thigh raised, her foot barely dipping into the

blue water. I remembered now that the raised thigh made
the same swan's-neck curve with the angle of the knee as
was made by the line of Albertine's thigh when she was
lying by my side on the bed, and I had often meant to tell
her that she reminded me of those paintings. But I had
refrained from doing so, for fear of awakening in her
mind the image of naked female bodies. Now I saw her,
side by side with the laundry-girl and her friends, recom-
posing the group which I had so loved when I was sitting
among Albertine's friends at Balbec. And if I had been an
art-lover responsive to beauty alone, I should have recognised that Albertine recomposed it a thousand times more
ravishingly, now that its elements were the nude statues
of goddesses like those which the great sculptors scattered
among the groves of Versailles or arrayed round the foun-
tains to be washed and polished by the caresses of their
waters. Now, beside the laundry-girl, I saw her, a girl at
the water's edge, in their twofold nudity of marble statues
in the midst of a grove of vegetation and dipping into the
water like aquatic bas-reliefs. Remembering Albertine as
she lay on my bed, I seemed to see the curve of her thigh,
I saw it as a swan's neck, seeking the other girl's mouth.
Then I no longer even saw a thigh, but simply the bold
neck of a swan, like the one in a stirring sketch seeking
the mouth of a Leda who is seen in all the specific palpi-
tation of feminine pleasure, because there is no one else
with her but a swan, and she seems more alone, just as
one discovers on the telephone the inflexions of a voice
which one fails to perceive so long as it is not dissociated
from a face in which one objectivises its expression. In
this sketch, the pleasure, instead of reaching out to the
woman who inspires it and who is absent, replaced by an

inert swan, is concentrated in her who feels it. At moments the contact between my heart and my memory was interrupted. What Albertine had done with the laundry-girl was indicated to me now only by quasi-algebraic abbreviations which no longer meant anything to me; but a hundred times an hour the interrupted current was restored, and my heart was pitilessly scorched by a fire from hell, while I saw Albertine, resurrected by my jealousy, really alive, stiffen beneath the caresses of the young laundry-girl to whom she was saying: "Oh, it's too heavenly."

As she was alive at the moment when she committed her misdeed, that is to say at the moment at which I myself found myself placed, it was not enough for me to know of the misdeed, I wanted her to know that I knew. Hence, if at those moments I thought with regret that I should never see her again, this regret bore the stamp of my jealousy, and, very different from the lacerating regret of the moments when I loved her, was only regret at not being able to say to her: "You thought I'd never know what you did after you left me. Well, I know everything—the laundry-girl on the bank of the Loire, and your saying to her 'Oh, it's too heavenly,' and I've seen the bite." Of course I said to myself: "Why torment yourself? She who took her pleasure with the laundry-girl no longer exists, and consequently was not a person whose actions retain any importance. She isn't telling herself that you know. But neither is she telling herself that you don't know, since she isn't telling herself anything." But this line of reasoning convinced me less than the visual image of her pleasure which brought me back to the moment in which she had experienced it. What we feel is the only thing that exists for us, and we project it into the past, or into the future, without letting ourselves be stopped by the fictitious barriers of death. If my regret that she was dead was subjected at such moments to the influence of my jealousy and assumed such a peculiar form, that influence naturally extended to my thoughts about occultism and immortality, which were no more than an effort to realise what I desired. Hence, at those moments, if I could have succeeded in evoking her by table-turning as Bergotte had at one time thought possible, or in meeting her in the other life as the abbé X thought, I would have wished to do so only in order to say to her: "I know about the laundry-girl. You said to her: 'Oh, it's too heavenly,' and I've seen the bite."

What came to my rescue against this image of the laundry-girl—certainly when it had lasted for some time—was that image itself, because we only truly know what is new, what suddenly introduces into our sensibility a change of tone which strikes us, what habit has not yet replaced with its colourless facsimiles. But it was above all that fragmentation of Albertine into many parts, into many Albertines, that was her sole mode of existence in me. Moments recurred in which she had simply been kind, or intelligent, or serious, or even loving sport above all else. And was it not right, after all, that this fragmentation should soothe me? For if it was not in itself something real, if it arose from the continuously changing shape of the hours in which she had appeared to me, a shape which remained that of my memory as the curve of the projections of my magic lantern depended on the curve of the coloured slides, did it not in its own way represent a truly objective truth, this one, namely that none of us is single, that each of us contains many persons who do not all have the same moral value, and that if a vicious Albertine had existed, it did not mean that there had not been others, the Albertine who enjoyed talking to me about Saint-Simon in her room, the Albertine who on the night when I had told her that we must part had said so sadly: "This pianola, this room, to think that I shall never see any of these things again" and, when she saw the distress which I had finally communicated to myself by my lie, had exclaimed with sincere pity: "Oh, no, anything rather than make you unhappy, I promise that I shall never try to see you again." Then I was no longer alone; I felt the barrier that separated us vanish. As soon as this good Albertine had returned, I had found once more the only person who could provide me with the antidote to the sufferings which Albertine was causing me. True, I still wanted to speak to her about the story of the laundry-girl, but no longer in order to score a cruel triumph and to show her maliciously how much I knew. I asked her tenderly, as I should have asked her had she been alive, whether the story about the laundry-girl was true. She swore to me that it was not, that Aimé was not very truthful and that, wishing to appear to have earned the money I had given him, he had not liked to return empty-handed, and had made the girl tell him what he wished to hear. No doubt Albertine had never ceased to lie to me. And yet, in the ebb and flow of her contradictions, I felt that there had been a certain progression due to myself. That she had not, indeed, confided some of her secrets to me at the beginning (perhaps, it is true, involuntarily, in a remark that escaped her lips) I would not have sworn. I no longer remembered. And besides, she

had such odd ways of naming certain things that they
could be interpreted one way or the other. But the impression she had received of my jealousy had led her afterwards to retract with horror what at first she had
complacently admitted. In any case, Albertine had no
need to tell me this. To be convinced of her innocence it
was enough for me to embrace her, and I could do so now
that the barrier that separated us was down, that impalpa-
ble but hermetic barrier which rises between two lovers
after a quarrel and against which kisses would be shattered. No, she had no need to tell me anything. Whatever
she might have done, whatever she might have wished to
do, the poor child, there were sentiments in which, over
the barrier that divided us, we could be united. If the
story was true, and if Albertine had concealed her tastes
from me, it was in order not to make me unhappy. I had
the comfort of hearing this Albertine say so. Besides, had
I ever known any other? The two chief causes of error in
one's relations with another person are, having oneself a
kind heart, or else being in love with that other person.
We fall in love for a smile, a look, a shoulder. That is
enough; then, in the long hours of hope or sorrow, we
fabricate a person, we compose a character. And when
later on we see much of the beloved being, we can no
more, whatever the cruel reality that confronts us, divest
the woman with that look, that shoulder, of the sweet nature and loving character with which we have endowed
her than we can, when she has grown old, eliminate her
youthful face from a person whom we have known since
her girlhood. I recalled the kind and compassionate look
in the eyes of that Albertine, her plump cheeks, the
grainy texture of her neck. It was the image of a dead

woman, but, as this dead woman was alive, it was easy for me to do immediately what I should inevitably have done if she had been by my side in her living body (what I should do were I ever to meet her again in another life), I forgave her.

The moments which I had lived through with this Albertine were so precious to me that I did not want to let any of them escape me. And occasionally, as one recovers the remnants of a squandered fortune, I recaptured some of them which I had thought to be lost: for instance, tying a scarf behind my neck instead of in front, I remembered a drive which I had never thought of since, during which, in order that the cold air might not reach my throat, Albertine had arranged my scarf for me in this way after first kissing me. That simple drive, restored to my memory by so humble a gesture, gave me the same pleasure as the intimate objects belonging to a dead woman who was dear to us which are brought to us by her old servant and which we find so precious; my grief was enriched by it, all the more so as I had never given another thought to the scarf in question. As with the future, it is not all at once but grain by grain that one savours the past.

Moreover my grief assumed so many forms that at times I no longer recognised it; I wanted to experience a great love; I wanted to find a woman who would live with me; this seemed to me to be the sign that I no longer loved Albertine, whereas it meant that I loved her still. Now, freed, she had taken flight again; men, women followed her. But she lived in me. I realised that this need to experience a great love was, quite as much as the desire to kiss Albertine's plump cheeks, merely a part of my regret.

And at heart I was happy not to fall in love with another woman; I realised that this continuing love for Albertine was like the ghost of the feeling I had had for her, reproducing its various stages and obeying the same laws as the sentimental reality which it reflected on the further side of death. For I was well aware that if I could extend the intervals between my thoughts of Albertine, I should have ceased to love her if the gap had been too wide; I should have become indifferent to her as I was now indifferent to my grandmother. Too much time spent without thinking of her would have broken, in my memory, the continuity which is the very principle of life, though it may recover and resume after a certain lapse of time. Had not this been the case with my love for Albertine when she was alive, a love which had been able to revive after a quite long interval during which I had not given her a thought? My memory must have been obedient to the same laws, must have been unable to endure longer intervals, for it simply went on reflecting, like an aurora borealis, after Albertine's death the feeling I had had for her; it was like the phantom of my love. It was when I had forgotten her that I might think it wiser and happier to live without love. Thus my regret for Albertine, because it was it that aroused in me the need of a sister, made that need unassuageable. And as my regret for Albertine grew fainter, the need of a sister, which was only an unconscious form of that regret, would become less imperious. And yet these two residues of my love did not follow the same rate of progress in their gradual decline. There were hours when I was determined to marry, so completely had the former been eclipsed, while the latter on the contrary remained very strong. And on the other hand, later on, my jealous memories having died away, suddenly at times a feeling of tenderness for Albertine would well up in my heart, and then, thinking of my own love affairs with other women, I told myself that she would have understood, would have shared them—and her vice became almost a reason for loving her. At times my jealousy revived in moments when I no longer remembered Albertine, although it was of her that I was jealous. I thought that I was jealous of Andrée, apropos of whom I heard at that time of an amorous adventure she was having. But Andrée was to me merely a substitute, a by-road, a connecting link which brought me indirectly to Albertine. So it is that in dreams we give a different face, a different name to a person as to whose underlying identity we are not mistaken. When all was said, notwithstanding the continuing ebb and flow which upset in these particular instances the general law, the sentiments that Albertine had bequeathed to me were more difficult to extinguish than the memory of their original cause. Not only the sentiments, but the sensations. Different in this respect from Swann who, when he had begun to cease to love Odette, had not even been able to re-create in himself the sensation of his love, I felt myself still reliving a past which was now no more than the story of another person; my personality was now somehow split in two, and while the upper part was already hard and chilled, it still burned at its base whenever a spark made the old current pass through it, even after my mind had long ceased to conceive of Albertine. And as no image of her accompanied the painful palpitations that were substituted for it, and the tears that were brought to my eyes by a cold breeze blowing as at Balbec through apple-trees already

pink with blossom, I came to wonder whether the renewal
of my grief was not due to entirely pathological causes
and whether what I took to be the revival of a memory
and the final period of a lingering love was not rather the
first stage of heart-disease.

There are in certain affections secondary symptoms
which the sufferer is too apt to confuse with the malady
itself. When they cease, he is surprised to find himself
nearer to recovery than he had supposed. Of this sort
had been the suffering caused me—the "complication"
brought about—by Aimé's letters with regard to the
bathing establishment and the laundry-girls. But a spiritual healer, had such a person visited me, would have
found that, in other respects, my grief itself was on the
way to recovery. Doubtless, since I was a man, one of
those amphibious creatures who are plunged simultaneously in the past and in the reality of the present, there
still existed in me a contradiction between the living
memory of Albertine and my consciousness of her death.
But this contradiction was in a sense the converse of what
it had been before. The idea that Albertine was dead,
which at first used to contest so furiously with the idea
that she was alive that I was obliged to run away from it
as children run away from an oncoming wave, by the very
force of its incessant onslaughts had ended by capturing
the place in my mind that a short while before was still
occupied by the idea of her life. Without my being precisely aware of it, it was now this idea of Albertine's
death—no longer the present memory of her life—that
for the most part formed the basis of my unconscious
musings, with the result that if I interrupted them suddenly to reflect upon myself, what surprised me was not,

as during the first days, that Albertine, so alive in me, could be no longer existent upon the earth, could be dead, but that Albertine, who no longer existed upon the earth, who was dead, should have remained so alive in me. Built up and held together by the contiguity of the memories that followed one another, the black tunnel in which my thoughts had lain dreaming so long that they had even ceased to be aware of it was suddenly broken by an interval of sunlight, bathing in the distance a blue and smiling universe where Albertine was no more than a memory, insignificant and full of charm. Was it she, I wondered, who was the true Albertine, or was it the person who, in the darkness through which I had so long been travelling, seemed to me the sole reality? The person I had been so short a time ago, who lived only in the perpetual expectation of the moment when Albertine would come in to say good-night and kiss him, was now made to appear to me, by a sort of multiplication of myself, as no more than a faint fragment of me, already half stripped away, and, like a flower unfolding its petals, I felt the rejuvenating refreshment of an exfoliation. However, these brief illuminations succeeded perhaps only in making me more conscious of my love for Albertine, as happens with every idea that is too constant, needing opposition to make it affirm itself. People who were alive during the war of 1870, for instance, say that the idea of war ended by seeming to them natural, not because they did not think enough about the war, but because they thought of it all the time. And in order to understand how strange and momentous a fact war is, it was necessary that, something else wrenching them out of their permanent obsession, they should forget for a moment that a state of war prevailed and should find themselves once again as they had been in peacetime, until all of a sudden, against that momentary blank, there stood out clearly at last the monstrous reality which they had long ceased to see, since there had been nothing else visible.

If only this withdrawal of my different impressions of Albertine had at least been carried out not in echelon but simultaneously, evenly, frontally, along the whole line of my memory, the recollections of her infidelities receding at the same time as those of her sweetness, forgetting would have brought me solace. It was not so. As upon a beach where the tide recedes unevenly, I would be assailed by the onrush of one of my suspicions when the image of her tender presence had already withdrawn too far from me to be able to bring me its remedial balm.

The betrayals had made me suffer because, however remote the year in which they had occurred, to me they were not remote; but I suffered from them less when they became remote, that is to say when I pictured them to myself less vividly, for the remoteness of a thing is in proportion rather to the visual power of the memory that is looking at it than to the real duration of the intervening days, as the memory of last night's dream may seem to us more distant in its imprecision and dimness than an event which is many years old. But, although the idea of Albertine's death made some headway in me, the reflux of the sensation that she was alive, if it did not arrest that progress, obstructed it nevertheless and prevented its being regular. And I realise now that during this period (doubtless because of my having forgotten the hours in which she had been cloistered in my house, hours which, by dispelling my anguish at misdeeds which seemed to

me almost unimportant because I knew that she was not
committing them, had become tantamount to so many
proofs of her innocence), I underwent the martyrdom of
living in the constant company of an idea quite as novel
as the idea that Albertine was dead (until then I had always started from the idea that she was alive), with an
idea which I should have supposed it to be equally impossible to endure and which, without my noticing it, was
gradually forming the basis of my consciousness, substi-
tuting itself for the idea that Albertine was innocent: the
idea that she was guilty. When I thought I was doubting
her, I was on the contrary believing in her; similarly
I took as the starting point of my other ideas the certainty—often proved false as the contrary idea had been
—of her guilt, while continuing to imagine that I still felt
doubts. I must have suffered a great deal during this period, but I realise that it had to be so. One is cured of
suffering only by experiencing it to the full. By protecting
Albertine from any contact with the outside world, by
creating for myself the illusion that she was innocent, and
also, later on, by adopting as the basis of my reasoning
the thought that she was alive, I was merely postponing
the hour of recovery, because I was postponing the long
hours of necessary suffering that must precede it. Now
with regard to these ideas of Albertine's guilt, habit, were
it to come into play, would do so in accordance with the
same laws as I had already experienced in the course of
my life. Just as the name Guermantes had lost the significance and the charm of a road bordered with red and purple flowers and of the window of Gilbert the Bad,
Albertine's presence that of the blue undulations of the
sea, the names of Swann, of the lift-boy, of the Princesse

de Guermantes and so many others, all that they had
meant to me—that charm and that significance leaving
me with a mere word which they considered big enough
to stand on its own feet, as a man who comes to set a
subordinate to work gives him his instructions and after a
few weeks withdraws—similarly the painful knowledge of
Albertine's guilt would be expelled from me by habit.
Moreover between now and then, like an attack launched
from both flanks at once, in this action undertaken by
habit two allies would mutually lend a hand. It was because this idea of Albertine's guilt would become for me
more probable, more habitual, that it would become less
painful. But at the same time, because it would be less
painful, the objections against my certainty of her guilt,
which were inspired in my mind only by my desire not to
suffer too acutely, would collapse one by one; and, one
action precipitating another, I should pass quickly enough
from the certainty of Albertine's innocence to the certainty of her guilt. I had to live with the idea of Albertine's death, with the idea of her misdeeds, in order for
these ideas to become habitual, that is to say in order to
be able to forget these ideas and in the end forget Albertine herself.

I had not yet reached this stage. At one time it was
my memory, made clearer by some intellectual excitement—such as reading a book—which revived my grief;
at other times it was on the contrary my grief—when it
was aroused, for instance, by the anguish of a spell of
stormy weather—which raised higher, brought nearer to
the light, some memory of our love. Moreover these re-
vivals of my love for Albertine might occur after an interval of indifference interspersed with other curiosities, as,

after the long interval which had begun with her refusal
to let me kiss her at Balbec and during which I had
thought far more about Mme de Guermantes, about Andrée, about Mlle de Stermaria, it had revived when I had
started seeing her regularly again. But even now various
preoccupations could bring about a separation—from a
dead woman, this time—in which she left me more indifferent. All this for the same reason, that she was a living
person for me. And even later on, when I loved her less,
it remained nevertheless for me one of those desires of
which we quickly tire, but which revive when we have allowed them to lie dormant for a while. I pursued one living woman, then another, then I returned to my dead one.
Often it was in the most obscure recesses of myself, when
I could no longer form any clear idea of Albertine, that a
name would come by chance to stimulate painful reactions
which I supposed to be no longer possible, like those dying people whose brain is no longer capable of thought
and who are made to contract their muscles by the prick
of a needle. And, during long periods, these stimulations
occurred to me so rarely that I was driven to seek for myself occasions for grief, for a pang of jealousy, in an attempt to re-establish contact with the past, to remember
her better. For, since regret for a woman is only a recrudescence of love and remains subject to the same laws,
the keenness of my regret was intensified by the same
causes which in Albertine's lifetime had increased my love
for her and in the front rank of which had always appeared jealousy and grief. But as a rule these occasions—
for an illness or a war can always last far longer than the
most prophetic wisdom has calculated—took me unawares and caused me such violent shocks that I thought

far more of protecting myself against suffering than of appealing to them for a memory.

Moreover a word did not even need to be connected, like "Chaumont," with some suspicion (even a syllable common to two different names was sufficient for my memory—as for an electrician who is happy with any substance that is a good conductor—to restore the contact between Albertine and my heart) in order to reawaken that suspicion, to be the password, the "Open sesame" unlocking the door of a past which one had ceased to take into account because, having seen more than enough of it, literally one no longer possessed it; one had been shorn of it, had supposed that by this subtraction one's own personality had changed its form, like a geometrical figure which by the removal of an angle would lose one of its sides; certain phrases, for instance, in which there occurred the name of a street or a road where Albertine might have been, were sufficient to incarnate a potential, non-existent jealousy, in quest of a body, a dwelling, some physical location, some particular realisation.

Often it was simply during my sleep that these "reprises," these "da capos" of one's dreams, which turn back several pages of one's memory, several leaves of the calendar at once, brought me back, made me regress to a painful but remote impression which had long since given place to others but which now became present once more. As a rule, it was accompanied by a whole stage-setting, clumsy but striking, which, giving me the illusion of reality, brought before my eyes, voiced in my ears, what thenceforward dated from that night. Besides, in the history of a love-affair and of its struggles against forgetfulness, do not our dreams occupy an even larger place than

our waking state, since they take no account of the infinitesimal divisions of time, suppress transitions, oppose
sharp contrasts, undo in an instant the web of consolation
so slowly woven during the day, and contrive for us, by
night, a meeting with her whom we would eventually
have forgotten, provided always that we did not see her
again? For whatever people may say, we can perfectly well
have in a dream the impression that what is happening in
it is real. It would be impossible only for reasons drawn
from our waking experience, an experience which at that
moment is hidden from us. With the result that this sup-
posititious life seems to us real. Sometimes, by a defect in
the internal lighting which spoiled the success of the play,
my well-staged memories giving me the illusion of life, I
really believed that I had arranged to meet Albertine, that
I was seeing her again, but then I found myself incapable
of advancing to meet her, of uttering the words which I
meant to say to her, of relighting in order to see her the
torch that had gone out—impossibilities which were simply in my dream the immobility, the dumbness, the
blindness of the sleeper—as suddenly one sees a huge
shadow which ought not to be visible obliterate the figures on the screen of a magic lantern, a shadow which is
that of the lantern itself, or that of the operator. At other
times Albertine was present in my dream, and proposed
to leave me once again, without my being moved by her
resolve. This was because a warning ray of light had managed to filter into the darkness of my sleep, and what
deprived Albertine's future actions, her threatened departure, of any importance for me was the knowledge that
she was dead. But often, even more clearly, this memory
that Albertine was dead was combined, without destroy-

ing it, with the sensation that she was alive. I chatted to
her, and while I was speaking my grandmother moved to
and fro at the back of the room. Part of her chin had
crumbled away like a corroded statue, but I found nothing
unusual in that. I told Albertine that I had various questions to ask her with regard to the bathing establishment
at Balbec, and to a certain laundress in Touraine, but I
would put them off till later since we had plenty of time
and there was no longer any urgency. She assured me that
she was not doing anything wrong and that she had
merely, the day before, kissed Mlle Vinteuil on the lips.
"What? Is she here?" "Yes, in fact it's time for me to
leave you, as I have to go and see her presently." And
since, now that Albertine was dead, I no longer kept her a
prisoner in my house as in the last months of her life, her
visit to Mlle Vinteuil perturbed me. I did not want to
show it; Albertine told me that she had done no more
than kiss her, but she was evidently beginning to lie again
as in the days when she used to deny everything.
Presently, no doubt, she would not be content merely
with kissing Mlle Vinteuil. Doubtless from a certain point
of view I was wrong to let myself be disturbed like this,
since, according to what we are told, the dead can feel
nothing, can do nothing. People say so, but this did not
alter the fact that my grandmother, who was dead, had
continued nevertheless to live for many years, and at that
moment was walking to and fro in my room. And no
doubt, once I was awake, this idea of a dead woman who
continued to live ought to have become as impossible for
me to understand as it is to explain. But I had already
formed it so many times in the course of those transient
periods of madness which are our dreams, that I had be-

come in time familiar with it; our memory of dreams may become lasting, if they repeat themselves often enough. And long after my dream had ended, I remained tormented by that kiss which Albertine had told me she had given in words which I thought I could still hear. And indeed they must have passed very close to my ear since it was I myself who had uttered them. All day long, I continued to talk to Albertine; I questioned her, I forgave her, I made up for my forgetfulness of the things which I had always meant to say to her during her life. And all of a sudden I was startled by the thought that the creature invoked by memory to whom all these remarks were addressed no longer bore any relation to reality, that death had destroyed the various parts of the face to which the continual thrust of the will to live, now abolished, had alone given the unity of a person.

At other times, without my having dreamed, as soon as I awoke I felt that the wind had changed in me; it was blowing coldly and steadily from another direction, issuing from the remotest past, bringing back to me the sound of a clock striking far-off hours, of the whistle of departing trains which I did not ordinarily hear. One day I tried to interest myself in a book. I reopened a novel by Bergotte of which I had been especially fond. Its congenial characters appealed to me greatly, and very soon, reconquered by the charm of the book, I began to hope, as for a personal pleasure, that the wicked woman might be punished, while my eyes grew moist when the happiness of the young lovers was assured. "But then," I exclaimed in despair, "I cannot conclude, from the fact that I attach so much importance to what Albertine may have done, that her personality is something real which cannot be destroyed, that I shall find her one day in her own likeness in heaven, if I invoke with so many entreaties, await with such impatience, welcome with tears the success of a person who has never existed except in Bergotte's imagination, whom I have never seen, whose appearance I am at liberty to imagine as I please!" Besides, in this novel, there were seductive girls, amorous correspondences, deserted paths in which lovers meet, and all this, reminding me that one may love clandestinely, revived my jealousy, as though Albertine had still been able to stroll along deserted paths. And the novel also pictured a man who after fifty years meets a woman whom he loved in her youth, fails to recognise her, is bored in her company. And this reminded me that love does not last for ever and distressed me as though I were destined to be parted from Albertine and to meet her again with indifference in my old age. If I caught sight of a map of France, my fearful eyes took care not to fall upon Touraine so that I might not be jealous, nor, so that I might not be miserable, upon Normandy, where would certainly be indicated at least Balbec and Doncières, between which I could situate all those places we had traversed so many times together. In the midst of other names of towns or villages of France, names which were merely visible or audible, the name of Tours, for instance, seemed to be differently composed, to be made up, not of intangible images, but of venomous substances which acted instantaneously on my heart, making it beat faster and more painfully. And if this force extended to certain names, making them so different from the rest, how, when I stayed closer to myself, when I confined myself to Albertine herself, could I be astonished that this force which I found irresistible, and to produce which any other woman might have served, had been the result of an entanglement, of a bringing into contact of dreams, desires, habits, affections, with the requisite conjunction of alternating pains and pleasures? And this continued her life in death, memory being sufficient to sustain the reality of life, which is mental. I recalled Albertine alighting from a railway carriage and telling me that she wanted to go to Saint-Mars-le-Vêtu, and I saw her again before that, with her "polo" pulled down over her cheeks; I thought of new possibilities of happiness, towards which I sprang, saying to myself: "We might have gone on together to Infreville, to Doncières." There was no watering-place in the neighbourhood of Balbec in which I did not see her, with the result that that country, like a mythological land which had been preserved, restored to me, living and cruel, the most ancient, the most charming legends, those that had been most obliterated by the sequel of my love. Ah, what anguish were I ever to have to sleep again in that bed at Balbec around whose brass frame, as around an immovable pivot, a fixed bar, my life had moved and evolved, bringing successively into its compass gay conversations with my grandmother, the nightmare of her death, Albertine's soothing caresses, the discovery of her vice, and now a new life into which, looking at the glazed bookcases in which the sea was reflected, I knew that Albertine would never come again! Was it not, that Balbec hotel, like the single set of a provincial theatre, in which for years past the most diverse plays have been performed, which has served for a comedy, for first one tragedy, then another, for a purely poetical drama, that hotel which already stretched quite far back into my past? The fact that this part alone, with its walls, its bookcases, its mirror, remained invariably the same throughout new epochs of my life, made me better aware that all in all it was the rest, it was myself, that had changed, and thus gave me that impression that the mysteries of life, of love, of death—which in their optimism children believe they have no share in—are not set apart, but one perceives with sorrowful pride that they have formed an integral part of one's own life through the course of the years.

I tried at times to take an interest in the newspapers. But I found the act of reading them repellent, and moreover by no means innocuous. The fact is that from each of our ideas, as from a crossroads in a forest, so many paths branch off in different directions that at the moment when I least expected it I found myself faced by a fresh memory. The title of Fauré's melody *Le Secret* had led me to the Duc de Broglie's *Secret du Roi*, the name Broglie to that of Chaumont;[26] or else the words "Good Friday" had made me think of Golgotha, Golgotha of the etymology of the word which is, it seems, the equivalent of *Calvus Mons*, Chaumont. But, whatever the path by which I had arrived at Chaumont, at that moment I received so violent a shock that I was far more concerned to ward off pain than to probe for memories. Some moments after the shock, my intelligence, which like the sound of thunder travels less rapidly, produced the reason for it. Chaumont had made me think of the Buttes-Chaumont, where Mme Bontemps had told me that Andrée used often to go with Albertine, whereas Albertine had told me that she had never seen the Buttes-Chaumont. After a certain age our memories are so intertwined with one another that what we are thinking of, the book we are reading, scarcely matters any more. We have put something of ourselves everywhere, everything is fertile, everything is dangerous, and we can make discoveries no less precious than in Pascal's *Pensées* in an advertisement for soap.

No doubt a fact such as the one about the Buttes-Chaumont, which at the time had appeared to me trifling, was in itself far less serious, far less decisive evidence against Albertine than the story of the bath-attendant or the laundry-girl. But in the first place, a memory which comes to us fortuitously finds in us an intact capacity for imagining, that is to say in this case for suffering, which we would have partly used up had it been, on the contrary, we who had deliberately applied our mind to re-creating a memory. And then to these latter memories (those that concerned the bath-attendant and the laundry-girl), ever present albeit obscured in my consciousness, like the furniture placed in the semi-darkness of a gallery which, without being able to see, one avoids knocking into, I had grown accustomed. Whereas it was a long time since I had given a thought to the Buttes-Chaumont, or, to take another instance, to Albertine's scrutiny of the mirror in the casino at Balbec, or to her unexplained delay on the evening when I had waited so long for her after the Guermantes party, or any of those parts of her life which remained outside my heart and which I would have liked to know in order that they might become assimilated, annexed to it, merged with the sweeter memories formed therein by an interior Albertine, an Albertine genuinely possessed. Lifting a corner of the heavy curtain of habit (stupefying habit, which during the whole course of our life conceals from us almost the whole universe, and in the dead of night, without changing the label, substitutes for the most dangerous or intoxicating poisons of life something anodyne that procures no delights), such memories would come back to me as at the time itself with that fresh and piercing novelty of a recurring season, of a change in the routine of our hours, which, in the realm of pleasures also, if we get into a carriage on the first fine day in spring, or leave the house at sunrise, makes us observe our own most trivial actions with a lucid exaltation which makes that intense minute worth more than the sum-total of the preceding days. Days in the past cover up little by little those that preceded them and are themselves buried beneath those that follow them. But each past day has remained deposited in us, as in a vast library where, even of the oldest books, there is a copy which doubtless nobody will ever ask to see. And yet should this day from the past, traversing the translucency of the intervening epochs, rise to the surface and spread itself inside us until it covers us entirely, then for a moment names resume their former meaning, people their former aspect, we ourselves our state of mind at the time, and we feel, with a vague suffering which however is endurable and will not last for long, the problems which have long ago become insoluble and which caused us such anguish at the time. Our ego is composed of the superimposition of our successive states. But this superimposition is not unalterable like the stratification of a mountain. Incessant upheavals raise to the surface ancient deposits. I found myself once more after the party at the Princesse de Guermantes's, awaiting Albertine's arrival. What had she been doing that evening? Had she been unfaithful to me? With whom? Aimé's revelations, even if I accepted them, in no way diminished for me the anxious, despairing in-

terest of this unexpected question, as though each different Albertine, each new memory, set a special problem of
jealousy, to which the solutions of the other problems
could not apply.

But I would have liked to know not only with what
woman she had spent that evening, but what special
pleasure it represented to her, what was happening inside
her at that moment. Sometimes, at Balbec, Françoise had
gone to fetch her, and had told me that she had found her
leaning out of her window with an anxious, questing air,
as though she were expecting somebody. Supposing I
learned that the girl she was awaiting was Andrée—what
was the state of mind in which Albertine awaited her, that
state of mind concealed behind the anxious, questing
gaze? How important were those tastes to Albertine? How
large a place did they occupy in her thoughts? Alas, remembering my own agitation whenever I had caught sight
of a girl who attracted me, sometimes when I had merely
heard her spoken of without having seen her, my anxiety
to look my best, to show myself to advantage, my cold
sweats, I had only, in order to torture myself, to imagine
the same voluptuous excitement in Albertine, as though
by means of the apparatus which, after the visit of a certain practitioner who had shown some scepticism about
her malady, my aunt Léonie had wished to see invented,
and which would enable the doctor to undergo all the sufferings of his patient in order to understand better. And
already it was enough to torture me, to tell me that, compared with this other thing, serious conversations with me
about Stendhal and Victor Hugo must have counted for
very little with her, to feel her heart being drawn towards
other people, detaching itself from mine, implanting itself

elsewhere. But even the importance which this desire must have for her and the reserve with which she surrounded it could not reveal to me what it was qualitatively, still less how she referred to it when she spoke of it to herself. In physical suffering, at least we do not have to choose our pain ourselves. The malady determines it and imposes it on us. But in jealousy we have, so to speak, to try out sufferings of every shape and size, before we arrive at the one which seems to fit. And how much more difficult this is in the case of a suffering such as that of feeling that she whom we loved is finding pleasure with beings who are different from us, who give her sensations which we are not capable of giving her, or who at least by their configuration, their aspect, their ways, represent to her something quite different from us! Ah, if only Albertine had fallen in love with Saint-Loup, how much less, it seemed to me, I should have suffered!

It is true that we are unaware of the particular sensibility of each of our fellow-creatures, but as a rule we do not even know that we are unaware of it, for this sensibility of other people is a matter of indifference to us. So far as Albertine was concerned, my misery or happiness would have depended upon the nature of this sensibility; I was well aware that it was unknown to me, and the fact that it was unknown to me was painful in itself. Once, I had the illusion of seeing these unknown desires and pleasures of Albertine's, another time, of hearing them. Of seeing them when, some time after her death, Andrée came to see me.

For the first time she seemed to me beautiful. I said to myself that her almost frizzy hair, her dark, shadowed eyes, were doubtless what Albertine had loved so much, the materialisation before my eyes of what she pictured in her amorous day-dreams, what she saw with the expectant eyes of desire on the day when she had so suddenly decided to leave Balbec. Like a strange, dark flower brought back to me from beyond the grave, from the innermost being of a person in whom I had been unable to discover it, I seemed to see before me, the unlooked-for exhumation of a priceless relic, the incarnate desire of Albertine which Andrée was to me, as Venus was the desire of Jove. Andrée regretted Albertine's death, but I sensed at once that she did not miss her. Forcibly removed from her friend by death, she seemed to have easily reconciled herself to a final separation which I would not have dared to ask of her while Albertine was alive, so afraid would I have been of failing to obtain her consent. She seemed on the contrary to accept this renunciation without difficulty, but precisely at the moment when it could no longer be of any advantage to me. Andrée abandoned Albertine to me, but dead, and having lost for me not only her life but retrospectively a little of her reality, now that I saw that she was not indispensable and unique to Andrée who had been able to replace her with others.

While Albertine was alive, I would not have dared to ask Andrée to confide in me about the nature of their friendship both mutually and with Mlle Vinteuil's friend, being uncertain, towards the end, whether Andrée did not repeat to Albertine everything I said to her. But now such an inquiry, even if it were to prove fruitless, would at least be unattended by danger. I spoke to Andrée, not in a questioning tone but as though I had known all the time, perhaps from Albertine, of the fondness that she herself, Andrée, had for women and of her own relations

with Mlle Vinteuil. She admitted it all without the slightest reluctance, smiling as she spoke. I could not help
drawing the most painful conclusions from this avowal;
first of all because Andrée, so affectionate and coquettish
with many of the young men at Balbec, would never have
been suspected by anyone of practices which she made no
attempt to deny, so that by analogy, when I discovered
this new Andrée, I felt that Albertine would have confessed them with the same ease to anyone other than myself, whom she felt to be jealous. But at the same time,
Andrée having been Albertine's best friend, and the
friend for whose sake she had probably returned in haste
from Balbec, and Andrée having admitted to these tastes,
the conclusion that was forced upon my mind was that
Albertine and Andrée had always indulged them together.
Of course, just as, in the presence of a stranger, we do not
always dare to examine the gift he has brought us, the
wrapper of which we shall not unfasten until the donor
has gone, so long as Andrée was with me I did not retire
into myself to examine the pain she had brought me. Although I could feel that it was already causing my bodily
servants, my nerves, my heart, the greatest turmoil, out of
good manners I pretended not to notice, chatting away on
the contrary with the utmost affability to the girl who was
my guest without diverting my gaze to these internal incidents. It was especially painful to me to hear Andrée say
of Albertine: "Oh, yes, she always loved going to the
Chevreuse valley." To the vague and non-existent universe in which Albertine's excursions with Andrée occurred, it seemed to me that the latter, by a subsequent
and diabolical act of creation, had just added to God's
work an accursed valley. I felt that Andrée was going to

tell me everything that she had been in the habit of doing with Albertine, and, as I went on trying, from politeness, from canniness, from pride, perhaps from gratitude, to appear more and more affectionate, while the space that I had still been able to concede to Albertine's innocence became smaller and smaller, it seemed to me that, despite my efforts, I presented the paralysed aspect of an animal round which a bird of prey is wheeling in steadily narrowing circles, unhurriedly because it is confident of being able to swoop on its helpless victim whenever it chooses. I gazed at her nevertheless, and, with such liveliness, naturalness and assurance as a person can muster who is trying to make it appear that he is not afraid of being hypnotised by someone's stare, I said casually to Andrée: "I've never mentioned the subject to you for fear of offending you, but now that we both find pleasure in talking about her, I may as well tell you that I found out long ago all about the things of that sort that you used to do with Albertine. And I can tell you something that you will be glad to hear although you know it already: Albertine adored you."

I told Andrée that it would be of great interest to me if she would allow me to see her (even if she simply confined herself to caresses which would not embarrass her unduly in my presence) performing such actions with those of Albertine's friends who shared her tastes, and I mentioned Rosemonde, Berthe, each of Albertine's friends, in the hope of finding out something.

"Apart from the fact that not for anything in the world would I do the things you mention in your presence," Andrée replied, "I don't believe that any of the girls whom you've named have those tastes."

Drawing closer in spite of myself to the monster that was mesmerising me, I answered: "What! You don't expect me to believe that of all your group Albertine was the only one with whom you did that sort of thing!"

"But I never did anything of the sort with Albertine."

"Come now, my dear Andrée, why deny things which I've known for at least three years? I see nothing wrong in them, far from it. For instance, that evening when she was so anxious to go with you the next day to Mme Verdurin's, you may remember perhaps . . ."

Before I had completed my sentence, I saw in Andrée's eyes, which it sharpened to a pinpoint like those stones which for that reason jewellers find it difficult to use, a fleeting, worried look, like the look on the face of a person privileged to go behind the scenes who draws back the edge of the curtain before the play has begun and at once withdraws in order not to be seen. This anxious look vanished and everything was back in place, but I sensed that whatever I saw from now on would have been artificially arranged for my benefit. At that moment I caught sight of myself in the mirror, and was struck by a certain resemblance between myself and Andrée. If I had not long since ceased to shave my upper lip and had had only a faint shadow of a moustache, this resemblance would have been almost complete. It was perhaps on seeing my moustache at Balbec when it had scarcely begun to grow again that Albertine had suddenly felt that impatient, furious desire to return to Paris.

"But I still can't say things that aren't true simply because you see no harm in them. I swear to you that I never did anything with Albertine, and I'm convinced that she detested that sort of thing. The people who told you that were lying to you, probably with some ulterior motive," she said with a questioning, defiant air.

"Oh, very well then, since you won't tell me," I replied, pretending to appear to be unwilling to furnish a proof which in fact I did not possess. However, I mentioned vaguely and at random the Buttes-Chaumont.

"I may have gone to the Buttes-Chaumont with Albertine, but is it a place that has a particularly evil reputation?"

I asked her whether she could not raise the subject with Gisèle who had at one time been on intimate terms with Albertine. But Andrée told me that because of a vile thing that Gisèle had done to her recently, asking a favour of her was the one thing that she must absolutely decline to do for me. "If you see her," she went on, "don't tell her what I've said to you about her; there's no point in making an enemy of her. She knows what I think of her, but I've always preferred to avoid having violent quarrels with her which only have to be patched up afterwards. And besides, she's dangerous. But you must understand that when one has read the letter which I had in my hands a week ago, and in which she lied with such absolute treachery, nothing, not even the noblest actions in the world, can wipe out the memory of such a thing."

On the whole I felt that if, in spite of the fact that Andrée had those tastes to the extent of making no pretence of concealing them, and the fact that Albertine had felt for her the great affection which she undoubtedly had felt, Andrée had none the less never had any carnal relations with Albertine and had never been aware that Albertine had those tastes, this meant that Albertine did not have them, and had never enjoyed with anyone those relations which, rather than with anyone else, she would have enjoyed with Andrée. And so when Andrée had left me, I realised that her categorical assertion had brought me some peace of mind. But perhaps it had been dictated by a sense of the obligation, which Andrée felt that she owed to the dead girl whose memory still survived in her, not to let me believe what Albertine, while she was alive, had doubtless begged her to deny.

Having thought for a moment, contemplating Andrée, that I could actually see these pleasures of Albertine's which I had so often tried to imagine, on another occasion I received an intimation of them otherwise than through the eyes: I thought I heard them. I had had two young laundry-girls, from a district where Albertine had often gone, brought to a house of assignation. One of them, beneath the caresses of the other, suddenly began to utter sounds which at first I found difficult to identify; for one never understands precisely the meaning of an original sound expressive of a sensation which one does not experience oneself. Hearing it from a neighbouring room without being able to see, one may mistake for uncontrollable laughter the noise which is forced by pain from a patient being operated on without an anaesthetic; and as for the noise emitted by a mother who has just been told that her child has died, it can seem to us, if we are unaware of its origin, as difficult to translate into human terms as the noise emitted by an animal or by a harp. It takes us a little time to realise that those two noises express what, by analogy with the (very different) sensations we ourselves may have felt, we call pain; and it took me some time, too, to understand that *this* noise expressed what, by analogy with the (very different) sensations I myself had felt,

I called pleasure; and the pleasure must have been very great to overwhelm to this extent the person who was expressing it and to extract from her this strange utterance which seemed to describe and comment on all the phases of the exquisite drama which the young woman was living through and which was concealed from my eyes by the curtain that is for ever lowered for other people over what happens in the mysterious intimacy of every human creature. In any case these two girls could tell me nothing, as they had no idea who Albertine was.

Novelists sometimes pretend in an introduction that while travelling in a foreign country they have met somebody who has told them the story of another person's life. They then withdraw in favour of this chance acquaintance, and the story that he tells them is nothing more or less than their novel. Thus the life of Fabrice del Dongo was related to Stendhal by a canon of Padua. How gladly would we, when we are in love, that is to say when another person's existence seems to us mysterious, find some such well-informed narrator! And undoubtedly he exists. Do we not ourselves frequently relate the story of some woman or other quite dispassionately to one of our friends, or to a stranger, who has known nothing of her love-affairs and listens to us with keen interest? Such a person as I was when I spoke to Bloch about the Princesse de Guermantes or Mme Swann, such a person existed, who could have spoken to me of Albertine, such a person exists always . . . but we never come across him. It seemed to me that if I had been able to find women who had known her I should have learned everything I did not yet know. And yet to strangers it must have seemed that nobody could have known as much about her

life as I did. Indeed, did I not know her dearest friend,
Andrée? Thus one imagines that the friend of a minister
must know the truth about some political affair or cannot
be implicated in a scandal. From his own experience the
friend has found that whenever he discussed politics with
the minister the latter confined himself to generalisations
and told him nothing more than what had already appeared in the newspapers, or that if he was in any trouble,
his repeated attempts to secure the minister's help have
invariably been met with an "It's not in my power"
against which the friend is himself powerless. I said to
myself: "If I could have known such and such
witnesses!"—from whom, if I had known them, I should
probably have been unable to extract anything more than
from Andrée, herself the custodian of a secret which she
refused to surrender. Differing in this respect also from
Swann who, when he was no longer jealous, ceased to feel
any curiosity as to what Odette might have done with
Forcheville, I found that, even after my jealousy had subsided, the thought of making the acquaintance of Albertine's laundry-girl, of people in her neighbourhood, of
reconstructing her life in it, her intrigues, alone had any
charm for me. And as desire always springs from an initial glamour, as had happened to me in the past with
Gilberte and with the Duchesse de Guermantes, it was
the women of Albertine's background, in the districts in
which she had formerly lived, that I sought to know, and
whose presence alone I could have desired. Whether or
not I could learn anything from them, the only women towards whom I felt attracted were those whom Albertine
had known or whom she might have known, women of
her own background or of the sort with whom she liked

to associate, in a word those women who had in my eyes
the distinction of resembling her or of being of the type
that might have appealed to her. Recalling thus either Albertine herself or the type for which she doubtless had a
predilection, these women aroused in me a painful feeling
of jealousy or regret, which later, when my grief subsided,
changed into a curiosity that was not devoid of charm.
And among these last, especially girls of the working
class, because of that life, so different from the life that I
knew, which is theirs. No doubt it is only in one's mind
that one possesses things, and one does not possess a picture because it hangs in one's dining-room if one is incapable of understanding it, or a landscape because one lives
in it without even looking at it. But still, I had had in the
past the illusion of recapturing Balbec, when in Paris Albertine came to see me and I held her in my arms, and
similarly I established some contact, restricted and furtive
though it might be, with Albertine's life, the atmosphere
of workrooms, a conversation across a counter, the spirit
of the slums, when I embraced a seamstress. Andrée, and
these other women, all of them in relation to Albertine—
like Albertine herself in relation to Balbec—were to be
numbered among those substitute pleasures, replacing one
another in a gradual declension, which enable us to dispense with the pleasure to which we can no longer attain,
a trip to Balbec or the love of Albertine, pleasures which
(just as going to the Louvre to look at a Titian consoles
us for not being able to go to Venice where it originally
was), separated one from another by indistinguishable gra-
dations, convert one's life into a series of concentric, con-
tiguous, harmonic and graduated zones, encircling an
initial desire which has set the tone, eliminated everything

that does not combine with it, applied the dominant colour (as had, for instance, occurred to me also in the cases of the Duchesse de Guermantes and of Gilberte). Andrée and these women were to the desire, which I knew I could no longer gratify, to have Albertine by my side, what had been, one evening, before I knew Albertine except by sight and felt that she could never be mine, the writhing, sun-drenched freshness of a cluster of grapes.

Associated now with the memory of my love, Albertine's physical and social attributes, in spite of which I had loved her, oriented my desire on the contrary towards what at one time it would least readily have chosen: dark-haired girls of the lower middle class. Indeed what was beginning partially to revive in me was that immense desire which my love for Albertine had been unable to assuage, that immense desire to know life which I used to feel on the roads round Balbec, in the streets of Paris, that desire which had caused me so much suffering when, supposing it to exist in Albertine's heart also, I had sought to deprive her of the means of satisfying it with anyone but myself. Now that I was able to endure the idea of her desire, since that idea was at once aroused by my own desire, these two immense appetites coincided; I would have liked us to be able to indulge them together, saying to myself: "That girl would have appealed to her," and led by this sudden detour to think of her and of her death, I felt too unhappy to be able to pursue my own desire any further. As, long ago, the Méséglise and Guermantes ways had laid the foundations of my taste for the countryside and prevented me thereafter from finding any real charm in a place where there was no old church, where there were no cornflowers or buttercups, so it was by linking them in my mind to a past full of charm that my love for Albertine made me seek out exclusively a certain type of woman; I was beginning once more, as before I loved her, to feel the need for overtones from her which would be interchangeable with a memory that had become gradually less exclusive. I could not have found pleasure now in the company of a golden-haired and haughty duchess, because she would not have aroused in me any of the emotions that sprang from Albertine, from my desire for her, from my jealousy of her love-affairs, from my grief at her death. For our sensations, in order to be strong, need to release inside us something different from themselves, a sentiment which cannot find its satisfaction in pleasure, but which adds itself to desire, swells it, makes it cling desperately to pleasure. Gradually, as the love that Albertine may have felt for certain women ceased to cause me pain, it attached those women to my past, made them somehow more real, as the memory of Combray gave to buttercups and hawthorn blossom a greater reality than to unfamiliar flowers. Even of Andrée, I no longer said to myself with rage in my heart: "Albertine loved her," but on the contrary, in order to explain my desire to myself, in an affectionate tone: "Albertine was fond of her." I could now understand the widowers whom we suppose to have found consolation and who prove on the contrary that they are inconsolable because they marry their deceased wife's sister.

Thus my waning love seemed to make new loves possible for me, and Albertine, like those women long loved for themselves who later, feeling their lover's desire fade, preserve their power by contenting themselves with the role of procuresses, provided me, as the Pompadour provided Louis XV, with fresh damsels. In the past, my time had been divided into periods in which I desired this woman or that. When the violent pleasures afforded by one had subsided, I longed for the other who would give me an almost pure affection until the need of more sophisticated caresses brought back my desire for the first. Now these alternations had come to an end, or at least one of the periods was being indefinitely prolonged. What I would have liked was that the newcomer should take up her abode in my house, and should give me at night, before leaving me, a familial, sisterly kiss. So that I might have been able to believe—had I not had experience of the intolerable presence of another person—that I regretted a kiss more than a certain pair of lips, a pleasure more than a love, a habit more than a person. I would have liked also that the newcomer should be able to play Vinteuil's music to me like Albertine, to talk to me as she had talked about Elstir. All this was impossible. Her love would not match up to Albertine's, I thought; either because a love which embraced all those episodes, visits to picture galleries, evenings at concerts, a whole complicated existence which allows correspondence, conversations, a flirtation preliminary to the more intimate relations, a serious friendship afterwards, possesses more resources than love for a woman who can only offer herself, as an orchestra possesses more resources than a piano; or because, more profoundly, my need of the same sort of tenderness as Albertine used to give me, the tenderness of a girl of a certain culture who would at the same time be a sister to me, was—like my need for women of the same background as Albertine—merely a recrudescence of my memory of Albertine, of my memory of my love for her.

And once again I discovered, first of all that memory has no power of invention, that it is powerless to desire anything else, let alone anything better, than what we have already possessed; secondly that it is spiritual, in the sense that reality cannot provide it with the state which it seeks; and lastly that, stemming from a dead person, the resurrection that it incarnates is not so much that of the need to love, in which it makes us believe, as that of the need for the absent person. So that even the resemblance to Albertine of the woman I had chosen, the resemblance of her tenderness, if I succeeded in winning it, to Albertine's, only made me the more conscious of the absence of what I had been unconsciously seeking, of what was indispensable to the revival of my happiness, that is to say, Albertine herself, the time we had lived together, the past in the search for which I was unwittingly engaged.

Certainly, on fine days, Paris seemed to me innumerably aflower with all the girls, not whom I desired, but who thrust down their roots into the obscurity of the desire and the unknown nocturnal life of Albertine. It was of one such that she had said to me at the outset, when she had not yet begun to be wary of me: "She's ravishing, that girl. What pretty hair she has!" All that I had wanted to know about her life in the past when I knew her only by sight, and at the same time all my desires in life, merged into this one sole curiosity, to know in what manner Albertine experienced pleasure, to see her with other women, perhaps because thus, when they had left her, I should have remained alone with her, the last and the master. And seeing her hesitations as to whether it would be worth her while to spend the evening with this or that girl, her satiety when the other had gone, perhaps her disappointment, I should have elucidated, I should have restored to its true proportions, the jealousy that Albertine inspired in me, because seeing her thus experience them I should have taken the measure and discovered the limit of her pleasures. Of how many pleasures, of what an agreeable life she deprived us, I said to myself, by that stubborn obstinacy in denying her tastes! And as once again I sought to discover what could have been the reason for that obstinacy, all of a sudden the memory came back to me of a remark that I had made to her at Balbec on the day when she gave me a pencil. As I reproached her for not having allowed me to kiss her, I had told her that I thought a kiss just as natural as I thought it revolting that a woman should have relations with another woman. Alas, perhaps Albertine had remembered it.

I took home with me the girls who would have appealed to me least, I stroked sleek virginal tresses, I admired a small and well-shaped nose or a Spanish pallor. True, in the past, even with a woman I had merely glimpsed on a road near Balbec or in a street in Paris, I had felt the individuality of my desire and that it would be adulterating it to seek to assuage it with another person. But life, by disclosing to me little by little the permanence of our needs, had taught me that failing one person we must content ourselves with another, and I felt that what I had demanded of Albertine could have been given to me by another, by Mlle de Stermaria. But it had been Albertine; and between the satisfaction of my need for tenderness and the distinctive characteristics of her body, such an inextricable network of memories had been woven that I could no longer detach all that embroidery from any new physical desire. She alone could give me that happiness. The idea of her uniqueness was no longer a metaphysical *a priori* based upon what was individual in Albertine, as in the case of the women I passed in the street long ago, but an *a posteriori* created by the contingent and indissoluble overlapping of my memories. I could no longer desire physically without feeling a need for her, without suffering from her absence. Hence the mere resemblance of the woman chosen, the caresses sought, to the happiness I had known only made me the more conscious of all that they lacked wherewith to revive it. The same vacuum that I had found in my room since Albertine had left, and had supposed that I could fill by taking women in my arms, I regained in them. They had never spoken to me, these women, of Vinteuil's music, of Saint-Simon's memoirs, they had not sprayed themselves with an overpowering scent before coming to see me, they had not played at intertwining their eyelashes with mine, all of which things are important because they seem to enable one to weave dreams round the sexual act itself and to give oneself the illusion of love, but in reality because they formed part of my memory of Albertine and it was she whom I wanted there. What these women had in common with Albertine made me feel all the more strongly what was lacking of her in them, which was everything, and would never exist again since Albertine was dead. And so my love for Albertine, which had drawn me towards these women, made me indifferent to them, and my regret for Albertine and the persistence of my jealousy, which had already outlasted my most pessimistic calculations, would perhaps never have altered appreciably if their existence, isolated from the rest of my life, had been subjected merely to the play of my memories, to the actions and reactions of a psychology applicable to immobile states, and had not been drawn into a vaster system in which souls move in time as bodies move in space.

As there is a geometry in space, so there is a psychology in time, in which the calculations of a plane psychology would no longer be accurate because we should not be taking account of Time and one of the forms that it assumes, forgetting—forgetting, the force of which I was beginning to feel and which is so powerful an instrument of adaptation to reality because it gradually destroys in us the surviving past which is in perpetual contradiction with it. And I really ought to have discovered sooner that one day I should no longer be in love with Albertine. When I had realised, from the difference that existed between what the importance of her person and of her actions was to me and what it was to other people, that my love was not so much a love for her as a love in myself, I might have drawn various conclusions from this subjective nature of my love and in particular deduced that, being a mental state, it might survive the person for some time, but also that, having no real connexion with that person, having no support outside itself, it must, like every mental state, even the most lasting, find itself one day obsolete, be "replaced," and that when that day came everything that seemed to attach me so sweetly, indissolubly, to the memory of Albertine would no longer exist for me. It is the tragedy of other people that they are merely showcases for the very perishable collections of one's own mind. For this very reason one bases upon them projects which have all the fervour of thought; but thought languishes and memory decays: the day would come when I would readily admit the first comer to Albertine's room, as I had without the slightest regret given Albertine the agate marble or other gifts that I had received from Gilberte.

Chapter Two

MADEMOISELLE DE FORCHEVILLE

It was not that I did not still love Albertine, but I no longer loved her in the same fashion as in the final phase. No, it was in the fashion of the earlier days, when everything connected with her, places or people, made me feel a curiosity in which there was more charm than suffering. And indeed I was well aware now that before I forgot her altogether, before I got back to the initial stage of indifference, I should have to traverse in the opposite direction, like a traveller who returns by the same route to his starting-point, all the sentiments through which I had passed before arriving at my great love. But these stages, these moments of the past are not immobile; they have retained the tremendous force, the happy ignorance of the hope that was then soaring towards a time which has now become the past, but which a hallucination makes us for a moment mistake retrospectively for the future. I read a letter from Albertine in which she had announced her intention of coming to see me that evening, and I felt for an instant the joy of expectation. In these return journeys along the same line from a place to which one will never return, when one recognises the names and the appearance of all the places through which one passed on the outward journey, it happens that, while one's train is halted at one of the stations, for an instant one has the illusion of setting off again, but in the direction of the place from

753

which one has come, as on the first occasion. The illusion vanishes at once, but for an instant one had felt oneself being carried towards it once more: such is the cruelty of memory.

And yet if, before returning to the state of indifference from which one started, one cannot avoid covering in the reverse direction the distances one had traversed in order to arrive at love, the itinerary one follows, the line one takes, are not necessarily the same. They have this in common, that they are not direct, because the process of forgetting is no more regular than that of love. But they do not necessarily take the same routes. And on the route which I followed on my return journey there were three stages, when I was already well on the way towards my destination, which I remember particularly, doubtless because I perceived in them things that had no part in my love for Albertine, or at most were linked to it only to the extent to which what existed already in one's heart before a great love becomes associated with it, whether by fostering it, or by combating it, or by offering contrasts with it or images of it for one's intelligence to analyse.

The first of these stages began early one winter, on a fine Sunday, which was also All Saints' Day, when I had gone out. As I approached the Bois, I remembered sadly how Albertine had come back to join me from the Trocadéro, for it was the same day, only without Albertine. Sadly and yet not without pleasure all the same, for the repetition in the minor, in a melancholy key, of the same motif that had filled that earlier day, the very absence of Françoise's telephone message, of Albertine's return, which was not something negative but the suppression in reality of what I remembered, gave the day a certain sadness, made of it something more beautiful than a simple, unbroken day, because what was no longer there, what had been torn from it, remained as it were etched upon it. In the Bois, I hummed a few phrases of Vinteuil's sonata. The thought that Albertine had so often played it to me no longer saddened me unduly, for almost all my memories of her had entered into that secondary chemical state in which they no longer cause an anxious oppression of the heart, but rather a certain sweetness. From time to time, in the passages which she used to play most often, when she was in the habit of making some observation which at the time I thought charming, of suggesting some reminiscence, I said to myself: "Poor child," but not sadly, merely investing the musical phrase with an additional value, as it were a historical, a curiosity value, like that which the portrait of Charles I by Van Dyck, already so beautiful in itself, acquires from the fact that it found its way into the national collection because of Mme du Barry's desire to impress the King. When the little phrase, before disappearing altogether, dissolved into its various elements in which it floated still for a moment in scattered fragments, it was not for me, as it had been for Swann, a messenger from a vanishing Albertine. It was not altogether the same associations of ideas that the little phrase had aroused in me as in Swann. I had been struck most of all by the elaboration, the trial runs, the repetitions, the gradual evolution of a phrase which developed through the course of the sonata as that love had developed through the course of my life. And now, aware that, day by day, one element after another of my love was vanishing, the jealous side of it, then some other, drifting gradually back in a vague remembrance to the first tentative beginnings, it was my love that, in the scattered notes of the little phrase, I seemed to see disintegrating before my eyes.

As I followed the paths through thickets whose gauzy screen of leaves grew thinner each day, the memory of a drive during which Albertine was by my side in the carriage on the way home with me, and during which I felt that my life was wrapped up in her, now floated round about me, in the vague mist of the darkening branches in the midst of which the setting sun lit up the tenuous horizontal strips of golden foliage so that they seemed suspended in the empty air. My heart kept fluttering from moment to moment, as happens to anyone who is haunted by an obsession which gives to every woman standing at the end of a path the resemblance or even the possible identity with the woman he is thinking of. "Perhaps it is she!" One looks round, the carriage continues on its way, and one does not go back. I did not simply contemplate this foliage with the eyes of memory; it interested me, touched me, like those purely descriptive pages into which an artist, to make them more complete, introduces a fiction, a whole romance; and this work of nature thus assumed the sole charm of melancholy which was capable of reaching my heart. The reason for this charm seemed to me to be that I still loved Albertine as much as ever, whereas the true reason was on the contrary that oblivion was continuing to make such headway in me that the memory of Albertine was no longer painful to me, that is to say had changed; but however clearly we may discern our impressions, as I then thought that I could discern the reason for my melancholy, we are unable to trace them back to their more distant meaning. Like those symptoms which the doctor hears his patient describe to him and with the help of which he works back to a deeper cause of which the patient is unaware, similarly our impressions, our ideas, have only a symptomatic value. My jealousy being kept in abeyance by the impression of charm and sweet sadness which I was feeling, my senses reawakened. Once again, as when I had ceased to see Gilberte, the love of women arose in me, relieved of any exclusive association with a particular woman already loved, and floated like those essences that have been liberated by previous destructions and stray suspended in the springtime air, asking only to be reunited with a new creature. Nowhere do so many flowers, "forget-me-nots" though they be styled, germinate as in a cemetery. I looked at the girls with whom this fine day was so multitudinously aflower, as I would have looked at them long ago from Mme de Villeparisis's carriage or from the carriage in which, on a similar Sunday, I had come there with Albertine. At once, the glance which I now gave one or other of them was matched immediately by the curious, furtive, speculative glance, reflecting unimaginable thoughts, which Albertine would surreptitiously have cast at them and which, duplicating my own with a mysterious, swift, steel-blue wing, wafted along these paths, so natural until then, the tremor of an unknown life with which my own desire would not have sufficed to animate them had it remained alone, for it, to me, contained nothing that was unfamiliar. At times the reading of a novel that was at all sad carried me suddenly back, for certain novels are like great but temporary bereavements, abolishing habit, bringing us back into contact with the reality of life, but for a few hours only, like a nightmare, since the force of habit, the oblivion it creates, the gaiety it restores through the powerlessness of the brain to fight against it and to re-create the truth, infinitely outweigh the almost hypnotic suggestion of a good book which, like all such influences, has very transient effects.

At Balbec, when I had first longed to know Albertine, was it not because she had seemed to me representative of those girls the sight of whom had so often brought me to a standstill in the streets of towns or on country roads, and because she might epitomise their life for me? And was it not natural that now the waning star of my love in which they had been condensed should disperse once again in this scattered dust of nebulae? All of them seemed to me Albertines—the image that I carried inside me making me find her everywhere—and indeed, at the bend of an avenue, a girl getting into a motor-car recalled her so strongly, was so exactly of the same build, that I wondered for an instant whether it was not her that I had just seen, whether people had not been deceiving me when they sent me the report of her death. I recalled her thus at the corner of an avenue, perhaps at Balbec, getting into a car in the same way, at a time when she was so full of confidence in life. And I did not merely record with my eyes, as one of those superficial phenomena which occur so often in the course of a walk, this other girl's action in climbing into the car: become a sort of sustained action, it seemed to me to extend also into the past by virtue of the memory which had been superimposed upon it and which pressed so voluptuously, so sadly against my heart. But by this time the girl had vanished.

A little further on I saw a group of three girls, slightly older, young women perhaps, whose elegant and energetic appearance corresponded so closely with what had attracted me on the day when I first saw Albertine and her friends that I hastened in pursuit of them and, when they stopped a carriage, looked frantically in every direction for another. I found one, but it was too late. I failed to overtake them. A few days later, however, on coming home, I saw emerging from the portico of our house the three girls whom I had followed in the Bois. They were absolutely typical, the two dark ones especially, except that they were slightly older, of those well-born girls who so often, seen from my window or encountered in the street, had made me form countless plans, had given me a taste for life, but whom I had never succeeded in getting to know. The fair one had a rather more delicate, almost an invalid air, which appealed to me less. It was she, nevertheless, who was responsible for my not contenting myself with gazing at them for a moment, having stopped dead, with one of those looks which, by their fixed absorption, their application as to a problem, seem to be concerned with something far beyond what meets the eye. I should doubtless have allowed them to disappear, as I had allowed so many others, if, as they walked past me, the fair-haired one—was it because I was scrutinising them so closely?—had not darted a furtive glance at me and then, turning round after having passed me, a second one that set me aflame. However, as she ceased to pay attention to me and resumed her conversation with her friends, my ardour would doubtless have subsided, had it not been increased a hundredfold by the following discovery. When I asked the concierge who they were, "They asked for Mme la Duchesse," he informed me. "I think only one of them knows her and the others

were simply accompanying her as far as the door. Here's
the name, I don't know whether I've taken it down properly." And I read: "Mlle Déporcheville," which it was
easy to correct to "d'Eporcheville," that is to say the
name, more or less, so far as I could remember, of the girl
of excellent family, vaguely connected with the Guermantes, whom Robert had told me that he had met in a
disorderly house and with whom he had had relations. I
now understood the meaning of her glance, why she had
turned round without letting her companions see. How
often I had thought about her, trying to visualise her from
the name that Robert had given me! And here I had just
seen her, in no way different from her friends, but for
that clandestine glance which established between herself
and me a secret entry into the parts of her life which were
evidently hidden from her friends and which made her
appear more accessible—already almost half mine—and
more soft-hearted than girls of the aristocracy usually are.
In the mind of this girl, she and I now had in common
the hours that we might have spent together if she was
free to make an assignation with me. Was it not this that
her glance had sought to express to me with an eloquence
that was intelligible to me alone? My heart beat wildly. I
could not have given an exact description of Mlle
d'Eporcheville's appearance, I could only picture vaguely
a fair-skinned face viewed from the side; but I was madly
in love with her. All of a sudden I realised that I was reasoning as though, of the three girls, Mlle d'Eporcheville
must be the fair one who had turned round and looked at
me twice. But the concierge had not told me this. I returned to his lodge and questioned him again. He told me
that he could not enlighten me on the subject, because

they had come today for the first time and while he was
not there. But he would ask his wife who had seen them
once before. She was busy at the moment scrubbing the
service stairs. Which of us has not experienced in the
course of his life exquisite uncertainties more or less similar to this? A charitable friend, to whom one describes a
girl one has seen at a ball, concludes from the description
that she must be one of his friends and invites one to
meet her. But among so many others, and on the basis of
a mere verbal portrait, is there not a possibility of error?
The girl you are about to see may well turn out to be a
different girl from the one you desire. On the other hand,
you may be about to see, holding out her hand to you
with a smile, precisely the girl whom you hoped that she
would be. This latter case is not infrequent, and, without
being justified always by a reasoning as convincing as
mine with respect to Mlle d'Eporcheville, arises from a
sort of intuition as well as from that wind of fortune
which favours us at times. Then, on seeing her, one says
to oneself: "She was the one." I remembered that, among
the little band of girls who used to parade along the
beach, I had guessed correctly which was named Albertine Simonet. This memory caused me a sharp but transient pang, and while the concierge went in search of his
wife, my chief anxiety—as I thought of Mlle d'Eporcheville, and since in those minutes spent waiting during
which a name or piece of information which we have for
some reason or other fitted to a face finds itself free
for an instant and floats between several, ready, if it belongs to a new one, to make the original face to which it
had applied retrospectively strange, innocent, elusive—
was that the concierge was perhaps going to inform me

that Mlle d'Eporcheville was, on the contrary, one of the two dark girls. In that event, the being in whose existence I believed would vanish, the being whom I already loved, whom I now thought only of possessing, that sly, blonde Mlle d'Eporcheville whom the fateful answer must then separate into two distinct elements, which I had arbitrarily united after the fashion of a novelist who blends diverse elements borrowed from reality in order to create an imaginary character, elements which, taken separately— the name failing to corroborate the supposed intention of the glance—lost all their meaning. In that case my arguments would be nullified, but how greatly, on the contrary, they found themselves strengthened when the concierge returned to tell me that Mlle d'Eporcheville was indeed the fair girl.

From then on I could no longer believe that it was a case of homonymy. It would have been too great a coincidence that of these three girls one should be named Mlle d'Eporcheville, that she should be precisely (and this was an initial, highly relevant corroboration of my supposition) the one who had looked at me in that way, almost smiling at me, and that it should not be she who frequented houses of assignation.

Then began a day of wild excitement. Even before setting out to buy everything in which I thought it proper to array myself in order to create a favourable impression when I went to call upon Mme de Guermantes two days later, when (the concierge had informed me) the young lady would be coming back to see the Duchess, in whose house I should thus find a willing girl with whom I would arrange a rendezvous (for I could easily find an opportunity of speaking to her alone in a corner of the drawing-

room), I decided, to make assurance doubly sure, to telegraph Robert to ask him for the girl's exact name and description, hoping to have his reply within forty-eight
hours (I did not think for an instant of anything else, not
even of Albertine), for I was determined, whatever might
happen to me in the meantime, even if I had to be carried
down in a chair because I was too ill to walk, to pay a call
on the Duchess at the appropriate hour. If I telegraphed
to Saint-Loup it was not that I had any lingering doubt as
to the identity of the person, it was not that the girl
whom I had seen and the girl of whom he had spoken
were still distinct personalities in my mind. I had no
doubt whatever that they were the same person. But in
my impatience at the enforced interval of forty-eight
hours, it was a pleasure to me, it gave me already a sort
of secret power over her, to receive a telegram concerning
her, filled with detailed information. At the telegraph office, as I drafted my message with the animation of a man
who is fired by hope, I remarked how much less helpless
I was now than in my boyhood, and in relation to Mlle
d'Eporcheville than I had been in relation to Gilberte. I
had merely had to take the trouble to write out my telegram, and thereafter the clerk had only to take it from
me, and the swiftest channels of electric communication to
transmit it, and the whole length and breadth of France
and the Mediterranean, together with the whole of
Robert's roistering life applied to the identification of the
person I had just met, would be placed at the service of
the romance which I had just sketched out and to which I
need no longer give a thought, for they would undertake
to bring it to a conclusion one way or the other before
twenty-four hours had passed. Whereas in the old days,

brought home by Françoise from the Champs-Elysées, brooding alone in the house over my impotent desires, unable to make use of the practical devices of civilisation, I loved like a savage, or indeed, for I was not even free to move about, like a flower. From this moment onwards I was in a continual fever; a request from my father to go away with him for a couple of days, which would have obliged me to forgo my visit to the Duchess, filled me with such rage and despair that my mother intervened and persuaded my father to allow me to remain in Paris. But for several hours my fury refused to be allayed, while my desire for Mlle d'Eporcheville was increased a hundredfold by the obstacle that had been placed between us, by the fear which I had felt for a moment that those hours of my visit to Mme de Guermantes, at the prospect of which I smiled in constant anticipation, as at an assured blessing of which nothing could deprive me, might not occur. Certain philosophers assert that the external world does not exist, and that it is within ourselves that we develop our lives. However that may be, love, even in its humblest beginnings, is a striking example of how little reality means to us. Had I been obliged to draw from memory a portrait of Mlle d'Eporcheville, to furnish a description of her, or even to recognise her in the street, I should have found it impossible. I had glimpsed her in profile, on the move, and she had struck me as being simple, pretty, tall and fair; I could not have said more. But all the reflexes of desire, of anxiety, of the mortal blow struck by the fear of not seeing her if my father took me away, all these things, associated with an image of which on the whole I knew nothing, and as to which it was enough that I knew it to be agreeable, already constituted a state of love. At last, on the following morning, after a night of happy sleeplessness I received Saint-Loup's telegram: "De l'Orgeville, *de* particle, *orge* barley, like rye, *ville*, like town, small, dark, plump, is at present in Switzerland." It was not the girl.

A moment later my mother came into my room with the mail, put it down carelessly on my bed as though she were thinking of something else, and withdrew at once to leave me on my own. And I, who was familiar with my dear Mamma's little subterfuges and knew that one could always read the truth in her face without fear of being mistaken, if one took as a key to the cipher her desire to give pleasure to others, I smiled and thought: "There must be something interesting for me in the post, and Mamma assumed that indifferent, absent-minded air so that my surprise might be complete and so as not to be like the people who take away half your pleasure by telling you of it beforehand. And she didn't stay with me because she was afraid that out of pride I might conceal my pleasure and so feel it less keenly." Meanwhile, on reaching the door, my mother had run into Françoise who was coming into the room, and forcing her to turn back, had dragged her out with her, somewhat alarmed, offended and surprised; for Françoise considered that her duties conferred upon her the privilege of entering my room at any hour of the day and of remaining there if she chose. But already, upon her features, astonishment and anger had vanished beneath a dark and sticky smile of transcendent pity and philosophical irony, a viscous liquid secreted, in order to heal her wound, by her outraged self-esteem. So that she might not feel herself despised, she despised us. Moreover she knew that we were masters, in

other words capricious creatures, who, not being conspic-
uously intelligent, take pleasure in imposing by fear upon
clever people, upon servants, in order to prove that they
are the masters, absurd tasks such as boiling water in
times of epidemic, washing down a room with a damp
cloth, and leaving it at the very moment when you
wanted to come into it. Mamma had placed the post by
my side, so that I might not overlook it. I could see however that it consisted only of newspapers. No doubt there
was some article by a writer whom I admired, which, as
he wrote seldom, would be a surprise for me. I went to
the window, and drew back the curtains. Above the pale
and misty daylight, the sky glowed pink, like the stoves
that are being lighted in kitchens at that hour, and the
sight of it filled me with hope and with a longing to
spend the night in a train and awake at the little country
station where I had seen the milk-girl with the rosy
cheeks.

I opened the *Figaro*. What a bore! The main article
had the same title as the article which I had sent to the
paper and which had not appeared. But not merely the
same title . . . why, here were several words that were
absolutely identical. This was really too bad. I must write
and complain. Meanwhile I could hear Françoise who, indignant at having been banished from my room, into
which she considered that she had the right of entry, was
grumbling: "It's a proper shame, a kid I saw brought into
the world. I didn't see him when his mother bore him, to
be sure. But when I first knew him, to say the most, it
wasn't five years since he was birthed!" But it wasn't
merely a few words, it was the whole thing, and there was
my signature . . . It was my article that had appeared at

last! But my brain which, even at that period, had begun to show signs of age and to tire easily, continued for a moment longer to reason as though it had not understood that this was my article, like an old man who is obliged to complete a movement that he has begun even if it has become unnecessary, even if an unforeseen obstacle, in the face of which he ought at once to draw back, makes it dangerous. Then I considered the spiritual bread of life that a newspaper is, still warm and damp from the press and the morning fog in which it is distributed, at daybreak, to the housemaids who bring it to their masters with their morning coffee, a miraculous, self-multiplying bread which is at the same time one and ten thousand, which remains the same for each person while penetrating innumerably into every house at once.

What I was holding in my hand was not a particular copy of the newspaper, but one out of the ten thousand; it was not merely what had been written by me, but what had been written by me and read by everyone. To appreciate exactly the phenomenon which was occurring at this moment in other houses, it was essential that I read this article not as its author but as one of the readers of the paper; what I was holding in my hand was not only what I had written, it was the symbol of its incarnation in so many minds. But then came an initial anxiety. Would the reader who had not been forewarned see this article? I opened the paper carelessly as would such a reader, even assuming an air of not knowing what there was this morning in my paper, of being in a hurry to look at the social and political news. But my article was so long that my eye, which was avoiding it (in order to be absolutely fair and not load the dice in my favour, as a person who is waiting counts very slowly on purpose) picked up a fragment of it in passing. But many of those readers who notice the main article and even read it do not look at the signature; I myself would be quite incapable of saying who had written the main article of the day before. And I now made up my mind always to read them, and the author's name too; but, like a jealous lover who refrains from being unfaithful to his mistress in order to believe in her fidelity, I reflected sadly that my own future attention would not compel, had not compelled the reciprocal attention of other people. And besides, there were those who would have gone out shooting, and those who would have left the house too early. But still, a few people would read it. I did as they would do: I began. Although I was well aware that many people who read this article would find it detestable, at the moment of reading it the meaning that each word conveyed to me seemed to me to be printed on the paper, and I could not believe that every other reader on opening his eyes would not see directly the images that I saw, assuming—with the same naïvety as those who believe that it is the actual speech they have uttered that proceeds just as it is along the telephone wires—that the author's thought is directly perceived by the reader, whereas quite other thoughts form in the latter's mind; at the very moment in which I was trying to be an ordinary reader, my mind was rewriting my article while reading it. If M. de Guermantes did not understand some sentence which would appeal to Bloch, he might, on the other hand, be amused by some reflexion which Bloch would scorn. Thus, a fresh admirer presenting himself for each section which the previous reader seemed to disregard, the article as a whole was lifted to the skies by a swarm of readers and prevailed over my own self-distrust, since I no longer needed to bolster it. The truth of the matter is that the value of an article, however remarkable it may be, is like that of those passages in parliamentary reports in which the words "We shall see," uttered by the Minister, only take on their full consequence when read thus: THE PRIME MINISTER, MINISTER OF THE INTERIOR AND OF RELIGIOUS AFFAIRS: "We shall see!" (*Loud exclamations on the extreme Left. "Hear, hear," from some Left and Centre benches*)—an ending better than the middle and worthy of the beginning. Part of the beauty—and it is the original flaw in this type of literature, from which the famous *Lundis* are not exempt—lies in the impression made on the readers. It is a collective Venus, of which we have but one truncated limb if we confine ourselves to the thought of the author, for it is fully realised only in the minds of his readers. In them it finds completion. And since a crowd, even a select crowd, is not an artist, this final seal which it sets upon the article must always retain a trace of the commonplace. Thus Sainte-Beuve, on a Monday, could imagine Mme de Boigne in her four-poster bed reading his article in the *Constitutionnel*, and appreciating some pretty sentence which he had taken a long delight in composing and which might never, perhaps, have flowed from his pen had he not thought it opportune to stuff it into his article in order to make a more far-reaching impression. Doubtless the Chancellor,[27] reading it too, would mention it during the visit he would pay to his old friend and mistress a little later. And when he dropped him home in his carriage that evening, the Duc de Noailles in his grey trousers would tell him what had been thought of it in society, if a note from Mme d'Arbouville had not already informed him.

And setting my own self-distrust against the ten-thousand-fold approbation which now sustained me, I drew as much strength and hope for my talent from reading the article at this moment as I drew misgivings when what I had written was addressed only to myself. I saw at that same hour my thought—or at least, failing my thought for those who were incapable of understanding it, the repetition of my name and as it were an embellished evocation of my person—shine on countless people, colour their own thoughts in an auroral light which filled me with more strength and triumphant joy than the multiple dawn which at that moment was blushing at every window. I saw Bloch, the Guermantes, Legrandin, Andrée, extracting from every sentence the images that it enclosed at the very moment in which I was endeavouring to be an ordinary reader, while reading as author, but not only as author. In order that the impossible creature I was endeavouring to be should combine all the opposites that might be most favourable to me, if I read as an author I judged myself as a reader, without any of the qualms that may be felt about a written text by him who compares it with the ideal which he has sought to express in it. Those passages which, when I wrote them, were so colourless in comparison with my thought, so complicated and opaque in comparison with my harmonious and transparent vision, so full of gaps which I had not managed to fill, that the reading of them was a torture to me, had only accentuated in me the sense of my own impotence and of my incurable lack of talent. But now, in forcing myself to be a reader, I transferred to others the painful duty of judging me, and I succeeded at least in making a clean sweep of what I had attempted to do in reading what I had written. I read the article while forcing myself to imagine that it had been written by someone else. Then all my images, all my reflexions, all my epithets taken in themselves, untarnished by the memory of the failure which they represented in relation to my aims, charmed me by their brilliance, their unexpectedness, their profundity. And when I became aware of too blatant a weakness, taking refuge in the spirit of the ordinary and astonished reader, I said to myself: "Bah! how could a reader possibly notice that? There may well be something lacking there, but good heavens, they ought to be pleased! There are enough good things in it to be getting on with, more than they usually get."

And thus, no sooner had I finished this comforting perusal than I who had not had the courage to re-read my manuscript wanted to start again immediately, for there is nothing of which one can say more aptly than of an old article by oneself that "it bears re-reading." I made up my mind to send Françoise out to buy more copies—in order to give them to my friends, I would tell her, but in reality to feel at first hand the miracle of the multiplication of my thought and to read, as though I were another person who had just opened the *Figaro*, the same sentences in another copy. It was, as it happened, a very long time since I had seen the Guermantes: I would go and pay them a visit in order to find out what people thought of my article.

I thought of some female reader into whose room I would have loved to penetrate and to whom the newspaper would convey, if not my thought, which she would be incapable of understanding, at least my name, like a eulogy of me. But eulogies awarded to somebody one doesn't love do not captivate the heart any more than the thoughts of a mind one is unable to penetrate attract the mind. With regard to other friends, however, I told myself that if the state of my health continued to grow worse and I could no longer see them, it would be pleasant to continue to write, in order thus to have access to them still, to speak to them between the lines, to make them share my thoughts, to please them, to be received into their hearts. I told myself this because, social relations having hitherto had a place in my daily life, a future in which they would no longer figure alarmed me, and because this expedient which would enable me to remain in the thoughts of my friends, perhaps to arouse their admiration, until the day when I should be well enough to begin to see them again, was a solace to me; I told myself this, but I was well aware that it was not true, that although I chose to imagine their attention as the object of my pleasure, that pleasure was an internal, spiritual, self-generated pleasure which they could not give me and which I could find not in conversing with them, but in writing far away from them, and that if I began to write in the hope of seeing them indirectly, in the hope they might have a better idea of me, in the hope of preparing for myself a better position in society, perhaps writing would relieve me of the wish to see them, and I should no longer have any desire to enjoy the position in society which literature might have given me, because my pleasure would be no longer in society but in literature.

After lunch, when I went down to Mme de Guermantes, it was less for the sake of Mlle d'Eporcheville, who had been stripped, by Saint-Loup's telegram, of the better part of her personality, than in the hope of finding in the Duchess herself one of those readers of my article who would enable me to form an idea of the impression that it had made upon those members of the public who were subscribers to or purchasers of the *Figaro*. It was not, incidentally, without pleasure that I went to see Mme de Guermantes. Although I told myself that what made her house different to me from all the rest was the fact that it had for so long haunted my imagination, by knowing the reason for this difference I did not abolish it. Moreover, the name Guermantes existed for me in many forms. If the form which my memory had merely noted down as in an address-book was not accompanied by any poetry, older forms, those which dated from the time when I did not know Mme de Guermantes, were liable to renew themselves in me, especially when I had not seen her for some time and the glaring light of the person with human features did not quench the mysterious radiance of the name. Then once again I began to think of Mme de Guermantes's dwelling as of something that was beyond the bounds of reality, in the same way as I began to think again of the misty Balbec of my early day-dreams as though I had not since then made that journey, or of the 1.22 train as though I had never taken it. I forgot for an instant my own knowledge that none of this existed, as we think at times of a beloved friend forgetting for an instant that he is dead. Then the idea of reality returned as I entered the Duchess's hall. But I consoled myself with the reflexion that in spite of everything she was for me the real point of intersection between reality and dream.

On entering the drawing-room, I saw the fair girl

whom I had supposed for twenty-four hours to be the girl
of whom Saint-Loup had spoken to me. It was she who
asked the Duchess to "reintroduce" me to her. And indeed, the moment I came into the room I had the impression that I knew her quite well, an impression which the
Duchess however dispelled by saying: "Oh! so you've met
Mlle de Forcheville before?" For, on the contrary, I was
certain that I had never been introduced to any girl of
that name, which would certainly have struck me, so familiar was it in my memory ever since I had been given a
retrospective account of Odette's love-affairs and Swann's
jealousy. In itself my twofold error as to the name, in
having remembered "de l'Orgeville" as "d'Eporcheville"
and in having reconstructed as "d'Eporcheville" what was
in reality "Forcheville," was in no way extraordinary. Our
mistake lies in supposing that things present themselves as
they really are, names as they are written, people as pho-
tography and psychology give an unalterable notion of
them. But in reality this is not at all what we ordinarily
perceive. We see, we hear, we conceive the world in a
lopsided fashion. We repeat a name as we have heard it
spoken until experience has corrected our mistake—something that does not always happen. Everyone at Combray
had spoken to Françoise for twenty-five years of Mme
Sazerat and Françoise continued to say "Mme Sazerin,"
not from that deliberate and proud perseverance in error
which was habitual with her, which was strengthened by
our contradictions, and which was all that she had added
of the egalitarian principles of 1789 to the France of
Saint-André-des-Champs in her make-up (she claimed
only one civic right, that of not pronouncing words as we
did and of maintaining that "hôtel," "été" and "air" were

of the feminine gender), but because she really did continue to hear "Sazerin." This perpetual error, which is
precisely "life," does not bestow its countless forms
merely upon the visible and the audible universe, but
upon the social universe, the sentimental universe, the
historical universe, and so forth. The Princesse de Luxembourg is no better than a prostitute in the eyes of the
judge's wife, which of course is of little consequence; what
is of slightly more consequence is the fact that Odette is
in Swann's eyes a difficult woman to conquer, whence he
builds up a whole romance which becomes all the more
painful when he discovers his error; what is of even more
consequence still, the French are thinking only of revenge
in the eyes of the Germans. We have of the universe only
inchoate, fragmentary visions, which we complement by
arbitrary associations of ideas, creative of dangerous illusions. I should therefore have had no reason to be surprised when I heard the name Forcheville (and I was
already wondering whether she was related to the
Forcheville of whom I had so often heard) had not the
fair girl said to me at once, anxious no doubt to forestall,
tactfully, questions which would have been disagreeable to
her: "Don't you remember that you knew me well long
ago . . . you used to come to our house . . . your friend
Gilberte. I could see that you didn't recognise me. I
recognised you at once." (She said this as if she had
recognised me at once in the drawing-room, but the truth
is that she had recognised me in the street and had
greeted me, and later Mme de Guermantes informed me
that she had told her, as something very comic and extraordinary, that I had followed her and brushed against
her, mistaking her for a tart.) I did not discover until after

her departure why she was called Mlle de Forcheville. After Swann's death, Odette, who astonished everyone by her profound, prolonged and sincere grief, found herself an extremely rich widow. Forcheville married her, after making a long round of country houses and ascertaining that his family would acknowledge his wife. (The family raised some difficulties at first, but yielded to the material advantage of no longer having to provide for the expenses of a needy relative who was about to pass from comparative penury to opulence.) Shortly after this, an uncle of Swann's, in whose hands the successive demise of innumerable relatives had accumulated an enormous inheritance, died, leaving the whole of his fortune to Gilberte who thus became one of the richest heiresses in France. But this was a time when in the aftermath of the Dreyfus case an anti-semitic trend had arisen parallel to a growing trend towards the penetration of society by Jews. The politicians had not been wrong in thinking that the discovery of the judicial error would be a severe blow to anti-semitism. But, temporarily at least, a form of social anti-semitism was on the contrary enhanced and exacerbated thereby. Forcheville, who, like every petty nobleman, had derived from conversations in the family circle the certainty that his name was more ancient than that of La Rochefoucauld, considered that, in marrying the widow of a Jew, he had performed a similar act of charity to that of a millionaire who picks up a prostitute in the street and rescues her from poverty and squalor. He was prepared to extend his bounty to Gilberte, whose prospects of marriage would be assisted by all her millions but hindered by that absurd name "Swann." He declared that he would adopt her. We know that Mme de Guermantes, to the astonishment of her friends—which she enjoyed and was in the habit of provoking—had refused, after Swann's marriage, to meet his daughter as well as his wife. This refusal had appeared all the more cruel inasmuch as what the possibility of marriage to Odette had long represented to Swann was the prospect of introducing his daughter to Mme de Guermantes. And doubtless he ought to have known, he who had already had so long an experience of life, that these scenes which we picture to ourselves are never realised for a diversity of reasons, among which there is one which meant that he seldom regretted his inability to effect that introduction. This reason is that, whatever the image may be—from the prospect of eating a trout at sunset, which makes a sedentary man decide to take the train, to the desire to be able to astonish the proud lady at a cash desk one evening by stopping outside her door in a magnificent carriage, which makes an unscrupulous man decide to commit murder or to long for the death of rich relatives, according to whether he is brave or lazy, whether he follows his ideas through or remains fondling the first link in the chain— the act which is destined to enable us to attain to it, whether the act be travel, marriage, crime or whatever, modifies us so profoundly that not merely do we cease to attach any importance to the reason which made us perform it, but the image conceived by the man who was not then a traveller, or a husband, or a criminal, or a recluse (who has set himself to work with the idea of fame and simultaneously lost all desire for fame), may perhaps never even once recur to his mind. Moreover, even if we are stubbornly determined to prove that our wish to act was not an idle one, it is probable that the sunset effect would

fail to materialise, that feeling cold at that moment we
would long for a bowl of soup by the fireside and not for
a trout in the open air, that our carriage would fail to impress the cashier who perhaps for wholly different reasons
had a great regard for us and in whom this sudden opulence would arouse suspicion. In short, we have seen
Swann, once married, attach importance above all else to
the relations of his wife and daughter with Mme Bontemps, etc.

To all the reasons, derived from the Guermantes way
of looking at social life, which had made the Duchess decide never to allow Mme and Mlle Swann to be introduced to her, we may add also that happy complacency
with which people who are not in love dissociate themselves from that which they condemn in lovers and which
is explained by their love. "Oh! I don't get mixed up in
all that. If it amuses poor Swann to behave idiotically and
ruin his life, that's his affair, but I'm not going to be
dragged into that sort of thing; it may end very badly; I
leave them to get on with it." It is the *suave mari magno*
which Swann himself recommended to me with regard to
the Verdurins, when he had long ceased to be in love with
Odette and no longer cared about the little clan. It is what
makes so wise the judgments of third persons with regard
to passions which they themselves do not feel and the
complications of behaviour which those passions bring
about.

Mme de Guermantes had in fact applied to the os-
tracism of Mme and Mlle Swann a perseverance that
caused general surprise. When Mme Molé and Mme de
Marsantes had begun to make friends with Mme Swann
and to bring a quantity of society ladies to her house,

Mme de Guermantes had not only remained intractable but had contrived to sabotage the lines of communication and to see that her cousin the Princesse de Guermantes followed her example. On one of the gravest days of the crisis during Rouvier's ministry when it was thought that there was going to be war with Germany, I dined at Mme de Guermantes's with M. de Bréauté and found the Duchess looking worried. I supposed that, since she was always dabbling in politics, this was a manifestation of her fear of war, as when, appearing at the dinner-table one evening looking similarly pensive and barely replying in monosyllables, upon somebody's inquiring timidly what was the cause of her anxiety, she had answered solemnly: "I'm worried about China." But a moment later Mme de Guermantes, herself volunteering an explanation of that preoccupied air which I had put down to fear of a declaration of war, said to M. de Bréauté: "I'm told that Marie-Aynard intends to launch the Swanns. I simply must go and see Marie-Gilbert tomorrow and get her to help me prevent it. Otherwise there'll be no society left. The Dreyfus case is all very well. But then the grocer's wife round the corner has only to call herself a nationalist and expect us to invite her to our houses in return." And this remark was in such frivolous contrast to the one I expected to hear that I felt the same astonishment as a reader who, turning to the usual column of the *Figaro* for the latest news of the Russo-Japanese war, finds instead the list of people who have given wedding-presents to Mlle de Mortemart, the importance of an aristocratic marriage having relegated the battles on land and sea to the back of the paper. Moreover the Duchess had come to derive from this immoderate perseverance of hers a self-

satisfied pride which she lost no opportunity of expressing. "Babal" she said, "maintains that we are the two most
elegant people in Paris because he and I are the only two
people who do not allow Mme and Mlle Swann to greet
us. For he assures me that elegance consists in not knowing Mme Swann." And the Duchess laughed heartily.

However, when Swann was dead, it happened that her
determination not to know his daughter had ceased to
provide Mme de Guermantes with all the satisfactions of
pride, independence, "self-government" and cruelty which
she was capable of deriving from it and which had come
to an end with the passing of the man who had given her
the exquisite sensation that she was resisting him, that
he could not compel her to revoke her decrees. Then the
Duchess had proceeded to the promulgation of other
decrees which, being applied to people who were still
alive, could make her feel that she was free to act as
she thought fit. She did not think about the Swann girl,
but, when anyone mentioned her, she would feel a certain
curiosity, as about some place that she had never visited, which was no longer suppressed by the desire to stand
out against Swann's pretensions. Besides, so many different sentiments may contribute to the formation of a single
one that it could not be said that there was not a lingering trace of affection for Swann in this interest. No
doubt—for at every level of society a worldly and
frivolous life paralyses the sensibility and robs people of
the power to resuscitate the dead—the Duchess was one
of those people who require a personal presence—that
presence which, like a true Guermantes, she excelled in
protracting—in order to love truly, but also, and this is
less common, in order to hate a little. So that often her

friendly feeling for people, suspended during their lifetime by the irritation caused her by some action or other on their part, revived after their death. She then felt almost a longing to make reparation, because she pictured them now—though very vaguely—with only their good qualities, and stripped of the petty satisfactions, the petty pretensions, which had irritated her in them when they were alive. This imparted at times, notwithstanding the frivolity of Mme de Guermantes, something rather noble—mixed with much that was base—to her conduct. For, whereas three-quarters of the human race flatter the living and pay no attention to the dead, she often did after their deaths what those whom she had treated badly would have wished her to do while they were alive.

As for Gilberte, all the people who were fond of her and had a certain respect for her dignity could rejoice at the change in the Duchess's attitude towards her only by thinking that Gilberte, by scornfully rejecting advances coming after twenty-five years of insults, would be able to avenge them at last. Unfortunately, moral reflexes are not always identical with what common sense imagines. A man who, by an untimely insult, thinks that he has forfeited for ever all hope of winning the friendship of a person whom he cares about, finds that, on the contrary, he has thereby assured himself of it. Gilberte, who remained fairly indifferent to the people who were kind to her, never ceased to think with admiration of the insolent Mme de Guermantes, to ask herself the reasons for such insolence; once indeed (and this would have made all the people who were at all fond of her die of shame on her behalf) she had thought of writing to the Duchess to ask her what she had against a girl who had never done her

any harm. The Guermantes had assumed in her eyes proportions which their birth would have been powerless to
give them. She placed them not only above all the nobility, but even above all the royal houses.

Some of Swann's former women-friends took a great
interest in Gilberte. When the aristocracy learned of her
latest inheritance, they began to remark how well brought
up she was and what a charming wife she would make.
People said that a cousin of Mme de Guermantes, the
Princesse de Nièvre, was thinking of Gilberte for her son.
Mme de Guermantes hated Mme de Nièvre. She spread
the word that such a marriage would be a scandal. Mme
de Nièvre took fright and swore that she had never considered such a thing. One day, after lunch, as the sun was
shining and M. de Guermantes was going to take his wife
for a drive, Mme de Guermantes was arranging her hat in
front of the mirror, her blue eyes gazing at their own reflexion and at her still golden hair, her maid holding in
her hand various sunshades among which her mistress
might choose. The sun was flooding in through the window and they had decided to take advantage of the fine
weather to pay a visit to Saint-Cloud, and M. de Guermantes, all ready to set off with his pearl-grey gloves and
topper, said to himself: "Oriane is really astounding still;
I find her delicious," and went on, aloud, seeing that his
wife seemed to be in a good humour: "By the way, I have
a message for you from Mme de Virelef. She wanted
to ask you to the Opéra on Monday, but as she's having
the Swann girl she didn't dare, and asked me to explore
the ground. I don't express any opinion, I simply convey the message. But really, it seems to me that
we might . . ." he added evasively, for, their attitude

towards people being a collective one, springing up identi-
cally in each of them, he knew from his own feelings that
his wife's hostility to Mlle Swann had subsided and that
she was curious to meet her. Mme de Guermantes settled
her veil to her liking and chose a sunshade. "Just as you
like. What difference do you suppose it makes to me? I
see no objection to our meeting the child. You know quite
well that I've never had anything *against* her. I simply
didn't want us to appear to be countenancing the dubious
establishments of our friends. That's all." "And you were
perfectly right," replied the Duke. "You are wisdom incarnate, Madame, and you are more ravishing than ever
in that hat." "You're very kind," said Mme de Guermantes with a smile at her husband as she made her way
to the door. But, before entering the carriage, she insisted
on giving him a further explanation: "Lots of people call
on the mother now. Besides, she has the sense to be ill for
nine months of the year . . . Apparently the child is quite
charming. Everybody knows that we were very fond of
Swann. People will think it quite natural." And they set
off together for Saint-Cloud.

A month later, the Swann girl, who had not yet taken
the name of Forcheville, came to lunch with the Guermantes. They talked about a variety of things, and at the
end of the meal, Gilberte said timidly: "I believe you
knew my father quite well." "Why, of course we did,"
said Mme de Guermantes in a melancholy tone which
proved that she understood the daughter's grief and with
a spurious intensity as though to conceal the fact that she
was not sure whether she did remember the father very
clearly. "We knew him very well, I remember him *very
well*." (As indeed she might, seeing that he had come to

see her almost every day for twenty-five years.) "I know quite well who he was, let me tell you," she went on, as though she were seeking to explain to the daughter what sort of man her father had been and to provide her with some information about him, "he was a great friend of my mother-in-law and he was also very attached to my brother-in-law Palamède." "He used to come here too, in fact he used to come to luncheon here," added M. de Guermantes with ostentatious modesty and a scrupulous regard for accuracy. "You remember, Oriane. What a fine man your father was! One felt that he must come of a very decent family. As a matter of fact, I once saw his father and mother long ago. What excellent people they were, he and they!"

One felt that if Swann and his parents had still been alive, the Duc de Guermantes would not have hesitated to recommend them for jobs as gardeners. And this is how the Faubourg Saint-Germain speaks to any bourgeois about other bourgeois, either to flatter him with the exception being made in his favour (for as long as the conversation lasts) or rather, or at the same time, to humiliate him. Thus it is that an anti-semite, at the very moment when he is smothering a Jew with affability, will speak ill of Jews, in a general fashion which enables him to be wounding without being rude.

But, queen of the present moment, when she knew how to be infinitely amiable to you, and could not bring herself to let you go, Mme de Guermantes was also its slave. Swann might have managed at times to give the Duchess the illusion, in the excitement of conversation, that she was genuinely fond of him, but he could do so no longer. "He was charming," said the Duchess with a

wistful smile, fastening upon Gilberte a soft and kindly
gaze which would at least, if the girl should prove to be a
sensitive soul, show her that she was understood and that
Mme de Guermantes, had the two been alone together
and had circumstances permitted, would have loved to reveal to her all the depth of her sensibility. But M. de
Guermantes, whether because he was indeed of the opinion that the circumstances forbade such effusions, or because he considered that any exaggeration of sentiment
was a matter for women and that men had no more part
in it than in the other feminine attributions, except for
food and wine which he had reserved to himself, knowing
more about them than the Duchess, felt it incumbent
upon him not to encourage, by taking part in it, this conversation to which he listened with visible impatience.

However, this burst of sensibility having subsided,
Mme de Guermantes added with worldly frivolity, addressing Gilberte: "Why, he was not only a *gggreat* friend
of my brother-in-law Charlus, he was also on very good
terms with Voisenon" (the country house of the Prince de
Guermantes), not only as though Swann's acquaintance
with M. de Charlus and the Prince had been a mere accident, as though the Duchess's brother-in-law and cousin
were two men with whom Swann had happened to become friendly through some fortuitous circumstance,
whereas Swann had been on friendly terms with all the
people in that set, but also as though Mme de Guermantes wanted to explain to Gilberte roughly who her father had been, to "place" him for her by means of one of
those characteristic touches whereby, when one wants to
explain how it is that one happens to know somebody
whom one would not naturally know, or to point up one's

story, one invokes the names of his particular social sponsors.

As for Gilberte, she was all the more glad to find the subject being dropped, in that she herself was only too anxious to drop it, having inherited from Swann his exquisite tact combined with a delightful intelligence that was recognised and appreciated by the Duke and Duchess, who begged her to come again soon. Moreover, with the passion for minutiae of people whose lives are purposeless, they would discern, one after another, in the people with whom they became acquainted, qualities of the simplest kind, exclaiming at them with the artless wonderment of a townsman who on going into the country discovers a blade of grass, or on the contrary magnifying as with a microscope, endlessly commenting upon and inveighing against the slightest defects, and often applying both processes alternately to the same person. In Gilberte's case it was first of all upon her agreeable qualities that the idle perspicacity of M. and Mme de Guermantes was brought to bear: "Did you notice the way she pronounces certain words?" the Duchess said to her husband after the girl had left them; "it was just like Swann, I seemed to hear him speaking." "I was just about to say the very same thing, Oriane." "She's witty, she has exactly the same cast of mind as her father." "I consider that she's even far superior to him. Think how well she told that story about the sea-bathing. She has a vivacity that Swann never had." "Oh! but he was, after all, quite witty." "I'm not saying that he wasn't witty, I'm saying that he lacked vivacity," said M. de Guermantes in a querulous tone, for his gout made him irritable, and when he had no one else upon whom to vent his irritation, it

was to the Duchess that he displayed it. But being incapable of any clear understanding of its causes, he preferred to adopt an air of being misunderstood.

This friendly attitude on the part of the Duke and
Duchess meant that from now on, if the occasion arose,
they would have said to her "your poor father," but this
would no longer do, since it was just about this time that
Forcheville adopted the girl. She addressed him as "Father," charmed all the dowagers by her politeness and distinction, and it was generally acknowledged that, if
Forcheville had behaved admirably towards her, the child
was very good-hearted and more than recompensed him.
True, since she was able at times and anxious to show a
great deal of naturalness and ease, she had reintroduced
herself to me and had spoken to me about her real father.
But this was an exception and no one now dared utter the
name Swann in her presence.

As it happened, on entering the drawing-room I had
caught sight of two sketches by Elstir which formerly had
been banished to a little room upstairs where I had seen
them only by chance. Elstir was now in fashion. Mme de
Guermantes could not forgive herself for having given so
many of his pictures away to her cousin, not because they
were in fashion, but because she now appreciated them.
For fashion is composed of the collective infatuation of a
number of people of whom the Guermantes are typical.
But she could not think of buying other pictures by him,
for they had now begun to fetch madly high prices. She
was determined to have something at least by Elstir in her
drawing-room and had brought down these two drawings
which, she declared, she "preferred to his paintings."

Gilberte recognised the technique. "They look like

Elstirs," she said. "Why, yes," replied the Duchess without thinking, "in fact it was your fa . . . some friends of ours who made us buy them. They're admirable. To my mind, they're superior to his paintings."

Not having heard this conversation, I went up to one of the drawings to examine it, and exclaimed: "Why, this is the Elstir that . . ." I saw Mme de Guermantes's desperate signals. "Ah, yes, the Elstir that I admired upstairs. It looks much better here than in that passage. Talking of Elstir, I mentioned him yesterday in an article in the *Figaro*. Did you happen to read it?"

"You've written an article in the *Figaro*?" exclaimed M. de Guermantes with the same violence as if he had exclaimed: "Why, she's my cousin."

"Yes, yesterday."

"In the *Figaro*, are you sure? I can't believe it. Because we each of us get our *Figaro*, and if one of us had missed it, the other would certainly have noticed it. That's so, isn't Oriane, there was nothing."

The Duke sent for the *Figaro* and only yielded to the evidence of his own eyes, as though up till then the probability had been that I had made a mistake as to the newspaper for which I had written.

"What's that? I don't understand. So you've written an article in the *Figaro*?" said the Duchess, making an obvious effort in speaking of something that did not interest her. "Come, Basin, you can read it afterwards."

"No, the Duke looks so nice like that with his great beard dangling over the paper," said Gilberte. "I shall read it as soon as I get home."

"Yes, he wears a beard now that everybody else is clean-shaven," said the Duchess. "He never does anything that other people do. When we were first married, he shaved not only his beard but his moustache as well. The peasants who didn't know him by sight thought that he couldn't be French. At that time he was called the Prince des Laumes."

"Is there still a Prince des Laumes?" asked Gilberte, who was interested in everything that concerned the people who had refused to acknowledge her existence during all those years.

"Why, no," the Duchess replied with a melancholy, caressing gaze.

"Such a charming title! One of the finest titles in France!" said Gilberte, a certain sort of banality springing inevitably, as a clock strikes the hour, to the lips of certain quite intelligent persons.

"Ah, yes, I'm sorry too. Basin would like his sister's son to adopt it, but it isn't the same thing; though it would be possible, since it doesn't have to be the eldest son, it can be passed to a younger brother. I was telling you that in those days Basin was clean-shaven. One day, at a pilgrimage—you remember, my dear," she turned to her husband, "that pilgrimage at Paray-le-Monial—my brother-in-law Charlus, who always enjoys talking to peasants, was saying to one after another: 'Where do you come from?' and as he's extremely generous, he would give them something, take them off to have a drink. For nobody was ever at the same time simpler and more haughty than Mémé. You'll see him refuse to bow to a Duchess whom he doesn't think duchessy enough, and heap kindnesses on a kennelman. So then I said to Basin: 'Come, Basin, say something to them too.' My husband, who is not always very inventive . . ." ("Thank you,

Oriane," said the Duke, without interrupting his reading of my article in which he was immersed) ". . . went up to one of the peasants and repeated his brother's question in so many words: 'Where do you come from?' 'I'm from Les Laumes.' 'You're from Les Laumes? Why, I'm your Prince.' Then the peasant looked at Basin's hairless face and replied: 'That ain't true. *You're* an English.' "[28]

In these little anecdotes of the Duchess's, such great and eminent titles as that of Prince des Laumes seemed to stand out in one's mind's eye in their true setting, in their original state and their local colour, as in certain Books of Hours one recognises amid the mediaeval crowd the soaring steeple of Bourges.

Some visiting-cards were brought to her which a footman had just left at the door. "I can't think what's got into her, I don't know her. It's to you that I'm indebted for this, Basin. Although that sort of acquaintance hasn't done you much good, my poor dear," and, turning to Gilberte: "I really don't know how to explain to you who she is, you've certainly never heard of her, she's called Lady Rufus Israels."

Gilberte flushed crimson: "No, I don't know her," she said (which was all the more untrue in that Lady Israels and Swann had been reconciled two years before the latter's death and she addressed Gilberte by her Christian name), "but I know quite well, from hearing about her, who it is that you mean."

Gilberte was becoming very snobbish. Thus a girl having one day asked her out of tactlessness or malice what the name of her real, not her adoptive father was, in her confusion and as though to euphemise the name a little, instead of pronouncing it "Souann" she said "Svann," a change, as she soon realised, for the worse, since it made this name of English origin a German patronymic. And she had even gone on to say, abasing herself with the object of self-enhancement: "All sorts of different stories have been told about my birth, but I'm not supposed to know anything about it."

Ashamed though Gilberte must have felt at certain moments, when she thought of her parents (for even Mme Swann represented for her, and was, a good mother), of such a way of looking at life, it must alas be borne in mind that its elements were doubtless borrowed from her parents, for we do not create ourselves of our own accord out of nothing. But to a certain quantity of egoism which exists in the mother, a different egoism, inherent in the father's family, is admixed, which does not invariably mean that it is superadded, nor even precisely that it serves as a multiple, but rather that it creates a fresh egoism infinitely stronger and more redoubtable. And ever since the world began, ever since families in which some defect exists in one form have been intermarrying with families in which the same defect exists in another, thereby creating a peculiarly complete and detestable variety of that defect in the offspring, the accumulated egoisms (to confine ourselves, for the moment, to this defect) must have acquired such force that the whole human race would have been destroyed, did not the malady itself engender natural restrictions, capable of reducing it to reasonable proportions, comparable to those which prevent the infinite proliferation of the infusoria from destroying our planet, the unisexual fertilisation of plants from bringing about the extinction of the vegetable kingdom, and so forth. From time to time a virtue combines with this egoism to produce a new and disinterested force. The combinations by which, in the course of generations, moral chemistry thus stabilises and renders innocuous the elements that were becoming too powerful, are infinite, and would give an exciting variety to family history. Moreover, with these accumulated egoisms, such as must have existed in Gilberte, there may coexist some charming virtue of the parents; it appears for a moment to perform an interlude by itself, to play its touching part with an entire sincerity. No doubt Gilberte did not always go so far as when she insinuated that she was perhaps the natural daughter of some great personage; but as a rule she concealed her origins. Perhaps it was simply too painful for her to confess them and she preferred that people should learn of them from others. Perhaps she really believed that she was concealing them, with that dubious belief which at the same time is not doubt, which leaves room for the possibility of what we wish to be true, of which Musset furnishes an example when he speaks of hope in God.

"I don't know her personally," Gilberte went on. Did she, in fact, when she called herself Mlle de Forcheville, expect that people would not know that she was Swann's daughter? Some people, perhaps, who, she hoped, would in time become everybody. She could not be under any illusion as to their number at the moment, and doubtless knew that many people must be whispering: "That's Swann's daughter." But she knew it only with that knowledge which tells us of people taking their lives in desperation while we are going to a ball, that is to say, a remote and vague knowledge for which we are at no pains to substitute a more precise knowledge based on direct observation. Gilberte belonged, during those years at least, to the most widespread variety of human ostriches, the kind that bury their heads not in the hope of not being seen, which they consider highly improbable, but in the hope of not seeing that they can be seen, which seems to them something to the good and enables them to leave the rest to chance. As distance makes things appear smaller, more indistinct, less dangerous, Gilberte preferred not to be near other people at the moment when they made the discovery that she was by birth a Swann. And as we are near the people whom we picture to ourselves, and we can picture people reading their newspaper, Gilberte preferred the newspapers to style her Mlle de Forcheville. It is true that with the writings for which she herself was responsible, her letters, she prolonged the transition for some time by signing herself "G. S. Forcheville." The real hypocrisy in this signature was made manifest by the suppression not so much of the other letters of the name "Swann" as of those of the name "Gilberte." For, by reducing the innocent Christian name to a simple "G," Mlle de Forcheville seemed to insinuate to her friends that the similar amputation applied to the name "Swann" was due equally to the necessity of abbreviation. Indeed she gave a special significance to the "S," extending it with a sort of long tail which ran across the "G," but which one felt to be transitory and destined to disappear like the tail which, still long in the monkey, has ceased to exist in man.

In spite of all this, there was something of Swann's intelligent curiosity in her snobbishness. I remember that, in the course of that same afternoon, she asked Mme de Guermantes whether she could meet M. du Lau, and that when the Duchess replied that he was an invalid and never went out, Gilberte asked what he was like, for, she added with a faint blush, she had heard a great deal about him. (The Marquis du Lau had in fact been one of Swann's most intimate friends before the latter's marriage, and Gilberte may perhaps even have caught a glimpse of him, but at a time when she was not interested in such people.) "Would M. de Bréauté or the Prince d'Agrigente be at all like him?" she asked. "Oh! not in the least," exclaimed Mme de Guermantes, who had a keen sense of these provincial differences and drew portraits that were sober and restrained but coloured by her husky, golden voice, beneath the gentle efflorescence of her violet-blue eyes. "No, not in the least. Du Lau was very much the Périgord squire, full of charm, with all the good manners and informality of his province. At Guermantes, when we had the King of England with whom du Lau was on the friendliest terms, we used to have a little meal after the men came in from shooting. It was the hour when du Lau was in the habit of going to his room to take off his boots and put on big woollen slippers. Well, the presence of King Edward and all the grand-dukes didn't disturb him in the last, he came down to the great hall at Guermantes in his woollen slippers. He felt that he was the Marquis du Lau d'Allemans who had no reason to stand on ceremony with the King of England. He and that charming Quasimodo de Breteuil, they were the two I liked best. Actually they were great friends of . . ." (she was about to say "your father" and stopped short). "No, there's no resemblance at all, either to Gri-gri or to Bréauté. He was the typical nobleman from Périgord. Incidentally, Mémé quotes a page from Saint-Simon about a Marquis d'Allemans, and it's just like him."

I recited the opening words of the portrait: "M. d'Allemans, who was a man of great distinction among the nobility of Périgord, through his own birth and through his merit, and was regarded by every soul alive there as a general arbiter to whom each had recourse because of his probity, his capacity and the suavity of his manners, as it were the cock of his province."

"Yes, that's it," said Mme de Guermantes, "all the more so as du Lau was always as red as a turkeycock."

"Yes, I remember hearing that description quoted," said Gilberte, without adding that it had been quoted by her father, who was, as we know, a great admirer of Saint-Simon.

She liked also to speak of the Prince d'Agrigente and of M. de Bréauté for another reason. The Prince d'Agrigente had inherited his title from the House of Aragon, but the family domains were in Poitou. As for his country house, the house, that is to say, in which he lived, it was not the property of his own family but had come to him from his mother's first husband, and was situated approximately halfway between Martinville and Guermantes. And so Gilberte spoke of him and of M. de Bréauté as of country neighbours who reminded her of her old home. Strictly speaking there was an element of falsehood in this attitude, since it was only in Paris, through the Comtesse Molé, that she had come to know M. de Bréauté, albeit he had been an old friend of her father's. As for her pleasure in speaking of the country round Tansonville, it may have been sincere. Snobbery is with certain people analogous to those beverages in which the agreeable is mixed with the beneficial. Gilberte took an interest in some lady of fashion because she possessed priceless books and portraits by Nattier which my former friend would probably not have taken the trouble to inspect in the Bibliothèque Nationale or the Louvre, and I imagine that, in spite of their even greater proximity, the magnetic influence of Tansonville would have had less effect in drawing Gilberte towards Mme Sazerat or Mme Goupil than towards M. d'Agrigente.

"Oh! poor Babal and poor Gri-gri," said Mme de Guermantes, "they're in a far worse state than du Lau. I'm afraid they haven't long to live, either of them."

When M. de Guermantes had finished reading my article, he complimented me in somewhat qualified terms. He regretted the slightly hackneyed style with its "turgid metaphors as in the antiquated prose of Chateaubriand"; on the other hand he congratulated me wholeheartedly for "keeping myself busy": "I like a man to do something with what God gave him. I don't like useless people who are always self-important or fidgety. A fatuous breed!"

Gilberte, who was acquiring the ways of society with extreme rapidity, declared how proud she would be to be able to say that she was the friend of an author. "You can imagine that I shall tell people that I have the pleasure, the *honour* of your acquaintance."

"You wouldn't care to come with us tomorrow to the Opéra-Comique?" the Duchess asked me; and it struck me that it would be doubtless in that same box in which I had first beheld her, and which had seemed to me then as inaccessible as the underwater realm of the Nereids. But I replied in a melancholy tone: "No, I'm not going to the theatre just now; I've lost a friend to whom I was greatly attached." I almost had tears in my eyes as I said this, and yet for the first time it gave me a sort of pleasure to speak about it. It was from that moment that I began to write to everyone saying that I had just experienced a great sorrow, and to cease to feel it.

When Gilberte had gone, Mme de Guermantes said to me: "You didn't understand my signals. I was trying to hint to you not to mention Swann." And, as I apologised: "But I absolutely sympathise: I was on the point of mentioning him myself, but I stopped short just in time, it was terrible. You know, it really is a great bore," she said to her husband, seeking to mitigate my own error by appearing to believe that I had yielded to a propensity common to everyone and difficult to resist.

"What am I supposed to do about it?" replied the Duke. "You'd better tell them to take those drawings upstairs again, since they make you think about Swann. If you don't think about Swann, you won't speak about him."

On the following day I received two congratulatory letters which surprised me greatly, one from Mme Goupil, the Combray lady, whom I had not seen for many years and to whom, even at Combray, I had scarcely ever spoken. A reading-room had given her the chance of seeing the *Figaro*. Thus, when anything occurs in one's life which makes some stir, messages come to one from people situated so far outside the zone of one's acquaintance, and one's memory of whom is already so remote, that they seem to be placed at a great distance, especially in the dimension of depth. A forgotten friendship of one's schooldays, which has had a score of opportunities of recalling itself to one's mind, gives us a sign of life, if in a negative sense. Thus for instance Bloch, whose opinion of my article I should have loved to know, did not write to me. It is true that he had read the article and was to admit it later, but as it were backhandedly. For he himself contributed an article to the *Figaro* some years later, and was anxious to inform me immediately of the event. Since what he regarded as a privilege had fallen to him as well, the envy that had made him pretend to ignore my article ceased, as though by the lifting of a compressor, and he spoke to me about it, though not at all in the way in which he hoped to hear me talk about his: "I knew that you too had written an article," he told me, "but I didn't think I ought to mention it to you, for fear of hurting your feelings, because one oughtn't to speak to one's friends about the humiliating things that happen to them. And it's obviously humiliating to write in the organ of the sabre and the aspergillum, of afternoon tea, not to mention the holy-water stoup." His character remained unaltered, but his style had become less precious, as happens to certain people who shed their mannerisms, when, ceasing to compose symbolist poetry, they take to writing serial novels.

To console myself for his silence, I re-read Mme Goupil's letter; but it was lacking in warmth, for if the aristocracy employ certain formulas which form a sort of palisade, between them, between the initial *"Monsieur"* and the *"sentiments distingués"* of the close, cries of joy and admiration may spring up like flowers, and their clusters spill over the palisade their adoring fragrance. But bourgeois conventionality enwraps even the content of letters in a tissue of "your well-deserved success," at best "your great success." Sisters-in-law, faithful to their upbringing and tight-laced in their respectable stays, think that they have overflowed into the most distressing enthusiasm if they have written "my kindest regards." "Mother joins me" is a superlative with which one is rarely indulged.

I received another letter as well as Mme Goupil's, but the name of the writer, Sanilon, was unknown to me. It was in a plebeian hand and a charming style. I was distressed not to be able to discover who had written to me.

Two days later I found myself rejoicing at the thought that Bergotte was a great admirer of my article, which he had been unable to read without envy. But a moment later my joy subsided. For Bergotte had written me not a word. I had simply wondered whether he would have liked the article, fearing that he would not. As I was asking myself the question, Mme de Forcheville had replied that he admired it enormously and considered it the work of a great writer. But she had told me this while I was asleep: it was a dream. Almost all our dreams respond thus to the questions which we put to ourselves with complicated statements, stage productions with several characters, which however have no future.

As for Mlle de Forcheville, I could not help feeling saddened when I thought of her. What? Swann's daughter, whom he would have so loved to see at the Guermantes', whom the latter had refused to give their great friend the pleasure of inviting—to think that she was now spontaneously sought after by them, time having passed, time that renews all things, that infuses a new personality, based upon what we have been told about them, into people whom we have not seen for a long time, during which we ourselves have grown a new skin and acquired new tastes. But when, to this daughter of his, he used from time to time to say, taking her in his arms and kissing her: "How comforting it is, my darling, to have a daughter like you; one day when I'm no longer here, if people still mention your poor papa, it will be only to you and because of you," Swann, in thus pinning a timorous and anxious hope of survival on his daughter after his death, was as mistaken as an old banker who, having made a will in favour of a little dancer whom he is keeping and who has very nice manners, tells himself that though to her he is no more than a great friend, she will remain faithful to his memory. She had very nice manners while her feet under the table sought the feet of those of the old banker's friends who attracted her, but all this very discreetly, behind an altogether respectable exterior. She will wear mourning for the worthy man, will feel relieved to be rid of him, will enjoy not only the ready money, but the real estate, the motor-cars that he has bequeathed to her, taking care to remove the monogram of the former owner which makes her feel slightly ashamed, and will never associate her enjoyment of the gift with any regret for the giver. The illusions of paternal love are perhaps no less poignant than those of the other kind; many daughters regard their fathers merely as the old men who leave their fortunes to them. Gilberte's presence in a drawing-room, instead of being an occasion for people to speak of her father from time to time, was an obstacle in the way of their seizing the opportunities that might still have remained for them to do so, and that were becoming more and more rare. Even in connexion with the things he had said, the presents he had given, people acquired the habit of not mentioning him, and she who ought to have kept his memory young, if not perpetuated it, found herself hastening and completing the work of death and oblivion.

And it was not only with regard to Swann that Gilberte was gradually completing the process of forgetting; she had accelerated in me that process with regard to Albertine. Under the influence of desire, and consequently of the desire for happiness which Gilberte had aroused in me during the few hours in which I had supposed her to be someone else, a certain number of miseries, of painful preoccupations, which only a little while earlier had obsessed my mind, had slipped away from me, carrying with them a whole block of memories, probably long since crumbling and precarious, with regard to Albertine. For if many memories, which were connected with her, had at the outset helped to keep alive in me my grief for her death, in return that grief had itself fixed those memories. So that the modification of my sentimental state, prepared for no doubt obscurely day by day by the continuous erosions of forgetfulness, but realised abruptly as a whole, gave me the impression, which I remember having felt that day for the first time, of a void, of the suppression in myself of a whole segment of my associations of ideas, such as a man feels in whose brain a long-impaired artery has burst, so that a whole section of his memory is abolished or paralysed. I no longer loved Albertine. At most, on certain days, when the weather was of the sort which, by modifying, by awakening one's sensibility, brings one back into relationship with the real, I felt painfully sad in thinking of her. I was suffering from a love that no longer existed. Thus does an amputee, in certain kinds of weather, feel pain in the limb that he has lost.

The disappearance of my suffering, and of all that it carried away with it, left me diminished, as recovery from an illness which has occupied a big place in one's life often does. No doubt it is because memories are not always true that love is not eternal, and because life is made up of a perpetual renewal of cells. But this renewal, in the case of memories, is nevertheless retarded by one's attention, which temporarily arrests and freezes what is bound to change. And since it is the case with grief as with the desire for women that one magnifies it by thinking about it, having plenty of other things to do should make it easier not only to be chaste but to forget.

By another reaction, if (though it was a distraction—the desire for Mlle d'Eporcheville—that had suddenly brought home to me the tangible reality of forgetting) it remains true that it is time that gradually brings forgetfulness, forgetfulness in its turn does not fail to alter profoundly our notion of time. There are optical errors in time as there are in space. The persistence within me of an old impulse to work, to make up for lost time, to change my way of life, or rather to begin to live, gave me the illusion that I was still as young as in the past; and yet the memory of all the events that had succeeded one another in my life (and also of those that had succeeded one another in my heart, for when one has greatly changed, one is misled into supposing that one has lived longer) in the course of those last months of Albertine's existence, had made them seem to me much longer than a year, and now this forgetfulness of so many things, separating me by gulfs of empty space from quite recent events which they made me think remote, because I had had what is called "the time" to forget them, by its fragmentary, irregular interpolation in my memory—like a thick fog at sea which obliterates all the landmarks—distorted, dislocated my sense of distances in time, contracted in one place, distended in another, and made me suppose myself now further away from things, now much closer to them, than I really was. And as in the new spaces, as yet unexplored, which extended before me, there would be no more trace of my love for Albertine than there had been, in the time lost which I had just traversed, of my love for my grandmother, my life appeared to me—offering a succession of periods in which, after a certain interval, nothing of what had sustained the previous period survived in that which followed—as something utterly devoid of the support of an individual, identical and permanent self, something as useless in the future as it was protracted in the past, something that death might as well put an end to at this point or that, without in the least concluding it, as those courses of French history in the sixth form at school which stop short indiscriminately, according to the whim of the curriculum or the professor, at the Revolution of 1830, or that of 1848, or the end of the Second Empire.

Perhaps then the fatigue and sadness that I felt arose not so much from my having loved in vain what I was already forgetting as from my beginning to enjoy the company of new living people, purely social figures, mere friends of the Guermantes, offering no interest in themselves. It was easier perhaps to reconcile myself to the discovery that she whom I had loved was no more, after a certain interval of time, than a pale memory, than to the rediscovery in myself of that futile activity which makes us waste time decorating our lives with a human vegetation which is robust but parasitic, which likewise will become nothing when it is dead, which already is alien to all

that we have ever known, but which nevertheless our gar-
rulous, melancholy, conceited senility seeks to cultivate.
The newcomer who would find it easy to endure the
prospect of life without Albertine had made his appearance in me, since I had been able to speak of her at Mme
de Guermantes's in the language of grief without any real
suffering. The possible advent of these new selves, which
ought each to bear a different name from the preceding
one, was something I had always dreaded, because of their
indifference to the object of my love—long ago in connexion with Gilberte when her father told me that if I
went to live in Oceania I would never wish to return,
quite recently when I had read with such a pang in my
heart the memoirs of a mediocre writer who, separated by
life from a woman whom he had adored when he was
young, meets her as an old man without pleasure, without
any desire to see her again. Yet he was bringing me on
the contrary, this newcomer, at the same time as oblivion
an almost complete elimination of suffering, a possibility
of comfort—this newcomer, so dreaded yet so beneficent,
who was none other than one of those spare selves which
destiny holds in reserve for us, and which, paying no
more heed to our entreaties than a clear-sighted and thus
all the more authoritative physician, it substitutes in spite
of us, by a timely intervention, for the self that has been
too seriously wounded. This process, as it happens, automatically occurs from time to time, like the decay and renewal of our tissues, but we notice it only if the former
self contained a great grief, a painful foreign body, which
we are surprised to find no longer there, in our amazement at having become another person to whom the sufferings of his predecessor are no more than the sufferings

of a stranger, of which we can speak with compassion because we do not feel them. Indeed we are unconcerned
about having undergone all those sufferings, since we
have only a vague remembrance of having suffered them.
It may well be that likewise our nightmares are horrifying.
But on waking we are another person, who cares little that
the person whose place he takes has had to flee from a
gang of cut-throats during the night.

No doubt this self still maintained some contact with
the old, as a friend who is indifferent to a bereavement
speaks of it nevertheless to the persons present in a suitable tone of sorrow, and returns from time to time to the
room in which the widower who has asked him to receive
the company for him may still be heard weeping. I too
still wept when I became once again for a moment the
former friend of Albertine. But it was into a new personality that I was tending to change altogether. It is not because other people are dead that our affection for them
fades; it is because we ourselves are dying. Albertine had
no cause to reproach her friend. The man who was usurp-
ing his name was merely his heir. We can only be faithful
to what we remember, and we remember only what we
have known. My new self, while it grew up in the shadow
of the old, had often heard the other speak of Albertine;
through that other self, through the stories it gathered
from it, it thought that it knew her, it found her lovable,
it loved her; but it was only a love at second hand.

Another person in whom the process of forgetting, as
far as Albertine was concerned, was probably more rapid
at this time, and indirectly enabled me to register a little
later a new advance which that process had made in myself (and this is my memory of my second stage before fi-

nally forgetting), was Andrée. I can scarcely indeed but cite this forgetting of Albertine as, if not the sole cause, if not even the principal cause, at any rate a conditioning and necessary cause of a conversation which occurred between Andrée and myself about six months after the conversation I have already reported, and in which her words were very different from those that she had used on the former occasion. I remember that it was in my room because at that moment I found pleasure in having semi-carnal relations with her, by reason of the collective aspect which my love for the girls of the little band had originally had and now assumed once more, a love that had long been undivided among them and only for a while associated exclusively with Albertine's person, during the months that had preceded and followed her death.

We were in my room for another reason as well which enables me to date this conversation quite accurately. This was that I had been banished from the rest of the apartment because it was Mamma's "at home" day. After some hesitation she had gone to lunch with Mme Sazerat, thinking that, since the latter always contrived, even at Combray, to invite one to meet boring people, she would be able without sacrificing any pleasure to return home in good time. And she had indeed returned in time and without regrets, Mme Sazerat having had nobody but the most deadly people who were in any case chilled by the special voice that she adopted when she had company, what Mamma called her Wednesday voice. My mother was none the less fond of her, and sympathised with her ill-fortune—the result of the indiscretions of her father who had been ruined by the Duchesse de X—which compelled her to live all the year round at Combray, with a

few weeks at her cousin's house in Paris and a long
"pleasure-trip" every ten years.

I remember that the day before this, after months of
entreaty from me, and because the Princess was always
begging her to come, Mamma had gone to call on the
Princesse de Parme, who paid no calls herself and at
whose house people as a rule contented themselves with
signing their names, but who had insisted on my mother's
coming to see her, since the rules of etiquette forbade Her
Highness to come to us. My mother had come home thoroughly cross: "You sent me on a wild goose chase," she
told me. "The Princesse de Parme barely greeted me. She
turned back to the ladies she was talking to without paying any attention to me, and after ten minutes, as she
hadn't addressed a word to me, I came away without her
even offering me her hand. I was extremely annoyed.
However, on the doorstep, as I was leaving, I met the
Duchesse de Guermantes who was very kind and spoke to
me a great deal about you. What a strange idea of yours
to talk to her about Albertine! She told me that you'd said
to her that her death had been a great blow to you." (I
had in fact said this to the Duchess, but I didn't even recall it, and I had hardly made a point of it. But the most
heedless of people often give remarkable attention to
words we let slip, words which seem quite natural to us,
and which excite their curiosity profoundly.) "I shall
never go near the Princesse de Parme again. You've made
me make a fool of myself."

The next day, which was my mother's "at home,"
Andrée came to see me. She did not have much time, as
she had to go and call for Gisèle with whom she was very
anxious to dine. "I know her faults, but she's after all my

best friend and the person for whom I feel most affection," she told me. And she even appeared to be slightly alarmed at the thought that I might ask her to let me dine with them. She was hungry for people, and a third person who knew her too well, such as myself, by preventing her from letting herself go, would prevent her from enjoying herself to the full in their company.

It is true that I was not there when she came; she was waiting for me, and I was about to go through my small sitting-room to join her when I realised, on hearing a voice, that I had another visitor. Impatient to see Andrée, and not knowing who the other person was (who evidently did not know her since he had been put in another room), I listened for a moment at the door of the small sitting-room; for my visitor was not alone, he was speaking to a woman. "Oh, my darling, it is in my heart!" he warbled to her, quoting the verses of Armand Silvestre. "Yes, you will always remain my darling in spite of everything you've done to me:

> The dead are sleeping peacefully beneath earth's crust.
> And so must sleep the feelings time effaces.
> Those relics of the heart, they also have their dust;
> Do not lay hands upon their sacred traces.[29]

It's a bit outmoded, but how pretty it is! And also what I might have said to you from the first:

> You will make them weep, child beloved and lovely . . .

What, you don't know it?

> . . . All those urchins, men of the future,
> Already they hang their youthful reverie
> Upon your eyelashes caressing and pure.

Ah! for a moment I thought I could say to myself:

> The very first night that he came here
> I had for my pride no further fear.
> I told him: 'You will love me, dear,
> For just as long as you are able.'
> In his arms I slept like an angel."

Curious to see the woman to whom this deluge of poems was addressed, even though it meant postponing for a moment my urgent meeting with Andrée, I opened the door. They were being recited by M. de Charlus to a young soldier whom I soon recognised as Morel, and who was about to set off for his fortnight's training. He was no longer on friendly terms with M. de Charlus, but saw him from time to time to ask some favour of him. M. de Charlus, who usually gave a more masculine style to his love-making, also had his tender moments. Moreover, during his childhood, in order to be able to feel and understand the words of the poets, he had been obliged to imagine them as being addressed not to faithless beauties but to young men. I left them as soon as I could, although I sensed that paying visits with Morel was an immense satisfaction to M. de Charlus, to whom it gave the momentary illusion of having married again. And besides, he combined in his person the snobbery of queens with the snobbery of servants.

The memory of Albertine had become so fragmentary that it no longer caused me any sadness and was no more now than a transition to fresh desires, like a chord which announces a change of key. And indeed, any idea of a passing sensual whim being ruled out, in so far as I was still faithful to Albertine's memory, I was happier at hav-

ing Andrée in my company than I would have been at
having an Albertine miraculously restored. For Andrée
could tell me more things about Albertine than Albertine
herself had ever told me. Now the problems concerning
Albertine still remained in my mind although my tenderness for her, both physically and emotionally, had already
vanished. And my desire to know about her life, because
it had diminished less, was now relatively greater than my
need of her presence. Moreover, the idea that a woman
had perhaps had relations with Albertine no longer
aroused in me anything save the desire to have relations
with that woman myself. I told Andrée this, caressing her
as I spoke. Then, without making the slightest effort to
make her words consistent with those of a few months
earlier, Andrée said to me with a lurking smile: "Ah! yes,
but you're a man. And so we can't do quite the same
things as I used to do with Albertine." And whether because she felt that it would increase my desire (in the
hope of extracting confidences, I had told her that I
would like to have relations with a woman who had had
them with Albertine) or my grief, or perhaps destroy a
sense of superiority to herself which she might suppose
me to feel at being the only person who had had relations
with Albertine, she went on: "Ah! we spent many happy
hours together; she was so caressing, so passionate. But it
wasn't only with me that she liked to enjoy herself. She
had met a handsome young fellow at Mme Verdurin's
called Morel. They came to an understanding at once. He
undertook—having her permission to enjoy them himself,
for he liked little novices, and as soon as he had set them
on the path of evil would abandon them—he undertook
to entice young fisher-girls in remote villages, or young

laundry-girls, who would fall for a boy but might not have responded to a girl's advances. As soon as a girl was well under his control, he'd bring her to a safe place and hand her over to Albertine. For fear of losing Morel, who took part in it all too, the girl always obeyed, and yet she lost him all the same, because, as he was afraid of what might happen and also as once or twice was enough for him, he would run off leaving a false address. Once he had the nerve to bring one of these girls, with Albertine, to a brothel at Couliville, where four or five of the women had her together, or in turn. That was his passion, and Albertine's too. But Albertine suffered terrible remorse afterwards. I believe that when she was with you she had conquered her passion and put off indulging it from day to day. Besides, her affection for you was so great that she had scruples. But it was quite certain that if she ever left you she'd begin again. Only I think that after having left you, if she succumbed to that overpowering urge, her remorse must have been even greater. She hoped that you would rescue her, that you would marry her. She felt in her heart that her obsession was a sort of criminal lunacy, and I've often wondered whether it wasn't after an incident of that sort, which had led to a suicide in a family, that she killed herself on purpose. I must confess that in the early days of her stay with you she hadn't entirely given up her games with me. There were days when she seemed to need it, so much so that once, when it would have been so easy elsewhere, she couldn't bring herself to say good-bye without taking me to bed with her, in your house. We were out of luck, and were very nearly caught. She'd taken advantage of the fact that Françoise had gone out to do some shopping, and you weren't yet home.

Then she'd turned out all the lights so that when you let yourself in with your key it would take you some time to find the switch; and she'd left the door of her room open. We heard you come upstairs, and I only just had time to tidy myself up and come down. Which was quite unnecessary as it happened, for by an incredible chance you'd left your key at home and had to ring the bell. But we lost our heads all the same, so that to conceal our embarrassment we both of us, without having a chance to consult each other, had the same idea: to pretend to dread the scent of syringa which as a matter of fact we adored. You were bringing a big branch of it home with you, which enabled me to turn my head away and hide my confusion. This didn't prevent me from telling you in the most idiotic way that perhaps Françoise had come back and would let you in, when a moment earlier I had told you the lie that we'd only just come in from our drive and that when we arrived Françoise hadn't yet left the house (which was true). But the big mistake we made—assuming that you had your key—was to turn out the light, for we were afraid that as you came upstairs you'd see it being turned on again; or at least we hesitated too long. And for three nights on end Albertine couldn't get a wink of sleep because she was constantly afraid that you might be suspicious and ask Françoise why she hadn't turned on the light before leaving the house. For Albertine was terribly afraid of you, and at times she maintained that you were treacherous and nasty and that you hated her really. After three days she gathered from your calm that you hadn't thought of asking Françoise, and she was able to sleep again. But she never resumed her relations with me after that, either from fear or from remorse, for she made out that she did really love you, or perhaps she was in love with someone else. At all events, nobody could ever mention syringa again in her hearing without her turning crimson and putting her hand over her face in the hope of hiding her blushes."

Like certain strokes of fortune, there are strokes of misfortune that come too late, and do not assume the magnitude they would have had in our eyes a little earlier. One such was the misfortune that Andrée's terrible revelation was to me. No doubt, even when a piece of bad news is bound to make us unhappy, it may happen that, in the involvement, the give and take of conversation, it will pass in front of us without stopping and, preoccupied as we are by all the things we have to say in reply, transformed into someone else by the desire to please our present interlocutors, protected for a few moments in this new context against the affections and the sufferings that we discarded upon entering it and will return to when the brief spell is broken, we do not have the time to take them in. However, if these affections and these sufferings are too predominant, we enter only distractedly into the zone of a new and momentary world, in which, too faithful to our sufferings, we are incapable of becoming other; and then the words that we hear said enter at once into relation with our heart, which has not been neutralised. But for some time past words that concerned Albertine, like a poison that has evaporated, had lost their toxic power. She was already too remote from me. As an afternoon stroller, seeing a misty crescent in the sky, thinks: "So that's the vast moon," I said to myself: "What, so that truth which I've sought for so long, which I've so dreaded, is nothing more than these few words uttered in

the course of conversation, words to which one cannot
even give one's whole attention because one isn't alone!"
Besides, it took me at a serious disadvantage, as I had exhausted myself with Andrée. Really, I would have liked to
have more strength to devote to a truth of such magnitude; it remained extraneous to me, but this was because I
had not yet found a place for it in my heart. We would
like the truth to be revealed to us by novel signs, not by a
sentence, a sentence similar to those which we have constantly repeated to ourselves. The habit of thinking prevents us at times from experiencing reality, immunises us
against it, makes it seem no more than another thought.
There is no idea that does not carry in itself its possible
refutation, no word that does not imply its opposite.

In any case, if it was true, it was by this time the sort
of useless truth about the life of a dead mistress that rises
up from the depths and reveals itself when we can no
longer have any use for it. Then, thinking doubtless of
some other woman whom we now love and with regard to
whom the same thing may occur (for to her whom we
have forgotten we no longer give a thought), we lament.
We say to ourselves: "If she were alive!" We say to ourselves: "If she who is alive could only understand all this
and realise that when she is dead I shall know everything
that she is hiding from me!" But it is a vicious circle. If I
could have caused Albertine to live, I should at the same
time have caused Andrée to reveal nothing. It is to some
extent the same thing as the everlasting "You'll see when
I no longer love you," which is so true and so absurd,
since one would indeed elicit much if one no longer loved,
but one would no longer be interested in eliciting it. In
fact it is precisely the same thing. For if the woman you

see again when you no longer love her then tells you all, it
is because it is no longer she, or because it is no longer
you: the person who loved has ceased to exist. There too
death has passed by, and has made everything simple and
pointless. I pursued these reflexions basing myself on the
assumption that Andrée was truthful—which was possible—and had been prompted to sincerity with me precisely because she had now had relations with me, from
that Saint-André-des-Champs side of her nature which
Albertine too had shown me at the start. She was encouraged in this case by the fact that she was no longer afraid
of Albertine, for the reality of other people survives their
death for only a short time in our minds, and after a few
years they are like those gods of obsolete religions whom
one offends without fear because one has ceased to believe
in their existence. But the fact that Andrée no longer believed in the reality of Albertine might mean that she no
longer feared (any more than to betray a secret which she
had promised not to reveal) to concoct a lie which retrospectively slandered her alleged accomplice. Had this absence of fear permitted her to reveal the truth at last in
telling me all that, or else to concoct a lie, if, for some
reason, she supposed me to be full of happiness and pride
and wished to cause me pain? Perhaps she was irritated
with me (an irritation that had been held in abeyance so
long as she saw that I was miserable, disconsolate) because I had had relations with Albertine and she envied
me, perhaps—supposing that I considered myself on that
account more favoured than her—an advantage which she
herself had never, perhaps, obtained, nor even sought.
Thus it was that I had often heard her say how ill they
were looking to people whose look of radiant health, and

in particular their awareness of it, exasperated her, and add, in the hope of annoying them, that she herself was very well, a fact that she never ceased to proclaim when she was seriously ill until the day when, in the detachment of death, it no longer mattered to her that others should be well and should know that she herself was dying. But that day was still remote. Perhaps she was angry with me, for what reason I had no idea, as long ago she had been filled with rage against the young man so learned in sporting matters, so ignorant of everything else, whom we had met at Balbec, who since then had been living with Rachel, and on the subject of whom Andrée poured forth defamatory remarks, hoping to be sued for slander in order to be able to formulate discreditable accusations against his father the falseness of which he would be unable to prove. Quite possibly this rage against myself had simply revived, having doubtless ceased when she saw how miserable I was. For the very same people whom, her eyes flashing with rage, she had longed to disgrace, to kill, to send to prison, by false testimony if need be, had only to reveal themselves to be unhappy or humiliated, for her to cease to wish them any harm, and to be ready to overwhelm them with kindness. For she was not fundamentally wicked, and if her unapparent, slightly deeper nature was not the niceness which one assumed at first from her delicate attentions, but rather envy and pride, her third nature, deeper still, the true but not entirely realised nature, tended towards kindness and the love of her fellow-creatures. Only, like all those people who in a certain state desire a better one, but, knowing it only through desiring it, do not realise that the first condition is to break away from the former state—like neurasthenics or drug-addicts who are anxious to be cured, but at the same time not to be deprived of their neuroses or their drugs, or like those world-loving religious or artistic spirits who long for solitude but seek none the less to envisage it as not implying an absolute renunciation of their former existence—Andrée was prepared to love all her fellow-creatures, but on the condition that she should first of all have succeeded in not having to visualise them as triumphant, and to that end should have humiliated them in advance. She did not understand that one should love even the proud, and conquer their pride by love and not by an even more overweening pride. But the fact is that she was like those invalids who wish to be cured by the very means that prolong their disease, which they like and would cease at once to like if they renounced them. But people wish to learn to swim and at the same time to keep one foot on the ground.

As regards the young sportsman, the Verdurins' nephew, whom I had met during my two visits to Balbec, it may be recounted here, incidentally and prematurely, that, some time after Andrée's visit, the account of which will be resumed in a moment, certain events occurred which caused a great sensation. First of all, this young man (perhaps in memory of Albertine with whom I did not then know that he had been in love) became engaged to Andrée and married her, to the despair of Rachel, of which he took no notice. Andrée no longer said then (that is to say some months after the visit of which I have been speaking) that he was a wretch, and I realised later on that she had said so only because she was madly in love with him and felt that he did not want her. But another fact made an even greater impression. This young man produced certain sketches for the theatre, with settings and costumes designed by himself, which effected in contemporary art a revolution at least equal to that brought about by the Russian ballet. In fact, the best-qualified critics regarded his works as being of cardinal importance, almost works of genius, and indeed I agree with them, confirming thus, to my own astonishment, the opinion long held by Rachel. The people who had known him at Balbec, intent only on seeing whether the cut of the clothes of the men with whom he associated was elegant or not, spending all his time at baccarat, at the races, on the golf-course or on the polo-ground, who knew that at school he had always been a dunce and had even been expelled from the lycée (to annoy his parents, he had gone to live for two months in the smart brothel in which M. de Charlus had hoped to surprise Morel), thought that perhaps his productions were the work of Andrée, who was prepared out of love to allow him all the glory, or that more probably he was paying, out of his huge personal fortune at which his excesses had barely nibbled, some inspired but needy professional to create them (this kind of wealthy society, unpolished by contact with the aristocracy and having no idea of what constitutes an artist—who to them is either an actor whom they engage to recite monologues at their daughter's engagement party, handing him his fee discreetly there and then in another room, or a painter to whom they make her sit once she is married, before the children come and when she is still at her best—are apt to believe that all the society people who write, compose or paint have their work done for them and pay to obtain a reputation as a creative artist as other men pay to secure a seat in Parliament). But all this was untrue, and this young man was indeed the author of those admirable works. When I learned this, I found myself torn between a number of different suppositions. Either he had indeed been for long years the "thickhead" that he appeared to be, and some physiological cataclysm had awakened the dormant genius in him, like a Sleeping Beauty; or else at the time of his turbulent schooldays, of his failures to matriculate, of his heavy gambling losses at Balbec, of his reluctance to get into the little "tram" with his aunt Verdurin's faithful because of their hideous clothes, he was already a man of genius, distracted perhaps from his genius, which he had left in abeyance in the effervescence of juvenile passions; or again, already a conscious man of genius, and at the bottom of his class only because, while the master was spouting platitudes about Cicero, he himself was reading Rimbaud or Goethe. True, there were no grounds for any such hypothesis when I met him at Balbec, where his interests seemed to me to be centred exclusively on turning out a smart carriage and pair and mixing cocktails. But even this is not an irrefutable objection. He may have been extremely vain—something that is not incompatible with genius—and have sought to shine in the manner which he knew was best calculated to dazzle in the world in which he lived, that is to say, not by showing a profound knowledge of *Elective Affinities*, but far rather a knowledge of how to drive four-in-hand. Moreover, I am not at all sure that later on, when he had become the creator of those fine and original works, he would have cared greatly, outside the theatres in which he was known, to greet anyone who was not in evening dress, like the "faithful" in their earlier manner, which would be a proof in him not of stupidity but of vanity, and indeed of a certain practical sense, a certain perceptiveness in adapting his vanity to the mentality of the imbeciles whose esteem he valued and in whose eyes a dinner-jacket might perhaps shine with greater brilliance than the gaze of a thinker. Who can say whether, seen from without, some man of talent, or even a man devoid of talent but a lover of the things of the mind, myself for instance, would not have appeared, to anyone who met him at Rivebelle, in the hotel at Balbec, or on the esplanade, the most perfect and pretentious fool? Not to mention that for Octave matters of art must have been something so intimate, inhabiting the most secret recesses of his being, that doubtless it would never have occurred to him to speak of them, as Saint-Loup, for instance, would have done, Saint-Loup for whom the arts had all the glamour that horses and carriages had for Octave. And then he may have had a passion for gambling, and it is said that he retained it. But all the same, if the piety which brought to light the unknown work of Vinteuil emerged from the murky environment of Montjouvain, I was no less struck by the thought that what were perhaps the most extraordinary masterpieces of our day had emerged not from the *concours général*, from a model, academic education in the manner of the Broglie family, but from the frequentation of paddocks and fashionable bars. In any case, in those days at Balbec, the reasons which made me anxious to know him, and which made Albertine and her friends anxious that I should not know him, were equally extraneous to his merit, and could only have illustrated the eternal misunderstanding between an "intellectual" (represented in this instance by myself) and society (represented by the little band) with regard to a social personality (the young golfer). I had no inkling of his talent, and his prestige in my eyes—like that of Mme Blatin long ago—had been that of being, whatever they might say, the friend of my girlfriends, and more one of their band than myself. On the other hand, Albertine and Andrée, symbolising in this respect the incapacity of society people to bring a sound judgment to bear upon the things of the mind and their propensity to attach themselves in that connexion to false appearances, not only thought me almost idiotic because I took an interest in such an imbecile, but were astonished above all that, golfer for golfer, my choice should have fallen upon the poorest player of them all. If, for instance, I had chosen to make friends with young Gilbert de Belloeuvre, apart from golf he was a boy who had a certain amount of conversation, who had almost succeeded in the *concours général* and was an agreeable versifier (as a matter of fact he was the stupidest of them all). Or again, if my object had been to "make a study for a book," Guy Saumoy, who was completely insane, who had abducted two girls, was at least a singular type who might "interest" me. These two might have been allowed me, but the other, what attraction could I find in him? He was the epitome of the "great lout," of the "thickhead."

To return to Andrée's visit, after the disclosure that she had just made to me of her relations with Albertine, she added that the main reason for which Albertine had left me was concern about what her friends of the little band, and other people as well, might think of her living like that with a young man to whom she was not married: "Of course I know it was in your mother's house. But that makes no difference. You can't imagine what that sort of girls' community is like, what they conceal from one another, how they dread one another's opinion of them. I've seen some of them being terribly severe with young men simply because they knew their friends and they were afraid that certain things might be repeated, and then I've happened by chance to see those very same girls in a totally different light, much to their chagrin."

A few months earlier, this knowledge which Andrée appeared to possess of the motives that swayed the girls of the little band would have seemed to me the most precious thing in the world. What she said was perhaps sufficient to explain why Albertine, who had given herself to me afterwards in Paris, had refused to do so at Balbec where I was constantly meeting her friends, a fact which I had absurdly supposed to be so advantageous for being on better terms with her. Perhaps indeed it was because she had seen signs of my confiding in Andrée, or because I had rashly told the latter that she was coming to spend the night at the Grand Hotel, that Albertine, who an hour earlier was perhaps ready to let me enjoy certain favours as though that were the simplest thing in the world, had abruptly changed her mind and threatened to ring the bell. But then, she must have been accommodating to lots of others. This thought rekindled my jealousy and I told Andrée that there was something that I wished to ask her.

"You did those things in your grandmother's empty apartment?"

"Oh, no, never, we'd have been disturbed."

"Why, I thought . . . it seemed to me . . ."

"Besides, Albertine chiefly liked doing it in the country."

"Oh! where?"

"Originally, when she hadn't time to go very far, we used to go to the Buttes-Chaumont. She knew a house there. Or else we would lie under the trees, there's never anyone about. In the grotto of the Petit Trianon, too."

"There, you see; how am I to believe you? You swore to me, not a year ago, that you'd never done anything at the Buttes-Chaumont."

"I was afraid of hurting you."

As I have said, I thought (although not until much later) that on the contrary it was on this second occasion, the day of her confessions, that Andrée had sought to hurt me. And this thought would have occurred to me at once, because I should have felt the need of it, if I had still been as much in love with Albertine. But Andrée's words did not hurt me sufficiently to make it essential for me to dismiss them immediately as untrue. On the whole, if what Andrée said was true, and I did not doubt it at the time, the real Albertine whom I now discovered, after having known so many diverse forms of Albertine, differed very little from the young bacchante who had loomed up and at once been detected that first day, on the front at Balbec, and who had offered me so many different aspects in succession, as a town alters the disposition of its buildings one after the other as we approach it, to the point of crushing, obliterating the principal monument which alone we could see from a distance, until finally, when we know it well and can judge it exactly, its true proportions prove to be those which the perspective of the first glance had indicated, the rest, through which we passed, being no more than that succession of lines of defence which everything in creation raises against our vision, and which we must cross one after another, at the cost of how much suffering, before we arrive at the heart. If, however, I had no need to believe absolutely in Albertine's innocence because my suffering had diminished, I can say that conversely, if I did not suffer unduly at this revelation, it was because, some time since, the belief in Albertine's innocence that I had fabricated for myself had been gradually replaced, without my realising it, by the belief, ever present in my mind, in her guilt. Now if I no longer believed in Albertine's innocence, it was because I had already ceased to feel the need, the passionate desire to believe in it. It is desire that engenders belief, and if we are not as a rule aware of this, it is because most belief-creating desires—unlike the desire which had persuaded me that Albertine was innocent—end only with our own life. To all the evidence that corroborated my original version, I had stupidly preferred mere assertions by Albertine. Why had I believed them? Lying is essential to humanity. It plays as large a part perhaps as the quest for pleasure, and is moreover governed by that quest. One lies in order to protect one's pleasure, or one's honour if the disclosure of one's pleasure runs counter to one's honour. One lies all one's life long, even, especially, perhaps only, to those who love one. For they alone make us fear for our pleasure and desire their esteem. I had at first thought Albertine guilty, and it was only my desire, by utilising the powers of my intelligence to construct an edifice of doubt, that had put me on the wrong track. Perhaps we live surrounded by electric, seismic signs which we must interpret in good faith in order to know the truth about people's characters. If the truth be told, saddened as I was in spite of everything by Andrée's words, I thought it fitter that the reality should finally turn out to

accord with what my instinct had originally foreboded
rather than with the wretched optimism to which I had
later so cravenly surrendered. I preferred that life should
remain on the same level as my intuitions. Those, moreover, that I had had that first day on the beach, when I
had believed that these girls were the incarnation of fren-
zied pleasure, of vice, and again on the evening when I
had seen Albertine's governess leading that passionate girl
home to the little villa, as one drives into its cage a wild
animal which nothing, later on, despite appearances, will
ever succeed in taming—did not those intuitions accord
with what Bloch had told me when he had made the
world seem so fair to my eyes by showing me, making me
quiver with excitement on all my walks, at every encounter, the universality of desire? Perhaps, when all was
said, it was better that I should not have found those first
intuitions verified afresh until now. While the whole of
my love for Albertine endured, they would have made me
suffer too acutely and it was better that there should have
subsisted of them only a trace, my perpetual suspicion of
things which I did not see and which nevertheless happened continually so close to me, and perhaps another
trace as well, earlier, vaster, which was *my love itself*. For
was it not, despite all the denials of my reason, tantamount to knowing Albertine in all her hideousness, actually to choose her, to love her? And even in the moments
when mistrust is stilled, is not love the persistence of that
mistrust and a transformation of it, is it not a proof of
clairvoyance (a proof unintelligible to the lover himself),
since desire, reaching out always towards what is most opposite to oneself, forces one to love what will make one
suffer? There is no doubt that, inherent in a woman's

charm, in her eyes, her lips, her figure, are the elements, unknown to us, most calculated to make us unhappy, so much so that to feel attracted to her, to begin to love her, is, however innocent we may pretend it to be, to read already, in a different version, all her betrayals and her misdeeds. And may not those charms which, to attract me, corporealised thus the raw, dangerous, fatal elements of a person, have stood in a more direct relation of cause and effect to those secret poisons than do the seductive luxuriance and the toxic juice of certain venomous flowers? It was perhaps, I told myself, Albertine's vice itself, the cause of my future sufferings, that had produced in her that honest, frank manner, creating the illusion that one enjoyed with her the same loyal and unqualified comradeship as with a man, just as a parallel vice had produced in M. de Charlus a feminine delicacy of sensibility and mind. In the midst of the most complete blindness, perspicacity subsists in the form of predilection and tenderness; so that it is a mistake to speak of a bad choice in love, since as soon as there is a choice it can only be a bad one.

"Did those excursions to the Buttes-Chaumont take place when you used to call for her here?" I asked Andrée.

"Oh! no, from the day Albertine came back from Balbec with you, except the time I told you about, she never did anything again with me. She wouldn't even allow me to mention such things to her."

"But my dear Andrée, why go on lying to me? By the merest chance, for I never try to find out anything, I've learned in the minutest detail things of that sort which Albertine did, I can tell you exactly, on the bank of a river with a laundry-girl, only a few days before her death."

"Ah! perhaps after she'd left you, that I can't say. She felt that she'd failed, that she'd never again be able to regain your trust."

These last words shattered me. Then I thought again of the evening of the syringa, and remembered that about a fortnight later, as my jealousy kept changing its object, I had asked Albertine whether she had ever had relations with Andrée, and she had replied: "Oh! never! Of course, I adore Andrée; I have a deep affection for her, but as I might have for a sister, and even if I had the tastes which you seem to suppose, she's the last person I should have thought of in that connexion. I can swear to you by anything you like, the honour of my aunt, the grave of my poor mother." I had believed her. And yet even if my suspicions had not been aroused by the contradiction between her former partial admissions with regard to certain matters and the vehemence with which she had afterwards denied them as soon as she saw that I was not indifferent to them, I ought to have remembered Swann, convinced of the platonic nature of M. de Charlus's friendships and assuring me of it on the evening of the very day I had seen the tailor and the Baron in the courtyard; I ought to have reflected that there are two worlds one behind the other, one consisting of the things that the best, the sincerest people say, and behind it the world composed of the sequence of what those same people do; so that when a married woman says to you of a young man: "Oh! it's perfectly true that I have an immense affection for him, but it's something quite innocent, quite pure, I could swear it on the memory of my parents," one ought one-

self, instead of feeling any hesitation, to swear to oneself
that she has probably just come out of the bathroom into
which, after every assignation she has with the young man
in question, she rushes in order not to have a child. The
spray of syringa made me profoundly sad, as did also the
thought that Albertine could have believed, and said, that
I was treacherous and hostile; and most of all perhaps,
certain lies so unexpected that I had difficulty in grasping
them. One day Albertine had told me that she had been
to an aerodrome where one of the airmen was a friend of
hers (this doubtless in order to divert my suspicions from
women, thinking that I was less jealous of men), and that
it had been amusing to see how dazzled Andrée was by
the said airman, by all the compliments he paid Albertine,
until finally Andrée had wanted to go up in his aeroplane
with him. Now this was a complete fabrication; Andrée
had never visited the aerodrome in question.

When Andrée left me, it was dinner-time. "You'll
never guess who has been to see me and stayed at least
three hours," said my mother. "I call it three hours, but it
was perhaps longer. She arrived almost on the heels of my
first visitor, who was Mme Cottard, sat still and watched
everybody come and go—and I had more than thirty
callers—and left me only a quarter of an hour ago. If you
hadn't had your friend Andrée with you, I'd have sent for
you."

"Well, who was it?"

"A person who never pays calls."

"The Princesse de Parme?"

"Why, I have a cleverer son than I thought. It's no
fun making you guess a name; you hit on it at once."

"Did she apologise for her coldness yesterday?"

"No, that would have been stupid. The visit itself was her apology. Your poor grandmother would have thought it admirable. It seems that about two o'clock she sent a footman to ask whether I had an 'at home.' She was told that this was the very day and so up she came."

My first thought, which I did not dare mention to Mamma, was that the Princesse de Parme, surrounded the day before by people of rank and fashion with whom she was on intimate terms and enjoyed conversing, on seeing my mother come into the room had felt an annoyance which she had made no attempt to conceal. And it was quite in the style of the great ladies of Germany, which for that matter the Guermantes had largely adopted—that haughtiness for which they thought to atone by a scrupulous affability. But my mother believed, and I came in time to share her opinion, that the Princesse de Parme, having simply failed to recognise her, had not felt bound to pay any attention to her, and that she had learned after my mother's departure who she was, either from the Duchesse de Guermantes whom my mother had met below or from the list of her visitors, whose names were requested by the ushers before they entered her presence and inscribed in a register. She had felt that it would be ungracious to send word or to say to my mother: "I didn't recognise you," and instead—and this was no less in keeping with the code of manners of the German courts and with the ways of the Guermantes than my original version—had thought that a visit, an exceptional action on the part of a royal personage, and what was more a visit of several hours' duration, would convey the explanation to my mother in an indirect but no less convincing form, which is just what did happen.

But I did not stay to hear my mother's account of the Princess's visit, for I had just recalled a number of facts concerning Albertine as to which I had intended but had forgotten to question Andrée. How little, for that matter, did I know, would I ever know, of this story of Albertine, the only story that really interested me, or was at least beginning to interest me again at certain moments. For man is that ageless creature who has the faculty of becoming many years younger in a few seconds, and who, surrounded by the walls of the time through which he has lived, floats within them as in a pool the surface-level of which is constantly changing so as to bring him within range now of one epoch, now of another. I wrote to Andrée asking her to come again. She was unable to do so until a week later. Almost as soon as she entered the room I said to her: "Very well, then, since you maintain that Albertine never did that sort of thing while she was staying here, according to you it was to be able to do it more freely that she left me, but for which of her friends?"

"Certainly not, it wasn't that at all."

"Then because I was too disagreeable?"

"No, I don't think so. I think she was forced to leave you by her aunt who had designs for her future upon that guttersnipe, you know, the young man you used to call 'I'm a wash-out,' the young man who was in love with Albertine and had asked for her hand. Seeing that you weren't marrying her, they were afraid that the shocking length of her stay in your house might prevent the young man from doing so. And so Mme Bontemps, on whom the young man was constantly bringing pressure to bear, summoned Albertine home. Albertine after all needed her uncle and aunt, and when she realised that they were forcing her hand she left you."

I had never in my jealousy thought of this explanation, but only of Albertine's desire for women and of my own surveillance of her; I had forgotten that there was also Mme Bontemps who might eventually regard as strange what had shocked my mother from the first. At least Mme Bontemps was afraid that it might shock this possible husband whom she was keeping in reserve for Albertine in case I failed to marry her.

So that it was possible that a long debate had gone on in Albertine's mind between staying with me and leaving me, but that her decision to leave me had been made on account of her aunt, or of that young man, and not on account of women to whom perhaps she had never given a thought. The most disturbing thing to my mind was that Andrée, who after all no longer had anything to conceal from me as to Albertine's morals, swore to me that nothing of the sort had ever occurred between Albertine on the one hand and Mlle Vinteuil or her friend on the other (Albertine herself was unconscious of her own proclivities when she first met them, and they, from the fear of being mistaken in the object of one's desire which breeds as many errors as desire itself, regarded her as extremely hostile to that sort of thing. Perhaps later on they had learned that her tastes were similar to their own, but by that time they knew Albertine and Albertine knew them too well for there to be any question of their doing those things together).

"But, my dear Andrée, you're lying again. Remember—you admitted it to me yourself when I telephoned to you the evening before, don't you remember?—that

Albertine had been so anxious, and kept it from me as though it was something that I mustn't know about, to go to the afternoon party at the Verdurins' at which Mlle Vinteuil was expected."

"Yes, but Albertine hadn't the slightest idea that Mlle Vinteuil was to be there."

"What? You yourself told me that she'd met Mme Verdurin a few days earlier. Besides, Andrée, there's no point in our trying to deceive one another. I found a note one morning in Albertine's room, a note from Mme Verdurin urging her to come that afternoon."

And I showed her this note which, as a matter of fact, Françoise had taken care to bring to my notice by placing it on top of Albertine's belongings a few days before her departure, and, I regret to say, leaving it there to make Albertine suppose that I had been rummaging among her things, to let her know in any case that I had seen it. And I had often wondered whether Françoise's ruse had not been largely responsible for the departure of Albertine, who saw that she could no longer conceal anything from me, and felt disheartened, defeated. I showed Andrée the note: *I feel no compunction, on the strength of this genuine family feeling* . . . "You know very well, Andrée, that Albertine used always to say that Mlle Vinteuil's friend was indeed a mother, an elder sister to her."

"But you've misinterpreted this note. The person Mme Verdurin wished Albertine to meet that afternoon wasn't Mlle Vinteuil's friend at all, it was the young man you call 'I'm a wash-out,' and the family feeling is what Mme Verdurin felt for the brute, who is after all her nephew. However, I think Albertine did hear afterwards that Mlle Vinteuil was to be there—Mme Verdurin may

have let her know incidentally. And of course the thought
of seeing her friend again gave her pleasure, reminded her
of happy times in the past, just as you'd be glad, if you
were going somewhere, to know that Elstir would be
there, but no more than that, not even as much. No, if
Albertine was unwilling to say why she wanted to go to
Mme Verdurin's, it was because it was a rehearsal to
which Mme Verdurin had invited a very small party, including that nephew of hers whom you met at Balbec, to
whom Mme Bontemps was hoping to marry Albertine off
and to whom Albertine wanted to talk. He was a real
blackguard . . ."

And so Albertine, contrary to what Andrée's mother
used to think, had had after all the prospect of a wealthy
marriage. And when she had wanted to visit Mme Verdurin, when she had spoken to her in secret, when she
had been so annoyed that I should have gone there that
evening without warning her, the intrigue between her
and Mme Verdurin had had as its object her meeting not
Mlle Vinteuil but the nephew who loved Albertine and
for whom Mme Verdurin, with that satisfaction of working towards the realisation of one of those marriages
which surprise one in some families into whose state of
mind one does not enter completely, did not desire a rich
bride. Now I had never given another thought to this
nephew who had perhaps been the initiator thanks to
whom I had received Albertine's first kiss. And for the
whole structure of Albertine's anxieties which I had built
up, I must now substitute another, or rather superimpose
it, for perhaps it did not exclude the other, a taste for
women not being incompatible with marriage. Was this
marriage really the reason for Albertine's departure, and

had she, out of self-respect, so as not to appear to be dependent on her aunt, or to force me to marry her, preferred not to mention it? I was beginning to realise that the system of multiple motives for a single action, of which Albertine showed her mastery in her relations with her friends when she allowed each of them to suppose that it was for her sake that she had come, was only a sort of symbol, artificial and premeditated, of the different aspects that an action assumes according to the point of view from which we look at it. It was not the first time I had felt astonishment and a sort of shame at never once having told myself that Albertine was in a false position in my house, a position that might give offence to her aunt; it was not the first, nor was it the last. How often has it happened to me, after having sought to understand the relations between two people and the crises that they entail, to hear all of a sudden a third person speak to me of them from his own point of view, for he has even closer relations with one of the two, a point of view which has perhaps been the cause of the crisis! And if people's actions remain so unpredictable, how should not the people themselves be equally so? Listening to the people who maintained that Albertine was a schemer who had tried to get one man after another to marry her, it was not difficult to imagine how they would have defined her life with me. And yet to my mind she had been a victim, a victim who perhaps was not altogether pure, but in that case guilty for other reasons, on account of vices which people did not mention.

But above all we must remember this: on the one hand, lying is often a trait of character; on the other hand, in women who would not otherwise be liars, it is a natural defence, improvised at first, then more and more organised, against that sudden danger which would be capable of destroying all life: love. Furthermore, it is not by mere chance that sensitive, intellectual men invariably give themselves to insensitive and inferior women, and moreover remain attached to them, and that the proof that they are not loved does not in the least cure them of the urge to sacrifice everything to keep such women with them. If I say that such men need to suffer, I am saying something that is accurate while suppressing the preliminary truths which make that need—involuntary in a sense—to suffer a perfectly understandable consequence of those truths. Not to mention the fact that, all-round natures being rare, a man who is highly sensitive and highly intellectual will generally have little will-power, will be the plaything of habit and of that fear of suffering in the immediate present which condemns to perpetual suffering—and that in these conditions he will never be prepared to repudiate the woman who does not love him. One may be surprised that he should be content with so little love, but one ought rather to picture to oneself the anguish that may be caused him by the love which he himself feels. An anguish which one ought not to pity unduly, for those terrible commotions that are caused by an unrequited love, by the departure or the death of a mistress, are like those attacks of paralysis which at first leave us helpless, but after which the muscles tend gradually to recover their vital elasticity and energy. What is more, this anguish does not lack compensation. These sensitive and intellectual persons are as a rule little inclined to falsehood. It takes them all the more unawares in that, however intelligent they may be, they live in the world of the possible, live in the anguish which a woman has just inflicted on them rather than in the clear perception of what she wanted, what she did, what she loved, a perception granted chiefly to self-willed natures which need it in order to prepare against the future instead of lamenting the past. And so these persons feel that they are betrayed without quite knowing how. Wherefore the mediocre woman whom we are astonished to see them loving enriches the universe for them far more than an intelligent woman would have done. Behind each of her words, they feel that a lie is lurking, behind each house to which she says that she has gone, another house, behind each action, each person, another action, another person. Of course they do not know what or whom, they do not have the energy, would not perhaps find it possible, to discover. A lying woman, by an extremely simple trick, can beguile, without taking the trouble to change her method, any number of people, and, what is more, the very person who ought to have discovered the trick. All this confronts the sensitive intellectual with a universe full of depths which his jealousy longs to plumb and which are not without interest to his intelligence.

Without being precisely a man of that category, I was going perhaps to learn, now that Albertine was dead, the secret of her life. Here again, do not these indiscretions which come to light only after a person's life on earth is ended prove that nobody really believes in a future life? If these indiscretions are true, one ought to fear the resentment of a woman whose actions one reveals fully as much in anticipation of meeting her in heaven as one feared it while she was alive and one felt bound to keep her secret. And if these indiscretions are false, invented because she is no longer present to contradict them, one ought to be even more afraid of the dead woman's wrath if one believed in heaven. But no one does believe in it.

On the whole, I did not understand any better than before why Albertine had left me. If the face of a woman can with difficulty be grasped by the eyes, which cannot take in the whole of its mobile surface, or by the lips, or still less by the memory, if it is shrouded in obscurity according to her social position, according to the level at which we are situated, how much thicker is the veil drawn between those of her actions which we see and her motives! Motives are situated at a deeper level, which we do not perceive, and moreover engender actions other than those of which we are aware and often in absolute contradiction to them. When has there not been some man in public life, regarded as a saint by his friends, who is discovered to have forged documents, robbed the State, betrayed his country? How often is a great nobleman robbed by a steward whom he has brought up from childhood, ready to swear that he was an excellent man, as possibly he was! And how much more impenetrable does it become, this curtain that screens another's motives, if we are in love with that person, for it clouds our judgment and also obscures the actions of one who, feeling that she is loved, ceases suddenly to set any store by what otherwise would have seemed to her important, such as wealth for example. Perhaps also it induces her to feign to some extent this scorn for wealth in the hope of obtaining more by making us suffer. The bargaining instinct may also enter into everything else; and even actual incidents in her life, an intrigue which she has confided to no one for fear of its being revealed to us, which many people might for all that have discovered had they felt the same passionate desire to know it as we ourselves while preserving a greater equanimity of mind and arousing fewer suspicions in the guilty party, an intrigue of which certain people have in fact not been unaware—but people whom we do not know and would not know how to find. And among all these reasons for her adopting an inexplicable attitude towards us, we must include those idiosyncrasies of character which impel people, whether from indifference to their own interests, or from hatred, or from love of freedom, or under the impulse of anger, or from fear of what certain people will think, to do the opposite of what we expected. And then there are the differences of environment, of upbringing, in which we refuse to believe because, when we are talking together, they are effaced by our words, but which return when we are apart to direct the actions of each of us from so opposite a point of view that no true meeting of minds is possible.

"Anyhow there's no need to seek out all these explanations," Andrée went on. "Heaven knows I was fond of Albertine, and she was a really nice creature, but, especially after she had typhoid (a year before you first met us all), she was an absolute madcap. All of a sudden she would get sick of what she was doing, all her plans would have to be changed that very minute, and she herself probably couldn't say why. You remember the year when you first came to Balbec, the year when you met us all? One fine day she got somebody to send her a telegram calling her back to Paris; she barely had time to pack her trunks. But there was absolutely no reason for her to go. All the pretexts she gave were false. Paris would be a deadly bore at that moment. We were all of us still at

Balbec. The golf club wasn't closed, indeed the heats for the cup which she was so keen on winning weren't finished. She'd certainly have won it. It only meant staying on for another week. Well, off she went at a gallop. I often spoke to her about it later. She said herself that she didn't know why she had left, that she felt homesick (the home being Paris, you can imagine how likely that was), that she didn't feel happy at Balbec, that she thought there were people there who sneered at her."

And I told myself there was this much truth in what Andrée said: that if differences between minds account for the different impressions produced upon one person and another by the same work, and differences of feeling account for the impossibility of captivating a person who does not love you, there are also differences between characters, peculiarities in a single character, which are also motives for action. Then I ceased to think about this explanation and said to myself how difficult it is to know the truth in this world.

I had indeed noticed Albertine's desire to go to Mme Verdurin's and her concealment of it: I had not been mistaken on that point. But then even if we do thus manage to grasp one fact, all the others, which we perceive only in their outward appearance, escape us, and we see only a succession of flat silhouettes of which we say to ourselves: it is this, it is that, it is because of her, or it is because of someone else. The revelation that Mlle Vinteuil was expected had seemed to me the true explanation, all the more so because Albertine, forestalling me, had spoken to me about it. And subsequently had she not refused to swear to me that Mlle Vinteuil's presence gave her no pleasure? And here, with regard to this young man, I re-

membered a point which I had forgotten. A short time
before, while Albertine was living with me, I had met
him, and he had been—in contrast to his attitude at Balbec—extremely friendly, even affectionate towards me,
had begged me to allow him to call on me, a request
which I had refused for a number of reasons. And now I
realised that it was quite simply because, knowing that
Albertine was living in my house, he had wanted to be on
good terms with me so as to have every facility for seeing
her and for carrying her off from me, and I concluded
that he was a scoundrel. Some time later, when I attended
the first performances of this young man's work, although
I continued to think that if he had been so anxious to call
on me, it was for Albertine's sake, and although I felt this
to be reprehensible, I remembered that in the past, if I
had gone down to Doncières to see Saint-Loup, it was really because I was in love with Mme de Guermantes. It is
true that the two cases were not quite the same: Saint-
Loup not being in love with Mme de Guermantes, there
was in my display of affection for him a trace of duplicity
perhaps, but no treason. But I reflected afterwards that
this affection which one feels for the person who possesses
the object of one's desire is something that one feels
equally even if he himself also loves that object. No
doubt, one ought in that case to resist a friendship which
will lead one straight to betrayal. And I think that this is
what I have always done. But in the case of those who
lack the strength to resist, we cannot say that the friendship they affect for their rival is a mere sham; they feel it
sincerely and for that reason display it with a fervour
which, once the betrayal has been accomplished, can cause
the betrayed husband or lover to say with amazed indig-

nation: "If you had heard the protestations of affection that the wretch showered on me! That a person should come to rob a man of his treasure, that I can understand. But that he should feel the diabolical need to assure him of his friendship first of all strikes me as a degree of ignominy and perversity almost impossible to imagine." No, in fact, there is no perverse pleasure in it, nor even an absolutely conscious lie.

The affection of this sort which Albertine's pseudo-fiancé had manifested for me that day had yet another excuse, being more complex than a simple by-product of his love for Albertine. It was only a short time since he had known himself to be, confessed himself to be, been anxious to be proclaimed an intellectual. For the first time, values other than sporting or hedonistic existed for him. The fact that I enjoyed the esteem of Elstir and Bergotte, that Albertine had perhaps told him of the way I talked about writers, which had led her to imagine that I might myself be able to write, meant that all of a sudden I had become to him (to the new man whom he at last realised himself to be) an interesting person whose friendship he would have liked to cultivate, to whom he would have liked to confide his plans, whom he might perhaps have asked for an introduction to Elstir. So that he was in fact sincere when he asked if he might call on me, expressing a regard for me to which intellectual reasons as well as a reflexion of Albertine imparted a certain veracity. No doubt it was not *for that* that he was so anxious to come and see me and would have dropped everything in order to do so. But of this last reason, which did little more than raise to a sort of impassioned paroxysm the two other reasons, he was perhaps unaware himself, and the other two existed really, as might really have existed in Albertine, when she had been anxious to go to Mme Verdurin's on the afternoon of the rehearsal, the perfectly respectable pleasure that she would feel in meeting again friends of her childhood who in her eyes were no more depraved than she was in theirs, in talking to them, in showing them, by the mere fact of her presence at the Verdurins', that the poor little girl whom they had known was now invited to a noted salon, the pleasure also that she might perhaps have felt in listening to Vinteuil's music. If all this was true, the blush that had risen to Albertine's cheeks when I had mentioned Mlle Vinteuil was due to the fact that I had done so in the context of that afternoon party which she had tried to keep secret from me because of the marriage proposal of which I was not to know. Albertine's refusal to swear to me that she would have felt no pleasure in meeting Mlle Vinteuil again at that party had at the moment intensified my torment, strengthened my suspicions, but proved to me in retrospect that she had wanted to be sincere, even over an innocent matter, perhaps simply because it was an innocent matter. There nevertheless remained what Andrée had told me about her relations with Albertine. Perhaps, however, even without going so far as to believe that Andrée had invented them solely that I should not be happy, or able to feel superior to her, I could still suppose that she had slightly exaggerated her account of what she used to do with Albertine, and that Albertine, by a mental reservation, also minimised slightly what she had done with Andrée, making use Jesuitically of certain definitions which I had stupidly formulated on the subject, judging that her relations with Andrée did not fall into the category of what she was obliged to confess to me and that she could deny them without lying. But why should I believe that it was she rather than Andrée who was lying? Truth and life are very difficult to fathom, and I retained of them, without really having got to know them, an impression in which sadness was perhaps actually eclipsed by exhaustion.

Chapter Three

SOJOURN IN VENICE

My mother had taken me to spend a few weeks in Venice, and—as beauty may exist in the most precious as well as in the humblest things—I received there impressions analogous to those which I had felt so often in the past at Combray, but transposed into a wholly different and far richer key. When, at ten o'clock in the morning, my shutters were thrown open, I saw blazing there, instead of the gleaming black marble into which the slates of Saint-Hilaire used to turn, the golden angel on the campanile of St Mark's. Glittering in a sunlight which made it almost impossible to keep one's eyes upon it, this angel promised me, with its outstretched arms, for the moment when I appeared on the Piazzetta half an hour later, a joy more certain than any that it could ever in the past have been bidden to announce to men of good will. I could see nothing else so long as I remained in bed, but as the whole world is merely a vast sundial, a single sunlit segment of which enables us to tell what time it is, on the very first morning I was reminded of the shops in the Place de l'Eglise at Combray, which, on Sunday mornings, were always on the point of shutting when I arrived for mass, while the straw in the marketplace smelt strongly in the already hot sunlight. But on the second morning, what I saw on awakening, what made me get out of bed (because they had taken the place in my mem-

ory and in my desire of the recollections of Combray),
were the impressions of my first morning stroll in Venice,
in Venice where everyday life was no less real than in
Combray, where as in Combray on Sunday mornings one
had the pleasure of stepping down into a festive street,
but where that street was entirely paved with sapphire-
blue water, cooled by warm breezes and of a colour so
durable that my tired eyes might rest their gaze upon it in
search of relaxation without fear of its blenching. Like the
good folk of the Rue de l'Oiseau at Combray, so also in
this strange town, the inhabitants actually emerged from
houses lined up side by side along the main street, but the
role played there by houses of casting a patch of shade at
their feet was entrusted in Venice to palaces of porphyry
and jasper, above the arched doors of which the head of a
bearded god (breaking the alignment, like the knocker on
a door at Combray) had the effect of darkening with its
shadow, not the brownness of the earth, but the splendid
blueness of the water. On the Piazza, the shadow that
would have been produced at Combray by the awning
over the draper's shop and the barber's pole was a carpet
of little blue flowers strewn at its feet upon the desert of
sun-scorched flagstones by the relief of a Renaissance
façade, which is not to say that, when the sun beat down,
one was not obliged, in Venice as at Combray, to pull
down the blinds, even beside the canal, but they hung between the quatrefoils and foliage of Gothic windows. Of
this sort was the window in our hotel behind the balusters
of which my mother sat waiting for me, gazing at the
canal with a patience which she would not have displayed
in the old days at Combray, at a time when, cherishing
hopes for my future which had never been realised, she

was unwilling to let me see how much she loved me. Nowadays she was well aware that an apparent coldness on her part would alter nothing, and the affection she lavished upon me was like those forbidden foods which are no longer withheld from invalids when it is certain that they are past recovery. True, the humble details which gave an individuality to the window of my aunt Léonie's bedroom seen from the Rue de l'Oiseau, the impression of asymmetry caused by its unequal distance from the windows on either side of it, the exceptional height of its wooden ledge, the angled bar which served to open the shutters, the two curtains of glossy blue satin tied back with loops—the equivalent of all these things existed in this hotel in Venice where I could hear also those words, so distinctive and so eloquent, which enable us to recognise from a distance the dwelling to which we are going home to lunch, and afterwards remain in our memory as testimony that, for a certain period of time, that dwelling was ours; but the task of uttering them had, in Venice, devolved not, as at Combray and most other places, upon the simplest, not to say the ugliest things, but upon the ogive, still half Arab, of a façade which is reproduced in all the architectural museums and all the illustrated art books as one of the supreme achievements of the domestic architecture of the Middle Ages; from a long way away and when I had barely passed San Giorgio Maggiore, I caught sight of this ogival window which had already seen me, and the thrust of its pointed arches added to its smile of welcome the distinction of a loftier, scarcely comprehensible gaze. And because, behind its multi-coloured marble balusters, Mamma was sitting reading while she waited for me to return, her face shrouded in a tulle veil as heartrending in its whiteness as her hair to me who sensed that, hiding her tears, she had pinned it to her straw hat not so much with the idea of appearing "dressed" in the eyes of the hotel staff as in order to appear to me to be less in mourning, less sad, almost consoled for the death of my grandmother; because, not having recognised me at first, as soon as I called to her from the gondola, she sent out to me, from the bottom of her heart, a love which stopped only where there was no longer any corporeal matter to sustain it, on the surface of her impassioned gaze which she brought as close to me as possible, which she tried to thrust forward to the advanced post of her lips, in a smile which seemed to be kissing me, within the frame and beneath the canopy of the more discreet smile of the arched window lit up by the midday sun — because of this, that window has assumed in my memory the precious quality of things that have had, simultaneously with us, side by side with us, their share in a certain hour that struck, the same for us and for them; and however full of admirable tracery its mullions may be, that illustrious window retains in my eyes the intimate aspect of a man of genius with whom we have spent a month in some holiday resort, where he has acquired a friendly regard for us; and if, ever since then, whenever I see a cast of that window in a museum, I am obliged to hold back my tears, it is simply because it says to me the thing that touches me more than anything else in the world: "I remember your mother so well."

And as I went indoors to join my mother who by now had left the window, on leaving the heat of the open air I had the same sensation of coolness that I experienced long ago at Combray when I went upstairs to my room;

but in Venice it was a breeze from the sea that kept the air cool, and no longer on a little wooden staircase with narrow steps, but on the noble surfaces of marble steps continually splashed by shafts of blue-green sunlight, which, to the valuable instruction in the art of Chardin acquired long ago, added a lesson in that of Veronese. And since, in Venice, it is works of art, things of priceless beauty, that are entrusted with the task of giving us our impressions of everyday life, it is to falsify the character of that city, on the grounds that the Venice of certain painters is coldly aesthetic in its most celebrated parts (let us make an exception of the superb studies of Maxime Dethomas), to represent only its poverty-stricken aspects, in the districts where nothing of its splendour is to be seen, and, in order to make Venice more intimate and more genuine, to give it a resemblance to Aubervilliers. It has been the mistake of some very great artists, from a quite natural reaction against the artificial Venice of bad painters, to concentrate exclusively on the Venice of the more humble *campi*, the little deserted *rii*, which they found more real.

It was this Venice that I used often to explore in the afternoon, when I did not go out with my mother. The fact was that it was easier to find there women of the people, match-sellers, pearl-stringers, glass or lace makers, young seamstresses in black shawls with long fringes, whom there was nothing to prevent me from loving, because I had to a large extent forgotten Albertine, and who seemed to me more desirable than others, because I still remembered her a little. Who, in any case, could have told me precisely, in this passionate quest of mine for Venetian women, how much there was of themselves, how much of Albertine, how much of my old, long-cherished desire to visit Venice? Our slightest desire, though unique as a chord, nevertheless includes the fundamental notes on which the whole of our life is built. And sometimes, if we were to eliminate one of them, even one that we do not hear, that we are not aware of, one that has no connexion with the object of our quest, we would nevertheless see our whole desire for that object disappear. There were many things that I made no attempt to identify in the excitement I felt as I went in search of Venetian women.

My gondola followed the course of the small canals; like the mysterious hand of a genie leading me through the maze of this oriental city, they seemed, as I advanced, to be cutting a path for me through the heart of a crowded quarter which they bisected, barely parting, with a slender furrow arbitrarily traced, the tall houses with their tiny Moorish windows; and as though the magic guide had been holding a candle in his hand and were lighting the way for me, they kept casting ahead of them a ray of sunlight for which they cleared a route. One felt that between the mean dwellings which the canal had just parted, and which otherwise would have formed a compact whole, no open space had been reserved; so that a campanile or a garden trellis vertically overhung the *rio*, as in a flooded city. But, for both churches and gardens, thanks to the same transposition as in the Grand Canal, the sea so readily served as means of communication, as substitute for street or alley, that on either side of the *canaletto* the belfries rose from the water in this poor and populous district like those of humble and much-frequented parish churches bearing the stamp of their necessity, of their use by crowds of simple folk, the gardens

traversed by the canal cutting trailed their startled leaves
and fruit in the water, and on the ledges of the houses
whose crudely cut stone was still rough as though it had
only just been sawn, urchins surprised by the gondola sat
back trying to keep their balance and allowing their legs
to dangle vertically, like sailors seated upon a swing-
bridge the two halves of which have been swung apart, allowing the sea to pass between them. Now and again
would appear a handsomer building that happened to be
there like a surprise in a box which one has just opened, a
little ivory temple with its Corinthian columns and an allegorical statue on its pediment, somewhat out of place
among the ordinary surroundings in the midst of which,
for all that we tried to make space for it, the peristyle
with which the canal had provided it retained the look of
a landing-stage for market gardeners. I had the impression, which my desire strengthened further, of not being
outside, but of entering more and more into the depths of
something secret, because each time I found something
new which came to place itself on one side of me or the
other, a small monument or an unexpected *campo*, keeping the surprised expression of beautiful things which one
sees for the first time and of which one doesn't yet perfectly understand the intended purpose or the utility.

I returned on foot through narrow lanes; I accosted
plebeian girls as Albertine perhaps had done, and I should
have liked to have her with me. Yet these could not be
the same girls; at the time when Albertine had been in
Venice, they would have been children still. But, after
having been unfaithful in the past, in a basic sense and
out of cowardice, to each of the desires that I had conceived as unique—since I had sought an analogous object

and not the same one, which I despaired of finding
again—now I systematically sought women whom Albertine had not known, just as I no longer sought those that
I had desired in the past. True, it often happened to me
to recall, with an extraordinary violence of desire, some
wench of Méséglise or Paris, or the milk-girl I had seen
early in the morning at the foot of a hill during my first
journey to Balbec. But alas! I remembered them as they
were then, that is to say as they certainly would not be
now. So that if in the past I had been led to qualify my
impression of the uniqueness of a desire by seeking, in
place of a convent-girl I had lost sight of, a similar convent-girl, now, in order to recapture the girls who had
troubled my adolescence or that of Albertine, I had to
consent to a further departure from the principle of the
individuality of desire: what I must look for was not those
who were sixteen then, but those who were sixteen today,
for now, in the absence of that which was most distinctive
in the person and which eluded me, what I loved was
youth. I knew that the youth of those I had known existed no longer except in my impassioned recollection, and
that it was not them, however anxious I might be to make
contact with them when my memory recalled them to me,
that I must cull if I really wished to harvest the youth and
the blossom of the year.

The sun was still high in the sky when I went to
meet my mother on the Piazzetta. We would call for a
gondola. "How your poor grandmother would have loved
this simple grandeur!" Mamma would say to me, pointing
to the Doges' Palace which stood contemplating the sea
with the thoughtful expression that had been bequeathed
to it by its architect and that it faithfully retained in its

mute attendance on its vanished lords. "She would even have loved those soft pink tints, because they are unmawkish. How she would have loved the whole of Venice, and what informality, worthy of nature itself, she would have found in all these beauties, this plethora of objects that seem to need no formal arrangement but present themselves just as they are—the Doges' Palace with its cubic shape, the columns which you say are those of Herod's palace, slap in the middle of the Piazzetta, and, even less deliberately placed, put there as though for want of anywhere better, the pillars from Acre, and those horses on the balcony of St Mark's! Your grandmother would have had as much pleasure seeing the sun setting over the Doges' Palace as over a mountain." And there was indeed an element of truth in what my mother said, for, as the gondola brought us back along the Grand Canal, we watched the double line of palaces between which we passed reflect the light and angle of the sun upon their pink flanks, and alter with them, seeming not so much private habitations and historic buildings as a chain of marble cliffs at the foot of which one goes out in the evening in a boat to watch the sunset. Seen thus, the buildings arranged along either bank of the canal made one think of objects of nature, but of a nature which seemed to have created its works with a human imagination. But at the same time (because of the always urban character of the impressions which Venice gives almost in the open sea, on those waters whose ebb and flow makes itself felt twice daily, and which alternately cover at high tide and uncover at low tide the splendid outside stairs of the palaces), as we should have done in Paris on the boulevards, in the Champs-Elysées, in the Bois, in any

wide and fashionable avenue, we passed the most elegant
women in the hazy evening light, almost all foreigners,
who, languidly reclining against the cushions of their
floating carriages, followed one another in procession,
stopped in front of a palace where they had a friend to
call on, sent to inquire whether she was at home, and
while, as they waited for the answer, they prepared to
leave a card just in case, as they would have done at the
door of the Hôtel de Guermantes, turned to their guide-
books to find out the period and the style of the palace,
being shaken the while, as though upon the crest of a blue
wave, by the wash of the glittering, swirling water, which
took alarm on finding itself pent between the dancing
gondola and the resounding marble. And thus any outing,
even when it was only to pay calls or to leave visiting-
cards, was threefold and unique in this Venice where the
simplest social coming and going assumed at the same
time the form and the charm of a visit to a museum and a
trip on the sea.

Several of the palaces on the Grand Canal had been
converted into hotels, and for the sake of a change or out
of hospitality towards Mme Sazerat whom we had encountered—the unexpected and inopportune acquaintance
whom one invariably meets when one travels abroad—
and whom Mamma had invited to dine with us, we decided one evening to try a hotel which was not our own
and in which we had been told that the food was better.
While my mother was paying the gondolier and taking
Mme Sazerat to the drawing-room which she had engaged, I slipped away to inspect the great hall of the
restaurant with its fine marble pillars and walls and ceiling that were once entirely covered with frescoes, recently

and badly restored. Two waiters were conversing in an Italian which I translate:

"Are the old people going to dine in their room? They never let us know. It's annoying; I never know whether I ought to keep their table for them (*non so se bisogna conserva loro la tavola*). Serve them right if they come down and find it's been taken! I don't understand how they can take in *forestieri* (foreigners) like that in such a smart hotel. They're not our sort of people."

Notwithstanding his scorn, the waiter was anxious to know what action he was to take with regard to the table, and was about to send the lift-boy upstairs to inquire when, before he had had time to do so, he received his answer: he had just caught sight of the old lady who was entering the room. I had no difficulty, despite the air of melancholy and weariness that comes with the weight of years, and despite a sort of eczema, of red leprosy that covered her face, in recognising beneath her bonnet, in her black jacket made by W—— but to the untutored eye exactly like that of an old concierge, the Marquise de Villeparisis. The place where I was standing, engaged in studying the remains of a fresco between two of the beautiful marble panels, happened by chance to be immediately behind the table at which Mme de Villeparisis had just sat down.

"Then M. de Villeparisis won't be long. They've been here a month now, and they've only once not eaten together," said the waiter.

I was wondering who could be the relative with whom she was travelling and who was named M. de Villeparisis, when a few moments later I saw her old lover, M. de Norpois, advance towards the table and sit down beside her.

His great age had weakened the resonance of his voice, but had in compensation imparted to his speech, formerly so reserved, a positive intemperance. The cause of this was perhaps to be sought in ambitions for the realisation of which he felt that little time remained to him and which filled him with all the more vehemence and ardour; perhaps in the fact that, cut off from a world of politics to which he longed to return, he imagined, in the naïvety of his desire, that he could turn out of office, by the savage criticisms which he launched at them, the men he was determined to replace. Thus do we see politicians convinced that the Cabinet of which they are not members cannot hold out for three days. It would, however, be an exaggeration to suppose that M. de Norpois had entirely forgotten the traditions of diplomatic speech. Whenever "important matters" were at issue, he became once more, as we shall see, the man whom we remember in the past, but for the rest of the time he would inveigh against this man and that with the senile violence which makes certain octogenarians hurl themselves at women to whom they are no longer capable of doing any serious damage.

Mme de Villeparisis preserved, for some minutes, the silence of an old woman who in the exhaustion of age finds it difficult to rise from recollection of the past to consideration of the present. Then, turning to one of those eminently practical questions that indicate the survival of a mutual affection:

"Did you call at Salviati's?"

"Yes."

"Will they send it tomorrow?"

"I brought the bowl back myself. You shall see it after dinner. Let us look at the menu."

"Did you send instructions about my Suez shares?"

"No; at the present moment the Stock Exchange is entirely taken up with oil shares. But there's no hurry, in view of the propitious state of the market. Here is the menu. As a first course there is red mullet. Shall we try them?"

"I shall, but you are not allowed them. Ask for a risotto instead. But they don't know how to cook it."

"Never mind. Waiter, some mullet for Madame and a risotto for me."

A fresh and prolonged silence.

"Here, I've brought you the papers, the *Corriere della Sera*, the *Gazzetta del Popolo*, and all the rest of them. Did you know that there is a strong likelihood of a diplomatic reshuffle in which the first scapegoat will be Paléologue, who is notoriously inadequate in Serbia. He may perhaps be replaced by Lozé, and there will be a vacancy at Constantinople. But," M. de Norpois hastened to add in a biting tone, "for an Embassy of such scope, in a capital where it is obvious that Great Britain must always, whatever happens, occupy the chief place at the council-table, it would be prudent to turn to men of experience better equipped to counter the subterfuges of the enemies of our British ally than are diplomats of the modern school who would walk blindfold into the trap." The angry volubility with which M. de Norpois uttered these last words was due principally to the fact that the newspapers, instead of suggesting his name as he had recom-

mended them to do, named as a "hot favourite" a young
minister of Foreign Affairs. "Heaven knows that the men
of years and experience are far from eager to put themselves forward, after all manner of tortuous manoeuvres,
in the place of more or less incapable recruits. I have
known many of these self-styled diplomats of the empiri-
cal school who centred all their hopes in flying a kite
which it didn't take me long to shoot down. There can be
no question that if the Government is so lacking in wisdom as to entrust the reins of state to unruly hands, at
the call of duty any conscript will always answer 'Present!'
But who knows" (and here M. de Norpois appeared to
know perfectly well to whom he was referring) "whether it
would not be the same on the day when they came in
search of some veteran full of wisdom and skill. To my
mind, though everyone may have his own way of looking
at things, the post at Constantinople should not be accepted until we have settled our existing difficulties with
Germany. We owe no man anything, and it is intolerable
that every six months they should come and demand from
us, by fraudulent machinations and under protest, some
full discharge or other which is invariably advocated by a
venal press. This must cease, and naturally a man of high
distinction who has proved his merit, a man who would
have, if I may say so, the Emperor's ear, would enjoy
greater authority than anyone else in bringing the conflict
to an end."

A gentleman who was finishing his dinner bowed to
M. de Norpois.

"Why, there's Prince Foggi," said the Marquis.

"Ah, I'm not sure that I know who you mean," muttered Mme de Villeparisis.

"But, of course you do—Prince Odo. He's the brother-in-law of your cousin Doudeauville. Surely you remember that I went shooting with him at Bonnétable?"

"Ah! Odo, is he the one who went in for painting?"

"Not at all, he's the one who married the Grand Duke N——'s sister."

M. de Norpois uttered these remarks in the cross tone of a schoolmaster who is dissatisfied with his pupil, and stared fixedly at Mme de Villeparisis out of his blue eyes.

When the Prince had drunk his coffee and was leaving his table, M. de Norpois rose, hastened towards him and with a majestic sweep of his arm, stepping aside himself, presented him to Mme de Villeparisis. And during the few minutes that the Prince was standing beside their table, M. de Norpois never ceased for an instant to keep his azure pupils trained on Mme de Villeparisis, with the mixture of indulgence and severity of an old lover, but principally from fear of her committing one of those verbal solecisms which he had relished but which he dreaded. Whenever she said anything to the Prince that was not quite accurate he corrected her mistake and stared into the eyes of the abashed and docile Marquise with the steady intensity of a hypnotist.

A waiter came to tell me that my mother was waiting for me. I went to join her and made my apologies to Mme Sazerat, saying that I had been amused to see Mme de Villeparisis. At the sound of this name, Mme Sazerat turned pale and seemed about to faint. Controlling herself with an effort: "Mme de Villeparisis who was Mlle de Bouillon?" she inquired.

"Yes."

"Couldn't I just get a glimpse of her for a moment? It has been the dream of my life."

"Then there's no time to lose, Madame, for she will soon have finished her dinner. But how do you come to take such an interest in her?"

"Because Mme de Villeparisis was, before her second marriage, the Duchesse d'Havré, beautiful as an angel, wicked as a demon, who drove my father to distraction, ruined him and then abandoned him immediately. Well, she may have behaved to him like the lowest prostitute, she may have been the cause of our having had to live, my family and myself, in humble circumstances at Combray, but now that my father is dead, my consolation is to think that he loved the most beautiful woman of his generation, and as I've never set eyes on her, it will be a sort of solace in spite of everything . . ."

I escorted Mme Sazerat, trembling with emotion, to the restaurant and pointed out Mme de Villeparisis.

But, like a blind person who looks everywhere but in the right direction, Mme Sazerat did not bring her eyes to rest upon the table at which Mme de Villeparisis was dining, but, looking towards another part of the room, said:

"But she must have gone, I don't see her where you say she is."

And she continued to gaze round the room in quest of the loathed, adored vision that had haunted her imagination for so long.

"Yes, there she is, at the second table."

"Then we can't be counting from the same point. At what I count as the second table there's only an old gentleman and a little hunchbacked, red-faced, hideous woman."

"That's her!"

Meanwhile, Mme de Villeparisis having asked M. de Norpois to invite Prince Foggi to sit down, a friendly conversation ensued among the three of them. They discussed politics, and the Prince declared that he was indifferent to the fate of the Cabinet and would spend another week at least in Venice. He hoped that by that time all risk of a ministerial crisis would have been avoided. Prince Foggi thought for a few moments that these political topics did not interest M. de Norpois, for the latter, who until then had been expressing himself with such vehemence, had become suddenly absorbed in an almost angelic silence which seemed capable of blossoming, should his voice return, only into some innocent and tuneful melody by Mendelssohn or César Franck. The Prince supposed also that this silence was due to the reserve of a Frenchman who naturally would not wish to discuss Italian affairs in the presence of an Italian. Now in this the Prince was completely mistaken. Silence and an air of indifference had remained, in M. de Norpois, not a sign of reserve but the habitual prelude to an intervention in important affairs. The Marquis had his eye upon nothing less (as we have seen) than Constantinople, after the prior settlement of the German question, with a view to which he hoped to force the hand of the Rome Cabinet. He considered, in fact, that an action on his part of international significance might be the worthy consummation of his career, perhaps even a prelude to fresh honours, to difficult tasks to which he had not relinquished his pretensions. For old age makes us incapable of doing but not, at first, of desiring. It is only in a third period that those who live to a very great age relinquish desire, as they have already

had to forgo action. They no longer even present themselves as candidates in futile elections where they have so
often tried to win success, such as that for the Presidency
of the Republic. They content themselves with taking the
air, eating, reading the newspapers; they have outlived
themselves.

The Prince, to put the Marquis at his ease and to
show him that he regarded him as a compatriot, began to
speak of the possible successors to the Prime Minister
then in office. Successors who would have a difficult task
before them. When Prince Foggi had mentioned more
than twenty names of politicians who seemed to him suitable for office, names to which the ex-Ambassador listened with his eyelids drooping over his blue eyes and
without moving a muscle, M. de Norpois broke his silence at length to utter the words which were to provide
the chancelleries with food for conversation for many
years to come, and afterwards, when they had been forgotten, would be exhumed by some personage signing
himself "One Who Knows" or "Testis" or "Machiavelli"
in a newspaper in which the very oblivion into which they
had fallen enabled them to create a fresh sensation. So,
Prince Foggi had mentioned more than twenty names to
the diplomat who remained as motionless and silent as a
deaf-mute, when M. de Norpois raised his head slightly,
and, in the form in which his most pregnant and far-
reaching diplomatic interventions had been couched, albeit
this time with greater audacity and less brevity, shrewdly
inquired: "And has no one mentioned the name of Signor
Giolitti?" At these words the scales fell from Prince
Foggi's eyes; he could hear a celestial murmur. Then at
once M. de Norpois began to speak about one thing and

another, no longer afraid to make a noise, as, when the last note of a sublime aria by Bach has died away, the audience are no longer afraid to talk aloud, to go and look for their hats and coats in the cloakroom. He made the break even more marked by begging the Prince to pay his most humble respects to Their Majesties the King and Queen when next he should see them, a farewell phrase corresponding to the shout for a coachman at the end of a concert: "Auguste, from the Rue de Belloy." We cannot say what exactly were Prince Foggi's impressions. He must certainly have been delighted to have heard the gem: "And has no one mentioned Signor Giolitti's name?" For M. de Norpois, in whom age had extinguished or deranged his most outstanding qualities, had on the other hand, as he grew older, perfected his bravura, as certain aged musicians, who in all other respects have declined, acquire and retain until the end, in the field of chamber-music, a perfect virtuosity which they did not formerly possess.

However that may be, Prince Foggi, who had intended to spend a fortnight in Venice, returned to Rome that very night and was received a few days later in audience by the King in connexion with certain properties which, as we may perhaps have mentioned already, the Prince owned in Sicily. The Cabinet hung on for longer than might have been expected. When it fell, the King consulted various statesmen as to the most suitable leader of a new Cabinet. Then he sent for Signor Giolitti, who accepted. Three months later a newspaper reported Prince Foggi's meeting with M. de Norpois. The conversation was reported as we have given it here, with the difference that, instead of: "M. de Norpois shrewdly inquired," one read: "M. de Norpois said with that shrewd and charming smile which is so characteristic of him." M. de Norpois considered that "shrewdly" had in itself sufficient explosive force for a diplomat and that this addition was, to say the least, excessive. He had even asked the Quai d'Orsay to issue an official denial, but the Quai d'Orsay did not know which way to turn. For, ever since the conversation had been made public, M. Barrère had been telegraphing several times hourly to Paris complaining of this unofficial ambassador to the Quirinal and describing the indignation with which the incident had been received throughout the whole of Europe. This indignation was non-existent, but the other ambassadors were too polite to contradict M. Barrère's assertion that everyone was up in arms. M. Barrère, guided only by his own reaction, mistook this courteous silence for assent. Immediately he telegraphed to Paris: "I have just had an hour's conversation with the Marchese Visconti-Venosta," and so forth. His secretaries were worn out.

M. de Norpois, however, had at his disposal a French newspaper of very long standing, which already in 1870, when he was French Minister in a German capital, had been of great service to him. This paper (especially its leading article, which was unsigned) was admirably written. But the paper became a thousand times more interesting whenever this leading article (styled "premier-Paris" in those far-off days and now, no one knows why, "editorial") was on the contrary badly expressed, with endless repetitions of words. Everyone sensed then, with great excitement, that the article had been "inspired." Perhaps by M. de Norpois, perhaps by some other man of the hour. To give an anticipatory idea of the Italian incident, let us show how M. de Norpois made use of this paper in 1870, to no purpose, it may be thought, since war broke out nevertheless, but most efficaciously, according to M. de Norpois, whose axiom was that one ought first and foremost to prepare public opinion. His articles, every word in which was weighed, resembled those optimistic bulletins which are at once followed by the death of the patient. For instance, on the eve of the declaration of war in 1870, when mobilisation was almost complete, M. de Norpois (remaining, of course, in the background) had felt it his duty to send to this famous newspaper the following "editorial":

"The opinion seems to prevail in authoritative circles that, since the afternoon hours of yesterday, the situation, without of course being of an alarming nature, might well be envisaged as serious and even, from certain angles, as susceptible of being regarded as critical. M. le Marquis de Norpois would appear to have had several conversations with the Prussian Minister, with a view to examining, in a firm and conciliatory spirit, and in a wholly concrete fashion, the various existing causes of friction, if one may so put it. Unfortunately, we have not yet heard, at the time of going to press, whether Their Excellencies have been able to agree upon a formula that may serve as the basis for a diplomatic instrument."

Stop press: "It has been learned with satisfaction in well-informed circles that a slight slackening of tension seems to have occurred in Franco-Prussian relations. Particular importance would appear to be attached to the fact that M. de Norpois is reported to have met the British Minister 'unter den Linden' and to have conversed with him for fully twenty minutes. This report is regarded as highly satisfactory." (There was added, in brackets, after the word "satisfactory" its German equivalent *"befriedigend."*) And on the following day one read in the editorial: "It would appear that, notwithstanding all the dexterity of M. de Norpois, to whom everyone must hasten to render homage for the skill and energy with which he has defended the inalienable rights of France, a rupture is now, one might say, virtually inevitable."

The newspaper could not refrain from following an editorial couched in this vein with a selection of comments, furnished of course by M. de Norpois. The reader may perhaps have observed in these last pages that the conditional was one of the Ambassador's favourite grammatical forms in the literature of diplomacy. ("Particular importance would appear to be attached" for "Particular importance is attached.") But the present indicative employed not in its usual sense but in that of the old "optative" was no less dear to M. de Norpois. The comments that followed the editorial were as follows:

"Never has the public shown itself so admirably calm" (M. de Norpois would have liked to believe that this was true but feared that it was precisely the opposite of the truth). "It is weary of fruitless agitation and has learned with satisfaction that the Government of His Majesty the Emperor would assume their responsibilities whatever the eventualities that might occur. The public asks" (optative) "nothing more. To its admirable composure, which is in itself a token of success, we shall add a piece of intelligence eminently calculated to reassure public opinion, were there any need of that. We are assured that M. de Norpois who, for reasons of health, was ordered long ago to return to Paris for medical treatment, would appear to have left Berlin where he considered that his presence no longer served any purpose."

Stop press: "His Majesty the Emperor left Compiègne this morning for Paris in order to confer with the Marquis de Norpois, the Minister for War and Marshal Bazaine in whom public opinion has especial confidence. H. M. the Emperor has cancelled the banquet which he was to give for his sister-in-law the Duchess of Alba. This action created everywhere, as soon as it became known, a particularly favourable impression. The Emperor has held a review of his troops, whose enthusiasm is indescribable. Several corps, by virtue of a mobilisation order issued immediately upon the Sovereign's arrival in Paris, are, in any contingency, ready to move in the direction of the Rhine."*

Sometimes at dusk as I returned to the hotel I felt that the Albertine of long ago, invisible to my eyes, was nevertheless enclosed within me as in the lead-covered cells of an inner Venice, the tight lid of which some incident occasionally lifted to give me a glimpse of that past.

Thus for instance one evening a letter from my stockbroker reopened for me for an instant the gates of the prison in which Albertine dwelt within me, alive, but so remote, so profoundly buried that she remained inaccessible to me. Since her death I had ceased to indulge in the speculations that I had made in order to have more money for her. But time had passed; the wisest judgments of the previous generation had been belied by the next, as had occurred in the past to M. Thiers who had said that railways could never prove successful; and the stocks of which M. de Norpois had said to us: "The income from them may not be very great, but at least the capital will never depreciate," were, more often than not, those which had declined most in value. In the case of my English Consols and Raffineries Say shares alone, I had to pay out such considerable sums in brokers' commissions, as well as interest and contango fees, that in a rash moment I decided to sell out everything and found that I now possessed barely a fifth of what I had inherited from my grandmother and still possessed when Albertine was alive. This became known at Combray among the surviving members of our family and their friends who, knowing that I went about with the Marquis de Saint-Loup and the Guermantes family, said to themselves: "Pride goes before a fall!" They would have been greatly astonished to learn that it was for a girl of Albertine's modest background, almost a protégée of my grandmother's former piano-teacher, Vinteuil, that I had made these speculations. Besides, in that Combray world in which everyone is classified for ever, as in an Indian caste, according to the income he is known to enjoy, no one would have been capable of imagining the great freedom that prevailed in the world of the Guermantes, where no importance was attached to wealth and where poverty was regarded as being as disagreeable as, but no more degrading, having no more effect on a person's social position, than a stomach-ache. Doubtless people at Combray imagined, on the contrary, that Saint-Loup and M. de Guermantes must be ruined aristocrats with heavily mortgaged estates, to whom I had been lending money, whereas if I had been ruined they would have been the first to offer, unavailingly, to come to my assistance. As for my comparative penury, it was all the more awkward at the moment, inasmuch as my Venetian interests had been concentrated for some little time past on a young vendor of glassware whose blooming complexion offered to the delighted eye a whole range of orange tones and filled me with such a longing to see her daily that, realising that my mother and I would soon be leaving Venice, I had made up my mind to try to create some sort of position for her in Paris which would save me from being parted from her. The beauty of her seventeen years was so noble, so radiant, that it was like acquiring a genuine Titian before leaving the place. But would the scant remains of my fortune be enough to tempt her to leave her native land and come to live in Paris for my sole convenience?

But as I came to the end of the stockbroker's letter, a passage in which he said: "I shall look after your credits" reminded me of a scarcely less hypocritically professional expression which the bath-attendant at Balbec had used in speaking to Aimé of Albertine: "It was I who looked after her," she had said. And these words which had never recurred to my mind acted like an "Open sesame!" upon the hinges of the prison door. But a moment later the door closed once more upon the immured victim—whom I was not to blame for not wishing to join since I was no longer able to see her, to call her to mind, and since other people exist for us only through the idea that we have of them—but who for a moment had been rendered more touching by my desertion of her, albeit she was unaware of it, so that for the duration of a lightning-flash I had thought with longing of the time, already remote, when I used to suffer night and day from the companionship of her memory. Another time, in San Giorgio degli Schiavoni, an eagle accompanying one of the Apostles, and conventionalised in the same manner, revived the memory and almost the suffering caused by the two rings the similarity of which Françoise had revealed to me, and as to which I had never learned who had given them to Albertine.

One evening, however, an incident occurred of such a nature that it seemed as though my love must revive. No sooner had our gondola stopped at the hotel steps than the porter handed me a telegram which the messenger had already brought three times to the hotel, for owing to the inaccurate rendering of the addressee's name (which I recognised nevertheless, through the corruptions introduced by the Italian clerks, as my own) the post office required a signed receipt certifying that the telegram was indeed for me. I opened it as soon as I was in my room, and, glancing through the message which was filled with inaccurately transmitted words, managed nevertheless to make out: "My dear friend, you think me dead, forgive me, I am quite alive, I long to see you, talk about marriage, when do you return? Affectionately. Albertine." Then there occurred in me in reverse order a process parallel to that which had occurred in the case of my grandmother. When I had learned the fact of my grandmother's death, I had not at first felt any grief. And I had been really grieved by her death only when certain involuntary memories had brought her alive again for me. Now that Albertine no longer lived for me in my thoughts, the news that she was alive did not cause me the joy that I might have expected. Albertine had been no more to me than a bundle of thoughts, and she had survived her physical death so long as those thoughts were alive in me; on the other hand, now that those thoughts were dead,

Albertine did not rise again for me with the resurrection of her body. And when I realised that I felt no joy at the thought of her being alive, that I no longer loved her, I ought to have been more shattered than a man who, looking at his reflexion in a mirror, after months of travel or sickness, discovers that he has white hair and a different face, that of a middle-aged or an old man. This is shattering because its message is: "the man that I was, the fair-haired young man, no longer exists, I am another person." And yet, was not the impression that I now felt the proof of as profound a change, as total a death of my former self and of the no less complete substitution of a new self for that former self, as the sight of a wrinkled face topped with a white wig instead of the face of long ago? But one is no more distressed at having become another person, after a lapse of years and in the natural sequence of time, than one is at any given moment by the fact of being, one after another, the incompatible persons, malicious, sensitive, refined, caddish, disinterested, ambitious which one can be, in turn, every day of one's life. And the reason why one is not distressed is the same, namely that the self which has been eclipsed—momentarily in this latter case and when it is a question of character, permanently in the former case and when the passions are involved—is not there to deplore the other, the other which is for the moment, or from then onwards, one's whole self; the caddish self laughs at his caddishness because one is the cad, and the forgetful self does not grieve about his forgetfulness precisely because he has forgotten.

I should have been incapable of resuscitating Albertine because I was incapable of resuscitating myself, of resuscitating the self of those days. Life, in accordance with its habit which is, by unceasing, infinitesimal labours, to change the face of the world, had not said to me on the morrow of Albertine's death: "Become another person," but, by changes too imperceptible for me to be conscious even that I was changing, had altered almost everything in me, with the result that my mind was already accustomed to its new master—my new self—when it became aware that it had changed; it was to this new master that it was attached. My feeling for Albertine, my jealousy, stemmed, as we have seen, from the irradiation, by the association of ideas, of certain pleasant or painful impressions, the memory of Mlle Vinteuil at Montjouvain, the precious good-night kisses that Albertine used to give me on the neck. But in proportion as these impressions had grown fainter, the vast field of impressions which they coloured with a hue that was agonising or soothing reverted to neutral tones. As soon as oblivion had taken hold of certain dominant points of suffering and pleasure, the resistance offered by my love was overcome, I no longer loved Albertine. I tried to recall her image to my mind. I had been right in my presentiment when, a couple of days after Albertine's flight, I was appalled by the discovery that I had been able to live for forty-eight hours without her. It had been the same as when I wrote to Gilberte long ago saying to myself: "If this goes on for a year or two, I shall no longer love her." And if, when Swann asked me to come and see Gilberte again, this had seemed to me as embarrassing as greeting a dead woman, in Albertine's case death—or what I had supposed to be death—had achieved the same result as a prolonged breach in Gilberte's. Death merely acts in the same way as absence. The monster at whose apparition my love had trembled, oblivion, had indeed, as I had feared, ended by devouring that love. Not only did the news that she was alive fail to revive my love, not only did it enable me to realise how far I had already proceeded along the road towards indifference, it at once and so abruptly accelerated that process that I wondered retrospectively whether the opposite report, that of Albertine's death, had not, conversely, by completing the effect of her departure, rekindled my love and delayed its decline. Yes, now that the knowledge that she was alive and the possibility of our reunion made her suddenly cease to be so precious to me, I wondered whether Françoise's insinuations, our rupture itself, and even her death (imaginary, but believed to be real) had not prolonged my love, to such an extent do the efforts of third persons, and even those of fate, to separate us from a woman succeed only in attaching us to her. Now it was the contrary process that had occurred. Anyhow, I tried to recall her image and perhaps because I had only to raise a finger for her to be mine once more, the memory that came to me was that of a somewhat stout and mannish-looking girl from whose faded features protruded already, like a sprouting seed, the profile of Mme Bontemps. What she might or might not have done with Andrée or with other girls no longer interested me. I no longer suffered from the malady which I had so long thought to be incurable, and really I might have foreseen this. Certainly, regret for a lost mistress and surviving jealousy are physical maladies fully as much as tuberculosis or leukaemia. And yet among physical maladies it is possible to distinguish those which are caused by a purely physical agency, and those which act upon the body only through the medium of the intelligence. Above all, if the part of the mind which serves as carrier is the memory—that is to say if the cause is obliterated or remote—however agonising the pain, however profound the disturbance to the organism may appear to be, it is very seldom (the mind having a capacity for renewal or rather an incapacity for conservation which the tissues lack) that the prognosis is not favourable. At the end of a given period after which someone who has been attacked by cancer will be dead, it is very seldom that the grief of an inconsolable widower or father is not healed. Mine was healed. Was it for this girl whom I saw in my mind's eye so bloated and who had certainly aged, as the girls whom she had loved had aged—was it for her that I must renounce the dazzling girl who was my memory of yesterday, my hope for tomorrow, to whom I could no longer give a sou, any more than to any other, if I married Albertine, that I must renounce this "new Albertine" whom I loved "not as Hades had beheld her . . . but faithful, but proud, and even rather shy"?[30] It was she who was now what Albertine had been in the past: my love for Albertine had been but a transitory form of my devotion to youth. We think that we are in love with a girl, whereas we love in her, alas! only that dawn the glow of which is momentarily reflected on her face.

The night went by. In the morning I gave the telegram back to the hotel porter explaining that it had been brought to me by mistake and that it was not for me. He told me that now it had been opened he might get into trouble, that it would be better if I kept it; I put it back in my pocket, but made up my mind to behave as though I had never received it. I had finally ceased to love Albertine. So that this love, after departing so greatly from what I had anticipated on the basis of my love for Gilberte, after obliging me to make so long and painful a detour, had ended too, after having proved an exception to it, by succumbing, like my love for Gilberte, to the general law of oblivion.

But then I thought to myself: I used to value Albertine more than myself; I no longer value her now because for a certain time past I have ceased to see her. My desire not to be parted from myself by death, to rise again after my death—that desire was not like the desire never to be parted from Albertine; it still persisted. Was this due to the fact that I valued myself more highly than her, that when I loved her I loved myself more? No, it was because, having ceased to see her, I had ceased to love her, whereas I had not ceased to love myself because my everyday links with myself had not been severed like those with Albertine. But if my links with my body, with myself, were severed also . . . ? Obviously, it would be the same. Our love of life is only an old liaison of which we do not know how to rid ourselves. Its strength lies in its permanence. But death which severs it will cure us of the desire for immortality.

After lunch, when I was not going to roam about Venice by myself, I went up to my room to get ready to go out with my mother and to collect the exercise books in which I would take notes for some work I was doing on Ruskin. In the abrupt angles of the walls I sensed the restrictions imposed by the sea, the parsimony of the soil. And when I went downstairs to join Mamma who was waiting for me, at that hour when at Combray it was so pleasant to feel the sun close at hand in the darkness preserved by the closed shutters, here, from top to bottom of the marble staircase where one could no more tell than in a Renaissance picture whether it was in a palace or on a galley, the same coolness and the same sense of the splendour of the scene outside were imparted thanks to the awnings which stirred outside the ever-open windows through which, upon an incessant stream of air, the warm shade and the greenish sunlight flowed as if over a liquid surface and suggested the mobile proximity, the glitter, the shimmering instability of the sea.

As often as not we would set off for St Mark's, with all the more pleasure because, since one had to take a gondola to go there, the church represented for me not simply a monument but the terminus of a voyage on these vernal, maritime waters, with which, I felt, St Mark's formed an indivisible and living whole. My mother and I would enter the baptistery, treading underfoot the marble and glass mosaics of the paving, in front of us the wide arcades whose curved pink surfaces have been slightly warped by time, thus giving the church, wherever the freshness of this colouring has been preserved, the appearance of having been built of a soft and malleable substance like the wax in a giant honeycomb, and, where on the contrary time has shrivelled and hardened the material and artists have embellished it with gold tracery, of being the precious binding, in the finest Cordoba leather, of the colossal Gospel of Venice. Seeing that I needed to spend some time in front of the mosaics representing the Baptism of Christ, and feeling the icy coolness that pervaded the baptistery, my mother threw a shawl over my shoulders. When I was with Albertine at Balbec, I felt that she was revealing one of those insubstantial illusions which clutter the minds of so many people who do not think clearly, when she used to speak of the pleasure—to my mind baseless—that she would derive from seeing works of art with me. Today I am sure that the pleasure does exist, if not of seeing, at least of having seen, a beautiful thing with a particular person. A time has now come when, remembering the baptistery of St Mark's—contemplating the waters of the Jordan in which St John immerses Christ, while the gondola awaited us at the landing-stage of the Piazzetta—it is no longer a matter of indifference to me that, beside me in that cool penumbra, there should have been a woman draped in her mourning with the respectful and enthusiastic fervour of the old woman in Carpaccio's *St Ursula* in the Accademia, and that that woman, with her red cheeks and sad eyes and in her black veils, whom nothing can ever remove from that softly lit sanctuary of St Mark's where I am always sure to find her because she has her place reserved there as immutably as a mosaic, should be my mother.

Carpaccio, as it happens, who was the painter we visited most readily when I was not working in St Mark's, almost succeeded one day in reviving my love for Albertine. I was seeing for the first time *The Patriarch of Grado exorcising a demoniac*. I looked at the marvellous rose-pink and violet sky and the tall encrusted chimneys silhouetted against it, their flared stacks, blossoming like red tulips, reminiscent of so many Whistlers of Venice. Then my eyes travelled from the old wooden Rialto to that fifteenth-century Ponte Vecchio with its marble palaces decorated with gilded capitals, and returned to the canal on which the boats are manoeuvred by adolescents in pink jackets and plumed toques, the spitting image of those avowedly inspired by Carpaccio in that dazzling *Legend of*

Joseph by Sert, Strauss and Kessler. Finally, before leaving the picture, my eyes came back to the shore, swarming with the everyday Venetian life of the period. I looked at the barber wiping his razor, at the negro humping his barrel, at the Muslims conversing, at the noblemen in wide-sleeved brocade and damask robes and hats of cerise velvet, and suddenly I felt a slight gnawing at my heart. On the back of one of the *Compagni della Calza* identifiable from the emblem, embroidered in gold and pearls on their sleeves or their collars, of the merry confraternity to which they were affiliated, I had just recognised the cloak which Albertine had put on to come with me to Versailles in an open carriage on the evening when I so little suspected that scarcely fifteen hours separated me from the moment of her departure from my house. Always ready for anything, when I had asked her to come out with me on that melancholy occasion which she was to describe in her last letter as "a double twilight since night was falling and we were about to part," she had flung over her shoulders a Fortuny cloak which she had taken away with her next day and which I had never thought of since. It was from this Carpaccio picture that that inspired son of Venice had taken it, it was from the shoulders of this *Compagno della Calza* that he had removed it in order to drape it over the shoulders of so many Parisian women who were certainly unaware, as I had been until then, that the model for it existed in a group of noblemen in the foreground of the *Patriarch of Grado* in a room in the Accademia in Venice. I had recognised it down to the last detail, and, that forgotten cloak having restored to me as I looked at it the eyes and the heart of him who had set out that evening with Albertine for Versailles, I was overcome for a few moments by a vague and soon dissipated feeling of desire and melancholy.

There were days when my mother and I were not content with visiting the museums and churches of Venice only, and once, when the weather was particularly fine, in order to see the "Virtues" and "Vices" of which M. Swann had given me reproductions that were probably still hanging on the wall of the schoolroom at Combray, we went as far afield as Padua. After walking across the garden of the Arena in the glare of the sun, I entered the Giotto chapel, the entire ceiling of which and the background of the frescoes are so blue that it seems as though the radiant daylight has crossed the threshold with the human visitor in order to give its pure sky a momentary breather in the coolness and shade, a sky merely of a slightly deeper blue now that it is rid of the glitter of the sunlight, as in those brief moments of respite when, though no cloud is to be seen, the sun has turned its gaze elsewhere and the azure, softer still, grows deeper. This sky transplanted on to the blue-washed stone was peopled with flying angels which I was seeing for the first time, for M. Swann had given me reproductions only of the Vices and Virtues and not of the frescoes depicting the life of the Virgin and of Christ. Watching the flight of these angels, I had the same impression of actual movement, literally real activity, that the gestures of Charity and Envy had given me. For all the celestial fervour, or at least the childlike obedience and application, with which their minuscule hands are joined, they are represented in the Arena chapel as winged creatures of a particular species that had really existed, that must have figured in the natural history of biblical and apostolic times. Constantly flitting about above the saints whenever the latter walk abroad, these little beings, since they are real creatures with a genuine power of flight, can be seen soaring upwards, describing curves, "looping the loop," diving earthwards head first, with the aid of wings which enable them to support themselves in positions that defy the laws of gravity, and are far more reminiscent of an extinct species of bird, or of young pupils of Garros practising gliding,[31] than of the angels of the Renaissance and later periods whose wings have become no more than emblems and whose deportment is generally the same as that of heavenly beings who are not winged.

On returning to the hotel I would meet young women, mainly Austrians, who came to Venice to spend the first fine days of this flowerless spring. There was one in particular whose features did not resemble Albertine's but who attracted me by the same fresh complexion, the same gay, light-hearted look. Soon I became aware that I was beginning to say the same things to her as I had said to Albertine at the start, that I concealed the same misery when she told me she would not be seeing me the following day because she was going to Verona, and that I immediately wanted to go to Verona too. It did not last—she was soon to leave for Austria and I would never see her again—but already, vaguely jealous as one is when one begins to fall in love, looking at her charming and enigmatic face I wondered whether she too loved women, whether what she had in common with Albertine, that clear complexion, that bright-eyed look, that air of friendly candour which charmed everyone and which stemmed more from the fact that she was not in the least interested in knowing about other people's actions, which interested her not at all, than that she was confessing her own, which on the contrary she concealed beneath the most puerile lies—I wondered whether all this constituted the morphological characteristics of the woman who loves other women. Was it this about her that, without my being able rationally to grasp why, exercised its attraction upon me, caused my anxieties (perhaps a deeper cause of my attraction towards her by virtue of the fact that we are drawn towards that which will make us suffer), gave me when I saw her so much pleasure and sadness, like those magnetic elements in the air of certain places which we do not see but which cause us such physical discomfort? Alas, I should never know. I should have liked, when I tried to read her face, to say to her: "You really should tell me, it would interest me as an example of human natural history," but she would never tell me. She professed an especial loathing for anything that resembled that vice, and was extremely distant towards her women friends. Perhaps indeed this was proof that she had something to hide, perhaps that she had been mocked or reviled for it, and the air that she assumed in order that people should not think such things of her was like an animal's instinctive and revealing recoil from someone who has beaten it. As for my finding out about her life, it was impossible; even in the case of Albertine, how long it had taken me to get to know anything! It had taken her death to loosen people's tongues, such prudent circumspection had Albertine, like this young woman, observed in all her conduct. And in any case, could I be certain that I had discovered anything about Albertine? Moreover, just as the conditions of life that we most desire become a matter of indif-

ference to us if we cease to love the person who, without
our realising it, made us desire them because they enabled
us to be close to her, to be in a position to please her, so
it is with certain kinds of intellectual curiosity. The scientific importance which I attached to knowing the particular kind of desire that lay hidden beneath the delicate pink
petals of those cheeks, in the brightness, a sunless brightness as at daybreak, of those pale eyes, in those days that
were never accounted for, would doubtless subside when I
had entirely ceased to love Albertine or when I had entirely ceased to love this young woman.

After dinner, I went out alone, into the heart of the
enchanted city where I found myself in the middle of
strange purlieus like a character in the *Arabian Nights*. It
was very seldom that, in the course of my wanderings, I
did not come across some strange and spacious *piazza* of
which no guidebook, no tourist had ever told me. I had
plunged into a network of little alleys, or *calli*. In the
evening, with their high bell-mouthed chimneys on which
the sun throws the brightest pinks, the clearest reds, it is
a whole garden blossoming above the houses, its shades so
various that you would have said it was the garden of
some tulip lover of Delft or Haarlem, planted on top of
the town. Moreover, the extreme proximity of the houses
made of every casement a frame from which a day-dreaming cook gazed out, or in which a seated girl was having
her hair combed by an old woman whose face in the dark
looked like a witch's—made of each humble quiet house,
so close because of the narrowness of the *calli*, a display
of a hundred Dutch paintings placed side by side. Packed
tightly together, these *calli* divided in all directions with

their furrows a chunk of Venice carved out between a canal and the lagoon, as if it had crystallised in accordance with these innumerable, tenuous and minute patterns. Suddenly, at the end of one of these alleys, it seemed as though a distension had occurred in the crystallised matter. A vast and splendid *campo* of which, in this network of little streets, I should never have guessed the scale, or even found room for it, spread out before me surrounded by charming palaces silvery in the moonlight. It was one of those architectural ensembles towards which, in any other town, the streets converge, lead you and point the way. Here it seemed to be deliberately concealed in an interlacement of alleys, like those palaces in oriental tales whither mysterious agents convey by night a person who, brought back home before daybreak, can never find his way back to the magic dwelling which he ends by believing that he visited only in a dream.

The next day, I set out in quest of my beautiful nocturnal *piazza*, following *calle* after *calle* which were exactly like one another and refused to give me the smallest piece of information, except such as would lead me further astray. Sometimes a vague landmark which I seemed to recognise led me to suppose that I was about to see appear, in its seclusion, solitude and silence, the beautiful exiled *piazza*. At that moment, some evil genie which had assumed the form of a new *calle* made me unwittingly retrace my steps, and I found myself suddenly brought back to the Grand Canal. And as there is no great difference between the memory of a dream and the memory of a reality, I finally wondered whether it was not during my sleep that there had occurred, in a dark patch of Venetian crystallisation, that strange mirage which offered a vast *pi-*

azza surrounded by romantic palaces to the meditative eye of the moon.

But, far more than certain places, it was the desire not to lose for ever certain women that kept me while in Venice in a state of agitation which became febrile when, towards the end of the day on which my mother had decided that we should leave, and our luggage was already on the way to the station in a gondola, I read in the register of guests expected at the hotel: "Mme Putbus and attendants." At once, the thought of all the hours of casual pleasure of which our departure would deprive me raised this desire, which existed in me in a chronic state, to the level of a feeling, and drowned it in a vague melancholy. I asked my mother to put off our departure for a few days, and her air of not for a moment taking my request into consideration, of not even listening to it seriously, reawakened in my nerves, exacerbated by the Venetian springtime, that old desire to rebel against an imaginary plot woven against me by my parents, who imagined that I would be forced to obey them, that defiant spirit which drove me in the past to impose my will brutally upon the people I loved best in the world, though finally conforming to theirs after I had succeeded in making them yield. I told my mother that I would not leave Venice, but she, thinking it wiser not to appear to believe that I was saying this seriously, did not even answer. I went on to say that she would soon see whether I was serious or not. The porter brought us three letters, two for her, and one for me which I put in my wallet among several others without even looking at the envelope. And when the hour came at which, accompanied by all my belongings, she set off for the station, I ordered a drink to be brought out to me on the terrace overlooking the canal, and settled down there to watch the sunset, while from a boat that had stopped in front of the hotel a musician sang *O sole mio*.

The sun continued to sink. My mother must be nearing the station. Soon she would be gone, and I should be alone in Venice, alone with the misery of knowing that I had distressed her, and without her presence to comfort me. The hour of the train's departure was approaching. My irrevocable solitude was so near at hand that it seemed to me to have begun already and to be complete. For I felt myself to be alone; things had become alien to me; I no longer had calm enough to break out of my throbbing heart and introduce into them a measure of stability. The town that I saw before me had ceased to be Venice. Its personality, its name, seemed to me to be mendacious fictions which I no longer had the will to impress upon its stones. I saw the palaces reduced to their basic elements, lifeless heaps of marble with nothing to choose between them, and the water as a combination of hydrogen and oxygen, eternal, blind, anterior and exterior to Venice, oblivious of the Doges or of Turner. And yet this unremarkable place was as strange as a place at which one has just arrived, which does not yet know one, or a place which one has left and which has forgotten one already. I could no longer tell it anything about myself, I could leave nothing of myself imprinted upon it; it contracted me into myself until I was no more than a beating heart and an attention strained to follow the development of *O sole mio*. In vain might I fix my mind despairingly upon the beautiful and distinctive curve of the Rialto, it seemed to me, with the mediocrity of the obvious, a bridge not merely inferior to but as alien to the notion I had of it as an actor of whom, in spite of his blond wig and black garments, we know quite well that in his essence he is not Hamlet. So it was with the palaces, the canal, the Rialto, divested of the idea that constituted their reality and dissolved into their vulgar material elements. But at the same time this mediocre place seemed distant to me. In the dock basin of the Arsenal, because of an element which itself also was scientific, namely latitude, there was that singularity in things whereby, even when similar in appearance to those of our own land, they reveal themselves to be alien, in exile beneath other skies; I felt that that horizon so close at hand, which I could have reached in an hour by boat, was a curvature of the earth quite different from that of France, a distant curvature which, by the artifice of travel, happened to be moored close to where I was; so that the dock basin of the Arsenal, at once insignificant and remote, filled me with that blend of distaste and alarm which I had felt as a child when I first accompanied my mother to the Deligny baths, where, in that weird setting of a pool of water reflecting neither sky nor sun, which nevertheless amid its fringe of cabins one felt to be in communication with invisible depths crowded with human bodies in swimming-trunks, I had asked myself whether those depths, concealed from mortal eyes by hutments which made their existence impossible to divine from the street, were not the entry to arctic seas which began at that point, in which the poles were comprised, and whether that narrow space was not indeed the open water that surrounds the pole; and in this lonely, unreal, icy, unfriendly setting in which I was going to be left alone, the strains of *O sole mio*, rising like a dirge for the Venice I had known, seemed to bear witness to my misery. No doubt I ought to have ceased to listen to it if I wished to be able to join my mother and take the train with her; I ought to have made up my mind to leave without losing another second. But this was precisely what I was powerless to do; I remained motionless, incapable not merely of rising, but even of deciding that I would rise from my chair. My mind, no doubt in order not to have to consider the decision I had to take, was entirely occupied in following the course of the successive phrases of *O sole mio*, singing them to myself with the singer, anticipating each surge of melody, soaring aloft with it, sinking down with it once more.

No doubt this trivial song which I had heard a hundred times did not interest me in the least. I could give no pleasure to myself or anyone else by listening to it religiously to the end. After all, none of the already familiar phrases of this sentimental ditty was capable of furnishing me with the resolution I needed; what was more, each of these phrases, when it came and went in its turn, became an obstacle in the way of my putting that resolution into effect, or rather it forced me towards the contrary resolution not to leave Venice, for it made me too late for the train. Wherefore this occupation, devoid of any pleasure in itself, of listening to *O sole mio* was charged with a profound, almost despairing melancholy. I was well aware that in reality it was the resolution not to go that I was making by remaining there without stirring, but to say to myself: "I'm not going," which in that direct form was impossible, became possible in this indirect form: "I'm going to listen to one more phrase of *O sole mio*"; but the practical significance of this figurative language did not escape me and, while I said to myself: "After all, I'm only listening to one more phrase," I knew that the words meant: "I shall remain by myself in Venice." And it was perhaps this melancholy, like a sort of numbing cold, that constituted the despairing but hypnotic charm of the song. Each note that the singer's voice uttered with a force and ostentation that were almost muscular stabbed me to the heart. When the phrase was completed down below and the song seemed to be at an end, the singer had still not had enough and resumed at the top as though he needed to proclaim once more my solitude and despair.

My mother must by now have reached the station. In a little while she would be gone. I was gripped by the anguish that was caused me by the sight of the Canal which had become diminutive now that the soul of Venice had fled from it, of that commonplace Rialto which was no longer the Rialto, and by the song of despair which *O sole mio* had become and which, bellowed thus beside the insubstantial palaces, finally reduced them to dust and ashes and completed the ruin of Venice; I looked on at the slow realisation of my distress, built up artistically, without haste, note by note, by the singer as he stood beneath the astonished gaze of the sun arrested in its course beyond San Giorgio Maggiore, with the result that the fading light was to combine for ever in my memory with the shiver of my emotion and the bronze voice of the singer in an equivocal, unalterable and poignant alloy.

Thus I remained motionless, my will dissolved, no decision in sight. Doubtless at such moments our decision has already been made: our friends can often predict it, but we ourselves are unable to do so, otherwise we should be spared a great deal of suffering.

But suddenly, from caverns darker than those from which flashes the comet which we can predict—thanks to the unsuspected defensive power of inveterate habit, thanks to the hidden reserves which by a sudden impulse it hurls at the last moment into the fray—my will to action arose at last; I set off in hot haste and arrived, when the carriage doors were already shut, but in time to find my mother flushed with emotion and with the effort to restrain her tears, for she thought that I was not coming. "You know," she said, "your poor grandmother used to say: It's curious, there's nobody who can be as unbearable or as nice as that child." Then the train started and we saw Padua and Verona come to meet us, to speed us on our way, almost on to the platforms of their stations, and, when we had drawn away from them, return—they who were not travelling and were about to resume their normal life—one to its plain, the other to its hill.

The hours went by. My mother was in no hurry to read her two letters, which she had merely opened, and tried to prevent me from pulling out my pocket-book at once to take from it the letter which the hotel porter had given me. She was always afraid of my finding journeys too long and too tiring, and put off as long as possible, so as to keep me occupied during the final hours, the moment at which she would seek fresh distractions for me, bring out the hard-boiled eggs, hand me the newspapers, untie the parcel of books which she had bought without telling me. We had long passed Milan when she decided to read the first of her two letters. At first I sat watching

her, as she read it with an air of astonishment, then raised
her head, her eyes seeming to come to rest upon a succession of distinct and incompatible memories which she
could not succeed in bringing together. Meanwhile I had
recognised Gilberte's handwriting on the envelope which I
had just taken from my pocket-book. I opened it. Gilberte
wrote to inform me that she was marrying Robert de
Saint-Loup. She told me that she had sent me a telegram
about it to Venice but had had no reply. I remembered
that I had been told that the telegraphic service there was
inefficient. I had never received her telegram. Perhaps she
would refuse to believe this. All of a sudden I felt in my
brain a fact, which was installed there in the guise of a
memory, leave its place and surrender it to another fact.
The telegram that I had received a few days earlier, and
had supposed to be from Albertine, was from Gilberte.
As the somewhat laboured originality of Gilberte's handwriting consisted chiefly, when she wrote a line, in introducing into the line above it the strokes of her *t*'s which
appeared to be underlining the words, or the dots over her
i's which appeared to be punctuating the sentence above
them, and on the other hand in interspersing the line below with the tails and flourishes of the words immediately
above, it was quite natural that the clerk who dispatched
the telegram should have read the loops of *s*'s or *y*'s in the
line above as an "-ine" attached to the word "Gilberte."
The dot over the *i* of Gilberte had climbed up to make a
suspension point. As for her capital *G*, it resembled a
Gothic *A*. The fact that, in addition to this, two or three
words had been misread, had dovetailed into one another
(some of them indeed had seemed to me incomprehensible), was sufficient to explain the details of my error and

was not even necessary. How many letters are actually read into a word by a careless person who knows what to expect, who sets out with the idea that the message is from a certain person? How many words into the sentence? We guess as we read, we create; everything starts from an initial error; those that follow (and this applies not only to the reading of letters and telegrams, not only to all reading), extraordinary as they may appear to a person who has not begun at the same place, are all quite natural. A large part of what we believe to be true (and this applies even to our final conclusions) with an obstinacy equalled only by our good faith, springs from an original mistake in our premises.

Chapter Four

NEW ASPECT OF
ROBERT DE SAINT-LOUP

"Oh, it's too incredible," said my mother. "You know at my age one has ceased to be astonished at anything, but I assure you that nothing could be more unexpected than the news I've just read in this letter."

"Well," I replied, "I don't know what it is, but however astonishing it may be, it can't be quite so astonishing as what I've learnt from mine. It's a marriage. Robert de Saint-Loup is marrying Gilberte Swann."

"Ah!" said my mother, "then that must be what's in the other letter, which I haven't yet opened, for I recognised your friend's hand."

And my mother smiled at me with that faint trace of emotion which, ever since she had lost her own mother, she felt at every event, however insignificant, that concerned human creatures who were capable of grief and recollection and who themselves also mourned their dead. And so my mother smiled at me and spoke to me in a gentle voice, as though she were afraid, by treating this marriage lightly, of belittling the melancholy feelings that it might arouse in Swann's widow and daughter, in Robert's mother who had resigned herself to being parted from her son, all of whom Mamma, in her kindness of

891

heart, in her gratitude for their kindness to me, endowed with her own faculty of filial, conjugal and maternal emotion.

"Was I right in saying that you wouldn't produce anything as astonishing?" I asked her.

"On the contrary," she replied in a gentle tone, "it's I who have the most extraordinary news, I shan't say the greatest or the smallest, for that quotation from Sévigné which everyone produces who knows nothing else that she ever wrote used to sicken your grandmother as much as 'What a pretty thing hay-making is.' We don't deign to collect such hackneyed Sévigné. This letter is to announce the marriage of the Cambremer boy."

"Oh!" I remarked with indifference, "to whom? But in any case the personality of the bridegroom robs this marriage of any sensational character."

"Unless the bride's personality supplies it."

"And who is the bride in question?"

"Ah, if I tell you straight away, that will spoil the fun. Come on, see if you can guess," said my mother who, seeing that we had not yet reached Turin, wished to keep something in reserve for me as meat and drink for the rest of the journey.

"But how do you expect me to know? Is it someone brilliant? If Legrandin and his sister are satisfied, we may be sure that it's a brilliant marriage."

"I can't answer for Legrandin, but the person who informs me of the marriage says that Mme de Cambremer is delighted. I don't know whether you will call it a brilliant marriage. To my mind, it suggests the days when kings used to marry shepherdesses, and in this case the shepherdess is even humbler than a shepherdess, charming as she is. It would have amazed your grandmother, but would not have displeased her."

"But who in the world is this bride?"

"It's Mlle d'Oloron."

"That sounds to me tremendous and not in the least shepherdessy, but I don't quite gather who she can be. It's a title that used to be in the Guermantes family."

"Precisely, and M. de Charlus conferred it, when he adopted her, upon Jupien's niece. It's she who's marrying the young Cambremer."

"Jupien's niece! It isn't possible!"

"It's the reward of virtue. It's a marriage from the last chapter of one of Mme Sand's novels," said my mother. ("It's the wages of vice, a marriage from the end of a Balzac novel," thought I.)

"After all," I said to my mother, "it's quite natural, when you think of it. Here are the Cambremers established in that Guermantes clan among which they never hoped to pitch their tent; what is more, the girl, adopted by M. de Charlus, will have plenty of money, which was indispensable since the Cambremers have lost theirs; and after all she's the adopted daughter, and in the Cambremers' eyes probably the real daughter—the natural daughter—of a person whom they regard as a Prince of the Blood. A bastard of a semi-royal house has always been regarded as a flattering alliance by the nobility of France and other countries. Indeed, without going so far back, to the Lucinges,[32] only the other day, not more than six months ago, you remember the marriage of Robert's friend and that girl whose only social qualification was that she was supposed, rightly or wrongly, to be the natural daughter of a sovereign prince."

My mother, without abandoning the caste ethos of Combray in the light of which my grandmother ought to have been scandalised by such a marriage, being anxious above all to show the validity of her mother's judgment, added: "Anyhow, the girl is worth her weight in gold, and your dear grandmother wouldn't have had to draw upon her immense goodness, her infinite tolerance, to keep her from condemning young Cambremer's choice. Do you remember how distinguished she thought the girl was, long ago, when she went into the shop to have a stitch put in her skirt? She was only a child then. And now, even if she has rather run to seed and become an old maid, she's a different woman, a thousand times more perfect. But your grandmother saw all that at a glance. She found the little niece of a jobbing tailor more 'noble' than the Duc de Guermantes."

But even more necessary than to extol my grandmother was it for my mother to decide that it was "better" for her that she had not lived to see the day. This was the culmination of her daughterly love, as though she were sparing my grandmother a final grief.

"And yet, can you imagine for a moment," my mother said to me, "what old Swann—not that you ever knew him, of course—would have felt if he could have known that he would one day have a great-grandchild in whose veins the blood of old mother Moser who used to say: 'Ponchour Mezieurs' would mingle with the blood of the Duc de Guise!"

"But you know, Mamma, it's much more surprising than that. Because the Swanns were very respectable people, and, given the social position that their son acquired, his daughter, if he himself had made a decent marriage,

might have married very well indeed. But everything had
to start again from scratch because he married a whore."

"Oh, a whore, you know, people were perhaps rather
malicious. I never quite believed it all."

"Yes, a whore; indeed I shall let you have some . . .
family revelations one of these days."

Lost in reverie, my mother said: "To think of the
daughter of a woman whom your father would never allow me to greet marrying the nephew of Mme de
Villeparisis on whom your father wouldn't allow me to
call at first because he thought her too grand for me!"
Then: "And the son of Mme de Cambremer to whom
Legrandin was so afraid of having to give us a letter of introduction because he didn't think us smart enough, marrying the niece of a man who would never dare to come
to our flat except by the service stairs! . . . All the same,
your poor grandmother was absolutely right—you remember—when she said that the high aristocracy did
things that would shock the middle classes and that
Queen Marie-Amélie was spoiled for her by the overtures
she made to the Prince de Condé's mistress to get her to
persuade him to make his will in favour of the Duc d'Au-
male. You remember too how it shocked her that for centuries past daughters of the house of Gramont who were
veritable saints had borne the name Corisande in memory
of Henri IV's liaison with one of their ancestresses. These
things may perhaps also occur among the middle classes,
but they conceal them better. Can't you imagine how it
would have amused your poor grandmother!" Mamma
added sadly, for the joys which it grieved us to think that
my grandmother was deprived of were the simplest joys
of life—an item of news, a play, or even something more

trifling still, a piece of mimicry, which would have amused her. "Can't you imagine her astonishment! But still, I'm sure that your grandmother would have been shocked by these marriages, that they would have grieved her; I feel that it's better that she never knew about them," my mother went on, for, when confronted with any event, she liked to think that my grandmother would have received an utterly distinctive impression from it which would have stemmed from the marvellous singularity of her nature and have been uniquely significant. If anything sad or painful occurred which could not have been foreseen in the past—the disgrace or ruin of one of our old friends, some public calamity, an epidemic, a war, a revolution—my mother would say to herself that perhaps it was better that Grandmamma had known nothing about it, that it would have grieved her too much, that perhaps she would not have been able to endure it. And when it was a question of something shocking like these two marriages, my mother, by an impulse directly opposite to that of the malicious people who are pleased to imagine that others whom they do not like have suffered more than is generally supposed, would not, in her tenderness for my grandmother, allow that anything sad or diminishing could ever have happened to her. She always imagined my grandmother as being above the assaults even of any evil which might not have been expected to occur, and told herself that my grandmother's death had perhaps been a blessing on the whole, inasmuch as it had shut off the too ugly spectacle of the present day from that noble nature which could never have become resigned to it. For optimism is the philosophy of the past. The events that have occurred being, among all those that were possible, the only ones which we have known, the harm that they have caused seems to us inevitable, and we give them the credit for the slight amount of good that they could not help bringing with them, for we imagine that without them it would not have occurred. My mother sought at the same time to form a more accurate idea of what my grandmother would have felt when she learned these tidings, and to believe that it was impossible for our minds, less exalted than hers, to form any such idea. "Can't you imagine," she said to me first of all, "how astonished your poor grandmother would have been!" And I felt that my mother was distressed by her inability to tell her the news, regretting that my grandmother would never know it, and feeling it to be somehow unjust that the course of life should bring to light facts which my grandmother would never have believed, thus rendering erroneous and incomplete, retrospectively, the knowledge of people and society which my grandmother had taken to the grave, the marriage of the Jupien girl and Legrandin's nephew being calculated to modify her general notions of life, no less than the news—had my mother been able to convey it to her—that people had succeeded in solving the problems, which my grandmother had regarded as insoluble, of aerial navigation and wireless telegraphy. But as we shall see, this desire that my grandmother should share in the blessings of our modern science was soon, in its turn, to appear too selfish to my mother.

What I was to learn later on—for I had been unable to keep in touch with it all from Venice—was that Mlle de Forcheville's hand had been sought both by the Duc de Châtellerault and by the Prince de Silistrie, while

Saint-Loup was seeking to marry Mlle d'Entragues, the Duc de Luxembourg's daughter.

This is what had occurred. Mlle de Forcheville possessing a hundred million francs, Mme de Marsantes had decided that she would be an excellent match for her son. She made the mistake of saying that the girl was charming, that she herself had not the slightest idea whether she was rich or poor, that she did not wish to know, but that even without a dowry it would be a piece of good luck for the most exacting young man to find such a wife. This was going rather too far for a woman who was tempted only by the hundred million, which made her shut her eyes to everything else. People realised at once that she was thinking of the girl for her own son. The Princesse de Silistrie went round protesting loudly, expatiating on Saint-Loup's social grandeur, and proclaiming that if he should marry the daughter of Odette and a Jew then it was the end of the Faubourg Saint-Germain. Mme de Marsantes, sure of herself as she was, dared not proceed further and retreated before the indignant protests of the Princesse de Silistrie, who immediately made a proposal on behalf of her own son. She had protested only in order to keep Gilberte for herself. Meanwhile Mme de Marsantes, refusing to own herself defeated, had turned at once to Mlle d'Entragues, the Duc de Luxembourg's daughter. Having no more than twenty million, the latter suited her purpose less, but Mme de Marsantes told everyone that a Saint-Loup could not marry a Mlle Swann (there was no longer any mention of Forcheville). Some time later, somebody having thoughtlessly remarked that the Duc de Châtellerault was thinking of marrying Mlle d'Entragues, Mme de Marsantes, who was the most punctilious woman in the world, mounted her high horse, changed her tactics, returned to Gilberte, made a formal offer of marriage on Saint-Loup's behalf, and the engagement was immediately announced.

This engagement was to provoke keen comment in the most different social circles. Several of my mother's friends, who had met Saint-Loup in our house, came to her "day," and inquired whether the bridegroom was indeed the same person as my friend. Certain people went so far as to maintain, with regard to the other marriage, that it had nothing to do with the Legrandin-Cambremers. They had this on good authority, for the Marquise, *née* Legrandin, had denied it on the very eve of the day on which the engagement was announced. I, for my part, wondered why M. de Charlus on the one hand, Saint-Loup on the other, each of whom had had occasion to write to me shortly before and had spoken in such friendly terms of various travel plans the realisation of which must have precluded the wedding ceremonies, had said nothing whatever to me about them. I came to the conclusion, forgetting the secrecy which people maintain until the last moment in affairs of this sort, that I was less their friend than I had supposed, a conclusion which, so far as Saint-Loup was concerned, saddened me. Though why, when I had already remarked that the affability, the egalitarian, "man-to-man" attitude of the aristocracy was all a sham, should I be surprised to find myself left out of it? In the establishment for women—where men were now to be procured in increasing numbers—in which M. de Charlus had spied on Morel, and in which the "assistant matron,"[33] a great reader of the *Gaulois*, used to discuss the social gossip with her clients, this lady, while conversing with a stout gentleman who used to come to her to drink bottle after bottle of champagne with young men, because, being already very stout, he wished to become obese enough to be certain of not being called up should there ever be a war, declared: "It seems young Saint-Loup is 'one of those,' and young Cambremer too. Poor wives! In any case, if you know these bridegrooms, you must send them to us. They'll find everything they want here, and there's plenty of money to be made out of them." Whereupon the stout gentleman, albeit he was himself "one of those," indignantly retorted, being something of a snob, that he often met Cambremer and Saint-Loup at his cousins' the Ardonvillers, and that they were great womanisers, and quite the opposite of "those." "Ah!" the assistant matron concluded in a sceptical tone, but possessing no proof of the assertion, and convinced that in our century the perversity of morals was rivalled only by the absurd exaggeration of slanderous tittle-tattle.

Certain people whom I no longer saw wrote to me and asked me "what I thought" of these two marriages, precisely as though they were conducting an inquiry into the height of women's hats in the theatre or the psychological novel. I had not the heart to answer these letters. Of these two marriages I thought nothing at all, but I felt an immense sadness, as when two parts of one's past existence, which have been anchored near to one, and upon which one has perhaps been basing idly from day to day an unacknowledged hope, remove themselves finally, with a joyous flapping of pennants, for unknown destinations, like a pair of ships. As for the prospective bridegrooms themselves, their attitude towards their own marriages was perfectly natural, since it was a question not of other people but of themselves—though hitherto they had never tired of mocking at such "grand marriages" founded upon some secret taint. And even the Cambremer family, so ancient in its lineage and so modest in its pretensions, would have been the first to forget Jupien and to remember only the unimaginable grandeur of the House of Oloron, had not an exception appeared in the person who ought to have been most gratified by this marriage, the Marquise de Cambremer-Legrandin. Being spiteful by nature, she reckoned the pleasure of humiliating her family above that of glorifying herself. And so, not being enamoured of her son, and having rapidly taken a dislike to her future daughter-in-law, she declared that it was a calamity for a Cambremer to marry a person who had sprung from heaven knew where, and had such bad teeth. As for young Cambremer, who had already shown a propensity towards the society of men of letters such as Bergotte and even Bloch, it may be imagined that so brilliant a marriage did not have the effect of making him more of a snob than before, but that, feeling himself to have become the successor of the Ducs d'Oloron—"sovereign princes" as the newspapers said—he was sufficiently persuaded of his own grandeur to be able to mix with anyone he chose. And he deserted the minor nobility for the intelligent bourgeoisie on the days when he did not confine himself to royalty. The notices in the papers, especially when they referred to Saint-Loup, invested my friend, whose royal ancestors were endlessly enumerated, with a renewed grandeur which, however, could only sadden me, as though he had become someone else, the descendant of Robert the Strong rather than the friend who, only a little while since, had taken the folding seat in the carriage in order that I might be more comfortable in the back; the fact that I had had no previous suspicion of his marriage with Gilberte—the prospect of which had appeared to me suddenly, in my letter, so different from anything that I could have expected of either of them the day before, as unexpected as a chemical precipitate—pained me, whereas I ought to have reflected that he had had a great deal to do, and that moreover in the fashionable world marriages are often arranged thus all of a sudden, as a substitute for a different combination which has come to grief. And the gloom, as dismal as the depression of moving house, as bitter as jealousy, that these marriages caused me by the accident of their sudden impact was so profound that people used to remind me of it later, congratulating me absurdly on my perspicacity, as having been, quite contrary to what it was at the time, a twofold, indeed a threefold and fourfold presentiment.

The people in society who had taken no notice of Gilberte said to me with an air of solemn interest: "Ah! she's the one who's marrying the Marquis de Saint-Loup," and studied her with the attentive gaze of people who not only relish all the social gossip of Paris but are anxious to learn and believe in the profundity of their observation. Those who on the other hand had known only Gilberte gazed at Saint-Loup with the closest attention, asked me (these were often people who scarcely knew me) to introduce them, and returned from the presentation to the bridegroom radiant with the joys of the festivity saying to me: "He's a fine figure of a man." Gilberte was convinced that the name "Marquis de Saint-Loup" was a thousand times grander than "Duc d'Orléans," but since she was very much of her knowing generation, she did not want to appear less witty than others, and delighted in saying *mater semita*, to which she would add in order to show herself wittier still: "In my case, however, it's my *pater*."

"It appears that it was the Princesse de Parme who arranged young Cambremer's marriage," Mamma said to me. And this was true. The Princess had known for a long time, through her charitable activities, on the one hand Legrandin whom she regarded as a distinguished man, on the other hand Mme de Cambremer who changed the subject whenever the Princess asked her whether it was true that she was Legrandin's sister. The Princess knew how deeply Mme de Cambremer regretted having remained on the threshold of aristocratic high society without ever being invited in. When the Princess, who had undertaken to find a husband for Mlle d'Oloron, asked M. de Charlus whether he knew anything about an amiable and cultivated man called Legrandin de Méséglise (it was thus that M. Legrandin now styled himself), the Baron first of all replied in the negative, then suddenly the memory recurred to him of a man whose acquaintance he had made in the train one night and who had given him his card. He smiled a vague smile. "It's perhaps the same man," he said to himself. When he learned that the prospective bridegroom was the son of Legrandin's sister, he said: "Why, that would be really extraordinary! If he took after his uncle, it wouldn't alarm me; after all, I've always said that they made the best husbands." "Who are *they*?" inquired the Princess. "Ah, madame, I could explain it all to you if we met more often. With you one can talk freely. Your Highness is so intelligent," said Charlus, seized by a desire to confide which, however, went no further. The name Cambremer pleased him, although he did not like the boy's parents; he knew that it was one of the four Baronies of Brittany and everything he could possibly have hoped for his adopted daughter; it was an old and respected name, with solid connexions in its native province. A prince would have been out of the question and, moreover, not altogether desirable. This was the very thing. The Princess then asked Legrandin to call. Physically he had changed considerably of late, on the whole for the better. Like those women who deliberately sacrifice their faces to the slimness of their figures and never stir from Marienbad, he had acquired the breezy air of a cavalry officer. He had taken up tennis at the age of fifty-five. In proportion as M. de Charlus had thickened and slowed down, Legrandin had become slimmer and brisker, the contrary effect of an identical cause. This velocity of movement had its psychological reasons as well. He was in the habit of frequenting certain low haunts where he did not wish to be seen going in or coming out: he would hurl himself into them.

When the Princesse de Parme spoke to him of the Guermantes family and of Saint-Loup, he declared that he had known them all his life, making a sort of compound of the fact that he had always known *by name* the proprietors of Guermantes and the fact that he had met *in person*, at my aunt's house, Swann, the father of the future Mme de Saint-Loup—although he had always refused to have anything to do with Swann's wife and daughter at Combray. "Indeed, I travelled quite recently with the brother of the Duc de Guermantes, M. de Charlus. It was he who spontaneously engaged me in conversation, which is always a good sign, for it proves that a man is neither a strait-laced fool nor a pretentious snob. Oh, I know all the things that people say about him. But I never pay any attention to gossip of that sort. Besides, the private life of other people is not my business. He gave me the impression of having a sensitive nature and a cultivated mind." Then the Princesse de Parme spoke of Mlle d'Oloron. In the Guermantes circle people waxed sentimental about the nobility of heart of M. de Charlus who, generous as always, was securing the future happiness of a penniless but charming girl. And the Duc de Guermantes, who suffered from his brother's reputation, let it be understood that, fine as this conduct was, it was wholly natural. "I don't know if I make myself clear, but everything in the affair is natural," he said, with calculated maladroitness. His object was to indicate that the girl was a daughter of his brother whom the latter acknowledged. This accounted at the same time for Jupien. The Princesse de Parme hinted at this version of the story to show Legrandin that after all young Cambremer would be marrying something in the nature of Mlle de Nantes, one of those bastards of Louis XIV who were scorned neither by the Duc d'Orléans nor by the Prince de Conti.

These two marriages which my mother and I discussed in the train that was taking us back to Paris had quite remarkable effects upon several of the characters who have figured in the course of this narrative. First of all upon Legrandin; needless to say, he swept like a hurricane into M. de Charlus's town house, for all the world as though he were entering a house of ill-fame where he must on no account be seen, and also, at the same time, to display his mettle and to conceal his age—for our habits accompany us even into places where they serve no useful purpose—and scarcely anybody observed that M. de Charlus greeted him with a smile which was hard to detect and harder still to interpret; this smile was similar in appearance—though in fact it was precisely the opposite—to the smile which two men who are in the habit of meeting in the best society exchange if they happen to meet in what they regard as disreputable surroundings (such as the Elysée where General de Froberville, whenever he met Swann there in the old days, would assume, on catching sight of him, an expression of ironical and mysterious complicity appropriate between two habitués of the salon of the Princesse des Laumes who were compromising themselves by visiting M. Grévy). But what was rather remarkable was the genuine improvement in Legrandin's character. For a long time past—ever since the days when I used to go as a child to spend my holidays at Combray—he had been surreptitiously cultivating relations with the aristocracy, productive at the most of an isolated invitation to a sterile house party. All of a sudden, his nephew's marriage having supervened to join up these scattered fragments, Legrandin stepped into a social position to which, retroactively, his former relations with people who had known him only in private but had known him well, gave a sort of solidity. Ladies to whom people offered to introduce him revealed that for the last twenty years he had stayed with them in the country for a fortnight annually, and that it was he who had given them the beautiful old barometer in the small drawing-room. It also transpired that he had been photographed in "groups" which included dukes who were now related to him. But as soon as he had acquired this social position, he ceased to take advantage of it. This was not merely because, now that people knew that he was received everywhere, he no longer derived any pleasure from being invited, but because, of the two vices that had long struggled for mastery in him, the less natural, snobbishness, was now giving way to another that was less artificial, since it did at least show a sort of return, however circuitous, towards nature. No doubt the two are not incompatible, and a nocturnal prowl may be undertaken immediately after leaving a duchess's party. But the dampening effect of age discouraged Legrandin from combining too many pleasures, from venturing out except well advisedly, and also made his enjoyment of the pleasures of nature fairly platonic, consisting chiefly in friendships, in time-consuming conversations, which, making him spend almost all his time among the people, left him very little for the life of society.

Mme de Cambremer herself became almost indifferent to the friendly overtures of the Duchesse de Guermantes. The latter, obliged to see something of the Marquise, had noticed, as happens whenever we come to see more of our fellow creatures, that is to say as combinations of good qualities which we eventually discover and defects to which we eventually grow accustomed, that Mme de Cambremer was a woman endowed with an intelligence and culture which were little to my taste but which appeared remarkable to the Duchess. And so she often went to see Mme de Cambremer in the late afternoon and paid her long visits. But the fabulous charm which her hostess imagined to exist in the Duchesse de Guermantes vanished as soon as she found herself sought after by her, and she received her out of politeness rather than pleasure.

A more striking change manifested itself in Gilberte, a change at once symmetrical with and different from that which occurred in Swann after his marriage. It is true that during the first few months Gilberte had been happy to open her doors to the most select society. It was doubtless only because of the inheritance that she invited the intimate friends to whom her mother was attached, but on certain days only when there was no one but themselves, segregated from the fashionable people, as though the contact of Mme Bontemps or Mme Cottard with the Princesse de Guermantes or the Princesse de Parme might, like that of two unstable powders, have produced irreparable catastrophes. Nevertheless the Bontemps, the Cottards and such, although disappointed to find themselves dining among themselves, were proud to be able to say: "We dined with the Marquise de Saint-Loup," all the more so because she sometimes went so far as to invite with them Mme de Marsantes, who showed herself emphatically the "great lady" with her tortoiseshell and ostrich-feather fan—also in the interests of the legacy. She merely made a point of paying tribute from time to time to the discreet people whom one never sees except when they are invited, a word to the wise after which she could bestow upon the Cottards, the Bontemps and their ilk her most gracious and lofty salutation. Perhaps because of my "Balbec girlfriend," by whose aunt I liked to be seen in these surroundings, I should have preferred to be included in that group. But Gilberte, in whose eyes I was now principally a friend of her husband and of the Guermantes (and who—perhaps even from the Combray days, when my parents did not call upon her mother—at the age when we do not merely add this or that to the value of things but classify them according to their species, had endowed me with the sort of prestige which one never afterwards loses), regarded these evenings as unworthy of me, and would say to me as I left: "It's delightful to have seen you, but you must come the day after tomorrow; you'll find my aunt Guermantes, and Mme de Poix; today it was just a few of Mamma's friends, to please Mamma." But this state of things lasted for a few months only, and then everything was totally transformed. Was this because Gilberte's social life was fated to exhibit the same contrasts as Swann's? However that may be, Gilberte had been for only a short time the Marquise de Saint-Loup (in the process of becoming, as we shall see, Duchesse de Guermantes)[34] when, having attained to the most brilliant and most rarefied position, she decided that the name Guermantes was now embodied in her like a lustrous enamel and that, whatever the society she frequented, from now onwards she would remain for all the world the Duchesse de Guermantes—sharing, in short, the opinion of the character in the operetta who declares: "My name, I think, dispenses me from saying more."[35] Wherein she was mistaken, for the value of a title, like that of stocks and shares, rises with the demand and falls when it is offered in the market. Everything that seems to us imperishable tends towards decay; a position in society, like anything else, is not created once and for all, but, just as much as the power of an empire, is continually rebuilding itself by a sort of perpetual process of creation, which explains the apparent anomalies in social or political history in the course of half a century. The creation of the world did not occur at the beginning of time, it occurs every day. The Marquise de Saint-Loup said to herself, "I am the Marquise de Saint-Loup," and she knew that, the day before, she had refused three invitations to dine with duchesses. But if to a certain extent her name aggrandised the very unaristocratic people whom she entertained, by an inverse process the people whom she entertained diminished the name that she bore. Nothing can hold out against such trends; the greatest names succumb to them in the end. Had not Swann known a princess of the House of France whose drawing-room, because anyone at all was welcomed there, had fallen to the lowest rank? One day when the Princesse des Laumes had gone to pay a brief duty call on this Highness, in whose drawing-room she had found only nonentities, arriving immediately afterwards at Mme Leroi's, she had said to Swann and the Marquis de Modène: "At last I find myself upon friendly soil. I have just come from Mme la Comtesse de X——, and there weren't three faces I knew in the room." At all events, Gilberte suddenly began to flaunt her contempt for what she had once so ardently desired, to declare that all the people in the Faubourg Saint-Germain were idiots, simply not worth meeting, and, suiting her actions to her words, ceased to meet them. People who did not make her acquaintance until after this period, and who, in the first stages of that acquaintance, heard her, by that time Duchesse de Guermantes, being very funny at the expense of the society in which she could so easily have moved, never inviting a single person from that society, and, if any of them, even the most brilliant, should venture into her drawing-room, yawning openly in their faces, blush now in retrospect at the thought that they themselves could ever have seen any glamour in the fashionable world, and would never dare to confess this humiliating secret of their past weaknesses to a woman whom they assume to have been, by an essential loftiness in her nature, incapable from the beginning of understanding such things. They hear her poking such delicious fun at dukes, and see her (which is more significant) matching her behaviour so entirely to her mockery! No doubt they do not think of inquiring into the causes of the accident which turned Mlle Swann into Mlle de Forcheville, Mlle de Forcheville into the Marquise de Saint-Loup, and finally into the Duchesse de Guermantes. Possibly it does not occur to them either that the effects of this accident would serve no less than its causes to explain Gilberte's subsequent attitude, association with commoners not being regarded in quite the same light in which Mlle Swann would have regarded it by a lady who is addressed by all and sundry as "Madame la Duchesse" and, by other duchesses who bore her so much, as "cousin." One is always ready to despise a goal which one has not succeeded in attaining, or has finally attained. And this contempt seems to us to form part of the character of people whom one did not know before. Perhaps, if we were able to go back over the years, we should find them devoured, more savagely than anyone, by those same weaknesses which they have succeeded so completely in disguising or conquering that we reckon them incapable not only of ever having been infected by them themselves but even of ever excusing them in others, because of their inability to imagine them. At all events, very soon the drawing-room of the new Marquise de Saint-Loup assumed its permanent aspect (from the social point of view at least, for we shall see what troubles were brewing in it in other respects). Now this aspect was surprising for the following reason. People still remembered that the most grandiose and glittering receptions in Paris, as brilliant as those given by the Princesse de Guermantes, had been those of Mme de Marsantes, Saint-Loup's mother. At the same time, in recent years Odette's salon, infinitely lower in the social scale, had been no less dazzling in its elegance and splendour. Saint-Loup, however, happy to have, thanks to his wife's vast fortune, everything that he could desire in the way of comfort, wished only to rest quietly in his armchair after a good dinner with a musical entertainment by good performers. And this young man who had seemed at one time so proud and so ambitious invited to share his luxury old friends whom his mother would not have admitted to her house. Gilberte, for her part, put into practice Swann's maxim: "Quality doesn't matter, what I dread is quantity." And Saint-Loup, very much on his knees before his wife, both because he loved her and because it was to her that he owed this extreme luxury, took care not to interfere with tastes that were so similar to his own. With the result that the great receptions that had been given year after year by Mme de Marsantes and Mme de Forcheville, principally with an eye to the establishing of their children in ostentatious splendour, gave rise to no receptions by M. and Mme de Saint-Loup. They had the best of saddle-horses on which to go out riding together, the finest of yachts in which to cruise—but they never took more than a couple of guests with them. In Paris, every evening, they would invite three or four friends to dine, never more; with the result that, by an unforeseen but at the same time quite natural retrogression, the two vast maternal aviaries had been replaced by a silent nest.

The person who profited least by these two marriages was the young Mlle d'Oloron who, already stricken with typhoid on the day of the religious ceremony, was barely able to crawl to the church and died a few weeks later. In the letter of intimation that was sent out some time after her death, names such as Jupien's were juxtaposed with some of the greatest in Europe, such as those of the Vicomte and Vicomtesse de Montmorency, H.R.H. the Comtesse de Bourbon-Soissons, the Prince of Modena-Este, the Vicomtesse d'Edumea, Lady Essex, and so forth. No doubt, even to a person who knew that the deceased was Jupien's niece, this plethora of grand marriage connexions could cause no surprise. The great thing, after all, is to have a grand marriage. Then, the *casus foederis* coming into play, the death of a simple little seamstress plunges all the princely families of Europe into mourning. But many young people of the rising generation, who were not familiar with the real situation, might, apart from the possibility of their mistaking Marie-Antoinette d'Oloron, Marquise de Cambremer, for a lady of the noblest birth, have been guilty of many other errors had they read this communication. Thus, supposing their excursions through France to have given them some slight familiarity with the country round Combray, when they saw that Mme L. de Méséglise and the Comte de Méséglise figured among the first of the signatories, close to the Duc de Guermantes, they might not have been at all surprised: the Méséglise way and the Guermantes way are cheek by jowl. "Old nobility of the same region, perhaps interrelated for generations," they might have said to themselves. "Who knows? It's perhaps a branch of the Guermantes family which bears the title of Comte de

Méséglise." As it happened, the Comte de Méséglise had no connexion with the Guermantes and was not even enrolled on the Guermantes side, but on the Cambremer side, since the Comte de Méséglise, who by a rapid advancement had remained Legrandin de Méséglise for only two years, was our old friend Legrandin. No doubt, if they had to choose between bogus titles, few could have been so disagreeable to the Guermantes as this one. They had been connected in the past with the authentic Comtes de Méséglise, of whom there survived only one female descendant, the daughter of obscure parents who had come down in the world, herself married to one of my aunt's tenant farmers named Ménager, who had become rich and bought Mirougrain from her and now styled himself "Ménager de Mirougrain," with the result that when it was said that his wife was born "de Méséglise" people thought that she must simply have been born at Méséglise and that she was "from Méséglise" as her husband was "from Mirougrain."

Any other sham title would have caused less annoyance to the Guermantes family. But the aristocracy knows how to tolerate such irritations, and many others as well, the moment a marriage is at stake which is deemed advantageous, from whatever point of view. Shielded by the Duc de Guermantes, Legrandin was, to part of that generation, and would be to the whole of the generation that followed it, the real Comte de Méséglise.

Yet another mistake which any young reader not acquainted with the facts might have been led to make was that of supposing that the Baron and Baronne de Forcheville figured on the list in the capacity of parents-in-law of the Marquis de Saint-Loup, that is to say on the Guermantes side. But on this side they had no right to appear since it was Robert who was related to the Guermantes and not Gilberte. No, the Baron and Baronne de Forcheville, despite these deceptive appearances, did figure on the wife's side, it is true, and not on the Cambremer side, not because of the Guermantes, but because of Jupien, who, the better informed reader knows, was Odette's first cousin.

All M. de Charlus's favour had been transferred after the marriage of his adopted daughter on to the young Marquis de Cambremer; the young man's tastes, which were similar to those of the Baron, since they had not prevented the Baron from choosing him as a husband for Mlle d'Oloron, naturally made him appreciate him all the more when he was left a widower. This is not to say that the Marquis did not have other qualities which made him a charming companion for M. de Charlus. But even in the case of a man of real merit, it is a quality not to be despised by the person who admits him into his private life, and one that makes him particularly useful if he can also play whist. The intelligence of the young Marquis was remarkable, and, as they had already begun to say at Féterne when he was barely out of his cradle, he "took" entirely after his grandmother, had the same enthusiasms, the same love of music. He reproduced also some of her idiosyncrasies, but these more by imitation, like all the rest of the family, than from atavism. Thus it was that, some time after the death of his wife, having received a letter signed "Léonor," a name which I did not remember as being his, I realised who it was that had written to me only when I had read the closing formula: *"Croyez à ma sympathie vraie."* The placing of that *vraie* infallibly added to the Christian name Léonor the surname Cambremer.

The train reached Paris before my mother and I had finished discussing these two pieces of news, which, so that the journey might not seem to me too long, she had deliberately reserved for the latter part of it, not allowing me to learn about them until after Milan. My mother had soon reverted to the point of view which for her was the only possible one, that of my grandmother. Mamma had first of all said that my grandmother would have been surprised, then that she would have been saddened, which was simply a way of saying that such a surprising event would have given her pleasure, and my mother, unable to accept that my grandmother should have been deprived of a pleasure, preferred to think that all was for the best, this news being of the kind that could only have caused her sorrow. But no sooner had we reached home than my mother felt that it was still too selfish of her to regret being unable to share with my grandmother all the surprises that life brings. She preferred to believe that this news would not have surprised my grandmother, since it merely confirmed her predictions. She wanted to see it as a confirmation of my grandmother's foresight, proof that she had been even more profound, more perceptive, more sagacious than we had thought. And so, in order to arrive at this attitude of pure admiration, it was not long before my mother was adding: "And yet, who knows whether your grandmother wouldn't have approved? She was so kind and tolerant. And then you know, for her, social status meant nothing; natural distinction was what mattered. And curiously enough, don't you remember, she liked both of them. Remember that first visit of hers to Mme de Villeparisis, when she came back and told us how common she thought M. de Guermantes was, and by comparison how full of praise she was for those Jupiens. Poor Mamma, do you remember her saying about the father: 'If I had another daughter, I'd give her to him as a wife, and his daughter is even nicer.' And the little Swann girl! She used to say of her: '*I* think she's charming; you'll see that she'll marry well.' Poor Mamma, if only she'd lived to see how right she was! Right up to the end she'll go on giving us lessons in goodness and foresight and judgment." And since the joys which we suffered to see my grandmother deprived of were all the humble little joys of life—an actor's intonation which would have amused her, a dish she would have enjoyed, a new novel by a favourite author—Mamma said: "How surprised she would have been! How it would have interested her! What a lovely letter she would have written in reply!" And my mother went on: "Just imagine, poor Swann who so longed for Gilberte to be received by the Guermantes, how happy he would be if he could see his daughter become a Guermantes!"

"Under another name than his, led to the altar as Mlle de Forcheville—do you think he would be so happy after all?"

"Ah, that's true, I hadn't thought of it."

"That's what makes it impossible for me to be happy for her sake, the thought that the little beast could have had the heart to give up her father's name, when he was so good to her."

"Yes, you're right; all things considered, it's perhaps just as well that he never knew." So difficult is it for us to know, with the dead as with the living, whether a thing would cause them joy or sorrow! "It appears that the Saint-Loups are going to live at Tansonville," my mother went on. "Old Swann, who was so anxious to show your poor grandfather his pond, could never have dreamed that the Duc de Guermantes would see it constantly, especially if he had known of his son's shameful marriage. And then, you've talked so often to Saint-Loup about the hawthorns and lilacs and irises at Tansonville, he'll see what you meant now. They'll be his property."

Thus there proceeded in our dining-room, in the lamplight that is so congenial to them, one of those long chats in which the wisdom not of nations but of families, taking hold of some event, a death, a betrothal, an inheritance, a bankruptcy, and slipping it under the magnifying glass of memory, brings it into high relief, detaches, thrusts back, and places in perspective at different points in space and time things which to those who have not lived through it seem to be juxtaposed on a single plane, the names of the deceased, successive addresses, the origins of a fortune and its vicissitudes, transfers of property. It is the wisdom inspired by the Muse whom it is best to ignore for as long as possible if we wish to retain some freshness of impressions, some creative power, but whom even those who have ignored her meet in the evening of their lives in the nave of an old country church, at a point when suddenly they feel less susceptible to the eternal beauty expressed in the carvings on the altar than to the thought of the vicissitudes of fortune which those carvings have undergone, passing into a famous private collection or a chapel, from there to a museum, then returning at length to the church, or to the feeling that as they walk around it they may be treading upon a flagstone almost endowed with thought, which is made of the ashes of Arnauld or Pascal, or simply to deciphering (forming perhaps a mental picture of a fresh-faced country girl) on the brass plate of the wooden prie-dieu the names of the daughters of the squire or the notable—the Muse who has gathered up everything that the more exalted Muses of philosophy and art have rejected, everything that is not founded upon truth, everything that is merely contingent, but that reveals other laws as well: the Muse of History.

Some old friends of my mother, who belonged more or less to Combray, came to see her to discuss Gilberte's marriage, which did not dazzle them in the least. "You know who Mlle de Forcheville is, she's simply Mlle Swann. And her witness at the marriage, the 'Baron' de Charlus, as he calls himself, is the old man who used to keep her mother at one time, under Swann's very nose, and no doubt to his advantage." "But what do you mean?" my mother protested; "in the first place, Swann was extremely rich." "One must assume that he wasn't as rich as all that if he needed other people's money. But what is there about that woman, that she hangs on to her old lovers like that? She managed to persuade the first to marry her, then the third, and she drags out the second when he has one foot in the grave to get him to be a witness at the marriage of the daughter she had by the first or by someone else—for how is one to tell who the father was? She can't be certain herself! I said the third, but I should have said the three hundredth. Mind you, even if the girl's no more a Forcheville than you or I, that puts her on the same level as the bridegroom who of course isn't noble at all. You can imagine that only an adventurer would marry a girl like that. It appears he's just a plain Monsieur Dupont or Durand or something. If it weren't that we have a Radical mayor now at Combray, who doesn't even lift his hat to the priest, I should know all about it. Because, you understand, when they published the banns, they were obliged to give the real name. It's all very nice, for the newspapers or for the stationer who sends out the invitations, to describe yourself as the Marquis de Saint-Loup. That does no harm to anyone, and if it can give any pleasure to those worthy people, I should be the last person in the world to object! What harm can it do me? As I shall never dream of going to call on the daughter of a woman who has let herself be talked about, she can have a string of titles as long as my arm for the benefit of her servants. But in an official document it's not the same thing. Ah, if my cousin Sazerat was still deputy-mayor, I'd have written to him, and he would certainly have let *me* know what name the man was registered under."

I saw a good deal of Gilberte at this time, as it happened, having renewed my friendship with her: for our life, in the long run, is not calculated according to the duration of our friendships. Let a certain period of time elapse, and you will see (just as, in politics, former ministries reappear, or, in the theatre, forgotten plays are revived) friendships renewed between the same persons as before, after long years of interruption, and renewed with pleasure. After ten years, the reasons which made one party love too passionately, the other unable to endure a too exacting despotism, no longer exist. The affinity alone survives, and everything that Gilberte would have refused me in the past, that had seemed to her intolerable, impossible, she granted me quite readily—doubtless because I no longer desired it. Although neither of us had ever mentioned the reason for this change, if she was always ready to come to me, never in a hurry to leave me, it was because the obstacle had vanished: my love.

Some time later, I went to spend a few days at Tansonville. This excursion was something of an inconvenience, for I was keeping a girl in Paris who slept in a bachelor flat which I had rented. As other people need the aroma of forests or the ripple of a lake, so I needed her sleep by my side during the night and, by day, to have her always by my side in the carriage. For even if one love has passed into oblivion, it may determine the form of the love that is to follow it. Already, even in the midst of the previous love, daily habits existed, the origin of which we did not ourselves remember; perhaps it was a moment of anguish early on that had made us passionately desire, then permanently adopt, like customs the meaning of which has been forgotten, the habit of those homeward drives to the beloved's door, or her residence in our home, our presence or the presence of someone we trust during all her outings. All these habits, which are like great uniform high-roads along which our love passes daily and which were forged long ago in the volcanic fire of an ardent emotion, nevertheless survive the woman, survive even the memory of the woman. They become the pattern, if not of all our loves, at least of certain of our loves which alternate among themselves. And thus my home had demanded, in memory of a forgotten Albertine, the presence of my mistress of the moment whom I concealed from visitors and who filled my life as Albertine had filled it in the past. And in order to go to Tansonville I had to obtain her consent to being looked after for a few days by one of my friends who did not care for women. I was going because I had heard that Gilberte was unhappy, in that Robert was unfaithful to her, though not in the fashion which everyone believed, which perhaps she herself still believed, which in any case she alleged. A belief that could be explained by pride, by the desire to hoodwink other people and to hoodwink oneself, not to mention the imperfect knowledge of infidelities which is all that betrayed spouses ever acquire, all the more so as Robert, a true nephew of M. de Charlus, went about openly with women whom he compromised, whom the world believed and whom Gilberte on the whole believed to be his mistresses. It was even thought in society that he was somewhat barefaced, never stirring, at a party, from the side of some woman whom he afterwards accompanied home, leaving Mme de Saint-Loup to return as best she could. Anyone who had said that the other woman whom he compromised thus was not really his mistress would have been regarded as a fool, incapable of seeing what was staring him in the face; but I had been pointed, alas, in the direction of the truth, a truth which caused me infinite distress, by a few words let fall by Jupien. A few months before my visit to Tansonville I had gone to inquire after M. de Charlus, in whom certain cardiac symptoms had been causing great anxiety, and having mentioned to Jupien, whom I found alone, some love-letters addressed to Robert and signed Bobette which Mme de Saint-Loup had discovered, I was stupefied to learn from the Baron's former factotum that the person who used the signature Bobette was none other than the violinist-journalist who had played so important a part in M. de Charlus's life![36] Jupien could not speak of him without indignation: "The boy was free to do whatever he liked. But if there was one direction in which he ought never to have looked, that was in the direction of the Baron's nephew. All the more so as the Baron loved his nephew like his own son. He has tried to break up the marriage—it's really shameful. And he must have gone about it with the most devilish cunning, for no one was ever more opposed to that sort of thing by nature than the Marquis de Saint-Loup. You've only to think of the follies he committed for the sake of his mistresses! No, however despicably—there's no other word for it—he deserted the Baron, that was his business. But to take up with the nephew! There are some things that just aren't done."

Jupien was sincere in his indignation; among so-called immoral people, moral indignation is quite as violent as among other people, only its object is slightly different. What is more, people whose own hearts are not directly involved always regard unfortunate entanglements, disastrous marriages, as though one were free to choose whom one loves, and do not take into account the exquisite mirage which love projects and which envelops so entirely and so uniquely the person with whom one is in love that the "folly" a man commits by marrying his cook or the mistress of his best friend is as a rule the only poetical action that he performs in the course of his existence.

I gathered that Robert and his wife had been on the brink of a separation (though Gilberte had not yet discovered the precise nature of the trouble) and that it was Mme de Marsantes, a loving, ambitious and philosophical

mother, who had arranged and enforced their reconciliation. She belonged to a world in which perennial inbreed-
ing and the impoverishment of patrimonies constantly
bring out, in the realm of the passions as in that of pecuniary interest, inherited vices and compromises. It was
with the same energy that in the past she had patronised
Mme Swann, encouraged the marriage of Jupien's niece
and arranged that of her own son to Gilberte, exercising
thus on her own behalf, with a pained resignation, the
same atavistic wisdom which she deployed for the benefit
of the entire Faubourg. And perhaps what had made her
at a certain moment expedite Robert's marriage to
Gilberte—which had certainly caused her less trouble and
fewer tears than making him break with Rachel—had
been the fear of his forming with another harlot—or perhaps with the same one, for Robert took a long time to
forget Rachel—a fresh attachment which might have been
his salvation. Now I understood what Robert had meant
when he said to me at the Princesse de Guermantes's:
"It's a pity your Balbec girlfriend hasn't the fortune that
my mother insists upon. I believe she and I would have
got on very well together." He had meant that she belonged to Gomorrah as he belonged to Sodom, or perhaps,
if he did not yet belong, that he had ceased to enjoy
women whom he could not love in a certain fashion and
together with other women. Gilberte, too, might have
been able to enlighten me as to Albertine. If therefore,
apart from rare moments of recollection, I had not lost
all my curiosity as to the life of my dead mistress, I could
have questioned not only Gilberte but her husband about
her. And on the whole it was the same thing that
had given both Robert and myself a desire to marry Al-

bertine—to wit, the knowledge that she was a lover of women. But the causes of our desire, as for that matter its objects, were the reverse of each other. In my case, it was the despair in which I had been plunged by the discovery, in Robert's the satisfaction; in my case to prevent her, by perpetual vigilance, from indulging her predilection; in Robert's to cultivate it, and by granting her her freedom to make her bring her girlfriends to him.

If Jupien traced back to a quite recent origin the new orientation, so divergent from their original course, that Robert's carnal pleasures had assumed, a conversation which I had with Aimé and which made me extremely unhappy showed me that the head waiter at Balbec traced this divergence, this inversion, back to a far earlier date. The occasion of this conversation had been a brief visit I paid to Balbec, where Saint-Loup himself, on long leave, had also come with his wife, whom during this first phase he never allowed out of his sight. I had been struck by the extent to which Rachel's influence over Robert still made itself felt. Only a young husband who has long been keeping a mistress knows how to take off his wife's cloak as they enter a restaurant, how to treat her with due attentiveness. He has received, during the course of his liaison, the education which a good husband requires. Not far from him, at a table adjoining mine, Bloch, among a party of pretentious young academics, was assuming a spuriously relaxed air, and shouted at the top of his voice to one of his friends, as he ostentatiously passed him the menu with a gesture which upset two carafes of water: "No, no, my dear fellow, you order! Never in my life have I been able to make head or tail of these documents. I've never known how to order dinner!" he repeated with

a pride that was obviously insincere and, blending literature with greed, decided at once upon a bottle of champagne which he liked to see "in a purely symbolic
fashion" adorning a conversation. Saint-Loup, on the
other hand, did know how to order. He was seated by
the side of Gilberte—already pregnant (subsequently he
did not fail to keep her continually supplied with offspring)[37]—as he slept by her side in their double bed in
the hotel. He spoke to no one but his wife; the rest of the
hotel appeared not to exist for him; but whenever a waiter
came to take an order, and stood close beside him, he
swiftly raised his blue eyes and darted a glance at him
which did not last for more than two seconds, but in its
limpid penetration seemed to indicate a kind of investiga-
tive curiosity entirely different from that which might
have inspired any ordinary diner scrutinising, even at
greater length, a page or waiter with a view to making hu-
morous or other observations about him which he would
communicate to his friends. This little glance, brief, disinterested, showing that the waiter interested him in himself, would have revealed to anyone who intercepted it
that this excellent husband, this once so passionate lover
of Rachel, had another plane in his life, and one that
seemed to him infinitely more interesting than the one on
which he moved from a sense of duty. But it was not otherwise visible. Already his eyes had returned to Gilberte
who had noticed nothing; he introduced her to a passing
friend and left the room to stroll with her outside. It was
then that Aimé spoke to me of a far earlier time, the time
when I had made Saint-Loup's acquaintance through
Mme de Villeparisis, in this same Balbec.

"Why, of course, Monsieur," he said to me, "it's

common knowledge, I've known it for ever so long. The first year Monsieur came to Balbec, M. le Marquis shut himself up with my lift-boy, on the pretext of developing some photographs of Monsieur's grandmother. The boy made a complaint, and we had the greatest difficulty in hushing the matter up. And besides, Monsieur, Monsieur remembers the day, no doubt, when he came to lunch at the restaurant with M. le Marquis de Saint-Loup and his mistress, whom M. le Marquis was using as a screen. Monsieur doubtless remembers that M. le Marquis left the room, pretending that he had lost his temper. Of course I don't suggest for a moment that Madame was in the right. She was leading him a regular dance. But as to that day, no one will ever make me believe that M. le Marquis's anger wasn't put on, and that he hadn't a good reason to get away from Monsieur and Madame."

So far as that day was concerned, I am convinced that, if Aimé was not deliberately lying, he was entirely mistaken. I remembered too well the state Robert was in, the blow he had struck the journalist. And, for that matter, it was the same with the Balbec incident; either the lift-boy had lied, or it was Aimé who was lying. At least so I believed; I could not be absolutely certain, for we never see more than one aspect of things, and had it not been that the thought distressed me, I should have found a certain beauty in the fact that, whereas for me sending the lift-boy to Saint-Loup had been the most convenient way of conveying a letter to him and receiving his answer, for him it had meant making the acquaintance of a person who had taken his fancy. For everything is at least dual. On to the most insignificant action that we perform, another man will graft a series of entirely different actions.

Certain it is that Saint-Loup's adventure with the lift-boy, if it occurred, no more seemed to me to be inherent in the commonplace dispatch of my letter than that a man who knew nothing of Wagner save the duet in *Lohengrin* would be able to foresee the prelude to *Tristan*. True, things offer men only a limited number of their innumerable attributes, because of the paucity of our senses. They are coloured because we have eyes; how many other epithets would they not merit if we had hundreds of senses? But this different aspect which they might present is made more comprehensible to us by the occurrence in life of even the most trivial event of which we know a part which we suppose to be the whole, and at which another person looks as through a window opened up on the other side of the house and offering a different view. Supposing that Aimé had not been mistaken, Saint-Loup's blush when Bloch spoke to him of the lift-boy had not perhaps been due after all to my friend's pronouncing the word as "lighft." But I was convinced that Saint-Loup's physiological evolution had not begun at that period and that he had then been still exclusively a lover of women. More than by any other sign, I could tell this retrospectively by the friendship that Saint-Loup had shown me at Balbec. It was only while he still loved women that he was really capable of friendship. Afterwards, for some time at least, to the men who did not attract him physically he displayed an indifference which was to some extent, I believe, sincere—for he had become very curt—but which he exaggerated as well in order to make people think that he was interested only in women. But I remember all the same that one day at Doncières, when I was on my way to dine with the Verdurins and he had just been staring rather hard at Morel, he had said to me: "Curious, that fellow reminds me in some ways of Rachel. Doesn't it strike you? They seem to me identical in some ways. Not that it can be of the slightest interest to me." And yet his eyes had afterwards remained for a long time gazing abstractedly at the horizon, as when we think, before returning to the card-table or going out to dinner, of one of those long journeys which we think we shall never make, but for which we have felt a momentary longing. But if Robert found something of Rachel in Charlie, Gilberte, for her part, sought to give herself some resemblance to Rachel in order to appear more attractive to her husband, wearing, like her, bows of scarlet or pink or yellow ribbon in her hair, which she dressed in a similar style, for she believed that her husband was still in love with Rachel, and so was jealous of her. That Robert's love may have hovered at times on the boundary which divides the love of a man for a woman from the love of a man for a man was quite possible. In any case, the memory of Rachel now played only an aesthetic role in this context. It is indeed improbable that it could have played any other. One day Robert had gone to her to ask her to dress up as a man, to leave a lock of hair hanging down, and nevertheless had contented himself with gazing at her, unsatisfied. He remained none the less attached to her and paid her scrupulously, though without pleasure, the enormous income which he had promised her and which did not prevent her from treating him in the most abominable fashion later on. This generosity towards Rachel would not have distressed Gilberte if she had known that it was merely the resigned fulfilment of a promise which no longer bore any trace of love. But love was, on the con-

trary, precisely what he pretended to feel for Rachel. Homosexuals would be the best husbands in the world if
they did not put on an act of loving other women. Not
that Gilberte made any complaint. It was the belief that
Robert had been loved, and loved for so long, by Rachel
that had made her desire him, had made her reject more
glittering matches; it seemed that he was making a sort of
concession to her in marrying her. And indeed, at first,
any comparison between the two women (incommensu-
rable though they were in charm and beauty) did not
favour the delightful Gilberte. But the latter subsequently
grew in her husband's esteem while Rachel visibly diminished.

There was another person, who changed her tune,
namely Mme Swann. If, in Gilberte's eyes, Robert before
their marriage was already crowned with the double
halo conferred on him on the one hand by his life with
Rachel, perpetually advertised by Mme de Marsantes's
lamentations, and on the other hand by the prestige which
the Guermantes family had always had in her father's
eyes and which she had inherited from him, Mme de
Forcheville for her part would have preferred a more brilliant, perhaps a princely marriage (there were impover-
ished royal families who would not have refused the
money—which incidentally proved to be considerably less
than the promised eighty million—laundered as it was by
the name Forcheville) and a son-in-law less depreciated in
value by a life spent outside the world of society. She had
been unable to overcome Gilberte's determination, and
had complained bitterly to all and sundry, denouncing
her son-in-law. One fine day her attitude changed completely; her son-in-law had become an angel, and she no

longer said anything against him except surreptitiously. The fact was that age had left Mme Swann (now Mme de Forcheville) with the taste she had always had for being kept, but, by the desertion of her admirers, had deprived her of the means. She longed every day for another necklace, a new dress studded with brilliants, a more sumptuous motor-car, but she had only a small income, Forcheville having squandered most of it, and—what Jewish strain influenced Gilberte in this?—she had an adorable but fearfully avaricious daughter, who counted every sou that she gave her husband, and naturally even more so her mother. Then suddenly she had sniffed out and found her natural protector in Robert. That she was no longer in her first youth mattered little to a son-in-law who was not a lover of women. All that he asked of his mother-in-law was to smooth down any little difficulty that might arise between Gilberte and himself, to obtain his wife's consent to his going on a trip with Morel. Odette, having applied herself thereto, was at once rewarded with a magnificent ruby. To pay for this, it was necessary for Gilberte to be more generous to her husband. Odette urged her in this direction with all the more fervour in that it was she herself who would benefit by her daughter's generosity. Thus, thanks to Robert, she was enabled, on the threshold of her fifties (some said her sixties), to dazzle every table at which she dined, every party at which she appeared, with an unparalleled splendour without needing to have, as in the past, a "friend" who now would no longer have coughed up, or even fallen for her. And so she had entered, permanently it seemed, into the period of final chastity, and yet she had never been so elegant.

It was not merely the malice, the rancour of the once poor boy against the master who has enriched him and has moreover (this was in keeping with the character and still more with the vocabulary of M. de Charlus) made him feel the difference of their positions, that had made Charlie turn to Saint-Loup in order to aggravate the Baron's sufferings. He may also have had an eye to his own profit. I had the impression that Robert must be giving him a great deal of money. After an evening party at which I had met Robert before I went down to Combray—and where the manner in which he flaunted himself by the side of a lady of fashion who was reputed to be his mistress, glued to her, never leaving her for a moment, enveloped publicly in the folds of her skirt, reminded me, but with something more hectic and jumpy about it, of a sort of involuntary repetition of an ancestral gesture which I had had an opportunity of observing in M. de Charlus, when he appeared to be wrapped in the finery of Mme Molé or some other lady, the banner of a gynophile cause which was not his own but which, without having any right to do so, he loved to sport thus, whether because he found it useful as a protection or aesthetically charming—I had been struck, as we came away, by the discovery that this young man, so generous when he was far less rich, had become so careful. That a man clings only to what he possesses, and that he who used to scatter money when he so rarely had any now hoards that with which he is amply supplied, is no doubt a common enough phenomenon, and yet in this instance it seemed to me to have assumed a more particular form. Saint-Loup refused to take a cab, and I saw that he had kept a tramway transfer-ticket. No doubt in so doing Saint-Loup was exercising, for different ends, talents which he had acquired in the course of his liaison with Rachel. A young man who has lived for years with a woman is not as inexperienced as the novice for whom the woman he marries is the first. One had only to see, on the rare occasions when Robert took his wife out to a restaurant, the adroit and considerate way he looked after her, his skill and poise in ordering dinner and giving instructions to waiters, the care with which he smoothed Gilberte's sleeves before she put on her jacket, to realise that he had been a woman's lover for a long time before being this one's husband. Similarly, having had to enter into the minutest details of Rachel's domestic economy, partly because she herself was useless as a housekeeper, and later because his jealousy made him determined to keep a firm control over her domestic staff, he was able, in the administration of his wife's property and the management of their household, to go on playing this skilful and competent role which Gilberte, perhaps, might have been unable to fulfil and which she gladly relinquished to him. But no doubt he did so principally in order to be able to give Charlie the benefit of his candle-end economies, maintaining him in affluence without Gilberte's either noticing it or suffering from it—and perhaps even assuming the violinist to be a spendthrift "like all artists" (Charlie styled himself thus without conviction and without conceit, in order to excuse himself for not answering letters and for a mass of other defects which he believed to form part of the undisputed psychology of the artist). Personally, I found it absolutely immaterial from a moral point of view whether one took one's pleasure with a man or with a woman, and only too natural and human that one should take it where

one could find it. If, therefore, Robert had not been married, his liaison with Charlie ought not to have caused me
pain. And yet I realised that the pain I felt would have
been as acute if Robert had been a bachelor. In anyone
else, his conduct would have left me indifferent. But I
wept when I reflected that I had once had so great an affection for a different Saint-Loup, an affection which, I
sensed all too clearly from the cold and evasive manner
which he now adopted, he no longer felt for me, since
men, now that they were capable of arousing his desires,
could no longer inspire his friendship. How could these
tastes have come to birth in a young man who had loved
women so passionately that I had seen him brought to a
state of almost suicidal despair because "Rachel when
from the Lord" had threatened to leave him? Had the resemblance between Charlie and Rachel—invisible to
me—been the plank which had enabled Robert to pass
from his father's tastes to those of his uncle, in order to
complete the physiological evolution which even in the
latter had occurred fairly late? At times, however, Aimé's
words came back to my mind to make me uneasy; I remembered Robert that year at Balbec; he had had a trick,
when he spoke to the lift-boy, of not paying any attention
to him which strongly resembled M. de Charlus's manner
when he addressed certain men. But Robert might easily
have derived this from M. de Charlus, from a certain
hauteur and a certain physical posture peculiar to the
Guermantes family, without for a moment sharing the
Baron's heterodox tastes. For instance, the Duc de Guermantes, who was wholly innocent of such tastes, had the
same nervous trick as M. de Charlus of turning his wrist,
as though he were straightening a lace cuff round it, and

also in his voice certain shrill and affected intonations, mannerisms to all of which, in the case of M. de Charlus, one might have been tempted to ascribe another meaning, to which he had given another meaning himself, the individual expressing his distinctive characteristics by means of impersonal and atavistic traits which are perhaps simply age-old characteristics ingrained in his gestures and voice. On this latter assumption, which borders upon natural history, it would not be M. de Charlus whom one described as a Guermantes affected with a blemish and expressing it to a certain extent by means of traits peculiar to the Guermantes stock, but the Duc de Guermantes who, in a perverted family, would be the exception whom the hereditary disease has so effectively spared that the external stigmata it has left upon him have lost all meaning. I remembered that on the day when I had seen Saint-Loup for the first time at Balbec, so fair-complexioned, fashioned of so rare and precious a substance, his monocle fluttering in front of him, I had found in him an effeminate air which was certainly not the effect of what I had now learned about him, but sprang rather from the grace peculiar to the Guermantes, from the fineness of that Dresden china in which the Duchess too was moulded. I recalled his affection for myself, his tender, sentimental way of expressing it, and told myself that this too, which might have deceived anyone else, meant at the time something quite different, indeed the direct opposite of what I had just learned about him. But when did the change date from? If from the year of my return to Balbec, how was it that he had never once come to see the lift-boy, had never once mentioned him to me? And as for the first year, how could he have paid any attention to the boy, passionately enamoured as he then was of Rachel? That first year, I had found Saint-Loup unusual, as was every true Guermantes. Now he was even odder than I had supposed. But things of which we have not had a direct intuition, which we have learned only through other people, are such that we no longer have the means, we have missed the chance, of conveying them to our inmost soul; its communications with the real are blocked and so we cannot profit by the discovery, it is too late. Besides, upon any consideration, this discovery distressed me too deeply for me to be able to appreciate it intellectually. Of course, after what M. de Charlus had told me in Mme Verdurin's house in Paris, I no longer doubted that Robert's case was that of any number of respectable people, to be found even among the best and most intelligent of men. To learn this of anyone else would not have affected me, of anyone in the world except Robert. The doubt that Aimé's words had left in my mind tarnished all our friendship at Balbec and Doncières, and although I did not believe in friendship, or that I had ever felt any real friendship for Robert, when I thought about those stories of the lift-boy and of the restaurant in which I had had lunch with Saint-Loup and Rachel, I was obliged to make an effort to restrain my tears.

NOTES · ADDENDA · SYNOPSIS

1 (p. 13) From Racine's *Esther*, Act I, Scene 3.

2 (p. 88) Famous Siamese twins who appeared in music halls and had a *succès de curiosité* at the 1900 World's Fair.

3 (p. 148) These words appear neither in the libretto of *Pelléas et Mélisande* nor in any of Rameau's operas, but in Gluck's *Armide* in this form: *"Ah, si la liberté me doit être ravie, est-ce à toi d'être mon vainqueur?"* Similarly, one or two of the phrases attributed to Arkel and Golaud in the next paragraph are a little fanciful: Proust invariably quoted from memory.

4 (p. 161) *Maquereau*=pimp.

5 (p. 170) Clarification of this expression can be found in an essay of Proust's entitled *En mémoire des églises assassinées*, in which, during a drive through Normandy, he compares his chauffeur with his steering-wheel to the statues of apostles and martyrs in mediaeval cathedrals holding symbolic objects representing the arts which they practised in their lifetimes or the instruments of their martyrdom—in this case a stylised wheel: a circle enclosing a cross. Cf. Vol. IV, *Sodom and Gomorrah*, p. 580.

6 (p. 205) Comic opera by Adolphe Adam (1836).

7 (p. 212) *Grue* means "crane" (in both the ornithological and the mechanical sense) and also, by analogy, "prostitute." *Faire le pied de grue*="to kick one's heels," "to stand around for a long time"—like a crane standing on one leg, or a street-walker in search of custom. Morel's use of the term is grammatically nonsensical.

8 (p. 249) Claude-Philibert Berthelot, Baron de Rambuteau: politician and administrator, *préfet* of the Seine in

1833, introduced public urinals with individual compartments.

9 (p. 275) Famous nineteenth-century tragedian.

10 (p. 288) This passage was obviously written before Proust composed his account of Bergotte's death and inserted it at an earlier point in this volume.

11 (p. 310) Mme Pipelet is the concierge in Eugène Sue's *Les Mystères de Paris*. Mme Gibout and Mme Prudhomme are characters in Henri Monnier's *Scènes populaires* and *Les Mémoires de Joseph Prudhomme*.

12 (p. 314) Famous Parisian caterers.

13 (p. 321) Cottard will nevertheless reappear—indeed at this same soirée (see p. 371)—to die during the Great War, in *Time Regained*.

14 (p. 367) The French has a play on the words *allegro* and *allègre*.

15 (p. 370) Mme Verdurin uses here the word *tapette*, no doubt unaware of its popular meaning (see Vol. IV, *Sodom and Gomorrah*, note 18 to p. 594).

16 (p. 382) The heroine of Victor Hugo's *Hernani*: the reference is to the final scene, which ends with Hernani's enforced suicide after the nuptial feast.

17 (p. 382) Thomas Couture, nineteenth-century French painter. The allusion is to his picture, *Les Romains de la Décadence*, shown in the Salon of 1847.

18 (p. 386) Auguste Vacquerie and Paul Meurice were two devoted disciples of Victor Hugo.

19 (p. 391) Mme de Villeparisis will reappear, extremely aged but very much alive, in *The Fugitive*.

20 (p. 406) To Condé's lament: "My dear friend La Moussaye,/Ah, God, What weather!/We are going to perish in the flood," La Moussaye replies: "Our lives are safe,/For we are Sodomites,/We have to die by fire." There is a marginal note by Proust in the manuscript at this point: "Stress the fact that homosexuality has never precluded bravery, from Caesar to Kitchener."

21 (p. 441) The *blancs d'Espagne* were a group of extreme legit-

imists who held that the true heirs to the French throne were the Spanish Bourbons who were descended in direct line from Louis XIV through his grandson Philip V of Spain.

22 (p. 457) Slang for anus. What Albertine had been about to say was "me faire casser le pot," an obscene slang expression meaning to have anal intercourse (passive).

23 (p. 510) There is a gap in Proust's manuscript at this point. For an illustration of the narrator's point, see Vol. II, *Within a Budding Grove*, p. 315.

24 (p. 555) Racine's *Esther* again.

25 (p. 590) *"Notre mal ne vaut pas un seul de ses regards"*—the line is from one of Ronsard's *Sonnets pour Hélène* (cf. Vol. IV, *Sodom and Gomorrah*, p. 738).

26 (p. 731) Albert, Duc de Broglie, the grandson of Mme de Staël, was exiled by Napoleon I and retired to Chaumont-sur-Loire—whence the association of ideas.

27 (p. 769) *Le chancelier* Pasquier, friend of Mme de Boigne, who ran a famous salon under the July Monarchy and whose *Mémoires* (published in 1907) suggested those of Mme de Beausergent which the narrator's grandmother loved to read. The Duc de Noailles was a friend and patron of Sainte-Beuve. Mme d'Arbouville was the latter's mistress.

28 (p. 790) Mme de Guermantes has told this story before, at the expense of the Prince de Léon (see p. 38).

29 (p. 808) "The dead are sleeping peacefully" comes from Musset's *La Nuit d'Octobre*, "You will make them weep . . . All those urchins" from Sully-Prudhomme's *Aux Tuileries*, and "The very first night" from Charles Cros's *Nocturne*.

30 (p. 873) The reference is to *Phèdre*, Act II, Scene 5, in which Phèdre declares her love for Hippolyte in cryptic terms: she loves him as she loved Thésée, *"non point tel que l'ont vu les Enfers . . . mais fidèle, mais fier, et même un peu farouche."*

31 (p. 879)   Roland Garros: famous French aviator.

32 (p. 893)   An illegitimate daughter of the Duc de Berry, son
              of Charles X, married a Lucinge-Faucigny.

33 (p. 899)   *Sous-maîtresse*: euphemism for a brothel-keeper or
              "madam."

34 (p. 909)   This passage is a little confusing. Proust never got
              round to marrying Gilberte to the Duc de Guer-
              mantes. In *Time Regained* she reappears as Saint-
              Loup's widow while Oriane is still alive and mar-
              ried to the aged Duke.

35 (p. 909)   Agamemnon in Offenbach's *La Belle Hélène*.

36 (p. 923)   This signature can be explained by the fact that
              Charles Morel was Bobby Santois in Proust's origi-
              nal manuscript.

37 (p. 926)   The widowed Gilberte, in *Time Regained*, appears
              to be the mother of an only daughter.

Addenda

Page 124.   *There is a brief passage inserted here in Proust's manuscript which interrupts the thread of the narrative:*

Lying is a very small matter; we live in the midst of it without giving it more than a smile, we practise it without meaning to harm anyone, but jealousy suffers because of it and sees more in it than it conceals (often one's mistress refuses to spend the evening with one and goes to the theatre simply to prevent us from seeing that she is not looking her best), just as it often remains blind to what the truth conceals. But it can elicit nothing, for women who swear that they are not lying would refuse even with a knife at their throats to confess their true character.

Page 128.   *The Pléiade editors (references in these Addenda are to the 1954 edition) have relegated to their "Notes and Variants" the following isolated passage which the original editors inserted, somewhat arbitrarily, after "for so long."*

The curious thing is that, a few days before this quarrel with Albertine, I had already had one with her in Andrée's presence. Now Andrée, in giving Albertine good advice, always appeared to be insinuating bad. "Come, don't talk like that, hold your tongue," she said, as though she were at the peak of happiness. Her face assumed the dry raspberry hue of those pious housekeepers who get all the servants sacked one by one. While I was heaping unjustified reproaches upon Albertine, Andrée looked as though she were sucking a lump of barley sugar with keen enjoyment. At length she was unable to restrain an affectionate laugh. "Come with me, Titine. You know I'm your dear little sister."

I was not merely exasperated by this rather sickly exhibition; I wondered whether Andrée really felt the affection for Albertine that she pretended to feel. Seeing that Albertine, who knew Andrée far better than I did, always shrugged her shoul-

ders when I asked her whether she was quite certain of Andrée's affection, and always answered that nobody in the world
cared for her more, I am convinced even now that Andrée's affection was sincere. Possibly, in her wealthy but provincial family, one might find the equivalent in some of the shops in the
Cathedral square, where certain sweetmeats are declared to be
"the best going." But I know that, for my part, even if I had
invariably come to the opposite conclusion, I had so strong an
impression that Andrée was trying to rap Albertine over the
knuckles that my mistress at once regained my affection and my
anger subsided.

Page 153. *In the place of this passage, the manuscript contains
the following*:

"What? You wouldn't kill yourself after all?" she said with a
laugh.

"No, but it would be the greatest sorrow that I could possibly imagine." And since, although living exclusively with me,
and having become extremely intelligent, she none the less remained mysteriously in tune with the atmosphere of the world
outside—as the roses in her bedroom flowered again in the
spring—and followed as though by a pre-established accord
(for she spoke to almost no one) the charmingly idiotic fashions
of feminine speech, she said to me: "Is it really true, that great
big fib?" And indeed she must, if not love me more than I
loved her, at least infer from my niceness to her that my tenderness was deeper than it was in reality, for she added:
"You're very sweet. I don't doubt it at all, I know you're fond
of me." And she went on: "Ah, well, perhaps it's my destiny to
die in a riding accident. I've often had a presentiment of it, but
I don't care a fig. I accept whatever fate has in store for me."

I believe that, on the contrary, she had neither a presentiment of nor a contempt for death, and that her words were
lacking in sincerity. I am sure in any case that there was no sincerity in mine, as to the greatest sorrow I could imagine. For,
feeling that Albertine could henceforth only deprive me of pleasures or cause me sorrows, that I would be ruining my life for

her sake, I remembered the wish that Swann had once formed apropos of Odette, and without daring to wish for Albertine's death, I told myself that it would have restored to me, in the words of the Sultan, my peace of mind and freedom of action.

Page 353. *There is an additional passage here, isolated by the Pléiade editors at the foot of the page. Saniette reappears further on (pp. 436–39).*

"Pretty well played, what!" said M. Verdurin to Saniette. "My only fear," the latter replied, stuttering, "is that Morel's very virtuosity may somewhat offend against the general spirit of the work." "Offend? What do you mean?" roared M. Verdurin while a number of the guests gathered round like lions ready to devour a man who has been laid low. "Oh, I'm not aiming at him alone . . ." "But the man doesn't know what he's talking about. Aiming at what?" "I . . . shall have . . . to listen to it . . . once again to form a judgment *à la rigueur.*" "*À la rigueur!* the man's mad!" said M. Verdurin, clutching his head between his hands, "he ought to be put away." "The term means 'with exactitude.' You ca . . . ca . . . can say 'with rigorous exactitude,' after all. I'm saying that I can't judge *à la rigueur.*" "And I'm telling you to go away," M. Verdurin shouted, intoxicated by his own rage, and pointing to the door with blazing eyes. "I will not allow people to talk like that in my house!"

Saniette went off zigzagging like a drunken man. Some of the guests, seeing him thus ejected, assumed that he had not been invited. And a lady who had been extremely friendly with him hitherto, and to whom he had lent a precious book the day before, sent it back to him next day without a word, scarcely even wrapped in some paper on which she had her butler simply put Saniette's address. She did not wish to be in any way "indebted" to someone who was obviously far from being in the good graces of the little clan. Saniette, as it happened, was never to know of this piece of rudeness. For scarcely five minutes had passed after M. Verdurin's outburst when a footman came to inform the latter that M. Saniette had had a stroke in the courtyard. But the evening was not yet over. "Have him taken home;

I'm sure it won't be serious," said M. Verdurin, whose *hôtel particulier*, as the manager of the hotel at Balbec would have said, thus became assimilated to those grand hotels where the management hasten to conceal sudden deaths in order not to frighten off their customers, and where the deceased is temporarily hidden in a meat-safe until the moment when, even if he has been in his lifetime the most distinguished and the most generous of men, he is clandestinely evacuated by the door reserved for the dishwashers and sauce chefs. In fact Saniette was not quite dead. He lived for another few weeks, but only intermittently regaining consciousness.

Page 628.   The Pléiade editors have inserted here as a footnote an additional passage which Proust placed a few pages later (clearly in error):

I was going to buy, in addition to the motor-cars, the finest yacht which then existed. It was for sale, but at so high a price that no buyer could be found. Moreover, once bought, even if we confined ourselves to four-month cruises, it would cost two hundred thousand francs a year in upkeep. We should be living at the rate of half a million francs a year. Would I be able to sustain it for more than seven or eight years? But never mind; when I had only an income of fifty thousand francs left, I could leave it to Albertine and kill myself. This was the decision I made. It made me think of *myself*. Now, since one's ego lives by thinking incessantly of all sorts of things, since it is no more than the thought of those things, if by chance, instead of being preoccupied with those things, it suddenly thinks of itself, it finds only an empty apparatus, something which it does not recognise and to which, in order to give it some reality, it adds the memory of a face seen in a mirror. That peculiar smile, that untidy moustache—they are what would disappear from the face of the earth. When I killed myself five years hence, I would no longer be able to think all those things which passed through my mind unceasingly, I would no longer exist on the face of the earth and would never come back to it; my thought would stop for ever. And my ego seemed to me even more null when I saw it as something that no longer exists. How could it be difficult to sacrifice, for the sake of the person to whom one's thought is constantly straining (the person we love), that other person of whom we never think: ourselves? Accordingly, this thought of my death, like the notion of my ego, seemed to me most strange, but I did not find it at all disagreeable. Then suddenly it struck me as being terribly sad; this was because, reflecting that if I did not have more money at my disposal it was because my parents were still alive, I suddenly thought of my mother. And I could not bear the idea of what she would suffer after my death.

Page 866. *Proust's manuscript has a different version of the Norpois–Villeparisis episode which the Pléiade editors print as an appendix. Passages that have become illegible are indicated by square brackets:*

Several of the palaces on the Grand Canal were transformed into hotels, and by way of a change from the one at which we were staying, we decided one evening to dine in another where the food was said to be better. While my mother was paying the gondolier, I entered a vast marble-pillared hall that had once been entirely covered with frescoes, [. . .]

One of the waiters asked if the "old couple" [. . .] were coming down [. . .], that they never gave any warning, and that it was most tiresome. Then he saw the lady appear. It was in fact Mme de Villeparisis [. . .] but bent towards the ground, with that air of dejection and bemusement produced by extreme fatigue and the weight of years. We happened by chance to be given a table immediately behind hers, up against the splendid marble walls of the palace, and fortunately, since my mother was tired and wanted to avoid introductions, we had our backs to the Marquise and could not be seen by her, and were moreover protected by the relief of a massive column with a [. . .] capital. Meanwhile I was wondering which of her relations was being referred to as M. de Villeparisis, when a few minutes later I saw her old lover, M. de Norpois, even more bent than she, sit down at her table, having just come down from their room. They still loved each other, and, now that he had given up his functions at the Ministry, as soon as the relative incognito which one enjoys abroad permitted, they lived together completely. In order to allow his old mistress a degree of respectability, he was careful not to give his name in hotels, and the waiters, ignorant at this distance of celebrated Parisian liaisons, and moreover seeing this old gentleman, even when he had gone out without her, invariably coming back to dine alone with the old lady, assumed that they were M. and Mme de Villeparisis. The matrimonial character of their relationship, which had been greatly accentuated by the carelessness of old age and travel, manifested itself at once in the fact that on sitting down to table M. de Norpois evinced none of those courtesies one shows towards a woman who is not one's wife, any more than she herself made any effort for him. More lively than Mme de Villeparisis, he related to her with a familiarity that surprised me what he had learned that day from a foreign ambassador he had been to see. She let a fair proportion of his words go by without answering, either from fatigue, or lack of interest, or deafness and a desire to conceal it. From time to time she addressed a few words to him in a faint voice, as though overcome with exhaustion. It was obvious that she now lived almost exclusively for him, and had long since lost touch with the social world—from which, with considerable volubility and in a rather loud voice (perhaps to enable her to hear him), he brought her the latest news—for she put to him, in a low-pitched, weary voice, questions that seemed strange on the lips of a person who, even though excluded from it for a long time, nevertheless belonged to the highest society. After a long silence [. . .] asked: "So this Bisaccia you [. . .] this afternoon, is he one of Sosthène's sons?" "Yes, of course, he's the one who became Duc de Bisaccia when Arnaud took the name Doudeauville. He's charming; he's a bit like Carnot's youngest son, only better-looking." And once more there was silence. What seemed most of all to be preoccupying the old woman, whose charming eyes in that ruined face no one could have identified through the mists which the distance from Paris and the remoteness of age accumulated round her, was a war over

Morocco. In spite of what the foreign ambassador had said to M. de Norpois, she did not seem reassured. "Ah, but you always see the black side," said M. de Norpois with some asperity. "I admit that Emperor William is often unfortunate in his choice of words and gestures. But the fact that certain things must be taken seriously doesn't mean that they should be taken tragically. It would be a case of Jupiter making mad those he wishes to destroy; for war is in nobody's interest, least of all Germany's. They're perfectly aware in the Wilhelmstrasse that Morocco isn't worth the blood of a single Pomeranian grenadier. You're alarming yourself about trifles." And again there was silence, prolonged indefinitely by Mme de Villeparisis, whose beauty, which was said to have been so striking, had been as thoroughly effaced as the frescoes that had decorated the ceiling of this magnificent hall with its broad red pillars, and whose personality was as well concealed, if not from the eyes of Parisians who might perhaps have identified her, at least from the hotel's Venetian staff, as if she had been wearing a carnival mask as in the old days in Venice. M. de Norpois addressed an occasional reproof to a waiter who had failed to bring something he had ordered. I noticed that he enjoyed good food as much as at the time when he used to dine with my family, and Mme de Villeparisis was as finicky as she had been at Balbec. "No no, don't ask them for a soufflé," M. de Norpois said, "they've no idea what it is. They'll bring you something that bears not the slightest resemblance to a soufflé. In any case it's your own fault, since you won't hear of Italian cooking." Mme de Villeparisis did not answer; then after a while, in a plaintive voice, as sad and faint as the murmur of the wind, she wailed: "No one knows how to make anything any more. I don't know whether you remember, in the old days at my mother's house, they used to bring off to perfection a dish called a *crème renversée*. Perhaps we could ask for one of those." "In fact it hadn't yet come to be called a *crème renversée*; it was called," said M. de Norpois, putting the phrase in inverted commas, "'creamed eggs.' What they give you here won't be up to much. Creamed eggs were so smooth and succulent, do you remember?" But, whether because she did not in fact remember, or because she had talked enough, Mme de Villeparisis said nothing. She relapsed into a long silence which did not offend M. de Norpois, presumably because it did not surprise him and because it must have been one of the characteristics, perhaps one of the charms, of his life with her. And while she laboriously cut up her beans, he went back to telling her how interesting, and on the whole optimistic, the foreign ambassador had been, meanwhile keeping an eye out for a waiter from whom he could order their dessert. Before this had been served, my mother and I rose from the table, and, while keeping my head turned away so as not to attract their attention, I could nevertheless still see the two aged lovers, seemingly indifferent to one another, but in reality bent by time like two branches which have developed the same tilt, which have drawn so close to each other that they almost touch, and which nothing will ever either straighten up or separate again.

This was perhaps what might have happened to me in the long run if Albertine had lived. And yet, comforting though it must after all be, since worldly men and women sacrifice social life and ambition for it, I felt no regret that what might have been had failed to come about, so impervious had I become to the memory of Albertine. I cannot however say that sometimes in the evening, when we returned to our hotel (for, since our encounter with the old Villeparisis–Norpois couple, my mother had decided against our dining elsewhere), I did not feel, in the nervous restlessness of nightfall, that the Albertine of long ago, invisible to myself . . . (cf. p. 866, line 17).

THE CAPTIVE

Life with Albertine. Street sounds (1). Albertine and I under the same roof (2). My mother's disapproval (6). My irregular sleeping habits (9). Françoise's respect for tradition (9). Intellectual development and physical change in Albertine (12). My confidence in Andrée (15). I advise against a trip with Andrée to the Buttes-Chaumont (16). I no longer love Albertine, but my jealousy subsists (16). Ubiquity of Gomorrah (20). The virtues of solitude (22). I long to be free of Albertine (26). Jealousy, a spasmodic disease (28).

Visits to the Duchesse de Guermantes (30). What survives of the magic of her name (32; cf. **III** 28). The Fortuny dresses (34). Attraction of the Duchess's conversation (34–39). Mme de Chaussepierre (41–42; cf. **IV** 98). Digression about the Dreyfus case (43–44).

M. de Charlus and Morel *chez* Jupien (48). "Stand you tea" (49). M. de Charlus receives a note from a club doorman (51). Natural distinction of Jupien's niece (55). M. de Charlus delighted at the prospect of her marriage with Morel (55). Morel's capricious sentiments and pathological irritability (59).

The syringa incident (64; cf. 812). Waiting for Albertine's return: pleasures of art (65). Change in her since she has sensed my jealousy (67). Andrée's defects; her calumnies about "I'm a wash-out" (70; cf. 815). Reports on her outings with Albertine (71). Albertine's taste and elegance (75). Variability of the nature of girls (77). Persistence of my desire for the fleeting image of Albertine at Balbec (81). Albertine asleep (84). Watching her sleeping (86), and waking (90). The soothing power of her kiss, comparable to that of my mother at Combray (93). My increasing resemblance to all my relations (95).

Changes of weather; their effect on my indolence (100) and on my jealous suspicions (103). Bloch's cousin Esther (105). Albertine's plan to visit Mme Verdurin (108). I suggest other expeditions (113). A "fugitive being" (113–16). Françoise's hostile prophecies about Albertine (122). Telephone call to Andrée about Albertine's visit to the Verdurins (124). But can I trust Andrée? (128). Albertine tries to dissuade me from accompanying her to the Verdurins' (130). I advise her to go to the Trocadéro instead (134). The anguish of being deprived of her customary good-night kiss (141). Her sleep again (142–45) and her charming awakening (145–46).

Spring morning (146). Street sounds; the musical cries of the street-vendors (146–51). Reflections on different kinds of sleep (153–60). Albertine's enthusiasm for the cries of Paris and the foodstuffs they offer (160); her eloquent disquisition on the subject of ices (165).

The chauffeur and the expedition to Versailles (168). Alone at the window, I listen to the sounds of Paris (174). Nostalgia for little girls (177). Françoise sends me one to do an errand: a pretty dairymaid whom I had noticed (178), but whose glamour quickly evaporates when she is in my presence (183). Léa is to perform at the Trocadéro (185). How to prevent Albertine from meeting her? (188). I send Françoise to fetch her (196). Deterioration in Françoise's speech (199); her inability to tell the right time (201). Awaiting Albertine's return, I play Vinteuil's sonata (204). Music and introspection (206). Reflections on the attitude to their work of nineteenth-century artists (207). Morel's mysterious occupations (210). His outburst against Jupien's niece: grand pied de grue (212). Drive to the Bois with Albertine (216). Similarities between desire and travel (222). Alternations of boredom and desire (225). Our shadows in the Bois (227). My servitude and hers (230). A meeting with Gisèle (231). The lies of the little band fit together exactly (233). Albertine admits a lie (235).

I learn of Bergotte's death (238). His illness, prolonged by medical treatment (238). At the Vermeer exhibition: the little patch of yellow wall. Dead for ever? (244). Albertine's lie about meeting Bergotte (247). Her technique of lying (247, 250).

The Verdurins quarrel with M. de Charlus. I set off for the Verdurins' in secret (253). Encounter with a repentant Morel (254;

cf. 255). His capriciousness and cynicism (212), and his rancour towards those to whom he causes pain (256). Meeting with Brichot (260). The death of Swann (260). Brichot evokes the Verdurin salon of old (265). Arrival of M. de Charlus, greatly changed (268). Brichot's attitude towards him (269). Homosexuality and the refinement of artistic tastes (270). M. de Charlus's conjugal behaviour with Morel (274). His detachment from social constraints (275). Morel's letter from Léa (280) M. de Charlus admires Morel's successes with women (284); and meanwhile tries to seduce other young men, in particular Bloch (285).

Arrival at the Verdurins' house (299). M. de Charlus and the footman (300). Saniette snubbed by M. Verdurin for announcing Princess Sherbatoff's death (302). Mme Verdurin obsessed with the desire to separate Charlus and Morel (305). Her reasons for resentment against the Baron: his veto on the society women she wanted to invite (306), in particular Mme Molé (310). The Verdurin salon and the Dreyfus Case (312), and the *Ballets russes* (314). Mme Verdurin and the death of Princess Sherbatoff (317). Her medical precautions against the effects of Vinteuil's music (320). Morel's improved manners (322). M. de Charlus's furtive exchanges with several important guests (323). Mme Verdurin draws up her plans (325). Rudeness of the Baron's guests (326), with the exception of the Queen of Naples (328).

The concert begins (331). An unpublished work by Vinteuil (332). Attitudes of Mme Verdurin, the musicians, Morel (334). Mysterious promise of the music (337). Art and life (339; cf. 259). Vinteuil's unique and unmistakable voice (340). The artist's "unknown country" (342). Music, language of souls (344). Final triumph of the joyful motif (347). The role of Mlle Vinteuil's friend in the revelation of this work (348).

The guests file past the Baron (353); his witty or caustic remarks (354). Mme de Mortemart puts out feelers for a musical *soirée* (357). M. d'Argencourt and inverts (362). Mme Verdurin's growing rage (364). The Queen of Naples' fan (365). M. de Charlus and General Deltour (371). Mme Verdurin asks Brichot to talk to the Baron while M. Verdurin tackles Morel (373). Brichot reluctantly complies (377). M. de Charlus's remarks on Morel's playing: the lock of hair (382–83). He appreciates Brichot's wit (385). His attendance at Brichot's Sorbonne lectures (387). Mme de Villeparisis's real social position (392; cf. III 244–45). Brichot and Charlus on homosexuality (395); M. de Charlus's statistic (397); Swann, Odette and her many lovers (399), M. de Crécy (402; cf. IV 657). General observations on sodomy (404 et sqq.)

M. Verdurin's revelations to Morel about the Baron (414); Mme Verdurin confirms and reinforces them (415–24). Morel repudiates the Baron, who remains dumbfounded (424). The Queen of Naples, returning to collect her fan, leads M. de Charlus away (430). The change in the Baron after this *soirée*; his illness (433); moral improvement followed by a new decline (434). The Verdurins' generosity towards Saniette (436). Unexpected side to M. Verdurin's character (439).

Disappearance of Albertine. Return from the Verdurins' with Brichot (440). The window streaked with light, symbol of my servitude (444). Albertine's anger (447). Her admission about the supposed three-day trip to Balbec (449). A mysterious and horrible Albertine reveals herself ("casser le pot") (453). My mendacious proposal that we should separate (459). Esther's photograph (461; cf. 107). I am intoxicated by my grief (475), Albertine and Léa (479), which I suddenly bring to an end by "a renewal of the lease" (483). Albertine's sleeping body: a mysterious allegory (485). A letter from my mother (490). Curiosity and sagacity of Françoise (492). Albertine's artistic tastes (496). The Fortuny gowns (497). Albertine plays me some music (501). The profound truth of Vinteuil's music (504). Reflections on genius (505). Key-phrases (506); the example of Dostoievsky (508).

Return of spring; vain resolution to change my way of life (522). Mme Bontemps's revelations about the Buttes-Chaumont and Albertine's readiness to leave Balbec with me (524). Two character traits: the multiple utilisation of a single action (526; cf. II 636), and the incapacity to resist the temptation of a pleasure (527). My outburst of anger (531). Interrogation of Albertine about her relations with Andrée (534). Reconciliation, but no good-night kiss (537). A presentiment of death (540). The noise of a window being opened in the silence of the night (541).

We go out together (544). The aeroplane (547; cf. **IV** 582). Albertine and the pastry-cook (548). Sounds and scents of spring (553); thirst for Venice (555). I resolve to leave Albertine immediately (557). Françoise informs me that she has just left (558).

THE FUGITIVE

Grieving and Forgetting. "Mlle Albertine has gone" (563). Albertine's letter (565–66). Hypotheses about the reasons for her departure (566). All my different "selves" must learn to live with my suffering (578–79). Albertine in Touraine (580). The little poor girl in my room (583).

Saint-Loup's mission to Touraine (587). His astonishment on seeing Albertine's photograph (589). Bloch's indiscretion and my anger (597). Summons from the Sûreté (597). First furtive hint of forgetting (603). My sleep is full of Albertine (604). First telegram from Saint-Loup: mission delayed (604); second telegram: Albertine has seen him (608). Furious, I cable to him telling him to return (610). A letter from Albertine (610). My mendacious reply (612). The declaration scene in *Phèdre* (617). The mystery of Albertine's rings (623; cf. 214). Another letter from Albertine (631). I ask Andrée to come and live with me, and tell Albertine (632). Saint-Loup's return; an overheard conversation shows him in a new light (634). His report on his mission (636).

A telegram from Mme Bontemps: Albertine's death in a riding accident (642). New and unprecedented suffering (642). Proliferation of memories (644–48). The baths at Balbec (663). Aimé's mission of inquiry (664). Alternation of odious suspicions and tender memories (665). Analogy between my love for Gilberte and my love for Albertine (677). Our mistresses are the daughters of our anguish (681). Lying words become prophetic truths (684). Aimé's letter confirming my suspicions (695). His mission to Touraine (705). Albertine and the laundry-girl (706); evocation of an Elstir painting (710). Revival in my memory of a sweet, kind and innocent Albertine (713).

Beginnings of recovery (718). I grow accustomed to the idea of Albertine's death (719–20). Intermittent revival of my love and my suffering (723 et sqq.). Andrée confesses her taste for women, but denies having had relations with Albertine (737). Renewal of desire for other women (745). The power of oblivion (751).

Mlle de Forcheville. Three stages on the road to indifference (754). A walk in the Bois on All Saints' Day (754). The three girls (758). Some days later, one of them gives me a look which rouses my passion (759). I identify her with Mlle d'Eporcheville, whom Robert had met in a house of assignation (760; cf. **IV** 126). Robert, in reply to a cable from me, tells me it is the wrong girl (765). My article in the *Figaro* (766–72). Visit to the Guermantes' (772). The blonde girl: Mlle de Forcheville (773–74), in other words Gilberte (775). Mme de Guermantes's changed attitude towards Swann's wife and daughter after his death (780); she entertains Gilberte and talks to her about her father (783). The Duke reads my article (788). Gilberte's snobbery (790). Two congratulatory letters (797). Gilberte helps to bury the memory of her father (800) and hastens the process of forgetting in me as regards Albertine (801). A new social self replaces the one that loved Albertine (803).

Second stage on the road towards indifference: second conversation with Andrée (806); her relations with Albertine (810); Albertine and Morel (810); the evening of the syringa (812; cf. 64). Andrée's different natures (815); her engagement to the Verdurins' nephew, "I'm a wash-out" (817), an artist of genius underneath his crude and frivolous exterior (818). The Princesse de Parme's visit to my mother (828). Third visit from Andrée (830); a new explanation for Albertine's departure (830). Albertine and "I'm a wash-out" (832). His attitude towards me (840).

Sojourn in Venice. Third stage towards indifference (844). Venice and Combray (844). Mme de Villeparisis and M. de Norpois, greatly aged (854–66). A telegram from Albertine telling me she is alive; it gives me no joy (869). The self that loved Albertine is dead (870). My outings in Venice, alone or with my mother (875). The Giotto chapel at Padua (878). Evening walks in Venice (881).

I ask my mother to postpone our departure (883); she refuses, and I decide to stay (884). Solitude, misery, *O sole mio* (884). The train (888). A letter from Gilberte announcing her engagement to Robert de Saint-Loup (889); the recent telegram was from her (889).

New Aspect of Saint-Loup. My mother tells me of another marriage, that of the Cambremers' son and Mlle d'Oloron, Jupien's niece (893). My mother's reflexions on the news, and thoughts of my grandmother (893). Ups and downs of Saint-Loup's engagement plans (898). Disapproval from Combray (899). Reactions of society people (902). Opposite effects of the same vice in Charlus and Legrandin (904). Roles of the Princesse de Parme, Charlus and Legrandin in Mlle d'Oloron's marriage (904). Change in Legrandin (906). Gilberte, at first happy in her new social position (908), becomes indifferent to it (909). Mlle d'Oloron's death (913). The Muse of History (919).

A visit to Tansonville (921). Saint-Loup's infidelity; his relations with Morel (922–23). Retrospective analysis of Robert's sexual tastes (924–30). Robert and Mme de Forcheville (930–31). My tarnished friendship (936).

THE MODERN LIBRARY IS PLEASED TO PUBLISH THE DEFINITIVE
TRANSLATION OF PROUST'S MASTERWORK, *IN SEARCH OF LOST
TIME*, IN BOTH HARDCOVER AND PAPERBACK

HARDCOVER:

Swann's Way, 0-679-60005-1, $21.95 (Canada $30.95)

Within a Budding Grove, 0-679-60006-X, $24.00 (Canada $33.50)

The Guermantes Way, 0-679-60028-0, $23.95 (Canada $33.50)

Sodom and Gomorrah, 0-679-60029-9, $21.00 (Canada $28.95)

The Captive & The Fugitive, 0-679-42477-6, $24.95 (Canada $34.95)

Time Regained & A Guide to Proust, 0-679-42476-8, $24.95 (Canada $34.95)

The Proust Six-Pack for $125.00, 0-679-60295-X

PAPERBACK:

Swann's Way, 0-375-75154-8, $12.95 (Canada $17.95)

Within a Budding Grove, 0-375-75219-6, $13.95 (Canada $19.50)

The Guermantes Way, 0-375-75233-1, $14.95 (Canada $20.95)

Sodom and Gomorrah, 0-375-75310-9, $13.95 (Canada $19.50)

The Captive & The Fugitive, 0-375-75311-7, $14.95 (Canada $20.95)

Time Regained & A Guide to Proust, 0-375-75312-5, $13.95 (Canada $19.50)

The Proust Six-Pack for $75.00, 0-676-58362-8

Available in bookstores everywhere, or call toll-free 1-800-793-BOOK
(credit card orders only and prices subject to change).

Reading Group Guide to *In Search of Lost Time* (676-57707-5) free, available
from your local bookseller, by calling 1-800-793-BOOK, or by visiting
www.modernlibrary.com

For even more information on Proust, visit our website at
www.modernlibrary.com